Judy Nunn's career has been long, illustrious and multifaceted. After combining her internationally successful acting career with scriptwriting for television and radio, Judy decided in the '90s to turn her hand to prose.

Her first three novels, *The Glitter Game*, *Centre Stage* and *Araluen*, set respectively in the worlds of television, theatre and film, became instant bestsellers, and the rest is history, quite literally, in fact. She has since developed a love of writing Australian historically based fiction and her fame as a novelist has spread rapidly throughout Europe, where she is published in English, German, French, Dutch, Czech and Spanish.

Her subsequent bestsellers, *Kal*, *Beneath the Southern Cross*, *Territory*, *Pacific*, *Heritage*, *Floodtide*, *Maralinga*, *Tiger Men*, *Elianne*, *Spirits of the Ghan*, *Sanctuary* and *Khaki Town*, have confirmed Judy's position as one of Australia's leading fiction writers.

In 2015 Judy was made a Member of the Order of Australia for her 'significant service to the performing arts as a script-writer and actor of stage and screen, and to literature as an author'.

Visit Judy at judynunn.com.au or on
facebook.com/JudyNunnAuthor

Books by Judy Nunn

The Glitter Game
Centre Stage
Araluen
Kal
Beneath the Southern Cross
Territory
Pacific
Heritage
Floodtide
Maralinga
Tiger Men
Elianne
Spirits of the Ghan
Sanctuary
Khaki Town

Children's fiction
Eye in the Storm
Eye in the City

Beneath the Southern Cross

JUDY NUNN

WILLIAM HEINEMANN

WILLIAM HEINEMANN

UK | USA | Canada | Ireland | Australia
India | New Zealand | South Africa | China

William Heinemann is part of the Penguin Random House group of companies whose addresses can be found at global.penguinrandomhouse.com.

First published by Random House Australia, 1999
This edition published by William Heinemann, 2020

Typeset by Midland Typesetters, Australia
Printed and bound in Australia by Griffin Press, part of Ovato, an accredited ISO AS/NZS 14001 Environmental Management Systems printer

A catalogue record for this book is available from the National Library of Australia

ISBN 978 1 76104 057 3

penguin.com.au

To Susan J. Mackie, the most understanding,
most encouraging and most demanding friend a
writer could have. Thanks Suzie, for the imprisonment,
for the delivery of writer's lunches and for
the homegrown blooms of inspiration.

Acknowledgements

I would like to especially thank my friend and researcher, Robyn Gurney, and my husband, Bruce Venables, both of whom have been with me every step of this long and interesting journey.

A special thanks also to Jane Palfreyman, Kim Swivel, Dr Grahame Hookway, William J Bailey and Colin Julin.

Of the many research sources explored by both Robyn Gurney and myself, I would like particularly to recognise the following publications:

The Sydney Language, Jakelin Troy, Australian Dictionaries Project/Australian Institute of Aboriginal and Torres Strait Islander Studies, 1993.

Sydney Cove, John Cobley, Angus & Robertson, 1987 edition.

Sydney, An Illustrated History, James Murray, Lansdowne Press, 1974.

This Was Sydney: A Pictorial History from 1788 to Present Time, Suzanne Mourot, Ure Smith, 1969.

The History of Australia, Volume 5, Manning Clark, Melbourne University Press, 1981.

The Official History of Australia in the War of 1914–1918, Volume 1, C. E. W. Bean, Angus & Robertson, 1921.

The House of Wunderlich, Susan Bures, Kangaroo Press, 1978.

Shopkeepers and Shoppers, Frances Pollon, The Retail Traders' Association of NSW, 1989.

The Australian People and The Great War, Michael McKernan, William Collins Pty Ltd, 1984 edition.

For Love or Money, Megan McMurchy, Penguin Books Australia, 1983.

Surry Hills, The City's Backyard, Christopher Keating, Hale & Iremonger Pty Ltd, 1991.

Kings Cross Album, Elizabeth Butel & Tom Thompson, Atrand Pty Ltd, 1984.

A Day Before Yesterday, Abe Davis, A. Davis, 1978.

CONTENTS

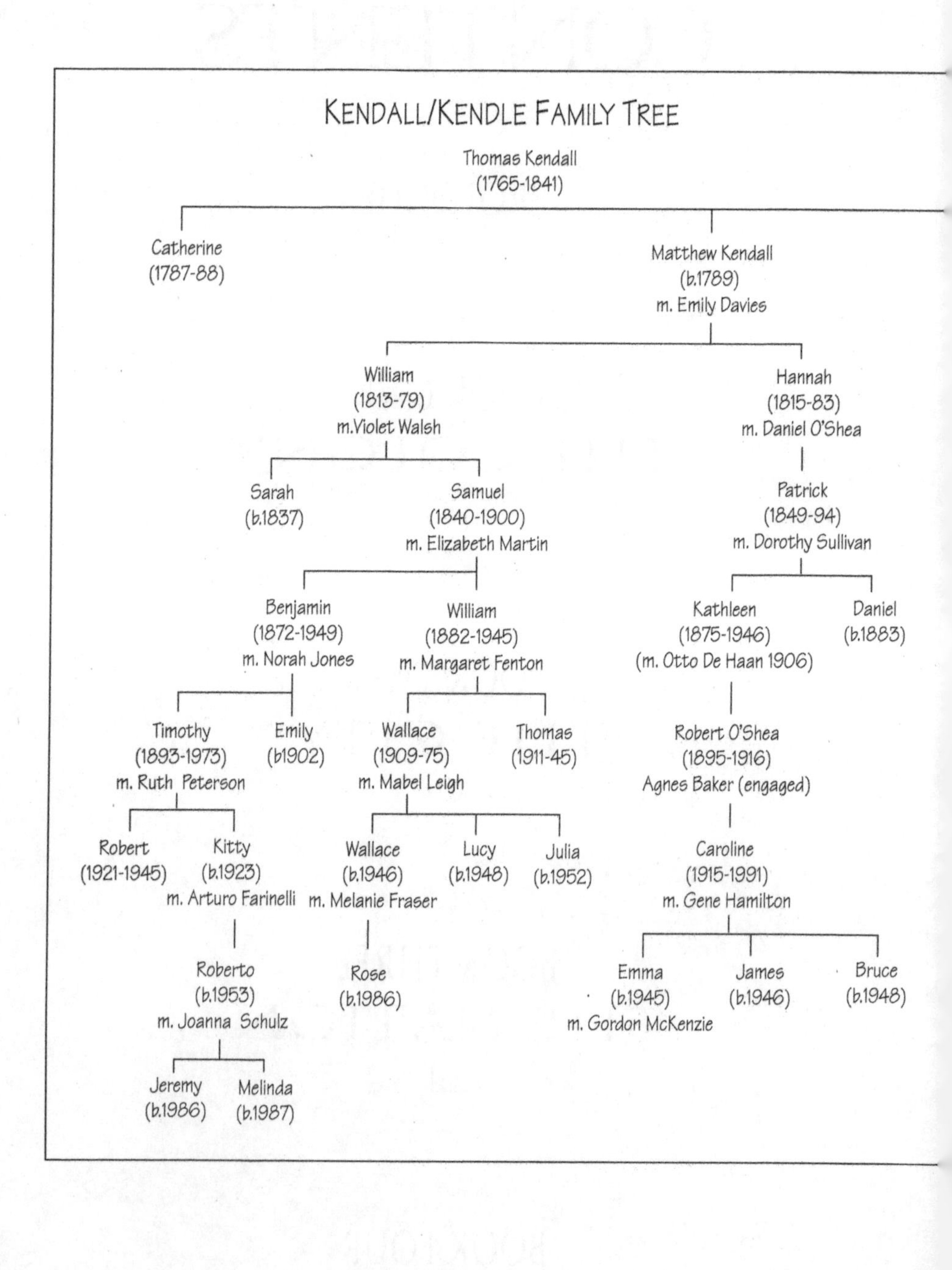
KENDALL/KENDLE FAMILY TREE
Thomas Kendall
(1765-1841)
Catherine
(1787-88)
Matthew Kendall
(b.1789)
m. Emily Davies
William
(1813-79)
m.Violet Walsh
Hannah
(1815-83)
m. Daniel O'Shea
Sarah
(b.1837)
Samuel
(1840-1900)
m. Elizabeth Martin
Patrick
(1849-94)
m. Dorothy Sullivan
Benjamin
(1872-1949)
m. Norah Jones
William
(1882-1945)
m. Margaret Fenton
Kathleen
(1875-1946)
(m. Otto De Haan 1906)
Daniel
(b.1883)
Timothy
(1893-1973)
m. Ruth Peterson
Emily
(b1902)
Wallace
(1909-75)
m. Mabel Leigh
Thomas
(1911-45)
Robert O'Shea
(1895-1916)
Agnes Baker (engaged)
Robert
(1921-1945)
Kitty
(b.1923)
m. Arturo Farinelli
Wallace
(b.1946)
m. Melanie Fraser
Lucy
(b.1948)
Julia
(b.1952)
Caroline
(1915-1991)
m. Gene Hamilton
Roberto
(b.1953)
m. Joanna Schulz
Rose
(b.1986)
Emma
(b.1945)
m. Gordon McKenzie
James
(b.1946)
Bruce
(b.1948)
Jeremy
(b.1986)
Melinda
(b.1987)

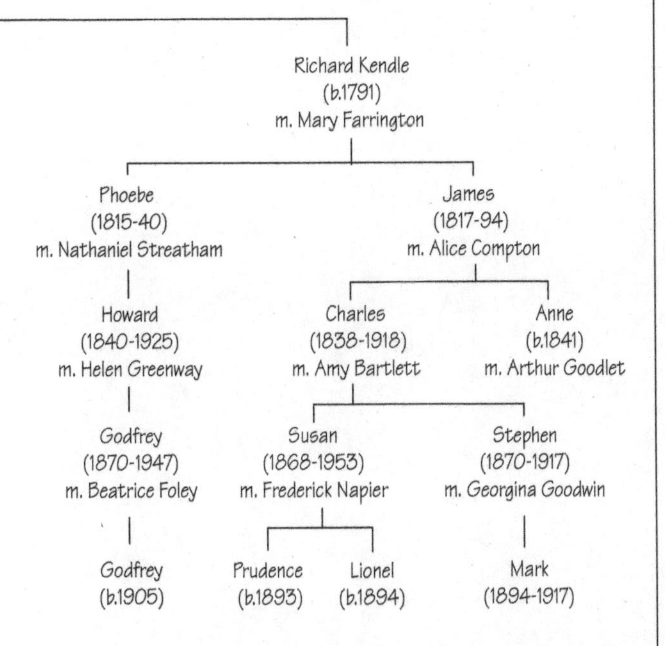

As researched by Rob Farinelli, 28 July 1999

Port Jackson I believe to be, without exception, the finest and most extensive harbour in the universe and at the same time the most secure, being safe from all the winds that blow. It is divided into a great number of coves, to which His Excellency has given different names. That on which the town is to be built is called Sydney Cove. It is one of the smallest in the harbour, but the most convenient, as ships of the greatest burden can with ease go into it, and heave out close to the shore. Trincomale, acknowledged to be one of the best harbours in the world, is by no means to be compared to it. In a word, Port Jackson would afford sufficient and safe anchorage for all the navies of Europe.

FROM THE RECORDS OF SURGEON GENERAL
JOHN WHITE, 1788

PROLOGUE

It was a moonless night, the night it happened. Which felt strange to young Thomas Kendall. The most successful forays for a warrener usually took place when the moon was full. Then the warrener could hunt out the burrows with ease, net the openings, send in the ferrets and set the lurcher on the rabbits, the dog, too, needing the light of the moon to pursue its quarry through the bracken.

But tonight Thomas and his father were not hunting rabbits. They were not wearing their warreners' smocks. And their lurcher, faithful old Jed, had been left at home.

'It be a bigger prize we hunt tonight, Thomas,' Jonathan Kendall had told his son, 'and you must say naught to your mother.'

Since the age of ten, Thomas had hunted with his father. He had learned how to press his ear to the earth and listen for the sounds of activity beneath the surface. He had learned to handle a shovel, to dig deep and fast, three feet in a matter of seconds, to get to the rabbit before the ferret moved off with it. And he had learned to huddle and gut his catch with swiftness and precision—the butcher was always pleased with the Kendall delivery. 'A pleasure to see,' he'd say, 'rabbits hulked proper—no mess, good and neat.'

Now, nine years on, young Thomas Kendall was a warrener as skilful as any on the Norfolk Brecklands. But this moonless night was different. As he crept along the banks of the Little Ouse River on the outskirts of the village of Thetford with his father and Bill 'Ferret' Bailey, young Thomas knew that a crime was about to be committed.

Beneath his ragged overcoat, tucked in the crook of his arm, was a large cloth bag. 'Hide it, lad, hide it,' his father had said as he handed it to him, and Thomas had noted both Ferret and his father stuffing similar bags inside their coats. 'Keep your eyes and ears open and your wits about you.'

They turned away from the riverbanks and cut through a grove of birch trees. Was it poaching they were up to, Thomas wondered. But they hadn't told him to bring his staff, he would need his staff if they were to go poaching.

He was distracted by a badger. Apparently oblivious to the presence of the men, it trotted along beside them, head down, hindquarters swaying flirtatiously side to side like an overweight coquette. Thomas liked badgers. After several moments, however, the badger paused to listen, body motionless, nose twitching, aware of danger present. They left the animal behind and Thomas's attention once more returned to the men. In the instant they broke out of the grove, he realised their intent.

The road to Norwich was to their left. In the darkness ahead was Burrell and Sons Works, and to their right, surrounded by lavish trees and gardens, was the home of the Widow Pettigrew. A brief thrill of shock ran through Thomas. So that was it! They were about to go thieving.

He said nothing as they straddled the low stone wall. He said nothing as they approached the house, keeping well under cover amongst the elms and oaks, maples and sycamores, but his mind was racing. This was a mad thing his father was contemplating. Was the widow at home tucked up in her bed? Were the servants in their quarters at the rear? There was no light visible, but that meant nothing. To rob this house was the action of a madman.

Thomas had few misgivings about the robbery itself, the widow could certainly afford to be relieved of some of her possessions, and if these were his father's instructions, Thomas was duty-bound to obey. But for the first time in his life he found himself questioning the wisdom of his father's actions.

'Saturday is the servants' night off,' Jonathan whispered, as if divining his son's thoughts, 'and the widow goes out to dine with friends in the village.'

'I've watched her,' Ferret added. 'She leaves at dusk and doesn't return till nigh on midnight.'

Prologue

They were around the side of the house where a large window-frame with small thick panes of glass was set into the knapped flintstone walls. Thomas watched with admiration as Ferret drew a cold chisel from his coat pocket and levered the window open with comparative ease. It was a skill born of long practice. Ferret was an expert, Thomas realised. Then, one by one, they clambered over the sill.

Inside the widow's house they crouched in the darkness while Jonathan struck the flint of his tinderbox and ignited three tallow candles. As the light filled the room each man stood, candle in hand, and looked about in silence.

On the mantel stood an ornate porcelain vase, several fine china ornaments and a pair of silver candlesticks. In a glass cabinet were a silver salver, a cutlery service and a set of goblets. A carved wooden chest in the corner was opened and revealed sets of linen and lace—sheets, towels, tablecloths and napkins.

'I told you so.' Ferret was the first to speak. He grinned greedily, his yellow teeth gleaming triumphant in the gloom. 'A haul fit for a king.' He crossed excitedly to the fireplace. 'Jonathan, look!'

On the table by the open hearth stood an ivory snuff box, a hand-carved humidor, a brass pipe-rack and a pewter jug with matching tankard. All preserved in memory of the widow's late husband who had died barely six months previously. Widow Pettigrew still wore black and, in church on Sundays, her mourning veil.

'She's even kept his coat,' Ferret cackled as he dropped his own threadbare garment and donned the heavy wool greatcoat which was draped over the armchair. 'A big man, old Pettigrew,' he added, the coat hanging off his scrawny frame.

'We'd best get to work.' Jonathan Kendall was already stuffing the silver candlesticks into his cloth bag. 'Thomas lad, you go upstairs. The widow's bedroom. It will be to the left.' Thomas hesitated. 'Ferret's kept watch these past three Saturdays,' Jonathan explained, 'he says that the upstairs light in the room on the left is the last to be snuffed at night.'

Thomas turned to do his father's bidding.

'Satin and lace and fine leather gloves fetch a good price,' Jonathan instructed. 'And feather bedding. And mind you check the dressing table,' he added, 'for that's where she'll be keeping her jewels and trinkets.'

Holding his candle aloft, Thomas stepped out into the main hall and up the stairway, each wooden step creaking alarmingly. Turning left at the top, he crept to the door at the end of the corridor and gently turned the knob.

As the door swung slowly inward, Thomas heard a noise. A noise he recognised. It was the noise he himself made when he was with Bertha in the little back room at the alehouse, passion mounting, nearing his release.

The light of the candle illuminated the room and he saw them. The naked man, buttocks pounding. Grunting. The woman pinioned beneath, invisible but for her bare parted legs high in the air and her hands clutching at the man's back.

The scene froze for one shocked instant. Then the grunting stopped. The man turned. The woman screamed. And Thomas dropped his candle and ran.

In the darkness he groped for the bannister railings and all but fell down the stairs. He heard the man in pursuit, saw the glow of candlelight ahead, thrust open the door to the lounge room and gasped, 'Run! Run!'

But Ferret and Jonathan had heard the commotion. Ferret was already halfway out the window and Jonathan, realising there was no time for all three of them to get out, grabbed his son. Together they pressed themselves against the wall by the door to the hall so when, with a howl of fury, the naked man appeared in the open doorway, he failed to see them in the half darkness.

'Now!' Jonathan yelled as the man entered the room, giving an angry growl at the sight of Ferret halfway out the window. Father and son dived into the hall and made for the main doors. 'Run, lad! Run!'

My God! Jonathan registered in the second he turned back to check that his son was close behind him. My God, but it's young Captain Pettigrew!

Fletcher Pettigrew also turned, momentarily indecisive as to whether to pursue the felons running for the main doors or the man escaping out through the window. Then he noticed that the man at the window was wearing his coat. With another furious roar he launched himself at Ferret.

Upstairs, in her bedroom, Mathilda Pettigrew clasped the fine linen bedsheets about her naked body and whimpered. She was not fearful for the safety of her lover. Fletcher Pettigrew was renowned for his skills in combat; the fact that he was naked and wore neither blade nor pistol was immaterial, fisticuffs would suffice. But did this mean that her secret was to be made public? Was the whole village about to know that she had been intimate with her dead husband's brother? That she had indeed been intimate with her husband's young brother for a full year before Ezekiel Pettigrew's tedious, lingering illness finally took him to his long-overdue grave?

They had been so careful, she and Fletcher. After Ezekiel's death, Mathilda had regularly visited her lover on Saturday nights when the servants were dismissed. She had dined publicly with friends, then gone to his rooms afterwards. And occasionally he had come to the house. On foot. After dark. Always entering through the servants' entrance at the rear. No-one had been any the wiser. And now, because of a common, grubby thief, her dreadful secret was sure to become public knowledge.

Mathilda Pettigrew had no cause for concern, however. When, three days later, Jonathan and Thomas Kendall, along with Bill Bailey, were arrested and held in Thetford Gaol to await sentence, the virtuous reputation of the Widow Pettigrew was of little concern to them. A crime such as theirs would demand one sentence and one sentence only. The gallows.

Their incarceration in the poky little gaolhouse on Market Street was not prolonged. Soon after their arrest the town of Thetford came alive, as it did these two special weeks of every year, for the Lent assizes.

People flocked from miles around. The local gentry returned to take up residence in their townhouses. Business was good. The hotels were full, copious amounts of ale and liquor were consumed, and numerous entertainments were held, the crowds delighting to the bawdy vaudeville and rustic classics performed at the theatre in White Hart Street. And throughout the festivities there was the constant excitement of men and women being sentenced to death, transportation or incarceration.

'General gaol delivery' poured into Thetford—waggons of prisoners transported from Norwich Castle Gaol for sentencing at the Lent assizes. Twenty-three in all this year.

Amongst the twelve prisoners charged with capital offences that

March of 1783 were Jonathan Kendall, his son Thomas and William Bailey.

Jonathan pleaded his son's case vociferously. 'The lad is only nineteen years of age, Your Honour,' he begged. 'He has never committed a crime. Indeed he knew nothing of our intention until the very night of the felony, I swear. The boy was simply obeying me, his father.' Jonathan's final plea was desperate and emotional. 'For the love of God, Your Honour, let him free!'

But his words fell on deaf ears and all three men were convicted and sentenced to the death penalty. A public hanging at Melford Common beside the road from London to Norwich.

'Where your bodies will remain for a time,' Judge Baron Eyre decreed, 'dangling from the hangman's rope, to serve as a lesson to passing travellers. And may the Lord have mercy on your souls.'

BOOK ONE

THE COLONY

Chapter One

'A night of debauchery it was.'

Thomas Kendall stood with his grandsons beside the massive sandstone walls of Fort Macquarie. He smiled as he looked out across Sydney Cove at the hustle and the bustle of pedestrians and soldiers and horse-drawn vehicles in the dusty streets of the busy town. It hadn't always been like that. Thomas could still see it as it had been all those years ago. Barren and unforgiving.

'Debauchery the likes of which will never be seen again, I swear, that night they brought the women convicts ashore.'

At sixty-five, Thomas preferred to view the old days with a sense of humour. It was more comfortable than dwelling on the grim realities of the past.

After languishing for a month in Thetford Gaol, young Thomas Kendall had escaped the hangman's noose only days before the execution of his father and Ferret Bailey. On the grounds of his youth, Judge Eyre had granted the lad a last-minute reprieve, and Thomas's sentence had been commuted to transportation, for a period of seven years.

He was transferred to Norwich to await his transportation, and there, for three long years, Thomas had withstood the brutality, squalor and depravity of Norwich Castle Gaol. Far from breaking his spirit, however, it had moulded him. From a simple, unquestioning lad into a resilient and resourceful young man, strong in mind and body. A man whom others learned to respect.

'The ships were hove to in the cove and the longboats collected the women and pulled in ashore yonder.' The old man pointed towards the Tank Stream on the western side of the bay. 'The livestock had been landed first, mind; cattle being more important than convict women. They'd landed the livestock a good ten days or so before, right here on this very point. They called it Cattle Point then. Course the fort wasn't here. Or the town. Nothing was here. Just scrawny trees that seemed to grow, God knew how, out of barren rock. And tents of course. By the time they brought the women convicts ashore there was a whole township of tents.

'Dressed in their finery, those women were,' Thomas continued, painting the picture for his grandsons, particularly young James who was enthralled. Unlike his cousin, William, James had never heard his grandfather's stories before. 'Leastways, they were pretending it was finery. Makeshift ribbons and bows they had in their hair. Primped and preened and saucy as could be. Excited too, every one of them, at the prospect of feeling solid land beneath their feet. We men had been living ashore for a week or more, see, clearing the land and setting up camp. But the women were hungry for the feel of the earth. Even the earth of that wretched God-forsaken wilderness, for it was a wilderness all right. Barren and hostile and downright fearsome.'

Thomas could still smell the fear of those early days, the fear of the unknown. He could remember the repugnance each and every one of the men had felt for the alien life that buzzed and crawled and slithered about them. The flies and spiders and snakes. And the birds. The demon birds. Some that screeched like banshees, others that cackled with the laughter of the devil himself, all of them chilling a man's blood each dusk and dawn.

Nowadays, of course, the cockatoos and kookaburras were considered amongst the more charming elements of the colony. William and James would laugh, Thomas realised, if he told them that insects and birds had been perceived as objects of terror by the hardened criminals of the first fleet. His grandsons were not to know that fear born of the unknown was the worst kind of fear to a lonely man in a foreign land.

'The soldiers and the sailors were accustomed to fearsome foreign parts,' he explained, 'but we who'd come, albeit in chains, from the civilised mother country found this to be a dreadful place.'

Seventeen-year-old William nudged his younger cousin. He'd told James about the old man's stories and James, wide-eyed with fascination, wasn't disappointed. James had met his grandfather on only one previous occasion, that he could remember anyway, and then it was in the company of his mother who refused to allow any discussion of her father-in-law's convict past.

The old man smiled again. It was easy, from his position of prosperity and comfort, to smile back down the years. For Thomas this was no longer a dreadful place. He looked at the boats in the bay. He could see one of his very own barges ferrying its load of passengers and provisions across the harbour to the village on the northern point. He looked at the thriving township; the five-storey-high Waterloo warehouse, the marketplace where the cries of the cockney seafood vendors rose above the bustle of human activity; he looked at George Street on the far side of the cove, the commercial centre of Sydney Town with its magnificent, wide-verandahed post office, its shops and taverns and cottages; at the traffic of the dusty streets, the men on horseback, the women in gigs and phaetons, the working horses and drays. And, amongst the endless procession, a gang of convicts being led to work at the stone quarries. Despondent, despairing. New arrivals, Thomas thought, and he wished them well.

He glanced out at the peak of the western point where the lighthouse stood. The latest allotment of land he had purchased was not far from the lighthouse. Soon he would be able to see his new cottage from here, high up there on the peak, overlooking the harbour and the whole of Sydney Town. Thomas felt proud. He had helped build this place, and this place, in return, had been good to him. Thomas loved Sydney Town with a fierce and personal pride.

'Those who had religion swore that God had visited his wrath upon us sinners that night.' Thomas turned to his grandsons, both of whom were waiting breathlessly for him to continue. 'For no sooner had the women's feet touched the soil of Sydney Cove than an almighty storm broke out. There was a crack like Satan's whip, an angry flash of gold, and in an instant the giant tree which stood in the very centre of the camp was split in two. It killed five sheep and a pig, which was a terrible thing in those days, livestock being highly valuable for future breeding.'

James nodded encouragingly. He wasn't really interested in the value of livestock. 'What about the people? Were any of the people killed?'

'Not by the storm they weren't. But there were many who met with floggings as a result of that night, and the floggings nigh on killed them. It's a wonder that some didn't meet the hangman's noose. No-one heeded the law, you see. There was brawling and riots and fornication throughout the camp; and whilst most were satisfying their lust, there were those who used the debauchery of the night as a cover for theft. And theft in those days,' Thomas added seriously, 'was punishable by hanging.'

'What about the soldiers?' James asked breathlessly. 'Didn't the soldiers try and stop it?'

'The soldiers were as lustful as the convicts,' Thomas declared. 'The soldiers were in the women's tents and the women were in the soldiers' tents and the sailors had all gone back to the ships to get drunk. The captains were relieved that the women were no longer their responsibility, see, for they had to pay a heavy penalty if a convict went missing. So they allowed the men grog and, above the thunder and the lightning, we could hear those sailors, drunk as lords, singing and carousing all through the night. Oh I tell you lads, everyone was a sinner that night.'

'What were you doing, Grandpa?'

William had tried to catch his cousin's eye, tried to warn him not to ask that question. The old man might have raved on for hours about rape and fornication, which was exactly what the boys wanted, had he not been asked about his own involvement. Too late.

'Me?' The mischievous smile faded and Thomas seemed a little saddened himself to be halted midstream. 'Ah, not for me the unbridled lust.'

James glanced at his cousin and William gave a wry shrug.

'How old are you, James?' Thomas asked, noting the brief exchange. 'I see you so little I lose track of your age.'

'Thirteen.'

'Well, it'll not be too long before you're a man. The day will come when you'll know women and lustful feelings.'

James flushed with the secret knowledge that he couldn't take his eyes from women's breasts, even his own mother's at times.

Thomas noticed the reaction and was sensitive enough not to make some ribald remark. James was a shy boy, he could tell, a lonely boy, and he was suffering the agonising guilt of pubescence. Well of course that mother of his wouldn't help. Surely Richard could be more of a confidant to his son though, Thomas thought critically. But then, Richard too was under the blasted woman's thumb.

'Don't misunderstand me, lad, I was a lustful young man myself in those days, as lustful as any that stormy night. The desire between men and women is as natural as breathing, young James, and nothing to be ashamed of, but the abandonment of that night meant nothing to me for, you see, I had my Anne.'

It had been in the third year of his incarceration in Norwich Castle Gaol that young Thomas Kendall had met Anne Simpson. Like him, Anne had escaped the death penalty due to her youth: she too had been nineteen years old when convicted of theft. But unlike Thomas, Anne had been no novice.

'Just the first time I got caught is all,' she openly admitted. 'Dear God in heaven, if they knew but a quarter of the thieving I've done, I'd have met the hangman long ago.'

She was a bold girl with a gypsy's face. Sensuous. Features too overgenerous to be beautiful, but wild hair and a mouth that beckoned. Thomas was smitten.

Both sexes were housed at the gaol and, discipline being a mixture of brutality and laxity, fornication was not uncommon. In fact, over the years many a child had been born as a result of couplings within the prison confines.

The cells having been built against the old walls of the roofless and dilapidated castle keep, it was not long before Thomas found a weak spot in the wall to the women's quarters. It didn't take him long to dislodge enough stone and dirt to wriggle his way through—as others had done before him—and, once there, his copulation with Anne was fast, fierce and lustful.

Mindless of the women around them, some urging them on, some fondling each other, some hissing obscenities and masturbating, Thomas and Anne fed on each other's passion. They soared above the prison walls, free of the squalor and confinement and, when they were spent, they kissed and laughed and made ribald comments to the others who were by then grumbling with envy and discontent.

When the news of imminent transportation finally spread throughout the gaol, Thomas and Anne prayed that they would be amongst those sent to a life in the colony of New South Wales.

Feeling amongst the other prisoners was uncertain. America having won its independence, the transportation was to be to the newly discovered south land. Half the world away. Surely it was better to serve out one's time in the old country, many said. The south land was a heathen place, hardly a land of opportunity like America.

But Thomas felt differently. 'They call it New South Wales, Anne,' he said. 'Just think, a whole new country! A whole new life!'

The union of Thomas Kendall and Anne Simpson had developed far beyond mere lustful congress. Together they nurtured each other's hopes and shared each other's strengths and, in the barren, dank gloom which was Norwich Castle Gaol, a genuine love had grown between them.

When they found that they were not only to be transported to New South Wales but aboard the very same ship as well, it was truly as if the gods had smiled upon them. And when Anne announced that she was with child, it seemed all the good fortune in the world had been laid at their feet.

'Ah, my Anne,' the old man murmured, unaware that his grandsons were waiting, spellbound, for the next instalment of the orgy. 'How it felt to hold her once more.' He could see her now, at the bow of the longboat, their child in her arms, the child he'd felt in her swollen belly but had never seen. He could feel Anne's lips against his and the softness of the baby's cheek against the stubble of his own. 'I'd not seen her since they'd transferred her from the *Friendship* to the *Charlotte* in Cape Town,' he said as he registered the boys' attention. 'Three long months it had been.'

Thomas had worried about Anne's condition and the hardship of the voyage, but she would have none of it. 'It's only a baby, Thomas, women bring babies into the world every day of the week.'

But it was hard. Thomas knew that it was hard. When the ship bucketed and rolled and the child in Anne's belly kicked, he would watch her try to hold down the victuals that would feed her unborn baby. He would help her press her hand to her mouth and watch as she tried to swallow her vomit.

When the fleet reached Cape Town and changes were made to accommodate the livestock boarded at this, their last port before Botany Bay, Anne and several other women were transferred to the *Charlotte*. Anne was near her time and Thomas, fearing for her safety, was all for demanding he be transferred with her, or they be offloaded to await the birth of the child. Again, Anne would not hear of it.

'You have earned the trust of the officers and the crew, Thomas,' she said. 'I have seen it. We can use this to our advantage in the colony; you must not cause trouble now.

'Listen,' she had insisted as he'd tried to argue, 'when my time comes I will be better attended by the women aboard the *Charlotte*.' Then she had kissed him. 'I'll see you in Botany Bay, my love, with a baby in my arms.'

But he didn't see her in Botany Bay. He didn't see her until Wednesday the 6th of February 1788, when the female convicts were finally landed on the shores of Port Jackson. It was then that Thomas saw his Anne, and, as she'd promised, she held their baby daughter in her arms.

The old man stood silent as he recalled their reunion that night they'd brought the women ashore. His coupling with Anne in the corner of the tent had been quiet, intense, oblivious to the raging storm and the threshing bodies about them. One week later, he and Anne, along with several other couples, had been the first convicts to be married by the Reverend Richard Johnson. As they had made their mark in the Register of Marriages, being able neither to read nor write, Thomas had whispered, 'This is just the beginning, girl, just the beginning.' The old man's eyes filled with tears as he recalled his joy that day.

James and William exchanged a glance but remained silent, respectful of the old man's reverie; they knew how much Grandpa Thomas missed his wife.

James had never met his grandmother, although she had died only four years ago, but William remembered Anne clearly. Having been brought up on their father Matthew's market gardens on the Surry Hills, a walkable distance from Thomas's house in the centre of town, William and his younger sister Hannah had seen a great deal of their grandparents. William remembered Anne as an unconventional old woman who, despite her physical frailty, was never shy of speaking her mind. He and Hannah had been very fond of Grandma Anne.

It was time to change the conversation, William decided. He didn't like to see his grandfather saddened by painful memories.

'May we go to Rushcutters Bay, Grandpa Thomas?' he asked. 'May we go and see Wolawara?'

Thomas knew why William was changing the subject and he appreciated the boy's good intentions. Of course the lad didn't realise that to think of Anne was never painful. The precious bitter-sweetness of her memory was a joy to Thomas always. He would treasure the taste and the touch and the smell of his wife until he drew his very last breath.

'Very well.' Thomas made a quick decision, knowing it would wreak havoc with his son and daughter-in-law. 'We shall go and see Wolawara.' It was time to extend young James's education. God alone knew when that wretched mother of his would once again allow the boy the company of his grandfather.

'I must warn you, James,' he said solemnly as they walked across the Government Domain towards Farm Cove, 'that Wolawara and his family are my friends. They are not oddities for you to boast of to your friends at school.'

'Yes, Grandpa Thomas.'

James couldn't believe his luck. He was going to meet Wolawara. Even his cousins, William and Hannah, didn't know the true story of Grandpa Thomas and Wolawara. The relationship between the two men was shrouded in mystery.

Several weeks previously, on a visit to James's family home in Parramatta, William and Hannah had boasted that Grandfather Thomas was best friends with an Aborigine.

'You must not listen to such nonsense,' James's mother had said when his cousins had departed. 'Your grandfather may have some passing acquaintance with the black servant of one of his friends or, knowing your grandfather, even one of the beggars in the streets of Sydney Town, but he is not "friends" with a native. No-one is "friends" with a native.'

Mary, aware of the presence of her husband Richard, knew she must soften her tone, but mentally she cursed the old man. Everything about her father-in-law grated with Mary. His common rural accent, his scruffy ill-kempt beard, his baggy breeches and shirtsleeves.

Thomas had no regard for personal appearances and was quite happy to wander about jacketless, which Mary considered disgraceful. He was a wealthy, successful man, he had a social position to uphold. But far more than his manner of speech and dress, it was the old man's pride in his ignoble past which Mary most abhorred.

'Grandfather Thomas is lonely, my dear,' she said as gently as she could, 'particularly since Grandmother Anne passed away, and he romanticises the past as if it were something of which to be proud.' She couldn't help it, the bite of disapproval returned to her tone. 'Believe me, it is not, James. It is a shameful thing.'

'Don't turn the boy against his grandfather, Mary.' Richard's remonstration was mild but it was there. He rarely questioned his wife, leaving the governing of the household and the upbringing of their two children in her capable hands. He agreed that it was only right, for the sake of the children, to distance themselves from his father's past; he had even agreed, ten years previously, to her suggestion that they change the spelling of their name to Kendle so it could not be traced to the shameful records of those who had arrived in the colony in chains. But Richard would not have his wife malign his father of whom he was not only fond, but to whom he was deeply grateful for the assistance given him upon his marriage. Indeed, without the family business and the lands at Parramatta which Thomas had transferred to his son's name, it was doubtful Mary's family would have agreed to the marriage at all. 'My father is a good man,' Richard insisted, 'and we owe him a great deal.'

'I am not turning the boy against his grandfather,' Mary replied a little tightly, 'and I am fully aware of the debt we owe, Thomas.'

There the discussion ended and, as usual, Mary had the last word.

But several weeks later Richard surprised her by insisting that James and his older sister, Phoebe, accompany her on a shopping expedition to Sydney Town.

'They are to meet their grandfather,' Richard announced. 'I must insist upon it, Mary.' He sensed that she was about to argue the case. 'They barely know him, it is not right.'

Mary wondered momentarily whether she should do battle, but reluctantly decided against it. Damn the old man, she thought.

If Mary Kendle could have had her way, her children would remain forever in Parramatta, and all ties with the Kendall side of the family would be severed. It was nothing personal, but for the good of her children's future they must be brought up as exclusives, of free British stock. Not only was their paternal grandfather an ex-convict, he believed in equality. Thomas Kendall maintained that prisoners who had served their sentences, and emancipists such as himself who through good conduct had been prematurely granted pardon, should be openly and immediately accepted into respectable society. Worse still, he believed in equality for the ticket-of-leavers, those convicts who had been granted a certificate from the Governor entitling them to seek their own employment and living quarters. The fact that applicants for a ticket of leave required a long record of exemplary behaviour, character references, letters of surety, meant little to the exclusivists. Ticket-of-leavers were still convicts. They were still serving their sentences, and it was a crime against society that they should be entitled to mingle freely.

To many in the colony, the views of Thomas Kendall and his ilk were outrageous and dangerous, and although Mary swore she bore Thomas himself no ill will, she was protective of her children and thoroughly convinced that no good could come of their connection with their grandfather.

Mary would allow her husband to have his way. Just this once. Her acquiescence would please him and maintain the peace, and a visit to the old man could do little harm, so long as the children were not left alone in his company. But she determined that such visits were not to become a habit.

'I shall not be accompanying you, my dear,' Richard announced to her further annoyance. 'The purchase of dresses and bonnets does not interest me as it does you and Phoebe. Besides,' he added, flashing her his most winning smile, 'I would be of little use, my taste is lamentable.'

Always elegantly attired, Richard's dress sense was faultless, and he knew it, just as he knew that his charm, as usual, would have the desired effect.

Mary laughed. 'You are shamelessly obvious, Richard.'

'Of course I am my dear. I am afraid I really am too busy to accompany you however,' he apologised, 'and I see Father and Matthew regularly on business trips to town. You don't mind *too* much do you?'

'I suppose I have no option.'

'And you will enjoy Emily's company,' he added, 'you always do.'

Richard had never quite been able to comprehend Mary's comfortable relationship with his brother's wife, they were such opposites. Not that Richard himself disliked Emily, far from it. Indeed, he found her an extremely attractive woman, in an untidy way—most men did. With little regard for convention or fashion, Emily prattled disarmingly, apparently unaware of her sensuality. In the early years of Matthew's marriage, Richard had even felt a little envious of his older brother. The foolishness of youth, he now thought, as he looked at his wife with comfortable affection. He had made a far finer match than his brother: Mary came from impeccable stock and was an exemplary wife and mother.

He winked at his daughter Phoebe. 'You and Hannah can play fine young ladies and have cakes at the teahouse in George Street.'

Fifteen-year-old Phoebe, pretty, fragile, her father's pride and joy, smiled excitedly. She liked her cousin. Despite the fact that Hannah was six months her junior, Phoebe deeply admired and envied her. There was a wild streak in Hannah.

And who exactly will be looking after my son, Mary wondered. The old man? She looked steadily back at her husband, once more considering battle, but Richard continued, apparently oblivious, 'And James will have William for company.' Before his wife could contest the arrangement, he added with a note of finality, 'The lad needs male companionship, my dear. Father and Matthew will entertain the boys whilst you do your shopping.' For once, it was Richard who had the last word.

The family gathering in Thomas's front parlour went smoothly enough. Matthew had not yet arrived, but to Mary's relief, the old man's conversation was perfectly harmless. They chatted about the weather and commented on the stirring sounds of the drums and fife which could be heard from the nearby garrison.

By the time she and Emily, together with their daughters, were preparing to take their leave, however, Mary was feeling distinctly agitated. Matthew had still not arrived.

'Matthew was to look after James and William,' she said rather pointedly to her sister-in-law.

'Oh good heavens no,' Emily declared, 'it's crop planting. He's far too busy. As a matter of fact, I had quite a time of it persuading him to allow William the day with his cousin. Poor Matthew needs all the hands he can get at the moment, particularly as he refuses to accept the government's offer of convict labour.'

'Why?' Mary was momentarily distracted from her dilemma. 'If the government sees fit to support the market gardeners, why in heaven's name should Matthew refuse cheap labour?'

'He is of the opinion that convict labour should be employed solely by the government,' Emily replied. She pointed a gloved finger forcefully at the ceiling, in imitation of Matthew in full tirade. '"It is up to the free settlers to provide work for the ticket-of-leavers and those who have served their sentences."' She punched the air with her fist. '"They are in need of employment to set themselves up in their new lives, and it is our bounden duty to assist them."' Emily smiled about at the assembled company, proud of her performance and of her husband.

'He's a good man, Matthew,' Thomas nodded approvingly.

It was the sort of conversation Mary did not wish to encourage in the presence of her children. 'But James and William . . .' she said, 'who will look after them?'

'I'm seventeen, Aunt Mary,' William laughed. 'I'm perfectly capable of showing James the sights.'

It was then that Thomas chimed in. 'I shall look after the lads, Mary,' he said with all the joviality of a favourite father-in-law. 'We shall go for a walk, just the three of us.'

The look of horror on Mary's face gave Thomas a rush of perverse pleasure. He despised the beliefs of Mary and her fellow exclusivists. In a new colonial society, the evils of class distinction should have been left behind in the old country. The fact that social injustice and racial intolerance abounded in a new land where equality should have free reign upset him deeply.

His smile was as benign as he could make it, which further irked Mary. 'We shall have a grand day, shan't we, lads?'

'Oh please may I come with you, Grandpa Thomas?' It was fifteen-year-old Hannah, the old man's unashamed favourite. Thomas glanced hopefully at Emily who shook her head and laughed.

'No, my darling, you may not.'

Emily had told Hannah as much before they'd left for Thomas's house. 'I don't want to go shopping with Aunt Mary,' the girl had said, 'she fusses so.' Emily had stated emphatically that Hannah was to accompany them, but she had known that her daughter would try again. Hannah was incorrigible.

'You can see Grandpa Thomas any time you wish, Hannah, you must let the boys have a day with him on their own. They can talk men's talk.' Emily winked at Thomas. 'Whatever that is.'

Mary turned her horrified gaze to her sister-in-law, but Emily was utterly oblivious to it. 'Now come along, Mary, the sooner we complete our shopping the sooner we can have tea and cakes and I am eager to hear all the gossip.' It was true the bond between the women was Mary's chatter, mostly slanderous, about the Parramatta landed gentry and her husband's wealthy business associates. Mary had the freedom of knowing that the stories would never get back to Richard's influential friends, and Emily the novelty of hearing people spoken of in a way no farming person on the Surry Hills would ever speak of their neighbour.

There was little Mary could do, but at the door she hissed to the old man, 'You are not to fill James's head with your nonsense, Thomas; he has led a sheltered life.'

It was then that Thomas had decided to tell the boys whatever stories they wanted to hear. The bawdier, the gorier, the better.

'You lads go on ahead,' he said as they walked through the Botanic Garden, 'I shall keep my own pace. And take your jacket off, James, 'tis far too hot to be wearing a jacket.'

He watched as the boy hesitated then took off his smart checked jacket and carefully folded it over his arm. Mary obviously didn't like her son being seen in public in his vest and shirtsleeves. He looked so vulnerable, Thomas thought, beside his older cousin. William, bareheaded, sleeves rolled up to his elbows, forearms well muscled and brown from toil in the sun, already had the body of a strong man. Like his father, Matthew. Both boys reminded Thomas of his sons, but James painfully so. James, awkward in his smart felt hat with its checked ribbon band matching his jacket, could have been Richard at the same age. Richard had always been painfully self-conscious, even as a boy.

Much as Thomas wanted to blame his daughter-in-law for the hurt his son had done him, he knew that Richard was equally at fault. Richard was too easily dictated to, by both society and his wife—which were much the same thing, Thomas thought grimly. To him, Mary typified the ignorance and bigotry of the British middle class.

Richard Kendall's denial of his family name had been one of the cruellest blows Thomas had ever been dealt. Crueller than his banishment from his mother country, for he had paid for his crime and embraced his new life. But to what crime did he owe his son's denial?

'Kendle sounds the same, Father,' Richard had said, 'so we are not really *changing* the name as such, merely the spelling. You cannot expect us to emblazon a convict name in gilt lettering on the sides of our coaches, it is simply not good business.' Richard misinterpreted his father's silence as misunderstanding. 'The coach service from Sydney Town to Parramatta is becoming famous,' he continued. 'Surely you must admit we need a name which can be respected.'

Nothing more was said on the subject, but it broke Thomas's heart.

Anne tried to soften the blow. 'Richard loves you dearly, Thomas; he intends no hurt.' And when Thomas refused to be mollified, she continued in her characteristically direct fashion. 'As his mother I should perhaps not say it, but Richard is a weak man. He always has been. He does not have your strength, my love, neither yours nor Matthew's. It is why I have always approved of his marriage; it is why I insisted you sign over the coach business and some of the Parramatta lands to him.' By now she had Thomas's undivided attention; in fact, his jaw was agape.

'Much as you may dislike Mary and much as we may both disagree with her views,' Anne continued, 'she is a strong young woman and Richard needs such strength. He's a superficial man with little depth of character, and I do not believe for one moment that he would survive with a weak wife.'

Thomas had finally found his voice. 'You always told me he was sensitive.'

'Yes, that is what I told you.' She had given him one of her impish smiles and kissed him. 'So do not let the weakness of his actions break your heart, my love, for that is all they are, the actions of a weak man. Forgive him.'

Try as he might, however, Thomas had not been able to find it in himself to forgive Richard, and from that day on he had seen his son through different eyes.

The old man and his grandsons left the mudflats of Woolloomooloo Bay behind them and started to climb the Darlinghurst Hill. The windmills which lined the Darlinghurst Ridge were picturesque, contributing to the description of Sydney as a town of windmills. Some of wood, some of stone, some operated manually, some mechanically, the windmills endlessly churned out the flour for a colony chronically short of adequate supplies.

As they walked, Thomas wondered whether young James was weak like his father. If so, how long would it take before self-consciousness became affectation, before social decree outweighed matters of principle? Not long, Thomas thought, living under the same roof as that woman. Well, today young James Kendle would learn a thing or two, the old man would make thoroughly sure of that.

Upon reaching Rushcutters Bay, Thomas led his grandsons beside the small stream which ran down to the harbour until it was lost in the swamp of rushes beside the bay. It was here, towards the eastern end of the cove, that Wolawara and his family lived in their hut amongst the reeds and spinneys.

They were at the edge of the clearing, twenty yards or so from the hut, when they were distracted by a rustling noise in a clump of nearby bushes. As they turned to investigate, a man leapt out at them with such swiftness and aggression that James gave an involuntary cry of alarm. Instinct told him to run, but Thomas and William were standing their ground, so the boy stifled his fear and edged closer to his grandfather instead.

The man rolled his eyes and, in the blackness of his face, the whites of his pupils shone with a madness that terrified James. Twice he sprang towards them, emitting a growl from the back of his throat like an animal intimidating its prey.

Thomas appeared unmoved and William, after a nervous glance at his grandfather, continued to stand his ground. James's feet were rooted to the spot; he doubted whether he could have run if he'd tried.

The man changed his tactics. Slowly he started to prance about them, knees bent, arms extended, palms upward, in a clumsy, uncoordinated dance. He was mumbling now, although the words were incoherent. And his manner was no longer aggressive, his eyes no longer mad. In his ragged shirt and breeches, and stinking of rum, he was in fact a pitiful figure.

'Massa, gim me rum. Rum merry good.'

The fear in James subsided. So this was Wolawara, he thought with a surge of disappointment. His mother had been right after all. Grandfather Thomas's native friend was no more than a drunken beggar.

'Good day, Yenerah,' Thomas said, although he made no move to give the man money.

The Aborigine did not heed the greeting, continuing to importune with his parody of a dance. 'Rum make me drunk like a gemmen. Rum merry good.'

'*Wuruwuru*!' The voice, with an angry edge, was one of authority, and the drunken man turned to face the figure which had appeared at the door of the hut. They all did. An imposing Aboriginal man in a red soldier's coat stood before them. In his middle sixties, grey-bearded and stern, he was not a big man, either in height or build, but there was a command about him which was impressive.

'*Wuruwuru*!' he repeated. '*Dadadadadadadada*!'

The drunken man stared back for a second, then turned his gaze to the ground. He scuffed his bare feet in the dirt for a moment or so. '*Yanu, yanu*,' he muttered, before shuffling pathetically off into the bushes.

There was silence as they all watched him go.

'Stay here,' Thomas muttered to the boys, then he walked up to the hut and offered his hand to the man in the red coat.

'Wolawara, *gamaradu*,' he said. The two men shook hands.

'*Ngandu*, Thomas,' Wolawara said, '*Ngandu*,' and there was an infinite sadness in his voice.

'No harm is done,' Thomas replied. '*Gamarada, gay, gay*.'

James watched, awestruck. 'Grandpa Thomas is speaking his language,' he whispered to William. Never before had James heard a white man talk to a native in anything other than New South Wales pidgin English. 'I've never seen anyone do that before.'

'And you never will again,' William replied quietly with obvious pride. 'It is the native tongue of the Gadigal people, a clan of the Dharug, Grandpa told me so.'

Ignoring the boys, the two men squatted on the ground beside the hut.

'We must stay here until we are asked to join them,' William instructed. 'And you are to tell no-one that Grandpa Thomas speaks their tongue, James. No-one. Only Hannah and I know, and now that he has let you into the secret, you must never breathe a word.'

James nodded, still staring, eyes like saucers, at his grandfather squatting in the dirt with Wolawara.

Thomas had been dismayed to witness the degradation of his old friend's son. Yenerah was Wolawara's only remaining boy, his other two having died of the smallpox many years previously.

It must be breaking the man's heart, Thomas thought; but recognising Wolawara's shame, he did not pursue the subject.

'I have not come to you for some time, Wolawara, but when I dream you are there.'

'When I dream you are there, Thomas.'

The men conversed in a mixture of pidgin and Dharug. These days it was rare for even Wolawara himself to converse purely in the native tongue of the Gadigal people. The language was dying out and, to his shame, much as he encouraged them, his own grandchildren spoke little Dharug.

'Wiriwa, she is well?' Thomas asked.

Wolawara nodded. 'Wiriwa, come!' he called to his wife. 'Thomas our friend is here.'

Wiriwa appeared at the door of the hut. She was dressed in a white cotton garment and carried an infant on one hip, her latest grandchild. She had known Thomas was there and had been waiting for her husband's call.

'*Gumal*, Wiriwa,' Thomas said. He smiled his greeting but did not rise.

Wiriwa smiled in return and nodded shyly before sitting on the ground at the opposite side of the entrance to the hut. She remained silently rocking her sleeping grandchild in her arms, pleased that she had been called into the presence of the men.

Thomas leaned forward and fingered the tattered lapel of Wolawara's coat. 'You have a jacket of fire,' he said. It was a personal observation and they both knew it. Wolawara had always loved the colours of fire. In Thomas's mind an image flashed briefly. The image of an excited young Aborigine with his new headband of yellow and red. '*Guwiyang*,' the young man was saying. '*Guwiyang*.'

Wolawara, pleased by the comment and proud of his new attire, explained that his daughter, who now served a military man's family, had brought home several articles of the soldier's old uniforms.

'And from his wife, dresses. Dresses white like the summer clouds for Wiriwa,' he added.

Wiriwa touched the lace yoke of her dress, which in actuality was a nightgown, and smiled back.

Emboldened by the fact that his grandmother and baby brother had been called to the company of the men, a ten-year-old boy had crept to the door of the hut. He had intended waiting until he too was called, but he had noticed William and James standing patiently at the edge of the clearing and couldn't resist.

Turumbah knew better than to run to the boys and make their acquaintance. His grandfather's rules regarding the meeting of menfolk were strict. But Turumbah also knew that he was his grandfather's favourite and that, if he pretended a patience he didn't have, his grandfather would eventually give in. He sidled out the door.

William and James watched as the boy crept up behind Wolawara. He was dressed in baggy trousers cut off above the knee and held up at the waist by twine from which hung several implements. He stood just behind his grandfather and gave them both a cheeky grin, but William nudged James, warning him not to react.

Fully aware of his grandson's presence, Wolawara continued his discussion with Thomas.

'Wiriwa holds my new grandson,' he boasted proudly and Wiriwa nodded once more, acknowledging the child as if he were her own. 'Four grandsons I now have. And three granddaughters.'

Thomas's eyes flickered to Turumbah who was shuffling in the sand behind his grandfather. The two men exchanged a smile.

'Two of my grandsons are now grown to manhood,' Wolawara continued. 'The fourth, I am not sure where he might be. Shall I call for him, Thomas?'

Thomas appeared to deliberate for a moment before agreeing. 'Yes. Call for him, Wolawara.'

Wolawara turned and pretended surprise as he bumped into the bare knees of his grandson.

'Ah, Turumbah. You remember our friend Thomas?' Turumbah nodded, but his eyes kept darting towards William and James. Particularly young James whose hat was becoming more fascinating by the second.

'Five years it has been,' Thomas said. 'You were a boy when last we met, Turumbah, now you are nearly a man.'

The boy shuffled about impatiently. When would the formalities be over? When could he play? He wanted to talk to the boy with the hat.

'These are your grandsons.' Wolawara indicated William and James. 'One I have not met.' It was the first time Wolawara had acknowledged the presence of the boys standing immobile at the edge of the clearing. 'They have fine manners,' he said approvingly, then glanced up at Turumbah. Turumbah, however, appeared not to have heard the admonishment, he was too busy grinning at the boys.

'May I greet your grandsons?' Wolawara asked.

'They would be honoured,' Thomas replied, and beckoned the boys to come forward.

After formal greetings were made in pidgin English and after much shaking of hands, it was finally time for Turumbah's introduction.

'Turumbah, this is Grandson William, and this is Grandson James,' Thomas said.

'Gran'sun William, Gran'sun James,' Turumbah repeated. There was more shaking of hands, and the boys were told they could go and play. Turumbah let out a whoop of excitement and started to skip about, until a sharp word of command from Wiriwa stopped him in his tracks.

All heads turned to her, it was the first time she had spoken. Her eyes met Wolawara's. She held his glance for a second or two until he nodded, then she returned her attention to the baby who had awoken at the sound of her voice.

'You are not to swim, Turumbah,' Wolawara commanded. The boy was about to argue back, but his grandfather continued, 'You have been sick, your grandmother says you are not to swim.' It was obvious that, for all her apparent compliance, it was Wiriwa's word that was law when it came to the health of the children.

Turumbah did not appear too upset. Instead, he grabbed James by the hand and dragged him in the opposite direction of the water. 'Gran'sun James come. Come, Gran'sun James.'

James was unaccustomed to such boisterous familiarity, but there was something so cheeky and likeable about Turumbah that it seemed pointless to resist. William followed after them with a regretful glance over his shoulder. He had hoped that he might be invited to join the men, but they were once more in deep conversation and took no note of the boys' departure.

'It was the ...' Wolawara was saying, searching for the word, '... the croup. Deep in his chest. Another white man's sickness.'

Talk of Turumbah's recent illness led Wolawara to discuss the plight of his people. He lowered his voice so that even Wiriwa might not hear but, intuitively, she knew what her husband was saying. Wolawara told Thomas that he should not have stayed so long, that he should have left Eora many years ago, as so many of his clan had. He should have fled inland to escape the white man's drink and disease.

Eora was the Dharug name for the coastal area which was the home of the Gadigal people, and, like many, Wolawara had found it hard to leave the waterways of his ancestors. 'We belong to the sea and to the rivers,' he had said when talk of leaving had first started. 'We are water people. It is wrong to take our families into the arid land.' And his stubbornness, he admitted now, had resulted in the deaths of two sons and a daughter. As for Yenerah, his last remaining son ...

The admission was difficult and Wolawara's gaze remained fixed on the ground. 'With your own eyes you have seen him, Thomas. He is possessed. Once a fine young man, now he begs in the streets for the rum to feed his demons.'

Wolawara raised his head and, behind the guilt in his eyes, was an angry resolve. 'This is not the fate which will befall my grandchildren. While there is strength enough left in this old man, it is Wolawara who must save them.'

Thomas paused for a moment before asking, 'What will you do?' He glanced briefly at Wiriwa who was listening intently for the answer.

'We will leave Eora.'

It was obvious from the fleeting shock visible in Wiriwa's eyes that Wolawara had not discussed his decision with her.

Thomas looked from one to the other. Wolawara and Wiriwa are old, he thought. Like me, they are old. Now was not the time for them to leave the home of their ancestors.

He said nothing. But, as Wolawara continued to talk, the seed of a plan germinated in the mind of Thomas Kendall.

'I've never seen anyone swim like that.'

James and William were lost in admiration as they stood watching young Turumbah's naked body cut through the water like a dolphin. One minute the boy had been submerged, the next he had leapt to the surface, emitted a squeal and disappeared again, only to reappear seconds later, twisting and rolling and diving like a creature delighting in its natural element.

When he had finished showing off, Turumbah swam closer to the point on which the boys stood and beckoned them to join him.

'Come massa! Come along! Come!'

For William the temptation was too great. The afternoon was hot, there was no-one about, so he took off his shirt.

'William!' James was horrified.

'No-one can see. Come on, James.'

Stripped to his undergarments, William flopped clumsily off the rocks. He could swim enough to keep himself afloat but he didn't venture too far from the point. Turumbah joined him and a splashing match ensued.

James wandered back along the point to the reedy shallows. Today had been a succession of shocks to him. From the fearful black man and his threatening dance, to Grandfather Thomas speaking in the native tongue and, finally, to the unashamed nakedness of Turumbah. That had been the biggest shock of all.

When Turumbah, signalling silence, had led James and William in a circle behind the hut to the water's edge and proceeded to strip to his bare skin in front of them, James's shock had left him speechless. No-one should be seen naked. For as long as he could remember, his mother had told him that nakedness was a sin. 'Cover yourself, James,' she would say when, as a very small boy, he emerged from the tin bathing tub, 'cover yourself.'

Shocking as today might have been, however, it was exciting

and unpredictable, a day like no other, and James wanted to be a part of it. He found a flat, dry rock, sat down and carefully took off his shoes and stockings. With equal care, he took off his vest, folded it with his jacket and placed his new felt hat on top. Then he pulled his trouser legs up to the knees and waded out into the shallows, enjoying the water, cool against his calves and the sand, coarse beneath his feet.

A shadow glided amongst the reeds ahead, then stopped. Too curious to be alarmed, James waded stealthily towards it. Just when he was convinced it was nothing, merely a play of light, the shadow reappeared right in front of him. About a foot in length and breadth, its sides appeared to gracefully curl, and once more it glided ahead of him, only to disappear in a brief flurry of sand.

James was fascinated. For a full ten minutes he followed the small stingray through the shallows until the creature retreated to the deeper water.

When he finally returned to the rock where he'd left his clothes, he found William and Turumbah dressed and sunning themselves as they waited for him.

'I saw a fish! A fish with a long tail!' James called excitedly. 'I followed it everywhere!'

'*Daringyan.*' Turumbah called back. 'Catch him towsan this place.' It was only then that James noticed, perched atop the Aboriginal boy's head, and at a rakish angle, his new felt hat.

James's dismay must have been evident, and he felt himself flush as William laughed loudly. 'Give it back to him, Turumbah, I told you he would be angry.'

Regretfully, the boy took off the hat. He examined it briefly to make sure it was unmarked—it was only a little damp inside—before handing it back with a mischievous smile.

James put the hat on and concentrated on the buttons of his vest, keeping his face averted. His shocked reaction had been instinctive. He didn't really mind Turumbah wearing his hat. He wished that William hadn't laughed.

As James knelt to put on his shoes and stockings, Turumbah stopped him. The boy repeated a word several times, a word which the other two didn't understand. '*Badangi, badangi,*' he said, then beckoned impatiently. 'Come, Gran'sun James, come along.'

They followed him, Turumbah unfastening a knifelike implement made from shell which dangled from the twine about his waist. It was time to shuck oysters from the healthy crop which grew along the rocks of the foreshore.

An hour later, when the boys returned to the hut—Turumbah ensuring that his hair and clothes were dry and that their approach was from the opposite direction to the bay—James's hands were scratched and bleeding and one trouser leg was torn. The big toe of his right foot was painful where he'd stubbed it on the rocks, and he knew that inside his shoe blood was oozing onto his stocking.

But James didn't care. He wiped his hands on the once pristine white handkerchief and returned it to his vest pocket. He savoured the sea-salt taste of the oysters on his tongue. The day had been the most exciting and memorable of his young life.

Thomas noticed James's dishevelled appearance but said nothing.

Wolawara rose to farewell them, and the two men shook hands.

'I beg of you, my friend,' Thomas said, taking both of Wolawara's hands in his, 'do nothing until I next come to you. I will return within seven days. Until then, please do not leave Eora.'

Wolawara nodded his consent and Thomas and his grandsons turned to go. But Turumbah would not leave it at that. He made a great show of shaking hands as vigorously as he could with William and James. Particularly James.

'You like Turumbah, Gran'sun James? Turumbah *budjerry* fellow.'

Before he knew what he was doing, James had taken off his new felt hat. He couldn't help himself. Holding it in both hands, he offered it to Turumbah.

The boy stared at the hat and the outstretched hands, bewildered.

'Take it, Turumbah,' James said. 'It's yours, a gift.'

No second bidding was necessary. In a moment the hat was on Turumbah's head, and when Thomas and his grandsons finally set off, the boy was still leaping about excitedly, dancing, waving and pointing to his new possession.

Thomas studied his younger grandson as they walked away from the clearing. There would be hell to pay when his mother found out he'd lost his new hat.

James felt his grandfather's eyes upon him. He looked up and smiled reassuringly. He had no regrets. He didn't quite know why he had done what he'd done, but he would weather the storm.

Thomas was pleased. More than pleased. It was a breakthrough. James was not yet entirely under the influence of his mother. It was time for him to learn some truths.

'Let's walk to the Common,' he said, 'and sit and talk. There is a story I wish to tell you both.'

He would tell them the story of Wolawara. But he would not tell them of his plan. Not yet. The boys would find out soon enough, for it would alienate him from his younger son forever. Now was the time for his grandsons to know the truth so they may judge his actions accordingly.

Much as Thomas railed against the exclusivists and their class system, the truly unpardonable sin in his eyes was the lamentable predicament of the native, who had been stripped of all he'd owned, including dignity. His numbers had been decimated by white man's diseases and he had been left to beg in the streets, his women to exchange their bodies for food. It was not the way Governor Phillip had wished it. It was not the way the King of England himself had instructed the colony be governed.

Thomas and his grandsons reached the vastness of Sydney Common where cattle and goats grazed and where, on misty mornings, groups of gentlemen regularly held swan-shooting parties. When they had settled themselves on a grassy hillock in the late afternoon sunshine, Thomas told them his story.

CHAPTER TWO

Food and shelter were the major priorities in the early days of the settlement. Heavy labour was assigned to the hardened criminals and, in chains and leg irons, they were mercilessly worked, their daily misery in the stone quarries and brick fields slowly producing the buildings of Sydney Town.

Those convicts considered less of a threat to the community were assigned work, under guard, at the government farm, and they soon learned that the trees of Port Jackson were tough and unyielding. The work was intense, many men labouring for several days to grub out just one swamp mahogany or one red gum. And when the land was finally cleared and cultivated, the soil proved too poor and too pest-ridden for the tropical plants acquired in South Africa, and the time unseasonal for the planting of fruit varieties brought from England.

Further delegation of labour was proving a problem. Whilst the navy and military were engaged in the navigation and exploration of rivers and terrain, who was to police the colony? It became evident that prisoners of good conduct who had proved themselves hardworking and reliable should be assigned positions of trust. Thomas Kendall, who had received a glowing report from the *Friendship*'s first mate, was deemed such a man.

'I was right, you see, Thomas,' Anne said, gratified by Thomas's improved status. 'I told you they would need men they could trust. Who knows but they might even grant you an early pardon.'

Anne had been ambitious for him from the very outset. When, occasionally, Thomas had returned from an expedition, angry at the brutality of a soldier or the unjustness of a situation, Anne had said, 'Do nothing, my love, do nothing.'

She was wise and cunning and Thomas knew she was right, although at times it had cost him considerable effort to keep his tongue in check.

By comparison to many in the colony whose miserable lives were spent in chains at the mercy of sadistic gaolers or guards, Thomas and Anne led a relatively comfortable existence. A married couple with a baby, both with good-conduct records, they were granted the comparative freedom of the camp's married quarters, and Anne was assigned daily service at the makeshift military barracks, washing, cleaning and cooking for the soldiers.

The work was hard but Anne never complained. She worried only about the health of her baby, whom they'd christened Catherine at an official ceremony conducted by the Reverend Johnson. The birth aboard the *Charlotte* had nearly killed both mother and child and Catherine had remained weak and fragile.

Sadly Anne's fears proved justified and on Saturday 8 March, 1788, Catherine Kendall, firstborn of Thomas and Anne, was laid to rest, three months of age, alongside others who had failed to withstand the rigours of life in the colony.

Since settlement Thomas had been assigned to working parties on expeditions up the Parramatta River and northward to Broken Bay, and he had even accompanied Captain Hunter's team on early surveys of the harbour. Furthermore, during each of these expeditions, Thomas had been surprisingly successful in communicating with the natives. Such a skill, coupled with his reliability, made him a perfect candidate for overseeing duties.

From the outset Thomas had been intrigued by the local people. Entirely naked, of slender build, dark black skin and short curly hair, they were ebullient and friendly. Curious, like children. Most of the men had a foretooth missing and scars on their bodies—results of manhood initiation ceremonies, it was later discovered—and many wore a short bone or stick through a hole in their nostrils.

On Thomas's first encounter with the natives, the men approached the longboats as soon as the working party had pulled ashore and, although each carried a spear or a club, their actions were not threatening. Indeed, they seemed fascinated by the strange visitors. Particularly, it appeared, by their clean-shaven faces.

They jabbered away in a harsh, staccato tongue and pointed towards the women who remained with their children in a cluster further down the shore—although, curiosity getting the better of them, they were inching gradually closer and closer to their menfolk—then they pointed at their own genitals. It was evident that the men were confused as to the sex of the clothed, and hairless, white intruders.

It was Second Lieutenant King who issued the order to one of his team and, as the soldier exposed himself, a great shout of admiration went up, not only from the men but from the women also.

Thomas was carrying the knapsack containing the gifts intended for the natives. He was instructed to open it. As he knelt and handed the trinkets, mirrors, baubles and beads to the various members of the working party to distribute, the natives, both men and women, clustered about like children around a Christmas tree.

Lifting two bright strips of cloth from the knapsack, Thomas was about to pass them to one of the soldiers when a black hand intercepted his. He looked up into the face of a young man about the same age as himself. The native poked himself in the chest, repeatedly asking for the cloth, and Thomas was uncertain—it was not really his place to distribute the gifts. But amongst the gabble of voices, the excitement of the natives jumping about, and the crew laughing at their antics, it didn't seem to matter. He nodded.

The man grinned, gap-toothed, with delight. '*Guwiyang*,' he said and, with slender fingers, dextrously wove the pieces of yellow and red cloth together. '*Guwiyang*,' he said over and over as he tied the woven cloth around his head.

Thomas couldn't help but smile back. He lifted out a string of bright blue beads, handed them to the man, and awaited the reaction. The man grinned again, nodded, and turned to the young woman who stood beside him. A three-month-old infant was at her hip, hanging comfortably off her naked body, watching the proceedings intently through bright, black, fascinated eyes. The man hung the string of beads over the woman's right ear. 'Wiriwa,' he said, pointing to the woman. 'Wiriwa.'

That was the first time Thomas met Wolawara. Several days later, their paths once again crossed.

On a survey of Shell Cove, again under the command of Captain Hunter, the working party came upon a group of natives in canoes, fishing. The canoes were small and flimsy, constructed of tree bark gathered at each end and secured by strong vine. The natives' skilful handling of such feeble craft drew admiration from the soldiers and the crew. With a two-foot paddle in each hand, legs tucked under them, bodies erect, not only could the men propel their craft at speed, they could stand at a moment's notice, aim their cumbersome pronged spears, ten or twelve feet in length, at the target of their choice and generally achieve success. One of the men, Thomas noticed, was wearing a bright red and yellow headband.

As the working party left the ship and set out in the longboat for shore, Thomas watched, enthralled. A number of women, too, were in canoes, fishing with hand lines. This in itself was not remarkable, but in the bows of several of the canoes burned a small fire. How they kept their fires constantly alight, without damaging their canoes in the process, remained a mystery; but it seemed the native always liked to travel with his fire.

As the team pulled for shore, the natives abandoned their fishing and joined the men on the beach. Gifts were again distributed. On previous expeditions, combs and mirrors had proved amongst the most popular offerings, and the crew laughed when a native, looking in a mirror for the first time, turned around to see who was standing behind him.

Thomas watched the man in the red and yellow headband. He had been given a comb. He scratched his arm with it. And when one of the crew demonstrated its use, he grinned affably and scratched his head with it.

As before, the clean-shaven faces of the white men fascinated the natives. 'Thomas,' the first officer commanded, 'shave one of them.' Thomas looked back at the officer, uncertain. 'It's been done before, man, very successfully. They like it. You just have to pick a bold beggar.'

The shaving equipment was brought ashore, and gestures were made as to which of the natives might want to be shorn of his beard. The first to step forward was the young man in the headband. A young woman, tending the fire in the bow of her canoe, rose to watch, concerned. Thomas recognised her. The man had given her the beads and said her name. What was it? He couldn't remember.

As Thomas approached him, the Aborigine grinned broadly. 'Aah,' he said, '*guwiyang*,' and he pointed to the headband, '*guwiyang*.'

Thomas repeated the word. '*Guwiyang?*' he asked and the man realised the question. '*Guwiyang*,' he repeated and pointed from the headband to the coals burning in the bow of Wiriwa's canoe. '*Guwiyang*.'

'Fire' was the first Dharug word Thomas learned.

As he shaved Wolawara, the natives nudging each other and chattering excitedly at the appearance of bare skin beneath the matted beard, Thomas spoke to him. 'Thomas,' he said, and he paused briefly to jab himself in the chest, 'my name is Thomas.'

'Tom-ass,' the man replied and, when Thomas nodded, he said 'Wolawara,' and pointed to himself.

'Wolawara,' Thomas repeated, and the man nodded in return, pleased with the introduction.

From that day on, Thomas always kept a lookout for Wolawara, the man in the headband of fire. And he memorised as many words of the Aboriginal language as he could glean from the excited exchanges which took place. When an inquisitive group of natives had gathered to watch the seine being hauled, there was much admiration as to the fine catch in the net, and that day Thomas learned that '*magura*' meant fish, a '*daringyan*' was a stingray, and that a '*walumil*' was a breed of shark, and that, for some strange reason, the natives would not eat shark.

Each time he encountered Wolawara, Thomas would test the latest word he'd acquired—often he was wrong and Wolawara would correct him—and on each encounter he greeted not only Wolawara by name but also Wiriwa, to whom he had been reintroduced. The greeting of his wife pleased Wolawara greatly.

Two months after he had first met Wolawara, Thomas received orders to depart with a team of six convicts and one armed guard for a period of one week to cut and bale the rushes which grew in the eastern bay and had proved ideal material for roof thatching.

As the boat pulled in to the rushcutting bay, Thomas studied his team of six workers. He did not know them personally but had seen them about the camp in each other's company, thuggish men, troublemakers, their undisputed leader a tough little cockney called Farrell. Such men would not have been recommended for a work detail like this, Thomas thought; Farrell must have bribed an officer. It was easily enough done, the military was rife with corruption.

Thomas hoped there would be no trouble, though he doubted the men were planning to escape. Although relatively easy for prisoners who worked unfettered by chains, escape was becoming less common as the convicts realised that there was nowhere for them to go. The French convoy, still at anchor in Botany Bay, refused them sanctuary under an agreement between Commander-in-Chief La Perouse and Governor Arthur Phillip, and many escapees, unable to survive in the wilderness, either met their death or eventually limped back to camp, half-starved and bleeding. No, Thomas decided, their plan would not be escape—Farrell was too smart for that.

They pitched camp and the soldier on guard duty, young Benjamin Waite, a strapping Lancashire lad of twenty-five, distributed the long-bladed knives with which the men were to cut the reeds. Private Waite's duty was not so much to guard the convicts as to guard their weapons. And it was not so much to guard the weapons from unlawful use by the convicts themselves—the weapons being stowed in Private Waite's tent at the end of each working day—as to guard the weapons from the nocturnal visits of thieving natives.

The Aborigines had outgrown their interest in baubles and beads. Even mirrors and combs had lost their attraction upon the discovery of hatchets and knives. Discriminate gifts of working implements were made here and there, the military not unduly worried about providing such potential weapons. The Aborigines had, after all, proved a peaceful people and, should they ever decide to turn hostile, they had weapons enough of their own.

The problem, however, was the Aborigines' inability to conceive the right of ownership. If they saw something they liked, they took it, be it food or hatchets or shovels or knives, and the only thing to send them on their way was a musket ball fired into the air. The duty of the amiable Benjamin Waite, therefore, was to protect camp property.

As the days passed uneventfully, it seemed to Thomas that his fears were ungrounded. The men were not out to cause trouble, it appeared, but were intent instead on having a good time. They were lazy, and he had to urge them on to make their daily work quota, but they took it in rough humour.

'We'll 'ave to get you a uniform, Kendall,' they'd say. 'You're a right soldier you are.' And Farrell would nudge his new-found friend, Private Waite, and say, 'Go on, Benny, give Mister Kendall your uniform, then you can be one of us.' And Private Benjamin Waite, big and burly and as simple as the men who followed Farrell, would laugh.

Benjamin liked Farrell. Farrell was funny. And generous. Around the campfire at night, as he told bawdy stories and made them all laugh, he gave each of the men a tot of his rum. 'Just a tot, mind,' he'd say. 'We don't want to run out of the stuff now, do we?'

Thomas felt hypocritical as he accepted the rum, he didn't like Farrell at all, and of course the rum was illicitly gained, but to refuse would alienate him from the men. Besides, the rum helped him sleep.

In teams of two, the men moved further and further afield each day, cutting fresh reeds to bring back to the camp for baling. In the midafternoon of the fifth day, Thomas noticed Red McGregor, his partner, in earnest conversation with Farrell.

McGregor was a flame-haired Scot with a fiery temper. Farrell kept him under control, but appeared the only man capable of doing so. Several times when Thomas had had cause to reprimand McGregor for slackness, it had been Farrell who had calmed the irate Scot. But Thomas knew only too well that Farrell was a cunning manipulator, and if it were to his advantage, he would be the first to fuel the Scotsman's rage.

Now, on observing the two men, Thomas decided to give them several minutes before breaking them up and ordering a return to work.

'We found a camp,' the Scot was whispering. 'Far east side, old hags tendin' babies.'

'Good,' Farrell replied, 'the young ones'll be back after the day's fishin'. If we can nick one of the women without too much trouble then we can 'ave us some fun.' Thomas was approaching. 'Pass the word around,' he muttered, 'we'll pay 'em a visit tonight.' Then, loudly, for Thomas's benefit, 'Now get back to work, Red, we don't want to upset Mister Kendall 'ere.' Red obediently trundled off and returned to his baling.

That night Farrell produced a full bottle of rum. 'Only two more nights to go,' he said, 'no point in takin' it back with us, is there?' He took a swig and passed the bottle on. 'Plenty more where this come from,' he boasted.

The men shook their heads in admiration. Farrell's constant liquor supply was a mystery and, rum being an excellent bartering commodity and therefore a power to those who could acquire it, he fiercely guarded his secret.

After a second swig, Thomas retired, leaving the men to their raucous campfire conversation.

Farrell passed the bottle again and again to Benjamin Waite. 'Come on, Benny me old mate, drink up, you're a big lad, you need your fuel.' And, when on the fifth swig, the rasping liquor caught in his throat and they all laughed, Benjamin joined in. He was having an excellent time.

Farrell looked a signal to Red McGregor, who quietly slipped away to steal the knives from the soldier's tent. When he returned, mission accomplished, Farrell insisted Benjamin take the final swig and the soldier obediently drained the bottle.

'Time to turn in,' Farrell announced.

As the men dowsed the fire and prepared to retire for the night, Private Benjamin Waite, happy and drowsy and just a little the worse for wear, weaved his way to his tent.

After noisily bidding each other goodnight, for the benefit of Thomas and Benjamin, Farrell silently signalled the others to follow and, away from the camp, they huddled to make their plans.

In the distance, they could see the Aborigines' campfire and, emboldened by the rum, one of the men was all for mounting a raid and storming the camp. Farrell was scathing in his reply.

'Want to get yourself killed, you fool? We don't know how many there are. Now listen.' The men squatted and awaited their orders. 'Red and me'll go out front,' he instructed, 'you lads keep well behind. Stay in the scrub and no noise, mind, the blacks are sharp. If we can get to the women without too much of a fight, then well and good; but if there's too many men, the deal's off. I'm not coppin' a spear from one of them black bastards.'

It was a cloudless spring night and from their vantage point amongst the trees Farrell and Red could easily make out the camp in the clearing. A series of bark lean-tos, women and children sleeping, curled up on beds of reeds, and to one side, gathered around the embers of their fire, a group of men talking. Farrell counted five in all. He shook his head. Too many.

Farrell and McGregor were about to creep back to the others when, as if in answer to their prayers, one of the sleeping women rose. She stood for a moment, stretched her naked body, then started to walk towards them.

They looked at each other, unable to believe their luck, and Farrell nodded to McGregor, his finger to his lips.

From the bark lean-to, where she sat suckling her child, Wiriwa watched her sister rise and walk to the edge of the clearing. Yenada squatted in the bushes to urinate and Wiriwa lost sight of her, returning her attention to the baby who, satisfied, had fallen asleep at her breast. As Wiriwa gently set the child down upon the bed of reeds, there was a brief scuffling noise from the bushes. She looked up, expecting to see Yenada returning to the camp. But there was nothing. She waited several seconds. Still nothing.

'Yenada,' she whispered softly, careful of waking those sleeping nearby. No answer.

Wiriwa rose to investigate. She would not call the men, they would be angry if she interrupted them for no purpose. She crossed to the edge of the clearing. The bushes where Yenada had squatted were flattened and there was a broken trail through the scrub. Wiriwa knew with a glance that the trail had been made by several people and she ran quickly to the men.

'Wolawara!' she urged in a whisper, again careful not to wake the others. There must be no outcry to warn the assailants. 'Wolawara, *barrawu*.'

She dragged him to the trail, the other men following soundlessly.

His hand clapped over her mouth, Red McGregor carried the terrified woman far from the Aboriginal camp. Farrell hissed at the others to quell their excitement and keep silent—the blacks had ears like dingoes.

They were not far from their own camp when they set the woman down. They laid her on her back and Farrell held a knife to her throat as McGregor released his grip. 'One sound and I'll slit you from ear to ear,' he threatened. Paralysed with fear, Yenada stared up at the men in silence.

Four of the convicts held an arm and a leg apiece and Farrell nodded magnanimously to Red McGregor. 'You get first go, Red.'

Yenada's head was threshing from side to side, a hissing sound coming from between her clenched teeth, as McGregor lowered his breeches and knelt between her thighs. He laid his body over hers, fumbling to find his mark, and Yenada kicked with all her might as she felt the man's hand on her private parts.

'Hold her still, damn it,' the Scotsman hissed, rising to his knees. 'Hold the whore . . .'

He was silenced as a spear ripped through his chest.

'*Djiriyay! Djiriyay!*' Screaming their war cry, the Aborigines were upon them.

Two hundred yards away, Thomas heard the cries and was up in a flash. He dragged Benjamin Waite from his tent. 'A raid!' he yelled. 'A raid!' As the soldier grabbed his musket, Thomas fumbled in the dark for a knife. There were none. The knives were gone. And so were the men. Thomas knew, in that moment, it was the convicts who had initiated the attack.

Clad in undergarments, firearm at the ready, instantly sober, Private Benjamin Waite charged into battle, Thomas Kendall close behind him.

Three convicts lay dead on the ground and, even as Benjamin and Thomas arrived on the scene, two Aborigines had set about a fourth with their clubs. The man dropped beside his fellows, his head a bloodied pulp. One of the convicts, wounded and whimpering, was dragging himself through the scrub in a bid to escape, but the Aborigines intended to leave none living. It was Wolawara whose spear was raised to deliver the mortal blow.

Benjamin aimed his musket directly at Wolawara's chest. The spear left the Aborigine's hand, piercing the convict through the heart, and Wolawara turned to confront the fresh aggressors.

In the split second which followed, Thomas flashed out instinctively and deflected the soldier's aim. Then the air was shattered with the musket's roar, and Wolawara fell to his knees.

Two spears hit Benjamin simultaneously, one in the leg and one in the side, but he was a big man. Strong. He staggered, then stood his ground and started to reload. He had already powdered his musket and was disconnecting his tamping rod when he was felled with clubs. It took two Aborigines many blows before Benjamin Waite finally lay still.

Only then did they turn their attention upon the unarmed man beside him. Thomas had not attempted to flee. Horrified at what he had done, he stood waiting for his turn to come.

One of the Aborigines wrenched a spear from the body of the soldier and was about to drive it into Thomas's chest.

'*Ngadu!*'

Spear poised, the man stopped midaction.

It was Wolawara who had spoken. He had staggered to his feet, in pain, holding his bleeding side. '*Gumal*,' he said to his clansmen.

The men muttered to each other, confused. How could Wolawara profess to a friendship with this white man? But Wolawara had seen Thomas lash out. He had seen the muzzle of the musket deflected in that second before the fire had ripped into his side, and he knew that Thomas had saved his life.

'Tom-ass.'

'Wolawara.' Thomas crossed to the Aborigine to inspect the wound as best he could in the moonlight.

Wolawara lay on the ground, as Thomas instructed, and the others gathered around. The white man had called Wolawara by name, he must be his friend, they muttered. Perhaps this was the man who had taken the hair from Wolawara's face. But in the darkness it was difficult to see the face of this man, and besides, the hairless white men all looked the same.

It was a flesh wound as far as Thomas could ascertain. The musket ball had hit Wolawara just above the left hipbone, but it had not lodged in the flesh. It had passed through, leaving an ugly wound which would need cauterising to avoid infection.

'*Guwiyang*, Wolawara.' He held his hands above the wound, then pressed them downward, making a hissing sound like fire on flesh. '*Guwiyang*.'

'*Guwiyang?*' Wolawara looked confused.

'*Guwiyang*.' Thomas made the same gesture with his hands as he racked his brain for the word he wanted.

There had been a day on the beach, he remembered. They'd hauled the seine. The natives had been excited, as usual. In the net there'd been the rotting carcass of a small kangaroo which had drifted in with the tide. They'd said a word, and at first he'd thought it was their name for kangaroo. He'd hopped about, miming a kangaroo and saying the word. They'd laughed loudly at him. Then they'd joined in the fun, jumping around saying the word over and over, holding their noses and making disgusted faces as they did so, and Thomas had realised that the word meant rotten, putrid. What was the word, damn it, what was the word?

'*Gudjibi*.' It came to him suddenly. '*Gudjibi*.' The men stood staring at him as if he were mad, but Wolawara's eyes were boring into his, he wanted to understand. Thomas mimed a musket and aimed it at Wolawara's wound. 'Boom,' he said loudly, and the men jumped, startled. He held his hands like claws over the wound. '*Gudjibi*,' he said and he worked his fingers like worms. '*Gudjibi*.' Slowly Wolawara nodded. '*Guwiyang*,' Thomas urged. '*Guwiyang*,' he mimed the pressing on of fire once again and shook his head. '*Guwiyang*, no *gudjibi*.'

Wolawara understood. As the Aborigines carried the injured man back to their camp, Wolawara beckoned Thomas to follow.

The men laid their clansman beside the campfire as the white man instructed, then stood in a circle watching as Thomas pulled one of the heavier sticks from the embers. He held the unburned end of the stick in his hand, squatted, and pointed the red-hot glowing tip towards the wound in Wolawara's side. The Aborigines muttered amongst themselves, but clearly their clansman was putting his trust in this white man.

Thomas placed his hand upon Wolawara's shoulder and gestured to one of the natives to do likewise. He repeated the gesture with Wolawara's leg, and the men realised that he wanted them to hold their comrade down. But Wolawara shook his head and they stood back at a respectful distance.

Thomas lowered the burning ember, praying that the pain would not cause the Aborigine to thresh about, risking further injury. Then he pressed the red-hot tip into the cavity of the wound.

Wolawara's muscles instantly spasmed with the pain, but he himself made no voluntary movement. As the sickly smell of burning flesh rose from his body, he remained rigid, hands in fists at his side, leg and stomach muscles locked hard. His teeth were clenched, he made no sound, and his eyes stared fixedly up at the clear night sky.

The surrounding men watched silently. They knew pain, and stoicism was respected in their community. Wolawara's courage was no more, no less, than was expected.

Thomas removed the burning ember and smoke continued to rise from the wound, the smell of burnt tissue now thick and acrid in his nostrils. He was astounded that the man had neither moved nor fainted during the procedure. Now, as Wolawara relaxed, which also was extraordinary for he must still have been in severe pain, Thomas realised that the Aborigine had induced in himself some form of trance. Some state beyond the normal threshold of human pain.

Wolawara held his fist to his heart then pointed to Thomas. '*Gamaradu*, Tom-ass,' he said.

Thomas offered his hand and they shook, the way Wolawara had seen the white men do. '*Gamaradu*, Wolawara,' Thomas replied. He had learned the Dharug word for 'comrade'.

As the Aborigines prepared to abandon their camp, Thomas returned to the scene of the massacre. He surveyed the carnage, identifying each man and checking each body for any sign of life, but there was none. It was only then he realised that Farrell was missing.

Thomas searched the nearby bush. Wounded, the man may have dragged himself off into the scrub. But there was nothing.

He knelt by the body of Benjamin Waite. Thomas knew that, with or without the death of Wolawara, the Aborigines would have killed Benjamin. There had simply been insufficient time for the soldier to reload his musket. But when Thomas had deflected his aim, Benjamin had turned for an instant before reloading and in his eyes had been a look which Thomas would never forget. A look of shock and disbelief and, above all, betrayal.

Thomas felt wretched for the part he had played in Benjamin's murder. For a long time he remained kneeling by the body and, although not a religious man, something inside him begged forgiveness.

At dawn he trudged the several miles back to the settlement, leaving behind him the slaughtered men where they had fallen, weapons in hand. There would be an investigation, he knew, and the scene would tell the truth with graphic clarity.

On Thomas's return a team was sent immediately to investigate the massacre, and detailed reports were made to a deeply concerned Governor Phillip.

There had been no Aboriginal raiding party, that much was clear—the convicts had died with their knives in their hands. After the slaughter the natives had not even taken the weapons from the corpses.

Thomas was called before the Governor to give his account of the events, which he did, omitting nothing, save his role in Private Waite's death.

'There were two native women present, sir,' Thomas could see them clearly, Wiriwa protectively holding the other woman close, 'which is unusual if the men are up to mischief. I don't believe they take their women on raiding parties. Leastways not to my knowledge, sir.'

Phillip said nothing but waited for Thomas to continue.

'It's my belief, sir, that the lads tried to interfere with the women.'

Phillip nodded. 'And why do you think you were left unharmed, Kendall?'

Thomas stared back at the slight man in the powdered wig. Although the eyes which met his were mild, benign, the authority behind them was unmistakable.

'I believe it to be because I was not part of the attack, sir.' It sounded a little lame even to Thomas. 'And they could see I was unarmed, sir.'

Thomas had decided that to mount a defence on Wolawara's behalf, to admit to their friendship and his personal belief in the man's good character, would not serve the Aborigine's cause. A soldier had been killed and there must be no identification of those involved. Governor Phillip was a humane man, sensitive to the plight of the natives, and if the attempted rape of their women by convicts had resulted in the deaths of those convicts, he would not exact punishment upon the Aborigines. But a soldier had been killed in the performance of his duty and that was not to be tolerated.

'Reports indicate that you have displayed a certain rapport with the natives, Kendall.' Phillip looked out the window of his makeshift office in the unfinished garrison. He gazed in silence across the expanse which would one day be a fine parade ground, and Thomas held his breath. Did the Governor suspect something? The killing of a soldier, or the interference in the performance of his duty, meant the hangman's noose.

'Communication with the natives is a good thing, Kendall.' Phillip turned to Thomas. 'We must make every effort to maintain good relations with them. This is not only my personal view but is contained in my Royal Commission, you understand?'

'Yes, sir.'

'King George himself has instructed that every endeavour be made possible to open an intercourse with the natives, and that all of His subjects are to live in amity and kindness with them.' Phillip quoted directly from his commission, the words indelibly etched in his mind. 'I am further instructed that, should any of His subjects wantonly destroy the natives, or give them unnecessary interruption, it is His Majesty's will that such offenders be brought to punishment.'

Thomas remained silent.

'Had it not been for the death of Private Waite,' Phillip continued, 'this matter would be closed, and whilst no recriminations will be brought upon the Aboriginal peoples in general, if the parties guilty of the murder of Private Waite are found, they will be punished accordingly.'

It seemed the interview was over but, as Thomas waited to be dismissed, Phillip added.

'Perhaps in your communications with the natives, Kendall, you could instil respect for His Majesty's Men. Fear if need be. Make it clear that the death of a soldier by a native hand will bring death upon that native's people.'

'Yes, sir.'

'You may go.'

Thomas left. Thankful. But confused by Governor Phillip's request. It sounded very much as if the Governor knew that the Aborigines had spared Thomas's life out of friendship. If so, why had Governor Phillip not demanded a fuller explanation? Why had he not demanded Thomas identify the attackers? Was he letting the matter rest because he did not wish to bring the natives to a white man's justice when they had simply been protecting their women?

A week later Farrell's body was discovered ten miles from the site of the attack, a spear staked through his heart in what appeared to be a ritual murder. Thomas was relieved that no witness remained to the events of that night, and for forty years he told no-one of his secret. Until the day he told his grandsons.

CHAPTER THREE

It was dusk when Thomas returned home with William and James, to find Mary in a barely controllable rage. She had been pacing the floor of his front parlour for two hours, refusing to be placated by Emily and the girls. When she finally laid eyes on her son, hatless, dishevelled, scratched and bleeding, she was at first speechless.

'We had a splendid time, Mother.' James had forgotten the hour and his appearance. 'Grandfather Thomas told us such stories of the old days . . .' James knew he mustn't mention Wolawara, but he couldn't contain the excitement of his afternoon, '. . . when the town was nothing but tents, and when they first brought the convicts ashore and . . .'

That was when Mary's anger reached the point of hysteria.

She had known this would happen, she screamed. She had known that by leaving James in Thomas's care, she was risking the very life of her only son. 'You disgusting old man, you care nothing for your kin,' she shouted. 'You will not be satisfied until you have dragged this whole family down into the gutter with you and your disreputable kind! You will be the ruin of us all.'

At first Thomas was amused to see Mary so uncharacteristically out of control. James and Phoebe, however, cowered at their mother's wrath, while William and Hannah stared at their aunt jaws agape, never having witnessed such rage.

'If the ruination of my family were my true aim, Mary,' Thomas replied mildly, 'surely it should be of little concern to you. You are no longer a Kendall.'

'And I never will be!' By now Mary's face was apoplectic with fury. 'Neither me, nor my husband, nor our children.'

Thomas's amusement evaporated, for this sounded suspiciously like a threat.

'If you continue to boast of your loathsome past,' Mary presented her ace with menacing triumph, 'you will never see your grandchildren again.'

Thomas interrupted, still calm but with a steely edge to his voice. 'Tell my son to come and see me tomorrow. I have business to discuss with him.'

The wind was taken out of Mary's sails for an instant. She'd expected apologies, even some grovelling. Perhaps the old man took her threat to be the idle ranting of a distraught woman. 'Look at James!' She dragged the boy, speechless, terrified, to her bosom. 'Just look at him! He's wounded, bleeding. Do you think for one minute that Richard, when he sees his son like this, will—'

'Tell Richard he is to see me tomorrow.' The old man's tone brooked no argument.

'My husband is not at your beck and call, Thomas,' she replied, fighting to recover her dignity. 'He has important work at hand. Meetings with people of standing in the community, people of influence. You can no longer click your fingers and expect—'

'He is to have a meeting with his father tomorrow. At noon. Tell him that if he does not come,' Mary was about to interrupt, 'he will be disinherited, and so will his children. Now get out of my house.'

'You cannot possibly be serious, Father.'

It was twelve-thirty in the afternoon and Richard stood in Thomas's front parlour on the very same rug upon which his wife had stood yesterday as she hurled her venom. Mary's instructions, however, had disappeared from Richard's mind. He was to have threatened the old man with the denial of his grandchildren's company unless he conformed to society's dictates; it had seemed relatively simple.

'You cannot be serious,' he repeated.

'I am in deadly earnest, Richard. My friend Wolawara and his family are to have the lands adjoining yours by the Parramatta River.' Richard was silent, shaking his head in disbelief as he stared back at his father. 'The land is useless for cultivation,' Thomas continued, 'which is why I did not include it in the property gifted to you on your marriage. I am sure Wolawara will be kind enough to grant you grazing rights for your domestic stock, should you wish it.'

Thomas could have laughed out loud at the sight of his son. Goggle-eyed, slack-jawed, the usually dapper Richard Kendall looked utterly foolish. Thomas pretended bewilderment. 'You appear worried, Richard.' Then realisation. 'Ah ... of course, I understand. I shall extract a promise from Wolawara that none of his clansmen are to kill and eat any of your livestock.'

'You are simply going to hand over the Parramatta land to this Aborigine and his kin?'

'Yes, I simply am. For as long as he and his descendants wish to live upon it.' Again Thomas pretended bewilderment. 'Do you have some objection, my boy?'

Thomas's only regret about his planned course of action had been the alienation of his younger son. However, Mary's threat had angered him so deeply that he now cared little for Richard's reaction. And if he were to be denied his grandchildren, he would live long enough, he swore to himself, to see those children of an age when they had minds of their own. Then, by God, he'd teach them a thing or two about the bigotry and intolerance of their wretched exclusivist upbringing.

'But, Father, our new house, which we built just last year, is by the water. You've not yet seen it, I realise, but you know that we built it there specifically for the river views.'

'Yes, I believe it's a grand home, quite a mansion I've heard.'

So that was it, Richard thought. The old man was piqued that he'd not been invited to see the new house. Richard had told Mary at the time that they should ask Thomas to come and stay for a day or so, but she'd ignored the suggestion. Damn it, he should have insisted. Now, after the heat of yesterday's row and Mary's melodramatic threats, the old man had decided to make these perverse intimidations in order to teach them a lesson.

'I'm sorry, Father, it's been very remiss of us not to have extended an invitation to you. You're most welcome to visit us, as you know, at any time. Perhaps next weekend?'

'I'd be delighted, my boy. I shall look forward to seeing your new home and spending some time in the company of my grandchildren.' Thomas took his hat from the brass hatstand which stood in the corner of the parlour. 'Now, if that concludes our business, and if you won't partake of the tea I offered earlier, I shall call on Wolawara and tell him the good news.' He opened the door to the hall and waited for the reaction which he knew would come.

'Father, in God's name you cannot be serious!'

'That is the third time you have said that, Richard.'

'But we will be living right beside the natives.' Richard dropped all pretences, forgetting to choose his words with care. 'Mary won't have it.'

'Then Mary can build another new house,' Thomas replied, 'somewhere else, where the view will not offend her.'

For the first time Richard recognised the hurt and anger beneath his father's resolution. He crossed to Thomas and rested his hand upon the old man's shoulder. 'She didn't mean it, Father. You will never be denied your grandchildren, you have my assurance of that.'

'She meant it.' Thomas knew that, despite his son's genuine concern, if Mary decided upon a course of action, there would be little Richard could do about it. He was a pitifully weak man with not a shred of his wife's strength. Mary had guts and a will of iron, Thomas had to give her that. 'My decision regarding Wolawara has nothing to do with your wife's threats, however. It was a decision I made before her ridiculous outburst.'

'Why? Why make such a decision?'

'Because the man is my friend. And if I cannot address the terrible wrongs done to his people, which I obviously cannot, then I can at least help a man to whom I owe my life.'

Richard realised that he must somehow assuage the old man's cantankerousness, 'Father,' he said gently, 'I understand and admire your feelings regarding the natives, it is a shocking state to which they have been reduced. Believe me, if there were some practical way of addressing their plight, I would lend my own assistance, I swear I would.'

In that instant Thomas despised his son. He wanted to call him a liar. He wanted to accuse him of being a shallow man. A spineless man. One with no true human depth whatsoever. But instead, as disappointment overwhelmed him, the old man let his son lead him to his favourite armchair and he sat wordlessly as Richard spoke with all the earnestness of a teacher trying to communicate with a backward ten-year-old.

'You don't understand, Father. Governor Macquarie himself attempted to settle several of the Aboriginal clans years ago. He provided land for them, and implements, and farming instruction. But it was useless.'

'And you remember that, do you, Richard? Remarkable. You were only a lad at the time.'

Old Thomas Kendall remembered the experiment clearly. It had been under the governorship of Lachlan Macquarie that Thomas, like so many others, had been granted his pardon, had acquired lands at Parramatta, and had been encouraged, along with other emancipists, to contribute to the colony as farmers, architects and builders of the new Macquarie towns. It was under the governorship of Macquarie that many emancipists had become valued citizens of the colony of New South Wales. But, much as Thomas admired Macquarie's governorship and humanity, the Aboriginal experiment had been a mistake. The Europeanisation of a nomadic race had been, from the outset, doomed to failure.

'I remember hearing of it, Father,' Richard replied patiently. He found his father's sarcasm offensive, but he took pains to hide his annoyance. 'And it didn't work. These people will never become farmers.' Thomas was silent. Richard started again. Patiently. Reasonably. 'You don't understand. You see—'

'No, Richard. *You* don't understand.' Thomas heaved himself out of his armchair. Today was one of those rare days when he was feeling his age. 'If my friend Wolawara did indeed wish to become a farmer I would have chosen to give him arable land. Perhaps the land further to the west which, as you know, is currently being held in trust for your children.'

It was an unnecessary barb—Thomas had no intention of disinheriting his grandchildren—but he was in the mood to shock. Futility and frustration, he was worn out by both. The futility of finding a true solution to Wolawara's predicament—certainly, the land would be a salve in old age to both Wolawara and Wiriwa, but it was no solution to the problems of their children and their children's children—and the frustration of attempting to communicate with the pig-headed, self-righteous members of colonial society, such as his son. 'But Wolawara does not wish to be a farmer,' Thomas assured his horrified son, 'so he will receive the marshy land by the river which will be far more to his liking. I am tired now, my boy, I am going to lie down, excuse me.'

'Parramatta,' Thomas said, '*Baramada*, the place where the eels lie down.'

Wolawara smiled and nodded, he knew Baramada well. The fishing was good there.

It had taken Thomas some time to explain his offer to Wolawara, that the land would truly belong to him and to his clanspeople. He had insisted that Wiriwa join them, and together they sat beside the hut in Rushcutters Bay and the men spoke their strange mixture of Dharug and pidgin, Wiriwa concentrating on their every word, her brown eyes darting from face to face, scarcely daring to believe her ears.

'But what am I to do with the land, Thomas? My people do not farm like the English man.'

'I understand this. It is not what is expected of you.

'You will do with the land as you have always done, Wolawara. You will fish and hunt and visit your sacred sites. And when the time comes, you will die in peace on the riverlands of your ancestors.'

The men embraced upon parting. '*Gamaradu*,' they said as they swore allegiance.

'When I dream you are there, Thomas.'

'When I dream you are there, Wolawara.'

Thomas was sad as he walked back to town. A deep sadness, as if a part of his life were over. Something told him he would not see Wolawara again. As he reached the top of the hill and looked down over Sydney, Thomas Kendall felt very alone.

'Your father is deranged,' Mary insisted. 'We must enlist the help of the family. Together we must convince him of the insanity of such an act.'

'Matthew is as radical as Father,' Richard argued. 'He will approve the old man's decision, you know he will. He approves of all of Father's causes. Dear God, they even go to the emancipists' meetings together!'

'So what exactly do you propose we do?'

'Nothing.'

They were sitting on the upstairs balcony of their grand new sandstone house which overlooked the river, the late afternoon breeze rising, welcome, from the water. Mary stared long and hard at her husband and there was criticism and accusation in her gaze.

'I am not merely giving in to pressure, Mary,' Richard said defensively. 'Old as Father may be, he is still very active in business. His connections with both the military and the private quarter are invaluable to us.'

Mary listened as Richard rambled on about the importance of Thomas in their water transport service, the barges which daily plied their trade between Parramatta and Sydney Town, delivering grain and supplies to the military and the merchants.

They didn't need Thomas Kendall at all, she thought. They should sell their share of the business back to the old man and buy into a partnership with Leyland Harvey, the shipping man. Imported quality goods, that was where the future lay.

Richard was saying something about the loyalty they owed his father for the farmlands and the coach service gifted them upon their wedding. Rubbish, she thought. It was through her social connections that the coach service had become the success it was today. And as for the farmlands, why, they had been barely cultivated! Successful businessman he may be, but Thomas Kendall was no farmer. Had Richard forgotten the invaluable assistance given them by Captain John Macarthur and his wife Elizabeth, perhaps the wealthiest and most successful farmers in the colony? And how had the relationship with the Macarthurs come about? Through none other than Mary's own father, Captain Robert Farrington.

She had been about to interrupt but, at the thought of her father, Mary realised, yet again, as she had so many times in the sixteen years of her marriage, how she longed to return to the simple, clear-cut dictates of military life. The ever-changing rules of colonial society, the lack of a clear class structure, the growing power of the emancipists and their democratic beliefs, all were disruptive and threatening.

She no longer listened to her husband. And Richard, without her interruption, convinced that his arguments were making an impact, went on. And on. Whilst Mary's mind wandered.

A detachment of the 73rd Regiment had accompanied Lachlan Macquarie, the new governor, to the colony in 1809. Amongst the ranks of the officers was Robert Farrington, and with him his wife Jane and nineteen-year-old daughter Mary. The 73rd Regiment's specific orders were to quell the military riot in the colony, the New South Wales Rum Corps, so named because of its illegal import of spirits from Calcutta, having rebelled against the previous governorship of William Bligh.

Amongst the key figures in the Rum Rebellion was one Captain John Macarthur. A warrant had been issued for Macarthur's arrest, and it was a particular irony that Robert Farrington might well prove to be the arresting officer. He would do his duty, as he always did, but he hoped such duty would not prove necessary, for he and his wife Jane had befriended John and Elizabeth Macarthur many years previously. As young married couples they had shared neighbouring quarters at Chatham Barracks in England, and Macarthur and Farrington still corresponded. Indeed, judging by his friend's reports, Robert Farrington secretly agreed that Bligh was a tyrant who had deserved the treatment meted out by the Rum Corps. But then Robert had always believed in the power of the military, in his opinion too often restrained by the authority of incompetent governors.

Robert soon discovered, however, that John Macarthur had fled to England with his two young sons, so Robert was saved the embarrassment of arresting his friend. But he and Jane visited the Macarthurs' farm at Parramatta which, during her husband's absence, Elizabeth administered with great success.

Two years after their arrival in the colony, young Mary Farrington met and fell instantly in love with Richard Kendall. It was impossible not to, he was dashingly handsome. Furthermore, he possessed a mischievous wit and charm which Mary had not previously encountered. Compared to Richard Kendall, the serious young officers with whom she had been encouraged to socialise suddenly seemed sadly lacklustre.

Her parents' disappointment knew no bounds. Young Kendall was good-looking certainly; it was understandable that he could set a young girl's pulse racing. But he was the son of an emancipated convict. They tried to talk sense to their daughter, they cajoled, and finally they threatened, but to no avail.

Three years later Richard and Mary wed, and there was little the good captain and his wife could do but give their blessing. At least the young man had land and monies, they acceded, albeit land in poor condition.

Help was needed, and once again Robert Farrington visited Elizabeth Macarthur at Parramatta, this time with his daughter and new son-in-law. In the years during her husband's exile, Elizabeth's introduction of agricultural improvements had earned the respect of Governor Macquarie himself who, in recognition of her services to the colony, had granted her six hundred acres near Elizabeth Farm.

Slender-necked, fine-boned and well bred, Elizabeth Macarthur impressed young Mary Kendall. And, strangely enough, young Mary Kendall impressed Elizabeth Macarthur.

Elizabeth was a good woman. Kind, strong, intelligent and, above all, unswerving in her loyalty. Perhaps she recognised a kindred spirit in the girl. She certainly recognised strength and loyalty. And Mary would need all of that to overcome the weakness of her husband, Elizabeth thought, seeing immediately the flawed character beneath Richard Kendall's charm. She also saw that Mary loved him deeply. Elizabeth herself was married to a difficult man. A brilliant man, but one of black moods and aggression and, although there appeared no blackness in Richard, his young wife could well find herself alone when it came to doing battle. Elizabeth knew only too well what it was like to do battle on one's own.

Elizabeth Macarthur's advice on the growing of wheat, barley and oats, and her practical assistance, most important of which was the appointment of an expert overseer, were invaluable to the Kendalls. But, to Mary, during those awkward years as one of the few free settlers in rural Parramatta, most of which was farmed by emancipated convicts, it was Elizabeth's friendship and commonsense which was most valuable of all, particularly when Mary's parents returned to England.

When, in 1817, John Macarthur was finally permitted to return to the colony after an exile of eight years, Mary discovered a hero. Like her father, Macarthur strongly disapproved of Governor Macquarie's emancipist programme and the offers of government assistance to convicts who had served their sentences. The convicts should be kept landless, Macarthur maintained. They should be assigned to the settlers who would feed and clothe them in exchange for free labour. Thus the government would be saved the expense of maintaining and providing for the criminal classes. Macarthur's vision of New South Wales as a colonial aristocracy fitted perfectly with Mary's own.

Macarthur himself, a vain, handsome man of vast egocentric proportions, found it only fitting that his wife's young friend should see in him a figure of heroic proportions. Charmed by her obvious admiration, he even presented Mary with two olive plants and several vine cuttings from amongst the supply he had brought back from Europe. Years later, the greatest pride on Mary Kendle's property was the olive grove in the eastern corner, 'Macarthur's Grove', she called it.

It was John Macarthur who suggested Mary change her family name to 'Kendle'. 'No offence to your father-in-law, my dear,' he said, although the disdain in his voice and the curl of his lip spoke otherwise. 'It is simply far wiser from a business standpoint.' Mary was in thorough agreement.

Sadly, these days Mary Kendle saw little of John Macarthur. Over the past years the man had become unbalanced, given to violent displays of rage in public, and to boastings of megalomaniacal proportions. He had even been quoted as saying that he had the means of sending home every governor of the colony, having indeed been the instigating force behind the removal of Lachlan Macquarie.

Mary convinced herself that such bouts of madness were proof of Macarthur's genius—all great men were touched with insanity—but she no longer visited him for fear of finding him in one of his demented moods.

Now, as Mary listened to her husband's ineffectual arguments as to why they needed Thomas Kendall, she found herself becoming irritated.

'No Richard, we have no need of your father,' she finally interrupted. 'Our achievements have been our own doing, and they shall continue to be ours.' Ours? she thought. Mine. But she did not say it. Mary would never knowingly humiliate her husband. For all of his weaknesses, perhaps because of them, Mary still loved Richard Kendle.

'But what of his threat to disinherit us?' Richard countered. 'Both us and the children. You surely cannot ignore that.'

'He would not dare, he cares too much for James and Phoebe.' Mary was a little uncertain, however. Would he dare? Thomas Kendall was tough. In fact, if he were not so pig-headed in his erroneous beliefs, she could admire his strength. Well, if Thomas was tough, so was she, Mary decided.

When Wolawara and his extended family, twenty in all, took over the adjoining land and built their huts down by the riverbanks, Mary watched them from her front balcony convinced that the old man was waiting for her outrage, for her to rant and rave like a fishwife and threaten him with the denial of his grandchildren. Well, she would not. She would do and say nothing. She would not give Thomas the satisfaction.

But, as the weeks passed, it became more and more difficult for Mary to remain silent. At night she watched the Aborigines gather around the campfire and listened to the men's corroborees; by day she watched the women, half naked, feeding their babies; and all the while she seethed at the fact that, through no fault of her own, she found herself, and her home and her family, neighbours to a tribe of natives. It was intolerable. But still she would not give in.

'Gran'sun James!' Turumbah yelled up to James one sunny Saturday morning.

James was standing on the balcony, looking longingly at the Aboriginal camp. He and Phoebe had been ordered to keep well away from the camp, to have no contact with the natives and to invite no exchange from the children amongst the clan. The rule presented no hardship to Phoebe who was instinctively intimidated by the strangeness of the black people, but to James, normally an obedient boy, the sight of Turumbah was a constant temptation.

'Gran'sun James! Come!' Turumbah stood directly below the big balcony of the grand house, ignoring his grandfather's orders not to intrude upon the Kendle property. He waved the hat as a symbol of his bond with James and held aloft a length of fishing twine. 'Come! Catch him eel towsan this place!'

James's heart lurched painfully. The hat! Grimy, bedraggled, but still recognisable. If his mother were to see it now, she would know the truth of that day James had spent with his grandfather.

'Turumbah,' he hissed, 'ssshh.' He pressed a finger to his lips and gestured for the boy to hide in the bushes.

Assuming it was some kind of game, Turumbah did as he was told and crouched amongst the mangroves near the riverbanks, watching whilst James ran from the balcony to join him.

Downstairs, James checked that his mother was still out in the backyard with Peg and Timothy O'Shaugnessy, the Irish ticket-of-leave couple who served as housekeeper, gardener and general dogsbodies for free board and very little remuneration. Mary worked them mercilessly.

Phoebe, who was at her mother's side, sorting out the kerchiefs and undergarments destined for Peg's laundry tub, looked up and saw James at the back door. She was about to say something, but James shook his head. Phoebe watched silently as he crept towards the front door.

Once outside James sprinted down to the riverbank where, amongst the mangroves, Turumbah was waving the battered hat about in wild enthusiastic greeting.

'Aah,' he said as James took it from him, 'Turumbah hat go way.' He patted his head, crestfallen at his loss, but apparently accepting the fact that James was demanding a return of the precious gift.

'No, it's yours, Turumbah.' James thrust the hat back into the boy's hands. 'I gave it to you, it is a gift.' As Turumbah jumped about, once again waving the hat, James shushed him, finger to lips, and mimed hiding the offensive hat behind his back or stuffing it down the front of his baggy shorts. 'But it is a secret. You must hide the hat, no-one must see it.'

It was an impossible instruction, and quite beyond the Aboriginal boy's comprehension. The hat was his badge of honour, a proof of great friendship, no other child in his clan owned such a hat. What was the point of hiding it?

James gave up. So long as he met his friend at the border of the two properties, down by the river amongst the mangroves, there was no reason to fear his parents might see the hat. Before long, a bond grew between the two and, delighting in the Aboriginal boy's uninhibited manner and infectious laughter, James soon found his barriers crumbling.

The day he stripped naked and swam amongst the mangroves

was a day of such joy and freedom that young James did not believe his actions could possibly be sinful. His toes trailed in the softness of the mud, and he felt the gentle suction of the tide as he eased himself along beside the riverbanks, the silken water caressing every inch of his body. Beneath the silent canopy of mangroves which protected him from prying eyes, he was at one with the river. The gnarled mangrove trunks formed a maze of mysterious tunnels waiting to be explored. Alone in a secret magic land, nakedness could surely not be sinful, in a secret magic land, surely normal rules did not apply.

As the weeks grew into months, emboldened by the strength of their friendship, Turumbah appeared to forget the boundaries which separated him from James. He had taught Gran'sun James how to catch the mud crabs which lived amongst the mangroves. His mother, Murrumuru, had shown him how they cooked the eels. Turumbah had even taught him how to paddle a canoe, laughing when James repeatedly capsized the light vessel. Turumbah was eleven years of age now; in less than one year he would be a young man, and young men were free to choose their friends. His grandfather, most respected of the elders, had himself welcomed Gran'sun James to the cooking fire. Why then should Turumbah hide such a friendship as if it were something that brought him shame?

It happened late one Sunday afternoon, when the family returned from a visit to their cousins on the Surry Hills.

Upon agreeing to the expedition, Mary had made it quite clear that Thomas was not to be present.

'I have Matthew's assurances on that, Mary,' Richard had assured her for the third time, 'although he honestly cannot fathom why you and Father—'

'Then you must tell him to stop trying,' Mary had interrupted. 'Neither he nor Emily will ever fathom the differences between your father and me.' She hadn't meant to snap, and with an apologetic smile, she explained as patiently as she could. 'Both your brother and his wife have far too much of the wild streak in them to begin to comprehend what is proper, Richard.' Her husband had been about to defend his brother, but Mary had been in no mood for debate. 'No matter, no matter, my dear. I agree that such differences should not in any way threaten the children's relationship with their aunt and uncle and cousins. Inform Matthew that we shall be pleased to stay overnight. I shall look forward to shopping with Emily and Hannah, and James can help young William on the farm. I must say,' she had added with some pride, 'William will be surprised at how fit and strong his cousin has become lately, James has grown sturdy over these past few months, quite the young man.'

On the Saturday night, around the large family dining table which Matthew himself had lovingly constructed and which was his pride and joy, the forbidden conversation was broached. Over a shoulder of beef with Yorkshire pudding, a mountain of baked vegetables and a large jug of gravy, Matthew and Emily attempted to bring up the subject of Thomas and the rift in the family. As Richard had warned them, it was to no avail.

'Beef,' Mary exclaimed at the first mention of her father-in-law, 'I am most impressed, how did you come by such a handsome shoulder of beef? It is surely one of the most expensive commodities in the colony.' Mary flashed a warning glance in Richard's direction. She had expected such an attempt from Emily and Matthew—despite the fact that they had been warned—both of them were socially gauche in Mary's opinion, and Richard had promised, under threat of an unpleasant scene, to come to her rescue.

'Matthew has an excellent arrangement with Godfrey Streatham, the storekeeper,' Richard proffered quickly—a scene was the last thing he wanted—'you know, Streatham and Son, the family retailers.'

'I most surely do.' Mary forgot that her query had been by way of distraction. 'Streatham and Son.' Her attention was caught in an instant. 'They have recently extended their business, I believe. They have advanced from the sale of basic commodities and barter transactions to the import of quality goods. Drapery and furnishings in particular. Did Leyland Harvey not tell you this, Richard?'

'Yes my dear,' Richard said with some relief, the immediate danger averted, 'you were quite right, imported quality goods are the way of tomorrow.'

'But the beef is not imported, Mary,' it was Emily, as usual ignoring the danger of the situation, 'it is top quality Blaxland beef, and was exchanged for several boxes of vegetables as fine as these you see upon this table, and we deliberately ordered a full shoulder hoping that perhaps we might invite Thomas to partake . . .'

Even Matthew flashed a warning, it was a bit late to invite Thomas now, his look said. But Emily had imbibed a little too much of the rough red wine which Mary and Richard had brought from their neighbours' new vineyard at Parramatta.

'. . . it is only a twenty-minute walk to Pitt Row,' she insisted, ignoring the warning, 'William could be back with the old man within the hour . . .'

'And Mary could be gone within the hour, my darling.' Matthew leaned across the table, grasped her hand and grinned. The only way out was to make a joke of it, he thought, sensing that Mary was about to spring to her feet. 'I am sure father will be happy with cold cuts tomorrow.'

'Grandpa Thomas is very fond of cold beef.' Under the table, Hannah kicked out at her brother William's foot, 'especially with mother's home-made horseradish sauce.' Having spent a fussy and interminable afternoon shopping with her aunt, Hannah would have welcomed a scene. 'Perhaps we could call upon him tomorrow, the whole family. We could lunch together.'

Hannah had never forgotten that day in Grandpa Thomas's front parlour when Aunt Mary had dropped all pretences and screamed like a banshee. Not that Hannah had approved of the reasons—what matter if cousin James was a little tattered and bleeding—but she had developed a new-found respect for her aunt's passion. In Hannah's opinion, all people should be passionate, whether right or wrong. Hannah intended to spend her entire life being passionate about everything.

Unfortunately Hannah's foot had missed its mark and Mary's ankle caught the blow. 'Yes, it is an excellent horseradish, Emily,' she said to her sister-in-law. 'May I?' As Richard hurriedly passed the bowl of sauce to his wife, Mary glared at her niece. The girl was rebellious beyond endurance.

Hannah, realising she had kicked the wrong person, awaited her aunt's accusation and her father's command to leave the table. But no accusation was made.

'You must give me the recipe, I insist.' Mary was determined there would be no scene, and Hannah, having met her aunt's withering glare with a bold return, was forced to look away. She was not yet a match for her Aunt Mary, but one day she would be. One day Hannah Kendall would be a match for anyone.

It was late Sunday afternoon when the family returned to Parramatta, and James, seated beside Phoebe in the rear seat of the carriage, did not see Turumbah as they turned from the dirt road through the open gates of the property, then up the winding track to the sandstone house. He and his sister had both been nodding off, lulled by the motion of the carriage and the steady clip-clop of the two-in-hand.

'I will not have this, Richard,' Mary said as she noticed the Aboriginal boy squatting beside the entrance to the harnessing yard. 'You must have words with the natives. They have not encroached upon our property to date and they are not to start now.'

As the carriage drew to a halt, Mary gave an imperious wave. 'Away with you, boy!'

Turumbah rose to his feet, and James looked about drowsily to see what was causing the commotion.

'Gran'sun James!' Turumbah stood, waving the hat like a flag, as he always did, and James watched in horror. 'Gran'sun James! I wait!'

Turumbah had been waiting for hours. When his friend James had not been at their meeting place by the mangroves, he had crept closer and closer to the grand house. Even the servants had not been there to shoo him away. And the big carriage and horses had gone. Turumbah had settled down to wait. At the sight of his friend, he had forgotten all the rules and begun jumping up and down, waving his precious hat as if his life depended on it.

Mary recognised the hat in an instant. As her husband helped her from the carriage and turned away to tend the horses, she whipped the offending article from the boy's hands. 'Where did you get this?' She dared not look at her son, for already she knew the truth.

Turumbah was startled. He was not by nature a nervous boy, but the sudden action caught him unawares. He edged away, wary, uncertain.

James had jumped down from the carriage, Phoebe beside him.

'I said where did you get this?' Mary wielded the bedraggled felt hat over the boy's head as if it were a cat-o'-nine tails and she were about to beat the life out of him with it.

It was then that young James Kendle did the boldest thing he had ever done, probably the boldest thing he would ever do in his entire life. He stepped forward and stood beside Turumbah.

'I gave it to him, Mother. As a gift. His name is Turumbah.'

Turumbah's uncertainty vanished in an instant. 'Gift,' he said. 'Turumbah, gift.' He grasped James's hand. 'Gran'sun James *budjerry* fellow. Turumbah friend.'

There was a long pause. Phoebe watched, frightened by her mother's anger; Richard stopped tending the horses, at a loss as to what to do, and James stared at the ground, unable to meet his mother's eyes. Only Turumbah seemed unaffected. He grinned at Mary, grinned at James, shuffled his feet and, apart from wishing that the missus would give him back his hat, felt perfectly happy.

'Turumbah?' Mary queried, and the edge had gone from her voice. The boy nodded. 'Here is your hat.' She handed it to him and he grabbed it eagerly. 'Go home now, go home.'

Turumbah nodded, waved and was gone in an instant, hoping that no-one would tell his grandfather he had been caught out of bounds.

'I do not blame you, James, I blame your grandfather.' Mary glanced briefly at Richard who made no comment. 'We will say no more about it.'

But Mary was angry. Very angry. For months now she had regretted the scene she had caused that day in Thomas's front parlour. She had lost her dignity, made a fool of herself. But the discovery of the hat changed everything. The boy had not merely been playing in the bush with his cousin, he had spent the entire day in the company of black heathens. Encouraged, furthermore, by his own grandfather to give away a valuable possession!

Mary felt sick with the anger which churned in the very pit of her stomach. The old man had treated her like a ranting, foolish woman that day, all the while knowing that her rage had been entirely justified. Dear God in heaven, what good Christian mother would not lose control under such circumstances? And now, with the natives living at her very doorstep, Thomas's reprehensible act had resulted in a friendship between her only son and one of the heathen children.

The following day Mary's rage had so deepened that she nearly broke her vow of silence. She paced the floor of the drawing room, on the verge of demanding that Richard take her to town that very morning so that she could tell Thomas Kendall that he could keep his inheritance and she would keep his grandchildren. She would tell him . . .

'There is a black woman at the front door, ma'am.' It was Peg, a basket of washing under her arm, tapping at the side windows of the drawing room. 'She has a boy with her. I told her to begone but she wants to see the mistress of the house. She speaks very proper for a native.'

'Very well, Peg. Tell her to go around to the back.'

A woman whom Mary judged to be in her thirties stood at the back door, the boy with the felt hat by her side.

'I am Murrumuru, missus,' she said.

Mary nodded and silently looked her up and down. The woman's skin was jet black and her ebony hair coarse and wiry, but Mary could not help observing that she was handsome in her own way, there was a bearing about her. Furthermore, she seemed respectable for a native; her skirt and blouse were clean and she wore slippers, which although worn and thin had once been fine.

'He say sorry,' she said, nudging the boy who twisted the hat self-consciously in his hands. 'We catch him come big house. Elders angry.' She nudged Turumbah again. 'Say sorry.'

Turumbah had cursed his indiscretion time and again during the night. He had been so excited at the return of his hat and the kindness in the missus's voice when she had simply told him to go home that he had forgotten to sneak back into the camp through the mangroves. He had not been clever. Now his mother insisted that he say sorry to the missus. His mother was always telling him to say 'sorry', or 'thank you', or 'please'. She was very proud of the English she had been taught by the military man's wife whom she had served in Sydney Town.

'Sorry, missus,' the boy mumbled.

Aware that Peg had come around to the back of the house, put down the washing basket and was watching the proceedings, possibly awaiting orders to shoo the intruders away, Mary decided to be gracious.

'Turumbah,' she leaned down to the boy, 'do you go to school?'

The boy looked up, first at Mary, then at his mother. 'Do you go to the mission school?' Mary repeated.

'I take him, missus,' Murrumuru said, proud that the missus knew her son's name. She didn't add that she had taken Turumbah to the mission school on only one occasion, that he'd refused to stay, and that she had given up on the exercise. Murrumuru had her reasons for wanting to impress the missus. 'Learn quick. Boy clever.'

'That is good,' Mary replied, not believing the woman.

'You need servant?' Murrumuru took the plunge. It was the reason she had dragged Turumbah to the big house in the first place. She had been wishing to make contact for quite some time, despite Wolawara's objections. To be a slave to the white people was not the plan, her father had insisted. It was not the reason Thomas Kendall had given them the land beside his clanspeople.

But during her two years in service, despite the hard toil involved, Murrumuru had adapted to household life. She missed the English food and the regular presents Lieutenant Hookway's wife gave her, the cast-off garments, hats and shoes. Not only for herself but for her children and her family. Her father had been proud of his red soldier's coat; why, then, should he be so adamant about returning to the old ways? It was a much harder life. Murrumuru could make it so much easier for all of them. And she would be given money too. Very little, it was true, but they could buy white man's things with money. It was better than begging in the streets as her brother Yenerah was doing once again, though she dared not tell their father.

Murrumuru took a deep breath and clearly enunciated her very best phrase, the one Missus Hookway had taught her when she had reluctantly resigned from service. 'I seek employment, missus,' she said.

Her announcement was met with silence, and Murrumuru hoped she hadn't offended the Missus who was staring at her, transfixed. 'I work good. Servant two year for army man. Lieutenant Hookway,' she announced with pride.

The woman was a godsend, Mary thought. In Murrumuru, she saw with instant clarity the solution to her dilemma. Thomas Kendall would be appalled to discover that one of his precious Wolawara's kin was in servitude to her rather than living a free life. And to keep a black servant was perfectly respectable, so long as the black servant could be taught to adhere to British standards of dress and decorum, which this woman obviously could. Furthermore, to convert a black servant was considered a positive triumph, the action of a truly Christian person. And that was exactly what Mary would do.

'Murru . . . ?' she queried.

'Murrumuru,' the woman answered quickly. 'I am Murrumuru.'

'Yes. Murrumuru. A pretty name.' She would insist the woman's child attend the mission school regularly, and the two of them would accompany Mary to church on Sundays. Mary would be seen to be a caring and civilising influence upon the family of her servant. Perhaps, in time, she could Christianise others amongst the clan. It was certainly her duty to try.

She would play Thomas Kendall at his own game. The old devil professed an understanding and a caring for the Aboriginal people. What had he done for them? Given them a parcel of marshy, non-productive land so they could return to their heathen ways. Mary would do far more. So long as they abided by her rules. For any who sent their children to school, she would provide food; to any who attended church, she would give cast-off clothes; to any who showed an inclination to utilise the land, she would provide basic gardening implements.

Not only would her treatment of the Aborigines be judged more proper and more Christian than Thomas's, her actions would drive the old man insane. She would undermine, at every turn, his well-laid plans for his native friends.

'Yes, Murrumuru, I do believe I could offer you employment.' The woman flashed a radiant smile, but Mary did not smile back. 'There will be conditions of course,' she added briskly, aware that Peg was scowling from the sidelines. Familiarity from the native woman must be firmly discouraged. 'I suggest you return tomorrow and we will discuss the arrangements.'

'Thank you, missus, thank you.' Murrumuru nudged her son. 'Say thank you, Turumbah.'

'Thank you, missus.' Turumbah beamed up at Mary. He was out of trouble and perfectly happy again. 'Turumbah see Gran'sun James?'

'No, Turumbah. Not now.' Not ever, Mary thought. The friendship between her son and the heathen black boy was terminated forever. 'I shall see you tomorrow morning, Murrumuru.' Mary gave a brusque nod to the woman, another brusque nod to Peg and went inside. But she left the door ajar and heard Peg stride up to Murrumuru.

'You listen to me, missy,' Peg said, 'and you listen good and proper. You learn your place. If the mistress wishes to employ you, and God knows why she should, you'll be answerin' to me, do you understand that?'

When Murrumuru had gone, and Peg had picked up her washing basket preparing to return to her duties, Mary confronted her 'You must mind *your* place, Peg.' Peg looked at her mistress, bewildered. 'That woman is, after all, a free woman,' Mary said. 'Unlike many in this colony, she has committed no crime. You must not forget that, Peg.'

Chapter Four

'Do not involve yourself too deeply with these people, Mary,' Elizabeth Macarthur advised. 'Not only for your own sake, my dear, but for theirs as well. You may do them more harm than good.'

Mary Kendle's plan had progressed slowly but, after a year of perseverance, she was finally making some headway in the education and betterment of her native neighbours. Much as he hated it, young Turumbah now regularly attended the mission school at nearby Black Town, and he and his mother accompanied Mary and her children to church on Sundays, Murrumuru occasionally bringing her elderly aunt, Yenada, with her.

The church outings were the only times Turumbah was allowed in the presence of his friend, Gran'sun James. And even then Gran'sun James barely acknowledged him. Whilst Turumbah pulled faces and tried to attract his attention, James would remain staring fixedly at the priest, concentrating on the interminable sermon.

Murrumuru would nudge her son, slapping his hand, fearful that his antics could cost her her employment. The missus had threatened that it might. And, all the while, Mary Kendle remained rigid, staring at the priest just as she had instructed her son to do. The native boy would learn eventually. His mother would teach him.

Young James Kendle was not happy. He missed his friendship with the Aboriginal boy, but fear of his mother's wrath overrode any desire to rebel. He never once attempted to sneak off to the riverbank where he knew Turumbah would be waiting. And now he was a prisoner in his home, his mother his gaoler. He no longer swam naked amongst the mangroves. He no longer watched Murrumuru cook the eels. Young James Kendle had lost the one brief taste of freedom he had ever known.

James had always been frightened of his mother, just as he was frightened of most things. In fact he had surprised himself with the boldness of his friendship from the very outset. The gift of his hat to Turumbah and the acknowledgement to his own mother of his action had been for James, a timid child by nature, acts of great bravery. Acts he would neither regret nor forget, but which he would never be able to repeat.

To Mary's great frustration, none of the Aboriginal menfolk could be persuaded to attend the church services, but she had employed several of them from time to time to repair fencing around the property. And once a week a growing number of Aborigines lined up, in orderly fashion, outside the servants' quarters for the bread, flour and sugar which, upon Mary's instruction, Timothy O'Shaugnessy dispensed amongst them.

Mary would have preferred a speedier conversion of the natives but, all in all, she was proud of her efforts, and Elizabeth Macarthur's words of warning were unwelcome.

Her displeasure was quite evident. 'Oh Mary,' Elizabeth assured her, 'I know your intentions are honourable, but you must be aware that others have experimented along these lines. The government itself has made repeated attempts to convert the natives to our way of life, with little success.'

Mary looked sullenly back at her friend. She so admired the older woman, so desperately sought her approbation, that she was hurt and disappointed at the note of censure in Elizabeth's warning. She had expected encouragement, even congratulations.

Elizabeth knew she was being a disappointment, but she continued nonetheless. 'Missionaries have tried, Mary. Men of faith, clergy trained in such matters. All have attempted it at one time or another, and all have failed.'

'But the clergy had no true feeling for these people,' Mary argued defensively. 'Why, the Reverend Samuel Marsden himself said that there would be no good done until we were rid of the natives. What Christian care is there in that attitude? And I do care for Murrumuru and her family, Elizabeth, I swear I do.'

Mary cared nothing for Murrumuru personally—the woman

was a black servant, no more, no less—but she had persuaded herself that her mission to Christianise and educate the natives surely meant that she cared in principle.

'I am sure you care for the woman, Mary. And if she wishes to be cared for, and if you can help her, then it does you credit. But you cannot take on her entire tribe. It will further neither your cause nor theirs.' Elizabeth felt obliged to fully spell out the dangers, remembering only too well as she did, the terrible European and Aboriginal conflicts of Parramatta's early days.

'You are supplying the natives with food, you say?'

'Those who show proper decorum and courtesy, yes. They are most polite when they queue up on Sundays, there is no unruliness amongst them . . .'

But Elizabeth appeared not to have heard. 'The word will spread,' she warned. 'It will be only a matter of time before they will come in numbers for the free food you are offering. Then there will be the odd theft of stock. A chicken here and there. Then they will start on the sheep of the nearby farms. And then the army will be called in. Be aware of the dangers, Mary. The dangers not only to yourself and your property, but to these people for whom you profess to care.'

Mary took her leave ten minutes later, courteously, wishing Elizabeth well. She had heard that John's illness had worsened of late, that he had been declared medically insane. But she couldn't help feeling, for the first time, a little superior to Elizabeth Macarthur.

Wolawara was deeply disturbed by the turn events had taken. He and Wiriwa had been happy in their new home. Content. Their family was healthier, their son was no longer begging in the streets of Sydney Town.

When his daughter had boldly announced that she was going to seek work at the big house, Wolowara had tried to dissuade her but, wisely, had not forbade her to do so. He could see that Murrumuru was bored, restless. She had grown accustomed to working in a white man's house. The fact that she had enjoyed such a life had always been a mystery to Wolawara. Servitude was not a part of his people's culture. To be a servant was to be a slave, and a person should be a slave to no-one.

Wolawara had decided that, if it would make Murrumuru happy to work in the big house, he would not stand in her way. But at times it troubled him to watch her, dressed in her grand new clothes, affecting the manners of the English missus.

When some of his clansmen accepted work digging fence posts at the big house, Wolawara could not blame them. They were paid a small amount of money and given as much food as they could eat. And he could not blame the others of his family when they lined up on Sunday to accept the bread and flour and sugar offered. But it did not bode well.

He was getting too old to make the decisions for the clan on his own, Wolawara thought, and lately the pain in his stomach seemed to attack more often and with greater ferocity. Even the healing potions Wiriwa gave him—the leaves and plant roots she ground and boiled in water—which normally provided comfort, now offered little relief when the pain twisted like a demon inside him.

So Wolawara did nothing. He and Wiriwa kept mainly to themselves, and during the days when he was free of the pain, he felt a great sense of peace. In his hut by the river, upon the land which he knew to be his own, Wolawara felt a sense of contentment greater than he had known in years.

Despite his reclusive behaviour, Wolawara still had a stabilising effect upon his clanspeople, the mere knowledge of his disapproval keeping an orderliness within the camp. Those who joined the Sunday queues outside the servants' quarters conducted themselves with 'decorum and courtesy' not so much to please the missus, but because they were concerned that Wolawara might be watching.

Occasionally, two or three of the young men stole into the township in search of rum, which they paid for from the money they had earned from their honest labour, but they never brought liquor back to the camp. And there was only one amongst them who regularly visited the streets of Parramatta to beg from the passers-by in order to feed his craving for rum and gin.

No-one told Wolawara about his son. No-one had the heart.

It was nearly five years after the clan's move to Parramatta that Wolawara mysteriously disappeared during the night. He had sat with the elders at the campfire the preceding evening but, come morning, he had gone, Wiriwa with him, and the younger members of the clan wondered at his absence. The elders, however, appeared to find no mystery in Wolawara's disappearance and when, four days later, Wiriwa returned to the camp, tired and drawn, they grieved with her for the loss of their kinsman.

Thomas Kendall was informed of Wolawara's death, strangely enough, through his daughter-in-law. Indirectly, of course. He had not seen, much less spoken to Mary since that day in the front parlour of his old house in Pitt Row.

The day Richard told him that Wolawara had died, Thomas was seated in the back garden of his cottage, high on the point near the windmill. His young granddaughter Hannah, who visited him regularly, was sitting with him, enjoying the warm sunshine.

Thomas's had been the first residential dwelling to be built on the point. Below, on the banks of the bay, seethed the taverns and brothels and gambling dens of The Rocks, where sailors and fishermen vied for whores' favours, drank rum together, then fought each other for the sheer pleasure of it. The cottage looked over this colourful potpourri of vice to the harbour beyond, where Fort Macquarie stood, ever vigilant, on the opposite headland, and where fishing boats nestled comfortably in the bay. It was a view of which he never tired.

'Mary asked me to tell you,' Richard said awkwardly, as his father stared out across the water. 'It happened several days ago. He had been ill for some time, I believe.

'He and his wife left the camp apparently, and four days later she came back with the news of his death,' Richard continued. 'Evidently it was quite expected.'

Of course Wolawara would have left the camp, Thomas thought, if he had had the option. Dying on the property would have affected his clanspeople—Aborigines would not live or camp at a death site. It was good that he had had the company of Wiriwa, and Thomas hoped that his old friend's death had not been too painful.

Richard waited for a reply from his father but none was forthcoming. 'I'm not even sure if Mary ever met the fellow, he kept very much to himself. I certainly never met him. She has met quite a number of the others though. She's been very good to them, Father, you'd be surprised.'

Richard knew he was gabbling, but he couldn't seem to stop.

He looked to Hannah for help, but his niece had simply taken the old man's hand in both of hers, seemingly unaware of the awkwardness of the situation.

'Mary has formed a relationship with the Aborigines over the past few years,' Richard continued. 'She's given them medicine for their children and so on . . .' Richard faltered. In truth, Mary no longer seemed interested in her Aboriginal cause, and for months now things had not been right in the Kendle household. Richard knew he was to blame, but for how long must he pay?

At first she had kept her hurt and anger to herself, presumably for the sake of the children, but over the past month she had been openly hostile. Even when he went out of his way to please her, which he did regularly. Richard didn't know what to do. The childen were being neglected and the natives were becoming more and more unruly.

Their numbers had been increasing ever since Wolawara's death; the queues at the servants' quarters had grown longer and rowdier, Mary no longer bothering to maintain control. Previously, at the first sign of disorderly conduct, she would have the food withdrawn. Now she was not even present at the Sunday disbursements, Timothy simply doling out the supplies as a matter of custom. Drunkenness had become evident in the camp and Richard told himself he would have to order Timothy to cease the disbursement of supplies, for his wife was too caught up in her own unhappiness to care.

'Anyway, Father,' Richard resumed lamely, wishing that Thomas would at least look at him, 'as I say, Mary wanted me to tell you the news as soon as possible. Which of course I would have done without her bidding,' he added quickly. 'I know this man was your friend.'

'Thank you, Richard.' There was an awkward pause.

'Is there any message you wish me to convey?' To whom, Richard wondered even as he asked. The man's wife? There were several elderly women at the camp, Richard had no idea which one might be Wolawara's wife.

Thomas finally seemed shaken from his reverie. He patted Hannah's hand, smiled briefly at her, and turned to his son.

'Thank Mary for me,' he said. 'I'm obliged for the news.'

Richard left minutes later, relieved to be gone, and Hannah sat silently with her grandfather, understanding his grief. She knew the importance of Wolawara in her grandfather's life. She had not only met the man when she was a child, but her brother William had related to her every detail of the day Grandpa Thomas had sat upon the Sydney Common and told his grandsons his story.

Hannah remembered being jealous at the time—she should have been there to share in the event. She had even written the story in her journal, the impressive leather-bound diary which her mother had given her upon her sixteenth birthday.

'Every young girl needs a diary, Hannah,' Emily had said with a conspiratorial wink, 'to record her innermost secrets.'

But to Hannah it was not a girlish diary at all, it was a journal for the recording of special events. Boldly, she had told Grandpa Thomas that she had written his story, and boldly she had waited, prepared to shoulder the burden of his anger. But, to the contrary, he had given her a hug and told her he was proud of her. 'I have learned my lesson, Hannah,' he had said. 'I promise I shall not exclude you in future.'

'Would you like a cup of tea, Grandpa Thomas?' she now asked.

'Thank you, my dear, an excellent idea.'

He watched her fondly as she went inside. Hannah was still his favourite. At twenty years of age, an able-bodied, strong-willed young woman with a rebellious streak just like his own, she was more like a son to him than a granddaughter.

It was sad, Thomas thought, very sad, that he had not seen Wolawara for so many years. He turned to stare unseeingly across the bay.

'I must visit Wiriwa and offer my condolences,' he said to Hannah when she returned with the tea. 'In a month or so's time when the mourning period is over.'

'May I come with you?' It was a rather bold request.

'Yes, Hannah, you may, if you wish.'

Thomas could have hugged her. It was not a trip he was looking forward to, and her presence would make all the difference.

Thomas Kendall did not announce his arrival at Parramatta to his son and daughter-in-law, he saw no occasion to do so for he did not intend to visit them. With Hannah in the trap beside him, he drove directly to the Aborigines' property, and it was midafternoon as, together, they walked from the track high on the ridge down into the camp to find Wiriwa.

Thomas was appalled and saddened by what he saw. Empty bottles and refuse littered the camp, and the first drunken person he encountered was Yenerah. That should not have surprised him, he supposed, but the lad at Yenerah's side, sharing the bottle with him. Mumbling. Incoherent. Reeling in his drunkenness.

'Turumbah?' Thomas queried. The lad could be no more than fifteen, perhaps sixteen, years old. Turumbah turned at the sound of his name, and Thomas ripped the bottle from his hand. Instinctively, the boy made to grab it back.

'Massa rum, gimme rum.' The words he'd heard his uncle saying to passers-by in the town.

Thomas cuffed the side of the boy's face with the back of his hand. Not hard, but Turumbah lost his balance and fell into the bushes. Yenerah giggled foolishly and squatted down beside him.

'Turumbah!' Thomas repeated.

The shock of the blow and the anger in the man's voice had a sobering effect. Turumbah stared up at the old man with the white beard who stood glowering over him, and he knew, through the blur in his brain, who it was.

'Thomas Kendall,' he said. The name he had heard his grandfather say over and over. 'Thomas Kendall,' he repeated, then he started to babble. 'Gran'sun James, Turumbah friend, Gran'sun James, Turumbah friend . . .'

Thomas dragged the boy to his feet. 'Where is your grandmother?' he demanded. 'Where is Wiriwa?'

The prospect of facing his grandmother in his present state had an immediately sobering effect on Turumbah. His grandmother was an old woman, wise the way the old were, and she would know in an instant. 'Rum,' she would say, and she would spit on him the way he had seen her spit on Yenerah.

He shook his head and mumbled.

Thomas wrested the boy to his feet. 'I want to see your grandmother, take me to see her.'

The old man's steel-like grip was as frightening as the prospect of his grandmother's wrath and Turumbah realised he had no option. He led the way to the hut by the river, Hannah silently following.

But Wiriwa did not spit on her grandson. The old woman shook her head sadly and waved him inside the hut, beckoning Thomas and Hannah to join her where she sat cross-legged at the door, Murrumuru by her side. Murrumuru no longer worked at the big house during these troubled times.

Wiriwa and Thomas introduced their daughter and granddaughter respectively, Murrumuru raising her eyes for barely a second before returning her gaze to the ground, but Thomas was accustomed to the shyness of Aboriginal women amongst strangers. He and Wiriwa chatted quietly, he offering his condolences and she explaining that Wolawara's death had been expected and that he had met it as bravely as she knew he would. She was glad, she said, that he had died without knowing the extent of his son's shame. She had disowned Yenerah, she told Thomas. He had been her only remaining son, but he was her son no more.

Guilt rested heavily upon Thomas. He took her hand and she looked at him, surprised. 'Forgive me. *Ngandu.*'

'*Ngandu*, Thomas Kendall?' Wiriwa looked bewildered.

'This place . . .' How could Thomas express his guilt? How could he tell this old woman, his friend, that perhaps he had been misguided? Much as he had meant to do good for her people, perhaps his interference had brought more trouble to their lives. 'This place, *wiri* place.'

She smiled a toothless smile. 'No, no. This place, *budyari* place.' It was clear she had understood and wanted to set him at ease. 'This place, no *wiri* place. *Wiri balagaman*, no *wiri* place.' She smiled again and boldly patted the hand that rested upon hers. 'Wolawara *gurigurang*, this place.'

'Thank you.' Thomas smiled, grateful for her words of comfort. It meant a lot to know that Wolawara had been happy on the land which was his. He and Wiriwa spoke a little longer, then Thomas rose, his body stiff and sore—he was no longer accustomed to sitting on the ground. 'Hannah, we must leave now.'

As Wiriwa rose to bid them farewell, Thomas told her that the land remained her property. He didn't have the words to tell her it was legally deeded as such, and he knew that she would not understand if he did. But he told her that, no matter how far she travelled, the land would always belong to her people, to the people of the Gadigal tribe. If she ever wished to return to this place, he said, this place would be hers.

She offered her hand, as Wolawara had always offered his upon parting with his friend. '*Gumal*, Thomas Kendall,' she said, and they shook hands like men.

'*Gumal*, Wiriwa.'

As they walked back through the camp, Hannah glanced sideways at her grandfather. It was a steep trek up from the riverbanks to the track where they had left the trap, and his breath was a little laboured. She was longing to know what had transpired, but she did not want to intrude on his thoughts. To her surprise as soon as they had gained flatter ground and Thomas had recovered his breath, he began to talk.

'Wiriwa told me that she is leaving with her daughter, grandson and some of her relatives before dawn tomorrow morning,' he said. 'I have assured her that this land belongs to the Gadigal people. It is hers to return to whenever she wishes. It belongs to her grandchildren and to her grandchildren's children should they wish to return to it. I would like you to write all of this in your journal, Hannah.'

Hannah looked at him; she had no idea he took her journal as seriously as she did herself.

'Someone must record their story, Hannah.' Thomas was in deadly earnest. 'Even their language is dying. Someone must record their story.'

They talked little in the trap on the long return to town, Hannah insisting upon taking the reins, for her grandfather looked very old and tired.

Parramatta had grown into a thriving township she was surprised to note as they trotted along Church Street where pedestrians promenaded in the early evening, and street-stall vendors touted, and shops and businesses did a brisk trade. Then they were out in the countryside where the smell of the eucalypts was strong in the nostrils; where sulphur-crested cockatoos screeched in the trees, and wallabies came out to graze in the cool of the gathering dusk.

Her grandfather seemed unaware of the surrounding beauty of the bush. He was not only tired, Hannah thought. He was sad. Even though the old woman, Wiriwa, had said something which had made him smile. Shortly before they had said goodbye. Hannah wondered what it could have been.

Before they alighted at the Surry Hills, it was as if Thomas had read her mind. 'I shall tell you everything, Hannah. I shall tell you everything, and you shall record it in your journal.'

It was not long before every one of Elizabeth Macarthur's predictions proved correct. Following the damage to property, the theft of chickens and corn, and finally the unforgivable disappearance of a number of sheep and cattle from nearby properties, the farmers rebelled and the army was called in.

Shortly after dawn's first light, from her balcony overlooking the Aborigines' property, Mary Kendle watched the arrival of the soldiers high on the ridge behind the camp. She recalled Elizabeth's words. But she felt no guilt. She could have done some good for these people, but she had been betrayed. Had she not been betrayed, she would have taken the situation under control before it had become so volatile. And if Elizabeth were here now, that is exactly what she would tell her. But Mary had seen her friend only once since that day at Elizabeth Farm, and then briefly, two years ago, at Camden Park, on the occasion of John Macarthur's funeral.

Everything had changed, Mary thought, as she watched the redcoats leave their horses and drays up on the track, and start their march down into the camp. She would tell Richard tomorrow that they were moving from Parramatta. Their business was mainly in Sydney Town these days, and she no longer liked this house.

Mary had known the army was mounting its raid this morning, all the local property owners had been warned, the Kendle family in particular having been told to leave at dawn or to keep within the safety of their home.

James and Phoebe had accompanied their father into Sydney Town, but Mary had insisted on staying.

'It could be dangerous,' her husband had warned.

'Nevertheless, I intend to watch, Richard. Can you blame me?' And, once more defeated, he'd said nothing.

Mary could barely see the redcoats now. They had disappeared amongst the bush, making their way towards the river. Flashes of red, glimpsed briefly amongst the trees. As she waited for the sound of a musket shot, that awful day came flooding back.

It was a Sunday. The house was empty, the servants at church. She herself had been at church with the children, but had returned home because Phoebe, as always during her time of the month, was ill.

As she unharnessed the horse, she told Phoebe to go into the house and lie down, she would presently bring her a warm compress. It was a hot day and the horse needed to be watered and stabled.

As she opened the stable door she heard a woman laughing. Quietly, she stepped inside, closed the door behind her and waited whilst her eyes adjusted to the gloom.

She saw them, half naked, on the fresh straw bedding at the end of the stalls. But they did not see her. Her husband, bare-chested, the whiteness of his skin stark against the bare black breasts he fondled. Murrumuru laughed again as he fumbled with her skirts, pulling them high above her naked black thighs. She was still laughing as Mary silently opened the stable door and stepped outside. Back into the glare of the day.

While she prepared the warm compress for Phoebe, she fought the desire to vomit. Her mind was a blank. There was nothing but the image of their bodies and the knowledge of her betrayal.

When Murrumuru presented herself for work the following day, Mary told her that her services were no longer required. She didn't look at the woman as she said, 'I am employing a ticket-of-leave worker. I have decided, after all, that I prefer the services of a white person.'

And to her husband she simply said, 'I am no longer happy with the woman's work.' She was unable to say Murrumuru's name out loud. Richard seemed quite content with the explanation.

It took a week or so for him to realise that his wife knew of his infidelity, though he had no idea how. Nothing else could explain her constant coldness, the looks of pure loathing which met his every attempt at charm.

Finally, one night when he had decided to make a more intimate approach in the hope that that might win her, she turned on him, sickened with hurt and rage.

'I saw you, Richard,' she hissed. 'I saw you with her.'

In a way he was relieved that the truth was out. It was just the one time, he swore to her. The woman had teased and taunted and he had been unable to resist. He begged her forgiveness. He loved her. He would devote his life to making her happy if she would only forgive him his one moment of weakness.

Mary knew she would never forgive him, but if he was telling the truth, at least she could see a way of returning to a semblance of their previous life together. Without the trust of course, but she would allow him to woo her forgiveness. There was a certain merit in that.

The ambush was unexpected. The young Aboriginal men who had been stealing livestock from the local farms had met with violence before. A number of times their raiding parties had been chased by angry farmers, and several had narrowly escaped a musket ball. But no white man, farmer or soldier, had as yet ventured upon their land.

Redcoats swarmed into the camp, where huts and lean-tos nestled by the river. Panic broke out. Women screamed and clutched their babies and children. Men, most of whom had been sleeping, grabbed for their spears and clubs.

Lieutenant Brewster fired his pistol into the air as a warning. His orders had been to keep the exercise as peaceful as possible. The camp was to be cleared, the huts burned to the ground, and all children to be taken for placement in missionary institutions.

The warning shot served its purpose. There was a startled silence. Women stared, shocked; men, clubs and spears in hand, halted as they saw the numbers of soldiers and guns, aware that their weapons were of little use against the fire from a musket's muzzle.

'Clear these huts!' Lieutenant Brewster shouted to his men. 'Round up the children and take them to the drays!'

Men, muttering rebelliously, were shunted about with the butt of a rifle or the shove of a hand. Women wailed as infants were torn from them. They grabbed back at their children, only to be pushed away by rough hands and yelled at by rough voices.

In Yenerah's drink-diseased brain, the voices which spoke to him told him these were *wiri wiri* men, demon men. And they had been sent to murder him in his sleep. But they had failed, he thought triumphantly. Yenerah held his *ngalangala*, ready to kill.

Squatting low, club in hand, he looked wildly about at the chaos. He would fight them all. He would kill any *wiri wiri* man who touched him. He would kill every single one of them if he
had to.

The butt of a musket prodded him on the shoulder. 'I said move along there.'

Yenerah screamed as he whirled. From his squatting position, he rose to his feet, swinging his *ngalangala* with both hands. The knobbed head of the club caught the soldier under the chin, smashing his jaw and laying open the side of his face.

'*Djiriyay!*' Yenerah shrieked as the soldier fell in agony. '*Djiriyay!*'

Yenerah's war cry was enough to inflame several of the others. Even as a musket ball exploded Yenerah's chest, a number of Aborigines turned on their captors. A soldier was speared through the leg, another clubbed to the ground, and panic abounded on both sides. The soldiers started backing away, firing indiscriminately.

Five of the men who had turned on the soldiers were shot dead in the barrage of gunfire, and several wounded. An old man, clawing for the return of his grandchild, was shot through the head. A young woman who ran at the soldier carrying her infant was shot through the chest. It was only when eight Aborigines lay dead, and the others had fled into the bush, leaving the elderly, the women and the children moaning and wailing and crying, that the mayhem ceased.

Yenada knelt staring at the body of her husband as the blood poured from his head in a steady stream towards the river. Why did they kill Nowinah? He had been begging them to return his grandson, nothing more. Numb with shock, Yenada did not wail and moan with the others, but she rocked on her heels as she knelt. They should have gone with her sister Wiriwa, she thought over and over. For the sake of their grandson, they should have gone. Wiriwa had said that bad things were going to happen, the white missus had told Murrumuru. 'Take your family and go,' that's what the missus had said. But Nowinah had refused to leave. He was an elder and it was his duty to stay and advise his people. That was what he had told her, but Yenada knew it was because he had grown too used to the easy life.

As the soldiers collected the children and took them away, Yenada waited to be herded up the hill with the others. To watch as they set fire to the huts.

She was old now; soon she too would be dead. Death held no fear for her. But killing did.

Yenada could still remember the terror of the night at the bay of rushes, the night when the convicts had dragged her from the camp. That night had been a night of killing, and her people had not been outnumbered then. But the slaughter had given her no joy. She had hoped she would not witness another such killing.

'Come along. Come along now, grandma.' The voice was not unkind. 'We have to get you up the hill where it's safe.'

The old man should not have been killed, the young private thought, taking Yenada's arm as gently as he could and helping her to her feet. Terrible things had happened here this morning. 'Come along, grandma.'

Upon government orders, a military investigation was held as to the necessity for such wholesale slaughter of the natives, but nothing untoward was found, particularly as two soldiers had been severely wounded. As a result, it was found unnecessary for reports of the killings to be made public. Renegade Aborigines had been routed from the area, the community was informed. Disease-ridden campsites had been burned to the ground, and sickly, malnourished children had been taken to missionary institutions where they would be housed, nurtured and educated. For their own good.

The Aborigines did not return to the death place, and the property remained vacant. When James and Mary sold their grand house and moved to Sydney Town, the buyers made an offer to Thomas Kendall for the sale of the adjoining land. But it was not within his power, Thomas informed them, the land was no longer his to sell. It was a cause of frustration to the new owners of the big house.

'Wolawara's family never returned,' Mary said. 'They never even attempted to reclaim the property.'

Thomas had not seen his daughter-in-law for ten years, and he was astounded that, upon such a sad occasion, her first words to him should be of the massacre four years previously.

It was at the wake, following her daughter Phoebe's funeral, that

Mary approached Thomas. Not once during the graveside ceremony had she cast a look in his direction. She had stood stiffly, her husband on one side, her son on the other, watching the lowering of the casket without shedding a tear.

Phoebe had died of typhoid at just twenty-six, leaving behind a one-year-old son and a devoted young husband. As Thomas looked at Nathaniel Streatham openly weeping over his wife's grave, he felt a weary sense of guilt. It is high time I died, he thought. At seventy-six years of age it was obscene to witness the burial of one's grandchild.

Thomas Kendall was amazed that he was still alive. Who would ever have thought that he would see the year 1840 nearly at a close? He stood at the graveside with Matthew and Emily, who themselves were grandparents now, their son William holding his secondborn in his arms. He longed to be reconciled with his younger son's family before he died. Kendall or Kendle, what did it matter? They were blood. He did not wish to die with bad feeling between them.

Thomas had wandered around the elegant house in Elizabeth Bay, waiting for the right opportunity to approach his daughter-in-law. But Mary had been surrounded by her family, accepting the condolences of friends, and Thomas had not been able to break into the conversation without appearing clumsy. James had stood beside his mother, his young wife who had not been present at the ceremony for the obvious reasons of her advanced pregnancy, next to him, holding the hand of a small boy. Thomas had heard they'd had a son.

Even as he had stood watching, he had seen Mary make her excuses. He was heartened as he watched her approach, and his condolences had been sincere. 'It is a sad day, Mary. You have my deepest sympathy,' he had said. But she had appeared not to have heard.

'. . . Surely the fact that the Aborigines have not returned is proof that the gift of land was wasted on them,' she suddenly declared, her tone triumphant. Thomas was at a loss for words.

'Did you ever think you could solve the problem of those people?' Mary was relentless in her pursuit. 'You not only ruined their existence, you cost a number of them their lives.'

Her words tore at him. For years Thomas had lived with the

burden of the Parramatta slaughter, as if the dead had been slain by his own hand.

'I believe that Wolawara spent his final days in peace,' he replied weakly; it was all he could think of to say.

'You have given peace to no-one, Thomas. Least of all your family.'

Mary's aim had been to hurt. She had wanted to destroy the old man. He looked as if he was not long for this life. Good, she had thought as she had surreptitiously glanced at him in the cemetery, fully aware that he was studying her. Let him go to his death knowing that he has ruined our lives.

Now the hurt and horror in his face robbed her of her victory. He was already beaten; just as she herself was beaten.

'And as for me . . .' Mary turned to stare at her husband. Richard was standing at the far side of the room, talking animatedly to Hannah, who was looking with some concern in their direction. 'It was your actions, Thomas, which ruined my marriage.' She studied her husband a moment longer, then turned back to face him. In her eyes Thomas could see the years of bitterness. 'For that I will never forgive you.'

With that, she walked away, once again circulating amongst the guests, accepting their condolences and encouraging them to drink a cup of tea or a glass of wine. Thomas stood still, utterly bewildered. How had he wreaked such havoc upon his family? What was it he had done?

'Can I get you something to drink, Grandpa Thomas?' It was Hannah, as always with an eye to his comfort. He did not respond, so she continued encouragingly, 'The red wine is excellent, I believe, from the vineyards of Aunt Mary's friends at Parramatta.'

She had witnessed the exchange between her aunt and grandfather. What in God's name had Mary said to him? The old man looked shocked, pale.'Come and sit down. Let me fetch a glass for you.'

From the far side of the room Mary watched as the old man allowed himself to be seated. He and Hannah were inseparable according to Emily.

'She writes down all of his stories in the diary I gave her,' Emily had said, 'and she won't let anyone see. It's for posterity, she says. Well, that doesn't seem right to me at all,' Emily had laughed affectionately as she'd prattled on, 'a girl should write about beaus in her diary. But then Hannah doesn't seem particularly interested in beaus.'

It was probably the beaus who were not interested in Hannah, Mary thought as she watched her niece return with the wine. A bold, brawny girl, one who made few concessions to femininity, it would be a rare breed of man who would take on Hannah Kendall. So unlike her mother, Mary thought, as she caught sight of Emily comforting Nathaniel. Even in middle-age, and even at a wake, Emily fluttered her fan coquettishly at Godfrey Streatham as she offered condolences to his son. And Matthew, standing beside his wife, smiled fondly, proud of her femininity.

Theirs was a good marriage, Mary thought with envy. A good marriage bound by love, support, trust, a happy family surrounding them ... She must not get maudlin, she told herself. The Kendalls, after all, would amount to nothing. The market farm had long since been subdivided and sold, the family keeping several small allotments which they rented to tenants. No longer a scattered village, Surry Hills was becoming the backyard of Sydney, providing low-rental housing for the working class. As landlords, the Kendalls earned enough to keep their family clothed and healthy, but they would have little to leave their children and their children's children.

The descendants of the Kendle line, however, would inherit wealth, power and station. She, Mary Kendle, had been the driving force behind a legacy unequalled in the colony. Her children would inherit Kendle and Streatham, soon to become the finest emporium in Sydney. What need had she for envy?

But try as she might, Mary could not shake off her despondency. It was a wake she told herself, the funeral of her only daughter, she was supposed to be despondent. But she had accepted Phoebe's death. During the two weeks it had taken Phoebe to die, mother and daughter had never been closer.

Mary's one worry had been that Phoebe might have married Godfrey Streatham's son simply to please her. The Kendle partnership with Streatham and Son, the well-known family retailers, had certainly been the business coup of the decade, and Phoebe had always done as her mother wished. But theirs had been a true love match. On her very deathbed, Phoebe had told her so.

'Look after him for me, Mother,' she had whispered in the dead of night when the fever had subsided, Mary spending every minute at her bedside. 'Look after Nathaniel, I do so love him.' They had clung to each other and wept and never in her life had Mary felt so close to another human being.

'I will love him like my own son, my darling, I promise,' she had whispered.

'And the baby. Look after the baby.'

'Your baby will have the world, Phoebe. I will give Howard Streatham the world, I promise you that too.'

The memory of her promises made Mary strong. So why did she feel so sad, so defeated?

She could live without the happiness she saw in her sister-in-law's marriage. That was a small enough price to pay for the legacy she would leave her grandchildren.

No, it was the look on Thomas Kendall's face which filled her with despondency. She had wanted him to bear the brunt of her hurt; it was his fault, she had told herself that for years. If Wolawara had never been his friend, if he had not given the land to the Aborigines, if he had not placed temptation in her husband's path . . .

But her accusations had only brought back the past. The look on the old man's face, the shock and the query in his eyes re-opened the old wound, and the humiliation was as stinging, the pain as fresh now as it had been then.

'There will soon be trouble,' she remembered saying. 'Take your mother and Turumbah and leave the camp.'

It had been barely a month after her dismissal that Murrumuru had come to her in tears. At first Mary had not believed her.

'I sleep with the massa for twelve month now,' she had said, 'I sleep with no other man.'

Mary wanted to strike the woman. She did not believe her, she could not believe her. She must believe her husband. The two had never been lovers. 'Just the once', he had said, 'just the once.' The woman had teased and taunted, that's what he had told her.

She ordered Murrumuru out of her house.

'Please, missus,' Murrumuru had begged, tears coursing down her cheeks. 'I know I do wrong. I know. But I love Richard. And he tell me too, he love me, he tell me too.'

That was when Mary knew it was the truth. When, sickeningly, she heard Murrumuru call her husband by name. Perhaps she had always known it was the truth, she thought as she fetched the money.

'You must leave this place, Murrumuru,' she said. 'There will be trouble. Take this money and leave with your family. For the sake of your unborn baby you must leave this place.'

She didn't tell Richard about Murrumuru's visit and the fact that the woman was with child. What was the point—he obviously cared nothing for his Aboriginal mistress. But any remnant of love which existed within Mary died that day, and from then on she looked at her husband with loathing.

The years had passed and she had never told him about his child, but she made him suffer a contemptible marriage. He must be made to carry the burden of his guilt.

And tonight, as she had looked at the old man, Mary had decided that he too must share the guilt. She wondered what Thomas Kendall would do if he knew that he shared a grandchild with his friend Wolawara. He would never know, but as she had watched him, the old bitterness had crept back like bile. He should suffer along with her husband. Both of them should suffer, both of them should know that they were the cause of her unhappiness.

But the old man's suffering had not eased her pain. It had only brought back the past.

'And these are your children.' Thomas's voice was weak but still authoritative. 'Remind me, James, it is easy to forget when one is dying.' The old man's health had not been good for some years, but following Phoebe's funeral, he had fallen into a rapid decline. He pointed a fragile finger at the little boy who stood dutifully beside the bed. 'Charles, and . . .' He couldn't remember the name of the baby James's wife was cradling. But then he couldn't remember the name of James's wife either.

'Anne, Grandfather, we named her after Grandmother.'

'Christen her Anne,' Mary had said the instant she had discovered the new baby was a girl. 'It is both politic and practical, James. You must not forget that your grandfather is still a man of property.'

'Good, good,' muttered Thomas, distracted. He was proud of

his great-grandchildren, five in all with the new baby, but he needed to talk to James alone. He gestured for the others to leave and Alice Kendle backed towards the door with the baby, grasping three-year-old Charles's hand as she did so.

'You too, Hannah,' Thomas said gently. 'Go along, my dear.'

Hannah, who had remained silent in the bedside chair for the duration of her cousin's visit, rose and held the door open for Alice. Pretty little Alice gave her one of those superior, pitying looks she always gave her, and as usual Hannah had to fight back the urge to hit her. Clearly Alice felt sorry for Hannah. Plain, without a beau at twenty-six, Hannah was obviously destined for an old maid's life.

'No, not you, James,' Thomas said as his grandson followed the family out. 'I want to talk to you.'

It was with some reluctance that James closed the door and sat down beside his grandfather's bed. Fifteen minutes later, he closed the bedroom door behind him and entered the sitting room where the others were waiting. He looked shaken, and Hannah rose to her feet, concerned.

'Is he all right?' she asked.

'He wants to see you,' James said. 'He's rather agitated.'

'Did you upset him, James?' she barked.

'No, no, he upset himself, I swear it.' James was visibly upset and his wife rose to pacify him. 'I don't have the answers for him, Hannah. I don't know what he expects of me. I don't have the answers ...' But Hannah had disappeared into the hall.

Inside the bedroom she took her grandfather's hand in both of hers, as she had always done when she'd sensed he was troubled.

'He doesn't know, Hannah,' Thomas said, his voice feeble now. He was tiring, and the breath wheezed from his lungs with the effort of talking. 'He doesn't know.'

'It doesn't matter, Grandpa, it doesn't matter.' Gently, she stroked his hand, the soft raised veins and the translucent skin like silk beneath her fingers, and as she did so, she cursed Mary Kendle. Thomas himself had told her of the hideous accusations her aunt had flung at him the night of Phoebe's funeral. Hannah wished she knew the answers herself, she wished she could make them up so that her grandfather could die in peace. 'It doesn't matter,' she said again.

'It does, it does. It matters very much to me.'

'I know it does. I know. Ssh now, it's time you slept.' His agitation was keeping him awake, and that was not good for his heart.

'I must know the answers.' the old hand tensed around hers, and the breathing was laboured. 'I must know what happened, what it was that I did.'

'I will find out for you, Grandpa,' she promised, although she knew it was not possible. 'I will find out for you, I swear I will.' She had never lied to anyone, least of all to her grandfather, but she didn't flinch as the old eyes, dim and faded, met hers. 'I will find out and I will write it all down in the journal, I promise.'

'Ah, Hannah,' he sighed thankfully, 'we're a good team, you and I.' He believed her, Hannah never lied.

'Sleep now, Grandpa Thomas, please try and sleep. I'll be here when you wake up.' Her voice was gentle, and Thomas could feel his eyelids closing. 'Go to sleep now. Go to sleep.'

'He said that you had condemned him.' Shaken by the exchange at his grandfather's bedside, James confronted his mother that same evening. 'He was desperate to know why.'

'The wanderings of an old man's mind,' Mary said dismissively.

'But you told him he'd ruined your marriage. You told him he'd given peace to no-one, least of all his family. He's tormented, Mother. What did you mean?'

'For goodness' sake, James, the man is dying. Who knows what tricks a dying man's mind plays on him.' Abruptly, Mary terminated the conversation. 'Now go home to your family, it is getting late.'

Thomas died in the early hours of the following morning. In his sleep. Peacefully, Hannah hoped.

She never found out the answers her grandfather so desperately sought. But, fifty years later, James did.

BOOK TWO

THE CITY

Chapter Five

From their vantage point at Mrs Macquarie's Chair, the harbour promontory once favoured by Governor Macquarie's wife, Charles Kendle and his cousin Howard Streatham trained their binoculars on the two twenty footers. *Wings of Honour* was vying for first place with *Merlin's Magic.*

Amidst a flotilla of yachts, the two were charging home, and the harbour was a mass of canvas as sails flapped on the final turn, skippers screamed orders, swingers leaned so far out for the homeward run that their backs skimmed the water, and hundreds of onlookers roared out the name of their favourite.

Merlin's Magic had the edge, the crisp breezes favouring her lighter hull, just as the experts had predicted. 'If the winds are strong over the harbour tomorrow,' Christopher Pearce, popular columnist for the *Sydney Morning Herald*, had written, 'my money will be on *Merlin's Magic.*'

Pearce wandered over to Charles and Howard, champagne glass in hand. 'It appears I was right, gentlemen.'

'Anything can happen yet, Chris,' Charles said, 'anything at all.' The company of Kendle and Streatham was a major advertiser with the *Sydney Morning Herald* and the men had become good friends, Charles with an eye, as usual, to his advantage. Christopher Pearce was a powerful man, popular with his readers, and Charles had quickly realised that in these modern times the power of the press reached considerably further than the advertisement pages.

Howard, of course, was sceptical. But he was a Streatham and they were all the same. Honest, trustworthy and dependable, certainly, but predictable, unadventurous and, at times, downright boring.

'I have a feeling something's about to happen,' Charles muttered to Christopher. 'A change of wind perhaps.' He smiled roguishly as he glanced sideways at the columnist. He had told Pearce to put his money on *Wings of Honour*, regardless of prevailing winds or popular opinion.

Out on the harbour, aboard *Merlin's Magic*, the skipper was hurling abuse at his crew as he always did, even when they were winning. He screamed at a laggard who was straining himself to the limit; he kicked the bailer who was puffing and sweating; then, to the swingers as the yacht reached for home, he bawled, 'Out on her! Get your ugly carcasses out on her!'

Paddy O'Shea leaned out as far as he could. He was a powerful man, six feet tall, weighing sixteen stone, and two thirds of his body was out of the boat. He was clinging to the gunwales with his knees, and he could feel the waves flicking his back as the boat surged through the choppy waters. He was bearing half the weight of the swinger beside him and suddenly it appeared he could take the strain no longer. In a second, he was swept overboard. The other swinger went over the side too, and together they clung to the boat, their combined drag slowing it to a crawl.

The sails of *Merlin's Magic* luffed uselessly in the wind as *Wings of Honour* ploughed past the floundering vessel and raced to victory.

'I told you so, Chris.' Charles's smile was smug and confident as his sister topped up his champagne glass. 'Thank you, Anne.'

Christopher Pearce was glad he had done as Charles had suggested and put his money on *Wings of Honour*. He didn't know how Kendle had managed it but, as usual, his tip was a good one, and, as usual, one favour deserved another. Already he had his leader for tomorrow's column. 'Charles Kendle's yacht flew home to victory in yesterday's spring regatta, proving that she is worthy of the proud store motto after which she is named. *Kendle and Streatham, Trading on the Wings of Honour*.'

In the back rooms of the Hero of Waterloo, Paddy O'Shea pocketed the five pounds Colin 'Cocky' Shaw handed him.

'We'll keep you on ice for a while, Paddy me old mate,' the cockney said. 'Don't want the word gettin' round. P'raps the Autumn Race Carnival, what do you say?'

'That's fine by me, Cocky,' Paddy agreed, and off he went to collect his winnings from the bookie with whom he'd placed a whole six quid, more than a fortnight's wages. But then *Wings of Honour* had been a sure bet.

These odd jobs were the cream on top of the milk, Paddy thought as, half an hour later, he walked up Windmill Street. A hell of a lot more lucrative than working the docks, and a lot more fun into the bargain. Now he could take his girls out for a Saturday night on the town, and he could give his old mother some ready cash to buy herself something nice. Not that she ever did, but they always shared the fun of his latest windfall.

'You rascal, Patrick O'Shea,' she'd say. 'What have you been up to this time?'

He never told her. 'Ask me no questions and I'll tell you no lies, Ma,' he'd say with a smile and a wink.

Today was no exception. She opened the door of her cottage, he thrust two one-pound notes into her hand, and she said, 'Where in God's name did this come from? I don't need this money. You take it right back, Patrick O'Shea.'

'Come on now, where's a hug?' She was a big, bulky woman, despite her sixty-seven years, but he lifted her bodily off the ground. 'Where's a hug for your only son?'

'Put me down!' she protested. 'Put me down, Paddy,' but she returned the embrace with equal fervour. Hannah Kendall O'Shea loved her son. He was an incorrigible, impetuous, reckless young man, just like her Daniel had been, and the adventurous spirit in Hannah loved him for it.

It had been that very spirit which had so attracted Daniel O'Shea to Hannah Kendall. He had recognised instantly a kindred soul.

'You won't find better than me, Hannah,' he'd said when he'd asked her to marry him. 'I'm amongst the best Mother Ireland has to offer.'

'Oh, is that so, Daniel?' she'd laughed. 'Then I should certainly hate to see her worst.'

'You'd not regret marrying an Irishman, I swear.' It sounded like another boast, but the banter had left his tone. 'We're a poor country with little to offer those outside, except our very selves.' Daniel had left his beloved Ireland only the previous year, like many hundreds of others, to escape the potato famine. 'And to those who take us into their hearts, we can bring magic.'

Hannah looked at him sceptically, he was a mercurial man, it was difficult to tell whether or not he was serious.

'I tell you, girl, I'll make you laugh and I'll make you cry, but I'll never bore you. And you're a woman, Hannah, who should never be bored. You will marry me, won't you?'

The following day, just one month after their initial meeting, Hannah announced her impending marriage. Everyone, with the exception of her brother William in whom she had confided, was astounded. Her Aunt Mary was openly scathing when she heard the news.

'The woman's mad to even consider marrying an Irishman,' she said to anyone who would listen. 'Chances are he'll murder her in her bed.' Mary suffered the anxiety prevalent amongst the English upper class regarding the Irish. Then to William, upon his brief visit to the Elizabeth Bay mansion, she added 'besides, the man's as poor as a church mouse, he's marrying her for her money.'

'If that were the case, Aunt Mary, he could do a lot better,' William protested, 'Hannah's hardly wealthy. None of we Kendalls are wealthy.' They saw little of the Kendle side of the family these days, which suited William. He found the Kendles' obsession with money and power made for boring conversation.

'She has the cottage,' Mary retorted. Then, sensing her nephew's disapproval, she added, 'Oh well, I suppose it's better she marry a ne'er-do-well, and an Irish one at that, than remain an old maid.'

When he was introduced to the family, Daniel didn't help matters by boasting, 'I'm a happy man, 'tis a woman of property I'm marrying.' And Hannah laughed, knowing it was a deliberately provocative statement. Daniel cared nothing for the fact that her grandfather Thomas had bequeathed her his cottage in the Rocks. 'Although,' he said to her privately, ''tis a convenient place to hang my hat.' Preferable, he admitted, to his one-room lodgings off the South Head Road. Daniel was employed as a labourer on the building of the new Victoria Barracks nearby.

Despite their own generous legacy, the Kendles had been critical of Thomas's last will and testament. The cottage should not have been left to Hannah—property was never left to female descendants, certainly not when there were male heirs. But Hannah knew the bequest was a declaration of love. Her grandfather had given her his precious cottage, the cottage where they had sat together in the little back garden overlooking the water, he dictating his stories and she recording them in her journal.

Now she sat in the same little back garden with her son, looking out over the same water but at a very different view. Massive tall ships rested in the haven of Sydney Cove—the great wool-clippers which she loved to watch race into the harbour—and dozens of windjammers were berthed beside the horseshoe-shaped sea-wall of semi circular quay. The sea-wall, which served as a quay along the entire waterfront of Sydney Cove, was a masterpiece of engineering construction but Hannah found it quite absurd that these days it was referred to as Circular Quay; the term really didn't make sense at all.

Directly below the cottage lay the tangled mess of the Rocks. Still a den of vice, still home to drinking and gambling and whoring, it was home also to the many who now lived in the tiny terrace houses which marched in rows down the hill. Washing was strung from garden to garden; neighbours exchanged produce grown in their little vegetable plots, a carrot here for a turnip there, a tomato or two for a lettuce. A strong community spirit existed amongst the residents of the Rocks.

'Do you want to join us tonight, Ma?' Paddy strode about, looking oversized in the small courtyard of the garden. He was elated, and Hannah wondered just exactly what it was he'd been up to. She hoped he wasn't gambling again, his wife would leave him if he was. Dorothy was a tough little woman and she'd threatened to do so before. Hannah knew her son could survive without his wife, but she would take the child, and the loss of his little girl would destroy him.

'Just the four of us,' he said. Then, arms wide as if he were about to burst into song, 'Dotty, the light of my life; Kathleen, the jewel in my crown; and you, the best mother a man ever had. Me and my three girls, out for a Saturday night on the town.'

Hannah laughed loudly, as Paddy had known she would. The pose and the brogue were pure Daniel O'Shea. But even when it was not a deliberate ploy to delight his mother, there was an Irish lilt to Paddy's voice. Born and bred in Sydney, he was Australian all right, and proud of it, but he was proud of the half of him that was Irish too.

'Come along, Ma, what do you say?'

'No, no, dear. All that walking, it would be more than my knees could take. Besides,' she added before her son could insist, 'there is an orchestral recital this evening, to celebrate the third anniversary of the Garden Palace, and I am to accompany Anne.'

'Ah,' Paddy mocked, 'fraternising with a Kendle, as I live and breathe.'

'She may be Charles's sister but she is not a Kendle,' Hannah insisted. 'She is a Goodlet.'

For thirty years Hannah had disassociated herself from the Kendles. She hadn't even attended the funerals of Mary and Richard. If Daniel O'Shea was not good enough for the Kendles, then the Kendles were not good enough for her. They were money-grabbing and power-hungry, and she disliked both her cousin James and, from the little she'd seen of him, his son Charles. She felt sorry for James's daughter Anne, however, and from time to time arranged outings with her. Daniel had died three years ago, around the same time as Anne's husband. The tenuous bond of widowhood existed between the two women but little else, apart from Hannah's genuine sympathy. Barely over forty, Anne was a tragic figure. Lonely and isolated. Living with her brother Charles and his family, she was totally reliant upon his charity.

'Ah well, Mother,' Paddy felt an urgent desire for a large foaming glass of ale, 'if you wish to play the good Samaritan, and to a Kendle of all people, I shall leave you to it.'

Hannah felt lonely when he'd gone. Or perhaps it was simply boredom. If her knees weren't so painful she would venture out more. She hauled her bulk out of the chair, she'd make herself a nice cup of tea and stop feeling maudlin.

The trouble was, for all of her life Hannah had felt useful. Needed. She'd been useful on the farm, working alongside her brother. 'As good with a pick and shovel as any man,' William had told her often enough. But then the farm had gone and William had sold up and headed for Ballarat, joining the hundreds in their mad rush for gold. No matter. By then she'd been needed by Daniel. 'I'd be lost without you, girl—' how many times had he said that? But now it seemed to Hannah that there was nobody who needed her. Oh, Paddy loved her right enough, but he had a family of his own.

No wonder she'd grown fat and lazy, she chastised herself as she plonked the old iron kettle on the wood stove and stirred the glowing embers in the grate. She really should make some effort. Perhaps she'd go and see her brother William's son. Surry Hills wasn't far away and she had always been fond of her nephew Samuel. But then Samuel Kendall, too, had a family and was busy carving a life of his own since his return from the goldfields, why should he welcome a fat old lady on his doorstep?

Hannah sat staring at the harbour long after her cup of tea had grown cold. She hardly noticed the changing light until the grandfather clock in the hall chimed seven and there was barely time enough to wash, dress and get to the Garden Palace for her meeting with Anne.

After a number of ales with the Irish contingent at the Lord Nelson, it was approaching dusk when Paddy set out for his home in Woolloomooloo. Down the hill, past the Sailors' Home, a right-hand turn and he was in the heart of George Street.

The block boys, or sparrow starvers as they were commonly termed, were already at work as he passed old one-eyed John Cadman's cottage. The boys, each assigned a city block, and each with broom and long-handled shovel, collected the horse manure, ensuring the streets would be clean for the Saturday-night revellers. Cheeky young larrikins for the most part, the block boys were employed by the City Council, which had realised that lads were cheaper to hire than men.

As always, George Street was bustling with activity. Amongst the pedestrians, an endless array of newspaper hawkers, bootblacks, fruit vendors, and Chinamen with vegetable baskets slung on poles across their shoulders paraded the sidewalks. Hansom cabs, traps and drays crowded the rough pavements, the wiry ponies of messenger boys darting in and out amongst them. All hurriedly cleared the way, however, upon the arrival of a double-decker steam tram. Horses shied and people dived for cover as the fearsome vehicle thundered along the crowded thoroughfare.

Paddy ducked into a side lane away from the traffic, wove his way through the backstreets, cut across the Botanic Gardens and fifteen minutes later was in Woolloomooloo.

They were waiting for him when he walked in the front door. 'Where have you been, Paddy,' Dorothy demanded. 'I thought you were coming home for tea.'

'Forget the tea, Dotty,' he said. 'Tis dinner out on the town for us tonight.' His six-year-old daughter squealed with delight as he swung her up onto his shoulders. 'Kathleen, Kathleen, the jewel in my crown,' he sang as he waltzed around the tiny kitchen, his wife trying to steer him away from the breakables. Paddy's exuberance could be expensive, she knew to her cost.

Finally he put down his daughter and, with equal ease, picked up his wife. 'Dotty, my Dotty, the wife a man dreams of ...'

'Have you been drinking, Paddy O'Shea?'

'No, no, I swear ... Well, only one small ale with the lads at the Rocks.' It had been four full pints which Paddy had scoffed at the Lord Nelson, but a little white lie never hurt anyone.

'And I had a tiny win on the boat race, so it's a night on the town for my girls.'

He caught the glint in his wife's eye and hastily added, 'I haven't been gambling, I swear, just a small wager on a sure bet.' It was true, Paddy's heavy gambling days were over. He still felt the yearnings, but he kept well away from the Randwick Racecourse and he knew better than to venture into the back rooms of the Darlinghurst pubs where poker was played in earnest.

'There you go, girl,' he handed Dorothy the four one-pound notes he'd separated from the wad in his top pocket, 'put those in your housekeeping jar, and spend one on something nice for yourself.'

'Paddy ...'

'I swear to you, Dot,' he gathered Kathleen in his arms again, 'I swear to you on my daughter's life, just a small sure bet on a boat race is all it was.' He kissed the little girl and put her down, kissed his wife and patted her bottom. 'Now you two get into your party dresses, I've another two pounds will give us a night on the town to remember.' He wouldn't tell her about the seven pounds in his top pocket, it would only worry her. Besides, who knew what luck might come his way, the seven pounds could well become seventy over the next several weeks. He wouldn't gamble heavily of course, just the odd little wager here and there. And the odd little wager did a man no harm.

Dorothy knew better than to nag any further. It wouldn't be fair, he'd brought his wages home regularly for a full six months now, and there'd been no heavy drinking. But she prayed he was telling the truth. Much as she loved Paddy, she would carry out her threat and leave him if he returned to his old ways.

It was the drink she feared as much as the gambling. There was no harm in a pint or two, she had no trouble with that, but Paddy in the rum was another matter. He was a different man, violent. Not to her or to Kathleen, but to any man who would take him on. Rage, uncontrollable, consumed him when he was in the rum, and many a time she had locked him out of the house when he'd staggered home in the wee hours to smash on the doors and shutters and bellow in the street like an enraged bull. She could not live with a man like that.

She must give him the benefit of the doubt, she thought now as she took Kathleen off to get changed. 'Put on a jacket, Paddy,' she called back to him. 'We're not going out with you dressed like that.'

Paddy stepped outside, lit up a smoke and sat on the steps of the front porch. He looked up the street at the rows of poky, little terrace houses, identical in design, but each one bearing the distinctive stamp of its tenant. Green shutters here, yellow railings there, a tub of flowering geraniums in a porch corner or a window box. It was an attractive street.

He waved to Tiny O'Rourke who was sitting on his chair on his own front porch, enjoying the early evening as he always did. There was room for no more than the chair and Tiny's bulk between his front door and the porch railing.

Paddy drew heavily on his cigarette, then called to Betty McCall who had stepped out of her front door in her bright purple dress, feathers in her hair.

'Evening, Betty.'

'Evening, Paddy. And a lovely one it is too.' She trotted down the hill towards the docks, where the pubs and the brothels did a brisk trade. Betty was a professional girl, but she was very polite and very discreet and no-one minded in 'the Loo'. Residents there were only too ready to live and let live in the knowledge that if you needed a hand there would always be one offered.

Paddy gazed up at the fine houses of Potts Point high on the ridge overlooking Woolloomooloo Bay. The finest of them all, its gas lights burning brightest in the gathering dusk, belonged to Charles Kendle. Surrounded by pillared verandahs, with an upper balcony of fine-laced ironwork, Kendle Lodge boasted a magnificent garden which extended down to the wall of rock in Victoria Street. Not only did the house command superb views across the Woolloomooloo valley to the city beyond, but from both the valley and the city, Kendle Lodge itself dominated the skyline.

Aware of the seven pounds in his top pocket, Paddy silently thanked Charles Kendle. He had not been told directly, but he was quite sure it had been Kendle who had rigged the race. It certainly wouldn't have been his partner and co-owner of *Wings of Honour*. Howard Streatham was said to be an honourable man.

Paddy looked about, with irony, at the dusty streets of the Loo, then up at the gaslit mansion above. Strange to think that he was related to Charles Kendle. The man was a bastard by all accounts, but tonight Paddy bore him no ill will. Tonight Paddy O'Shea would swap places with no man.

'Where's your jacket, Paddy?'

He turned. She'd lit the gas lamp in the front room and he could see them, pretty as a picture, standing there. His raven-haired daughter with her sapphire eyes. And Dot. Dot, not pretty by conventional standards, her body too slight, her face too thin, but to Paddy she was beautiful.

'Pretty as a picture,' he said as he stood and admired them. 'Pretty as a picture, my two girls.'

Dotty had put on a little weight, he thought as he kissed her. It suited her, there was an unaccustomed fullness to her breasts.

'Stop it, Paddy,' she said as his hand lingered, but he could tell she enjoyed it.

Dorothy could feel the love in him and she could feel herself responding. She wondered whether she should tell him tonight that she was pregnant. Perhaps not. She would start to show soon enough anyway, and it might bring bad luck to announce it. After two miscarriages she wanted to be sure that this one would last.

Paddy O'Shea and his wife and daughter stepped out into the evening to join the countless swarms who thronged the streets of

Sydney on a Saturday night. Barrel organs pumped out melodies on every corner; cheapjacks yelled themselves hoarse in the crowded marketplace, and shopfronts gleamed enticingly in the garish glitter of gas.

It was during Ludwig van Beethoven's symphony *Eroica* that Hannah started to feel decidedly ill. She glanced sideways at Anne, whose rapt attention was on the orchestra, and decided to say nothing. Gently, she dabbed the perspiration from her forehead with her handkerchief and breathed deeply. It was just the warmth of the evening, she told herself, and the overpowering music. She didn't like Beethoven, she decided. Not that she knew anything about music, the rare occasion she attended a concert or recital was really only to keep Anne company.

She always enjoyed coming to the Garden Palace, however, and she looked about the giant interior of the dome by way of distraction as she prayed for the dizzy spell to pass. The central dome, towering ninety feet high, was the grandest feature of the impressive Garden Palace which had been built three years ago to house the Sydney International Exhibition and stood in the centre of the Botanic Gardens.

Around its central stained glass skylight, the dome's ceiling was painted blue and scattered with stars, and circling its cornice was a verse printed in gold lettering: 'The Earth is the Lord's and the fulness thereof, the World, and they that dwell therein.'

The massive circular interior was a series of arches and pillars, above which the walls were patterned with endless and intricate friezes, paintings and tiles of all fashion and design. And on its central pedestal, in pride of place, stood the bronze statue of Queen Victoria.

The dizzy spell began to fade but Hannah wished the music would stop, for her head was beginning to ache.

Again she tried to distract herself from the relentless swell of the orchestra. She thought of the basement, which housed the offices and archival storage areas. The basement was possibly Hannah's favourite part of the Garden Palace. She had made friends with an employee there who was very obliging, and she derived a great deal of pleasure from looking at the land occupancy records, and the maps and plans of the colony's early days, proudly noting the name of Kendall which featured prominently in the first land grants.

She found it strangely moving to see her grandfather's signature on the deed transferring Thomas Kendall's Parramatta lands to the people of the Gadigal tribe, and remembered with great clarity that day when she had visited the camp with him. She wondered what had happened to the land, and to the people who had been so brutally evicted. She should visit Parramatta and see, for herself, she often thought. But she never did.

Hannah glanced anxiously at Anne. She needed some air. 'I might pop outside for a moment,' she whispered, fumbling for her walking stick.

Anne looked up horrified. 'Oh Hannah,' she whispered back, 'you cannot. We are seated in the front, it would be so rude.' Her horror was swiftly replaced by concern. 'Are you not well?'

'A little dizzy,' Hannah murmured, dabbing once more at her forehead, 'and it's so warm in here.'

'Oh dear,' Anne said. 'Oh dear.' It wasn't warm at all. 'There will be an interval at any moment, I know there will.' She took her friend's hand, it was clammy to the touch. 'Oh dear.'

By the time the interval came ten minutes later, Hannah was unsure as to whether she could even stand. 'Wait with me, Anne,' she said faintly. 'Wait until the people have gone.'

'Oh dear, shall I fetch someone? Someone to help?'

'No, no.' If she could just get out into the air, Hannah thought, everything would be all right.

When the majority of the audience had gone, she took her walking stick in one hand and grasped Anne's arm with the other. 'I shall need your help, my dear.'

Frail as she was, Anne was of little assistance in getting Hannah's bulk out of the chair, and they both nearly toppled over as, with a mighty heave, Hannah hauled on her stick and Anne's arm to get herself upright.

'Slowly, slowly.' Hannah was muttering more to herself than Anne as she shuffled clumsily towards the archway which led to the exit. Just as she reached the columns of the arch, however, she stopped.

'Are you all right, Hannah?' Anne was terrified—Hannah's face was a chalky white.

Hannah said nothing, but shook her head. Then she gave a small, startled cry and fell heavily to the tiled floor.

Anne screamed. People ahead at the exit turned. 'Help! Help me, please!' She knelt by Hannah as a man rushed to her aid. 'Oh please, help her,' she started to sob. 'Please help her.'

But no-one could help Hannah Kendall O'Shea. She had suffered a massive stroke. She never regained consciousness, and two days later she died.

Paddy was grief-stricken. Whilst his mother lay in a coma, he would come home from the hospital, via the pub, drunk. Not violently so, he'd not been in the rum, Dot could tell, but it took a lot of ale to get Paddy that drunk. She could hardly blame him, whilst his mother lay dying, but she wondered where he was getting the money. When she tentatively questioned him, he said that the lads were helping him to drown his tears, they were buying him drinks, and where was the harm in that?

'No harm, Paddy, no harm.' And she supposed there wasn't.

But Paddy's friends were not buying him drinks. It was Paddy who paid the bill at the bar. 'Drink to the best mother a man ever had,' he'd say as he told the barman to line them up.

The seven pounds had served him well. A winning hand in a poker game, and a quick visit by steam tram to the Randwick Racecourse had more than tripled his money. But he'd only done it to take his mind off Hannah, lying as if dead in that hospital bed. You could hardly call it gambling. And the copious ales he downed with the lads, you could hardly call that drinking. Ale wasn't liquor, ale was mother's milk.

The afternoon of Hannah's funeral, two days after her death, was a different matter altogether. Paddy spent the morning in the pub. And he didn't drink ale, it was rum he ordered from the bar.

'Paddy, how could you? It's disrespectful!' Dot was shocked when he walked in the door half an hour before they were due to leave for the cemetery, dishevelled and reeking of rum.

'I know, I know, I've been bad, I've been bad, but it's a terrible thing to see her go in the ground.'

He was remorseful, not violent, and Dot had to forgive him. But she hoped he wouldn't disgrace them at the cemetery. Hannah O'Shea was a highly respected woman, heaven knew who would be at the funeral.

She bathed his face with a cold flannel and brushed his hair, then changed his shirt and put on his vest, jacket and tie. The trousers and boots were too difficult to master as he sat on the bed mumbling, 'The best mother a man ever had', so she left them as they were and hoped people would be too busy grieving to notice.

'Hannah's funeral?' Charles Kendle was quite astounded by his father's suggestion. 'Why in God's name should I go to Hannah's funeral?'

They were in the showroom of the Kendle and Streatham Emporium. Three hundred feet in length, with splendid displays of imported goods and, more recently, those from the local market. It had been Howard Streatham's idea to support local industry; it was their duty, he said. And, after initial misgivings, Charles had found that Sydney's factories and mills successfully eliminated the middlemen and ensured a handsome profit.

The wall at the far end of the hall bore the emblem of gull's wings and the motto 'Kendle and Streatham, Trading on the Wings of Honour'. The yacht in full sail had been added beneath, two years previously.

'I barely knew her.' Charles wandered amongst the furnishing displays, checking a mantelpiece here, a dresser there, ensuring not a speck of dust could be found. His father was forced to follow. 'Why should I go to her funeral?'

'Because she was family,' James replied, 'and it is the done thing.'

'But you didn't even like her, Father. And she certainly never liked you.'

James wondered why the words hurt so. They were true enough, although deep down he had admired Hannah, everyone had. Even Mary Kendle, much as she would have been loath to admit it. But Hannah had not liked him, and James had often wondered why. He had never done anything particularly bad to anyone in his entire life, and yet nobody really liked him. Nobody particularly disliked him either. They simply didn't notice him. Yet he'd done well with the business. He'd taken over the reins from his father Richard—well, from his mother Mary really—and, together with his brother-in-law Nathaniel Streatham, he had built it into the success it was today. Why did no-one respect him for it?

'I would like you to come to the funeral with me, Charles.' He tried to keep an even edge to his voice, but it threatened to quaver. And he stroked his trim, grey beard, as he always did when he was nervous.

Dear God, but his father was pathetic, Charles thought. He'd never had much time for the old man. Even as a youngster being trained in the family business he had hated working with him, preferring the more ruthless attack of his grandmother, Mary.

'Anne is going to attend, and Howard too, I believe,' Charles said as he centred a vase of flowers on a mahogany dining table. Sloppy placement, he must have a word with the design and decoration department. 'They will be more than adequate company for you.'

James, as usual, sensed his son's contempt and, mustering every ounce of strength he could, said firmly, 'Neither Anne nor Howard is my son, Charles. You are.'

Surprised by the insistence in his father's voice, Charles turned, brow lifted enquiringly, and gave the old man his full attention.

James wilted a little—most people did when Charles Kendle turned his focus upon them, metal grey eyes defying opposition—but he managed to stand his ground. 'I would deem it a favour.'

The inference was not lost on his son. Well bless my soul, Charles thought, Father is calling in favours. Ah well, he supposed he owed the old man a few. Not least for his early retirement ten years previously.

James had not wanted to retire, he'd been barely fifty-five at the time, there was plenty of work left in him yet. But Charles had promised that his position on the board of directors would be most influential, that he would still be very much a part of the store, and that he, Charles, would deem it a personal favour. Charles had been sick to death of fighting Howard Streatham's dogmatic policy of customer service and James Kendle's indecision. At least with his father out of the way, the fight would be strictly between him and Howard. And, in a one-to-one situation, Charles usually came out on top.

'Very well, Father,' Charles smiled indulgently. 'I shall accompany you.'

'Thank you, Charles.'

'But I shan't stay long.'

Outside, in the Haymarket, as James Kendle stepped into his carriage, he wondered how it had all happened. Systematically, it seemed, piece by piece, everything he cared about had been taken from him. He no longer even bothered to attend the directors' meetings—his seat on the board was a token gesture and it was humiliating when no-one listened to him. His wife Alice and his partner Nathaniel had died; his son didn't like him, and his widowed daughter, Anne, could not be persuaded to live with him.

'I am needed at Charles's, Father,' she said. 'He works so hard, he is rarely home, and he doesn't trust the servants with the children . . .'

What about his wife, James wondered, why can't his wife look after her own children?

'. . . And Amy is constantly busy with her charitable works. They need me with them at all hours.'

There was nothing left in his life, James thought, looking out of the carriage window as they passed the busy promenade of Hyde Park. No store, no wife, no children. Perhaps that was why he was so desperate for Charles to accompany him to Hannah's funeral.

With his cousin Hannah dead, James was the last of his generation remaining in Sydney, and there would be family members present at the funeral, he knew. Family whom he'd not seen in years, and he wanted to prove his place in the scheme of things. He wanted to be seen with his son at his side.

At the cemetery James Kendle barely recognised the family he so wished to impress, but he could guess who they were.

Paddy O'Shea, whom he'd met only briefly years ago, could be none other than Hannah and Daniel's son. With his mother's big, brawny frame and his father's dark Celtic brow, he towered over the priest by his side. A woman who must be his wife was holding his arm, and in his big hands, along with his battered bowler hat, he clutched a red rose. There were tears in his eyes, and he was swaying a little.

Meticulous as he was about appearances, James disapproved strongly of Paddy's brown trousers and boots. He sympathised with the man's grief, certainly, but brown trousers and boots! At a funeral! Even in grief, such apparel was unpardonable.

The man standing beside them must be Samuel Kendall,

William's son, and with him his wife and their two children, a baby and a boy around ten years of age.

Howard Streatham stood at the end of the grave, pushing his spectacles up the bridge of his nose then reclasping his hands in front. Sombre and respectful. It was good that Howard had come to pay his respects, but then Howard had always refused to enter into the family feud. 'I am a Streatham, Grandmother,' he would say to Mary when she tried to turn him against the Kendalls.

It had always infuriated his mother, James recollected, that she did not have Howard under her complete control. 'But I promised Phoebe,' James had heard her say to her husband, 'on her deathbed, I promised Phoebe I would give young Howard the world.'

'And so you can, my dear,' Richard had replied with some enjoyment, 'but as a Streatham, it would appear, not a Kendle.'

As the priest's voice droned on, James looked at the gathering around the graveside, and felt proud. The Kendles were without a doubt the only truly respectable family there. Certainly they were the only ones in correct, formal, funeral attire. Apart from himself, Charles and Howard, not one gentleman present was wearing a black top hat. An omission which, in polite society, would be quite unforgivable.

He had made his statement, he thought, and he was glad. Glad that the others could see him for the success he truly was. A father who had sired a daughter of elegance and breeding, although James did wish Anne could control her tears as she sniffed and dabbed beneath her mourning veil, and a stylish, affluent son.

Charles, as always impeccably attired, back ramrod straight, was bored and intensely irritated. When would this interminable episode end, and why did he have to admit that these shabby people were in any way connected to his family?

Paddy O'Shea, whom on their one brief meeting he had found to be an oaf, was disgustingly drunk, disgracefully dressed, and his wife was propping him up. The poor little woman in the cheap cotton dress was straining with the effort. Any moment they might both topple into the grave. Well, at least that would provide some amusement.

Sensing he was being observed, Paddy looked up and, for a brief moment, the men's eyes met across the grave, Paddy's bleary with tears and rum, Charles's frosty with disapproval. Then Charles looked away in disgust, mentally tabulating a list of the business affairs to which he could have attended this afternoon had he not been coerced into this sordid little ceremony to celebrate the life and death of a woman for whom he cared nothing.

Despite his drunkenness, or perhaps because of it, Paddy O'Shea registered every nuance of Charles Kendle's disgust and irritation. At the outset, through the blur of alcohol and emotion, Paddy had been vaguely surprised by the man's presence; but he'd concluded hazily that anyone who wished to pay homage to the finest woman who ever lived was welcome at her funeral, and he'd thought no more about it.

Now Paddy felt the blur of alcohol lifting, to be replaced by a slow burning anger. Beside him, Dorothy became aware that her husband had straightened his back and was breathing deeply. Thank God, she thought, Paddy was sobering up. It often happened quite quickly. He could stand on his own now, she decided and, gratefully, she removed the hand she'd had crooked through his arm and surreptitiously rubbed her shoulder which was sorely cramped.

Black eyes smouldering, Paddy stared at Charles Kendle across the open grave.

The coffin was lowered, the straps were removed. 'Ashes to ashes,' the priest intoned as he emptied the small trowel of earth into the grave.

Still Paddy stared at Charles, whose impatient gaze remained on the horizon.

'Paddy,' Dorothy whispered, nudging her husband. The priest was offering him the fresh trowel of earth. Paddy took it and emptied the earth into the grave.

'Dust to dust,' the priest intoned. Paddy handed back the trowel and once more stared at Charles.

'The rose,' Dorothy hissed. He glanced at her. 'The rose,' she said again. He dropped the flower into the grave and returned his gaze to Charles.

'... and certain hope of resurrection to eternal life ...'

Paddy saw Charles dip his hand into his fob pocket and remove his watch. He saw him glance at it briefly, frown with annoyance, tuck it back in his pocket and put on his top hat as he turned to go.

'... through our Lord Jesus Christ ...'

It was all Paddy needed. His anger was at fever pitch, and as

Charles Kendle turned his back on Hannah's grave and started walking briskly away, Paddy's fury exploded.

'... who shall change our vile body that it may be like—'

'Where's your respect, man?' Paddy charged behind the priest, who staggered and nearly fell into the grave. 'Where's your respect?' In several strides he had reached Charles who had turned, bemused.

'I beg your pardon,' Charles said. He could smell the rum on the man's breath, it was disgusting. 'Are you addressing me?'

The insolence in the voice and the contempt in the eyes compounded Paddy's fury and he grabbed the man's collar. 'Would you spit on my mother's grave, would you?' he yelled, shaking him with all his might, Charles's top hat tumbling to the ground. 'Would you spit on my mother's grave?'

'Easy, Paddy, easy.' Samuel Kendall was at his side. He was not a big man like Paddy, but he was strong, a strength born of hard physical labour. He grabbed Paddy's arm to pull him away. 'Let him go, Paddy. Let him go.'

Samuel's strength was not enough, however, and Paddy would not let go. Then Howard Streatham was on his other side and between the two of them they managed to break Paddy's grip.

Charles stepped back and straightened his collar.

'You're a bastard, Kendle!' Paddy roared, Samuel and Howard holding his arms tight. 'You're a bastard!'

'And you are a fool, O'Shea.' Charles paused for a moment before bending to retrieve his top hat. He flicked the dust from it. 'A disgusting fool,' he added with contempt, 'and I advise you to keep well away from me ...'

He didn't look at the others who were staring in shock, his father, James, most horrified of all. '... well away, do you understand?' Beneath the tight measure of control, a murderous anger glinted, cold as steel, in Charles's grey eyes. 'If you come near me or my family or my property, even once, you will regret it, I warn you, Paddy O'Shea.'

He donned his top hat, turned and walked from the graveside.

The Kendles did not attend the wake at the little house in Woolloomooloo and Dot was glad of their absence as she scurried about filling glasses of ale and offering trays of cured ham. A whole leg they'd bought—only the best Paddy had said, and the corner butcher had agreed to waive the bill till the following month—and there was tea and rich fruitcake for those who wanted it.

It had taken a good hour to erase Paddy's scowl, and several jugs of ale to wash away the anger. But eventually, as the Irish contingent sang all the old favourites and neighbours popped in with posies of flowers and bottles of ale, it was Paddy himself who was singing the loudest.

Front and back doors were open and people crammed the porch and the yard out the back. When fresh mourners arrived, the little house could contain no more, and the party spilled into the street where it continued on through the night. They sang until their throats ached and voices were hoarse, and then they sang some more. All the old songs Daniel O'Shea had sung to Hannah. And no neighbours complained, they all joined in. From porch to porch they encouraged the singers, until it seemed the whole of the Loo was celebrating the life of Hannah Kendall O'Shea. Paddy had never felt so proud.

High above, at Kendle Lodge, Charles stood, pyjama-clad, on his balcony. In the terraced garden immediately below, captured in the glow of strategically positioned gas lamps, bloomed the glorious confetti of spring. Vivid red and white camellias, delicate honeysuckle, the misty blue of wisteria, all riotously assembled amongst a series of trellises and arbours, fountains and statues.

Upon Charles's instruction, the lamps burned throughout the night. The garden being his pride and joy, it was necessary the world should see and admire his personal masterpiece. It never seemed to occur to Charles that the creation was nature's, and that the masterpiece was the work of a team of gardeners who tirelessly orchestrated that creation.

But tonight his attention was directed beyond the garden to the valley of Woolloomooloo, where it appeared every house was a blaze of light and every person was giving full voice to the drunken caterwauling which was keeping him awake. It was after four in the morning, he thought angrily. When in God's name were they going to shut up?

'Send for the police, Charles,' his wife Amy had said two hours previously when she and Anne had joined him on the balcony, they too unable to sleep.

'No, Charles, you mustn't.' Anne had been aghast. 'You mustn't send for the police. It is Hannah they are celebrating. It is her wake, you would destroy it.'

All the more reason to send the police in. They could arrest Paddy O'Shea and his wretched layabout Irish companions. Charles recalled the grimy paws on his collar, the stench of rum in his nostrils, the humiliating sight of his top hat rolling in the dust. He would never forgive the filthy assault of Paddy O'Shea.

He realised, however, that should he send for the police, Paddy and his company of larrikins would make it widely known, possibly even to the press, that he, Charles Kendle, had sabotaged the wake of a member of his own family. He could not afford such adverse publicity.

'Go to bed,' he had instructed the women. 'They must stop soon, they can't sing all night.'

It appeared they could, he thought now, over two hours later, as he went inside to pour himself a mild Scotch and water. He returned to the balcony where he sat and watched and listened, angered, but strangely fascinated by the voices of Woolloomooloo.

It was well after five o'clock in the morning when the last of the revellers staggered home to bed, and by that time Charles Kendle had dozed off in his chair.

Paddy sat on the porch steps, drained the last drop from the whisky bottle, and reluctantly decided it was time for bed. What a night it had been. A night to remember.

He walked inside a little unsteadily, but in relative control, all things considered. Inside, Tiny O'Rourke was sitting bolt upright on the small two-seater divan, fast asleep and snoring gently, his bulk taking up every inch of the space.

'Tiny!' He shook the man by the shoulders. 'Wake up, Tiny!'

A brief snort, a shake of the head and Tiny was wide awake. 'Where've they gone?' he said looking around, wild-eyed. 'Where've they gone?'

'Home. Do you want a nightcap?'

'Sure, and why not? Will you give us a hand? Tis a tight fit this sofa of yours.'

Paddy levered him up, the divan coming with him for part of the way. 'We'll go outside,' he said, 'it stinks like a brothel in here.'

The stench of cigarettes and spilt ale was enough to make a man gag, he thought happily. Clearly a good time had been had by all.

Charles Kendle awoke with a start. There was a spring nip in the air and, despite his warm flannel pyjamas, he was decidedly cold. How foolish of him to fall asleep in the damp night air, he could catch pneumonia that way.

The servants had extinguished the gas lamps in the garden, and the first filtered light of dawn was in the sky. Perhaps he would stay up and watch the sunrise, but he must fetch a dressing gown first.

Something attracted his attention as he turned to go. In the Botanic Gardens. A strange radiance. It was the dome of the Garden Palace. It was glowing from within. Gleaming, flickering. Second by second becoming more incandescent. Then he noticed the smoke. Thin spirals, coiling their way up into the air.

'My God!' he said out loud. 'The Garden Palace is on fire!'

Paddy and Tiny, bottles of ale in hand, were weaving their way down to the bay to watch the sunrise over the water. They had arrived at the mudflats and were standing, amongst the fishing dories when Tiny, glancing to his left, suddenly said, 'Sweet Jesus, will you look at that!'

Paddy turned a bleary eye to see the Botanic Gardens flooded with light.

'Tis the Garden Palace!' Tiny cried. 'Tis the Garden Palace, Paddy, she's on fire!'

The blaze, which had roared captive within the dome, suddenly made its escape. Sheets of flame burst through the skylight and spread greedily in every direction. North, south, east, west, the fire rippled along the roofing, heading as if by command for the corner towers.

'Let's go and watch!' Paddy yelled. 'Come on!' He sprinted up the hill, yelling, 'Wake up! Wake up! The Garden Palace is on fire!'

Tiny lumbered along behind, others joining him, passing him, racing on to join Paddy up ahead. In minutes, people were flocking from all directions.

From up on his balcony, Charles had a bird's-eye view. At his side, Amy, their two children, and Anne watched, mesmerised, as the flames reached the towers. In seconds it seemed the entire building was fringed with a bright red frill of fire.

A series of angry explosions like the discharge of firearms split the air. Then an ominous roar thundered across Sydney. A drum roll heralding the final moment.

A massive flame leapt into the sky. It towered there for a moment, a giant with a life of its own, then it was clouded by dense black smoke billowing in volumes up into the morning air. There was an almighty crash, like a peal of thunder. And, finally, the great dome fell.

The current of air created by the fall wreaked havoc. As if carried by a whirlwind, red-hot galvanised iron and clouds of burning embers were hurled across the inner suburbs of Sydney, as far as Elizabeth Bay. In Macquarie Street, windowpanes were cracked by the heat, and for hours ashes fell upon Woolloomooloo and Potts Point.

Paddy and the hundreds of others who had flocked to the scene stayed to watch, despite the rain of debris. Miraculously, no-one was killed or seriously injured as they stood and gazed in awe.

For a full three hours they watched whilst the rising sun fought its way through a haze of smoke and multicoloured flames of carmine and green, yellow and blue, creating a dawn of their own. They watched along with the fire brigades which had arrived from all quarters. There were the steam fire engines, and the manual fire engines, with reels and all the equipment to hand. But they were powerless. And, along with Paddy and the citizens of Sydney, the firemen stood and watched as the noble Garden Palace was razed to the ground.

Paddy was witnessing the blaze of his mother's funeral pyre. Hannah Kendall O'Shea had died there, he thought. Four days ago she had died in the great dome, and now on this, the very day of her funeral—to Paddy it was still the same day—the dome had become her funeral pyre. He was overwhelmed by the sight and the notion.

By nine o'clock in the morning little remained of the Garden Palace. Along with the building itself, unique objects and documents were lost—paintings, hung for the New South Wales Art Society's annual exhibition, the colonial collection of statuary, the

Linnean Society's library, the Department of Fisheries' collection of illustrations. And the people of Sydney lost their land occupancy records from the beginning of the colony, along with many documents of deed and title. All of which had been housed in the basement.

So passed the Garden Palace. According to Christopher Pearce of the *Sydney Morning Herald*, 'leaving only a few crumbling brick piers, and heaps of black and smoking cinders, to mark the spot where stood, the day before, one of the finest and most graceful structures to be found south of the Equator'.

CHAPTER SIX

'Wunderlich their name is. Ernest and Alfred, they're brothers.'

'Huns I take it.'

Howard Streatham tried to ignore the sneer in his cousin's voice. 'They were born in London, I believe. Educated in Switzerland.' He loathed Charles's bigotry. 'And these men are artists, Charles,' he emphasised, 'not tradesmen at all. Their ceilings are works of art.'

'I realise that. I've seen the Centennial Hall. Did you get a quote from them?' he asked impatiently.

'They need to view the showroom and make an assessment first.'

'But surely you gave them the measurements?'

'Yes, Charles, I gave them the measurements.' Howard, as always, refused to be provoked by his cousin's peevishness, 'but as I said, they are artists and it is not as simple as you might wish it to be. There are styles and designs Mr Wunderlich needs to discuss with us, which he will do tomorrow at noon.'

Alfred Wunderlich was not a remarkable looking man. Tall, lean, clean-shaven but for a neatly cropped moustache, his hairline was receding and he wore steel-rimmed spectacles. But there was something about him. Something, Howard noticed, which appeared to impress even Charles. It was breeding, he decided. Alfred Wunderlich was a man of refinement. Cultivated. Well bred. In fact everything that Charles himself claimed to be but wasn't quite.

Wunderlich commented flatteringly on the impressive displays behind the huge glass window-panels of the store's ground floor.

The windows themselves, set in copper trim with cedar woodwork, had been imported at great expense, Charles boasted proudly.

When Wunderlich suggested, in his slightly clipped voice, that he would be most interested in seeing the entire store, Howard cast a wary glance at Charles and waited for the outburst. The Kendle and Streatham Emporium was four storeys high and encompassed almost an entire city block.

'Only a glimpse at each floor,' Wunderlich added upon noticing Howard's apprehensive glance, 'and of course if time is scarce, then I am happy to proceed directly to the showroom.'

'We are completely at your disposal, Mr Wunderlich,' Charles said expansively, 'and I should be most proud to show you around our store.'

Howard was dumbstruck as he followed the two men up the main stairway, Wunderlich remarking upon the ornately carved wood and highly polished brass trimmings. 'If time is scarce,' Wunderlich had said. Time was always scarce to Charles Kendle, there were never enough hours in the day for him. If he felt someone was robbing him of even ten minutes, he flew into a rage. Alfred Wunderlich had certainly made a favourable impression.

The guided tour took an entire hour, during which they visited each department on each level of the store, including even the top floor which was devoted to workrooms. There, young women sat at endless tables, sewing beautiful imported silks, beading fine crepe de Chine and weaving ribbons and feathers into millinery works of art.

As the men entered the huge showroom, the conversation between Charles and Alfred Wunderlich had progressed to music.

'Do you play an instrument, Mr Kendle?' Alfred Wunderlich was an accomplished musician himself, with a fine bass voice.

'No, no, not in any true sense, I leave that to those with a talent far greater than I possess.'

This humble reply, which somehow managed to infer he did indeed play an instrument but preferred to leave the performing to those more gifted, amused Howard. To his certain knowledge Charles's fingers had never once strayed across a piano keyboard, his hand had never once held the bow of a violin, and his lips had at no time been introduced to the mouthpiece of a brass or wind instrument.

Howard wondered why Charles was trying so hard to impress Wunderlich. It was so uncharacteristic of him.

'You will be interested to learn, Mr Kendle, I am sure, that . . .' Alfred Wunderlich stopped abruptly, suddenly mindful of Howard's presence. 'Do please forgive our rudeness Mr Streatham, we have been a little distracted in our musical discussion.'

'Not at all,' Howard assured the man, 'I am no musician myself, but I frequently attend concerts and am most interested in things musical. Please continue.'

It was true, Howard regularly accompanied his cousin Anne to orchestral concerts and operatic performances, much to Charles's chagrin.

'She has no-one else to accompany her, Charles,' he would insist and, indeed, since Hannah's death eight years ago it appeared poor widowed Anne Goodlet had not one friend in the entire world. 'Besides,' Howard added, 'I find I very much enjoy our musical outings, they are most uplifting.'

Charles could do little about the situation. With his youngest child now well and truly grown to adulthood, Anne's duties as a nanny were no longer required. But it annoyed him nonetheless. He wasn't quite sure why, but he told Anne that it was not dignified that she, a widowed woman, should be seen gallivanting about the town with a married man.

'I have been widowed for nearly twenty years, Charles,' she reminded him when she had recovered from the shock of his insinuation, 'and the married man with whom I am supposedly "gallivanting" is my cousin.'

There was a sharpness to her tone which quite surprised Charles, unaccustomed as he was to any form of retaliation from his sister. He decided not to pursue the subject any further with her, but broached it with Howard instead. Very brusquely. 'Doesn't Helen take offence at your squiring Anne with such regularity?' he asked.

Howard laughed out loud, which was unusual for him. 'Good heavens, Charles, what are you intimating? I am fifty years old, the woman is my cousin, she is desperately lonely, and Helen is not only a trusting wife, she too feels sorry for Anne.'

Charles had dropped the subject altogether, but he couldn't rid himself of the unreasonable resentment he felt when, over the breakfast table on a morning following one of her musical outings,

Anne still glowed with the pleasure of the preceding night. It was disloyal of her, he decided. Anne owed her very existence to his generosity. If she were to glow it should be with gratitude, and in his direction.

'You will be interested to learn,' behind his glasses, Alfred Wunderlich's eyes shone with excitement, 'that the Centennial Hall, the ceiling of which you have most graciously commented upon, was never designed as a concert hall at all.'

'Really?' Howard was most interested to learn of such a fact. 'But I have attended a number of recitals there and have always presumed that the hall was specifically designed to house the dimensions and the sound of the great organ.'

'Many others have been of the same opinion, but this was never so.'

Who would care, Charles thought. He was bored now. And irritated. The three of them were standing in the middle of the vast showroom, his pride and joy, and Wunderlich, in the excitement of his own tedious conversation, had passed no flattering remark.

'The organ was obviously an afterthought,' Wunderlich continued. There was no stopping him now. 'For, you see, the architects had specified a plaster ceiling. One with pendentives and console. A very elaborate affair.'

God the man was pedantic, Charles thought.

'Yes?' Howard was interested, but confused.

'Well, such a plaster ceiling would have been disastrous,' Wunderlich concluded triumphantly. 'As soon as the organ's sixty-four foot, lower-C pipe sounded, such a plaster ceiling would most certainly have fallen upon the audience.'

'Good heavens above!' Howard was as impressed as Wunderlich had intended him to be.

'Exactly.' Alfred Wunderlich nodded, gratified by the response. 'My brother Ernest and I managed to induce the City Council to substitute stamped zinc for the ceiling and its decoration. A vastly superior material, not only in composition, but in acoustic value. More resonance, you see.'

'Ah.' Howard nodded encouragingly.

'So,' Wunderlich concluded, 'now we have a Centennial Hall which is structurally sound and acoustically splendid.'

'Why call the thing "Centennial" Hall in the first place? It wasn't even finished until '89.' Charles's interruption was abrupt, and jarringly rude. 'Damn silly calling it Centennial Hall; it's the Town Hall, that's what it is.'

'Yes, and I'm sure it will become known as exactly that in time to come.' Alfred Wunderlich concluded that, beneath the stylish exterior, Charles Kendle was a boor. Despite the man's patrician face, fine carriage and imperious manner, he was a philistine. 'Now, let us attend to a ceiling design for this impressive showroom of yours, Mr Kendle.'

Things were not going well for Paddy O'Shea. They should have been. He was a man of property. He owned a cottage in the Rocks. Furthermore, he had a fine seven-year-old son whom he'd christened Daniel after his father, and a daughter who, at fifteen, was already a beauty. He had a faithful wife who loved him and mates who would see him through thick and thin. Things should have been going well for Paddy O'Shea. But they weren't.

He couldn't understand how it had come to this. He couldn't even remember how it had started, not in earnest anyway.

Paddy and Dotty O'Shea had led a life of ease following the death of Hannah. At least it certainly seemed that way to Dotty. For the first time in their marriage she didn't have to scrimp and save and fret over money.

They had decided not to live in Hannah's cottage. It was a joint decision, they wanted to stay in the Loo. But it had been Dotty's idea not to sell the cottage, which was much grander than their little terrace.

'It would fetch twice the rent we pay here, Paddy,' she told him. 'Just think, love, we'd be landlords.' Then she giggled self-consciously at the thought—it didn't seem right somehow. 'We'd pay our rent and have as much again left over.'

And there was the additional money to be made from the sale of Hannah's furniture, very little of which would fit into the tiny Woolloomooloo terrace. Paddy kept mementos of course—Hannah's favourite chair, an etching which she loved, a vase with a dragon embossed on the side which he remembered from childhood. And, most important of all, her journal.

In sorting through Hannah's belongings, Paddy had stumbled

upon the impressive leather diary. 'This journal is the property of Hannah Kendall', he read on the opening page, 'given her by her mother, Emily, on her sixteenth birthday, the 13th of April in this year of 1831'.

It didn't seem right that he should read it, but it was somehow fitting that his daughter should.

'I have a precious gift for you, Kathleen,' he said when he returned home that evening. And he presented her with the journal. 'It's a diary. It belonged to your grandmother.'

'It's beautiful, Pa.' Kathleen stroked the cover admiringly.

'Smell the leather,' he said, 'it's very old.' He opened the journal to the first page. 'Do you want to add your name?'

Hannah would like that, he thought. With her love of writing, Hannah had always been most insistent upon her son acquiring literacy skills at an early age. Paddy had not inherited his mother's devotion to the written word, but he had certainly followed her example in the schooling of his daughter.

Kathleen nodded and he gave her a pencil. In her seven-year-old hand, beneath Hannah's entry, she painstakingly printed, 'Kathleen O'Shea, 1 October, 1882'. It was a laborious and clumsy exercise, with much prompting from Paddy, but when the little girl had completed the task he felt very proud, knowing that this was what his mother would want.

Kathleen treasured the diary, it was a beautiful thing, and she was very proud of her name in the front. She put it away in the cardboard box under her bed where she kept her most precious things and, from time to time, she would take it out and smell the leather, carefully polishing it with her handkerchief.

Each Saturday morning, Paddy personally collected the rent from his tenants, after which, regular as clockwork, he popped into the real estate office in William Street and paid his own rent, then he went straight home and doled out half the remaining money to Dotty who put it in the housekeeping jar. She didn't have to ask what he did with the money he kept, it was obvious. These days, when they stepped out of a Saturday night, Paddy O'Shea was dressed smartly in a high-collared shirt, a new checked suit and shiny black boots. But he didn't spend the money just on himself. There were new dresses and bonnets for her and Kathleen, and presents and treats and outings.

Never in his life had Paddy had such sums of money to play with. The sale of the cottage furnishings had realised ten times more than he had expected. He said nothing to Dotty of the small hoard he'd kept for himself, justifying himself with true gambler's logic. Why, with such cash to hand, he could make them a fortune! She'd thank him one day when they were wealthy and owned a house like Charles bloody Kendle's up there on the ridge.

He was cautious to start with. Don't be greedy, he told himself, play it safe, back the easy bets, win more often than you lose, Paddy my lad. It paid off, and the stockpile which he kept in the tin hidden beneath the back steps grew as the months passed.

But as the months became years, caution became increasingly difficult. Why be cautious, the voice would whisper. When a man has close to a thousand pounds sitting under his back step he can afford to gamble for fun. Nothing serious, of course, nothing that would threaten his fortune, or his marriage.

Paddy no longer reported to the docks, as Dotty thought he did. He caught the Elizabeth Street tram which travelled direct to Randwick Racecourse instead, and there he met his mates from nearby Irish Shanty Town. He was careful to do nothing to arouse his wife's suspicions, he never touched the hard liquor and he always arrived home on a Friday night with exactly the amount of money he would have earned from a week's work on the wharves.

As time passed, however, the bets grew bigger and the risks grew greater and the money slowly dwindled. So he raised the rental on the cottage—without telling Dotty of course—and that helped for a while, but the inevitable day came when the tin box was close to empty. No need to panic, he told himself, he'd win it back. One day you're up, the next you're down, life's like that.

Credit with the bookies was easy. Paddy was known to them as a heavy gambler, and he had property as a guarantee. Sometimes he won and paid off a debt. More often he lost, and borrowed from one source to pay back another, until eventually he owed money everywhere. And then came the run of bad luck. Not a horse, not a poker hand, not even a friendly wager seemed to go his way, and the bookies began to get demanding.

It was late one Friday night when Cocky Shaw approached him at the bar of the Lord Nelson. The pub was crowded, but most of Paddy's mates had left an hour or so previously to take their pay packets home to their families. He knew he should leave too, but he was staving off the moment. It was the second week in a row he would have to go home without a pay packet. On a number of occasions, when he'd had only a few pounds to give Dotty, he'd told her work had been slow that week. He'd stood in a queue with the others, for hours and hours, he swore, then they'd all said what the hell and gone to the pub for an ale. It had happened three days in a row, he said, but he hadn't had the heart to tell her.

'Never mind, love,' Dotty had said, 'there's the rent from the cottage, we'll manage, we're better off than most.'

Thank God, Paddy thought, that he'd never touched the money from the cottage. He'd been tempted at times, but religiously he'd stuck to his Saturday routine. Perhaps he could tell her he'd lost his pay packet, but that was the excuse he'd used in the bad old days and she'd know for sure he was lying.

'Paddy me old mate.' It was Cocky Shaw in his trademark derby hat.

'Evening, Cocky.'

'Got a little job for you. Interested?'

'I might be, Cocky, yes, I might be.' Paddy's spirits lifted. Cocky paid good money.

'Good lad.' Cocky winked and jabbed a thumb in the direction of the door at the side of the bar. 'Let's go out the back, eh? Bit crowded in 'ere.' Cocky never discussed business in public.

Cocky Shaw was a well-known figure around Sydney, with a finger in every pie. A middle man for many a shady deal, no-one ever knew who his employers were, which was why he was in such constant demand. They paid for his discretion.

Paddy followed the cockney through the back room of the pub. A stroke of luck this was, he told himself. Saved in the nick of time. He wondered briefly what the job was, not that it mattered of course, when a man was as desperate as he was. He followed Cocky into the lane at the back. Whatever it was he'd do it, so long as it wasn't violent of course. Paddy wouldn't be in any of that standover business.

A giant fist smashed into his face and he felt the sickening crunch of broken cartilage. Simultaneously, two men, one on either side, pinioned his arms behind him.

Paddy roared and fought back, swinging his shoulders from side to side with such force that the men were thrown off balance.

'That's enough, Paddy me lad. We don't want you hurting yourself.'

There was a knife at his throat. Paddy could feel the point of the blade tucked tightly under his chin. He could feel the gentle trickle of blood as it wound its way down his neck. He stopped struggling and peered through the gloom at his attackers.

He didn't think he knew the big man who held the knife, although even at this close range, through the darkness and his already swelling eyes, it was difficult to tell. And he daren't turn his head to look at the others who held him—one move and his throat would be slit. But he could easily make out Cocky Shaw, arms folded, legs astride, silhouetted against the hazy light of the gas lamp which reached them from the end of the lane.

'That's better,' Cocky said when Paddy stopped struggling. 'Now you mustn't take this personally, me old mate. There'll be many a time we'll do business again, I'm sure. Once you've cleared up your present predicament, that is. But you've got yourself in a bit of strife at the moment, and I'm here to remind you that there are people who need to be paid. You understand me, don't you?'

With a blink of his eyes Paddy acknowledged that he did.

'That's good, that's good,' Cocky nodded approvingly, 'we understand each other. My instructions, however, are to ensure that you understand fully the seriousness of your situation. So that's what the boys are here for. Nothing personal, you understand.' He gestured to the man with the knife. 'Nothing personal at all, Paddy me old mate.'

The knife disappeared and in the same instant a fist of iron rammed itself into Paddy's solar plexus. His breath exploded and with a rasping grunt he crumpled to his knees, the two men dropping beside him, keeping his arms pinned behind.

As he gasped through aching lungs, his head bowed to the ground, all Paddy could think of was the force of the blow. No fist was built like that, there was metal around those knuckles. Then the knife was back in position, forcing his head up.

'Now, these people who need to be paid,' the cockney waited a few seconds for Paddy to regain his breath, 'they want their money, with interest, and they want it now. You understand me?'

The knife was again drawing blood, and Paddy didn't dare nod, but again he blinked.

'Good, that's good. These people are aware that you have property, and they are willing to wait until you sell that property, but they expect you to sell that property immediately. And if these people find that that property is not on the market first thing Monday morning, then it won't be just a little lesson like this you'll be copping, do you get my drift?'

Paddy blinked again.

'Good, good, that's good. Well, we'll leave you with another little reminder.' He nodded to the men before assuring Paddy, 'Just my instructions, Paddy, you understand, nothing personal.' Then to the men: 'Leave him enough strength to get home, boys. We don't want him lying in the street all night.'

The knife disappeared once again and the metal fist slammed into his ribs. The men released his arms and Paddy fell on his side. Then the boots came in. Dozens it seemed, raining merciless blows from every direction. Paddy didn't even attempt to fight; he covered his head and curled into a ball, and that was all he remembered.

It was nearly dawn when he regained consciousness. He staggered down the laneway and into the street. The sparrow starvers were at work already, and the market gardeners were arriving to set up their kerbside stalls, but no-one took any notice of Paddy. Casualties of drunken brawls were commonplace in the Rocks, even at this hour of the morning.

The ten-minute walk to Woolloomooloo seemed to take forever but finally he was home. Dotty was in her nightdress, sitting at the kitchen table with a cup of tea. She hadn't been able to sleep for worry. Not once had she felt anger, not once had it occurred to her that Paddy might be out on the drink, scoffing back his wages. Paddy didn't do that any more. But when he staggered through the door that was the first thing she thought—Paddy's on the rum again—and her heart sank. Then she saw his face.

'Oh dear God!' She sat him at the table and fetched a bowl of warm water, a cloth and the disinfectant.

'I'm sorry, Dotty,' he mumbled, 'I'm sorry, I'm sorry . . .'

'Don't talk,' she said as she bathed his face. 'Don't talk, you can tell me about it later.'

He did. That same day, after he'd slept, lying on the bed, his cracked ribs aching, he told her everything. And then he waited for the diatribe. There was no holding Dotty back when she was angry.

But Dottie was strangely quiet. Eventually she said, 'Well, you'll have to sell the cottage.' When he shook his head, she felt a surge of irritation. 'Of course you'll sell the cottage, Paddy,' she snapped. 'Either that or you'll be dead, and a dead husband's no good to me.'

Dotty was irritated but she was not angry. She was weary, weary with disappointment. These last years of blissful, unquestioning happiness had been a lie. Every single day he had lied to her. She would have liked to have cried, that would have been a relief, but she couldn't, she was too disappointed to cry.

Paddy sold the cottage. There was no trouble in getting a buyer, it was snapped up on the very first day. The real estate man said he'd got a good price too, which was a relief to Paddy who wouldn't have had a clue as to the value of the property.

He did everything else that Dotty instructed him to do. After he'd paid back the bookies, he deposited the two hundred pounds left over from the sale in the Standard Bank of Australia. Then he gave her the deposit book. Between the bank and Dotty's governing hand, their future would be secure. The money was never to be touched, she said, it was to remain in the bank, their nest egg, to be called upon only in a case of dire emergency.

Meekly, Paddy agreed to everything. Time and again he told Dotty he was sorry. And he was. He felt sick with contrition. Something had gone from their marriage and it was all his fault. He would give anything to see the trust once more in her eyes and to hear her say, 'It's all right, love, we'll manage, we're better off than most.' But she didn't.

Charles Kendle was pleased with his latest acquisition. Not because the cottage in Windmill Street had once belonged to his great-grandfather—he couldn't have cared less about that—but because Paddy O'Shea had been taught a lesson, and a long-overdue lesson it was, in Charles's opinion. He'd seen Paddy from time to time, strutting about in his vulgar new clothes, and the sight of the man's cockiness and new-found affluence had been irksome.

Upon the discovery, through Cocky Shaw, that Paddy O'Shea was deeply in debt with the bookies, it had been simple enough to make use of the cockney's services. Charles had had a number of dealings with Cocky over the years. An unpleasant little man, but a useful one.

Charles had wondered why the bookies hadn't called their debts in earlier, but Cocky had assured him that they were prepared to let Paddy get in a bit deeper, knowing that his cottage was worth a tidy sum.

In his opinion, Charles, by employing Cocky and his heavies, had done a favour for a number of people, all of whom should be grateful to him. The bookies had received their payment; the real estate agent, in doubling his percentage at Charles's suggestion, had made a very good deal; and Charles himself had acquired a nice little property at far less than its market value. The most pleasing part of the exercise, of course, was the blow dealt to Paddy O'Shea; the only disappointment being that the man didn't know by whom, though it was probably safer that way.

Having told the real estate agent to put the cottage up for rent, Charles promptly forgot he owned the place. But one Saturday morning, when he was alone in the breakfast room, his sister Anne tentatively approached him about it.

'I believe you have purchased Hannah's cottage, Charles,' she said.

'How did you know that?' Charles was irritated. He didn't like anyone knowing his business.

'Amy told me.'

His irritation turned to anger. He would have to have words with his wife. Her loose tongue had caused trouble in the past. 'So what of it, Anne? Of what interest is it to you?'

'She says you are going to lease the cottage.'

'It is in the hands of the agent, yes.'

She could sense his annoyance and it made her nervous. Nevertheless she soldiered on. 'I should very much like to apply for tenancy.'

Charles was shocked. Deeply shocked. Though he tried not to show it. 'I see.' He rose and crossed to the servery where he poured himself a cup of tea from the large silver teapot. 'You wish to renounce my care and support,' he said, his back to her, 'after all these years.'

'It is not that I am ungrateful, Charles,' she insisted. 'Believe me, I am fully aware of how deeply indebted I am to you and I shall always be thankful for your generosity.'

He returned to his seat at the head of the breakfast table, but did not invite her to join him.

Anne steeled herself to continue. 'In six months time I shall be fifty years of age, and I wish for some solitude in my declining years.'

He sat, cup and saucer in hand, sipping his tea in silence.

'Your children have been grown up for a number of years now; indeed, little Susan is to be married in six months, so she certainly has no further need of me. I feel I serve no purpose here, Charles, and I should like to have a house of my own.' There. She had said her piece.

Charles looked her up and down. Feet tidily together, the toes of her highly polished shoes pointed neatly from beneath the hem of her long-sleeved brown dress with its high chokered collar. Anne was always dressed in some shade of brown. A deep brown, or a tan, or a mustardy beige, but always brown, the colours of the earth, as if she wanted to sink into the ground and disappear completely. It was a pity really, Charles thought. In her quiet way, with a little added colour here and there, his sister could have been an attractive woman.

'Sit down, Anne,' he said. 'Sit down, please.' His voice was kindly enough and she did as she was told. 'You are wrong, my dear, very wrong. You are much needed in this house. What would Father do without you? For the past five years, James Kendle, now in his dotage, had lived at Kendle Lodge. His body frail, his mind wandering, James was completely dependent upon his son, rarely leaving his upstairs rooms.

It was the argument Anne had known her brother would present, and she was ready for it. 'I have spoken at length with Father and he is in agreement. Besides, he knows I will visit him here daily.'

The old fool, Charles thought. James Kendle's mind was so addled he'd agree to anything. 'I see,' he said thoughtfully. 'And why the cottage in Windmill Street?'

'Because it belonged to Hannah.' There was a warmth and a

vitality in Anne's eyes that Charles had not seen before. 'And Hannah was happy there. Oh Charles, it is a beautiful cottage,' she exclaimed, 'with views as lovely as those we have here, and it is a home. A real home ...'

She stopped as she registered his displeasure and realised what she'd said. Her brother had forbidden her to visit Hannah at her cottage. The Rocks was too rough a neighbourhood, he had told her.

Anne stared at the lace cloth on the breakfast table. 'I am sorry, Charles, but she was my friend ...' Her voice petered out.

Her betrayal outraged him, but he quelled his anger; he must not frighten her, he needed her to stay with him. For some unknown reason, inexplicable even to himself, the presence of his widowed sister in his house was of the utmost importance to Charles Kendle.

'I forgive you, Anne, that was many years ago. And I do not believe you have made a habit of disobeying me.'

'No, Charles,' she murmured, concentrating upon the lace.

He put down the cup and saucer. 'However, my reservations about the Rocks remain unchanged. It is not an area in which a woman of quality should reside.'

'Hannah lived there, and she was very happy.' Anne looked up from the tablecloth and again her eyes implored him.

'You are hardly Hannah, my dear.' He couldn't help the edge to his voice. Her eyes darted away, startled, and he softened his tone immediately. 'For which you should be very grateful. Would you like a cup of tea?'

She shook her head. 'No thank you.'

'Anne,' he leaned forward, concerned, 'there is one factor I believe you have not considered.' She looked at him questioningly. 'Where exactly would you find the funds to lead a life of independence?'

Her reply was animated. 'Oh Charles, I would not come to you with such a request. You have been more than generous to me for more years than I can count, I could not possibly ... would not ever expect you to ...'

'Then where exactly?' The steely eyes were focused on her like a snake's upon a rabbit.

Anne looked back at him, surprised. 'Why, from Father of

course. He has kindly offered me a generous weekly allowance.'

There was a moment's pause before Charles sat back in his chair and began laughing with mirthless relief.

'Why, Charles? Why do you laugh? He is more than happy to help me.'

'Oh Anne, Anne, my dear Anne.' He leaned forward once more and his smile was indulgent. 'Father could not give you even a penny.'

'But Father is very wealthy.'

'Father has lost his mind.'

'Well, yes, I know he wanders occasionally, but often when we talk he is lucid, and when we spoke of the cottage, he said he—'

'*Father has lost his mind, Anne.*' She stared back at him uncomprehending. 'Don't you know what that means? It means he is incapable of handling his affairs and is completely dependent upon me for guidance. I have had his enduring power of attorney for three years now; he cannot even sign a cheque.'

Anne looked down at the tablecloth again as she fought back the sting of tears. She concentrated on the patterns in the lace, willing herself not to cry. It wasn't just for herself she was crying, or for the loss of her dream. She cried for James Kendle.

'We all have a dream, Anne,' her father had said when she had told him about the cottage. 'I had many dreams,' his thin voice always quavered now, 'some of which came true. The store was one. Nathaniel Streatham and I, we were such a team ...'

When the conversation eventually came back to the cottage, he told her she should fight for it. 'Confront Charles,' he said, 'the way I never could. Tell him I will pay the bills, tell him that.' The voice was stronger now, quaver and all. 'I am rich, Anne. I will give you a weekly allowance, you will have a life of your own. You tell Charles that. You tell him.'

Anne and her father had become friends over the past years. Weak and wandering as he was, she had been closer to him in his illness than she had ever been before, and it hurt her deeply to think of him as having lost his mind. Though in her heart she knew her brother was right.

Charles rose from his chair and circled the table to stand beside his sister. He stroked her hair, pulled back into a tidy bun at the nape of her neck. It felt velvet to the touch. Anne had beautiful hair. 'I didn't mean to be cruel, my dear.' The kindess in his voice released tears which flowed freely down her cheeks.

He knelt beside her chair, one hand upon her knee, the other offering a handkerchief. 'There, there, don't cry.' She tried to take the handkerchief from him. 'No,' he said, 'let me,' and he gently dabbed the tears from her face. 'Anne, dear Anne.' She sobbed afresh; she'd never known Charles to be so kind.

He gave her the handkerchief to blow her nose and, when she'd regained control, remained kneeling beside her, gently stroking her knee. 'You see, my dear, Father needs you so, how could you think of leaving him?' She nodded, clutching the handkerchief to her mouth, not daring to speak. 'And I need you too, Anne. I need you too.'

She looked down at him. It was strange to see Charles, so concerned, kneeling beside her. He reached up and stroked her hair once more. 'You won't leave us, will you, my dear?' She shook her head and sniffed into the handkerchief. 'There's a good girl. Now, I insist you have a cup of tea.'

'Really, Charles, I know nothing of menus and decorations.' Anne was confused. And uncomfortable. Ever since their discussion at the breakfast table, Charles had been conciliatory towards her, and embarrassingly brusque to his wife. Now he was even deferring to Anne's opinion in regard to his daughter Susan's forthcoming nuptials.

Anne looked with some embarrassment at Susan who simply smiled and shrugged, she had long relinquished any say in her wedding arrangements. Not through any lack of spirit on her part, Susan was indeed a feisty young woman. But she hadn't wanted a lavish affair in the first place so, if her mother wished to fret and fuss, as she obviously did, and if her father wished to spend a fortune, which he apparently saw as his right and duty, then let them. She too was a little bewildered, however, by her father's deferral to Anne's taste and judgement, he'd never done so before.

'Rubbish, my dear, you have impeccable taste.'

Amy herself fumed. Charles was ignoring her again. Surely he wasn't still angry about that cottage business. 'I really think, Charles,' she ventured, 'that we can leave the reception details to Monsieur Phillipe, he is the expert after all.'

'I am fully aware of that, Amy.' His tone was civil enough but she could tell he was irritated. 'However, I appreciate Anne's contribution with regard to decoration—she has the eye of an artist.' His attention again returned to his sister. 'And most certainly, my dear, you must attend to the musical accompaniment, you are the only member of the family with a true musical ear.'

Several days later Amy tried a more intimate approach. In their bedroom. Anne could hardly compete with her there.

She excused herself from the gathering around the piano a little earlier than usual in order to prepare herself. Besides, the sight of Charles proudly watching his sister and daughter playing a duet infuriated her. In the past, when the women had gathered at the piano after dinner, Charles had always retired to his study. Lately, he not only stayed, brandy balloon in hand, he encouraged Anne to play solo, and on the weekends when Stephen was home from College, Charles would encourage applause at the conclusion of Anne's piece and Stephen, always eager to please his father, would obediently clap his hands and cry 'bravo'. When a duet was performed Charles was even rude enough to wave his wife away from the piano stool and say, 'No, no, Amy, Anne must play with Susan, she's far more musical.' Amy was left not knowing whether to scream with rage at Charles' insensitivity, or burst into tears and run from the room.

Upstairs, Amy dressed herself in her most alluring satin and lace nightgown, one of the several Charles had had imported from Paris especially for her. She released her shoulder-length fair hair from its coiffure and brushed it until it shone, then she applied her favourite scent, the jasmine fragrance Charles so liked.

When he finally joined her in their bedroom, the lights were dim and she was posed alluringly at her dressing table, having decided that to pose upon the bed might be a little vulgar.

Charles immediately recognised her intentions; how could he fail to do so? The signals were hardly subtle. She might as well have been lying there naked, he thought. But then subtlety had never been Amy's strongest suit. She was wearing one of those sample nightdresses he'd had sent from France. He always found it helpful to experiment on his family. Amy's delight in the nightdresses had proved an excellent indicator and the line was now most popular amongst Sydney's wealthier set.

She stood. 'I've been waiting for you,' she purred.

'You look lovely, my dear.'

It was what she wanted him to say, and he had to admit that for a forty-five-year-old she was impressive. She'd certainly kept her figure: her breasts were full, her waist was slim. In the subdued lighting she could well have passed for a woman ten years her junior.

He returned her embrace. She was wearing far too much of that scent he'd made the mistake of telling her he liked. He found it very cloying. However, he felt himself respond as she expertly removed his jacket without breaking the rhythm of her body which undulated invitingly against his. It had been some time since their last sexual union, possibly months, Charles thought; he had been very busy.

She lifted her face as she unbuttoned his shirt, and her eyes closed gently. 'Darling,' she murmured. It was time for the kiss.

Her seduction techniques were predictable. Predictable now, but in the early days they had seemed bold and unbelievably exciting. When had her predictability become boring, he wondered as their mouths met. So long ago now it was difficult to remember. Not that it bothered Charles, to whom the daily thrust and parry of business had become far more of an adventure than the occasional thrust and parry of his libido. Besides, other women were readily available, as they always were to men of wealth and power, if he felt the need for fresh excitement. But he rarely did.

He felt her fingertips glide over his nipples beneath the open shirt. He took her head in his hands and ran his fingers up through the golden locks. Then he clasped a fistful of her hair the way he knew she liked it.

Fleetingly, he thought of Anne's hair, thick brown and luscious. Released from its captivity Anne's hair quite possibly reached right down to her waist . . .

With just the right mixture of care and brutality, he eased Amy's head back and lowered his mouth to the vulnerable base of her throat. She moaned with pleasure as she always did.

Charles wondered what Anne's throat would look like. She had a slender, elegant neck, he could tell, beneath the high-collared blouses and dresses she wore. But he had never seen her throat . . .

He slid the thin straps of the nightdress from Amy's shoulders.

The satin fabric caressed every curve of her body as it slowly slithered its way to the floor.

She moaned again, her pleasure palpable as he released his grip on her hair, his hand travelling down her back, over her hip, across her belly, then up. Up to cup the curve of her breast.

Anne's breasts would be smaller, Charles couldn't resist thinking. He didn't know why he thought it, he simply found the fact interesting. Amy's breasts were a little vulgar when all was said and done, just as Amy herself was a little vulgar. Anne naturally had a more refined, a more elegant body, Anne was a Kendle after all . . .

Amy had expected to go through her normal routine of pretence that night, but for the first time in years she enjoyed their lovemaking. Right from the very start. When he'd made a fist of her hair and pulled back her head, she hadn't had to fight the gasp which accompanied the pain. It had been the way he used to do it, when they were first married and she'd told him she liked it like that.

Charles had not been Amy's first lover, but she had been his. His energy having been focused upon the family business and the pursuit of wealth, Charles had remained a virgin until he was twenty-eight; and Amy, a sensual woman, had enjoyed teaching him the balance of tenderness and passion which aroused her. The first year or so of their marriage had been exciting for them both. But it had not been long before Charles's obsession with the burgeoning family empire once more consumed him, and Amy found herself marooned, with no outlet for her sexuality.

She had worked hard to resurrect her husband's passion, and for a year or so she had succeeded. But after a while even her wanton advances had failed to titillate, and it humiliated her when he said, with the tired edge of irritation to his voice, 'Not now, Amy, for God's sake, not now.'

So she left him alone and waited for him to come to her, which he did, on average, about once a month. For the first ten years or so anyway. After that, months and months could go by before he felt the urge. And when he did, he performed the erotic lessons she'd taught him perfunctorily, by rote, which she hated. She wished that he would stop and just satisfy his carnal lust; there was no pleasure in their foreplay, and quite often there was pain.

Twice during their marriage Amy had taken a younger lover,

which had assuaged her frustration, but she had lived in such terror of discovery or blackmail, or both, that she had quickly ended the affairs. These days, on the rare occasions when she and Charles made love Amy fantasised about her young lovers. But it was sometimes difficult when Charles got the balance wrong. When he pulled her hair too hard, or pinched her nipple too forcefully, or drew blood as he bit her lip.

The balance had been perfect tonight, she thought as she lay beside him, sated. She stretched herself like a cat then curled to lie in the crook of his shoulder. She hadn't had to simulate her pleasure tonight. The tiny gasps which had fluttered from her throat, the thrusting motion of her loins, the clasping, grasping of her hands, the guttural moans, had all been real. She had been pretending for so long that she had forgotten the pure joy of being awakened. She lightly kissed her husband's breast.

Charles was not aware of her lips upon his skin. He, too, had enjoyed their lovemaking; it had been more than a mere release, there had been an added dimension. His thoughts of Anne perhaps? Interesting that she should have been so much in his mind. Protectiveness of course. And the fact that he was only just now coming to know his sister, previously a shadow in his life. He must look after Anne. He owed it to her. They were kin after all; they shared the Kendle blood. He rolled over to go to sleep.

'Charles,' Amy whispered.

'Mmm?'

'About Susan's wedding . . .' She stroked his back lightly with the tips of her fingernails. 'I do so wish you would allow me to oversee the arrangements, my darling.' She kept stroking his back and her voice was gentle. 'After all, she is my daughter.'

Charles tried to curb his irritation. He was tired, the last thing he wanted was conversation. 'You're arranging the gowns, my dear, the bridesmaids and the flower girls, surely—'

'But Anne is in charge of everything else.' A slight whinge had crept into her voice, Charles loathed it when she whinged. She waited for a response but there was none. 'Well, it's not right, Charles, surely you must see that.' She stopped stroking his back and leant up on one elbow. 'It is not right that Anne should be responsible for Susan's wedding. Anne is not her mother. I am.'

The repetition of his sister's name further irritated Charles.

'Concentrate upon the gowns, Amy,' he snapped. 'It's where your talent lies. Now go to sleep, for God's sake.'

He knew she was crying as she rolled away from him but he couldn't be bothered mollifying her. The image of Anne was in his mind as he drifted off to sleep.

The day before James Kendle's seventy-third birthday, a visitor arrived at Kendle Lodge. Old Spike Monroe let her in through the garden side gate. If she'd arrived at the front door, the butler would never have admitted her, and even at the servants' entrance she would have been turned away by Mrs Marett, the housekeeper. But Spike was a strange fellow. Despite the fact that he was head gardener, and as such a very important member of the Kendle staff, he never saw himself as a figure of authority.

So when the Aboriginal woman called to him through the ornate iron gate, it didn't occur to him to order her away.

'Hey there, mister,' she said, and he crossed to the gates.

She was not a beggar, Spike could tell that immediately. She was quite a nice-looking woman, he thought, in her mid-thirties perhaps, and her smile was pleasant, if a little nervous.

'Mr James Kendle, he lives here, don't he?'

'Yep. He does.' Spike was surprised that she should know of James Kendle, the old man had kept to himself for years now.

'Can I see him? Mr Kendle?'

'I don't know,' Spike shrugged. 'He's sick, keeps to his bed.'

'Please,' the woman begged, and there was an urgency in her eyes, 'please can I see him?'

'Not up to me,' Spike said, 'I'm only the gardener.' But he felt sorry for the woman, there was a desperation about her. 'Come in,' he said and opened the gate. 'Come in and we'll ask.'

She followed him through the gardens and across the tiled verandah, standing respectfully behind him as he approached the main back doors. Spike was about to knock for Mrs Marett but, even as he raised his hand, the door opened and the master's sister stood there, dressed in a bonnet and cape.

'Oh.' Anne was startled to open the door and find the gardener and an Aboriginal woman standing before her.

'Begging your pardon, ma'am,' Spike removed his cloth cap, 'but there's a person here wants to see Mr Kendle.'

'My name's Milly, missus,' the woman stepped forward and bobbed a sort of curtsy. 'And I'm not begging, I swear.' Anne, too, could see the desperation in her. 'Can I see him? Can I see Mr Kendle?'

'I shall enquire for you,' Anne said, 'but you must understand, he is a very busy man.' She hoped that Charles would be civil to the woman. 'Wait here one moment.'

Spike had been about to correct her. 'It's the old Mr Kendle she wants to see,' he'd been about to say, but Anne was gone. 'Well, I'll leave you to it,' he said to the woman. The master would be none too happy that he'd let a stranger in through the side gate, and Spike didn't want to be around to cop a reprimand.

'Thank you,' the woman said as he left. And she stood, nervously twisting her small cloth handbag.

'I'm so sorry, but my brother Charles is busy,' Anne said upon her return. It had been just as she had expected. 'What do I want to see a black for?' Charles had snapped. 'She'll only be after money, send her away.' It was better like this, Anne supposed. At least this way the woman wasn't being insulted to her face.

'No.' The woman shook her head. 'The old master, that's who I want to see. Mr James Kendle.'

'I'm sorry, but he is not well, he is bedridden.'

'Please, missus,' the woman implored, clearly agitated, twisting the bag in her hands. 'Please.'

'May I ask what business you feel you have with my father?' Anne enquired gently. She felt sorry for the woman.

Milly stared at her mutilated handbag and wondered how she could tell this neat woman in her bonnet and cape and dainty gown.

'We are kin,' she finally mumbled.

'I beg your pardon?' Anne wasn't sure if she had heard correctly.

'We are kin.' She said it louder this time. The words were out and she felt bolder now. 'My name is Milly,' she looked directly into Anne's eyes. 'Milly Kendle.'

Anne felt a shock of outrage. It was a blasphemous thing for the woman to have said. Outrageous. Unbelievable. Preposterous.

Milly could see the shock and incredulity; she hadn't wanted to tell anyone but the old man. 'Please, missus, please let me see him. Old Mr James is the only one who will know. He is the only one who can help me.' There were tears in her eyes. She tried to fight them back, not wanting to lose control.

'What exactly is it you want from him?' Anne managed to ask.

'They are going to take my babies.' Milly couldn't help it, there was no stemming the tears now. 'They say I can't look after my babies.' She sniffed and wiped at her face with her cloth handbag. 'The Protection Board is going to take my two babies. They are going to take them far away and change their names and put them with a white family and I'll never see them again.'

Milly wiped her runny nose with the back of her hand, the tears under control now. 'If I show the Protection Board that I can look after my babies, then they'll let them stay with me on the reservation.'

'So it is money you're after.' Anne's voice was hard and cold. Charles had been right, she thought.

The missus was going to send her away, Milly knew it. She was very calm now. 'My father's name was Jackie Kendle,' she said. 'His mother was called Murrumuru and his father was called Richard Kendle.'

At the mention of her grandfather's name, Anne felt a fresh sense of shock. But it was the shock of plausibility. How could the woman know of Richard Kendle? How could she invent such a preposterous lie? At the same time Anne recognised that the woman was not an Aborigine of full blood, her skin was too light, her features too European. It was suddenly imperative to Anne that she find out the truth.

'Come with me,' she said.

Inside the house, Milly stood on the huge Persian carpet, feeling it plush beneath the thin, worn soles of her shoes, and stared up at the moulded ceiling high above, the gleaming crystal chandelier hanging from its centre. She had never dreamed a house could be so grand. There were gold-framed paintings on the walls, and a statue in the corner, and a massive fireplace set in tiles with a carved wooden mantelpiece over the top. And a piano. Milly had never seen a piano, not a real one, only a picture of one in the newspaper.

Anne beckoned Milly to follow her up the grand staircase. It was as well Amy and Susan were at the dressmaker for a final wedding gown fitting, she thought. Her eyes darted to Charles's study which led off from the downstairs sitting room. The door was ajar and she prayed that he wouldn't appear.

When they reached upstairs she breathed a sigh of relief. But as she walked along the landing to her father's bedroom, she was startled by a voice behind her.

'Excuse me, ma'am.' Anne turned, as did Milly, to confront Mrs Marett, who had stepped out from one of the bedrooms. 'May I be of any assistance?'

'Thank you no, Mrs Marett.' Anne could see the censure in the housekeeper's eyes.

'My father has a visitor,' Anne replied as boldly as she could. 'We will be brief, and you do not need to inform my brother, I shall do so myself.'

'Very good, ma'am.'

Anne ushered Milly into the bedroom.

It was a large room, with French windows which, if opened, would have permitted the grandest view from the balcony across Woolloomooloo Bay to the city skyline. But the windows were not open now, the red velvet drapes were drawn and the room was gloomy. So gloomy that Milly barely noticed the person asleep in the four-poster bed to her right.

Anne crossed to the windows and drew open the heavy curtains. Mrs Marett would have closed them, she thought with irritation. She had asked the woman not to do so, but then Charles's house-keeper never listened to a word she said. She opened the French windows, and the afternoon sun shone through the lace curtains.

James stirred from his drowsiness. 'Anne?' he murmured.

'Yes, Father, I'm here. And you have a visitor. Come along now, let's sit you up.' She took the spare pillows from the cupboard and propped them behind him, then she poured water from the jug into the porcelain bowl on the marble washstand beside the bed and bathed his face with a flannel. 'Pull the chair to the bed where he can see you,' she instructed Milly.

Milly did as she was told and then sat wondering what to do next. The old man looked so frail.

'Tell him everything, exactly as you told me,' Anne said, squeezing the flannel dry and draping it over the side of the basin.

'My name is Milly, sir,' she said.

'Milly, that's nice.' The voice was frail too. Everything about the old man was frail, from the waxlike skin of his thin, thin face, to the fragile claw of his hand which rested gently on the bedcover. 'A visitor,' James said, 'we don't have many visitors, do we, Anne? How very pleasant.'

'That's right, Father, and Milly has something to tell you. Something which is very important, so you must listen carefully.' She sat on the bed and took the clawlike fingers in her hand. 'Go on,' she said to Milly, 'everything, just as you told me.'

Milly took a deep breath. 'My name is Milly, sir. Milly Kendle. And my father was Jackie Kendle—'

'Kendle,' the old man interrupted, smiling delightedly, 'Kendle, that is my name.' He turned to his daughter. 'That is our name, Anne, Milly shares our name. Is that not extraordinary?'

Milly halted, confused.

'Go on,' Anne said.

'Jackie Kendle's mother was called Murrumuru. And his father was called Richard Kendle.'

'Richard Kendle.' James seemed even more delighted. 'My father's name, extraordinary, quite extraordinary.' His voice quivered with excitement, he would start to ramble any minute now, Anne thought. 'How charming you should visit us. Will the tea be long, Anne? How charming, I do so like having visitors, although visitors are few and far between these days, are they not, Anne?'

'Yes, Father, we have few visitors, but Milly is trying to tell you that she is more than a visitor. She believes she is a Kendle, you see.'

'A Kendle? Well, yes, she is, she is. She says she is.' James smiled, it was nice to have a visitor. Someone other than Anne. Albeit a native. Nice to have a visitor.

'No, Father, she is telling you that she is kin, or so she believes.'

'Kin?' James looked bewildered. 'Kin?'

'Yes, Father. She believes that she is family.'

'But how can she be family?' He looked from Milly to Anne, then back to Milly. 'How can she be family? She is black.'

'Yes. And she is saying that Grandfather Richard sired a child by an Aboriginal woman, a woman called Murrumuru.' The baldness of the statement sounded brutal, but she needed to shock him, to keep his concentration focused.

'Murrumuru ... Murrumuru ...' James murmured the name, savouring the sound. Vaguely he remembered it from somewhere. 'Murrumuru. Murrumuru.' It reminded him of the gentle, haunting sounds the black men made through their long wooden pipes. Murrumuru. Suddenly he remembered. Of course. Murrumuru cooked eels. At Parramatta, in the camp beside the river, he had watched her cook eels. She was the mother of his friend. The boy to whom he had given his hat. What was the boy's name?

'You remember Murrumuru do you, Father?' The old man was nodding as he murmured the name. He nodded again and Anne knew she must be direct, there was no time to spare, soon he would disappear once more into his twilight world. 'Did Murrumuru bear a child by Richard Kendle?' she asked firmly.

Turumbah, that was the boy's name, James recalled. Turumbah. Turumbah and Gran'sun James, they had been such friends. Turumbah had taught him to swim. Ah, those were the days. The days of freedom, secret and forbidden. The freedom of swimming naked and alone amongst the mangroves. The old man smiled at the memory.

'Please try and concentrate, Father. Did Murrumuru and Richard Kendle have a child? Please, Father. Try.'

Anne was gently and methodically squeezing his hand, James realised. She only did that when she wanted him to concentrate. James tried. He tried hard. He would do anything for Anne.

'Murrumuru and Richard Kendle,' he whispered.

'Yes, Father, well done. Murrumuru and Richard Kendle, did they have a child?'

James shook his head. What an outrageous remark, how could Anne suggest such a thing? His own father and the black housemaid! For James recalled now that Murrumuru had been a servant in their house.

'But could they have done so, Father, would it have been possible?' Anne was persistent, she would not let him drift away. 'Could she have been his mistress?'

Suddenly the memories flooded in. A kaleidoscope of images. How old would he have been—fifteen? sixteen?—when he and Phoebe had noticed a rift between their parents. It had been around that time that Murrumuru had left the household. 'I prefer white servants,' had been his mother's only explanation. Most vivid in the myriad of pictures which tumbled through James's brain was the face of Grandfather Thomas, head upon the pillow of his deathbed, begging for an answer. 'What did I do to your mother, James? How did I ruin her marriage? Why has she condemned me?' It had been Thomas Kendall who had brought Wolawara and his clan to Parramatta. It had been Thomas Kendall who had given them the land. And, of course, it had been Thomas Kendall whom Mary had blamed for the ruin of her marriage.

Everything was falling into place. James fought to retain his concentration, but was tiring from the effort. It all made sense now. Shocking sense, most certainly, but . . .

'How unlike you, Anne, to be so cruel.'

Anne and Milly had both been so focused upon the old man, they had failed to hear the door open. Anne wondered how long her brother had been standing there.

'Stop torturing the man, let him be.' Charles crossed to the bed and disengaged Anne's hand from her father's. 'You must not squeeze his fingers so, he is very fragile. You of all people should know that.'

Anne rose guiltily from the bed and Charles took her place, stroking James's brow, crooning to him gently. 'Rest now, Father, rest.'

'So much to remember, Charles.' The old man was agitated. 'So much to remember.'

'Sssh, there, there. You must not distress yourself. Relax, Father, relax.'

The softness of his son's voice and the gentle touch of his fingers were soothing. James closed his eyes. He had been somewhere peaceful only moments ago. Where, he wondered. Ah yes, that was it. Swimming. Naked. Alone in his magic land beneath the silent canopy of mangroves, his toes trailing in the softness of the mud, the gentle suction of the water caressing his body . . .

'That's it, Father, relax . . .' Charles's steel-grey eyes belied his soothing tone. Even as he stroked his father's brow, he glared hate at Milly who sat frozen on the edge of the chair.

As soon as Charles sensed that his father's mind had slipped away, he dropped all pretence. He rose from the bed and addressed Milly, quietly but with such menace that she dared not move.

'My housekeeper is waiting for you on the landing, she will see you out the servants' entrance, and you will never show your face here again, do you understand me?'

It was not only Milly who was frightened. Anne had seen Charles like this before, and it always terrified her. But something deep inside lent her strength. 'Charles, we must know the truth,' Anne heard herself protest, amazed at her own boldness. 'It is important for us all.'

'We know the truth, Anne.' His eyes did not leave Milly's. 'The truth is this woman wants money, is that not so?'

Milly nodded, petrified but desperate. 'Yes, sir, for my babies.'

'Exactly,' he mocked her with his scorn, 'for your babies.'

'It is true, Charles,' Anne insisted, 'everything she says —'

'Anne, my dear,' he turned to his sister and spoke reassuringly, albeit with an air of condescension, 'I am sympathetic to this woman's plight, you must believe me, and Mrs Marett will give her money, I have instructed her to do so.' He smiled his assurance. 'Now we must let the poor creature go, we have terrified her quite enough.' To Milly: 'You may go.' It was an order.

Milly slid from her chair and sidled out through the door as quickly as she could.

'Charles, I don't know how much you heard but —'

'I heard quite enough, my dear, and you must trust me in my judgement.' He stepped close to her and took her face in his hands. She felt like a mouse in a trap. 'I am the head of this family, am I not?' She nodded, but her glance flickered nervously towards the door. 'The woman will be recompensed, have no fear.' His eyes were boring into her.

'You must obey me, Anne,' he said with infinite tenderness, 'I have your best interests at heart.' Her face locked between his hands, her eyes locked to his, there was nothing she could do but stand, paralysed, feeling the warmth of his breath as he bent to her. 'You must always remember that, my dear.' And he kissed her softly upon the lips. 'Always,' he whispered as their mouths parted. Then he left her there, standing at her father's bedside, frozen, shocked into submission.

Milly did not receive any recompense. These were not Mrs Marett's orders. Terrified, she was bundled out the servants' entrance and told never to return.

Six months later her children were taken from her. She never saw them again.

Chapter Seven

Tis the hope of something better than the present or the past—
Tis the wish for something better—strong within us to the last.
Tis the longing for redemption as our ruined souls descend;
Tis the hope of something better that will save us in the end.

As the commercial depression of 1892 spilled over into 1893, the voice of Henry Lawson, the boy from Grenfell, urged his fellow countrymen to be strong. No longer were they second-rate Europeans; he told them through his pen, they were Australians and should be proud of it.

For many it was difficult though. As yet more banks crashed and more companies became insolvent, as yet more rock-solid businessmen filed bankruptcy petitions in the courts and more pillars of society were charged with fraud, pride was a luxury many could ill afford. Particularly the burgeoning numbers of unemployed who, in the streets of Melbourne and Sydney, staged demonstrations to draw attention to their plight.

On Sunday 19 November, Paddy O'Shea and a number of his mates joined the three hundred strong who were gathered at the Queen Victoria statue in the centre of Sydney. The crowd milled for an hour or so, gathering forces before the march to the Centennial Hall, and the babble grew bitter as men voiced their opinions on the cause of the economic ruin.

The public service was overmanned, some said. The government departments were so clogged with red tape that public works were at a standstill. Others said it was the politicians getting fat on the taxpayers' money whilst families starved. Some said the depression was caused by flash speculation. Others maintained it was a punishment for the folly of excessive overseas borrowing. Everyone had an opinion, and by the time the march set off, the voice of disillusionment was vociferous and loud.

Paddy was amongst those at the head of the procession, behind the leader, who carried a huge wooden cross, nailed to which was the effigy of a man with the wounds of Christ smeared in red paint upon it. Above the head was a placard on which was written 'Humanity crucified'.

As the procession started to march off, some of the bystanders voiced their outrage at the blasphemy, whilst others, sympathetic to the victims of the crisis, shouted their approval. But the bickering posed no threat of violence and, aside from a brief scuffle with police, the demonstration progressed peacefully to Centennial Hall. There voices were raised in protest and, at the culmination of the proceedings, the Reverend Bavin assured the gathering that God was sympathetic to their predicament, and to remember always that God loved them.

For Paddy it was not enough. God's love had done little for him, he thought. Like many, Paddy was angry. Very angry. The latest bitter pill he'd had to swallow had not been one of his own making.

He had not been responsible for the closure of the Standard Bank of Australia. And whilst many banks had closed, only to reopen again once order had been restored, the Standard Bank of Australia had not been one of them. It had closed its doors for good, it had gone forever, and with it had gone Paddy's money. His and Dotty's nest egg, their security for the future. And Paddy was powerless to do anything about it.

But he would not stand by and see young Daniel, ten years of age, taken from school, deprived of an education because he, Paddy O'Shea, could not buy books for his son. He would not stand by and see his beautiful eighteen-year-old daughter, Kathleen, dressed in rags. And, above all, he would not stand by and see his loyal wife grow thinner and more worn with each day, fretting, scraping together the pennies to feed her family.

Paddy was going to take matters into his own hands. He had a plan.

Paddy would not listen to any more empty promises of God's love. He would commit a crime, and he knew exactly who was to be his victim. Charles Kendle. He had made the choice several months previously. The day he'd bumped into Charles's sister, Anne Goodlet.

Every so often Paddy would walk up the hill from the pub to look at his mother's cottage. Just for old time's sake. On this particular day, huddled against a lamp post, the collar of his work shirt turned up against the light drizzle of rain, he watched as a neat woman, tucked beneath an umbrella, opened the gate. She stepped up onto the porch, shook out the umbrella and set it down to dry. It was then, as she took the front-door key from her purse, that Paddy realised, to his surprise, who the woman was.

He called her name. 'Anne! Anne Goodlet!'

She turned, and he crossed to the gate. 'Paddy O'Shea?' she queried.

'The very same.'

'I've not seen you since Hannah's funeral.'

He nodded. 'You are living in her cottage?'

'I own it now. I have done so for nearly a year.'

It was not a boast, there was no triumph in her tone and Paddy felt neither anger nor envy. He had long accepted that he had lost his mother's cottage through his own stupidity.

'That's good,' he said simply. 'Ma would be pleased.'

Anne found it a very generous statement. Touching too. 'For goodness' sake, come on out of the rain,' she said, 'it's going to pour down any minute.' He joined her on the front porch. 'Would you like a cup of tea?'

'It would be a pleasure.'

She opened the door into the hall and he followed her through the formal front parlour and into the living room. In one corner stood a dressmaker's dummy clothed in a girl's pretty ball gown, beside it a table with boxes of beads, fine satin ribbons and lace. Against the far wall was a large desk upon which sat books and papers, inkwells and pens.

'You are a dressmaker, Anne?' Paddy asked.

'Goodness no, I do not have the skill.' It was modesty speaking—Anne had a good eye for design and was a talented embroiderer with a number of regular customers. Customers who would have their daughters' ball gowns and wedding dresses embroidered by no-one other than Anne Goodlet, whose work was known for its detail and delicacy. Anne's wealthy clients were referred to her by Howard Streatham; it was the least he could do as she refused to accept his financial assistance. 'No, Paddy, I merely embroider and lacework the finished article.'

'And you are studying, I see.' Paddy gestured to the desk.

'No, I take notation.' He appeared a little bemused. 'There are many people who cannot write and who will pay to have their letters written for them.' She was aware that he was surprised to discover she was working. 'And I teach reading and writing,' she continued, 'just the basic skills, as my pupils are mostly children, and immigrants with a poor knowledge of English.' It was important to Anne that Paddy should know she earned her own living. 'It does not make me a rich woman but I manage to get by.'

Paddy was indeed surprised, he had presumed that her brother Charles was supporting her. He declined her offer to sit in the front parlour whilst she made the tea. 'I should feel far too grand,' he said, 'and I'm in my work clothes, it wouldn't be right.' He gestured to his clumsy boots and heavy duty trousers.

Paddy was always in his work clothes these days, but it didn't mean he was working. Each morning he would queue up with the others, sometimes for hours, only to be turned away with, 'Nuthin' today, fellas, sorry.' Every now and then he'd be one of the few lucky ones to get a day's work, but more often than not he'd miss out, most of them did.

He followed her into the kitchen and watched her bustling around efficiently. What a remarkable change, he thought. Where was the timid colourless creature she had once been? There was an animation about her now, a healthy bloom in her cheeks, a strength of purpose in her actions. Anne Goodlet was a woman no longer unsure of herself.

'How is your family, Paddy?' Anne enquired, deciding that Paddy O'Shea did not look at all well. Although his body was still huge, still strong, it was apparent that he had lost weight. His face was gaunt and there was worry in his eyes.

'Fine, fine. I have a son since last we met. Ten he is now. I called him Daniel after Pa, but he gets called Dan mostly.'

They talked about his family whilst she made the tea and then they sat by the living-room windows looking out at the rain which was coming down in sheets now. So heavy was it that they could barely see past the little courtyard to the harbour beyond. Strange, they agreed, how summer was Sydney's wettest season.

Talk of the weather and other niceties dwindled as Paddy stared, distracted, out of the window. What was he thinking, Anne wondered, and she decided to be direct. It was an ability she had only recently acquired.

'Is something troubling you, Paddy?' He looked at her. 'You seem a little worried.'

'These are hard times, everyone's worried.' He realised that his reply had been brusque, even rude, and that she was genuinely concerned. 'I'm sorry,' he said gently, and he told her about the bank.

Anne was so obviously sympathetic to his plight that Paddy found himself pouring out the whole story. The stupidity of his gambling, the forced sale of the cottage, the collapse of the bank. It was a relief to talk so openly.

'Tis a devil of a thing, Anne, the gambling lust. Had I not succumbed to it, I would have had no need of the bank, never did trust them anyway. I would still own this very cottage.' He realised how insensitive his remark must have sounded. 'No offence intended, I assure you,' he hastily added. 'If I can't own the place myself, you're the first person I'd wish to see have it, I swear.'

Anne smiled, no offence had been taken. 'It must have angered you dreadfully when Charles purchased it,' she said. 'I was always surprised that you did not refuse his offer and wait for another.' She didn't register his stunned reaction as she continued, 'But now of course I realise—the demands of the bookies would have necessitated a swift transaction.'

'Kendle purchased it?'

'Why yes of course. Surely you knew?'

'No. The real estate fellow said it was a businessman. I didn't enquire any further.'

Anne wondered whether she should tell Paddy the truth. Yes, she decided, he had a right to know. 'I am very much afraid,

Paddy, that you were the sole reason Charles made the acquisition. He boasted of it to his wife. "I have taught Paddy O'Shea a lesson", that's what he told Amy.'

Paddy stared blankly at her. It had been late on a Friday night when Cocky's heavies had done him over. The cottage had been snapped up first thing Monday morning. He'd blessed his good luck at the time. But it had not been good luck at all. Charles Kendle had known all the while that the cottage would be on the market that very day. The realisation overwhelmed Paddy. It had not been the bookies who called in Cocky. It had been Charles Kendle.

'I don't know how he did it,' Anne was continuing, 'but he said that he had planned it, he boasted to Amy that he had. He hates you, Paddy, ever since you attacked him at Hannah's funeral. You humiliated him, and he won't have that.' She sensed his anger, and hoped she would have no cause to regret telling him all this.

'You must not think of revenge, Paddy. Charles is a vindictive man, and powerful. It will do you no good to retaliate.'

Paddy wasn't listening. He had made a decision. Paddy would steal from Charles Kendle everything that was owed to him, and then he would steal more.

'Please, Paddy, promise me,' Anne implored.

'Promise you?' He forced his mind back to the present. He must not rush things, such a crime must be carefully planned, there was plenty of time. 'Promise you what, Anne?'

'That you will not attempt revenge. Charles could destroy you. And he would, believe me.'

'Don't you worry, Anne,' he smiled his reassurance. 'Don't you worry for one minute. Now tell me,' he changed the subject, 'how did you come by ownership of the cottage? Your brother didn't give it to you, surely.' It was quite obvious from the tone of her voice when she spoke of him that Anne despised her brother.

'Yes,' she answered after a moment's pause, 'he gave it to me.'

'What,' Paddy said scornfully, 'from the goodness of his heart?'

'No. Not from the goodness of his heart. But he gave it to me.' Paddy had been so open with her that Anne felt she owed him an explanation, but she could give him none. She could not tell him the truth. She could tell no-one the truth. 'Would you like some more tea?'

'No, thank you.' Her face was flushed, Paddy noticed, as she fiddled with the teapot. He had no wish to distress her. 'The rain has eased,' he said, looking out of the bay windows. 'I must be on my way.'

They parted warmly at the door, Paddy promising to visit her again. And Anne watched him from the front porch as, shoulders hunched, collar turned up, he walked down Windmill Street through the rain.

She thought of him a lot that night as she lay in her bed unable to sleep, and she wished she could do something for him. But even if she wanted to, she could hardly give Paddy back his cottage. It was all she had. Not only was it her one financial asset, it was her very sanity. Living alone in the cottage, Anne had come to know a freedom she had never before experienced. And she had come to know a person whom she had never known existed. A person called Anne Goodlet, who was no longer a mere shadow existing on the periphery of other people's lives.

Anne was convinced that the cottage had saved her life, for during the two years prior to her move, there had been days of such black despair that she had found the task of living almost beyond endurance.

It had all started the day of Milly Kendle's visit, when Charles had kissed her and left her standing beside her father's bed, paralysed with shock and shame.

Anne did not know for how long she remained standing there, all she knew was the hideous realisation that her brother desired her. 'I have your best interests at heart, Anne,' he'd said, but she had seen far more in his eyes than sibling affection. As he had lowered his face to hers, she had seen lust in his eyes. Then his lips had brushed hers with a lover's touch, leaving her in a state of dazed horror.

In the months that followed, she studiously avoided her brother. Whenever he addressed her, she stared at the floor. Each morning she prayed that she would not encounter him at the back door or in the main hall when she was leaving the house. Her daily walks grew longer, her outings to the galleries, to concerts and the theatre grew more frequent and, finally, she insisted that she take her meals with her father in his room. Mealtimes were the most awkward she had found. Susan was now married and living in

Melbourne, and Anne was marooned with Amy and Charles, feeling his eyes upon her, aware that he desired her more than he desired his own wife who was making empty conversation across the table.

Charles Kendle was obsessed. His sister, the creature over whom he had had total power, was withdrawing more and more from him and, as she did, so the need to bring her back under his control grew stronger and stronger.

He was not disturbed by the fact that Anne was in his thoughts when he made love to his wife. It was not unnatural, he told himself, to love his sister. She was reliant upon him, he must protect her, she must love him equally in return.

At night, as Charles felt his body meld with Amy's, he and Anne were one. And when Amy sighed her satisfaction, it was the acquiescence of his sister which Charles experienced. Only then could he find pleasure in his own release.

'You have taken your evening meal with Father every night for the past two weeks, Anne.' Charles's anger was evident. 'I consider it extremely rude.'

She had popped into the dining room as Charles and Amy were seating themselves at table and made her announcement as a matter of courtesy, as she had for the past fortnight. Each time Charles had simply said, 'If you must', and she had disappeared upstairs for the ensuing two hours, after which she had returned to bid her brother and his wife goodnight before retiring.

Charles would have no more of this. How dare she deprive him of her company. She owed him far more than she owed their father.

'I am sorry you consider it rude, Charles.' She focused upon the floor as she always did when addressing him these days. 'But Father has become more feeble of late, and if he is not supervised, I fear he will not eat properly.'

'Mrs Marett can supervise his feeding. She can feed him by hand if need be.'

'Mrs Marett is not his daughter.'

Amy looked up, surprised. There was no insolence in Anne's tone, but she was answering back to Charles.

'I am his daughter,' Anne continued, her gaze still directed at the floor, 'and much as I do not wish to displease you, I must insist that I take my meals with him, for the sake of his health.' It was not altogether a lie, James's health was indeed deteriorating, as was his interest in food.

Amy waited for the outburst of anger.

'I see.' Strangely enough, Charles was calm. Although he wanted her to look at him, he found her subservient attitude attractive, even as she took a stance against his wishes. He did not wish to frighten her. He wished her to admire him. 'I do not mean to be inconsiderate, Anne. Your care of the old man is admirable.' Amy's eyes flickered from one to the other, she couldn't believe her ears. 'Perhaps you will take your Sunday evening meals with us, that would not be too much to ask, surely?'

'Of course, Charles.' She nodded obediently. 'May I go to Father now?'

'You may.'

The Sunday evening meals became an endurance test for Anne. When Charles personally filled her wine glass, ignoring the butler, she knew he did so in order to feel the touch of her fingers as he passed it to her. Constantly he queried her about her activities, ensuring that the entire mealtime conversation revolved around her, and that she would be forced to look up from the table. When she did, and caught his eyes feasting upon her, she flushed and looked back down at her untouched plate.

Anne served her time like a prisoner at Kendle Lodge, her only respite the old man upstairs, her only moments of peace spent in the gloomy room of her dying father.

There was just one light at the end of the tunnel and, for Anne, the weeks could not pass quickly enough. Charles, Amy and their son, Stephen, were shortly to depart for Europe, the trip being Charles's graduation present to Stephen who, at twenty-three, had recently completed his Bachelor of Arts degree at Sydney University.

'How very ungrateful of you, Anne,' Charles had said when she had steadfastly refused to accompany them.

'I know it must appear so Charles, but father's condition is deteriorating so rapidly I could not possibly leave him.'

At first, Charles had cursed his father. Ineffectual to the last, James Kendle couldn't even die efficiently.

Upon consultation with James's physician, however, Charles discovered that the old man was likely to die at any minute.

'He's failing fast, I'm afraid,' Dr Muggleton said.

'How long?' Charles demanded.

'Well,' the doctor shook his head gravely, 'I doubt whether he will last longer than a fortnight or so. I've not told Mrs Goodlet,' he added. 'Her own condition is somewhat delicate, I fear, she really must look after her health.'

'She will be in good hands, I assure you,' Charles replied. 'We leave for Europe in six weeks and the change of scenery will be just what she will need to ease the grief of her tragic loss.' And Charles concerned himself no more with the irritation of his father's lingering death.

Upon Stephen's return home from St Paul's College a month prior to their departure for Europe, life at Kendle Lodge resumed a semblance of normality.

'Richard Windeyer eh?' Charles was most gratified to hear of Stephen's friendship with the son of so prominent a man as the recently knighted William Charles Windeyer, Supreme Court judge.

'Yes sir, Richard also rooms at St Paul's,' Stephen boasted enthusiastically, enjoying the unaccustomed attention from his father. 'He's a grand fellow and we've become very good friends.'

'Excellent, excellent. I should like to meet the Windeyer boy.'

As he listened to his son talk of college life and the friends he had made, Charles felt his old envy resurface. The envy he had always felt for the automatic social status granted those with a university education. He cursed himself for refusing the opportunity when his father had offered it; he'd been so eager to join the family business.

Howard Streatham had been Oxford educated, Charles often thought bitterly, which explained why Howard was socially acceptable to people like the Wunderlichs. Despite the fact that every major room in Charles's house now boasted a Wunderlich ceiling he had not as yet been welcomed into the Wunderlichs' artistic circle of friends, a fact which constantly irked him.

'You must bring young Windeyer home and introduce him to us,' he said, 'when we return from Europe.'

Anne was thankful for the distraction of Stephen's presence, but she nonetheless counted the days until she would be free of Charles. For a whole six months she would have the house to herself, just she and her father and the servants. She might even persuade the butler to carry James downstairs, he had always so enjoyed sitting in the garden. Although he was very fragile these days, perhaps it would not be wise.

Despite the fact that Anne continuously worried about her father, she refused to accept the imminence of his death. She hung on the doctor's words. 'He's bearing up well enough, Mrs Goodlet,' he said. 'You must not stress yourself so, you have your own health to consider.'

Only two weeks to go. Charles was becoming impatient. Muggleton's prognosis had proved incorrect. Charles was angry with the doctor and livid with his father. The old man should have been in his grave by now.

It was Saturday. Amy was lunching with friends, Stephen was sailing his yacht on the harbour and Charles returned home in the late afternoon from several hours' work at the office to find Dr Muggleton waiting for him in the drawing room. He knew in an instant.

'Mr Kendle,' the doctor said, rising from his armchair, 'I'm afraid I have some bad news.'

Thank God, Charles thought, at last.

'Mrs Goodlet sent for me at around two o'clock, but I'm sorry to say there was nothing I could do. He passed away about a half an hour ago.'

But Charles wasn't listening, he was already halfway up the stairs.

Anne was sitting in the chair, hands clasped, wrists leaning against the bed as if she had been praying. She was quietly contained, but had obviously been weeping. Charles crossed to stand beside her and look down at his father.

Emaciated, paper-thin skin stretched over a skull which appeared as fragile as egg-shell, James nevertheless seemed at peace. His eyes were closed beneath sunken lids and his withered hands were gently crossed upon the counterpane.

'It was very peaceful,' Anne said without looking up. 'He didn't awake, but he whispered as he was sleeping. He seemed to be dreaming. Of his childhood, I think.'

Well, of course he would be, Charles thought. The old man had been in his second childhood for years. 'It's a relief to know he was not in pain,' he replied dutifully. 'I shall tell the doctor to make the necessary arrangements.'

He was about to leave but Anne, horrified, stopped him. 'You can't possibly mean to take him away now.'

'Of course.'

'But people will wish to pay their respects.'

'What people?'

'Well, Amy for one. And Stephen.'

'You're right, Anne.' Charles knew that the prospect of staring at a cadaver, even for the requisite minute or so, would be the last thing Amy would wish. But of course she must be seen to do the right thing. 'I shall send them both up as soon as they arrive home.'

'And there's Howard,' Anne added. 'Howard would wish to pay his respects.' Sadly, she could think of no-one else.

'Very well,' Charles reluctantly conceded, 'I shall have Howard informed immediately, and tomorrow morning I shall have the . . .' he stopped himself from saying 'the body removed', '. . . the necessary arrangements carried out.'

Anne stayed by her father's bedside for most of the night. She thought of her own life, and she thought of his. They had a lot in common, she realised. What lonely lives they had both been.

Before he'd died, when the doctor had tactfully left her alone with her father, she had knelt by the bed, her head nearly resting on the pillow beside his, to catch his whispered words in case he should be calling for her. But he wasn't.

She heard the word 'Turumbah' a number of times. Was it a name, she wondered. Then 'Murrumuru'. Yes, she knew the name Murrumuru. The Aboriginal woman who had come to the house that day . . . Milly. Milly had spoken of Murrumuru. Of Murrumuru and Richard Kendle. Anne knew at that moment, without a doubt, that Milly had been telling the truth. But then she had known it that day. She had known it and she had done nothing. It had been a terrible thing, she thought, to send the woman away.

Her father whispered of eels. Of eels and Murrumuru. And then he made soft shushing sounds and gently rolled his head upon the pillow. At first, Anne was alarmed. Was he distressed?

'What is it, Father? Is something wrong? Is there something I can do?'

He must have heard her, for he seemed to want to answer. 'The river,' he whispered, 'the river,' and she could swear there was the touch of a smile upon his lips, 'the water against the skin.' Then, once more, he made the soft shushing sounds.

Was he a child again? Was he swimming in the river? She would never know, but Anne was glad that her father died in a world where he had once been happy.

The days which followed James's death were amongst the blackest of Anne's life. Not since the death of her husband had she known such despair. Whilst her father had been alive she had served a purpose, but now there was nothing. Nothing but the loathsome anticipation of six months in Europe with Charles dancing attendance upon her.

'Cheer up, Anne,' he said. 'Just think, you'll soon be in Italy, you always wanted to go to Italy. And I'll buy you such beautiful things. Do smile for me, dear, I hate to see you so miserable.'

Once again he was ignoring his wife and Anne could sense Amy's hurt and bewilderment. He barely even acknowledged the presence of his son. His sole attention was focused upon her.

Several days before their departure, when Stephen was spending the night with a friend Anne escaped the claustrophobia of the house and the prospect of an evening meal alone with Charles and Amy to attend a concert at the Town Hall.

Howard and his wife Helen had insisted on supper following the recital and it was well after midnight when she slipped in the front door of Kendle Lodge.

Only the downstairs night lights illuminated the house, all else was in darkness, and Anne was thankful that the household had retired. She crossed the main living room towards the stairs.

'Anne.' His voice came from out of the gloom and she looked about, startled. 'Come and join me for a drink.'

He was seated in one of the large armchairs by the bay windows. She couldn't see his face, only the silhouette of his legs, crossed, the brandy balloon in one hand resting upon his knee.

'Oh. Charles, you startled me.'

'Come and join me.' The brandy balloon waved towards the other armchair in the window recess. 'Tell me about your evening.'

'No, thank you, it is very late and I am tired.'

He leaned forward and she could see his face. 'I said come and join me.' It was an order. 'Come and spend a little time with your brother.'

His words were not slurred but his manner was aggressive and Anne knew he was drunk.

'I am sorry, Charles,' she said, 'but I really must retire, I am very weary.'

He put his brandy balloon down on the coffee table and crossed to her at the stairs. 'Too weary to talk to your own brother?' He was close to her now, his voice belligerent, his eyes angry, and she could smell the cognac on his breath. 'Come, come, Anne, it's been a long time since we've talked as brother and sister should.'

She edged away slightly, feeling the wooden column of the stairs and the bannister railing against her back. There was nowhere else she could go. For the first time she felt genuinely frightened of him.

'What is there we should speak of as brother and sister, Charles?' She tried to keep her voice steady, efficient. 'Is there family business to discuss?'

'We should speak of our love for each other,' he said, moving closer, one foot upon the lower step, one hand upon the bannister railing, locking her close to him. 'You are the only family I have left in the world.' The belligerence and anger had faded. 'And I am the only family you have left, Anne; surely you realise that?'

'Yes. Yes, I do, Charles.' She couldn't help it. Steady as she tried to keep her voice, the breath caught in her throat and she gasped the words.

She loved him, Charles thought. The emotion in her voice was proof. He had known it all along. 'Anne,' he murmured, 'my own Anne.' His love for her overwhelmed him. 'You are the only person upon this earth who matters to me.' As he lowered his face to kiss her, he placed his hand upon her breast.

Anne's fear vanished in an instant, replaced once more by the repulsion and shame she had known for years. He had shown his true colours at last; even Charles could not disguise such an action as a display of brotherly affection.

With a violence and a strength she didn't know she possessed, she pushed him from her. He swung away, comically, off balance, his hand gripping the railing to save himself from landing on his backside upon the stairs.

'You disgust me!' she screamed. 'You disgust me!'

She raced past him up the stairway, and Charles looked about, nervous that Amy might appear any moment. What had he done that was so very wrong? He had another cognac and went to bed, falling into a drunken, untroubled sleep.

Anne did not sleep. All night she lay wondering what to do. There could be no further pretence, she must leave the house, but where could she go? If only she could end her life. Surely tonight must lend her the courage. She recalled the drunken lust in his eyes and the hand upon her breast. Over and over she relived his actions and her humiliation, urging herself to find the strength to make the decision. To end it all. And gradually she felt her resolution grow. But it was a resolution born of anger and, in the morning hours, she had made her decision. She would not kill herself. There would be no need, there was another way out.

She stayed in her room and avoided breakfast, venturing downstairs shortly before Charles usually departed for his business meetings. He was still in the dining room with Amy, lingering over his coffee.

'Good morning, Amy. May I see you, Charles? In your study?'

Amy looked taken aback, but Charles agreed meekly enough. 'Of course,' he said, and led the way.

'Would you like to sit down?' he asked as he closed the door behind them.

'No thank you, I shall not take up much of your time.' She remained standing in the centre of the room, and Charles was uncertain as to whether or not he should sit behind his desk and take control of the situation as he normally would. She didn't allow him the opportunity. 'I shall be leaving the house and I have a proposition to put to you.'

'Where will you go?' Charles was so stunned he could think of nothing else to say.

'To Hannah's cottage. You will give me the cottage. I shall ask nothing more. I shall support myself.'

Charles could remember the events of the previous night, but he had successfully persuaded himself that he had done no wrong, he had been drunk, that was all. Now, in the cold hard light of morning, the thought that his sister might have misconstrued his actions horrified him. If she were to think for one moment that he would betray her trust, that he would violate his sacred position as her brother and benefactor . . .

'Anne, last night . . . Please, do not misunderstand, I was drunk, I meant nothing. The way I touched you, it was simply an accident.' He was begging. She said nothing. 'I swear. I would do nothing to offend you. I swear I will never —'

'We will not speak of it, Charles. We will never speak of it. Not one word. For as long as we both live.'

'I promise,' he said desperately. 'I promise you, Anne, I shall not —'

'But there is something else I shall speak of, something I shall make public to whomsoever I can, if I have to. And it will ruin you, Charles.' He waited, speechless, for her to continue. 'If you do not give me the cottage,' her voice was as steady as a rock, the strength of her resolve unshakable, 'I shall make it known that there is an illegitimate line in the Kendle family, a line of Aboriginal descent.'

Charles stared at his sister in disbelief, and Anne found, to her astonishment, that she was relishing the moment. 'Just think, Charles, black bastards bearing the Kendle name. You will be a social outcast.'

He was powerless, as she had known he would be, and one week after the family had left for Europe, Anne moved into Hannah's cottage in Windmill Street.

'What a grand one it is this evening.' Paddy clinked his bottle against Spike Monroe's and together, huddled in their winter coats, they swigged their ale as they watched the vivid pinks and reds of the sunset which fanned the sky over Woolloomooloo Bay.

They were sitting in the gardens of Kendle Lodge. In the arbour near the wall, right at the very end. 'The master never comes down here,' Spike had assured Paddy.

In the six months since he had seen Anne and decided on his plan, Paddy O'Shea had been busy. It had been easy to befriend the old gardener, easier than Paddy could ever have hoped. Simply a matter of admiring the garden through the big iron gates at the side.

Spike had invited him in and the two men had struck up a friendship that very day. Spike had taken immediately to Paddy's

Irish charm. 'The master will have no Irish in his employ,' he confided, 'but little does he know he has one right here in his own gardens. I was born in Killarney,' the old man chortled. 'Course I was only a babe when Pa came out to the new country, so the brogue is gone, but I'm Irish through and through.'

Paddy didn't have the heart to tell Spike that he'd never set foot upon the Emerald Isle, that he'd been born in the Rocks in the heart of Sydney. 'Dublin,' he said, 'we hail from Dublin.' Well, his father Daniel had, hadn't he, Paddy thought, and as he talked, his brogue grew thicker. 'Tis a beautiful garden, it does you credit.' Spike glowed with pride and nodded agreement. 'I've looked up at it often from down there in the Loo,' Paddy continued, gazing out over the valley, 'and thought how I'd love to watch a sunset from this very spot.'

'Then you shall, you shall.' Spike's weather-beaten face cracked into a grin. 'Come back this evening and we'll watch it together.'

It had become a habit after that. Each Friday—the night the master went to his club, Spike confided—Paddy arrived with two bottles of ale just prior to sunset, and they sat side by side in the arbour admiring nature's brilliance.

Paddy took his time gleaning information from the old gardener, asking few questions, waiting for answers to present themselves naturally. There was no hurry, he told himself as he perused the layout of the house and made his plans. He would have no trouble scaling the wall, and the lock on the inside of the gates was simple to operate. He would open them first to allow for a quick escape. The vine-covered trellis by the side of the balcony looked strong enough to support his weight. That would give him access to what he learned was the master bedroom.

'The mistress is home,' Spike had whispered one evening, pointing up to the open French windows and hustling Paddy out of sight. 'Come quickly,' he said as they scurried down to the arbour, 'most often she steps out onto the balcony to watch the sunset.'

Over the next several months, Paddy observed that Amy Kendle, when at home on a Friday, more often than not went back inside once the sun had disappeared below the horizon, extinguished the bedroom light then presumably went downstairs to dine in her sitting room. And, when she did so, she did not close the French windows.

Each evening, after whispering a hurried goodnight to Spike at the gate, Paddy remained in the shadows and watched. He watched the butler light the lamps in the garden, and he flattened his back against the wall as the man checked the lock on the side gate. Then he watched as the butler disappeared through the servants' entrance, presumably to check all the locks from within. And each time he watched, he noted that not once, when the mistress was at home, were the French windows at the far end of the balcony closed. They remained open, as she had obviously instructed they should.

Two hours later the bedroom lights were once more lit, and the French windows closed. By Amy Kendle. He could see her clearly. A further half hour later the lights were again extinguished—the mistress had retired for the night.

The windows became an obsession with Paddy. They were the way into the house. And they were open for just two hours, and then only on a Friday when the mistress was home.

As balmy autumn slid into winter and the evenings grew chilly, Paddy started to worry that perhaps, on the next Friday night Amy stayed at home, the windows would not be left open.

'Getting a wee bit cold, Spike,' he said one evening. 'I'll not be coming much longer, not until the spring.' Paddy was paving the way. If, following a burglary, and with no plausible explanation, he failed to arrive for their weekly rendezvous, the old man would put two and two together. Spike was naive, but he was not a fool.

'Get away, a young man like you, and an Irishman at that, where's your spine? A bit of cold does a man no harm.' Paddy's visits had become the highlight of Spike's week and he didn't want them to end. 'It's a tot of rum we want these nights,' he said, swigging the last of his ale, 'a tot of rum'd warm you up.' But Paddy kept hinting that the next time he came might be the last as he watched for the open windows on the balcony and pretended to shiver beneath his heavy winter coat with the large false pockets sewn inside. He didn't like the cold, he said to Spike. It was the one thing he didn't miss about Ireland, he'd gotten used to the Australian sun.

Paddy blessed his luck. There they were, the open windows. He nearly hadn't come tonight, there was the threat of a storm in the air, and surely she wouldn't leave the windows open during a storm.

'Quick,' Spike pointed up to the balcony, 'she's home,' and they hurried to the end of the garden. 'I didn't think you'd come, what with the weather and all.'

'I came to say goodbye,' Paddy replied. 'Only till the spring,' he added, noting Spike's disappointment. He'd grown fond of the old man. 'Let's toast to it,' he said, handing Spike his ale. 'To the spring.'

They clinked their bottles and drank. 'What a grand one it is this evening,' Paddy said and they swigged again from their bottles as, huddled against the chill night air, they watched the brilliance of the setting sun captured amongst the gathering storm clouds.

Amy Kendle pulled her wrap around her shoulders and stepped out onto the balcony to admire the view for a moment or two. She noticed the clouds gathering and wondered briefly whether she should close the windows, then decided not to.

She found the bedroom airless and claustrophobic and Charles refused to allow her to open the windows at night, fearing a chill. Friday evenings, when her husband was at his club, were the only times she could open the room up to a breeze.

She wished that she had the courage to leave the windows open all night, the chances being that upon his return Charles would sleep in the spare room adjoining his study anyway. But she daren't take the risk. If he came to their bed after a night at the Australian Club, he would be affected by alcohol and prone to aggression.

Outside, in the garden, Spike Monroe reluctantly locked the gate and retired to his room in the servants' quarters. He would miss his friend. An Irishman who loved sunsets. Why, he and Paddy were soulmates, they were. Spike decided he would have a tot of rum or two after his dinner and drink to an early spring.

In the shadows, Paddy watched as the butler went about his nightly duties. The lamps were lit, the gate was checked and the man disappeared through the servants' door.

Paddy collected the rocks he'd stored in the nearby bushes over the past month or so and, placing them beside the six foot high stone wall, stepped up, grasped the top and scaled it with ease.

He dropped to the ground on the other side and remained crouched for several seconds, trying to choose a shadowed path through the glare of light from the gas lamps. There was none. The whole garden was illuminated. Including the trellis. Too late to worry about that. Paddy had planned this night for months and he was not backing out now.

He unlocked and opened the iron gates, then sprinted through the blaze of the gardens. Ducking and weaving amongst the statues and shrubs, dodging behind the fountains and arbours, expecting an outcry at any moment. But there was none. When he reached the trellis on the far side, he knew he was safe for a moment or two, out of sight of those in the house. He checked that the trellis would take his weight. It was strong and secure. He started to climb.

The flowering vine which grew upon the trellis had thorns that pricked his hands, but Paddy didn't heed them. He must get into the shade of the balcony as soon as possible. The nightly radiance of Kendle Lodge was admired by many from afar and, ten feet above the ground, halfway up the side of the house, he felt like a monkey in a spotlight.

He gripped onto the balcony railing and hauled himself over. As he did, a streak of lightning flared in the sky and for a split second the balcony was flooded with light; it appeared nature itself was determined to expose him. Quickly, he slipped through the open French windows and into the master bedroom.

He stood beside the drapes, praying that Amy Kendle had gone downstairs as was her custom. What if she had not felt well? What if she had retired instead? He crept to the four-poster bed—it was empty—and breathed a sigh of relief.

Paddy looked about him in the half light cast through the windows from the garden lamps below. This was far more than a bedroom. The massive four-poster bed was to the left, and to the right was a mahogany desk and chair, two armchairs and a sofa. Gilt-framed pictures and elaborate mirrors adorned the walls; two large brass tubs, ablaze with pink and white petunias, flanked the windows, and on a pedestal in the corner stood a statuette in bronze. A nude female, fine and delicate.

Beyond, to the right, through a wide arch in the wall, was another room altogether. A decorative room, feminine. A vanity table with ornately framed mirror and matching chair, two wardrobes and several chests of drawers, all lacquered white and trimmed with gold. A grooming set laid out upon the table. Silver-backed hand mirrors, hairbrushes and combs, silver-topped jars of perfumes and powders, solid silver glove hooks and boot hooks. The silver alone would fetch a tidy sum. And this would be where she would keep her jewellery, Paddy told himself as he stepped through the archway.

Downstairs, Amy toyed with her poached salmon, lonely and depressed. She wished Stephen would visit more often, but then he was engaged to be married so she supposed it was understandable. And she wished yet again that Anne was still living in the house. She would never have thought she would so miss her sister-in-law, unobtrusive as Anne had been, but at least she had had another female to talk to apart from the maids.

If only Anne were here now, Amy thought, as she pushed the poached salmon to one side and sipped at her glass of wine.

There was the crash of thunder. The storm had travelled quickly, it was nearly overhead. The windows, she thought as she heard the sudden downpour of rain. The drapes would be soaked if she didn't hurry. She stood, pushing back her chair, just as Mrs Marett appeared at the door, tray in hand.

'You do not wish for dessert Madam?' she enquired disapprovingly. The mistress could have told her, Mrs Marett thought.

'Yes. Thank you, Mrs Marett, I would like dessert.' Why did the woman unnerve her so? 'I need to fetch something from the bedroom, however. A magazine.' As if she should need to explain herself.

'Very well, Madam.' Mrs Marett collected the salmon and placed the creme caramel upon the table whilst Amy left the room.

Paddy had found what he was looking for in the top drawer of the vanity table. Diamond bracelets, earrings, strings of pearls, gold clasps and hatpins, brooches of precious stones. Some were wrapped in velvet, some were in boxes, but most were lying carelessly loose in the drawer. The nonchalance of a wealthy woman. It was all too easy, he thought, stuffing them into his pockets. He could simply take the jewels, along with the silver grooming set, and leave. He was already carrying a fortune in his old winter coat.

But it was not enough to hurt Charles Kendle. He must rob the man of something more precious than his wife's ornaments. Paddy needed revenge.

Suddenly there were footsteps in the hall. The knob of the bedroom door turned. Paddy dived for the archway and pressed himself into the corner, watching as Amy Kendle crossed to the windows. If she were to light the lamps, if she were to come into her dressing room, she would see him. But she did neither.

Outside, the storm was raging and, driven by the howling wind the rain was whipping at the windows. Amy struggled for a moment, then finally got them closed. She looked about in the gloom, picked up a magazine from her bedside table, closed the drapes, and left the room in darkness as she pulled the door closed behind her.

Paddy waited for several minutes before creeping to the bedroom door and opening it slightly. He looked along the landing, illuminated by lamps set in alcoves beside each bedroom door. The main staircase was up ahead. Creeping to the railings, he peered down at the main lounge below. No-one was in sight. He must decide on an avenue of escape and wait until the household had retired. There would be time enough then for him to explore downstairs, to find Charles Kendle's personal treasures.

He crept along the landing and tentatively opened the door to the next bedroom. No light shone from within, but could someone be sleeping? Surely it was far too early. Spike had not mentioned any visiting family members, and Paddy knew that the servants' quarters were downstairs. The room must be empty.

It was. Paddy closed the door behind him, crossed to the French windows and opened them. This would be his escape.

Outside, the storm was raging. Angry thunder roared above; lightning cracked the sky, and the gardens of Kendle Lodge were whipped into a frenzy by the wild, windswept rain.

Paddy sat on the floor, the windows ajar, and looked down the balcony to the master bedroom. Amy Kendle would soon light the lamps in that room, then a half an hour later she would extinguish them. Paddy would wait for one more hour after that, and then he would venture downstairs.

Charles Kendle sat in the armchair by the windows of his sitting room on the sixth floor of the Australia Hotel and looked out over Martin Place as the two waiters set down their trays, one of them opening the champagne in the ice bucket whilst the other laid the table.

When they had gone, the adjoining bedroom door opened and Harriet peeped out.

'They have gone,' he said, 'may I pour you a glass?' He made to rise.

'No, please, my dear, let me.' She poured two glasses of champagne and brought his to him. He liked the way she waited on him.

They had been occasional lovers for five months now, although they never discussed their relationship. Every so often, and only on a Friday, Charles invited Harriet to dine with him. Always in his suite of rooms at the Australia Hotel, and always, after they had eaten, they would make love as if by accident, as if it were not a foregone conclusion.

Charles had been surprised to find the seduction of Harriet Winterman so easy. Certainly, her surrender had not been wanton, indeed had it been so he would not have found her attractive. She demurred at first, she murmured that she mustn't, she tried, feebly, to resist his advances, but it soon became apparent that her own desire was her undoing, which excited Charles at the time. Now, although they never spoke of it, he was sure that she was in love with him.

It was Harriet's subservience which had attracted Charles. It reminded him of Anne. She even looked a little like Anne, he thought. Slim, demure in her dress, she wore her hair tied back in a bun. Her mannerisms, too, were similar. Eyes, shy, cast downward at times, hands genteelly clasped at her waist.

His sister's departure and the humiliation of her unjustified suspicions had eaten away at Charles for months. He had worked sixteen hours a day at the store in order to distract himself, he had got drunk on Fridays at the Australian Club, but he had not been able to erase the image of Anne from his mind.

Not until the Kendle and Streatham quarterly meeting attended by the heads of each department. How come he had never really noticed Harriet Winterman before, he wondered? And his attraction quickly became obsession. He started to court her. Subtly at first. Business meetings to discuss the women's haberdashery lines, lunch or coffee at the Wintergarden rooftop restaurant to discuss still more business, then finally the invitation to dine.

These days Harriet was the answer to his problems and Charles was no longer tormented by the image of his sister. He even toyed vaguely with the notion of setting Harriet up in a small place of her own, making her officially his mistress, the idea had its appeal. But then, if he tired of her, it could become complicated. As it was, all he had to do to get rid of her was to dismiss her from his employ. No, he decided. No house. Too risky.

'Shall I serve for you, Charles?' she asked, removing the silver dome of the heating dish.

'Please, my dear.'

At Kendle Lodge, a shaft of light shone through the slit in the drapes of the master bedroom. Paddy watched it from further along the balcony. A half hour later, the light was extinguished and the room was in darkness. One more hour to wait.

Harriet Winterman knew how to please men. She knew how to pander to their egos and make them feel like kings. How to excite them in bed by feigning her own pleasure, just as she was doing now. She moaned with simulated ecstasy as she felt Charles approach his climax.

Harriet was thirty-eight years old. She had been in the employ of Kendle and Streatham for twenty years and was now not only in charge of women's haberdashery, but was the only female in any position of authority within the company. She had learned how to play the game. Subservient, modest and respectful to the men who were her superiors, and a martinet to the employees under her control.

She had never married but there had been a number of lovers. Two of them wealthy. Both married men. One had even talked of setting her up in her own little house. But that's all it had been, talk, three years later he had gone back to his wife. Harriet was hoping that Charles Kendle would be different.

The hour was up. Paddy opened wide the French windows of the guest bedroom in preparation for his escape, then crossed to the door and stole out onto the landing. He crept down the main staircase, aware that he was clearly visible in the glow of the night lights which remained lit in the downstairs living room. He circled the room. Wary. Tentatively checking each door, prepared at any second to dive behind a sofa or beneath a table. It was still relatively early. Not yet eleven o'clock. The housekeeper and the butler might well be up, although presumably they were in the servants' quarters to the rear of the house.

Charles had seen Harriet into a hansom cab and hailed one for himself. He wondered whether or not to go to the Australian Club, it was still early, only eleven, then decided against it. It was a filthy night. Besides, he was content, sated. He felt like a nightcap but he didn't need to get drunk.

'Potts Point,' he said to the driver and settled back into his seat as they trotted through the storm. Perhaps he would wake Amy when he got home. They could have a liqueur together and talk of the family. She would enjoy that, and he felt like being nice to Amy. He didn't find her sexually attractive any longer it was true, but she had been a good enough wife, putting up with his tantrums all these years. He had to admit he was ill-humoured at times, he really should make more of an effort.

Paddy had found Charles's study. Through the open door, in the dim light, he could see that the walls were hung with paintings and photographs. A closer inspection revealed that the photographs were of the Kendle and Streatham Emporium in all its various stages. From the early days to its present glory, each photograph was enlarged, ornately framed and cased in glass. Amongst the paintings, some collectors' items, some personally commissioned, was a striking watercolour of Kendle Lodge, a family portrait of a young Amy Kendle with her two children and, in pride of place behind the desk, a large portrait in oils of Charles himself.

The shelves were lined with yachting trophies and hand-carved models of Kendle's prized sailing craft. Yet more carved yachts, some large, some small, but all impressive, stood atop bookcases and on plinths around the room. Each was to scale, the larger ones with canvas sails, sturdy shining masts and booms, the smaller ones with gossamer stays and ropework as delicate as the thread of a spider's web. It was a precious collection. The man's pride and joy, Paddy thought triumphantly.

The desire to destroy outweighed the desire to steal and,

throwing caution to the winds, Paddy closed the door, lit the gas lamp in the wall bracket and took the knife from his inner pocket.

He started on the portrait first. As he plunged his knife between the eyes, it was Kendle himself he was destroying. He slashed again. This is for spitting on my mother's grave. Another slash. This is for having me done over by Cocky and his mates. A third slash. This is for stealing my cottage. And then he was slashing for no other reason than the sheer pleasure of killing Charles Kendle.

The portrait in shreds, Paddy came to his senses. He must be more methodical. Destroy the man's treasures and get out, he told himself. No need to steal anything further, the jewels in his pockets were more than enough.

He took the first of the framed photographs from the wall. He daren't smash the glass, but it was easy to hack the backing apart with his knife, pull out the picture and rip it to pieces. There were six in all, it didn't take long.

The watercolour of Kendle Lodge, despite its size, took barely ten seconds to demolish. The portrait of Amy and her children Paddy left intact—he had no quarrel with them. Then, finally, leaving the choicest till last, he turned his attention to the models.

Works of art each and every one, but Paddy knew which was most precious of all. It wasn't the biggest or the grandest, in fact it was the smallest of the carvings which stood upon the shelves. The name, etched in gold on the wooden base, was *Wings of Honour I*. The first proud yacht that Kendle had owned. Paddy lifted it down. This was the prize. Grasping the base in one hand, with his other he embraced the delicate, polished masts and the billowing sails of paper-thin crafted wood, and slowly he crumpled them. They dropped like so much ash and kindling to the floor of Kendle's study. Then he picked up the next model.

Charles cursed the rain as he dashed from the hansom cab to the front porch. It was only twenty yards but the downpour was so heavy he was soaked when he got there. His good mood had evaporated as he unlocked the front door.

He hung his coat and hat on the stand, crossed the tiled entrance hall and opened the door to the main living room. He stopped. There was a lamp lit in his study to the left. He could see the light spilling from beneath the closed door. His irritation turned to anger. No-one, neither the servants nor his wife, was allowed to enter his study. Even the maid when she cleaned it had to seek his permission.

It couldn't be a burglar surely, he thought. What burglar would have the audacity to light the lamp? What burglar would close the door, denying himself an escape route? It had to be one of the servants.

Charles approached quietly, turned the knob, and the door swung silently open. He stood shocked, confronting the desecration of his study.

Paddy sensed, rather than heard, the presence behind him. He turned. Charles Kendle stood frozen in the open doorway.

Paddy held a yacht in his hands. The final model, the biggest one. With his huge hands he broke the hull in two. Then he crushed the mast, the boom and the spars. He shredded the canvas sails. And all the while he watched Charles Kendle as slowly, one by one, he dropped the pieces to the floor. Paddy was glad he had been caught in the act. This way he could relish the horror in Kendle's eyes.

'They are irreplaceable,' Charles said, staring at the shattered remnants of his prized collection strewn at Paddy O'Shea's feet. He would kill the bastard.

'I had rather hoped they would be.'

Charles stepped slowly into the room, wondering if the man would attack him, knowing that he would be no physical match for Paddy's bulk and strength, but he needed to buy time, to get closer to the desk where he kept the revolver.

'You'll go to Darlinghurst Gaol for this,' he said. Even if Paddy had rifled the desk, he would not have found the Webley .476 revolver. The gun was in a secret compartment at the side.

'I'll surely go to Darlinghurst Gaol,' Paddy replied, 'if you can prove it was me. I'll have many an alibi to back me up.' And he would, his mates would stand by him.

Paddy felt no fear—Charles Kendle was no match for him physically. And far from raising the alarm, he was actually entering the room, allowing Paddy access to the door as he confronted him with empty threats. The man was bold, Paddy would give him that.

'I came to rob you,' Paddy said, his eyes on the door, 'but I must admit this has been far more satisfying.'

'You'd leave empty-handed?' Charles had eased his way to the side of the desk in the pretence of viewing the damage. He studied the tattered portrait on the floor, the image of his face ripped to shreds. 'This is enough?' He edged his hand towards the hidden desk panel.

'I helped myself to some of your wife's valuables upstairs,' Paddy said. 'They'll suffice nicely, thank you.'

'My wife's valuables!' Charles laughed. 'You fool, do you seriously think I would let her strew her precious jewels about in the drawers of her dressing-room table?' That was exactly what Amy did, and a constant source of annoyance to Charles it was too, but he needed to distract Paddy's attention. 'It's French paste she keeps upstairs,' he lied, 'you'll be walking away with nothing.' He noted the flicker of annoyance in Paddy's eyes. 'Her precious gems are locked in the safe behind that bookcase.'

It worked. Instinctively, Paddy glanced at the bookcase. Charles pressed the spring-loaded panel on the side of the desk. It slid back and he grasped the heavy revolver.

Paddy registered, from the corner of his eye, the sudden movement and turned to launch himself upon Charles, but stopped as he saw the gun aimed at his chest. He cursed himself.

'Well, it seems you have the upper hand,' he said, assessing the distance between them, wondering if he could launch himself upon Kendle before he pulled the trigger. Impossible, the man's hand was steady, his aim direct. 'It would seem that perhaps it's Darlinghurst Gaol for me after all.'

'Either that or I kill you.'

'Not a wise move.' Paddy started to feel uneasy, there was a murderous intent in Kendle's eyes. Surely the man would not shoot him down in cold blood. 'It would be very bad publicity for Kendle and Streatham,' he said, his mind racing. 'The public would not relish reading that one of its most eminent citizens had killed a man. Even a burglar,' he continued, pre-empting Charles's interruption. 'And if the burglar happened to be a family man, upon hard times as many are, and if the newspapers were to discover, as they quickly would, that the thief was kinsman to the eminent citizen . . .'

Paddy gave an eloquent shrug, aware now that Kendle was listening to him, assessing his every word.

'Can you not see it?' Paddy urged. 'To kill me would attract notoriety; the name Kendle would be forever associated with the killing of an unarmed man, albeit a common thief. Sure, you'd not be guilty of a crime yourself,' he concluded, 'but could the Kendle name afford such infamy?'

Charles studied Paddy thoughtfully for a moment or so, then smiled. The garrulous fool of an Irishman appeared to honestly believe he had talked his way out of death. Paddy O'Shea should have known that his life was over the moment he had destroyed Charles's priceless collection.

The Irishman had taken pleasure in tormenting him, now it was Charles's turn. 'Infamy for shooting a madman who attacked me with a knife?' Charles indicated the knife which Paddy had left on the desk after slashing the paintings. 'Notoriety for killing the man who brutally assaulted my wife? For Amy will swear that you did so.'

'No, my friend,' he continued, 'I will be neither infamous nor notorious, I will be lauded, and quite correctly so, as a man who protected his home and avenged his wife's honour.'

Charles had no intention of allowing the press to publish the events of this night. Paddy had been quite right in his assessment. Charles Kendle would go to whatever ends necessary to prevent such tawdry publicity. He would pay whatever it took. But it was too easy to simply shoot the man, Paddy must be made to squirm. 'The press will ensure that the Kendle name, as always, remains a source of pride to those who bear it.'

Nervous sweat beaded Paddy's brow. Despite Kendle's reputation as a ruthless businessman, Paddy had not thought the man capable of murder. Charles Kendle was a proper man, a pillar of society. He never dirtied his own hands, he employed others to dirty theirs for him. As the steel-grey eyes mocked him and the gun remained steadily aimed at his chest, Paddy realised his mistake. Kendle was more than capable of cold-blooded murder.

'I told you once you were a fool, Paddy O'Shea,' Charles said, 'and I was right. You're a fool who has dug his own grave.'

In the second Charles pulled the trigger, Paddy threw himself forward. The bullet tore through his chest and he crashed to the floor. But he took Kendle with him, burying the man beneath his body as he fumbled for the gun. If this were to be his moment of death, then Paddy was determined that it would be Charles Kendle's too.

There was sudden commotion about the house. The sound of footsteps racing up from the servants' quarters, a shrill scream from upstairs.

Charles fought to free himself from Paddy's embrace, but even in the throes of death Paddy was strong. The gun was wedged between the two of them, grasped in both their hands, the muzzle slowly turning towards Charles's throat as Paddy exerted every last ounce of his fading strength. Nearly there. Nearly there. His finger edged for the trigger.

Then numbness embraced him. Drained of strength, Paddy was powerless to resist as Charles struggled from beneath him. Powerless as he felt himself rolled onto his back to lie useless and spent like a landed fish.

Paddy looked dimly up at Charles who had risen to his feet, the gun in his hand. He saw that Kendle was covered in blood. His blood, Paddy realised. Their eyes met. Then Paddy watched as the muzzle was slowly raised and aimed at his head. I'm sorry, Dotty, he thought.

There was a scuffle at the door. Amy had arrived, the butler at her heels, and the two stood transfixed as Charles took aim. Slowly, methodically.

I'm so sorry, Dotty, Paddy thought. Then the gun roared and Amy screamed again.

Chapter Eight

The death of Queen Victoria on the 22nd of January, 1901, mourned though it was, heralded a new era of fashion and frivolity in British society. The Edwardian era. Following the stolid style and dull fashions dictated by the aged and widowed Victoria, the reign of Edward VII and his Queen, the beautiful Alexandra, saw some of the most exotic years in British social history. And the changes were reflected no less in the City of Sydney than they were in London itself.

Sydney had further reason for a sense of exhilaration, as did the whole of Australia. The Federal Constitution of the new Commonwealth of Australia had been proclaimed in Sydney's Centennial Park on the 1st of January, 1901 and on 29 March, following the first national election, Edmund Barton became the country's first Prime Minister.

It was an exciting time. The new century. A time of social change, freedom, and a national pride fit to burst.

Benjamin Kendall, his eight-year-old son Timothy perched on his shoulders, stepped off the paddle-boat at Circular Quay and turned to assist his wife Norah from the gangplank. Then, arm in arm, they joined the milling crowd which surged its way to George Street and the markets and stores, taverns and tea gardens.

It was Saturday, a late spring morning, and Benjamin Kendall's twenty-ninth birthday. They were going shopping, he had announced the previous evening, but first they were going for a ferry ride on the harbour.

'Tim's never been on a ferry before,' he had insisted, noting his wife's reluctance, 'and there's a new paddle-boat ferry that does a round-trip.'

'It would be good for the boy, I know that, Ben,' she'd said, 'but perhaps you two should go on your own.' She patted the slight bulge of her stomach but he appeared not to notice.

'What sort of a wife refuses to celebrate a bloke's birthday?' he argued. 'I'd be better off going out with the mates and getting drunk, I would.'

She smiled, grateful in the knowledge that he wasn't serious. He was a good husband. A hard worker and an excellent provider. Benjamin's family was everything to him and he never drank away his wages as did many a Surry Hills man, leaving his wife sick with worry and wonder.

'It may not be proper,' she said, patting her stomach a little more ostentatiously this time, 'to parade myself in public.'

He laughed out loud. 'Is that all it is? Why, Nellie Putman paraded herself till she nigh on dropped the thing in the middle of Riley Street.'

'I'm not Nellie Putman,' she said primly, 'and that's hardly respectable talk, Benjamin.'

'No, you're not Nellie Putman, that's true enough.' Proud as he was of his neat and proper wife, Benjamin sometimes wished Norah was a little bit more like Nellie Putman. A stickler for convention, Norah's obsession with appearances was sometimes at odds with the neighbourhood, despite the fact that she'd lived in the heart of Surry Hills her whole life. It was a source of bewilderment to Benjamin. 'But it doesn't show at all, love, my word of honour it doesn't. You're only four months gone, when all's said and done.'

He'd persuaded her and, her best blue woollen shawl tightly clutched around her shoulders and across her belly, Norah had enjoyed the ferry trip around the harbour as much as Timothy had.

Now, upon reaching George Street, the crowd spilled its various ways, some heading for the taverns of the Rocks, others for the trams to Redfern Railway Station or Victoria Park or the University of Sydney. Benjamin swung Timothy from his shoulders and, turning south, the three of them, hand in hand, joined the throng that strolled the pavements of the broad boulevard. The centre of the street was a bustle of hansom cabs, traps and drays, as well as the omnipresent electric trams which passed relentlessly to and fro, ruling the road.

Beneath the endless verandahed shops they walked, pausing to admire a window display here and there. Past Martin Place and the stone magnificence of the General Post Office. Ahead loomed the massive dome of the Queen Victoria Building and, just beyond, the towers of the Town Hall and St Andrew's Cathedral rose majestically above the busy streets.

Top hats and picture hats mingled with cloth caps and straw boaters, Sydney was a city for the people and a fine spring Saturday brought them all out to play.

Finally, they came to the new Kendle and Streatham store. It had been opened to the public only six months previously and Norah had never been inside, although she had read about it in the *Sydney Morning Herald*.

She stood gazing up at the chandelier in the foyer. 'Electrically lit it is,' she whispered to her wide-eyed son who was equally impressed. Ahead was a huge oak-panelled staircase, on either side of which was a stand with signs pointing in every direction to every possible department, all spelled out in perfect copperplate.

'Let's go and buy you that hat, love,' Benjamin said. 'The millinery department, that's what we need.' He pointed to the sign which said 'Ladies' Millinery and Haberdashery, First Floor'.

'Can we ride to the top in the lift, Dad?' Timothy begged. 'You said we could.'

'After we've bought your mother a hat, I promise.'

But Norah had seen the sign to the right which said 'Mourning Department'. 'We'll go in here first,' she said.

'What? "The Mourning Department". Who's in mourning?'

'For goodness' sake, Benjamin,' she looked around, hoping that nobody had heard, 'everybody's in mourning. Now come along, Timmy, there's a good boy.' She took her son's hand and sailed ahead, Benjamin forced to comply.

Following the death of Queen Victoria, a special 'mourning department' had been quickly established in Kendle and Streatham's new seven-storey emporium. The citizens of Sydney having entered a period of respect for the old Queen's passing, mourning was big business, and decorative signs of reverence did a brisk trade; black armbands, black plumes, ribbons and bows. 'Widow's weeds', jet jewellery and garments heavily beaded with jet (the accepted trimming to signify the death of a loved one) were in such constant demand that ever-increasing stock was needed.

'What are we doing here Norah? We came to buy you a hat, love, and some gloves, and a toy for Tim, we did. What are we . . . ?'

'Sssh Ben,' she said, keeping her voice low and respectful as the ladies in black glided by, guiding the reverent customers to the wares on display. 'Show some respect.'

'Who for? Dad's been dead nearly a whole year.'

'For Queen Victoria,' she hissed, annoyed, 'that's who.'

Like his father Samuel before him, Benjamin was an eminently practical man. He couldn't see the sense in wasting good money on a display of mourning for a person he'd never met. But it was easier to keep the peace, he supposed. Besides, if she dilly-dallied for too long, he'd take Tim off for a ride in the hydraulic lift, a prospect which excited Benjamin as much as it did his son. He'd never been in an hydraulic lift.

But Norah did not waste time. She herself was practical. In fact her sense of practicality was very closely connected to her sense of propriety. There were 'specials' on display everywhere (discreetly labelled of course). She would be seen as a dutiful subject showing public respect for her deceased monarch, whilst at the same time availing herself of some very useful bargains which would no doubt be put to good use time and again in the future.

Gently, she fingered the black velvet armbands with matching hat ribbon and bow. She could certainly have used these over the past two years, she thought. First her baby, then barely twelve months ago Samuel Kendall himself. Samuel Kendall, Benjamin's father, as strong as a horse, who would have thought it? Dead, just like that. Bubonic plague. But then so many had gone the same way. The strong, the weak and the in-between. The plague did not discriminate.

Norah bought a set of armbands and hat ribbons for both herself and Benjamin, and a child's set for Timothy, careful to avoid those which had Victoria's insignia, or a profile of the Queen woven into the fabric. It would not be practical, and besides, the personalised sets were much more expensive. She insisted that they all put on their armbands and, carefully, she tucked the ribbons, wrapped in tissue paper, inside her purse.

The hydraulic lift was slow and cumbersome and the operator clanged the doors open and shut in a ferocious manner. Norah did not enjoy the experience, but she suffered it—they had promised Tim they would go all the way to the seventh floor. She distracted herself by looking at the armbands, they had put her in a slightly melancholic mood anyway, so it was easy to allow their distraction. She wondered when the next family occasion would arise necessitating their use, and prayed that it would not be the child she carried in her womb. The loss of her baby two years previously had nearly destroyed her. Six months old her little girl had been.

Norah looked at Tim who guffawed with excitement each time the lift came jarringly to a halt and the doors clanged open. To think that eight years ago she had prayed for a miscarriage, prayed for her son not to exist. It had seemed the easiest way out at the time. Well, she had paid since then for such sinful prayer; the death of a baby had been the price. Norah pulled her shawl closer around her and shivered slightly although it was not cold.

They stayed in the lift for the downward trip, the operator rattling off the names of the departments and wares housed on each floor. At the third floor, when Norah heard the words 'Toy department', she said, 'Let's get out here. We'll buy my hat later, Ben,' she insisted. 'Please. Let's get Timmy his toy first.'

Kendle and Streatham's toy department was a children's paradise. In the very centre, aglow with electric fairy lights, stood a carousel, its bright, bobbing wooden ponies inciting children to clamber aboard. On tinsel strands from the ceiling, fairies flew. Gnomes and goblins, pixies and nursery rhyme characters abounded, and everywhere shop assistants in fantasy costumes demonstrated the very latest in games and toys and mechanical inventions.

At the far end of the floor was a special play section with slides and swings, and train sets for the boys and dolls' houses for the girls. Here parents were encouraged to leave their children under supervised care so that they could shop unhindered.

Young Timothy Kendall, having had three rides on the carousel, dived on the complex toy train with all the enthusiasm of an eight-year-old who had never seen such sophistication in the whole of his life. It was impossible to drag him away so, assured by the attendant that their son was in excellent care, Benjamin and Norah set off to buy a hat.

Ladies' Millinery and Haberdashery, on the first floor, offered the latest trends in the new Edwardian fashion and Norah didn't know where to start. The picture hats were beautiful but they seemed too bold, too flamboyant.

She took off her own hat, careful of disarranging her hair which she had taken great pains to pin up that morning, and chose one of the more modest designs. It was still a little too colourful to be in good taste, surely. Although it was certainly attractive, she thought, self-consciously admiring her image in the oval gilt mirror. She looked very grand.

'It looks ever so nice, madam,' the young assistant with the adenoidal voice said, 'suits you to perfection.' The well-used phrase was trotted out with blatant insincerity, and Norah felt herself flush with embarrassment.

'She's right, love, you look pretty as a picture,' Benjamin nodded encouragingly. 'Let's buy it, and we'll get you some gloves to match.'

'No, no.' Flustered, Norah was already removing the hatpin.

'May I agree with your husband, madam, it is indeed a perfect choice.' Harriet Winterman materialised from nowhere. Doing her rounds, checking on staff with her ever-vigilant eagle eye, Harriet had noticed the ineffectual young assistant about to lose a sale. 'You may go,' she said coldly to the girl, she would have her fired tomorrow.

'Modern and stylish,' she continued, 'yet modest and in the very best of taste. May I?'

Norah meekly allowed the woman to take the hatpin from her and, in the oval mirror, she watched as the hat was firmly but gently repositioned, the pin tucked securely in place and the blue satin bow at the front given a tweak here and there.

'Yes,' Harriet gave a nod of satisfaction, 'a most refined choice.' Too refined, she thought. She had picked them instantly as working class, the plain and tidy wife in the well-worn gloves, and the husband with his labourer's hands. Still, in these affluent times, it was the workers who spent the money, one couldn't afford to offend them. And he was certainly a handsome fellow, Harriet couldn't help observing. In a weathered sort of way. Sandy-haired, rugged-faced, skin tanned from hours of toil in the sun, he was common, but there was an easy candid charm about him which was most attractive.

'Your husband is obviously a man of taste,' she added, smiling at Benjamin with just a touch of flirtation.

Benjamin didn't like the woman. He had registered immediately her condescension towards his wife. Norah, however, was most impressed. If anyone would know style, this woman would, she thought. Slim, straight-backed, perfectly coiffed and dressed in simple black, this woman was the picture of elegance.

'We'll take it, shall we?' she queried a little breathlessly into the mirror, and behind her Benjamin nodded.

'Of course we will, love.' Then brusquely he said to the woman, 'Get us some gloves to match.'

'Certainly.' Well, you couldn't expect manners from the working classes could you? 'I shan't be a moment,' and Harriet sailed away with her nose in the air.

Norah was mortified. 'How could you be so rude, Ben?' she whispered. 'She's a lady, she's very refined.'

'She's a saleswoman, that's what she is, and we're the ones who're buying.'

He had that look in his eyes which told Norah she mustn't argue. She gave an inward sigh. It was very hard keeping up appearances when Benjamin was in one of his defiant moods. 'I didn't look at the price,' she said, 'I hope we can afford it.'

He grinned, the mood broken. 'Course we can, love. We're doing well, remember?' He was referring to the raise he'd received at Wunderlich's the previous month.

'Yes, but it looks so expensive . . .'

'Sssh.'

Benjamin would brook no argument, and when the woman returned with a pair of ice-blue kid gloves, Norah was so distracted by their softness and perfection that, as she tried them on, she failed to notice either the exchange between Benjamin and Harriet Winterman, or the fact that they had both disappeared to the nearby service counter. She rested her gloved fingers against her cheek, relishing the velvety touch, and gazed at her image in the oval mirror. Was this really her in the picture hat with the blue satin ribbon and the ice-blue gloves to match?

Suddenly the woman was at her side again, and Norah felt herself once more flush with embarrassment. How vain she must have appeared.

'Shall I pack it for you, madam?' The woman carried a ribboned hatbox, and her tone was icy. Benjamin must have offended her again.

'Yes. Thank you,' she said a little nervously.

'No.' Benjamin took the hatbox from the woman. 'She'll wear it, won't you, Norah?' He opened the hatbox. 'Put those in here, thank you,' he said peremptorily, gesturing to Norah's hat and gloves which sat on the satin stool beside the mirror.

'Of course.' Harriet picked up Norah's straw hat with the beige tulle around the brim as if it was slightly suspect. Then, together with the cream cotton gloves, she gingerly placed it in the hatbox. 'I trust we will see you again, madam.' She smiled tightly.

'Yes. Thank you so much.' Norah took Benjamin's arm and they left to collect Tim from the toy department.

Harriet Winterman watched them go, furious with herself. How could she have allowed such a trivial incident to upset her? He was a common, vulgar, working man, yet he had successfully reminded her that, not only was she well past her prime and no longer attractive to men, she was on a social level comparable to his. She, who had been Charles Kendle's mistress, albeit for a short period of time.

Harriet watched the couple disappear up the stairs, then turned to survey her domain. For the rest of the morning, she prowled the Millinery and Haberdashery Department wielding her power and wreaking her vengeance upon those unable to fight back. Harriet Winterman was not a happy woman.

'I can't wear it, Ben, truly I can't. It's far too grand.' Norah's mortification at Benjamin's rudeness to the stylish saleswoman had been replaced by self-consciousness, and she stopped him as they were halfway up the stairs to the second floor. 'I'm going to take it off right now. I'll put it on again as soon as we get home, I promise.'

Benjamin looked at the women parading past, up and down the grand staircase. Many of them wore picture hats far more ornate than Norah's. He pointed them out, one by one. 'There,' he said. 'See? And there.'

'Stop it, Ben, it's so rude to point.' She started up the stairs once more, sure that they were conspicuous, loitering mid-level. 'It doesn't go with my dress,' she insisted.

'Yes, it does.'

'My dress is beige.'

'What colour is your shawl?'

'Blue,' she admitted after a moment's hesitation.

'A perfect match.' He stopped her as they reached the second floor. 'I want you to wear it, Norah. For me. As a birthday present. Please.'

Benjamin desperately wanted his wife to wear the hat. It was true that it didn't really go with the dress, Benjamin could see that himself, but he wanted Norah to assert herself. He wanted her to do something a little bit daring. Just this once.

Norah registered that it was important, for some unfathomable reason, that she wear the hat. She hesitated. Dare she? 'All right,' she said, steeling herself, shoulders back, head held high. This was Ben's birthday and she wanted to please him.

They collected Timothy and bought him a set of marbles. Impressive but not expensive.

'You'll be the envy of Surry Hills with those, Tim,' Benjamin said, and Tim nodded happily. He was a good-natured child and easy to please.

'We must buy a present for you now, Ben,' Norah said as, upon Tim's insistence, they headed once more for the dreaded lift.

'Not yet, love, it's lunchtime. After lunch we will. You hungry, Tim?' He hoped to avoid the issue altogether—there was no money left to buy him a present.

Benjamin had been astonished to discover that the cost of the hat was a full week's wages, more than they could afford, but not for one moment had he contemplated admitting as much to the patronising saleswoman.

The gloves had cost close to another week's wages and Benjamin had been left with three pounds in his pocket. Enough for a modest present for Tim, a picnic lunch in Hyde Park, and a little bit left to tide them over. He'd intended taking them somewhere posh for lunch, but the idea of a picnic in the park met with such delight from Tim that Norah readily agreed, unaware of its financial necessity.

The lift doors clanged open and they stepped out into the main foyer, Norah instinctively flinching as she caught sight of herself in one of the many wall mirrors. Benjamin noticed her reaction and, when he took her hand, she looked up at him, smiled, and her gloved fingers squeezed his. The expense had been worth it, he thought. She did look pretty in the hat but, far more important, she had quelled her inhibitions. Just for him. And he admired her for that. It wouldn't have been easy, Norah being Norah.

Of course she'd be furious when she found out the cost of the hat and gloves, and they'd have to scrimp on housekeeping for the next two weeks. But they were hardly going to end up in the poorhouse. Not for as long as he was employed by the Wunderlich Patent Ceiling and Roofing Company anyway. The Wunderlichs looked after their employees, particularly those who had worked for the company for a full eight years. Benjamin and his family were set for life.

As they crossed the foyer, he looked up at the huge emblem in pressed metal above the main doors of the store. The gull's wings and the sailing boat, and the motto, 'Kendle and Streatham, Trading on the Wings of Honour'. Strange to think that he owed his good fortune to none other than Howard Streatham himself.

Benjamin could vaguely remember having met Howard once, as a small boy, but his father must have known him quite well. In fact Benjamin recalled Samuel having once said that they were distantly related. Benjamin himself didn't know how, and he didn't much care, but he was deeply grateful to Howard Streatham.

Samuel Kendall's approach to Howard Streatham during the depression of 1893 had been a desperate last resort to help his son who, along with dozens of others, had lost his job due to the financial collapse of his employers.

'I realise that Benjamin is in the same boat as hundreds of others all over the country, Howard,' Samuel had said, finding the situation even more disconcerting than he'd expected. Perhaps it was the luxury of his surroundings, seated on the terrace of Streatham's mansion in Kirribilli, looking out over the immaculate lawn at the ferries crossing the harbour. Samuel, a builder's labourer, had worked on many a fine house in his time, but never one as grand as this. And here he was asking Howard Streatham to give his son a job. No wonder he felt awkward.

'But you see, the boy's got himself into a spot of trouble,' he explained. 'A girl.'

'Ah.'

'Yes, stupid young pup, only twenty-one he is. They're getting married within the month.'

'I can see your cause for concern.' Howard pushed his spectacles up his nose, a nervous mannerism he'd adopt when he felt uncomfortable.

Howard had seen little of Samuel since Hannah's funeral all those years ago, but he knew that although uneducated, even somewhat coarse, Samuel was an honest man, a man worthy of respect. 'But, as I'm sure you realise,' he continued with regret, sincerely wishing that he could be of help, 'Charles would refuse to employ your son.'

'Oh yes, I know that only too well,' Samuel growled. Charles employ a Kendall? He'd die first. 'That's why I've come to you instead of your cousin.' Samuel leaned forward in his chair. 'You employ so many, couldn't you give the boy some back-room job, anything that'll earn him a few quid, and Charles'd be none the wiser?'

'Regrettably no. Charles regularly examines the books and visits every department of the store. It would be only a matter of time before he found out.'

'I see.' Samuel took his hat from the table in front of him. He certainly wasn't about to beg. 'Thanks for your time,' he said as he stood.

Howard knew exactly what Samuel was thinking. The store's half yours, why don't you tell Charles to go to hell? But to employ a Kendall simply wasn't worth the trouble. Not since the killing of Paddy O'Shea. Since then Charles had become fixated.

'He was Hannah's son! A Kendall and a lunatic!' he would roar. 'The man had been out to ruin me for years! He attacked me at his own mother's graveside. If it weren't for the butler, my wife would be dead.'

Howard religiously avoided any discussion on the events of that night. They were simple enough, it appeared. A small paragraph in the newspaper had been enough to explain it all. An armed burglar, caught committing a felony in the home of Charles Kendle, had attacked the mistress of the house and the butler had

had the presence of mind to take the master's revolver from his desk and shoot the attacker dead.

'One moment, Samuel.' Howard rose from his chair. 'I have another idea. Your boy is a builder like yourself, is he not?' Samuel nodded. 'Any experience with roofing?'

'He's done the lot.' Samuel's reply was terse. Howard Streatham was a coward.

'Come and have a look at this.' Howard stepped from the porch onto the lawn and Samuel joined him as he strode several paces down towards the harbour then turned back. 'See that?' He pointed to the gabled roof of his magnificent Queen Anne style house. 'Terracotta roofing tiles from Marseilles. The Wunderlich brothers have recently become the sole agent for their importation.'

Samuel's belligerence turned to hope. 'You'd put in a word?' he asked, wondering, however, just how much influence Howard really had with the Wunderlich company. If he was afraid of his own cousin, how could he command the respect of men like the Wunderlichs?

Howard had nodded. 'I'm sure they'll take him, they need experienced roofing men.' And they had.

The picnic lunch having been an unmitigated success, Benjamin, Norah and Timothy alighted from their tram in Elizabeth Street outside the Tramway Hotel, turned the corner and walked up Wexford Street into the heart of Surry Hills, happily exhausted.

Although the City of Sydney Improvement Board had demanded the demolition of many hundreds of working-class houses in Surry Hills, the suburb had remained relatively unchanged. Thickly populated, tenanted mainly by working-class labourers and small freeholders who lived on the premises of their numerous pubs, workshops, stables and grocery stores, Surry Hills had a character uniquely its own.

The press, in eulogising the mayoral efforts to clean up inner-city suburbs, ran rampant with stories of Chinese gambling and opium dens, child whores, and the murderous push gangs that prowled the lanes and alleys of the slums of Surry Hills. But overlooked by the newspapers was the true resilience of the local residents. A network of neighbourly support, coupled with a common cynicism of authority, bred a close-knit community which rallied together in the face of adversity.

Benjamin, Norah and Timothy walked up the hill, past the small joss house where their nostrils were assailed with the odour of burning incense, past the gaming house and the sly grog shop, past the restaurant which boasted three-course meals for sevenpence. 'Soup, meat and sweets', the sign said, 'bread and butter and a cup of tea included'.

They stopped to say hello to Ping Kee, the Chinese storekeeper who was seated outside his shop. The Chinese had long been resident in Surry Hills and were recognised as a peaceable community, despite their fondness for gambling and opium.

They crossed over Exeter Place, a narrow lane running east of Wexford, and Norah shuddered as she always did. Exeter Place was a constant reminder of the plague. Mostly demolished during the cleansing operations of 1900, the houses which remained standing amongst the rubble were hovels of stone and rusty corrugated iron, where poverty was rife and families lived five to a room.

Not that Wexford Street was much better, but at least the congested rows of terrace houses had survived. And some even looked attractive, here and there an iron lace balcony, albeit rusty, or a wooden awning, albeit in need of a coat of paint. But many a family in Wexford Street lived on the poverty line and, like their neighbours, they had not escaped the plague.

Norah could remember only too vividly the months of quarantine during the cleansing operations, when gangs of ratcatchers and disinfectors had combed the crowded dwellings. Samuel Kendall and his sons, Benjamin and young Billy, along with many other locals trapped within the quarantined areas, were unable to go to work and had lined up for employment as ratcatchers. It was dangerous work, potentially fatal but, at seven shillings a day, eagerly sought after. Rumour had it that up to a thousand men had camped out in the backyards and lanes of the Darling Harbour goods yard in the hope that they would be quarantined and so obtain employment. Such was the desperation of the poor, Norah supposed; but she had watched daily, with sick foreboding, as her husband, together with his father and young brother, had joined the ranks of the professional ratcatchers.

It was the fleas that carried the plague, that's what the newspapers had said. The rats had come into the city on board ships from foreign ports and the rats brought the fleas.

Outbreaks of bubonic plague had seized the older and poorer neighbourhoods of Sydney and over three hundred people had been infected, one third of whom had died. It was no wonder that Samuel, strong as he was, had been taken. The wonder lay in the fact that his sons had escaped his fate, and Norah had been deeply thankful that the good Lord had seen fit to save her Benjamin. But her heart had gone out to Beth who had had to watch the hideous death of her husband.

'Beth,' she said as they arrived at the shabby door of number 22 which opened directly onto the pavement and where, overhead, the red climbing geraniums in the corner tub wove their way through the iron lacework of the balcony. Norah was very proud of her red geraniums. 'We should have bought a present for Beth.'

'Mum can live without,' Benjamin replied, opening the door. 'She can share Tim's marbles,' he grinned, winking at his son. 'I bet she'll beat you, you know how good she is at marbles.'

'I bet she won't.' The boy raced into the house yelling at the top of his voice. 'Gran! Come and look at my marbles!' They heard him inside, thundering up the narrow stairs to the little rear bedroom he shared with his grandmother and which doubled as Beth's sewing room. 'Gran,' they heard him yell as he went, 'do you want a game of marbles?'

It was only then Norah realised, with horror, 'Ben! We didn't buy you a present! It's your birthday, and we didn't buy you a present!'

'Well, what have we here?' a female voice interrupted from overhead. 'Royalty visiting Surry Hills,' and a loud guffaw followed. It was Nellie Putman, on the balcony adjoining theirs; she'd watched them walking up the street.

Benjamin and Norah stepped off the pavement and onto the street to look up at their neighbour who was dangling herself dangerously over the railing.

'Wondered who it was under that fancy hat.' There was no malice in the tone, but Benjamin could feel Norah cringe beside him.

Nellie Putman was a large, loud, vulgar woman. Married to a petty criminal who spent much of his life behind bars, her two older sons were the terrors of the neighbourhood, but Nellie herself had a heart as big as any to be found in Surry Hills and people respected her for it.

Not Norah, however. Norah found it embarrassing, having the Putmans as neighbours, and Benjamin found her embarrassment irksome.

'Must have cost a pretty penny,' Nellie yelled down at them.

'It did, but it was worth it,' Benjamin called back. 'Doesn't she look a treat?'

He glanced at his wife, praying that Norah wouldn't spoil their perfect day. She would not be outrightly rude to Nellie, he knew that. But sometimes her embarrassment caused her to be aloof, and aloofness in Surry Hills was interpreted as snobbery, one of the cardinal sins, a public brawl being far more acceptable than a social snub.

Norah had automatically winced at Nellie's raucous tone, and she was now painfully aware that strangers passing by, and neighbours peering from doorways and balconies, were all looking at her hat. She wished wholeheartedly that she could disappear but, conscious of her husband's scrutiny, she bravely stood her ground and smiled up at the balcony.

'He bought me these beautiful gloves too, Nellie, look,' she held up her hands, 'and he bought some marbles for Timmy. But it's his own birthday. It's Ben's birthday, and we didn't even get him a present.'

'You'll be his present in that hat, lovey, you mark my words you will.'

Pleased by Norah's unexpectedly friendly response, Nellie Putman gave them a wave before she went inside. 'Happy birthday, Ben, we'll share a beer before tea, what do you say?'

'Good-o. See you out the back at six then.' Benjamin returned the wave, then pulled Norah close to him. 'She's right, love,' he kissed her lightly, 'you're my birthday present.'

'For goodness' sake, Ben, not in the street.' But she smiled as they went inside.

The door from the street led directly into the sitting room which was small and crammed with an assortment of second-hand furniture. To the left was a narrow staircase leading to the two upstairs bedrooms, and the wall to the right was given over to a large grey-pink sofa, the back of which was covered with several lace-worked antimacassars which hid the moth holes. The sofa was far too big for the room but it doubled as a bed for Benjamin's young brother Billy.

The fireplace beneath the wooden mantel in the corner was framed by green tiles with, here and there, a flower motif. Several of the tiles were cracked and chipped, but they were attractive nonetheless. The tiles were kept glossy and shining, and always there was a small vase of flowers on the mantelpiece, violets or pansies or even sweetpeas, whatever was available from the street vendor on the corner. The fire in the little iron grate gave off a good strong heat too, and the family was cosy in the colder months, unlike many of their neighbours who lived in damp and rotting dwellings.

Benjamin and Norah walked through to the kitchen where they found Beth and Timothy seated at the table, admiring the set of marbles. The kitchen was where the family invariably gathered, and most of the space was taken up by the old, scarred wooden table which Samuel had made. Pots and pans hung from hooks screwed into the yellowing plaster walls, and utensils dangled from nails driven into the big wooden beam above the stove.

'Well, well, well,' Beth said, rising to admire the hat closely, 'now that's what I call posh.' She felt the texture of the blue satin bow. A seamstress by trade, employed as an outworker by the Goulburn Street tailor, J Cohen, Beth certainly knew her fabrics. 'Very, very posh.'

Norah fumbled with the hatpin. 'Try it on, Beth. Do. You can borrow it whenever you wish. It can be ours to share if you like.'

Knowing how hard Beth slaved away in her little sewing room, the second-hand machine Samuel had bought her whirring away till well past midnight, young Timmy all the while sleeping soundly in the upper bunk, Norah once more felt a wave of guilt that she had not insisted upon buying a present for her mother-in-law.

'Put it on,' she urged. 'Please.'

Benjamin watched, puzzled as he often was by the genuine affection between them. He remembered a time when Beth had been highly critical of Norah. 'Above herself,' he could remember his mother saying to Samuel. 'She's just a Surry Hills lass like the rest of them, who does she think she is?' But somewhere along the line, she had changed her tack. 'Shy she is,' Beth would say in defence of her daughter-in-law. 'Shy that's all,' when the neighbours insinuated that Norah was a bit stuck up. Benjamin was grateful that the two had become friends, but it only confirmed his confusion about the female sex. Much as he loved and admired the look and the smell and the touch of them, their minds remained a mystery to him.

'Fine piece of craftsmanship, I must say.' Beth turned the hat in her hands, examining it from every angle. 'Very nicely worked.'

'Here, let me help you.' Norah sat Beth down and tucked the stray wisps of grey hair back up into the untidy chignon. She placed the hat on Beth's head and secured the pin. 'There. Now come and look in the mirror.'

Benjamin and Timothy followed as Norah dragged her mother-in-law into the sitting room, and together they all looked in the mirror over the mantelpiece.

The hat was totally at odds with the colourless face which peered from beneath its brim. It mocked the once blue eyes, now a faded grey, and emphasised the sunken cheeks which had once been rosy. Beth was fifty-five years of age, but in that hat she could have been seventy.

'Now, there's a sight for sore eyes,' she said, her weary face cracking into a smile. 'It's a younger woman should wear this hat, and that's a fact.' She laughed out loud as she took it off.

The flash of humour revealed a strength which belied the aged face beneath the hat. There was plenty of life left in Beth Kendall. The fight for survival might have drained the colour from her, but survive she had. She would never admit defeat, although the death of her husband had brought her close to it. In the thirty-three years of their marriage she had weathered two miscarriages, given birth to a stillborn baby, and lost two, one to scarlet fever at ten months, and a three-year-old to measles. None of which had prepared her for the death of her husband.

For the first week or so they had persuaded themselves that he had caught a chill. His high temperature, his headaches, his dry cough. 'Just a chill,' Samuel had said, and she'd believed him. Then, overnight, the plague had struck with a passion and within three days he was dead. Mercifully quick some might say, but it was a hideous death to behold. Daily Beth had watched her Samuel wasting before her eyes, coughing up blood-stained sputum, his skin turning blue. Delirious. Vomiting. And when the end finally came, withered to a husk, skin ulcerated, abscesses covering his body.

She had nurtured him throughout, washing him, caressing him, lying beside him and whispering her support. She'd held his decaying body close, the once strong body she had known and loved, and often she'd wished that the plague would take her too. But it hadn't. And she supposed she should be grateful, it was a death no-one should have to suffer. And there was more living to be done after all, she still served a useful purpose.

'You keep the hat for yourself, Norah,' she said, handing it back. 'I'll play with Tim's marbles, they suit me better.'

'Fancy a drink out the back?' Benjamin asked. 'Nellie said she'd join us.'

Beth caught the hopeful plea in her grandson's eye. 'You two go on,' she said, giving Tim a nod, 'we'll be out when we've had a game of marbles.'

The boy raced off into the kitchen and Beth smiled at her daughter-in-law. 'It's a lovely hat, Norah, it suits you well.'

Norah smiled back happily. 'Thank you,' she said.

Strange how transforming that smile was, Beth thought. For a relatively plain young woman, Norah looked very pretty when she smiled.

Norah's plainness had been included in Beth's litany of criticism during the early days. 'She's not even pretty,' she'd grumbled to Samuel. 'She's stuck up and she's not even pretty. Why, she's nowhere near as good-looking as the other girls Ben's courted.'

'Ben's never "courted" a girl in his life,' Samuel had replied with more than a touch of cynicism, 'and well you know it.'

Beth had known it. Only too well. Devilishly handsome with charm to boot, Benjamin was a magnet to women. And at his age, if girls wished to surrender themselves to him, who could blame him for enjoying his conquests? But it had been only a matter of time, despite his father's regular warnings. 'You be careful, boy,' Samuel had said time and again. 'Many a young ram's had to pay for his pleasure.' Only a matter of time. And then there she was. Norah Davis. Twenty-one years old. A full five months pregnant. And plain.

In Beth's eyes it had all added up to one thing. A trap. How come all the pretty girls Benjamin had bedded over the past five years had managed to keep themselves out of trouble? Well, two of them hadn't, she knew that for a fact, but they'd found the solution to their problem.

'There are ways, you know. Ways to get rid of it.' Beth had been cruelly direct with the girl. Didn't she know they were in the depths of a depression? The lad was too young and the times were too hard to be saddled with a wife and a baby. 'There are ways,' she said. Then she told the girl about hot baths and gin, about smashing her stomach against a chair or a railing. 'Did you try anything?' she demanded.

The girl shook her head, about to cry. 'I prayed,' she said, 'I prayed that I'd lose the baby.'

Prayer! Beth had little time for prayer, it had certainly never worked for her. 'Oh well, it's too late now. Five months. Nothing you can do about it now.'

The tears started then. Silently. Coursing down the girl's cheeks. Beth refused to be moved. The distress was genuine, she could see that. But her son was trapped. Why should she waste her sympathy?

'There's no need for that. Ben will do the right thing, you'll be married before the baby's born.' She rose from her chair. 'Now pull yourself together, I'll put the kettle on for some tea.'

After the marriage and the birth of the baby, Beth's attitude towards Norah softened a little. The girl loved her son, and was a good wife and mother, for that she should be grateful. And gradually she realised that Norah's reserve was not due to any snobbishness on her part, that she was indeed shy, and painfully self-conscious.

The death of Norah's second child, the little girl she had so longed for, finally sealed their relationship. Without Beth's strength and support, and above all understanding, Norah would never have survived her loss, Beth knew it. And from that moment on, she became protective of her daughter-in-law.

Following the game of marbles, which she let Tim win—the first game with his new set, it seemed only right—Beth and her grandson joined the others in the communal backyard shared by the Kendalls and the Putmans.

There had once been a dividing fence, but in the lean times

Samuel Kendall and Jack Putman had pulled it down and used it for firewood. No-one had told the landlord, but then he was unlikely to find out. Most landlords in the poorer areas of Surry Hills were disinterested in the living conditions of their tenants and, so long as the rent was paid, were rarely seen. Neither of the families had ever mentioned rebuilding the fence, although Norah always wished they would. The Kendalls and the Putmans preferred it that way. A communal backyard was neighbourly, they said.

'A grand age for a man, thirty.' Nellie toasted Ben yet again with her bottle of beer, then took another swig—she always drank from the bottle. 'A man's not a man till he's thirty, that's what I say.'

Nellie was flirting with Ben. She always did. Nellie flirted with every man she met and particularly with Ben because she liked him the best. She meant no harm, she was just as saucy with men in the presence of her own husband. More so at times, Jack Putman enjoying his wife's vulgar good humour, safe in the knowledge of her loyalty. But Jack Putman was not present at the moment, he was halfway through a six-month stint in Darlinghurst Gaol for petty pilfering. Nellie had been furious at the time. How could he have been so thoughtless, she'd roared, just before the baby was born, and all for the sake of a bloke's wallet in a pub.

'I tell you, Ben, when my Jack was thirty,' Nellie grinned and gave a growl of sexual innuendo, 'oh, a bull of a man he was! A bull of a man!'

There were times when Norah found Nellie Putman repulsive. And this was one of them. She looked away, pretending to be deep in thought, so that she didn't have to watch Nellie, seated at the rickety table outside her back door, intermittently sucking on her bottle of beer whilst her child sucked on her breast, every now and then throwing her head back to laugh her raucous laugh, her big frame heaving, the baby grabbing at the nipple which had escaped it.

'It takes a hell of a woman to bring the bull out in a man, Nell,' Benjamin deliberately flirted back, angered by his wife's disapproval. 'And you're one hell of a woman.'

Seated beside Ben on the bench outside their own back door, Norah felt his body stiffen and she knew she'd annoyed him, but she couldn't help it. It was disgraceful that Nellie Putman, at forty-two, should have had yet another child. The woman had two married daughters and three grown sons, and there was an eighteen-year age gap between the baby at her breast and her youngest boy. It was disgraceful that Nellie Putman openly displayed her great, sagging breast and suckled the child in the company of others. But more than anything it was disgraceful that Nellie, a middle-aged woman, fat and blowsy, should flirt with her husband. And that he should flirt back. Time and again Norah told herself the flirtation meant nothing. It was Surry Hills backyard banter. Boisterous, bawdy and utterly harmless. But she couldn't help it. The more she listened to them, the more she shrank into herself, convinced that Ben didn't love her, that he never had.

Norah had always been threatened by women's reactions to her husband. She could see the way pretty women looked at Ben. And she could see the way they looked at her. 'What a handsome man,' she could hear them thinking, 'why is he married to her?' Well if they'd asked, she could have told them. 'He married me out of a sense of duty,' she could have said, 'a sense of duty, that's all. He never loved me.' Oh, and she could just see their faces if she told them that. 'So you trapped him,' they'd think. 'You clever girl, you trapped the pick of the bunch.'

Well that's what Beth had believed, hadn't she? And in a way, Beth had been right. Norah had been so desperately in love with Benjamin that she had let him have his way. How else could she have held his interest? What else had she to offer? She wasn't beautiful, she wasn't even pretty. But she had never intended to become pregnant. She had been a virgin, with no idea how to guard against conception. And when she had discovered her pregnancy, she had genuinely prayed for a miscarriage, not wishing to force an unwanted marriage upon the man she loved. And in due time she had paid shockingly for such wicked prayer. The memory of her dead baby weighed perpetually upon Norah's conscience.

The banter between Benjamin and Nellie continued, but just as Norah was about to make her excuses and go inside, the back door slammed open and in walked nineteen-year-old Billy with his comrade-in-arms Mick Putman beside him, both dressed in their trademark bell-bottom trousers, bright bandanas and black slouch hats.

'Billy!' Tim yelled, his Uncle Billy was his hero. 'Wait till you see my new marbles,' and the boy dashed into the kitchen.

Nellie beckoned her youngest son to her. 'Fetch us some more beer from the ice chest, Mick, there's a good lad, it's Ben's birthday.'

'No, Nell, no, it's our shout. Fetch the beer, Billy, let's have a party.' As his young brother dived inside, Ben called after him, 'And bring out the kitchen chairs.'

Nellie was delighted. 'Go get your mouth organ, Mick,' she said, 'we'll have a singalong.'

The evening turned into a boisterous success, like many a backyard party at number 22. They ate outside around the Putmans' table, sharing Nellie's rabbit pie—she'd bought a pair from the rabbit-oh's cart for sixpence that very afternoon—and Beth's mutton stew, mopping up the rich, fatty gravy with home-made damper. There was tapioca pudding to finish up with, after which they dragged the chairs back inside and sat around the table in the Kendalls' kitchen, singing along to Mick's harmonica. When they ran out of beer, Nellie got into the gin, and by midnight, she was maudlin drunk and bemoaning the fact that her Jack wasn't there.

'Time for bed now, Timmy,' Norah insisted, 'and I'm going myself.' Beth had retired an hour previously and Norah had only stayed up to keep an eye on her son.

'Oh Mum,' Tim whinged as he followed Norah out of the kitchen, but it was a token protest only. He'd been fighting to stay awake for over an hour, trying desperately to hide his exhaustion. The sips of beer Billy had been surreptitiously feeding him must have amounted to two full glasses by now and he was feeling the effects.

Tim had had a wonderful night. He'd beaten his Uncle Billy twice at marbles. Unheard of! But then Billy had been pretty drunk. Tim wondered if that counted.

'I beat Billy twice, Mum,' he said on the way upstairs, 'and he's really good.'

'Shh, don't wake your grandmother.'

Norah waited whilst he undressed and climbed into the top bunk and, in a matter of seconds, he was asleep.

As Beth snored lightly in the bunk below, Norah studied her son. She worried about Billy's influence over the boy. Not that

Billy Kendall was bad, but he and Mick Putman together were a wild pair of lads.

'Billy and Mick are little more than boys themselves, Norah,' Ben had protested when she'd raised her fears with him. 'They're not yet twenty, stands to reason they're high-spirited.'

'But Timmy spends so much time with them.'

'Nothing wrong with that, every boy needs a hero.'

Benjamin had known full well that Billy and Mick Putman were members of the Gipps Street Gang, but he'd said nothing about that to Norah. Anyway, half the young men in Surry Hills belonged to one or another of the local larrikin pushes, it was necessary for their reputation. They lounged around outside the headquarters of their favourite pub or billiards hall, baiting police, conducting slanging matches with passers-by and generally making nuisances of themselves. Occasionally the more criminal element in a gang waylaid a toff who should have known better than to walk the Surry Hills backstreets alone at night. A quick smack to the skull with a sock filled with sand and the toff was relieved of his wallet to wake an hour later with an aching head.

In the prearranged venues of local paddocks and alleys, neighbourhood gangs staged occasional battles, resulting in black eyes and scratches and bruises, but rarely anything more. There was cause for concern, however, when a push moved outside its own territory. When the Darlinghurst push invaded Surry Hills, or the Woolloomooloo push took on the Rocks, then it was war, and sand-filled socks were exchanged for flick-knives and daggers.

Billy and young Mick were good enough lads though. They both had legitimate jobs. Mick was employed in a blacksmith's shop and Billy had regular shift work at the Toohey's Standard Brewery in Elizabeth Street.

Ben said as much to Norah. 'They're good lads, love, they go to work, they're not like Nellie's other two.'

Spotty and Geoff Putman were professionals. Burglars by trade. More ambitious and more proficient than their petty-thief father, they had never seen the inside of Darlinghurst Gaol, and quite possibly never would. Their downfall was more likely to come via the underworld, they had trodden on some toes in their time.

If Norah had known, as she studied her sleeping son, freckle-faced, sandy-haired, with the promise of his father's good looks, that Timothy 'Tiny Tot' Kendall was in fact the mascot of the Gipps Street Gang, she would have worried herself sick.

Tim had hated his nickname at first. 'Tiny Tot's bedtime, is it?' big 'Horse' Morgan had said loudly to Billy one day, and the other men had laughed. It was a Friday and Tim had called in to the Pig and Whistle on his way home from Crown Street School, as he did every now and then, to say hello to Billy and have a sip of his beer. A number of other young boys made a habit of hanging around the pub, relatives or fans of the push members, but they always left before it got dark. This particular time, however, Tim had stayed on too late.

Nobody had taken much notice of him, sitting quietly in the corner of the back room. He'd watched the lads smoke and drink beer and play darts, and he'd listened to their dirty stories and tales of bravado grow louder and wilder, and before he'd realised it darkness had set in. He'd be in big trouble when he got home.

Billy, suddenly recognising his nephew's dilemma, said, 'I'll come home with you, Tim. We'll tell them we were having a kick of the footie, we won't say a word about the pub.'

'Tiny Tot's bedtime, is it?' Horse Morgan said and the others laughed. Billy too. Good-naturedly of course, but Tim felt his face redden with rage and humiliation. He was acutely aware that he was small for his age, the smallest in his class. He'd been involved in many a skirmish to prove he wasn't the weakest, however, and they didn't tease him at school any more. Tim glowered as he left the pub.

To his horror, the nickname stuck. Not in its entirety; he was sometimes Tiny and sometimes the Tot to the members of the push, but never Tim like he used to be, and he hated it. He suffered in silence though, knowing that if he whinged he'd not only cop a terrible teasing, he'd lose the gang's respect. Even the most insulting of nicknames was better than being ignored.

Then one day, he was inadvertently rescued by none other than Ernie Morgan, Horse's nine-year-old brother.

'G'day, Tiny Tot,' Ernie yelled above the babble of the bar.

'What did you say?' Tim yelled back.

'Tiny Tot, that's what I said, I said g'day Tiny Tot.' Ernie jostled Tim with his shoulder, jealous of the attention the Kendall kid received from the push. Ernie himself didn't have a nickname. It wasn't fair, he should have had one, his big brother was one of the leaders of the Gipps Street Gang, he should have had a nickname.

'Tiny Tot! Tiny Tot,' he chanted. Then he gave one of his goofy grins which looked like a leer, his pug-dog mouth going down at the corners instead of up.

Tim launched himself at Ernie Morgan then and there, in the middle of the Pig and Whistle, and the fight was on. The men cleared the decks to make room for the boys as they rolled amongst the sawdust and cigar butts and fag ends. They roared their approval, all barracking for Tim. Even Ernie's big brother Horse was barracking for Tim. For Tim didn't stand a chance. Ernie Morgan was a year older, and big and solid for his age. He worked alongside his brother in their father's stables and he had the Morgan build.

But Tim was acquitting himself well, heroically in fact, and the men let the fight go on. Billy and Mick weren't there to stop it, they were in the back room playing darts.

'Go Tiny!'

'Come on the Tot!'

'Go Tiny Tot!'

The lads of the push roared and roared, until finally it became a chant. 'Tiny Tot! Tiny Tot! Tiny Tot!'

In the back room Billy and Mick could hear the noise from the bar, a fight was on, they agreed, but they couldn't hear what was being yelled so they didn't know who was copping it. They decided to finish their game of darts before they joined the fun. Then the door opened and the barman said, 'You better come out here, Billy, before Ernie Morgan murders that nephew of yours.'

Billy and Mick pushed their way through the crowd to discover Tim on his back on the floor of the bar, snotty-nosed, one eye bleeding, Ernie Morgan astride his chest.

'Do you give up?' Ernie yelled, looking a little the worse for wear himself.

'No!' Tim raised his head and his hand lashed out wildly, but without much force.

'Tiny Tot!' a number of the lads shouted—those who would have been happy to see the fight go through to the death; others, more sensible, had stopped yelling and were clearing the way for Billy, aware it was time to break it up.

'Do you give up?' Ernie demanded, grabbing Tim by the ears and bashing his head back into the sawdust.

'No!'

'He gives up, Ernie,' Billy said. 'You've won the fight.'

Horse Morgan stepped forward and dragged his baby brother off Tim. The crowd applauded as Billy gave Tim a hand to his feet and dusted him off. Young Tiny Tot had won the respect of the bar.

That was three months ago, and since then Tim had been adopted by the Gipps Street Gang. It was tacitly understood, much to the chagrin of the other boys, that he was their mascot, and that the members of the push were permitted to call him Tiny Tot but their baby brothers were not.

Christmas and New Year passed and, two months after his father's thirtieth birthday, Timothy Kendall turned nine years old. Turning nine was a step in the right direction. Nine was much closer to ten, much older than eight. But he still wasn't any bigger. It worried him.

Billy Kendall and Mick Putman were sensitive to the boy's problem. Neither was concerned about Tim playing the wag from school, hanging around with the push, playing billiards, drinking beer. It was normal, they'd both done it themselves in their time, and they'd turned out all right. Besides, Crown Street School was the quickest introduction to the push there was. The ten-year-olds at Crown Street had gangs of their own, they were merely rehearsing for the day when they would leave behind their pencils and books. But Billy and Mick were concerned when they discovered Tim's genuine worry about his size.

'Ernie Morgan's not ten yet,' Tim said the day after his birthday, 'he's only eleven months older than me, and he's twice as big.' Despite their wrestling match, or perhaps because of it, Ernie and Tim had become good friends.

'Of course he is,' Billy argued encouragingly, 'look at his father.' Tim's expression said 'so what'. 'Look at Horse,' Billy continued. 'Look at Ernie's other brothers. All three of them. They're huge. The whole family's built like that. Well, all of them except his sister,' he added (Horse's sister was a ravishing beauty, a fact which bewildered and fascinated the push), 'just as well, eh?' He grinned lasciviously at Mick who grinned back. Not that either of them had ever dared cast an eye in the direction of Horse's sister, Horse would kill them if they did.

The answer didn't satisfy Tim at all. 'So what about our family? You're not little. And Dad's sure not little.'

'I was once, I was a real runt.'

'Oh yeah.'

'Too right I was. I swear I didn't grow an inch till I was about fifteen.'

'Yeah, yeah,' Tim sneered again. Even more derisively this time. He didn't believe Billy for a minute and he was regretting the fact that he'd brought up the subject.

Billy and Mick were leaning against the lamp post outside the Pig and Whistle. It was late afternoon, changeover time for the day and night shifts at the nearby workshops and factories, and workers, old and young, male and female, passed to and fro in pairs or groups, demanding comment from the local push. Billy and Mick obliged as usual with admiring whistles for the girls and cheeky insults for the men.

Tim looked at his heroes. Beers in their hands, slouch hats at a rakish angle, Billy with neatly rolled fag in the corner of his mouth, and Mick with clay pipe in his, they made an impressive pair. Tim felt depressed. He'd never look like that. He dug his hands deep into the pockets of his baggy shorts and stared down at the dust. He should have kept his trap shut, he shouldn't have told them, he'd never told anyone else.

'It's a fact, Tim,' Mick said, tapping his pipe on the heel of his shiny-black shoe, he always did it with panache. 'Billy was a skinny little bugger.' Tim looked up, a glimmer of hope in his eyes. 'Short too,' Mick added, slipping the pipe back into the top pocket of his vest.

Mick didn't lie, Tim thought, his spirits lifting a little. Well, not when he didn't have to anyway. And Mick Putman had grown up with his uncle Billy, so Mick'd know.

'But he didn't take any lip about it, just like you don't,' Mick continued. 'He tried to bash me up once when I called him a scrawny chook. About ten we were . . .'

'*Tried* to! I did, you bugger.' Billy shoved Mick in the chest and Mick spilt some of his beer.

'Watch it, mate.'

Two pretty girls walked past. In their twenties, just finished their ten-hour shift at Newlands Brothers factory in Riley Street. 'Hello, love, fancy a beer?' Tim leered.

'Want a fag, love?' Like lightning, Billy whipped out his silver cigarette case, the one he'd bought for a quid at Leibman's Pawnshop in Little Riley and which he kept buffed and gleaming always. He flipped it neatly open. Inside were the four perfectly rolled cigarettes reserved for such occasions, he never smoked them himself or offered them to the lads. 'Help yourself,' he said, 'do.'

The girls shared a snigger, not alarmed, not threatened, and not interested. These were boys, and the girls had beaus.

'She looked back, did you see that, Mick?' Billy flipped the case closed and put it back in the pocket of his blue velvet jacket, 'definitely interested.'

Tim was glad of the distraction. He was feeling a little self-conscious and didn't want to talk about his problem any more. But he was pleased that he had, he felt much better for it.

One Friday afternoon Tim asked his mate Ernie Morgan if he wanted to come and kick the footie around with Billy and Mick. The boys were sitting on the kerbside outside the pub, Tim waiting impatiently for Billy and Mick to finish their beers inside.

Ernie ignored the invitation, appearing not to hear it as he announced dramatically, 'Horse is going to a two-up game tonight, and Billy and Mick are going with him. I heard the three of them talking.'

'So what?'

Ernie Morgan was a solemn-faced boy with bulldog-like features which ran in the family, Horse was the same. A small punched-in nose, heavy jowls, and a thuggish jaw, Ernie had yet to grow into his face.

'So what?' Tim repeated when Ernie remained mysteriously and irritatingly silent. 'They often play two-up.' It was true, even when times were hard, money regularly changed hands on the toss of two pennies in a deserted warehouse or a lamp-lit alley.

'Not in the Loo they don't. Not with the Dockers' Gang.'

'Hell,' Tim said, and Ernie was gratified by the response.

'Yep,' he nodded. 'Midnight. Bottom of the Butler Stairs. There'll be a fight all right. Shall we go and watch?' Ernie's eyes gleamed, he loved nothing more than to watch a good stoush. A bit of blood, the crunch of knuckle and bone, men wrestling in the mud. Ernie couldn't wait to be older.

But Tim was concerned. 'Just the three of them? Just Horse and Billy and Mick? Going to a Dockers' two-up game?'

'Yep. It's got nothing to do with the gang, Horse says. He's got a score to settle with Snaky Ryan, and he wants Billy and Mick for his seconds. I couldn't hear any more,' Ernie shrugged. 'They shut up when they saw me listening and Horse belted me one on the ear.'

'Rightio,' Tim said, trying to sound nonchalant. He'd go with Ernie to watch the midnight fight between Horse Morgan and Snaky Ryan, course he would. 'Rightio,' he said again, and excitement blended with fear as he nodded his agreement.

Tim was not the only one with mixed feelings. As he crept out the front door of number 22 at half past eleven that night, Billy Kendall felt exactly the same way. He'd exchanged his sand-filled sock for a dagger. The blue-handled dagger which was his pride and joy, but which he rarely carried. He'd never knifed anyone and he didn't relish the prospect, but if others were carrying knives, then he needed to be prepared.

Mick was waiting for him out in the street. Collars up, hat brims down, they turned the corner and marched up Goulburn Street. Horse was standing on the corner of Goulburn and Brisbane, and as the three men walked in silence through the streets of Surry Hills, two small figures followed in the darkness.

Tim and Ernie knew the way to the Butler Stairs, but it was more exciting to follow their heroes going off to war. To fearlessly confront the enemy. Tim grinned at Ernie. Any trepidation he'd had was gone, this was the thrill of a lifetime.

The Butler Stairs linked Potts Point and Kings Cross with Woolloomooloo. Cut into the rock of the hillside, the Stairs led from fashionable Victoria Street, leafy and broad, to the working houses and cobblestones of Brougham Street far below.

During the day the Stairs were safe enough. Pedestrians used them as a convenient, albeit tiring, short cut; children used them as a playground, and Chinamen with baskets full of produce hanging either side of the poles slung across their shoulders used them as a main thoroughfare, trudging laboriously up and down the endless stone steps.

At night it was a different matter. At night the Butler Stairs were a favourite meeting place for thieves and cutthroats, and members of the push planning a raid. The perfect place to be coshed and robbed if a man was foolish enough to walk alone.

At the base of the Stairs a metal arch linked the stone pillars on either side, and atop the arch in the very centre was a gas lamp. Tonight, however, Brougham Street was flooded with a far brighter light. Lanterns stood on the pavements and, amongst the crowd gathered for the game, several men held lamps aloft.

A canvas tarpaulin was spread on the ground, half bricks and lumps of gravel anchoring it at the corners and pieces of paling weighting down the sides. Two men stood in the centre and thirty or more others, wearing the trademark cloth caps of the Dockers, gathered around in a circle.

'Come in spinner!' the boxer called when the side bets had been placed. Then he stood back whilst the other man in the centre of the ring tossed the coins from the wooden kip in his hand and the two pennies were sent spinning high in the air. The babble of chatter ceased. Lamps were raised. The onlookers watched in silence.

As the coins fell on the canvas, the boxer's assistant stepped in with his lantern. 'No throw,' the boxer said when he saw the pennies, one heads, one tails, and the assistant nodded affirmation to the others.

The babble of voices started up again, and men swigged from bottles, rolled cigarettes or puffed on their cigars as they waited for the next spin.

Horse, Billy and Mick stood watching from their vantage point, ten yards or so up the hill of Brougham Street, their eyes raking the crowd for a sign of Snaky Ryan. Meanwhile, unnoticed, Tim and Ernie ducked around the side of the mob to crouch on the steps. Tucking themselves into the shadows, the boys huddled against the wall of the Stairs and waited in breathless anticipation.

'Come in spinner!' the boxer called and the man with the kip stepped into the centre. He raised his arm chest high, and all eyes were on the narrow strip of wood he held in his hand, the two pennies resting on top. He lowered his hand, about to throw, then stopped mid-action, his gaze directed to the three men standing beyond the crowd, just up the hill.

'Horse Morgan!' he called. 'You've got a nerve.'

All heads turned, annoyed that the game had been momentarily halted.

'Just my luck,' Horse muttered to the others. They'd been searching the crowd for Snaky and hadn't thought to look at the spinner.

'What are you doing on our turf, you mongrels?' Snaky Ryan tipped the pennies into his left hand and started to cross the pit.

There were boos and snarls from the assembled men. 'Shove off!' some of them growled at the intruders. 'Go back to your rat holes.' But the rest were deriding Snaky. 'Toss the bleeding things!' they yelled. 'Sort it out later, Snaky, get back in the game!' There was money riding, and a few uninvited guests from a rival push were no reason to hold up play.

'Come in spinner!' the boxer called above it all, trying to re-establish order.

Snaky Ryan stood undecided; he knew why Horse Morgan was there, and he was willing to do battle. But he had just one more pair of heads to spin before he could collect his winnings and pass the kip to the next man. Besides, he didn't fancy taking on his own angry mob if he held up the game. He'd sort out Horse Morgan later, he decided and, turning his back on the members of the Gipps Street Gang, returned to the centre of the pit.

Horse had a terrible temper when roused. Under normal circumstances he would have known better than to interrupt the play of a Dockers' two-up game, but he'd been boiling with rage for two whole days now. And the disdain with which Snaky turned his back and sauntered away was more than Horse could stand.

'You keep your filthy paws off my sister!' Horse screamed at the top of his voice. 'Do you hear me, you slimy bastard?'

In the split-second silence which followed, Billy and Mick exchanged glances. Horse's sister!

'A matter of honour,' Horse had told them. He'd been no more explicit than that and, proud that he'd asked them to act as his seconds, they'd respected his privacy and the gravity of his cause, whatever it may be. But his sister? They should have guessed! Horse was always protecting the dubious honour of his only sister, regularly taking on any member of his own gang he thought was trifling with her virtue. But no-one took him seriously. No-one took his sister's virtue seriously, least of all his sister.

If Horse had left his challenge until Snaky Ryan had completed his run as spinner, or if Snaky had ignored the challenge and continued with the game, trouble would have been averted. But the gauntlet had been thrown and Snaky grabbed it. No man, particularly one from the Gipps Street Gang, called Snaky Ryan a slimy bastard.

Snaky hurled the kip and pennies into the crowd and charged across the pit. Bets, placed upon the ground in orderly fashion, were scattered as he dived through the mob to get at Horse. The game was disrupted and the Dockers screamed their angry abuse.

Knives glinted in the lamplight. The intruders were about to learn a serious lesson. Horse and Snaky were locked together, rolling on the ground, trying to strangle each other, and the irate men turned their attention on Billy and Mick.

'Run, Mick!' Billy yelled, but Mick, knife drawn, had nowhere to go, and as Billy turned, he realised they were trapped. The Dockers had formed a circle and were taunting them with their knives.

Young Ernie Morgan and Tim Kendall had but one route of escape. 'Come on!' Ernie yelled and he started to sprint up the Butler Stairs. Heart pumping, Tim followed, but before they reached the first landing they heard the cry from above.

'Coppers!' the cockatoo standing lookout in Victoria Street yelled and, seconds later, a young member of the Dockers' Gang sprinted down the steps, nearly bowling them over. He stopped for an instant, surprised by the sight of the boys. 'Coppers,' he said again, 'move it,' and raced down into the street, Tim and Ernie following. Above them they could hear the shrill squeal of police whistles and the urgent sound of men's voices and the scuffle of boots at the top of the Stairs.

In Brougham Street, the warning had gone unheard. The Dockers were too busy trying to rally their humiliated leader—Horse Morgan was winning the fight. Giant hands around Snaky's throat, Horse was squeezing with all his might, whilst the surrounding men yelled for Snaky to fight back. But it was evident to all that the cause was lost.

Billy and Mick remained trapped in the circle of men, no longer the centre of attention but still unable to escape. If they tried, they copped another nick on the cheek or a slash to the arm. Their jackets were already in shreds, their faces and hands bleeding. They stood together, powerless, watching the two men locked in combat. The mob would surely turn on them once Horse had defeated Snaky.

'Coppers!' The young Docker burst through the mob. 'Coppers! Coming down the Stairs!'

The warning had an instant effect. The police were the enemy of the push. Rival gangs had even been known to team up in the presence of their common foe. Men quickly sheathed their knives, snuffed their lamps and gathered their money which lay scattered on the ground.

Horse released his grip on Snaky Ryan.

Through the crowd, as it dispersed, young Ernie Morgan saw his brother on his knees. He couldn't see the man lying on the ground. 'Horse!' he called, hoping his brother wasn't hurt.

Horse turned.

Still on his back, Snaky fumbled inside his jacket for his knife. Ignoring the warning of police and the panic of men fleeing about him, Snaky was bent on one thing—revenge for his dishonour. Horse Morgan would pay for the humiliation he'd suffered.

'Horse!' Ernie called again and, Tim Kendall beside him, he ran to his brother.

Amazed at the sight of the boys, Horse started to rise to his feet. As he did so, Snaky scrambled to one knee and lunged with the knife. Just as Ernie reached Horse.

The blade intended for Horse ripped through the boy's back and into his heart. It took him only a second or so to die. His mouth was open. 'Are you all right, Horse?' he'd been about to say, and his eyes were wide with surprise as he crumpled into his brother's arms.

It all happened in an instant. Billy Kendall and Mick Putman stood dumbfounded, staring as Horse clutched his dead brother. Young Tim Kendall stood staring at the shudder of Ernie's head and the twitch of his body in its death throes.

'Jesus Christ,' the young Docker who'd called the warning whispered, 'he's only a kid.'

Then Horse let out a howl and dropped to his knees, cradling Ernie to him. As if his anguish were a signal, Brougham Street came alive. Police burst upon the scene, whistles squealing, truncheons flailing as men scuttled down alleys and slid behind open doorways of friendly houses. Snaky Ryan was the first to vanish into the night.

Mick Putman fled. Billy grabbed young Tim and made to follow, but Tim was rooted to the spot. He was staring down at Ernie lying in a pool of blood, big Horse Morgan kneeling beside him, rocking back and forth on his heels.

Billy looked about wildly. They were hemmed in. Police were coming from the other end of Brougham Street now.

'Come with me.' It was the young Docker, urging them to follow. Billy half dragged and half carried Tim as they ducked into Windeyer Street, a tiny lane which led into the heart of Woolloomooloo.

In a state of shock, Tim was a dead weight. Billy hoisted the boy over his shoulder as they dodged through alleys and laneways, stumbling now and then, the sound of police whistles sometimes nearby, sometimes from afar. They clambered through holes in fences and straddled low stone walls, they fought their way through lines of washing hanging in backyards, until Billy had lost all sense of direction.

Then, finally, they crossed a street, turned a corner and the young man made for a terrace house with a small porch and yellow shutters. 'In here,' he hissed, opening the front door and ushering Billy inside.

'You're safe here,' he said, closing the door and drawing the living-room curtains. He lit the lamp in the wall bracket. 'Put him down there,' he gestured to the sofa. 'How is he?' he asked as Billy knelt beside Tim.

'He's in shock, I think.'

'What's going on?' It was a woman's voice. In her nightdress, she stood framed in the doorway, and even in the dim glow of the lamp Billy could tell she was beautiful.

'There's been an accident,' the young man said. 'The boy's not hurt, but he's in shock.'

The woman took control immediately. 'Keep him warm,' she said, 'get a blanket,' and she disappeared.

A minute or so later she reappeared, a lamp in one hand and a glass of brandy in the other. She set the lamp down on the table beside the sofa and sat next to Tim, forcing him to drink the fiery liquid. He was starting to shake now. 'That's a good sign,' she said to the others. 'Just one more sip.' And then Tim started to cry.

'He'll be all right.' She rose from the sofa. 'I'm not so sure about you,' she said to Billy. 'Let's have a look at those cuts.'

She pulled a chair up beside the table and Billy sat down gratefully, suddenly aware that he was feeling very shaky. 'Thanks,' he said, taking off his slouch hat and placing it beside him.

Whilst she fetched a bowl of water to bathe his wounds Billy looked closely at the young man for the first time. He was no older than Billy himself. Eighteen, nineteen, he couldn't have been twenty. Dark-haired, heavy-browed, a brooding sort of face. 'Thanks, mate,' Billy said, 'I'll owe you for that.'

The young man took off his cloth cap and hung it on one of the brass pegs on the back of the door. 'You were fools to turn up at the Dockers' game. What did you think you were playing at?' He'd recognised the slouch hats and bandanas—the badges of the Gipps Street Gang—the moment he'd seen Mick and Billy.

'We were only there as seconds for Horse.' Billy didn't need a lecture, he was feeling decidedly sick. He looked with concern at Tim who was gulping for air. 'You all right, mate?'

Tim nodded. He wished he could stop crying, he was trying his hardest, but no amount of air into his lungs seemed to help and he was starting to feel dizzy.

The woman returned. 'Put your head between your knees,' she said to Tim. Then to Billy: 'This might sting a bit.'

Whilst she bathed the cuts on his face, Billy studied her. Late twenties, he guessed, and one of the most beautiful women he'd ever seen. Far too classy for him, even Billy knew that. Full-bodied. Dark hair, loose to her shoulders. And amazing eyes. Such a vivid blue.

She was aware he was studying her. She was used to that. Young and old, most men did. 'So what happened?' she asked.

Before Billy could answer, a boy appeared in the doorway. Dark-haired like the woman and young man, he was dressed in his nightshirt.

'What's happened?' he asked, blearily repeating his mother's words, still half asleep.

'This is my son.' The woman ushered the boy to the sofa. 'This is Robbie,' she said to Tim, 'he's seven, about your age, I reckon.'

Tim shook his head. He wanted to introduce himself, to say, 'No, I'm nine.' He tried desperately to stem his tears but to his embarrassment he couldn't and, as he didn't dare speak, he offered his hand instead.

Robbie shook it. 'G'day,' he said, bewildered but fascinated. The handshake was firm and the boy on the sofa didn't look like a cry-baby. Something terrible must have happened.

'This is Tim.' Billy made the introduction. 'And I'm Billy,' he added, addressing the woman. 'Billy Kendall.'

'Kendall,' she replied with sudden interest. 'Where do you live?'

'He's one of the Gipps Street Gang,' the young man said with a the touch of a sneer to his voice. 'There were three of them there tonight. They busted the Dockers' two-up game.'

The woman gave a shrug of annoyance—she had little time for the push. 'You're from Surry Hills then?'

Billy nodded.

One of the Surry Hills Kendalls, she thought. This must be Samuel and Beth's boy. She'd not seen her father's cousin and his wife since she was a child. She wondered whether she should tell him that they were related, but decided not to bother, there seemed no point.

'I'm Kathleen.' She held out her hand. 'This is my brother Dan, and this is my son Robbie. Robbie O'Shea.'

Chapter Nine

The slaying of young Ernie Morgan shocked the push. But they closed ranks, as they always did upon police investigation and, despite numerous enquiries conducted around Woolloomooloo and Surry Hills, the boy's death remained a mystery. The constabulary, while infuriated, were not surprised, accustomed as they were to the push's code of silence. Even big Horse Morgan swore he hadn't seen his brother's murderer.

'It was dark,' he said, and they could get nothing more out of him.

Two weeks later, when Snaky Ryan was discovered in a Kings Cross alleyway, his throat cut from ear to ear, the police concluded that justice had been served and investigations came to a halt.

Billy Kendall, sickened by the child's death, left the Gipps Street Gang. He applied for a job with the Wunderlich Company, his brother had been urging him to do so for years and, through Benjamin's influence, Billy was quickly accepted. Gone now were the slouch hat and bandana, and he no longer carried a sock filled with sand in the pocket of his jacket. Billy still enjoyed his mates' company, however, sharing a beer at the pub, kicking the footie around, accepting good-naturedly their ragging about his having gone soft.

Billy and Mick had told their families nothing. Their shredded clothing and the cuts to their faces and hands were the result of 'a bit of a stoush with the Riley Street mob'. But when the police arrived on the doorstep, and they were summoned to Darlinghurst Station for questioning, it was obvious that Billy and Mick had both been there that terrible night.

Norah worried about young Tim, who was obviously affected by the news. 'Well of course he knew the Morgan boy,' she said to Beth, 'they played footie together on Fridays, Timmy says. He's so quiet. Keeps to himself all the time. It's not like him, Beth, what should I do?'

'Stop fretting, that's what you should do. It's not good for the baby.' Norah was nearly seven months pregnant now and, healthy as she was, she became easily distressed. 'Let the boy grieve for his friend,' Beth said, 'it's only natural.'

Tim didn't dare tell anyone of what he had seen, but he couldn't erase the images which burned in his brain. Ernie's mouth. Open, about to call a question. Ernie's eyes. Startled, taken by surprise. And then the awful shuddering. First Ernie's head, then his body, twitching, conceding its death.

Billy had tried to help. After the warning instructions. 'Say nothing, Tim,' he'd made Tim promise, 'you've got to button your lip, not a word about that night.' Then he'd said, 'But you can talk to me. If you want to. Would it help?'

Tim shook his head. He wanted to talk. Desperately. But he couldn't.

'I wanted to say thank you,' Billy said, holding out the bunch of flowers he'd bought from the Dutchman's fruit and veg cart at the end of the street. It was a Saturday afternoon and he and Tim were paying a visit to Kathleen O'Shea.

Kathleen wiped her hands on her apron and, with just a touch of suspicion, took the flowers. Men who gave her flowers usually wanted something. Then she smiled, he was little more than a lad after all, and he wasn't wearing his larrikin gear. He looked nice, she thought, clean-shaven, spruced up in his plain brown jacket and clean white shirt. And he'd brought the boy with him. Fair-haired, freckle-faced, the boy was more handsome than she'd realised.

'Hello, Tim,' she said.

'I wanted to say thank you, too.'

'Come inside, I'll put the kettle on.'

They sat in the kitchen, a homey room not unlike their own with pots and utensils hanging from the walls, and Kathleen stoked the stove.

'Robbie's out the back,' she said to Tim. 'He's got a puppy, do you want to go and look?'

'Yep.'

'I'll call you both in when the tea's ready.' As the back door slapped shut behind him, she asked, 'How's he been?'

'Hard to tell,' Billy answered. 'He keeps it locked up inside.'

'Terrible thing for a young boy to see.' She started to fill the kettle.

Billy nodded. She was even more beautiful in the daytime, he was thinking. In her apron, her thick, dark hair pinned untidily up, escaped tendrils resting against her slender neck as she bent over the sink. 'Ernie was his friend.'

'Oh.' She turned around, concerned. And the vivid eyes, circled in the blackest of lashes, met his mesmerised stare.

'Um . . .' Billy looked away, caught out.

Kathleen laughed, she couldn't help it, he was so blatant, and so gauche.

Billy didn't mind. In fact he liked it. Hers was an honest laugh. He felt encouraged, maybe she found him attractive. He grinned back. 'Sorry. Fair cop. I was staring.'

She changed the subject. 'Do you know we're related?'

'What?'

'Sort of. My grandmother was a Kendall.'

'You're having a lend of me.'

'I'll prove it.' She put the kettle on the stove. 'Stay there,' she ordered and trotted upstairs.

Outside in the little backyard, Tim and Robbie were sitting on the ground playing with the pup, a mongrel of indeterminate breed.

'He's a stray,' Robbie explained. 'He followed me home from the park. At least that's what I told Mum,' he admitted. 'I really got him from Johann, the Dutchie's kid down the street. Their bitch had a litter and they drowned the rest. Mum reckons if he gets too big we can't keep him, but I'll get around her.'

The puppy jumped at Tim, smacking its skull against his nose. It hurt, but Tim laughed. For the first time in a month, briefly, the images had left him.

Robbie studied his new friend for a moment or so. There was something he'd been longing to ask. 'I heard them talking about that night,' he said. 'You saw him die, didn't you?'

The images were back. Tim held the pup at arm's length as he stared at Robbie.

'I heard them talking. They said he was only a kid. Only a kid our age.' The heavy brow and the black eyes, in a face older than its years, were intense. 'What was it like watching him die?'

The pup squirmed closer, Tim pushed it away, he didn't want to play any more.

Robbie took the pup into his lap and stroked it gently, calming it. 'Tell me,' he said, sensing Tim's reluctance. 'We'll share secrets. I've got a secret too. You tell me yours and I'll tell you mine.'

'He was my friend,' Tim said, his voice a whisper.

'Yeah.' Robbie's attention was riveted and his calming hand on the pup was lulling the animal to sleep. 'That'd make it worse. Much worse.'

Inside the kitchen Kathleen placed the heavy, leather-bound journal on the table and opened the cover. 'There,' she said, 'see?'

Billy read out loud the childish hand. ' "This journal is the property of Hannah Kendall." '

'Hannah Kendall,' Kathleen announced, 'my grandmother.'

He was very aware of her shoulder touching his as she bent over the table, and he tried to keep his eyes from the generous swell of her breasts beneath the apron's bib. He concentrated on the journal.

' "Kathleen O'Shea," ' he went on. ' "October, 1882." And that's you.'

'That's me.'

He turned the page.

'No,' she said, 'that's all.' She closed the journal and picked it up. 'It's a woman's diary, men aren't supposed to read it.'

'Oh, I see,' his grin was suggestive, 'we're not supposed to read it but I bet it's all about us.' He gave a lecherous wriggle of his eyebrows, which was Billy's way of flirting. 'I bet old Hannah's written a few things in there that'd make a bloke blush.' He probably didn't stand a chance, he thought, but what the hell, a man could only try. He wondered what had happened to Kathleen's husband. Dead probably. She'd have to be a widow, no man would walk out on a woman like Kathleen O'Shea.

She bristled. 'You think it's all about men, do you?'

'Yeah, it's a woman's diary.' He was too naive to read the warnings.

'It's not about men at all,' she replied tartly, 'it's about Sydney in the old days. These are stories told to my grandmother by her own grandfather, she wrote them all down.'

'Oh.' Put in his place, Billy looked dutifully chastened. 'Sorry.'

Kathleen was defending neither her grandmother nor the diary; she herself would have enjoyed sharing her grandmother's intimate girlish gossip. But the little she had read of the journal's contents had in fact been rather heavy going, and she'd added nothing to its pages herself, apart from recording the deaths of her father and mother and the date of her son's birth.

Billy's words did not offend Kathleen, but the manner in which he said them did. He was making a play for her and she was disappointed. She instinctively liked young Billy Kendall and, whilst his open admiration was flattering and harmless, she did not welcome his lewd suggestions—she received enough of those from other quarters.

'I showed you the diary because you're a Kendall,' she added, talking primly to him as a schoolmistress might to a wayward child, 'not in order for you to make smutty remarks.'

'I'm sorry, really I am.' Billy cursed himself. He'd acted like she was a factory girl outside the Pig and Whistle, no wonder she'd found him insulting. A classy number like Kathleen O'Shea wouldn't be used to that sort of treatment. 'I didn't mean to . . . you know . . .' he stammered. 'I wasn't really trying to . . .'

His voice trailed off miserably, reminding her again that he was just a gauche lad.

She'd over-reacted, she told herself. She'd been doing that quite a bit lately. Fed up with men, that was the problem.

'It's all right, no offense taken. The kettle's boiling. Will you fill the pot while I put this back, then give the boys a yell?'

Billy willingly jumped to his feet, glad that all was forgiven. 'So how are we related?' he called up the stairs. 'Fifty-sixth cousins or what?'

'I don't know, I haven't worked it out, but it doesn't much matter does it?'

''Spose not.' Billy started to fill the teapot.

In the yard Tim had left out nothing. In a monotone, he'd recounted to Robbie every step of Ernie's death and, as he'd said the words out loud, one image replacing another, he had found great relief. To his amazement, when he'd finished and there was nothing left to describe, his mind was blissfully blank.

Robbie had breathed not a word, but sat cross-legged, the sleeping pup in his lap, staring at Tim, transfixed with a child's ghoulish fascination.

He remained silent for a moment after Tim had finished. Then, 'No wonder you were in shock that night,' he said. 'That's what I heard them say,' he added. "He's in shock", that's what Billy said, I was listening on the stairs.' Another pause. 'Do you have nightmares?'

'Yep.'

'I would too.'

The back door opened and Billy yelled, 'The tea's ready, boys.'

Robbie rolled the pup off him and they got to their feet.

'So what's your secret then?' Tim asked.

'You remember my Uncle Dan? The bloke who brought you and Billy home that night?' Tim nodded. 'Well, he's an O'Shea too.'

'So?'

'So he's my mother's brother,' Robbie announced importantly and a second or two passed whilst Tim looked blank. 'So it means my mum's not married,' Robbie explained impatiently.

'Oh.'

'Yeah. I'm a bastard.'

'And that's your secret?' Tim laughed. 'Hell, Robbie, that's not a fair trade.'

They'd finished their tea and Billy and Tim were about to leave when Dan O'Shea arrived home. He didn't look too happy to see Billy. Despite the common stand taken against the police enquiries, there was still no love lost between the Dockers and the Gipps Street Gang. Particularly since the murder of Snaky Ryan. The Dockers all knew Horse Morgan had done it, and there had been no retribution. If a Docker had lost his baby brother the same way Horse Morgan had, it was accepted that he'd seek revenge too. But the fact remained that if the Gipps Street Gang boys had not trespassed on the Dockers' turf that night, there would have been no police investigation. And the Dockers, like all push gangs, did not like to be investigated.

Dan said as much when Billy tried to thank him. 'I owe you for that night, Dan,' Billy said, 'and I wanted to say thanks.'

'You made a lot of trouble for us,' Dan growled. 'The Dockers didn't like it, they didn't like it at all.'

Kathleen glared at her young brother. He was being rude, and she didn't like any discussion of the push in her house, certainly not in the presence of her son. Robbie was going to be kept well away from the gangs if Kathleen O'Shea had anything to do with it.

'Fair enough, we did wrong,' Billy accepted the rebuke.

Dan scowled. It was difficult to pick a fight with a bloke who didn't want one. 'You look like a toff,' he said.

'Yeah.' Billy fingered the lapel of his conservative brown jacket. 'I've left the gang,' he smiled self-deprecatingly, 'gone real straight, working for Wunderlichs even.'

Dan didn't smile back. 'Better leave before it gets dark. Walking around here dressed like that, people might get the wrong idea.' It was a threat and Billy knew it.

'That's enough, Dan,' Kathleen said.

Billy didn't rise to the bait. 'Thanks anyway, for that night,' he said, but he didn't offer his hand, knowing that Dan didn't want it. 'Thanks for the tea, Kathleen.'

'Any time, Billy,' she said pointedly, looking at her brother. 'You're welcome any time.'

Kathleen saw them to the front door whilst Dan sat in the kitchen, his feet on the table, drinking a cup of tea.

'Do you want to come back and play with the pup?' Robbie asked Tim.

'Yep. When?'

'Tomorrow. We can take him to the park.'

When they'd gone, Kathleen confronted her brother. 'Why did you have to be so rude? He only came to thank us.'

'He came because he fancies you, just like all the others.'

There was contempt in his voice and Kathleen felt angry. What right did he have to scorn her? But she tried to answer reasonably. 'What's happened to you, Dan? We used to be good friends. Why have you changed? What have I done?'

He didn't answer but lifted his feet from the table, rose, and put on his cap and the jacket he'd draped over the chair.

'What's wrong with you, tell me!' His sullen silence was annoying her beyond measure. 'It's the damn push, isn't it?' she snapped when he still refused to answer. 'That Dockers' Gang'll be the death of you, they're turning you into a thug.'

He walked out of the kitchen. 'I'm going to the pub to meet the lads.' His tone was surly. He wished to God that she'd stop nagging. She'd nagged him since he was eleven years old and he used to like it then, in the days when she'd been more mother than sister, as well as best friend and hero to boot. But her loyalties lay elsewhere these days, and she'd lost the right to nag.

She followed him through the front room and grabbed his arm as he opened the door. 'Haven't any of you learned from the death of that boy?' she hissed with anger and frustration. 'Are you all that stupid?'

'I won't be back till late, the lads have got some plans.' He patted the pocket of his jacket meaningfully, intimating he was carrying a knife. He wasn't, but he wanted to annoy her. He hadn't liked the way Billy Kendall had looked at her, and he wondered whether she had encouraged him.

'Don't be a fool, Dan.' She pulled at his arm as he turned to go. 'Don't be a fool. Listen to me!'

He wrenched his arm from her grip. 'Why?' he snarled. 'Why should I listen to a whore!' The words were out before he could stop himself, and he regretted them immediately. 'I'm going, Kath.' And he left, avoiding the hurt in her eyes.

As Kathleen boiled the kettle again, for hot water to wash the cups, she tried to erase the words from her mind, telling herself he hadn't meant them. But he had, she knew it. And there was anger beneath her hurt. So what if, over the years, she'd accepted the odd gift from a man, did that make her a whore? She'd never walked the streets and sold her body. She'd never slept with a man if she didn't wish to. Well, no, that wasn't quite true, but it still didn't make her a whore.

She banged the teacups into the wash bowl, chipping the side of one. And if she was a whore, as her brother said, then what did that make him? A pimp surely. A pimp lived off the earnings of a whore, didn't he? Kathleen seethed with moral indignation. She worked hard, legitimately, for the money that kept them alive! By God, she thought, if Dan was here now, if he hadn't run off to the pub to escape her, she'd have a thing or two to tell him.

Kathleen O'Shea had been nineteen years old, and her young

brother Dan eleven, when their mother Dotty had died. It had been less than a year after the killing of Paddy O'Shea, but his death was not the cause, Dotty had not given up. Dotty had fought on to support her family, slaving away in a milliner's workshop, her daughter by her side. Young Dan was to stay in school, she maintained, no block boy's job for him.

It was the smallpox which claimed Dotty, as it had so many others. Just a rash on her body at first. It didn't show on her face, and Dotty kept quiet about it in case it was something infectious. She couldn't afford to be sent to the quarantine hospital and lose her pay, or worse, lose her job. It might not be there when she got better, there were too many queuing for employment.

But a week later, when the sores erupted, she could no longer hide her predicament. The doctor told her it was only a matter of days before she'd be highly infectious and her family would be at risk.

'Do you people not know of the vaccination?' Doctor Davies said as he treated the pus-filled sores. 'Do you not read the newspapers? Do you not see the notices? Do you not know that this can be prevented?'

Dotty nodded. 'I've seen the notices,' she said, 'but no-one around here gets the vaccination.'

It was a typical reaction and Hector Davies, a passionate Welshman, was exasperated. People took no note of warnings and heeded no advice. The government was greatly to blame, in Hector's opinion, physicians had been lobbying for compulsory vaccination laws since his own grandfather's time. But to no avail.

In England in the 1790s the British physician, Edward Jenner, had observed that many of the local milkmaids appeared to be immune to one of the most deadly diseases known to man. Tests proved that the milkmaids were infected with the milder virus, cowpox. Jenner's resulting vaccine, hailed as the most profound medical discovery of the century, was made instantly available, and shipments of the cowpox vaccine had arrived in Sydney as early as 1804. Doctors had been loudly vocal in promoting its use, but the government had remained unconvinced of the necessity of compulsory vaccination laws.

For nigh on ninety years the vaccine had been available, and yet still people were dying of smallpox. By the hundreds. To Hector Davies, the situation was ludicrous.

Like his grandfather before him, Hector was an agitator for medical reform, and a deeply frustrated man. But he would not give in to apathy. He would draw up yet another petition and, with the support of his fellow physicians, he would present it yet again to the government.

'You must be transferred to the Coast Hospital for Infectious Diseases,' he said wearily, doubtful that the woman would survive.

Dotty nodded. She prayed that her job at the workshop would still be there when she got better.

'You may go with your mother,' the doctor said. 'Kathleen, is it not?' The girl nodded. She was a beauty, Hector thought, and educated to a degree—she had written down his instructions—but what would her fate be without a mother to guide her? 'In several days, however, when your mother is in her most dangerous state, you will not be allowed in her company, for that is when the disease will be at its most contagious, do you understand?'

Dotty died in the hospital two weeks later, the bacteria which had infected her sores causing damage to her heart and lungs. She was buried in the Coast Cemetery and Kathleen, young Dan with her, regularly travelled by tram to visit Dotty's grave overlooking the rocky coastline of Botany Bay.

Kathleen continued to work her ten-hour shifts at Abraham's Millinery but her salary barely covered the rent and their food and clothing. Dan begged to be allowed to leave school, he could earn good money as a block boy, he insisted, or working on the newspaper delivery drays. But Kathleen refused to listen. 'Mum and Pa wouldn't like it,' she said. 'You'll stay at school.'

When Mr Abraham himself singled her out from the fifteen women employed in the workshop, Kathleen felt very privileged.

'Receptionist work requires a pleasant manner and appearance above all else, my dear,' he said in his perfect, clipped voice with its trace of Polish origin. 'You have the necessary qualifications, and I am sure you will not let me down.'

'Yes, Mr Abraham,' she bobbed a sort of curtsy, eager to please.

Then the words which were magic to her ears. 'Of course there will be a substantial rise in your wages befitting your new position.'

'Thank you, Mr Abraham.'

On receipt of her first week's wages, Kathleen visited the bargain basement of Kendle and Streatham's Emporium and bought herself two new blouses and a tailored jacket and skirt. She was riddled with guilt as she did so, but it was necessary, she told herself. She must look smart and respectable now that she was in daily contact with the buyers and with Mr Abraham's business associates.

Kathleen was aware that her rise in station met with the deepest of disapproval from Elsa Duckworth, the martinet in charge of the women who slaved away in the workshop. At the end of each day, when Elsa delivered the quota sheets to the reception desk, she looked Kathleen up and down and gave a derisive snort which openly said that Kathleen had been selected for her looks alone.

Elsa's disdain, however, only served to spur Kathleen on, and she quickly learned not only the filing system and the paperwork required, but the names and personal details of all the regular buyers. 'Mr Saxon,' she'd say, 'and how is your new baby?' Or, sympathetically, 'I hope Mrs Littlemore will be better soon.'

All of which pleased Mr Abraham. Kathleen had seen little of him when she'd worked in the back room but now she saw him every day and he was always exceedingly courteous. 'Is that a new bolero, my dear?' he'd say in a fatherly way. 'Most attractive.' He always noticed what she was wearing, and Kathleen went to great pains to look her best. It was the least she could do, she told herself, for Mr Abraham was a man of great style. Always impeccably dressed, with a neatly trimmed goatee, Mr Abraham even held a monocle to his right eye when he was studying his paperwork. The monocle deeply impressed Kathleen.

David Abraham had indeed employed young Kathleen O'Shea because of her appearance. Under normal circumstances he would have instructed Elsa Duckworth to place an advertisement seeking someone with the proper qualifications, but he had noticed Kathleen in the back room. He had no ulterior motive beyond the pleasure of her appearance—he liked beautiful things. And if it proved that the girl could not handle the job then he could easily have her returned to the workshop.

But as the days and weeks passed, David Abraham found himself mesmerised, watching her through the glass windows of his office as she busied herself at her desk. Kathleen O'Shea was more than pleasing to look at, Kathleen O'Shea was a true beauty.

He couldn't help himself. It hadn't been his original plan at all but, 'Do you enjoy theatrical performances, Miss O'Shea?' he asked her one Friday night.

'I don't know, Mr Abraham, I've never been to one.' The sapphire eyes met his with disarming honesty.

'Mr Coles has kindly supplied me with two tickets to a performance tomorrow night and I wondered whether you might like to accompany me.'

William Coles was the proprietor of the Bohemians, a theatrical company named after the cultural movement which had recently been embraced by Sydney's artistic circles. His company performed at the circus and entertainment centre on the west side of George Street. Modelled on Buffalo Bill Cody's American venture, the performances were staged in an enormous marquee, with tiered seating around the canvas walls. Wild West shows, circuses and melodramas, including many Australian plays, were staged there, all proving immensely popular with the general public. As Abraham's Millinery supplied the headwear used in the productions—anything from Red Indian headdresses and cowboy hats, to police helmets and damsels' bonnets—David Abraham had any number of seats at his beck and call.

'Oh yes,' overwhelmed as she was by the invitation, Kathleen didn't hesitate for a minute, 'I'd like that very much.'

'Shall I call for you?'

'No, no, I'll meet you out the front.'

'Excellent.' Probably better that way, he thought. 'At seven o'clock, shall we say?'

'Yes, Mr Abraham. Thank you.'

Kathleen saw *The Mystery of the Hansom Cab* that Saturday night and, as she fell in love with the world of entertainment, David Abraham fell in love with her.

One month and many outings later, including an evening at the Theatre Royal, a performance at the Tivoli, a vaudeville show and a production of *Ned Kelly* by the Bohemians, David summoned up the nerve to kiss her. Outside her own front door. He'd dropped her home in a hansom cab and the driver was waiting.

He didn't know why he was nervous. He was fifty years old, he'd been married, and he'd had affairs, though not many, since the death of his wife fifteen years previously. He was not inexperienced with women. But she was so young, and so nubile, surely she must find him unattractive. The kiss was tentative as he awaited her response.

Kathleen was a virgin, but she was accustomed to kissing. She'd kissed and fumbled before and was an expert at knowing when to stop. She was not at all offended by Mr Abraham's show of intimacy—despite his insistence, she still had trouble calling him David. She liked him and she wanted to be nice and, besides, she owed him a lot. She returned his kiss with grateful fervour, instinctively opening her mouth to his and pressing her body against him.

For a moment David lost himself. His hand fumbled for her breast. His eyes were closed, his breathing heavy, he hadn't intended for it to happen like this but he didn't want it to stop.

Kathleen was instantly aroused; for some time now she'd been longing to know what it was like to be with a man, and she was more than ready to find out. She responded to his passion with equal intensity and, her arousal driving him mad, David grabbed at her skirts and ground his body against hers like a twenty-year-old on fire. He wanted to take her up against her own porch railing, right there in the lamplit street.

Then he opened his eyes and saw the hansom cab driver. The man, from his perfect viewpoint atop the cab, was grinning. He saluted David with his whip as if to say, 'Good on you, guv', and David broke away, mortified.

His heart was beating wildly and he felt a little dizzy. He turned his back on the cab driver and sat on the railing as he fumbled for the phial of laudanum he kept in the pocket of his vest. He hoped he wasn't going to have one of his turns, he wasn't used to this sort of excitement.

'Are you ill?' Kathleen asked, concerned.

'No, no, my dear,' he assured her, waving the phial under his nose, his head quickly clearing.

Moments later he made his farewell as if nothing had happened, and Kathleen thanked him for a most enjoyable evening as she always did. When he got out of the cab in Glebe Point Road, David refused to look at the driver.

The die was cast, however, and Kathleen and David both knew it. After a performance of *The Squatter's Daughter* he asked her home for supper, and their sexual union was a foregone conclusion.

She was a virgin, she told him, a fact which, given their encounter on the porch, David had not expected, and which at first he found a little unnerving. He made love to her as gently as he could, taking care to cause her as little pain as possible, but after the initial hurdle had been passed and her sexuality unleashed, it appeared Kathleen's passion knew no bounds. They made love twice that night and again in the morning when her hands awoke him from a deep sleep, playing on his body, demanding pleasure. It had been twenty years since his virility had been put to such a test and David was exhausted. Exhausted, but deeply, passionately and obsessively in love.

It was difficult to disguise their affair at work, particularly for David whose feelings were clearly readable every time he looked at Kathleen, and Elsa Duckworth quickly spread the word in the back room that Kathleen O'Shea was a slut.

Although she dared say nothing out loud, Elsa Duckworth tut-tutted and sneered in Kathleen's presence, making her disgust apparent in numerous ways, all of which Kathleen ignored. She was blissfully content and she refused to allow any unpleasantness to encroach upon her ideal existence.

She was not in love with David Abraham, but she was very fond of him, and immensely grateful for the change in her circumstances. No longer did she need to scrimp and save in order to support herself and her brother. David had increased her salary handsomely, and he regularly gave her gifts, the more expensive of which she sold, salting the added revenue away for a rainy day.

Each Saturday they went to a performance. Sometimes to the theatre, sometimes to the vaudeville, but most often to the Bohemians. Kathleen loved the magic of their colour and pageantry, the world of excitement and make-believe. After the performance, and sometimes supper with Mr Coles and his players, they would return to David's house and make love, though Kathleen refused to stay with him more than one night a week. She needed to be with her young brother, she said, she was like a mother to Dan.

They'd been lovers for four months when Kathleen discovered she was pregnant. She was dismayed, it was all her own fault, she told herself, she should have been more careful. But she did not agonise over her decision; there was one option and one only.

Her gratitude to David Abraham for his kindness and generosity demanded that she bring him no shame. Besides, commonsense told her that no man would desire a mistress with a child. She must leave both David and her position at Abraham's Millinery. But she would keep her condition a secret for as long as possible. She would need to squirrel away all the money she could in order to see her through her confinement, and to support herself and Dan until she was able to work again.

David Abraham, in the meantime, was in a terrible quandary. He desperately wanted to marry Kathleen, but dared not ask for fear of frightening her away. She was only just twenty, why should a young girl, and one of such beauty, agree to share her life with an old man like him? He knew she was fond of him, but her affection was bought with gifts and a salary far beyond that of an office worker. Even his money would not keep her for long; she would meet a young man and be swept off her feet. It could happen any day now.

A month went by, and another, and he wondered whether perhaps, after all, there was room for hope. He started to pluck up the courage. Next Saturday, he told himself. But then Saturday came and went, the courage he'd summoned up during the week deserting him as he found himself once again in awe of her vibrancy, her youth and her beauty.

Kathleen was nearly four months pregnant and the swell of her belly was evident. She reported for work on Monday knowing that she would have to leave at the end of the week. She would collect her wages on the Friday and leave a note on her desk, sealed and addressed to Mr Abraham, explaining that she had met someone else. It seemed cruel, but it was the only way, she knew, otherwise he would call on her to discover why she had gone.

David did not come into the office that Monday morning, though no-one knew why, for he'd left no message as he usually did. Then, in the late afternoon, the employees of Abraham's Millinery were called together in the workroom and informed by the company's solicitor of the terrible news.

'It is with great regret I must inform you,' he said, 'that Mr Abraham has passed away. A heart attack it is believed. On Sunday, in the evening.'

On Sunday! Kathleen stared at the solicitor, shaking her head in disbelief. It was not possible. She had been with David that very morning.

Beside her, Elsa Duckworth was staring at Kathleen. She could see the girl's reaction and she knew what it meant.

'There will be no more work today,' the solicitor informed them, 'you may all go home. But you will report as usual tomorrow when Mr Abraham's sister and nephew will have arrived from Melbourne. Mrs Bloomfield and her son are to take over the business and will instruct you all accordingly. I am sure you need fear no changes in your employ. As a mark of respect, the workshop will be closed on Wednesday for Mr Abraham's funeral. I am informed that no salaries will be docked and employees are welcome to attend the service. Thank you for your attention.'

The crowd dispersed, some girls in tears, others muttering their shock. Elsa Duckworth, herself in tears, her face white with grief, hissed under her breath at Kathleen. 'Hussy.' Elsa Duckworth had been in love with David Abraham for the twenty years of her employ.

But Kathleen didn't hear her. She walked back to the front office, numb with disbelief.

A week later she found herself summoned to Mr Abraham's office.

'Your services will no longer be required, Miss O'Shea. You will oblige me by clearing the front office of your belongings as soon as possible.'

Irene Bloomfield, seated authoritatively behind David's desk, her hands spread on the tabletop before her, did not look the least bit like her brother. A big woman with spongy features, she had none of David's dapper style. Her clothes, though expensive and fashionable, sat awkwardly on her bulky frame, creases and bulges appearing here and there as if the fabric were seeking a shape which did not exist.

Her son, hovering beside her, would probably end up the same way. He was a pallid young man whose skin appeared never to have been exposed to the sun.

Mrs Bloomfield continued, 'In fact, given your lack of qualifications, I find it remarkable that my brother selected you for a position of such responsibility in the first place.'

Oscar Bloomfield did not find it at all remarkable. He did, however, find it nothing short of incredible that old Uncle David had bedded such a glorious young creature, for if they were to believe the forewoman, that was exactly what had happened.

'Perhaps we are being a little hasty, Mother,' he interjected. 'Uncle David would not have suffered sloppiness or inefficiency, perhaps Miss O'Shea . . .'

His mother did not so much as cast a glance in his direction. 'That will be all,' she concluded. 'Miss Duckworth will assist you in the clearing of your belongings,' Elsa Duckworth had intimated that the girl might well steal items of value if she were not supervised, 'and she will see you from the premises. Good day.'

Kathleen did not look at Elsa Duckworth as she collected her few meagre items from the front desk. A mirror, a comb, two handkerchiefs. She did not even take the fine-tipped pen and the little brass inkwell David had given her, for fear she would be accused of stealing.

'He was never a well man,' Elsa Duckworth said, her eyes swollen from last night's weeping, 'and then you had to come along. It was you who killed him. He'd still be alive if it wasn't for you.'

Kathleen walked out of the front office and down the stairs. 'Good riddance!' she heard Elsa Duckworth call out behind her. 'Harlot! Slut!'

She left without looking back.

Four and a half months later Kathleen gave birth to her son in the little upstairs bedroom of her house in Woolloomooloo. As the months passed, the money she had saved dwindled alarmingly. With reluctance she allowed Dan to leave school—the baby must come first, they both agreed—but his meagre pay working on the newspaper delivery was not enough and Kathleen knew she must find a job.

One Friday night she left baby Robbie, now six months old, in Dan's care, and visited Mr Coles backstage after the Bohemians' evening performance.

'I wondered if you might give me a job, Mr Coles.' She got straight to the point. 'I am at present unemployed.'

William Coles looked her up and down; he remembered her of course, he'd always been impressed by her beauty. 'Can you sing, my dear?'

'Not that I know of.'

'Can you dance?'

'No.'

'Can you act?'

'I've never tried.'

None of which mattered, William Coles thought, looks like hers were always good stage dressing.

'I thought I might perhaps work behind the scenes,' Kathleen pleaded. 'I could help sew the costumes and make the scenery. I am not afraid of hard work.'

'That would be sheer waste, my dear, we shall give you a try.'

Kathleen's talent was not vast, but she proved co-ordinated enough to manage simple dance routines, and her voice, though not strong, was tuneful enough.

William Coles was pleased with his latest acquisition and before long Kathleen had a strong following of ardent admirers who were convinced that beauty was talent. Even the odd newspaper critic was duped. 'In a minor role, the gifted Miss Kathleen O'Shea brings a refreshing fillip to the ranks of the Bohemian players,' said the variety columnist of the *Sydney Morning Herald*.

Kathleen quickly realised that the world of entertainment was not the magic fairyland which had once so enchanted her, but sheer hard work for those employed in it. She enjoyed her moments onstage, the boisterousness of the audience as it booed the villain, cheered the hero and shrilly whistled its approval at the appearance of beauty—more often than not Kathleen's—but she was never onstage for very long, her roles always being minor. William Coles was no fool, he knew the difference between beauty and talent. When Kathleen was not actually performing, she was busily helping others with their quick costume changes, assisting the backstage workers or setting up the properties for the next scene.

She liked the members of the company, an energetic, rowdy lot in the main and, as she was not competitive, she was popular with her co-workers. In awe of those with true talent, and aware of her own limitations, Kathleen was forgiven her beauty by the women and admired for it by the men, a number of whom tried, without success, to seduce her.

Kathleen's refusal to succumb to the actors' advances was not due to any timidity on her part. It wasn't even because she found them unattractive; indeed several male members of the company she found most sexually appealing. But her discovery that work in the theatre was arduous had been quickly followed by her discovery that actors were not particularly wealthy or stable. In fact actors had very little to offer Kathleen, who needed a father for her child.

It was amongst the ranks of her admirers that she searched, accepting invitations to the Athenaeum Club, the Cafe Français, the Dawn and Dusk Club, all the fashionable nightspots where, in the social potpourri of after-show suppers, artistes mingled with the aristocracy of Sydney and anyone could meet anyone, and most hoped that they would.

After several such suppers with an admirer whom she decided she liked, Kathleen would accompany him to his home or hotel and sleep with him. Over the ensuing weeks such a relationship more often than not resulted in at least one expensive gift. Sometimes two, or even three, all of which she took to the pawnbroker in Pitt Street.

Eventually, when she thought the time was ripe, and when she felt a genuine affection for her benefactor, Kathleen would invite him home to meet her child. That was inevitably the end of the relationship.

Kathleen looked down at the chipped cup in her hand and wondered whether she should keep it, it was one of the good ones. No, damn it, she could afford to buy more, she could buy a whole new set if she wanted to. How dare Dan call her a whore! But her initial anger had abated, and he was probably right, she thought, when all was said and done.

She peered through the door at the clock on the living-room wall. Time to get Robbie his tea before she left for the theatre.

Kathleen no longer worked for the Bohemians. She was now employed at the Tivoli Theatre in Castlereagh Street. Her talent being insufficient to get her into the chorus, she served more as stage dressing, a term which she'd learned over the past several years applied to those with no more to offer than beauty. The work was boring and, with constant costume changes, tiring. Furthermore, the Tivoli was far more regimented than Mr Coles had been. Dress codes were strict. Members of the company were expected to arrive and depart the stage door smartly dressed; shabby appearances would not be tolerated, the queues of fans waiting to see the performers expected glamour. And if a member of the company was late, as Kathleen often was, there was a shilling's fine to be paid to the stage manager.

The Tiv, however, paid twice as much as the Bohemians and attracted a more sophisticated clientele, so Kathleen had little option but to accept its rules. At twenty-eight years of age she was running out of time. She doubted a woman of thirty would be employed as stage dressing. Besides, she needed the admirers the Tivoli offered.

Kathleen had long given up finding a father for Robbie amongst her stage-door Johnnies, but the gifts she received from them augmented her income so dramatically that she could not afford to ignore them. She wondered if Lewis Carlingford would be in the audience tonight. She supposed he would, he'd been there each Saturday night for the past six weeks. She didn't particularly like Lewis Carlingford but she'd recently broken her rule about sleeping with only those whom she liked. The brooch he'd given her last week had fetched twenty pounds at the pawnbroker's.

The back door slapped open and Robbie appeared with the puppy in his arms. He'd gone outside as soon as his mother and Dan had started arguing. They argued a lot these days and Robbie hated it.

'Put him out the back,' she said automatically. 'The pup stays out the back, you know the rules. And wash your hands, tea'll be ready in a few minutes.'

He sat at the table whilst she heated the stew. 'Can me and Tim take the pup to the park tomorrow?' he asked.

'I've an even better idea,' she said. 'Mr De Haan has offered to take us out in his trap. We could go all the way to Watsons Bay if you like. We'll take a picnic and you can ask Tim along.'

Robbie nodded. 'That'd be good.' She ladled the stew onto his plate. 'Dan doesn't like the Dutchie.'

'Then we won't ask Dan along, there won't be room for him anyway. And don't call Mr De Haan the Dutchie.'

'Why not? Everybody else does.'

'Because I don't want you to, that's why not.'

'He doesn't mind,' Robbie muttered under his breath as he tucked into his stew.

Could Otto De Haan be the reason for her brother's outburst, Kathleen wondered. And suddenly it all made sense. Of course, that was it, Dan was jealous. He'd been like a father to Robbie for all these years, and then Otto De Haan had come along. Kathleen smiled to herself, relieved to have discovered the answer. She'd have to have a serious talk with Dan—Otto De Haan was no threat to their lives. He was a lonely widower and she felt sorry for him, that was all. Otto's wife had died during the sea voyage from Holland, and he had been left with a six-year-old son to bring up on his own in a new country. Kathleen enjoyed his company well enough, but she wasn't sleeping with him. What was the point? He had no money. Poor dear Dan. He'd called her a whore because of the one innocent relationship she'd had in her life. My goodness, she thought, if only he knew the half of it!

'Not long to go by the looks of things, you're about ready to pop, you are.'

Norah gave an involuntary start and turned to confront Posie Brown. Posie lived in Wexford Street a half a block down from the Kendalls and was vociferous in her criticism of Norah. 'Miss High-and-Mighty. Who does she think she is?' she'd proclaim to all and sundry, and she had good reason, for it was plainly evident that Norah considered Posie common.

Posie Brown lived openly with a man to whom she was not married, she dyed her hair a ginger-gold, and she worked behind the bar of the Crown and Anchor. Not that there was any harm in that, Norah would hastily add when she caught Ben's disapproving look, there were good women working behind bars, she was sure, but not the way Posie did. Not drinking and smoking and spitting like a man, at least that's the way rumour had it. Norah preferred not to be associated with Posie Brown, and Posie Brown knew it.

'Thought you'd be shy of parading yourself like that. You of all people.'

If Norah had taken the time, she might have registered the note of approval in Posie's voice. Pregnancy must have mellowed Norah Kendall, Posie thought, it was good to see her out with her huge, fat belly. But as it was, covered with confusion and embarrassment, and furious at having been caught out when she'd thought she'd be able to pop up to the corner cart without being seen, Norah turned her back on the woman. She accepted her bag of turnips and chokos from the greengrocer and clasped her shawl about her. When she turned to face Posie, she was composed, although a little flushed in the cheeks.

'I have indeed remained at home during the period of my confinement.' It was her intention to sound superior, which was always Norah's way of defence, but profound embarrassment lent an unpleasant icy edge to her tone. 'I consider it only proper.' And she started to move off down the street.

Posie, outraged that her pleasant greeting had been so deliberately snubbed, followed. 'Con-fain-ment,' she said mockingly, her voice shrill, 'oon-ly propp-aar, well, listen to you Miss Hoity-Toity.'

Norah hastened her pace, her face now crimson, her heart beating quickly. A man and woman passing by had turned to look at her. Only a block to go, but it seemed so far away.

'A person tries to exchange the time of day and she doesn't get so much as a nod in her direction.' Posie was performing for the passers-by, enjoying Norah's humiliation. It was time Norah Kendall copped a dressing-down, she'd been asking for it for long enough.

Posie trotted along beside Norah, a skip to her step. 'Now I aa-sk you, is that po-laite bee-haviour?' She gave a raucous laugh, pleased with herself, noting Nellie Putman on her balcony, watching. Good, Posie liked an audience.

Norah couldn't help herself, she was only several steps from her front door, she should have dived inside without a word. But she didn't. She whirled on Posie Brown.

'Get away from me!' she cried with a touch of hysteria. 'Get away from me, you common, awful woman!'

Posie had only been having fun, teaching Miss Stuck-Up a bit of a lesson, but Miss Stuck-Up had gone too far, and Posie was suddenly angry.

'Just who the bleedin' hell do you think you are?' she hissed, thrusting her face close to Norah's, her voice ugly now. 'You reckon you're too good for the likes of us, don't you?'

Norah took the last couple of steps and fumbled with the front-door handle. She had to escape, two women had stopped in the street and were openly watching.

'Well, you listen to me, Lady Muck.' Posie followed her, right to the door. 'Your husband isn't above us common lot, you ask Maureen at the Crown and Anchor.'

Norah heard the words and froze. She felt sick as she turned.

'Saw him myself I did,' Posie enjoyed the shock on Norah's face, 'coming downstairs with Maureen McLaughlan, late on Saturday night, you ask him!' And she left as Norah once more fumbled with the door handle, her eyes blinded by tears.

Nellie Putman had watched the proceedings from her balcony, but hadn't been able to hear what Posie had said. A mixture of curiosity and a genuine desire to help led Nellie downstairs and through the kitchen to knock at the Kendalls' back door.

As she closed the front door, Norah was gasping, she couldn't seem to get her breath, and she hoped she wasn't going to be sick. She ran to the kitchen for a glass of water.

Beth was there. She'd just that minute come downstairs from her sewing room to make a pot of tea. 'You've been out, Norah,' she said surprised, 'that's not like you.' She stoked the coals in the grate. 'Not that I think there's any harm in a bit of a walk in your condition . . .'

Norah sat at the table, swallowing hard, trying to control herself. She'd expected Beth to be upstairs and the house deserted. 'Just to the corner cart,' she managed to say. Then she burst out sobbing.

'Good God, girl, what's wrong?' Beth quickly filled a glass of water and forced Norah to drink it.

Between sips, she coughed and choked and sobbed. 'Posie Brown,' she said, 'Posie Brown said that Ben . . .' but she couldn't go on.

'Drink it all down, there's a good girl,' said Beth, giving her a clean tea towel to blow her nose. 'Drink it all down and then you can tell me.'

But Norah had to say the words, she couldn't keep them inside. 'Posie Brown said that Ben slept with Maureen McLaughlan,' it came out in a rush, 'at the Crown and Anchor on Saturday night.'

'Drink the water, there's a good girl.' Beth was buying time, she wasn't sure how to tackle this one, it had the ring of truth. She knew that Ben had come home late on Saturday night, and a little the worse for wear by the sounds of things—she'd heard him clumping up the stairs more heavily than usual.

She saw Nellie Putman approaching the open back door and was grateful for the diversion. Nellie could be helpful at times like this, Beth wasn't good at telling lies and they needed to make light of the situation.

'He came home late on Saturday,' Norah mopped her eyes with the tea towel, 'and he was drunk.'

'A night with the boys, he said the next morning, and what's wrong with that on a Saturday? Why, Nellie, come in, I've just put the kettle on.' The older women exchanged glances, Beth's eyes asking for help.

'What's the matter, lovey?' Nellie plumped herself down in one of the chairs and Beth had to edge around her bulk to put the cups and the dish of biscuits on the table. 'I saw Posie Brown giving you a hard old time of it all the way down the street.'

Norah sat primly up in her chair, wishing that Nellie would go away. She needed to talk to Beth, Beth was the only person she could talk to, the only person she'd ever been able to talk to. Why had Nellie intruded? Why had Beth asked her in? Then, to her horror, Norah heard her mother-in-law say, 'Posie Brown reckons that Ben slept with Maureen McLaughlan, at the Crown and Anchor on Saturday night.'

Beth didn't look at Nellie as she lifted the tea canister down from the shelf, she just hoped that Nellie would know what to say.

The statement was so brutal that Norah once more lost control. Despite the presence of Nellie Putman and regardless of maintaining appearances, she buried her face in the tea towel and sobbed.

'Ah. I see.' Nellie smiled at Beth, but it wasn't a smile of complicity, not the exchange that Beth had expected, Nellie obviously saw no problem. 'That Posie Brown, she's a one all right.' She leaned her heavy elbows on the table. 'She's never liked you, Norah.'

Norah blew her nose on the tea towel as discreetly as she could, wishing that Nellie Putman would go away.

'And she's always fancied your Ben,' Nellie added, 'most of them do, you know.'

Norah stopped concentrating on the tea towel and looked at Nellie. What an outrageous thing to say!

'You do know that, don't you, lovey?' Deadly serious, Nellie was demanding an answer. 'All the girls, they fancy your Ben, you do know that.'

Norah found herself nodding, as the tears gathered once more. She couldn't even hate Nellie for saying it, she was only telling the truth.

Beth watched intently. Nellie wasn't going about this the right way at all, Norah was insecure enough as it was, the last thing she needed to be told was that women were queuing up for her husband.

'And Posie's just one of them, Norah, she lusts after your Ben. And when you're snooty to her that's the way she causes trouble, 'cos she knows that if your husband was a lecher he could choose whoever he wanted, and I'll bet my last quid Posie wishes he'd choose her.

'And I'll tell you something else for nothing, Norah,' Nellie continued. 'I've been around in my time. I've been with a lot of men, and that may shock you or not and I don't really care if it does . . .' The kettle was boiling by now but nobody noticed. 'Course I've never cheated on my Jack,' she added, 'not even when he was inside. But when I was a girl, Norah, I had more men than you could poke a stick at. Lived with my first one when I was fifteen, I did.'

It was not a boast but a statement, and Norah found herself staring at Nellie Putman, and for some strange reason hanging on her every word.

'So you see, lovey, I know men. And I can spot a lecher from a hundred yards. I can tell by his walk, I can see it in his face. I can smell it on him, so help me God I can, I've known so many in my time.' She leaned over and patted Norah comfortingly on the knee. 'And your Ben isn't one, lovey, I'd swear it on my mother's grave I would.'

Beth picked up the kettle and burned her hand. She gave a sharp gasp, quickly put it down and reached for the oven mitt. Was Nellie naive? Did she believe what she was saying, or was she spinning a yarn? It was impossible to tell, Beth thought as she filled the teapot. But if it was lies Nellie was coming out with, then she had a nerve swearing on her mother's grave. That was asking for trouble.

'There, Norah.' She brought the pot to the table, sat beside Nellie and started to pour the tea. 'You just listen to Nellie. She's the wise one. She knows what it's all about, don't you, Nell?'

'I certainly do.' Nellie picked up the cup of tea and Beth looked again for some sign of duplicity in the woman's eyes, but there was none. 'You've got a good man in your Ben and you shouldn't listen to some little floosie who tells you otherwise just because she fancies him and because she wants to get back at you for being snooty.' She handed the cup to Norah. 'It's not fair to Ben it's not. Now you drink your tea, lovey, there's a good girl.'

'It's true, I was rude to her.' Calm now, Norah dutifully sipped. 'I didn't really mean to be, but I was embarrassed.'

'Course you were. Thank you, Beth.' Nellie accepted her cup of tea and took a biscuit from the plate.

'Ben'll be cross when he finds out I snubbed Posie. He always gets cross when he thinks I've been rude.'

'Well then, we won't tell him, eh? We'll keep our lips buttoned up and say nothing at all. What do you reckon?'

'Yes, I think that would be best.' Norah nodded.

Nellie was pleased with her victory, and she knew that she was right. Of course she wouldn't swear on her mother's grave that Ben had not been with Maureen McLaughlan on Saturday night, but during the last week or so of a woman's pregnancy her husband could be forgiven for seeking sexual satisfaction elsewhere. It certainly didn't make him a lecher. Nellie would swear on her mother's grave to that.

'It wasn't the first time either, I bet.' Beth read her son's silence as acknowledgement that she was correct. 'Oh Ben, how could you? Norah's about to have the baby any day.'

'I know, I know.' Although part of him wanted to tell his mother that it was none of her business, Ben couldn't stand the disappointment in her eyes. He felt that he'd let her down. 'I went with Maureen three times, Mum. Honest. Three times, that's all.'

She wondered if he was lying. He looked like a ten-year-old caught with his finger in the pie. 'Well, if you can't control yourself, you'll just have to be more careful. Norah's delicate, you know she is. She could throw a fit and lose the baby, finding out something like that. You're only lucky Nellie was here to talk her round. I don't know how she did it, Nellie's a genius.'

'I have been careful, Mum,' Ben said defensively, his annoyance starting to show.

'But Posie Brown saw you.'

'Only because she was spying. She's been spying on me for a month now, ever since I knocked her back.'

Benjamin was not vain enough to invent such a lie. So Nellie had been right. Perhaps Nellie had been right about the rest too. Beth chose to believe so. She chose to believe that her son was not a lecher.

'I'm sorry to interfere, Ben, I know it's not my place. I just worry about Norah, you understand?'

'Yeah, Mum, I understand.'

Ben lay awake for much of that night, aware of Norah beside him, fitful in her sleep. He wondered whether she would bring up the subject the following morning. Beth's confrontation had come as a shock to Ben, it had been so unexpected. There had been nothing in Norah's manner, when he'd come home from work, to intimate the afternoon's drama. Over tea, when he'd asked why she was so quiet, she'd simply said she felt queasy and might go to bed early.

'She'll keep her lip buttoned just like Nellie told her to,' his mother had said, 'and you can thank your lucky stars for that.'

It appeared that Beth was right. The following morning Norah said nothing as she prepared breakfast for him and Billy. The Kendall brothers always left for the Wunderlich factory a good hour before young Tim needed to be woken for school, and throughout her pregnancy Norah had insisted upon getting up early and, still in her nightdress and dressing gown, she would cook them a hot breakfast.

'Billy and me can get our own breakfast, love,' Ben had said on a number of occasions, and each time she'd smile indulgently. The men were not accustomed to getting their own food and they really wouldn't know how. 'Well, Mum can,' Ben would add with a grin.

'Beth gets the evening meal as it is,' Norah would adamantly reply. 'The least I can do is see that you boys are well fed before a hard day's work.'

This morning she was pale and quiet, and Ben was silent, concentrating on his mug of tea.

But Billy wasn't to know. 'You all right, Norah?' he asked as he mopped up his bacon fat with a lump of bread. 'You don't look too good.'

'I'm well, Billy, really, I'm well, just a little bit tired that's all.'

'You should have slept in, love,' Ben said. 'We can get our own breakfast.' There was nothing in the smile she returned him which denoted displeasure, and it only added to Ben's guilt.

He'd never do it again, he told himself. There'd be no further straying. He'd not been lying to his mother either. He had only slept with Maureen McLaughlan three times, no more, and then only in the last month of his wife's pregnancy.

'You should go back to bed, love,' he said, concerned at how very pale she was.

'Yes, I think I might. When you've gone and I've done the dishes, I might just have a little lie-down.'

Norah's contractions had started, but it was still early and they were far apart, no cause to sound the alarm yet. And there was certainly no need to inform the men, men had no place at the birth of a child.

However, she thought, it would be a fine thing, if when Ben came home from work in the late afternoon, he could be presented with a fine, healthy baby. She tried to close her mind to all else, to rid herself of her anxieties. For months she had been unable to escape the horrifying, nagging fear that her child might be stillborn, that she might give birth to a baby with terrible deformities. There were sins to be accounted for, and Norah lived in fearful agony that she would be called upon to answer them. A healthy baby, that's all she must think of now.

She saw the men off at the front door and tended to the dishes. She could hear Beth and Tim stirring upstairs. No point in raising the alarm with Beth just yet, she decided. Midwives cost money, and her labour with Tim had lasted sixteen hours. She'd wait until her time was ready.

'I'm just popping upstairs for a little lie-down, Beth,' she said as her mother-in-law entered the kitchen.

'Oh?' There was a definite question in Beth's eyes.

'No, no, I'm just feeling a little queasy, that's all.'

She did look tired, Beth thought. But then, after the dramas of yesterday afternoon, the poor girl probably hadn't slept a wink. 'All right, Norah, you give me a call if there's anything you need.'

Norah lay on the bed and tried to blank out her mind as she

listened to the sounds of the day. Beth farewelling Tim at the door, then the raucous return of the Putman boys.

'Got a present for you, Ma,' Norah heard Spotty say, then a guffaw from Nellie, a cheer from Geoff, and the cry of the baby. You'd swear there were twenty people next door.

The sounds were comforting and, between each spasm of pain, Norah drifted in and out of a fitful doze. She was so very tired, exhausted in fact, and grateful that her body was allowing her these intermittent moments of rest. She would need all the strength she could muster soon.

Twice she was aware of Beth's gentle tap on the door, her head appearing and the whisper, 'You all right, Norah?' And the second time, 'You want some lunch, dear?' But she feigned sleep, although by now the contractions were closer together and she was no longer dozing.

Two hours later, as each spasm seized her, Norah clutched the head of the old brass bedstead and clenched her teeth against the pain. Then, as it receded, she counted the minutes until the next one came. Soon. She would call Beth soon.

Downstairs, Beth boiled the kettle. It was two o'clock in the afternoon, she would take Norah a cup of tea and some fresh-baked bread and cheese, the girl had to eat something.

Norah felt a trickle of moisture between her legs. But her waters could not have broken, she thought, it was not yet time. She pulled aside her dressing gown, lifted her nightdress and reached down to touch herself. Feeling the wetness, she withdrew her hand and inspected it, to find her fingers covered in blood.

She lifted herself onto her elbows and looked down at her parted thighs. Dear God, what was happening? She was aware of no added pain beyond that of the contractions, and yet blood was pouring from her vagina. Not a trickle, but a steady stream. Her nightdress, her dressing gown, the bed, all were soaked in her blood.

She panicked and tried to call out. 'Beth!' But her voice was weak. Why couldn't she call louder? 'Beth!' Beth was obviously unable to hear her above the sound of the sewing machine. But Norah could not hear the swift click-clack of the machine—Beth must be downstairs.

She struggled to her feet, feeling weak and faint as she opened the bedroom door, and she stood for a moment on the little top landing, trying to gain her balance. At the bottom of the stairs Beth appeared in the open door to the kitchen, a plate in one hand and a mug of tea in the other.

'Beth,' Norah opened her mouth to call, but the words didn't come out. The world spun for one dizzying moment, and then, it seemed in slow motion, the stairs rose up to meet her.

Beth dropped the mug and the plate and stood frozen, horrified and helpless, as Norah pitched headfirst down the narrow stairway, a tumble of arms and legs, her belly bumping shockingly on every step. Then Beth flung herself forward onto her knees in a desperate attempt to cushion the final blow of landing.

Norah's head struck her painfully in the ribs and Beth fell onto her side, holding the girl to her, as Norah's body crumpled and slithered to a halt at the bottom of the stairs.

'Norah?' Beth struggled to her knees. Gently she rested Norah's head on the floor and searched for signs of life, but the girl seemed shockingly still. 'Norah?' Oh God, don't let her be dead.

A guttural sound escaped Norah's throat, and her body spasmed. The baby, Beth thought, the baby was coming.

It was then she noticed the blood on the lower steps. She pulled aside Norah's dressing gown. Both it and her nightdress were soaked in blood.

Beth was shocked but she kept her voice steady. 'Don't you worry, girl,' she said, just in case Norah could hear her, 'don't you worry.' And she raced out through the kitchen to the Putmans' back door.

She was back in a matter of seconds, Nellie lumbering behind her, and behind Nellie were the Putman boys, Spotty and Geoff, dragged from their beds and still half asleep.

Delirious, barely conscious, Norah was moaning and clutching her belly.

'Get the midwife, Spotty,' Nellie ordered.

'Don't bother with the midwife,' Beth countermanded, 'it's old Mack we need. And as quick as you can.' Wide awake now, Spotty dived for the front door. 'Tell him she fell down the stairs, and tell him she's bleeding,' Beth called. 'There's a lot of bleeding, tell him.'

'Gently, gently,' Nellie said as, upon Beth's instruction, Geoff lifted Norah onto the old grey-pink sofa. Then, 'Sweet Jesus,' she whispered as she saw the blood, 'I hope Mack gets here soon.'

'Scissors from the sewing room upstairs, Geoff, and cotton,' Beth ordered. 'Nellie, there's hot water on the stove.'

'I'll get a bowl, and I'll fill the kettles and saucepans for more.' With uncharacteristic speed, Nellie made for the kitchen.

Beth pulled Norah's nightdress well up over her belly. If old Mack didn't arrive in time, then she and Nellie must deliver the baby. They knew what to do, they'd both assisted at births before.

But there was no baby coming. There was nothing coming out of Norah but blood. Was the baby dead? Was Norah dying? She was still breathing but she'd lost all consciousness now. Dear God, please let Mack be at home, Beth silently prayed. Get here quick, they're both dying, I know it.

To the working class of Surry Hills Old Mack was a hero. He'd ceased working long hours in 1900, the year he'd turned sixty-five, and his practice was no longer open ten hours a day, but Dr Alastair McBurney was always available to those in need. In the poorer streets of Surry Hills, it was sometimes hours before a doctor arrived at the scene of an emergency, by which time the patient was often dead, but Old Mack was different. Old Mack dropped everything and was there in minutes.

Geoff charged downstairs and handed Beth the scissors and thread, averting his eyes as he did so. It made him feel sick, all that blood coming out of a woman.

'Go and get Ben,' Beth said. 'He should be here.' Unseemly as it was for a man to be present at the birth of his child, he should certainly be present at the death of his wife.

'Right.' Geoff was out the door in a flash.

The women bent Norah's knees up and parted her legs. They looked for a sign of the baby but they couldn't see a thing for the blood. The old grey sofa was crimson by now, and as fast as Nellie sponged between Norah's legs, the blood kept pumping out. Beth and Nellie, both strong women, reliable in a crisis, were sick with helpless panic.

'Dear God in Heaven, Nell, what do we do?'

The front door opened and Old Mack stood there, Spotty Putman at his side.

'Put her on the floor,' Mack panted, taking his Gladstone bag from Spotty. He'd run three blocks in two minutes. A body his age wasn't used to it.

They did as they were told, and Mack opened his bag as he knelt beside the woman. His decision had been instant. The moment he'd seen the blood gushing from her he'd known that he had no choice.

'Boiling water, and lots of it,' he said to Spotty.

'Already hot on the stove, Spotty,' Nellie instructed her son, and she and Beth watched as the doctor set to work.

Old Mack took his scalpel from his bag. No point in wasting time with chloroform, the mother was unconscious, in profound shock. It was highly unlikely she would live anyway, and every second counted if he was to save the baby.

He made his midline incision, cutting from the umbilicus to the pubic area, exposing and folding apart the section of yellow fat. Then he started to cut his way through to the wall of the uterus.

The two women stood watching in horror.

'Dear Father in Heaven,' Nellie crossed herself, 'he's murdering her.'

'We have here,' Old Mack said, his voice calm but his hands working quickly and efficiently, 'either a ruptured uterus or a placenta praevia. I am hoping for the latter.'

Beth nodded, not understanding a word he was saying, but reassured by the sound of his voice. She watched, shocked, unable to take her eyes from the gruesome spectacle.

The wall of the uterus was now exposed. It was intact. Good, Mack thought, some hope remained. If the uterus had been ruptured, the abdomen would have been filled with blood and the baby's chances for survival would be minimal, the mother's most certainly nil.

'The baby's head has bumped onto the head of the placenta,' he continued as he began cutting his way through the uterine wall, 'and the placenta is leaking blood and blocking the passage from the womb.'

He could see the baby now, curled limp amongst the blood and gore, but he couldn't tell if it was dead or alive. 'A placenta praevia, we call it. Not an uncommon event, but a most unfortunate one.' He finished cutting. 'A Caesarian section is the only way.'

He reached his hands inside and lifted out the baby. Holding it upside down by the ankles, he smacked it sharply on the bottom and handed it up to Beth. 'Upside down and keep smacking,' he instructed as he clamped the cord. Then he turned his attention once more to the mutilated woman on the floor. There was little chance of her survival, but as yet she was still alive. There had even been moments of semiconsciousness throughout the operation, when she'd emitted low groans and moved her head slightly.

Beth held the baby upside down and slapped its bottom. It was blue. Quite blue. And flaccid. It was dead, surely. She heard a faint gurgle. Material dribbled from the baby's mouth. Breathe, Beth begged, breathe, and she slapped it again.

Then, miraculously, there was a loud squawk, like an angry chicken, and the baby squirmed. It breathed. And Beth held a living creature in her hands.

'It's a girl,' Nellie whispered.

'Good, good,' Mack said without looking up. He'd removed the placenta, dumping it in a bloody mess on the floor beside him and, with the flat of his hand, was cleaving a plain in the uterus. 'Beth, tend to the baby. Nellie, I need that hot water, and clean hand towels and tea towels, whatever you can get.'

They formed a line, Spotty and Nellie kneeling beside the doctor, Spotty plunging the hand towels into boiling hot water, scalding his hands as he did so, then partially squeezing the towels dry and handing them to Nellie, who squeezed them again and handed them to Mack. Mack then packed them into the uterus.

Throughout the procedure the old doctor kept checking Norah's vital signs, expecting any moment to call a halt to the proceedings. She must have lost half her blood volume, they needed to get fluid into her. She was dying, and it was doubtful she would reach the hospital alive. Even if she did, Mack thought, she would die there. Of blood loss or infection. But in the meantime, somehow, the girl was hanging on and Mack was doing everything he could.

Norah was floating now. Somewhere beyond pain. A number of times she'd been shocked from her oblivion by a pain so unbearable that she'd prayed for death. And she'd gratefully accepted it, sinking into comfortable darkness. Then, only moments later, the agony had returned. When would it end? Let me die, she'd prayed and begged as she'd drifted on the border of life and death.

In the instant, however, that she'd heard the cry of her baby, Norah's prayer had changed. She would embrace death happily but, please God, not until she had seen her child. Please God, let her live long enough to see that the baby she had borne was healthy.

Drifting in her blackness, Norah talked to God. And the two of them made a bargain. God told her that He had given her a healthy baby. A girl, He said. She'd wanted a girl. And He promised her He would let her hold her baby. In return, she promised Him her life. It was a very good bargain and, as if to shake hands on the deal, God took away the pain and Norah sank into blissful, pain-free unconsciousness.

Ben sat at Norah's bedside, holding her hand, praying the only way he knew how. Not directly to God, that would be hypocritical, he'd never done it before, why should God listen to him now? But he begged forgiveness and promised to be a better man if only Norah could live.

She'd been in Sydney Hospital for over a week, barely conscious, in a fever, no-one expecting her to live through each day. But somehow she had.

Ben hadn't realised how much he loved her. He hadn't even been sure that he did. He certainly hadn't loved her in the beginning. He'd resented having to marry at the age of twenty-two, and he'd resented the fact that his wife seemed to think she was above the common herd of Surry Hills. There'd even been times when he'd thought, as his mother had, that Norah had trapped him into marriage.

Nevertheless, he'd done all the right things by his new-found family, worked hard and supported them well, but for the first two years of his marriage, he'd not been faithful to his wife. His sexual liaisons had been more a rebellion than anything; they'd meant little to him and he'd kept them discreet, but they'd been his way of showing his resentment, if only to himself.

Then, shortly after his son's second birthday, Ben had suddenly realised that he was happy. He loved young Tim more than life itself, and Norah was a good mother and a good wife who had given him a fine son. As the years passed, his fondness for Norah grew to a deep affection. But he'd not recognised it as love. Not until now.

Ben looked down at the thin pale face, almost as white as the pillow upon which it rested. 'You can do it, Norah girl,' he whispered. 'You can do it, I know you can.' He said it every five minutes or so. The nurses and doctors told him that she couldn't hear, but he said it anyway, just in case.

The doctors and nurses were right, she couldn't hear him. She couldn't hear him because, during her moments of semiconsciousness, she was too busy talking to God.

I must see my baby, she was saying. You promised me. I cannot die until I've seen my baby.

At the end of the second week, her eyelids flickered open. She studied the room. A white ceiling, white walls. Where was she? Someone was holding her right hand. She turned her head and there was Ben, leaning back in the bedside chair looking tired, very nearly asleep.

'Where's my baby?' she whispered.

Ben heard a sound, something more than the rasping of her breath as she struggled for daily survival. He was jolted awake. He looked at his wife. Her eyes were open.

'Norah?'

'Where's my baby?'

They brought her baby to her, positioning it in the crook of her left shoulder. She couldn't move her arms, so they bent her left elbow and placed her left hand on the baby's chest. Then they draped her other arm over her body so that she was embracing the child. She turned her head on the pillow and looked down at her baby.

It did not matter at all to Norah that she could not move her arms, for she could move her fingers. And she touched the skin of her little girl's face, and felt the tiny hand clutching hers.

The nurses left the mother and father and baby alone. Just for a little while. It was a miracle, they said. A miracle that she'd regained consciousness at all.

Ben watched his wife silently. Then, 'I love you, Norah,' he whispered. The words were more to himself than to her.

But Norah heard him. Ben's voice. He was sitting on the other side of the bed, she could turn her head towards him if she wished. She was loath to take her eyes from the baby, but Ben had told her that he loved her. He'd never said that before. Slowly she turned her head.

Good heavens, he's crying, she thought. She'd never seen him do that before either.

'I do,' he said. 'I love you, girl.'

She smiled as she closed her eyes. God had given her much more than they'd agreed upon in their bargain. How very kind of Him. But frustrating too. She really didn't want to die now.

'There was blood everywhere. Spotty Putman told me. They had to throw out the old sofa. Red with my mum's blood it was, that's what Spotty told me.'

Robbie O'Shea was deeply impressed. Tim had known he would be, Robbie was always enthralled by stories of blood and gore.

They were sitting on the grass in Hyde Park, the pup gambolling about them, chasing the sticks they threw. Except the pup wasn't a pup any more, he was fully grown. Huge and gawky and clumsy, and far bigger than Kathleen had ever anticipated. 'If he gets too big, we have to get rid of him,' she'd threatened, but Robbie had got round her, as he'd known he would.

'She was in hospital for a whole two months,' Tim said proudly. 'They said it was a miracle that she lived. After she lost all that blood,' he added, to impress Robbie further.

'Yeah.' Robbie was dutifully impressed. 'She's lucky all right, your mum.'

Tim wrested the stick from the dog's mouth and hurled it into the bushes. 'Go get it, boy!' he yelled. It was a competition between him and Robbie to see who could throw the stick the furthest.

'So what are they calling her?' Robbie asked as the dog lumbered off and disappeared amongst the undergrowth. 'Your baby sister, what are they calling her?'

'Emily. It was my dad's great-grandmother's name and Mum reckons she likes it.'

'Do you like it?'

'What? The name?'

'No, the baby.'

'I dunno,' Tim shrugged. 'I suppose. It's hard to tell, she cries a lot.'

The dog crashed its way back through the bushes, the stick in its mouth, and stood looking about, momentarily disoriented.

'Here, boy!' Robbie called. 'Here, boy, over here!' As the animal romped towards them, something suddenly occurred to Robbie. 'Hey, Tim,' he said.

'What?'

'We ought to give the pup a name.'

Tim wondered why they hadn't thought of it before. 'Yep,' he agreed. It was high time the pup had a name.

They both thought for a while. Tim wasn't sure if it was the talk of blood which brought Ernie Morgan to mind. He hadn't thought of Ernie as he'd boasted about the bloodied sofa, but suddenly Ernie was there, as he was every now and then and probably always would be.

'We could call him Ernie,' he suggested. Robbie looked at him and Tim felt he owed an explanation. 'Ernie was big,' he said. 'All the Morgans are big.'

But Robbie didn't need any explanation. 'Ernie's a good name,' he agreed. 'We'll call him Ernie.'

BOOK THREE

THE NATION

Chapter Ten

'It's a ridiculous situation and we should have kept well out of it from the very beginning. Why should the death of an obscure Austrian duke have anything to do with us? And where in God's name is Sarajevo anyway?'

Charles Kendle was holding forth at his dinner table as he always did. And, as always, his son, Stephen, and his grandson, Mark, were offering little opposition. Stephen because he disliked confrontation and still lived in fear of his father, and Mark because he disliked the old man and didn't want to give him the pleasure of an argument. Twenty-year-old Mark, who invariably disagreed with his grandfather's views, had often spoken out in the past, only to discover that was exactly what the old man was after.

'You see, Stephen,' Charles would triumphantly crow to his son, 'the boy's got the guts to stand up to me. Something you've never done.'

Mark hated to see his father humiliated, but he hated far more the way his father accepted his humiliation. 'Why do you take it, Dad?' he'd ask. 'Why do you let him bully you?'

'It's more peaceful that way,' was Stephen's simplistic reply. 'He'll always win, why bother fighting him?'

It seemed a fair enough answer, Mark supposed, and for his father's sake, he stopped rising to the old man's bait. When his grandfather made outrageous statements in a deliberate attempt to arouse debate, just as he was doing tonight in talking so of the imminent war in Europe, Mark held his tongue and said nothing. But it didn't mean that he'd given in to the old man. Not for one minute.

'If there is a war, then of course we must fight, Charles, and you know it.'

It was old Howard Streatham who spoke out, for tonight the three generations of Kendle men were not clustered alone, as they usually were, at one end of the vast dining table of Kendle Lodge, the butler and maid hovering attentively. Tonight there was quite a party in progress. Mark's eccentric Aunt Susan, whom he rather admired, was present, along with Howard Streatham, his wife Helen and their eldest son, Godfrey.

'It has gone far beyond the assassination of Archduke Ferdinand. The Germans have declared war on France! They've threatened to invade Belgium!' Howard knew full well he'd been teased into debate, but he couldn't help it, the crisis in Europe demanded a passionate response. He adjusted his spectacles and continued. 'The British are duty-bound to deliver an ultimatum. If the Kaiser continues to run rampant, why, then the British Empire itself could be at stake.'

Howard's false teeth had an unfortunate way of clacking slightly as he spoke, which always reduced the impact of his argument. Unprepossessing in appearance, he was frail, wizened, completely bald, and looked every bit of his seventy-four years. But Mark had always admired the way he talked back to Grandfather Charles. Howard Streatham was obviously undaunted by his old partner, and was still active in the family firm, despite having retired four years ago. Kendle and Streatham not only boasted the two biggest emporiums in Sydney but also maintained three supply factories, producing ironmongery, woollen and leather goods, and Howard was strenuous in voicing his opinions on each and every aspect of the company's concerns.

As the maid cleared the sorbet dishes, Charles signalled the butler to pour the claret which would accompany the main course.

'Then let the British look after their Empire,' he said provocatively. 'We're half the world away here.'

'What an appalling thing to say.' There was sheer outrage in Godfrey Streatham's voice. 'We are *part* of the British Empire.'

That was the trouble with Godfrey, Charles thought. He had no sense of humour, just like his father. He shared his father's tenacity too, and his stubbornness and strong moral sense, which in Charles's opinion was dangerous for business.

Charles Kendle, unlike his cousin Howard, had no intention of retiring. And certainly not whilst the other two co-directors of Kendle and Streatham were his and Howard's sons. Boring and dogmatic as he was, Godfrey Streatham would eat Stephen Kendle for breakfast.

Charles's son was a vast disappointment to him. A spineless man, he had many years ago concluded. One who possessed a moderate talent at the piano keyboard, a passable skill as a yachtsman (which was not surprising, he had been brought up amongst the yachting fraternity) and one who, in all other areas, was ineffectual and lacking any shred of leadership ability. Should the day ever come when he wished to retire, Charles had decided he would hand over the reins to his grandson. He sensed a strength and a leadership in Mark which reminded him a little of himself. His vanity chose also to believe that the lad looked like him, for Mark was a handsome young man. Dark of hair and brow, slim of build and with the bearing of an aristocrat, he could have been the young Charles Kendle, and although Charles suspected the boy didn't much like him, he wasn't overly bothered. His grandson would one day admire him; in the meantime, fear and respect were enough.

'And as the most distant *part* of the British Empire,' Charles mocked the pomposity of Godfrey's tone, 'we should have more sense than to waste manpower and money on a war which will not affect us.'

'Ah yes, Father,' Susan interjected, 'money! There lies the key. Money! Be honest now, if there were money to be made, you'd be all for the war, would you not?'

A shocked silence ensued. Susan had not intended to enter the conversation, quite aware of the fact that her father was deliberately provoking argument; but Helen Streatham had exchanged a conspiratorial look which had intimated 'Men's talk, dear, we must keep well out of it', and such a look was, as always to Susan, like waving a red rag at a bull.

To everyone's surprise Charles gave one of his short barks of laughter. 'But of course, my dear, I would look far more favourably upon this war if it were a sound financial investment.' He noted, with pleasure, that his remark had offended. 'Why do you look so shocked, Godfrey? Many a sensible businessman will make a great deal of money out of this war. It will not, however, be businessmen like us who live on the other side of the world, more's the pity.'

Stephen concentrated intently on his wine glass as the butler poured his claret. 'Thank you, Arthur,' he muttered. He dared not look up. If he did, he might meet the challenge in his father's eyes, defying him to speak out. Or Godfrey might see the guilty flush in his cheeks. For it had been Stephen Kendle's signature which had accompanied his father's on the agreement to supply leather and woollen goods to the military in the advent of war. The government had not approached Kendle and Streatham, Charles had initiated the deal himself when the first rumblings of conflict in Europe had reached Australian shores.

The transaction had been far from ethical. Money had changed hands, no questions had been asked, and Charles had beaten any possible competition well before general tenders had been invited. For appearances' sake, however, tenders, when they arrived, were given due consideration.

The contract had required the signatures of two of the senior directors of Kendle and Streatham, and Stephen had ventured to suggest that Godfrey would not approve.

'So he'll call me a warmonger, so what?' his father had snarled. 'If we don't grab the chance, somebody else will. By the time Godfrey finds out, there'll be no moral decision to be made, the money will be rolling in and he'll be only too happy to take it. Now just sign the damn thing, Stephen!'

And of course Stephen had.

Charles glanced across the table at his daughter, rather wishing he could boast to her of his government contract, though he knew for the moment it must remain a secret. It was Susan who had inherited his strength, Charles thought; it showed in her face. The set of her jaw, the determination of her brow, not a marshmallow face like her brother's. Even in her midforties she was a handsome woman, although a little on the weighty side. But then both she and Stephen had inherited their mother's fleshiness and grown bulky in their middle years.

Charles wished it had been his son rather than his daughter who had inherited his strength. He never trusted strong women. And he certainly did not approve of his daughter. She had done the most appalling things with her life, and her behaviour was at times most embarrassing. She even smoked in public.

A divorced woman, Susan had years ago left her husband and two children in Melbourne to return to Sydney and set up a small art gallery and handicrafts shop. In Manly of all places. Charles had thought of disinheriting her at the time—for propriety's sake—until he'd discovered that she had reverted to her maiden name.

'It is a sorry enough state of affairs, Father,' she had stiffly remarked, 'that, upon her marriage, a woman is required to relinquish all rights to her family name. But, should her marriage fail, it is nothing short of loathsome that she be expected to continue to bear the name of a man she no longer loves, in fact quite possibly abhors.'

It was a radical statement, and quite shocking, but Charles had been secretly delighted. The more Kendles the better, he thought, and he made veiled hints at monetary rewards for her two children, Lionel and Prudence, should they wish to follow their mother's example and change their name. But Susan appeared uninterested.

Although Charles did not approve of his daughter, he could not fail but respect her. She was outrageous. She had a far greater ability to shock than he, for he was too bound by social protocol. Furthermore, she stood up to him like a man. Susan had guts.

The claret had been poured and, unable to garner his daughter's attention and, like her, bored with the diatribe Godfrey Streatham had embarked upon half an hour ago, Charles rose to his feet.

'Well said, Godfrey!' he loudly announced, and Godfrey was forced to stop midsentence.

Charles stood for a second or so at the head of the table, not only to survey his guests, but in order that he should be surveyed by them. He looked imposing and knew it. He'd weathered the storm far better than Howard. At seventy-six, he still had a striking head of hair, silver-white now, and beneath the aged eyelids the steel-grey eyes still glinted powerfully.

'A toast!' he said and he raised his glass. 'To King and Country.'

They all rose. 'To King and Country.'

Two hours later, when their guests had departed, Charles insisted Stephen and Mark join him for a coffee and port. He seemed in a most affable mood. 'My word, but we set a cat or two amongst the pigeons tonight, didn't we?' he laughed.

Mark glanced at his father. Both of them had said barely a word all evening.

'Well, Susan and I did,' Charles added, noting the exchange. 'And you could certainly have stirred them up a great deal more, Stephen, had you wished. A right old hornets' nest it would have been, had you dredged up your nerve and spoken out.'

'You made me promise, from the outset, to say nothing, Father.' Stephen heaved an inner sigh. He could tell that his father still wished to play games. Stephen hated it when Charles goaded him in front of his son.

'Of course, of course, and you were quite right to keep your mouth shut.' The old man leaned forward and poured himself another glass of port from the decanter on the coffee table. He would probably regret having a second, but he had so enjoyed himself tonight that he didn't want the evening to end. 'And I'm sure it must have cost you such effort to do so,' he said with gleeful spite. He had seen Stephen hiding behind his wine, praying that no-one would notice his guilty flush. 'You must have been positively biting your tongue.' Charles sipped his port teasingly, 'But we might perhaps tell Mark of our little secret, what do you say?'

Stephen apparently had nothing to say, as he stared at the empty coffee cup in his hands. Charles had expected as much. 'After all,' he continued, 'when Mark leaves university at the end of next year he will be part of Kendle and Streatham. Perhaps it is time he learned of our more nefarious activities.'

Mark and Stephen exchanged a look, and there was a query in Mark's eyes.

'Well, Stephen,' Charles insisted with a touch of impatience, 'shall we tell him or shall we not?'

'He already knows.' Stephen savoured the moment. The look of surprise in his father's eyes, the fleeting knowledge that, for just one second, he had bested the old man. His life would be made hell for the next few days, but he must remember this moment, he told himself, he must not regret it.

'He knows?' Charles put down his glass, the port no longer interested him. 'About the government contract?'

'Yes.'

'But I told you to tell no-one.'

'I did not take that to mean Mark, Father.' Stephen looked to his son and was pleased to see the encouragement in Mark's eyes. 'I tell my son most things. He is very discreet.'

'I see.' After a moment's pause the old man turned to his grandson. 'And what do you think of the transaction, Mark?' His voice was cold, his displeasure evident.

'I think it is an excellent business coup, Grandfather.' Mark didn't. He thought it was sheer warmongering greed but, not wishing to cause more trouble for his father, he was happy enough to humour the old man.

'Yes,' Charles was slightly mollified, the boy showed sound judgement, 'it is.' He was still annoyed, however, that the wind had been taken out of his sails. Why was it that the only time Stephen showed any character was in the presence of his son, why couldn't he do it in a boardroom?

'I am delighted there is such a bond of trust between you and your son, Stephen,' he said archly as he eased himself out of the armchair, his left hip was aching now, 'but your abuse of our confidentiality speaks poorly of your character. You are not a man of your word. I am tired now, I'm going to bed.'

Circular Quay was busy, as it always was on a Saturday night. Brightly lit ferries of all shapes and sizes churned the black waters of Sydney Harbour; small passenger ferries beetled back and forth from Milsons Point and Kirribilli and the other stops on the nearby northern side; large ocean-going ferries surged across the open waters of Port Jackson to the picturesque suburb of Manly on the far northern headland; and, dwarfing them all, were the behemoths, the gigantic vehicular ferries which transported all manner of vehicles. Sydney was still a city of horses, and daily, along with the queues of motor cars awaiting transportation, were the queues of horse-drawn vehicles of every description.

It was a bleak July night and the wind was whipping up. It would be a rough crossing to Manly, Susan thought. She hugged her heavy winter coat about her and hoped there would be a seat inside.

There wasn't, so she stood on the port side and looked out at Dawes Point as the ferry slid away from Circular Quay. It had been announced in the newspaper some time ago that the Public

Works Committee had accepted a proposal for an electric railway system, including a traffic bridge, to be built across the harbour from Dawes Point to Milsons Point. Of course they'd been talking about a bridge for years, but they would have to build one some day, the harbour was choked with ferries. The only alternative route from the city to the rapidly expanding northern suburbs was the five bridges road, a detour of ten miles or more around the head of the harbour, crossing bridges at Pyrmont, Glebe Island, Iron Cove, Gladesville and Fig Tree. And, having travelled the detour, to then continue all the way to Manly was unthinkable. Manly residents were totally reliant upon the ferries. Which was probably why she so loved Manly, Susan thought. Away from the influence of the city, the place had a character all its own. Ah well, if the war came, the government would probably put paid to the idea of a bridge.

It was inevitable, wasn't it, the war. Any moment now, they said. She wondered what it would mean, and she thought of the glib conversation over dinner. The Streathams with their complacency and she with her desire to shock, just like her father. She knew he thought they were two of a kind. They were not, and they never would be. Strong as she was, Susan was not cruel like her father, she was not vindictive.

She had always been strong. Well, she supposed she had. But she had not always been cynical; as a girl she had not been suspicious of people's motives as she was now. She remembered a time when life had been simple. Her wedding to Frederick for instance. A wealthy Melbourne lawyer and aspiring politician, the family had approved of Frederick Napier. 'A pillar of society,' her father had called him. She'd been in love too, or so she'd thought. And her wedding day could not have been a more glamorous affair, befitting the spoilt daughter of a wealthy man and his frivolous wife. She remembered Amy's fussing over the bridal gown, the length of the veil, the size of the bouquet. Susan, who had not wanted a grand wedding in the first place, had delighted in her mother's pleasure, and had never been closer to Amy than she had been then. So what had gone wrong? Everything. Her mother had died a tragic death. Fifteen years ago now. A distracted woman ever since the death of Paddy O'Shea, she was reliant upon drugs to keep her madness at bay. And Susan and her marriage? Equally tragic. The pillar of society had proved to possess an ugly side, never displayed to his business associates nor to his political colleagues, but reserved solely for his wife.

Frederick Napier was a man who would brook neither argument nor disagreement, nor even a differing opinion. Not when it came to running a household and raising a family. Life with such a husband was difficult for a spirited girl like Susan, but she learned to govern her tongue, and she dutifully bore him two children in two years, hoping that perhaps fatherhood might mellow him. It didn't.

The first time he struck her she remembered feeling strangely glad. Perhaps this would be the turning point. Perhaps the remorse he would suffer would form a bond between them and they would talk about their marriage. But he did not suffer remorse and they did not talk, and the bouts of violence became regular. Always in the privacy of their bedroom. Never in front of the children. It was only his wife who suffered, and she invented excuses as to how she had come by the bruises on her face and arms. Until one day, five years into their marriage, she decided she had had enough.

He was shocked when she said she was leaving him, he had never expected that she would.

'Go if you wish,' he said, 'but you must be aware that by deserting your husband and your children you will bring great shame upon yourself.'

'I am not deserting my children, Frederick. Lionel and Prudence will be coming with me.'

'Oh, no they will not. The children will remain with their father. As in the eyes of the law they must.'

He was not violent towards her that night. He was cold and clinical as he informed her of the truth. 'In law, my dear,' he said, 'the child of the married woman has only one parent, and that is the father. Unless you can prove in a court of law that I am an incompetent parent,' and his tone defied her to do so, 'no judge will allow you to run off with your children.'

The next night, however, he was violent, and the next, assuming he'd worn her down and that she had no option but to stay. A week after their initial confrontation, Susan sought advice from a legal firm and was informed that Frederick was correct in his points of law. Furthermore, it was pointed out, her husband was a prominent and successful man and she could present no proof of his violent behaviour. Two days later, Susan Napier left her husband and her children and returned to Sydney.

Divorce proceedings ensued and Frederick, possibly fearful that she might divulge the reason for their marriage break-up, which could prove embarrassing, allowed her unlimited access to the children. However, as the years progressed, so strongly were Lionel and Prudence under the influence of their father that Susan's relationship with them changed. Try as she might, she felt like a stranger. The more love she displayed, the more politely remote they became, as if she were a distant relative to be tolerated. But she too had changed, and she knew it. She was not the mother they had known. She was harder, tougher, more outspoken. Furthermore, she had reverted to her maiden name, a fact her children found incomprehensible.

Incensed by the ultimate injustice of the law, Susan had become an ardent social reformer and a staunch campaigner for women's rights.

Surprisingly enough, in the early days following her return to Sydney, her father had not been averse to her devotion to the suffragette movement, for through the meetings of the Womanhood Suffrage League Susan became closely acquainted with Lady Mary Windeyer, a leader in the fight for women's rights.

Charles Kendle had always boasted of his family's connections with the Windeyers, one of Sydney's most prominent families. His son had attended Sydney University with the Windeyer boys, and indeed Stephen still socialised with Richard, both keen yachting enthusiasts and members of the Royal Prince Alfred Yacht Club. When, to Charles's delight, his daughter struck up a friendship with none other than Lady Mary herself, the Windeyer boys' mother, his views on the suffragette movement underwent a radical change. Previously loud in his insistence that women be denied the vote—'preposterous notion, women do not have the brains to vote intelligently'—Charles suddenly became most sympathetic to the cause. In fact, he even offered to put Kendle Lodge at the League's disposal.

Fully aware of her father's ulterior motives, Susan did not accept his offer, though she did suggest he support her in a more practical manner by assisting her to set up a business of her own. Susan desperately needed to get out of the family home. Life at Kendle Lodge was claustrophobic and depressing, and at times she felt she was being suffocated by the unhappiness which surrounded her.

She had not realised that her mother was so far gone. Floating on laudanum throughout the day, heavily sedated at night in order to escape the nightmares which plagued her, Amy Kendle was a creature in torment, and it broke Susan's heart to see her once pretty, flirtatious mother reduced to such a state.

And Stephen. Poor defeated Stephen.

His wife had died giving birth prematurely to their second child, and the doctors had been unable to save the baby, a girl. Stephen had been a broken man at the funeral, which was hardly surprising, but Susan had hoped that time might heal his wounds. He had a beautiful little son, barely three years old. He was not yet thirty, he was a successful businessman with his life ahead of him. But, always prone to give in to adversity even as a child, Stephen had now given up altogether. Life had defeated him and any shred of self-esteem that had survived had been systematically hounded out of him by his tyrant of a father.

Susan grew to hate their father as, each night, she looked at him across the dining table of Kendle Lodge amidst the ruin of his family. She defended Stephen whenever she could, and she prayed that his little boy would grow up strong enough to withstand the influence of his grandfather. It would be only a matter of time before the old man would try to get his hooks into the child and take over his life.

She had to get out, away from the misery of Kendle Lodge, and her father's money was the only way. 'A loan, Father,' she insisted. 'I shall pay you back when the business is established.'

Howard Streatham proved immensely helpful. His contacts were invaluable, and within only twelve months Susan's gallery and handicrafts shop had slowly and steadily become established.

'But in Manly!' Her father had been scathing, of course. 'Why Manly of all places? It's a backwater.'

'You're quite wrong, Father,' she had emphatically replied, 'Manly is a thriving community. Local enterprise is far more supported in the Village than it is in the inner suburbs. Besides,' she added, 'artists and craftspeople have moved to the Village for the sheer beauty of the place. It is high time they had a shop and a gallery in which to display their works.'

'And who the hell's going to buy them?' Charles had growled.

'Visitors. Tourists. Fellow artists. I advertise, you know, and the shop has gained quite a reputation already.'

The lights of Manly loomed ahead. Susan clung to the railings as the ferry pitched and rolled, finally pulling into calmer waters as it approached the wharf. The gangplank crashed into place and Susan was first off the ferry, striding ahead of the stream of disembarking passengers. It was late and she needed to be up early. She always spoke at the Domain on Sundays. In fact, of all the speakers who spruiked their causes at Sydney's open-air centre of free speech, Susan Kendle's following was invariably one of the largest. And so it should be, she contended. The women of New South Wales may have won the right to vote a full twelve years ago, but that was only the beginning, there was a long road ahead. They had yet to win the right to be elected to parliament, and in the meantime, the daily struggle went on. Women needed to be told of their rights, not only in the political arena, but in the home and workplace.

Such a lot of work to be done, Susan thought as she strode up Sydney Street through the wintry Saturday night.

At nine on the morning of 17 August, crowds of men gathered on the weather-worn asphalt of the Victoria Barracks parade ground, laughing and jostling each other and talking excitedly like children about to go on a picnic. Men of all shapes and sizes—tall, short, fat and thin. Men of all ages—youngsters fresh from school, those in their prime and those showing signs of age. Men of every type and from every walk of life, but they had one thing in common. The spirit of adventure did not discriminate, and each man's eyes shared with the next the eager light of anticipation.

Here and there, standing to attention, was a professional soldier in uniform, his taut military bearing only serving to highlight the disorderliness of the motley crowd. It would be his duty to train this unruly horde of excited volunteers who were to become the 3rd Battalion of the 1st Infantry Brigade.

them that winter isn't over yet?' Everyone agreed, but no-one cared, spirits were high and the men were in good humour.

The conditions improved, their training intensified and, as they were equipped with their uniforms and kits, the kindred spirit of adventure grew. As did the ranks, men pouring in from the city and the outlying suburbs, eager to be in on the action. Recruiting for the battalion had commenced in the country, and officers were sent to meet the trains and conduct the country recruits to the Racecourse where the battalion was now camped in tents.

By 3 September the battalion was complete—thirty-two officers and nine hundred and ninety-one men—and on 14 September it marched out for the first time to the heathland overlooking the sea at Maroubra. The battalion was now equipped with waggons, horses, two Maxim machine-guns, the brass band was practising daily and, by 20 September when the men's paybooks were compiled, everyone was raring to go. All they needed now were their orders.

'It's official, they say. Any day now.' Kathleen looked up from the newspaper, but Otto didn't reply as he downed his mug of tea and rose from the kitchen table. 'It's just as Robbie told us on the weekend,' she continued. 'They're hoping to set sail before the end of the month.'

Robbie O'Shea had warned his mother that the weekend might be the last leave he'd be granted. 'The officers don't tell us anything but there's a rumour going round that embarkation orders have been issued.'

'I must get back to the shop,' Otto said. 'Young Aggie will be wanting her lunch.'

Kathleen stood and, reaching up her hands, locked her fingers behind the bull-like neck of her husband. 'Don't, Otto,' she whispered, 'don't shut me out along with Johann.'

'*Mijn duif*,' he always called her his dove, 'never would I shut you out. Never.' He engulfed her in his embrace and, feeling the fullness of her body against him, wanted to make love to her. But then Kathleen had always had that effect on him and eight years of marriage had not lessened his desire.

Otto De Haan loved his wife passionately, he had from the moment he'd met her. Even when he'd been 'the Dutchie down the road' who took her out for a drive with her son—in the hired trap which he'd pretended had been his—even then he'd loved her. Never for one moment, not even in his wildest dreams, had he ever dared hope that she could be his.

But he'd never been good at explaining his feelings. He wanted to tell her now that he did not mean to shut his son, his only child, out. It was not anger at Johann he felt, it was fear. It was anger mixed with fear. And disappointment. And frustration, and helplessness. Otto couldn't explain it to himself, how could he explain it to her?

'I must go, *mijn duif*,' he said. 'It is unfair to Aggie that I am late.'

Kathleen felt sorry for him as she watched him leave. She knew he was in turmoil and she wished she could help, but Otto was a private man, not one to express his emotions. Not even to his son, who was his very life. No wonder young Johann had run away rather than face up to the father with whom he could barely communicate. The boy had left a note. He'd joined the army. 'I'm sorry, Dad,' he'd written, 'but I knew you'd try and stop me.'

Kathleen was disappointed that young Johann had not confided in her. As a child he had talked to her in a way, she suspected, he had talked to no-one else. A strange little boy who hid his vulnerability behind bravado, Johann ached to be just like all the other kids.

'I don't want to talk Dutch, Kathleen,' he told her. 'Dad talks Dutch to me in public and it's awful, people look at us. I'm Australian, I'm not Dutch. I don't even know where Holland is.'

Kathleen knew that for years following the death of his wife, Otto had clung to Johann. A foreigner, learning the language and the customs of a new land, his only son had been the most precious thing in Otto's life. And yet daily she watched as he alienated the boy.

On occasions she had been a successful buffer between the two, but not this time. Not now that Johann had run away. This time Otto refused to communicate with him altogether.

On his visits home, Robbie tried to ease the situation. Most of his leave he spent with his fiancée Aggie, who worked in Otto's shop down the street and lived in the room above, but on Sunday he lunched with his mother and stepfather.

'Don't you worry about Johann, Otto,' he said. 'Me and Tim are looking after him. He's doing fine.'

'He is seventeen.'

'I'm nineteen.'

'You are a man,' Otto said. 'You know what you do. Johann is a child. And he is a fool.'

Robbie couldn't really disagree with the Dutchman there. Johann had always been a bit crazy, even as a kid. Forever showing off, pretending to be a daredevil when everyone knew he wasn't. Of course he was always being teased for being a foreigner, which probably had something to do with it. But he was as Australian as the next bloke now. It was time he grew up.

'Don't you worry,' Robbie said again, 'the army'll make a man out of him, just you wait and see.'

'He will be killed.'

There wasn't much a bloke could say to that, Robbie thought, so he changed the subject and tried to brighten things up a bit, for his mother's sake at least. Otto could be a bit dour at times. But Robbie liked him, he always had. Otto was a man who kept his feelings inside and Robbie was like that himself, except with Tim of course, but then Tim was his best mate. Robbie felt that he understood Otto. In fact it had been Robbie who had set the wheels in motion all those years ago.

'He's shook on you, Mum,' he'd said. He'd been eleven years old at the time.

'Who?'

'The Dutchie. Otto.'

'Don't be silly, he's just a friend.'

'Sure. A friend who's mad for you.' A little later on he'd said to Otto in a moment of privacy, 'My mum really likes you. She likes you a lot.' He'd let them work it out from there, but somehow he'd known the Dutchie'd make a good dad.

As the weeks progressed, the situation regarding Johann did not get any easier.

'Johann gets a weekend leave like you, Robbie?' Otto said one Sunday lunch. It was a rhetorical question and Robbie didn't answer. 'And yet he does not come home.'

There was no point in lying and Robbie didn't try. 'I think he's too frightened,' he answered truthfully. He and Tim had tried to convince Johann to visit his father, but he never had.

'Maybe I will,' the boy would say airily when his leave came up, 'but I'm seeing this girl,' a suggestive wink and a leer, 'might not have the time.'

There was no girl, and Tim and Robbie knew it. Johann was always telling lies, stupid ones too. Neither Robbie nor Tim could quite work Johann out.

'It is right that Johann should be frightened,' Otto growled, and Robbie and Kathleen exchanged a look. They both knew it was Otto who was frightened.

Kathleen helped her husband the only way she could. By letting him know that, whatever happened, she would always love him. For, incongruous pair as they were, Kathleen did love Otto De Haan. Her love had been born through a series of surprises. The discovery that Otto desired her had been the first. A woman normally alert to the lust in men, Kathleen had been singularly unaware of Otto's desire. He was a widower, a devoutly religious man, and his life was devoted to his small son, he had no place in his life for a lover, or so she had thought.

When he had clumsily confessed his affection, she had allowed him to kiss her, and that had been the next surprise. She'd been aroused by his embrace, the strength of his body and the gentle passion of his kiss. She'd wanted him to make love to her, but he hadn't. He'd courted her instead, bringing her flowers from his corner cart, taking her for drives in his trap, always kissing her goodnight, always keeping his own passion in check whilst hers mounted to the extreme. She wanted to beg. She wanted to plead 'make love to me, Otto,' but she daren't for fear of shocking him.

Then, finally, his breathless proposal of marriage, his expectation of refusal obvious, but of course she had accepted him. Otto might not have been the husband she may once have hoped for, but she was thirty-one now, and deeply grateful to find an honest man who would support her and her child.

Then had followed the next surprise. Their wedding night. Otto De Haan proved to be the best lover Kathleen had ever experienced. He was gentle and considerate, attentive and passionate, energetic and powerful. All the love and desire he could not articulate, he expressed with his body and his lovemaking, and

Kathleen, a deeply sexual woman, was left exhausted by the gratification of her own passion.

But the greatest surprise was yet to come. In a matter of months Kathleen realised that she loved Otto. It was not only the sexual satisfaction which she loved, it was the man himself. The big, bullish Dutchman with the guttural accent and the greengrocer's cart on the corner. She loved him and she was content.

Otto, however, was not. A man with a corner greengrocer's cart was not good enough for Kathleen. So he worked hard and bought up the lease on a grocery shop at the end of Bourke Street near the docks.

The shop prospered and Otto built an extension to the old house in Woolloomooloo. It left them with no backyard, but a fine room for Robbie and Johann to share. And when Kathleen's brother Dan moved out, the boys had a bedroom of their own. An unaccustomed luxury for two young Woolloomooloo lads.

Kathleen watched Dan go with mixed emotions, saddened but also grateful. Dan mixed with a bad crowd now, no longer just the push. She supposed she had seen it coming and she wondered if she could have done more. But it was too late; neither she nor Otto could afford to have their young sons influenced by Dan and his criminal associates.

She saw little of her brother these days. He lived at the top of Kings Cross, and rumour had it that he and his woman ran a house of ill repute, and God knew what else besides. Kathleen felt sorry for Dan, but his anger had taken him along a dangerous path and she had the sense to let him go.

'It won't last long, the war, and we'll get married as soon as I come home. In a church.'

'And I'll have a white dress, and a long veil, and bridesmaids.' Robbie and Aggie said the same thing over and over, each Saturday of his weekend leave, after they'd made love in the little bedroom above the store and were lying, satisfied, in each other's arms.

'Oh Robbie, I wish you didn't have to go.' She always said that too.

'But I do, you know that.'

The planned dispatch of troops aboard the Aberdeen liner *Euripides* had been deferred. The lads were restless. September was drawing to a close, and still they'd not set sail. Robbie O'Shea wasn't sure how he felt about the delay. It meant he had another weekend leave, another night with Aggie but, like the others in camp, he longed to visit foreign parts and do battle with the enemy.

'I love you, Aggie.' Robbie kissed her and ran his fingers over the perfect little mounds of her young breasts. She was the first girl he'd ever made love to and there would never be another. 'I really do.'

The next day they had lunch with Kathleen and Otto. Little was said of the war, and Johann was barely mentioned.

Robbie tried to offer a comforting word, for Otto's sake. 'Johann's fine,' he said. 'They work us hard and he's getting very fit.' But Otto just grunted. Robbie decided to leave the subject alone, which was a pity, he thought, because he would have liked to have told Otto that the army was good for his son, that Johann was becoming a man.

'By crikey, Johann's a different bloke,' Tim Kendall had remarked. 'The army's doing him good I reckon.'

'Let's go to the Domain,' Kathleen suggested as they cleared away the dishes. Otto was in one of his dismal moods and it would do them all good to get out of the house.

'Will we take Ernie with us?' Robbie asked, patting the old dog whose head had rested on his knee throughout lunch.

'I don't usually these days,' Kathleen replied, 'not to the Domain, the walk's a bit much for him.'

Ernie was nearly fourteen, and he looked every bit of his age. He was mangy in summer and arthritic in winter; his eyes were rheumy and he was partially deaf, but still Kathleen refused to have him put down. It would break Robbie's heart, she said to Otto every time he suggested it. Besides, the dog didn't seem to be in much pain, except for the particularly cold days when his arthritis played up. Even then, he never complained, just sat on his rug in the kitchen, looking tired. Kathleen loved the old dog.

'Let's give it a go, Mum,' Robbie said. 'I'll bring him home if he gets crook.'

Otto didn't come with them; he wanted to put in some new shelving at the shop, he said, and Kathleen thought it was just as well. Otto was best left alone when he was in one of his moods.

He'd work off his ill-humour with hard physical labour as he always did.

Kathleen, Robbie and Aggie set off through the streets of Woolloomooloo, Robbie resplendent in his military uniform, old Ernie plodding behind. When they reached the steep hill which led to the Domain, they slowed down so the dog could catch up.

'You're a good old boy, aren't you,' Robbie said, squatting beside the dog and scratching his ears when Ernie came wheezing up to them.

'I don't know how you can do that,' Aggie screwed up her nose in distaste, 'he's so dirty.' Aggie never patted Ernie.

It had been the girl's repugnance towards Ernie which had first alienated Kathleen. A silly and shallow reaction, she knew, but she hadn't been able to help herself. Now, as they continued up the hill, Aggie refusing to hold Robbie's hand because he'd been scratching the dog—'He's got mange,' she complained—Kathleen felt irritated.

She was annoyed with herself for feeling so, but something about the girl rubbed her up the wrong way. Try as she might, Kathleen simply could not warm to Aggie, and she wished that Robbie had not settled upon his first love affair. But then that was typical of Robbie. Always deeply affected by the events in his life, his first sexual experience was bound to have had a profound impact.

She was certainly a pretty girl, Kathleen thought as she watched them up ahead, Robbie with his arm around Aggie's tiny waist. A little on the slim side in Kathleen's opinion, but a beautiful body, long slender back and well-shaped arms, and beneath her straw boater, her hair was the colour of corn, thick and curly, framing a pretty, pert face.

Kathleen had felt sorry for Aggie when she'd applied for the job at the shop. Just turned seventeen, the girl had had a hard life. Brought up by her widowed and destitute mother, the main influence in Aggie's young life had been the Christian workers at the Jubilee School, a charitable institution run by the Sydney Ragged School Movement. The Jubilee School was dedicated to the 'rescue and salvation' of children who would otherwise have been destined to a life on the streets, and Aggie had obviously been a model student. She was a well-mannered girl with an air of refinement about her. Kathleen had insisted that they give her the job, even though Otto had thought she was too young.

What a pity Aggie annoyed her, Kathleen thought, she would have so liked to feel affection for her future daughter-in-law. But then perhaps there was no girl good enough for her only son, she reprimanded herself. She really must try harder.

The Domain was more crowded than ever this sunny Sunday afternoon. Hundreds upon hundreds of people mingled in the vast public parkland, some wandering down the rocky peninsula to picnic at Mrs Macquarie's Chair, or to throw a fishing line off the wharf at Bennelong Point which was no longer a military area, old Fort Macquarie having been demolished to make way for tram-sheds. Others explored the Botanic Gardens, or visited the recently built Mitchell Library, or wandered through the Palace Garden where once had stood the magnificent but short-lived exhibition building with its famous giant dome. Most of those who came to the Domain on a Sunday, however, gathered to listen to the speakers.

In the early days the Governor's Domain had consisted of all the land from the Tank Stream east to Walla Mulla Bay—which shortly became known as Woolloomooloo—and south to an area later known as the Inner Domain. Some of the land was set aside for government buildings, but predominantly the Domain belonged to the people and, over the years it had become the centre of free speech for the citizens of Sydney, the more vocal of whom loudly expressed their views to the crowds, who agreed or disagreed, heckled or simply stood listening.

From their boxes and platforms and ladders—some even sat in Moreton Bay fig trees—the speakers ranted and raved about every imaginable topic from the Gospel and the salvation of the human race, to the damnation of mankind and the end of the world. There were those against capitalism, those against communism, and those against the current government. There were those for world peace, those for the rights of the working man, and those for women's liberation.

Always the Domain reflected the people's voice, and today, as Kathleen, her son and his fiancée mingled with the crowd, the people's voice spoke of war. Today the Domain was taken over by the zealous call for volunteers. 'Join the army, boys!' the speakers screamed. 'Fight for your King and your Country!'

'Come on lads! Britain needs you!'

'Be a man! Sign up today!'

The frenzy of this call to arms depressed Kathleen. Her son's military uniform was reminder enough that he would soon be going off to war. Now, as people gave Robbie's shoulder a hearty slap and pumped his hand effusively, saying, 'Good on you, son, we need lads like you,' or 'Kill one of those dirty Huns for me, boy', she found it offensive and disturbing.

The other soldiers amongst the crowd were receiving the same treatment, and the speakers used their presence to humiliate young men in civilian attire. 'Shame on you, lad, look at this fine young soldier. Get yourself into a uniform!'

'I might take Ernie home,' Kathleen said after an hour or so. 'He's very tired.'

During the slow walk home, the old dog bone-weary limping behind, Kathleen gave in to her feelings of melancholy. Please God let him come home, she prayed. Please God don't let them kill my son. For the first time Kathleen wished she had Otto's faith. In the early days she had accompanied him and Johann to the Catholic church on Sundays, taking Robbie with them, but the Mass had been foreign to her and she'd felt like a hypocrite amongst such devotion. Gradually she'd stopped going and, to his credit, Otto had never tried to foist his religious beliefs upon her.

It wasn't so much that she didn't believe in God. More that she hadn't given Him much thought. Despite the hardships in her life, and there had certainly been many, it had never occurred to Kathleen to seek God's help, she had always relied upon her own resourcefulness. That was not enough now. Now Kathleen wished that she'd persevered with the church services. Perhaps God listened more to those who prayed in churches.

Johann's letter arrived two days before the troops embarked for overseas.

> *Dear Dad*
> *You'll probably never forgive me for not coming to see you, and I can't say I blame you, it was a hurtful thing*

to do. But to tell you the truth, I was frightened. I was frightened that you'd stop me going. You can be a tough bloke at times and I wouldn't have been able to stand up to you. I have to go, you see, Dad. I don't expect you to understand why, I'm not sure I do myself. But I have to be a part of it.

The main thing I wanted to tell you, and this I know you'll understand, is that God is going with me. I've been to Mass each Sunday since I left home and I've prayed for you and Kathleen, and for all the lads of course. But most of all, I've prayed that you'll forgive me.

I'm sorry that I hurt you, and I promise that I'll write regularly while I'm away. Your loving son, Johann.

Kathleen watched as Otto read the letter. When he'd finished, he stood up from the kitchen table and nodded. 'Johann has grown up,' he said, passing the letter to her.

He took his mug of tea out onto the back porch. Kathleen didn't follow, she'd seen the tears in his eyes. But ten minutes later, when he came back inside, she smiled thankfully as he embraced her.

All over Australia the units of the first contingent of the Australian Expeditionary Force were marching through the city streets to the harbours and the transport ships which awaited to take them off to war.

The Australian government had chartered the largest suitable ships in ports. Passenger liners, great wool-carriers and meat-carriers, all had been fitted with mess tables and hammocks; the horse transports had been furnished with endless stalls, spread with coconut matting and secured against heavy weather.

A large fleet of troopships, numbering A1 to A28, had been lying in various ports throughout the country for many weeks now, awaiting embarkation.

Thousands lined the streets of Sydney to farewell their sons, their fathers, their lovers, their friends, or simply to wish the lads godspeed.

Onlookers stood on tram-stop benches or on boxes they'd brought themselves; others sat in the branches of trees or perched on the pedestals of statues, clutching at the bronze and stone limbs of bygone heroes in order to get a better view of the boys going off to the war. Along the route to the harbour, every office building window was crowded with well-wishers showering streamers and yellow wattle blossom upon the troops marching proudly below.

And march proudly they did, in their own special way. A jaunty way. Rifles over shoulder, slouch hats at an angle, chin straps drawn tight, their chests thrust out and their well-muscled arms swinging, theirs was an unconventional march. Neither ragged nor precise, but boyish and enthusiastic.

Every man kept a keen eye out for his loved ones, some even marched with their sweethearts by their side, and there were smiles and winks and waves and hurrahs exchanged as names were called from the crowds, children were raised onto shoulders to wave goodbye to their fathers, and wives and mothers blew frantic kisses.

Robbie O'Shea grinned and waved to Kathleen and Otto. He gave a special wink to Aggie who was crying, but she missed it as she buried her head in her handkerchief.

Tim Kendall and his uncle Billy had no trouble picking their family out from the crowd as they marched. Little Emily, now twelve years old, was perched on Benjamin's shoulders; Norah was waving wildly, and beside them stood Billy's wife Marge and their two little boys. If only his mother, Beth, could have been there to watch him march, Billy thought, she would have been so proud, but Beth Kendall had died two years ago.

Further down the line were the Putman boys, Mick and his older brother Geoff. Geoff was nearly forty now but, fit as a mallee bull, he hadn't even bothered to lie about his age. The army needed men like him. Their mother Nellie, in pride of place on the kerbside corner, having shoved her way through to the front, was giving her boys a grand old send-off. Shrieking at the top of her lungs, her husband on one side—Jack had been out of gaol for a whole two years on the trot—and her eldest son, Spotty, on the other, holding his little sister Lizzie's hand and not looking too happy. Spotty had wanted desperately to go to the war. He'd volunteered all right, but he hadn't passed the medical.

'It's just a cough,' he'd said, 'I've always had it, it doesn't make me sick.'

But they'd told him he had bad lungs—weakened by the smallpox which had nearly killed him as a child, they said. Just his luck. Spotty watched his brothers enviously. They were going to have all the fun, and he had to stay home just because of a bleeding cough.

Otto's eyes were searching frantically amongst the troops as they passed, he couldn't see Johann.

'Can you see him?' he asked Kathleen.

'Not yet. I'm looking. Not yet.' She prayed that they'd not missed him. He couldn't have passed them by. He couldn't. Then suddenly, 'There he is! Look, Otto. There he is!'

Johann has changed, she thought the instant she saw him. Robbie had been right. The skinny young boy was a man now, his body filled out and well formed. And, although his face was the same, deep-furrowed bridge to the nose, square-jawed, thin-lipped—the traits which had always set him apart and labelled him a foreigner—his expression was entirely different. There was a pride in his eyes now, and a joy in the curve of his mouth, there was an openness which had never been there. It was the pride of comradeship. Little Johann, the Dutchie's kid, had finally become one of the boys.

'Johann!' Otto raised his giant hand and bellowed as he waved. 'Johann!'

Johann heard his father's voice and their eyes met across the sea of faces.

'God go with you, my son!' Otto yelled.

Johann grinned, and as he marched past his father, he saluted.

Chapter Eleven

As soon as Godfrey Streatham found out about Kendle and Streatham's government contract, he knew immediately it had not been secured by any ethical means. He was astounded that Charles had managed to keep the secret for so long, but then the factories had remained principally his and Stephen's concern, Godfrey concentrating upon the emporiums and the retail side of the business.

Godfrey was outraged. He called a private meeting in the boardroom of the George Street store. Just Charles, Stephen, himself and Howard.

'We must even up the numbers, Father,' Godfrey insisted, although Howard required little persuasion, he was as appalled as his son by the news.

'Kendle and Streatham has enjoyed an unsullied reputation since your grandfather's time,' he said, his bony knuckles clenched upon the ivory handle of his walking stick as he and Godfrey stood in the store's grand foyer waiting for the lift.

He jabbed his walking stick into the air. 'Look,' he said as he pointed up at the emblem emblazoned in pressed metal above the main foyer doors. ' "Kendle and Streatham, Trading on the Wings of Honour", we have lived by that motto and now he has made a mockery of it.'

Howard was becoming seriously agitated. 'Calm down, Father,' Godfrey said as they stepped into the lift. 'You must not upset yourself, it is not good for your health.' An emotional outburst from his father would also not serve their purpose. The old man was there simply to back up Godfrey's plan of action. 'Calm down and leave it to me.'

The meeting in the giant oak-panelled boardroom of Kendle and Streatham went exactly as Godfrey had predicted it would. Charles ranted and raved; Stephen nodded a little from time to time, obviously agreeing with Godfrey but not daring to say so out loud; and Howard, in whom Godfrey had not confided, wildly applauded his son's suggestion.

The plan was simple enough. All goods supplied to the army were to be sold at cost price, and all profits made from any previous sales were to be donated to the war effort. 'As of now,' Godfrey said, 'before the press finds out and labels us profiteers.'

'Why the hell should the press find out?' Charles growled.

'It is not worth the risk,' Godfrey insisted. 'And besides, it is the honourable thing to do.'

Pompous and unprepossessing as he was, Godfrey Streatham could be a formidable force when set upon a course of action. Implacably he stood his ground, refusing to compromise in any way whatsoever, and eventually there was little Charles could do but look for a way to turn Godfrey's plan to his own advantage.

A fortnight after the meeting, a small item appeared in the *Financial Times*. It was rumoured, the journalist reported, that Kendle and Streatham had been anonymously donating considerable sums to the war effort. Several days later a full page article appeared in the *Sydney Morning Herald*, accompanied by a very flattering picture of Charles.

> *It is with reluctance that Mr Kendle agreed to this interview,* the article said, *and he has done so only because news of the philanthropic activities of Kendle and Streatham has already been leaked to the press. He would otherwise have preferred to maintain his silence.*

The reluctant Mr Kendle not only admitted to his company's contributions to the war effort, but was apparently willing to announce to the journalist Kendle and Streatham's plans for returned soldiers.

> *'All men will be guaranteed re-employment upon their*

return from the front,' Mr Kendle told this reporter. 'And should a longstanding employee of Kendle and Streatham make the ultimate sacrifice for his King and his country, then his widow and children shall be provided for from the special funds allocated for such a tragic event.

'Kendle and Streatham is a family,' Mr Kendle said, 'and as a family we look after our own.'

It had taken Godfrey a solid week of argument to convince Charles that they must set up a protection scheme for soldiers and their families. 'On a sliding scale,' he had suggested, 'for men who have been in our employ for upward of five years.'

'Why, in God's name?' Charles had actually laughed at the suggestion. 'If a man is fool enough to go off and get himself shot, why should it be any concern of ours?'

'Tell him about the Wunderlichs,' Howard had suggested to his son, 'that'll do it.'

'The Wunderlichs are leading the way in industrial and personal relations,' Godfrey told Charles, 'which is proving not only harmonious to the company, but also profitable. They have even set up a staff partnership and profit-sharing scheme which guarantees loyalty and productivity.'

'It's the first I've heard of it.' Charles's tone was belligerent, but Godfrey knew that he had the old man's undivided attention.

'The scheme has not been made known to the general public,' Godfrey explained, 'but you need only ask any one of their employees. And they most certainly intend to look after their returned soldiers. Alfred Wunderlich is most insistent upon it.'

It was the mention of Alfred Wunderlich that clinched Godfrey's argument. The man had never liked him, Charles knew it. He had never invited him to join his prestigious social set. Alfred Wunderlich was a thorn in Charles's side.

Mr Charles Kendle, the *Sydney Morning Herald* journalist concluded, *is to be congratulated as a man ahead of his time, one leading the way in industrial and personal relations. A true hero of the people.*

'Poppycock,' Charles said when Godfrey accused him of giving the story to the press. 'If an ethical journalist from an ethical publication approaches me for an interview—an interview which can only be for the good of the firm I might add—am I to refuse? Where are your wits man? We have press relations to maintain.'

Charles didn't care one bit about Godfrey's outrage and Howard's disapproval, he had far more important things on his mind.

'What do you mean Mark's joined the army!' Charles growled. 'No grandson of mine is going to war. I forbid it!'

'He enlisted last week, Father, he's already left for training camp.' Stephen remained frozen in the doorway of his father's study, and he found himself flinching as the old man slowly rose from the chair behind his desk. He couldn't help it, the ferocity of his father's rage had always terrified him.

'And you let him go! Without trying to stop him!' Charles's voice was shrill with anger, bordering on hysterical, as he approached his son. 'Without telling me!'

'Yes.'

Charles struck Stephen's face with all the force his age could muster, the gaunt flat of his right hand leaving a pink imprint upon his son's cheek.

For a second or two, the men stood staring at each other in silence, the blow having shocked them both. Stephen was taken aback by his father's sheer audacity more than anything. Charles Kendle was nearly eighty, white haired and wizened. Stephen was twice his size, he could have beaten the old man to a pulp. Yet, as he looked into the steel-grey eyes, he was helpless. He knew that he should turn his back on his father and simply walk away, but he couldn't. He knew that he should leave his father's house and never return, but he knew that he would never do that.

Stephen Kendle could do nothing but wonder, yet again, at his father's power, and at his own sickening weakness.

'Let me tell him, Dad,' Mark had said, 'at least then you won't have to bear the brunt of his insanity. Because he'll go mad, you know he will.'

'Yes, I know it.' Dear God, he had thought, what sort of a man am I, my own son feels the need to protect me. 'You are to leave your grandfather to me, I insist upon it, Mark,' he'd said. 'If you must go to the war, then you go with my blessing and the knowledge that your family is proud of you.' He'd felt proud himself, proud and strong as he'd embraced his son.

Charles gripped the handle of the open door for support, his strength suddenly waning. As he had struck his son, he had wanted to kill him, if there'd been a weapon in his hand he would probably have done so. Now all he felt was loathing and disgust.

'What sort of a father are you?' he demanded. 'You willingly send your own son off to his possible death.' When Stephen remained silent, Charles felt his anger grow once more. 'Why didn't you go yourself? You're expendable, we could well do without you . . .'

'The army doesn't want men in their forties.'

But Charles wasn't listening. '. . . why did you have to send my grandson. The only grandson who bears my name.'

'I didn't *send* him, Father . . .'

'You're a traitor to this family,' the edge of hysteria was once again creeping into the old man's voice. 'A traitor d'you hear?'

Stephen watched while, exhausted by his tirade, his father returned to collapse in the chair behind his desk. Charles Kendle looked old. Tired and defeated. Stephen knew of the old man's plans for Mark. The future of the Kendle dynasty rested upon the strong young shoulders of the only grandson who bore his name. Mark was to take on the mantle of Kendle and Streatham, the fourth generation to do so. But Stephen wanted to tell his father that such plans were pointless.

'I will never work for the family firm,' Mark had said, 'and if Grandfather wishes to disinherit me, then let him, he will not take over my life, as he has done everyone else's.'

The remark had not been intended to hurt, but the underlying inference had. Stephen had almost winced at its truth. 'I promise I'll stand by you, son,' he'd said. 'I'll not let you down. Please. Don't go to war in order to escape your grandfather.'

That was when Mark had made his desperate plea, appalled that he'd hurt his father, and appalled that his father had so misinterpreted his intentions. 'But that's not why I'm going, Dad, that's not why I'm going at all.'

He'd jumped up from the old garden bench in the arbour at the bottom of the garden, where they so often sat in solitude, and looked out over Woolloomooloo at the panoramic view of the city beyond. At the skyline which was forever changing, growing and expanding.

'You saw them march,' he said. 'You saw them march through those very streets. You can see the route from here. I have to be one of them, Dad. I have to march through the streets too. I have to know that my country's proud of me.'

'What would you have me do?' he begged, turning to his father, 'wait for the white feathers to arrive in the mail? That's what's happening, did you know? It's women mostly. Women whose sons and husbands have gone to war, they're sending white feathers to able-bodied men who haven't signed up. I won't be labelled a coward.'

'Sending white feathers is a cowardly act in itself,' Stephen protested, 'a man should not be so pressured into going to war.'

'That's not why I'm going either. Oh Dad, you must understand me! You must!' Mark insisted. 'I'm going because I *want* to go, because I'm *proud* to go. And I want you to be proud of me too.'

'I am,' he said, and it was true. He had always been proud of Mark. In fact Stephen had wished many times over the years that he had a strength of his own to match that of his son.

Now Stephen stood in his father's study wishing that he could tell the old man the truth. He summoned up every last ounce of his courage. 'Father,' he began, 'Mark told me before he left . . .'

'Get out.'

'. . . he told me that he would never work for the family . . .'

'Get out!' the old man screamed. He knew what his son was about to say and he refused to listen to such blasphemy. 'Get out of my sight, you disgust me!'

Like a craven dog, Stephen slunk from the room, hating himself and his inadequacy.

'Mothers are supporting fatherless families on a wage barely adequate to sustain themselves, let alone their babies,' Susan Kendle proclaimed from her platform in the centre of the Domain. Like many involved in the Women's Movement, Susan was passionate about the injustice displayed towards women who were doing men's work. 'Industry is either denying them work altogether or paying them less than half a man's wage.' Susan's voice was, as always, so strong and commanding that passers-by found themselves compelled to stop and listen.

'And educated women,' she continued emphatically, 'women with business college degrees. They are employed readily enough as clerks and secretaries. They are granted positions as bookkeepers and accountants. But they are paid a trifle in comparison to their male counterparts. Is this justice?'

Whilst strongly advocating a woman's right to work, and her right to 'an equal day's pay for an equal day's labour', Susan was sensible and balanced in presenting her case. She knew when to bow to the sensitive issues at hand.

'We do not wish to steal our men's jobs,' she insisted. 'When they come home, we will stand by them and help to rebuild their lives in the work force. Then, and then only, can we work together towards unity and equality.'

When Susan confined her argument to equal pay, the opposition she encountered was minimal. It was when she spoke out against the war that she ran into trouble. And speak out she did. Brazenly and, to many, shockingly. Along with other members of the Women's Political Association, she had joined the recently formed Women's Peace Army and, like her fellow members, was vociferous in her opinions.

She ran a risk in speaking out publicly against the war, for under the War Precautions Act, it was illegal to do so, a six-month sentence the penalty. But Susan felt that her letters to the major newspapers, and her articles which were published in *The Woman Voter*, the major agent for antiwar opinion, were not enough. She needed to speak directly to the people.

Amongst those who listened to Susan regularly was Kathleen O'Shea. Even before the war Kathleen had been impressed by the forceful advocate for women's rights who spoke regularly from her platform near the old Garden Palace grounds. A bulky woman, a little ill-kempt in her dress, her hair unruly, she had, however, a fine voice and a handsome face, and Kathleen could tell she was a woman of breeding.

Her arguments were well informed and intelligent and Kathleen had learned a lot as she'd listened, often thinking that she could have done with a little such knowledge in her youth. These days as she listened, however, Kathleen found herself confused. How was she to reconcile herself to the notion that her son had gone off to fight a war that was 'senseless', a war that 'should never have been fought by Australians'?

'Never should we have been called upon to make such a sacrifice!'

The woman's voice rang out across the crowd, clearly audible above the heckling and the booing of the many dissenters gathered about her.

'Never should our women have been called upon to give up their husbands and their sons! Never should our fine Australian men have been called upon to give up their very lives!' There was a frenzied reaction from the crowd.

'She should be locked up,' Aggie said loudly, which was exactly what the majority of the crowd was saying. Here and there a member of the Women's Peace Army, wearing the symbolic purple peace button with the white dove insignia, voiced approval but was quickly howled down.

'There'll be a riot any minute, let's go home,' Aggie said. And when Kathleen took no notice, she whinged, 'I'm not feeling well, I want to go home.'

'I told you not to come in the first place,' Kathleen replied a little snappily. Aggie invariably found something to complain about. Now more than ever, her pregnancy being the perfect excuse.

'Well, I thought the walk would do me good, didn't I?' Aggie looked sulky. 'I didn't know you were going to stand around for so long. It's not good for me, getting jostled about in a crowd like this, not in my condition.'

Kathleen wanted to stay, but the more Aggie's pregnancy had blossomed, the more she had demanded constant attention, forever blackmailing Kathleen with the precious burden of her grandson.

'Otto's at church, I'll be all on my own,' she'd said that morning when Kathleen had announced she was going to the Domain.

'So?'

'I don't want to be on my own.'

'You want to walk up the hill, do you? "In your condition"?' Kathleen couldn't resist the barb, but it didn't register with Aggie.

'Yes. The walk'll do me good.'

Kathleen looked about the Domain. The crowds gathered around those speakers calling men to arms were loudly voicing their approval. Union Jacks were being waved, a mob was singing 'Rule Britannia'. Patriotism, jubilation and a fervent belief in the war abounded. But here, gathered around the woman's platform, men were shaking their fists and women were yelling, 'Shame! Shame on you!' Aggie was not wrong, she thought, there might well be a riot any minute.

'All right,' she said with reluctance. 'All right, we'll go.' She glanced back at the woman as they walked away. Kathleen might not agree with her views, but she couldn't help but admire her courage in voicing them.

They walked slowly. Although it was April, the day was warm, more like summer than autumn, and Aggie was seven months pregnant and feeling the heat. Her ankles hurt, she said, and her back was sore.

Kathleen paid little regard to the girl's litany of complaint. There were certainly no grounds for concern, Aggie was as healthy as a horse. Kathleen kept Robbie well informed of the fact every time she wrote, never sure how much Aggie might have dramatised her condition in her letters to him.

Robbie O'Shea had been elated when he'd heard of his impending child. 'Look after my girl, Mum,' he'd written, 'and look after my baby when it comes. The two of them couldn't be in better hands, I know it, and that's such a good, safe feeling.'

Kathleen's initial reaction had not been as joyful as her son's. 'You're pregnant?' she'd queried abruptly when Aggie had told her the news in the privacy of the kitchen, Otto safely away at Mass. Aggie knew that he wouldn't approve. 'How far gone?'

'Between three and four months the doctor says.'

'Damn.' The girl should have been more careful, Kathleen thought. A young man fighting a war did not need the added distraction of an unborn baby and the worry over the safety of both mother and child. A young man fighting a war needed to concentrate on his own survival. Damn the girl.

Her face must have mirrored her thoughts, for Aggie looked suddenly distressed.

'I didn't mean for this to happen, Kathleen,' she begged. 'Truly I didn't. Please don't send me away.'

The severity of Kathleen's expression frightened Aggie. Disapproval was the last thing she had expected. Kathleen so doted on her son that Aggie had been certain the prospect of a grandchild would delight her. In fact that had been Aggie's guarantee, or so she'd thought.

Suspicious that her future mother-in-law did not particularly like her, Aggie had planned the conception. Should Robbie die in battle, it was quite possible that Kathleen would want nothing more to do with her. She'd be back on the streets in no time. But Kathleen O'Shea, Aggie was sure, would not abandon the mother of her grandchild. In the tragic event of her fiancé's death, Aggie and her baby would be assured of a comfortable life within the O'Shea household.

But her plan had clearly backfired, Aggie thought with a sudden rush of anxiety. 'Please, Kathleen, don't send me away.' Aggie could feel the advent of frightened tears, and she didn't try to stem them, tears were useful. 'I didn't mean it to happen.'

'Why on earth would I send you away?' Kathleen said, sitting beside Aggie and putting her arm around the girl's heaving shoulders whilst her whole body racked with sobs. 'What could make you say such a thing?'

Kathleen dug into the pocket of her apron and produced a handkerchief which the girl took, her sobs subsiding a little. 'Come along now, stop crying, you're Robbie's fiancée, you're the mother of my future grandchild.' Kathleen smiled comfortingly. 'How could I ever send you away?'

Aggie smiled wanly as she gulped back the last sob.

'You will move into the house,' Kathleen continued, 'into Robbie's old room. He'd like that.'

Aggie lifted her head from Kathleen's breast. 'What will Otto say?' She dabbed at her eyes with the handkerchief. 'He won't approve.'

'Otto will do as I ask him. And we will tell everyone that you and Robbie married before he left for the war,' she said. 'From now on you are Aggie O'Shea.'

Aggie smiled through the remnants of her tears, genuinely relieved and grateful. 'Thank you, Kathleen.' She hugged the older woman. 'Thank you, thank you.'

As Aggie's belly grew, so did her confidence. She was Aggie O'Shea, proud mother-to-be, and Robbie's letters, assuring her of Kathleen's devotion to her and the baby, gave her unlimited licence to demand special attention.

Robbie's were not the only letters to arrive from the training camp in Egypt. Johann too wrote regularly and from the outset his letters were boyishly enthusiastic.

> *You wouldn't believe Cairo, Dad, it's like a story from* The Arabian Nights. *We went to the bazaars, me and Robbie and Tim, and there were snake charmers, and women dancing in veils, and the smell of incense everywhere. And the people! So many people you wouldn't believe! All trying to sell you something. Carvings and jewels and good luck charms. I bought some beaut souvies.*

'What is this "souvies"?' Otto pointed the word out to Kathleen.

'Souvenirs?' she said after a moment's thought.

'Ah. Yes.'

> *... and you should see the pyramids, Dad. One of the seven wonders of the world all right. You wouldn't believe how big they are or how they made them like that.*
>
> *The work's been hard. Took us weeks clearing bloody great rocks out to make a campsite and a parade ground. And marching through the sand's a right bugger, I can tell you.*

'He swears too much,' Otto said.

'He's just being one of the boys,' Kathleen assured him as she peered over his shoulder.

Otto grunted and read on.

> *There's talk that we're leaving here soon. But no-one knows where we're going. At least, if they do they're not telling us. Some of the blokes reckon it might be Greece, some reckon it might be Turkey. Just furphs. Nobody really knows.*
>
> *I've made a lot of new mates in the army, Dad. Robbie and Tim are still my best cobbers of course, but you'd be surprised how many of the blokes here are Catholics, and we go to Mass together on Sundays. It's something we share, it makes us close. I know that, like me, they pray*

for their mates and their families back home. And it feels right that we're here. It feels that God's on our side and He'll look after us all. So don't you worry about me.
Your loving son, Johann.

Robbie's letter to Kathleen a month later made it clear why Johann's letter had been so vague about their destination.

Our ship's anchored at a British base, but we're not allowed to say whereabouts. They didn't even tell us where we were going until two days before we got here.

We've been at the base for nearly a month now, and we don't look like leaving in a hurry. Sometimes they exercise us ashore, but mostly we're confined to the ship, practising disembarkation drills. Belting up and down rope ladders and in and out of small boats carrying full gear is no joke, I can tell you. And I reckon they don't mean it to be either. I reckon they'll be landing us somewhere pretty soon.

Don't say any of this to Aggie, Mum, this is just for you and Otto. I've written her a letter that will go out with this mail, telling her I'm having a beaut time and that I miss her, the usual thing. I do too. She must be nearly seven months by now. How I'd love to see her. Puffed out, knowing that the baby inside her is mine. It's a wonderful thing.

Look after her, Mum, I know that you will. And if anything happens to me—well, I don't want to sound gloomy, and I don't want to make you unhappy, but I think it's not far away now, and we have to be realistic, don't we?

I love you, Mum. Second to my girl you're the dearest thing in my life. Write soon.
Robbie.

The horrifying news of the bloodbath at Gallipoli plunged Australia into a state of shock. Official numbers were not yet known, but the endless casualty lists published in the black-bordered newspapers were hideous proof of the extent of the slaughter.

Like countless others all over the country, Kathleen and Otto queued up every day to buy the newspaper, or joined the dozens clustered around the lists displayed at railway stations and various other public buildings.

Together they would scan the names, praying that they would not see their own. No De Haans or O'Sheas today, thank God, and they would go home to comfort Aggie who sat frozen at the kitchen table, holding her huge belly, waiting for the news.

In Surry Hills, Benjamin and Norah Kendall were doing the same thing. As were Nellie and Jack Putman, who lived a block away now. The Putmans and the Kendalls were no longer neighbours. Wexford Street, along with whole blocks of Surry Hills, had been destroyed to make way for the broad new Wentworth Avenue where the rents were so high that the area was effectively killed off as a residential neighbourhood.

Each morning Spotty Putman would fetch the paper, bringing it home to his parents so that the three of them could search the lists together. They never looked at the paper until Lizzie was safely off to school.

The first week went by and they were safe. Then, early in the second week, Nellie's finger froze on the spot as she was tracing her way down the list.

'"Putman, Geoffrey,"' she read. And, directly beneath, '"Putman, Michael."'

'Both of them,' she whispered. 'Oh sweet Jesus, no. Not both of them.' She turned to her husband. Her eyes, like raisins in the dough of her fleshy face, were brimming with tears of shock and disbelief. 'Not both of them, Jack. Not both of them. Not both of them.'

Jack Putman held his wife's huge body to him as she cried. Not loudly. For once Nellie was not loud. Her sobs were more gulps, deep, despairing gulps for air. Silent tears coursed down Jack's cheeks as he looked over his wife's shoulder at his son.

Spotty was not crying. Spotty was shaking his head at the newspaper as he read and reread his brothers' names.

'They were bound to cop it together,' he said. 'Geoff promised he'd look after Mick, d'you remember, Dad? He said, "Don't you worry about Mick, I'll stick right by his side every minute of the day", d'you remember?'

Jack pulled a seat out for Nellie at the kitchen table and sat beside her as she mopped her face and blew her nose on her apron.

Spotty was talking to himself now, but it didn't matter, he just went on. '"They get one Putman, they'll have to get us both," that's what he said. He reckoned it wouldn't happen, he reckoned the law of averages was on his side. Silly bugger, the law of averages doesn't count over there!' Spotty was getting angry. 'And his bloody brother's thirty-one years old, he doesn't need his hand held!' He sniffed and wiped his runny nose with the sleeve of his shirt. 'Silly buggers,' he said, 'they were bound to cop it together.'

Spotty left his parents to their grief and went out to get drunk.

Two months later a letter arrived from the front. It was addressed to Nellie and it was from Billy Kendall.

> *Dear Nell*
> *I don't know if this will be of much comfort to you, but I wanted to write and let you know. I was close by Geoff and Mick when it happened and they fought bravely right till the end. It came quickly, I honestly don't think they felt any pain. They died for their King and their Country, just like we are all prepared to do, and you have every right to feel proud of them.*
> *My love and sympathy to you all,*
> *Billy Kendall*

Nellie was grateful. 'He's a fine man your brother,' she said to Ben when she visited the Kendalls to show them the letter. 'His own life in the balance and he takes time out to comfort me like this.' She dabbed at her eyes with her ever-present handkerchief, she always seemed to be crying these days. Not sobbing or bawling, but tears streamed from her eyes at the oddest times. 'A very fine man. I hope he comes home safely, him and young Tim.'

Ben nodded and Norah said gently, 'Let me get you a cup of tea, Nellie.'

'That'd be nice, thank you Norah, I'll give you a hand. And don't you worry about this,' she sniffed and dabbed away, 'I'm fine, lovey, really I am, just can't seem to stop, that's all.'

Ben stepped out onto the back porch whilst the women made

the tea. He didn't want Nellie to see his face, for Nellie's letter was a tissue of lies.

Benjamin too had received a letter from his brother, delivered by a returned soldier in order to escape military censorship. It was several pages long, the first page being a brief note to Norah assuring her that her son Tim was alive and well. The rest of the letter was for Ben's eyes only.

Tear this up when you've finished it, it won't do anyone any good to read what it is that I want to say. I don't even know how I'm going to say it, all I know is that I have to, and you're the only one I can say it to. I can't talk to the blokes over here because a lot of them feel the same way, I can see it in their faces, but like me they're too scared to admit the truth. They don't dare, not even to themselves. They pretend that what's happening is right and that it's noble—men dying for King and Country and all that stuff.

But the truth is, it's not. It's not right and it's not noble. I saw the Putmans cop it and there was nothing noble about their deaths, I can tell you, just like there was nothing noble about all the others who copped it in the first landing. Half of them were shot in the back while they rowed ashore. The Putmans were. Mowed down before they could face the enemy.

Our boat was ten yards in front of Mick's and Geoff's and I don't know how we ever got to the beach, but we did. Three of our boys were shot, and we chucked them over the side and kept on rowing, we had to keep on rowing so as not to upset the rhythm, but any minute we expected to get it in the back. I just fixed my eyes on the boat coming in behind us and tried not to think about anything but heaving on the oars.

It was easy to see in the dark, the flares the Turks were firing turned the whole night into day, it was like we were all under one bloody great spotlight. Mick copped it first and they chucked him overboard, I think he was dead, I think it was quick. Then about four of their blokes copped it all at once and the boat capsized. The others tried swimming ashore but they didn't make it, they were picked off one by one. Geoff was wounded and he couldn't swim, but he was yelling at the top of his voice. I couldn't be sure what he was yelling, not above all the din, but I'd swear it was 'You bastards'. They shot him and he went under just as our boat hit the shallows and I don't remember anything after that except running like hell for the cover of the cliffs.

I remember an hour or so later though. When the sun came up and you could see all the bodies. Everywhere, they were. I couldn't pick out which ones were Geoff and Mick, but there were lots washed up in the shallows. Dozens of blokes whose boots hadn't touched dry sand. They never got a chance to play the hero, they never even fired a shot. What's bloody noble about that? And now we've heard that the whole thing was a bungle. We were landed in the wrong place. Fed to the Turks we were, like prize targets in a shooting gallery. What's bloody right about that?

I shouldn't be writing this to you, Ben, not with Tim over here, but there's no-one else I can talk to and I didn't want to die without getting it off my chest. I said in my note to Norah that I'd look after Tim, but to tell you the truth, he doesn't need looking after. He's much tougher than I am. He seems to be weathering the storm far better, and I hope that'll see him through. Remember when I was his age and belonged to the Push? I thought I was so tough, me and Mick Putman, we both did. Now Mick's dead and I'm over here scared out of my wits.

I'm going to send Nellie a letter saying all the right things. God forbid she should ever know that Geoff and Mick died so bloody uselessly. After that, apart from a note now and then to let Marge and the kids know I'm alive, I'm not going to write any more. I've had my say.

You've been a good big brother to me, Ben, more like a father really, after Dad died. I hope I see you again, but if I don't, thanks for everything.

Love Billy

Ben wasn't the only one receiving disturbingly frank news from the front.

There had been no word from Johann since the troops had left the safety of the British base on the island of Lemnos. Then, finally, a full five months after the landing at Gallipoli, Otto De Haan received a letter from his son.

> *Dear Dad*
> *I don't know how I've lasted this long, I don't know how any of us have, but I know that I won't last much longer, and I wanted to say goodbye. Thank Kathleen and give her my love, she's been a good mother to me when most of the time I didn't deserve it.*
> *I can still remember my real mum, even though I was only a kid when she died, and I'd like to think I was going to see her on the other side. But I know now that I won't. There's no life after death. There's nothing after death. I'm sorry to disappoint you, Dad, but the war's knocked all that out of me.*
> *If I have a chance, my last thoughts will be of you. I love you, Dad, and I'm grateful to have had you for a father. Goodbye.*
> *Your loving son, Johann*

The letter arrived two weeks after the priest's visit. The war office had settled upon a more humane way of informing families of their loss, and a visit from a clergyman now preceded the casualty lists published in the newspapers.

For Otto the knowledge that his son had lost his faith brought a profound anguish. The thought that Johann had died alone, without God's comfort, was agony to him. But he was only one of many who found themselves bereft.

General Sir Charles Munro's recommendation that the peninsula be evacuated, 'on purely military grounds', resulted in a visit to the Australian and New Zealand Army Corps by Lord Kitchener on 13 November. Orders ensued that the troops were to be removed from Gallipoli, and the evacuation of the Anzacs, as they were now known, commenced. The battle had lasted just over six months and the losses had amounted to 7,600 dead and 19,000 wounded.

Chapter Twelve

The enthusiasm with which the declaration of war had first been greeted and the jubilation with which the troops had been farewelled were quickly forgotten as the horror of Gallipoli reached home. No longer did the lackadaisical attitude that 'it would all be over in a few months' exist. The war was destined to grind remorselessly on, and thousands more were destined to lose their lives.

In August, 1916, whilst the disastrous battle of the Somme still raged in France, the British Army Council urgently demanded reinforcements from Australia. Prime Minister, William Morris Hughes, was presented with a problem. The rates of enlistment had been falling off throughout 1916 and, at the conclusion of the seven-week battle of the Somme, the Anzac casualties numbered approximately 25,000, a statistic which would no doubt serve as a further deterrent to prospective volunteers. The only method, Hughes therefore decided, which could guarantee the sustained supply of manpower was conscription.

Billy Hughes was an aggressive bantam rooster of a man. A patriotic militarist, he stood five feet six inches tall, was partially deaf, and commonly known as 'The Little Digger'. He liked the nickname, it suited his self-styled image as a 'battler' with a commitment to Australia's fighting men.

Despite opposition from his own Labor Party and from the very unions which he himself had helped form, Hughes forced the issue of conscription upon the people of Australia by popular referendum.

There ensued the most controversial political issue Australia had ever faced. It seemed no sector of the community was left undivided. Even amongst religious leaders there was conflict of opinion. The Roman Catholic Archbishop of Melbourne, Dr Daniel Mannix, was Hughes's most forceful antagonist, yet the Archbishops of Sydney, Perth and Hobart strongly supported conscription.

Within the arts, prominent figures lent their voices to the cause, both for and against. The great diva, Dame Nellie Melba, appealed to Australian women to vote 'yes', whilst the flamboyant Melbourne contralto Cecilia John publicly sang the plaintive:

I didn't raise my son to be a soldier;
I brought him up to be my pride and joy.
Who dares to put musket to his shoulder,
To kill some other mother's darling boy?

Artists and caricaturists were employed to join the fray, some even plagiarising the opposition's theme. 'I didn't raise my son to be a soldier,' a mother was pictured saying as she embraced her foppish boy, whilst, beside her, another mother said 'I did,' her hand on the shoulder of her strong young son in uniform. Above the four, the caption demanded 'Whose son are You? Enlist today!' The people of Australia were in a dilemma. Who should they listen to?

Strangely enough, the mothers, wives and sweethearts of the men who'd gone to war listened to little of the propaganda, they seemed to have made up their own minds. But, despite their common circumstances, they too held opposing views. There were women who vehemently believed that their men needed backup on the battlefields of France, 'stand by your brothers!' they cried. And there were others who said 'too many have died, don't send more of our sons to their death!' The country was in turmoil.

In Sydney, the turmoil found its voice, as it always did, on the Domain. There, in 1916, shortly before the referendum was put to the people, the Labor Party held an anti-conscription rally, the press later estimating attendance numbers as high as 100,000.

Billy wished he hadn't come. Marge had been right. 'You hate crowds, love,' she'd said gently, 'and they say there's going to be thousands there.' But he'd felt somehow obliged to attend.

He'd arrived early, the rally had only just started, yet throngs of jostling people seemed deliberately to impede his way as he wove through them in an attempt to escape. And the noise—the screech of the speaker's voice through the megaphone, the rousing cries from the crowd—Billy was getting a headache.

Billy Kendall was one of the thousands who attended the rally, as many a returned serviceman did. Men in uniform were prominent amongst the crowd, soldiers on crutches, or blind, or missing an arm. Many wondered which way such soldiers would vote.

Up on the platform the opening speaker was delivering a stirring speech. Beside him stood fellow Labor Party members and those waiting to lend their voices to the cause. A representative from the Women's Peace Army was present, her placard reading: 'A vote against conscription is a vote for peace!'

But not all the women amongst the crowd were there to lend their support. A large group had banded together to oppose the rally, and they were shaking their fists up at the platform. 'Shame!' they were yelling. 'Our boys need help! Shame on you!'

'I lost two sons!' one woman was bellowing angrily at the top of her voice. 'Why should my boys cop it while others stay home?'

Billy recognised the voice. He couldn't see through the crowd to the group of hecklers, but it was Nellie Putman all right. It was her constant theme these days. If she had to give up her two boys, then other women should risk losing theirs. Like the 'shrieking sisterhood' of women who were dedicated to forcing men into the army, Nellie had become quite a monster. She would accost any physically fit-looking man she saw in the streets. 'Get into uniform!' she'd demand. 'Be a man, go and fight for your country!'

As Billy forced his way through the crowd he heard the cries of the women Nellie was whipping into a frenzy. 'I lost my husband', 'I lost my brother', and even a young girl's voice, 'My father died at Gallipoli.'

He had to get away, he couldn't breathe. He'd cut through Woolloomooloo. More and more people were pouring into the Domain from every direction, he'd head home through the backstreets.

Billy breathed a sigh of relief as, the worst of the crowd behind him, he started down the hill. Amongst the many who were walking up from Woolloomooloo to the rally, he glimpsed a face he knew. He turned away quickly before she saw him, and when he was sure she was safely past, he turned once again and watched her disappear into the crowd. It was Kathleen O'Shea.

Billy hadn't seen Kathleen since the visit he'd paid her shortly after his return from the front. Two months ago now. He'd wanted to offer his sympathy. To Otto De Haan too, whom he'd never met. A tragic thing, both Kathleen and Otto losing their only sons. But then it was a tale all too common these days. Billy knew one family who had lost all three of their sons.

She hadn't recognised him at first, then it had slowly dawned. 'Billy Kendall?'

She's as beautiful as ever, he thought. She would have had to have been over forty, but even the dark circles of grief beneath her eyes couldn't mar her beauty. He wanted to embrace her. He'd always been a bit in love with Kathleen O'Shea, but then, he supposed, what man wouldn't be?

Kathleen put her hands on his shoulders and kissed his cheek, horrified at how much he'd aged. He couldn't be more than thirty-one, thirty-two, and yet he looked fifty.

'Come in, Billy, come in, come in.' She ushered him into the front room and sat him on the sofa. 'I'll put the kettle on and fetch Otto. You haven't met my husband, have you?'

'No. I've heard a lot about him though. From . . .' he gave a quick jerk of his head which seemed to indicate the war was just behind him, '. . . from over there.' They both knew that he meant from Johann.

Kathleen nodded. 'I'll fetch him, he's just home from church.'

Aggie was in the kitchen, rocking baby Caroline's cradle, and as Kathleen walked through to the porch she asked, 'Would you put the kettle on for me, Aggie? We have a visitor.' Out on the back porch she said to Otto, 'Billy Kendall's come to see us.' He didn't appear to hear her. 'He's young Tim Kendall's uncle,' she explained.

Otto nodded vaguely, still staring into space, as he did so often lately.

'He knew Johann and Robbie,' Kathleen prompted. 'He's just come home from the front.'

'Oh.' Otto put his arm around his wife as he rose. 'I am sorry, I do not mean to be rude.'

'I know. Come in and say hello.'

Billy jumped to his feet as they appeared, and Kathleen made the introductions. When Otto extended his right hand, Billy clumsily shook it with his left, and it was only then that they realised.

'Oh Billy,' Kathleen said, 'I'm so sorry, I didn't know.' The cuff of his right sleeve was neatly tucked into his jacket pocket and she'd not noticed that the pocket was flat.

Billy loathed introductions. Daily he cursed the fact that he'd lost his right hand and not his left. If it had been his left, he might have been able to talk to people for a while before embarrassing them, or seeing pity in their eyes. For a while he might have been normal, just like them.

'It's only the hand,' he said. 'They took it off at the wrist, I've got the rest of the arm.' It would only have been two fingers, the doctor had said, if they'd got him to the field hospital quicker. But he'd been stuck out in no-man's-land for two days and gangrene had set in. Just his luck.

'Would have been better off losing the whole arm,' he said with false bravado. 'They pay better compensation for an arm.'

He was clearly in a nervous state, talking too loudly, too quickly, and Kathleen tried to calm him. 'It's good to have you home, Billy. Sit down, please. Aggie's getting us some tea.'

Billy sat on the hardback chair beside the table, leaving the sofa for them, and fought to calm himself. He got the jitters a lot lately. For no apparent reason he'd get jumpy and tense. He hoped he wasn't about to have one of his turns.

'I wanted to offer my sympathy,' he said. 'To you both.'

Otto nodded, and Kathleen said, 'Thank you', and Billy wasn't sure what to say next. 'Johann spoke about you a lot, Mr De Haan.'

'Otto, please.'

'Otto. He was a good soldier, Johann was. Popular too. You would have been very proud of him.'

'I am. Thank you.' Otto's reply was brief but his gratitude was evident.

There was an awkward pause before Otto rose saying, 'I go to help Aggie with the tea.'

When he'd gone, Kathleen asked, 'And Robbie? How was Robbie when you saw him?' She wanted to ask how he'd died, whether it was quick, whether he was in pain, but she couldn't. She didn't know whether she'd be able to bear the answer.

Billy knew exactly what she was asking. 'Robbie handled the war pretty well,' he said, hedging. 'Both him and Tim. Strong young blokes. Good mates too, just like when they were kids.' Her eyes still begged the question. 'I wasn't with him when it happened, Kathleen.'

'Ah.' She looked away, both disappointed and relieved.

'Tim was, though. It was Tim who told me that Robbie had been killed, when he visited me at the field hospital. It was about the same time as . . .' Billy gestured at his missing hand.

'Was it quick?' Kathleen had blurted it out before she could stop herself.

Billy felt a surge of anger. What did the woman expect him to say? 'No, your son lay in the stinking mud for days, helpless, in agony, listening to death rattling in the throats of his nearby mates, knowing it'd be his throat rattling next?'

Billy didn't actually know how Robbie had died, Tim had not gone into detail. 'You just get yourself better, mate,' that's all Tim had said when he'd asked. But no death on the boggy battlefields of France was pretty. What the hell was he expected to say?

Tears glistened in Kathleen's eyes. She was holding her breath, Billy was sure, and he could see the artery in the side of her neck throbbing.

'Yep,' he said brusquely. 'It was quick. That's what Tim told me. "Robbie never even knew what hit him", they were Tim's exact words.'

Brutal as they were, those were words Kathleen was longing to hear, and she put her hands over her face, surrendering to the tears of relief which rolled down her cheeks.

Billy himself was not lying, but he believed that Tim had been. Why should he have to lie? Why should any of them have to lie? Countless men were dying hideous deaths and all people wanted were lies. Then Kathleen looked up at him and whispered, 'Thank you', and the anger drained from Billy to be replaced by an overwhelming despair. It was the deaths not the lies that were wrong.

'Are you feeling all right, Billy?' Kathleen leaned forward and put a hand on his knee.

Billy rose from his chair, agitated. 'This killing, it has to stop.'

The images crowded his brain as they always did when he was about to have one of his attacks. There wasn't enough room in his brain for all those mutilated bodies. He tried to will them away but they kept pouring in. 'It has to stop,' he said over and over, 'it has to stop.'

'Billy, please. Sit down. Please. I'll get you a glass of water.'

She ushered him back to the chair, her arm was firmly around him. Briefly, Billy regained his senses. 'I'm sorry, Kathleen. I'm fine. I'm fine.' Any minute the images would be back, he had to get out before he made a scene. 'Yes, I'd like a glass of water, thank you.'

The moment she had disappeared into the kitchen, Billy had dived for the door. He had to get home. Kathleen mustn't see him having one of his turns. No-one, least of all Kathleen, must be witness to his humiliation.

Billy's head was throbbing now as he watched her disappear into the crowds at the rally, her huge husband by her side. He would have liked to have said hello and to have apologised for his rudeness in disappearing that day. But he didn't dare, not with his head throbbing the way it was. A headache like this was precursor to an attack; he must get home to Marge.

When he got home he knew what would happen. He would bawl and blub like a baby and Marge would cradle him in her arms and rock him to and fro until the sobbing subsided and he was left drained and exhausted. Then he'd hate himself for his weakness, and he'd hate Marge for having witnessed it and, no matter how many times she told him that she loved him and that it didn't matter, Billy would remain convinced that his wife must surely despise him.

By the time Kathleen and Otto had fought through the crowds to a vantage point from which they could see the official platform, the speaker from the Women's Peace Army was addressing the rally.

'A vote against conscription is a vote for peace,' Susan Kendle proclaimed. Nellie Putman and her band of women booed loudly, but Susan ignored them. 'We must not send more of our men to their slaughter!' Through the megaphone, her voice rang out clearly across the expanse of the Domain. 'We should be bringing them home, not sending them to their deaths!'

Susan was walking a fine line. There were many present who, despite being anticonscription, were not antiwar, and there were mutterings of disapproval from many amongst the crowd. Kathleen, however, strongly agreed with the woman. At the outset she'd tried to convince herself that Robbie was risking his life for a noble cause, and she'd done what she could to make herself feel useful, collecting for the War Chest fund and joining one of the innumerable sewing and knitting circles which provided clothing for the troops.

Before Robbie's death, Kathleen had found the work fulfilling. The knowledge that, in her own way, she was serving her country had made her feel closer to her son. But although she worked even harder after his death, joining the Red Cross Society whose contribution was paramount to the war effort, she no longer believed that she was serving her country. She worked in order to distract herself. She no longer believed in the war.

The woman was right, Kathleen thought, and she wanted to applaud both her views and her boldness. She had never before thought to enquire about the woman's name, now she wanted to know. She edged her way through to one of the nearby policemen.

'Who is the speaker?' she yelled above the din.

'Susan Kendle,' the policeman yelled back. 'A troublemaker.' The police regarded Susan as an agitator with the potential to incite a riot. 'You'd think at her age and with her money she'd have something better to do with her time, wouldn't you?'

Kathleen stared at the policeman. 'Kendle?' she asked.

'Kendle and Streatham,' he shouted louder over the babble of the crowd. 'Her old daddy's a millionaire.'

Kathleen edged her way back to Otto. Susan Kendle. Good heavens above. All these years she had been admiring Charles Kendle's daughter. What would Paddy O'Shea have to say about that?

Kathleen had been eighteen when her father had died and, like her mother, she was convinced that Charles Kendle had killed him. 'Or if not,' Dotty had always insisted, 'he ordered it done.'

The crowd was starting to get angry. Several people were pushing and shoving at the platform, which was rocking dangerously; the policemen were disengaging their batons and calling for order. Otto took Kathleen's arm.

The sins of the fathers, Kathleen thought, and she looked back over her shoulder as Otto protectively cleared a way for her through the mob. All so much water under the bridge now.

'Stop the killing on the Western Front!' Susan bellowed. Fist raised, she continued to denounce the war, even as the police moved in.

Kathleen thought she'd like to meet Susan Kendle one day. Not to talk of the past—the woman wouldn't even know who she was—but to tell Susan Kendle that she was right. Right in every word she said. It was a senseless war.

On 28 October, 1916, 1,160,033 Australians voted against conscription and 1,087,557 voted for. Soldiers, including those on active service, voted 72,399 for conscription and 58,894 against.

The immediate result of the referendum was a split in the Labor Party. Prime Minister Billy Hughes stormed out of a Labor parliamentary meeting exclaiming 'let all who support me follow me', and twenty-three of the sixty-five members did.

Abandoning his past allies, Hughes formed a new party, the National Labor Party, a coalition of his followers and his former political opponents, and, in 1917, the National Labor Party came into power. In December of that year, the indomitable and dogmatic Hughes forced yet another conscription referendum upon the people.

The Commonwealth Government issued lurid posters portraying the 'Hun' as a bestial creature who, if he was not shooting soldiers, was murdering grandmothers and babies. The press, too, hounded the people. 'Remember,' the newspapers said, 'that every No vote is a vote to dishonour Australia, a vote to tarnish the glory that has been won by the Anzacs.'

But, as they had done the previous year, a majority of Australians voted no. And, this time, not only because they wished for freedom of choice; it was nearly 1918 and Australia was thoroughly war-weary.

Kathleen knew there was something going on. She'd known ever since the New Year's Eve party down at the docks.

'You're not going out again,' she said. Aggie had been out every Saturday night for the past three months.

'Just a gang of us going to the dance hall,' she answered petulantly. 'I'm allowed to have a bit of fun, aren't I?'

But Kathleen knew Aggie wasn't going to the dance hall. The dance hall didn't sell grog. Neither did the pubs for that matter, not at night any more. That was another change the war had brought about. Early closing. The 'six o'clock swill' now saw workers head from their offices and factories straight to the pubs to pour as much alcohol down their throats as they could and then stagger home well before the sun had set. So how come Aggie was getting in after ten o'clock, the worse for wear and stinking of cheap grog?

Kathleen had caught her out twice. 'Just a little drink at a friend's place' had been the girl's defensive response, but Kathleen had known better. And the other times, when Aggie's heavy-footed clumping in the downstairs rooms had woken her, Kathleen had known that the girl was drunk again.

So when Aggie brazenly said she was leaving, Kathleen was not at all surprised.

'You've met someone,' she said. It was not a question.

'What if I have?' Aggie's tone was belligerent. 'Why should I pretend to be a widow for the rest of my life? We weren't even married, when all's said and done.'

Kathleen bent over the large tin tub on the back porch table and concentrated on the washing. As usual Aggie had been careful with her timing, she thought as she scrubbed at the heels of Otto's woollen socks. Sunday morning, Otto was at church. Aggie was scared of Otto.

'So where are you going?' she asked, trying to sound indifferent. The prospect of Aggie disappearing from her life was neither here nor there, but her heart pounded at the thought of losing Robbie's child. She looked at little Caroline playing in the small courtyard with the wooden building bricks Otto had made for her. The little girl was two and a half years old now, a good-natured child, happy in her own company, and Kathleen adored her.

'He loves me.' Aggie's pert chin was tilted defiantly, as if she dared Kathleen to differ. 'He wants to marry me.'

'I'm sure he does and I hope you'll be happy.' Kathleen squeezed the socks dry, dumped them into the wicker basket and started on the collar of one of Otto's work shirts. 'So where are you going?'

'He's got a good job too, he works at Vicars Woollen Mills.'

'You'll be living in Sydney then,' Kathleen said, relieved. Vicars Woollen Mills was in Marrickville.

'Yes. Near the factory.'

'Well, that's good, I'll be able to visit Caroline.' Kathleen relaxed. 'And when she gets bigger she can come and see me,' she said, squeezing Otto's shirt dry and placing it in the wicker basket with the rest of the washing.

'Leo doesn't want the baby.'

Kathleen had picked up the tub of dirty washing water and was about to tip it down the drain beside the porch. Now she stood embracing the tub and stared disbelievingly at Aggie.

Aggie had anticipated Kathleen's contempt. She'd even considered leaving without telling her, but she had a begrudging respect for the older woman and she wanted Kathleen to understand. 'Men don't want a woman with a child,' she said.

The tub was heavy. Kathleen tipped the water over the side of the porch and into the drain.

'I have to find a husband, Kathleen.'

Kathleen turned to face her. 'You'd give up your little girl?'

'It's all right for you,' Aggie whined. How dare Kathleen act so self-righteous and judgemental; she hadn't been brought up by a slut of a mother and dumped in a charity school for the destitute. 'You've had it easy all your life, you've got a husband and a house, it's all right for you.'

Kathleen filled the tub with fresh water from the tap by the porch. There was no need to comment. And why bother to judge the girl when Aggie was bestowing upon her the greatest gift possible? The gift of her own son's child.

Aggie took Kathleen's silence as censure. 'My mother wasn't a widow,' she said. She'd tell Kathleen at least part of the truth. 'My mother was a whore.'

Kathleen stopped rinsing the clothes and gave the girl her full attention.

'I swore I'd never end up like her,' Aggie said. 'I swore I'd never sell myself, all I wanted was a kind man who'd make a good husband. Then I met Robbie.' She sniffed tearfully. 'We would have been happy. It's not fair.' It wasn't fair either, Aggie thought. All her well-laid plans had come to naught.

Robbie O'Shea had not been the first man Aggie had seduced,

nor had he been the first man to whom she had surrendered her 'virginity'. She'd had the deception down to a fine art by the time she'd met Robbie. Her mother had taught her the tricks when she was fifteen years old.

A young woman allowed a man to seduce her at the very end of her menstrual period, resulting in a small amount of blood left on the bedlinen. Men liked virgins, they paid more for virgins. And men were simple; they did not know that menstrual blood was a different colour. Aggie learned to angle her body slightly and feign pain as the man thrust into her. It was very easy, and Aggie was well remunerated with gifts. She never asked for money, she never considered herself a professional girl.

The refined manner which Aggie had assiduously acquired under the tutelage of the Christian workers at the Jubilee School had given her such an air of credibility that Robbie O'Shea, like the others before him, had been only too eager to accept the gift of her unquestioned virginity. But Robbie, unlike the others, had been eager, also, to accept the responsibility of such a gift. And the responsibility was marriage.

Aggie had told Kathleen the truth in one respect. Well tutored as she had been, she had never wished to follow her mother's path. When she had used the tricks her mother had taught her, it had always been with the prospect of gaining a husband. Once she had surrendered her 'virginity', however, the men had soon lost interest. Not Robbie though, her plan had paid off with Robbie. They were to have been married. And then he'd been killed and she'd been left with a baby. It wasn't fair.

'I would have been a good wife to him.' Aggie was weeping tears of self-pity by now. It was unfair of Kathleen not to sympathise with her. 'You don't understand, it's not easy for someone like me. No man wants another man's baby.'

'I understand, Aggie, of course you must find yourself a husband. I'll look after Caroline, and I'll do whatever I can to help you in your new life.'

'Thank you, Kathleen.' Aggie sniffed back her tears gratefully. 'You've been good to me, I'll never forget you.'

'But that's exactly what I want you to do, my dear.' The girl had been about to embrace her, but stopped, puzzled, as Kathleen continued. 'My granddaughter will be raised as an orphan. In time she will be told that her mother is dead. You are never to see her again.'

Aggie was confused. Kathleen's words were so cruel, but her tone was not. In fact she sounded kind, even sympathetic.

'But I do—' she started to protest.

'No you don't, Aggie,' Kathleen gently interrupted. 'You don't love your little girl. Those are my conditions. Do you accept them?'

Aggie knew it was a test. And she knew, just as Kathleen did, that it was a test she could not pass. She looked down at the toes of her shoes as she whispered, 'Yes.'

The day after Caroline's third birthday there was a knock at the front door and Otto answered it.

'Tim! Tim Kendall!' Kathleen heard her husband exclaim, 'Come quick, *mijn duif*, Tim Kendall is back,' and she ran in from the kitchen, little Caroline at her side.

As she embraced him, tears in her eyes, all she could think was thank God one of them had come home.

Tim was leaning heavily on a cane. 'It's nothing much,' he said when Kathleen started fussing. 'If it'd happened earlier, they probably would have fixed me up and sent me back to the front. I wouldn't have put it past them. But the war'll be over soon so they sent me home instead. Soon all the boys'll be home. Well, all that's left, that is.' Tim didn't believe in small talk any more. 'I'm sorry about Johann and Robbie.'

'We'll talk about Johann and Robbie as soon as you're sitting down and I've made you some tea,' Kathleen insisted, ushering him towards the sofa.

'Go easy, Kathleen, not the front room,' Tim said. 'A bloke who's a member of the family sits at the kitchen table.'

'And a bloke who comes home from the war, he has a beer,' Otto said as they walked through to the kitchen, Caroline skipping along beside them.

Kathleen smiled. It had been years since she had seen Otto so animated.

'So you're Caroline,' Tim said, sitting at the table while Otto fetched the beer from the icebox. 'I knew your dad, we were best mates.'

'What's the matter with your leg?'

'It's just busted,' he said. 'Be as good as new soon. The other one's all right though.' He lifted the little girl up onto his good knee and she sat there happily rocking backwards and forwards.

Kathleen started to cut up some thick slices of damper and cheese. 'It's early in the day for beer,' she said. 'You'll need to put something in your stomachs.'

'Is your beer,' Otto said, dumping a bottle and a glass on the table in front of Tim.

'I see your English hasn't got much better, Otto.' Tim had always enjoyed giving cheek to Otto; he'd always got away with it too.

'Ja. It get me into trouble. Some people, they think I am German.' He gave a guttural growl of anger. 'It make me so mad. I say to them, "My son, he die for this country, what right you have to call me Hun?"' He clenched his huge fist. 'I tell you, Tim, I come close to hit someone.'

Kathleen watched the men as they talked. That Otto could admit so freely to his anger was a merciful relief. There had been times when he had come home in the blackest of rages. Like the time someone had scrawled 'Hun' in white paint over his shopfront. Never had she seen her gentle Otto so incensed.

As the men talked, Kathleen studied Tim. He'd changed. He was as lean and lithe and handsome as ever, but the boyish young face was finally that of a man, and a tough man, she could tell.

'How is Billy, Tim?' she asked as she brought the damper and cheese to the table. 'We've only seen him the once since he's been home and that's a long time ago now.'

'Pretty crook.' Tim didn't beat about the bush. 'A bit jumbled up.' He tapped his forehead with his forefinger. 'A lot of the blokes went like that. Maybe he'll come good,' he shrugged, 'and maybe he won't. It's tough on his wife.'

There was a moment's silence, then, 'You drink your beer, Tim,' Otto said, and the men clinked glasses and drank.

'Do you want to see Millicent?' Caroline asked, pulling at Tim's shirt.

'Yes, I'd love to,' he said. The little girl scrambled off his knee and ran upstairs.

'Millicent's the new doll,' Kathleen explained when Tim raised a quizzical eyebrow at her. 'It was Caroline's birthday yesterday.'

The doll was presented to Tim and duly admired. 'So how old are you, Caroline?' he asked the raven-haired little girl with the big brown eyes. She thought for a moment before holding up three fingers.

'Darling, why don't you take Millicent out onto the porch?' Kathleen suggested. 'She's looking a bit pale, she needs some sun.'

'Three years old,' Tim said as he watched her go. 'It's been that long?'

'Yes, it's been that long.'

'She looks like him.'

Kathleen nodded, and the three of them sat watching the little girl through the open back door as she sat on the porch and chatted to her doll.

Tim momentarily let his guard down, something he rarely did these days. 'He was the best mate a bloke could have,' he murmured. 'I miss him.'

Neither Kathleen nor Otto said a word, but Kathleen could have wept for the vulnerability she saw in Tim's eyes.

Then, aware of their sympathy, Tim retreated behind his facade. It wasn't that he didn't trust Kathleen and Otto, but a bloke couldn't afford to let down his guard or he'd go under, just like Billy.

'I was with him when he copped it.'

'Yes,' Kathleen nodded, 'Billy told me.'

'He didn't feel a thing. No pain. He never knew what hit him.'

Kathleen nodded her thanks and Tim changed the subject. They talked about the good old days, and Otto fetched more beer and got slightly drunk. They talked about Johann and Robbie as if they were still alive and, every now and then, Otto wiped a tear from his eye or laughed out loud, and Kathleen could have hugged Tim Kendall. It was as if he'd brought her Otto back to life.

She did hug him, an hour later when he left. So did Otto, and Caroline too.

'It's so good to have you home, Tim,' Kathleen said. 'You'll come and see us often?'

'Of course I will. Have to keep an eye on the little princess here, don't I?' Caroline gave him a big wet kiss as he put her down. And then he had to kiss Millicent. And then he was out in the street walking home to Surry Hills.

His leg ached a little as he walked, but he needed to keep exercising it, so he didn't end up with a permanent limp. He tried to concentrate on each step, to think of nothing but his leg. He marched, ignoring the pain. Left, right, left, right. He must concentrate on marching. Left, right, left, right. But it wasn't working, his mind kept wandering. He turned the corner and doubled back through Woolloomooloo to the docks. He'd sit and look at the harbour for a while. He didn't want to go home to his mum and dad. Not just yet. He didn't feel like talking.

The visit to Kathleen and Otto had shaken Tim more than he'd cared to admit. The little girl, so like Robbie he could have been looking into Robbie's eyes, had brought it all back to him, the images he'd been so careful to shut out.

He hadn't lied to Kathleen. Or to Billy. Robbie had known no pain in death.

Tim could see him now, running up ahead, screaming as he ran, like he always did. Tim screamed too. Sometimes. He didn't quite know why, but sometimes it seemed to help. The noise of his own voice ringing in his ears sometimes helped block out, just a little, the distant roar from the batteries and the whistle of shells through the air and the hideous explosions which showered them with mud as they ran, clumsily, sometimes sinking up to their calves in the bog of the battlefield, sometimes tripping over the men who had fallen in front.

Tim didn't see Robbie fall; he was thrown to the ground himself by the peripheral force of the blast. He struggled groggily to his knees, amazed at the fact that he was still alive, and crawled over the bodies of the men in front to where Robbie lay.

His chest was ripped open and, through the coat of grey mud, Tim could see the white shards of shattered ribs and the mangled mess of entrails which lay shockingly exposed within. Robbie was dead. Just like that. A carcass. The same as dozens of others he'd seen. And Tim lay beside him, his mind a blank, nothing in his head but the vague hope that when he too copped it, he'd go quick like Robbie.

He lay in the mud, too weary to run, too drained to care, just wishing it all was over. Then Robbie groaned. Oh sweet Jesus no, Tim thought, don't let him gain consciousness, don't let him lie here in agony, not even for a minute.

Behind closed lids, Robbie's eyes were flickering. A rasping noise sounded from his throat. Tim clicked the bayonet free from his rifle and held the muzzle to Robbie's temple. It took no more than a second or so. A single shot and it was over. Then, shocked to his senses, he got up and ran. Through the mud and the blood and the gore of the battlefield he ran for his very life.

Tim looked out at the harbour. The blue waters were dotted with white. It was Saturday, a fine late September afternoon, and the rich people were sailing. Dozens of eighteen footers were racing under full canvas. The Sydney Flying Squadron's Saturday regatta. Other yachts, under light rig, and with ladies aboard, were enjoying a leisurely social outing. For some, it seemed, the war didn't exist.

Tim turned for home. He'd visited his ghosts. He could face Ben and Norah now. 'Saw Kathleen and Otto,' he'd be able to say, 'we talked about old times. Robbie's little girl's a real beauty.'

Maria Nina skimmed effortlessly across the water. With only a light rig hoisted, she was still a graceful boat, but under full sail she drew great admiration and was an impressive contender on race days. Custom designed and made in Tasmania, the eighteen footer was built of huon pine and was Stephen Kendle's pride and joy.

It had taken his father years to accept the eighteen footers. They were cheaper to build and to run, and Charles Kendle swore they'd belittle the sport. 'The eighteen footers are putting the ownership of sailing craft within the purse strings of the common herd,' was what he said. But once he'd realised they were the fastest yachts on the harbour, he'd changed his tune.

Today *Maria Nina* was not racing, however; Stephen was sailing single-handed. His sister Susan was with him, but Susan could hardly be counted as crew, she knew nothing about sailing and refused to learn.

'Why should I?' she'd insisted. 'You're the expert. In fact you'd never get me out in this thing if I didn't know you were one of the best.' In her strident way, Susan was always good for her brother's ego, and she intended to be.

'Don't put up too much sail, Stephen, please,' she'd asked when they'd set sail, 'not today. You know I don't like it when the boat leans too far.' There was a stiff breeze up and, with the regatta in full swing, Susan was, as usual, anxious. 'For God's sake don't bump into anybody,' she begged. Everywhere she looked there seemed to be yachts.

Stephen laughed. 'The fearless and ferocious Susan Kendle, nearly tarred and feathered by angry hordes, arrested for inciting a riot, afraid of a bit of a breeze.'

'Just sail the thing, Stephen, and get away from these boats,' Susan growled.

It was true that several of those who'd advocated peace in the early days of the war had been tarred and feathered. And the day of the rally in 1916 she'd been escorted to Darlinghurst Police Station and accused of inciting a riot, but she hadn't been charged. They'd let her go with a warning because old Charles Kendle was her father. She'd demanded they charge her but, much to her chagrin, they'd steadfastly refused.

Once they were away from the melee of boats, Susan relaxed. The prospect of collision genuinely made her nervous, and the possibility of capsizing terrified her. She was not a good swimmer, and if Stephen only knew the effort it had cost her the first time she'd accepted his invitation, perhaps he would not be so cavalier in his attitude. But she trusted him now, and as they sailed past Shark Island and away from the others, she breathed a sigh of relief and gave herself up to the beauty that was Sydney Harbour.

At first she'd agreed to go sailing as an offer of solidarity, aware that her brother desperately needed a friend. But as their relationship grew stronger, Susan found that she needed Stephen as much as he needed her. In fact Stephen was the only true family she had. She didn't see her children any more. Lionel and Prudence chose not to visit her these days and her father could hardly be considered a comfort. She and Stephen were an odd pair, she thought. The insecure boy in the man's body and the 'ferocious' Susan Kendle. But she loved her brother.

They turned about at Vaucluse Point and, with the wind behind them, it was a leisurely cruise home.

Susan leaned back in the cockpit and pulled her jacket about her. There was a chill in the spring breeze now. She watched the yachts as Stephen skilfully manoeuvred *Maria Nina* amongst them. It seemed obscene, somehow, that people could be so apparently oblivious to the war. 'Thank God it'll all be over soon,' she said.

'Yes.' Stephen had been thinking about his son. 'When Mark comes home,' he said, 'I'm going to buy him his own eighteen footer. Tasmanian huon pine, the very best.'

Back at the yacht club, with *Maria Nina* safely penned, Stephen insisted he and Susan share a bottle of champagne in the lounge as usual and, as usual, she agreed. She never drank more than a glass, whilst Stephen demolished the rest of the bottle. She didn't enjoy drinking and she didn't enjoy the yacht club. The frivolity of the mood and conversation was meaningless, the hearty masculinity of the men and the flirtatiousness of the women irritating. But Stephen liked the place and she was loath to spoil his afternoon ritual by declining.

When Stephen had drained the last of the champagne, he suggested another bottle, but Susan as always declined.

'I might have one quick drink with the boys in the bar then,' he said.

He drank far more than was good for him, Susan thought as she said goodbye, but then he was probably just buying time before going home to Kendle Lodge and the awful presence of their father. Susan could hardly blame him for that. Why on earth didn't he get out of the place, she wondered time and again, but she knew that he never would.

It was nearly dusk when Stephen arrived home. The three Scotches he'd had with Teddy and the boys were sitting quite happily on top of the champagne and he was feeling mellow. Plenty of time to change for dinner without annoying his father. It was only when he got home more than a little drunk and well after dark that he risked one of his father's moods.

'The cook waited dinner,' Charles would archly remind him.

'You don't need to wait for me, Father, you should go ahead and—'

'I do not like dining alone, Stephen. As you very well know.'

It had taken Stephen years to realise that his father deliberately waited dinner in order to be disagreeable. The old man enjoyed disagreeable scenes. At eighty years of age, physically frail and confined mostly to his home, disagreeable scenes added spice to Charles Kendle's otherwise tedious day.

The house was gloomy, the lights of the main hall had not been switched on. And where was the maid, Stephen wondered as he hung his coat and scarf on the brass pegs of the hall stand. Betty was normally there to take them from him.

Stephen crossed into the main lounge. To the left, his father's study door was ajar and a light shone from within, but the lounge, too, was dimly lit, only the wall brackets from the upper level illuminating the main stairs and casting shafts of light into the shadows below.

He wondered briefly whether he should pop his head into his father's study and let the old man know he was home. No, he decided, he'd go upstairs and dress for dinner first.

It was only when he was about to mount the stairs that he saw his father seated in the bay alcove, one of Charles's favourite spots, silhouetted by the dusk light which shone through the windows behind him.

'You're home,' Charles growled, 'drunk I suppose.' He'd dismissed the servants hours ago and, throughout the afternoon, had sat watching the hall door, waiting for Stephen.

'Where's Betty?' Stephen asked. His father had a brandy balloon in his hand, which in itself was unusual—his father never drank before dinner, and he certainly never drank alone.

'I sent her out for the night. Told her to leave. The cook too.'

Charles Kendle put down his glass and painfully pulled himself to his feet with the aid of his stick. He laboured his way, rheumatic hips aching with every step, across the room to the stairs.

In the spill of light from the upper wall brackets, Stephen saw his father's face. It was ghastly. Haggard and birdlike. Over the past several years, as age had claimed him, Charles had withered away to a skeleton. But it was not the cadaverous look of his face that shocked Stephen now, it was the hatred he saw there, the malevolence which glittered from the sunken eyes.

'You've been out drinking, having a fine old time, haven't you?' Charles said accusingly. His voice, the one thing which remained robust whilst the rest of him failed, quavered as he fought for control.

'But I'm not late home, Father, and I'm not drunk,' he protested. 'Now why don't you come and sit down . . .'

Charles shrugged away Stephen's helping hand and lifted his cane as if to ward him off. He stared up at his son's fleshy face and yet again wished he were twenty years younger. How he'd love to beat that useless, dissipated face to a pulp. But Charles knew, even through his own pain, that he could inflict a far greater agony on his son than any physical beating.

'While you were out getting drunk with your cronies, we had a visitor,' he said with malicious triumph, 'a visitor from the War Office.' He held up the crumpled telegraphic cable which was clutched in his right hand. 'Do you want me to read it to you?'

Stephen said nothing but stood staring at the cable.

'You killed him!' Charles spat it out with all the venom he could muster. 'The one and only son you ever managed to sire and you killed him!' But Stephen wasn't listening, he was walking away.

'You're useless to this family, you always have been!' Charles screamed, demented in his rage. He tried to follow his son as Stephen strode into the hall, but he fell at the doorway. Heedless of the pain which seared through his leg, he lay there, still screaming. 'Useless, d'you hear! Useless!'

But Stephen didn't hear one word. His mind was too busy trying to encompass the fact that his son was dead.

Half an hour later, having lit the kerosene lamp aboard *Maria Nina* and hoisted the mainsail, his mind was still numb with shock. For years he'd lived in constant fear, as had all those whose sons had gone to war, but lately, with the talk that it would all so soon be over, he'd been lulled into a false sense of security. Mark was dead, his brain kept telling him, but something deep inside his being could not believe it.

A strong north-easterly was blowing. He snuffed the lamp and sailed well out into the harbour in the direction of Manly, then tacked to starboard and headed for Watsons Bay. He had to tack two more times before he reached the heads of Sydney Harbour and the open sea.

By then, as *Maria Nina* whipped through the water at a crazy tilt and he leaned well out over the side, automatically and expertly using the weight of his bulky frame, the realisation had hit with a vengeance and tears were streaming down Stephen's face, only to be whisked away in the wind.

The moon was out in all its brilliance. Behind him, on the southern headland, the Watsons Bay lighthouse flashed its warning, and beyond that shone the lights of Sydney, but he didn't look back. He followed the shaft of moonlight across the black sea, with nothing but thoughts of Mark in his mind.

Mark as a baby, when their family had been happy. Stephen had been so proud of his wife, and of himself too, for presenting the first male heir to the Kendle throne. Then three years later she'd died, and the boy had grown up looking after the emotional cripple who was his father. Stephen wondered at the fact that Mark had never given up on him, but his son had loved him throughout and had grown to be the man Stephen could never be.

The waves loomed, black and fearsome, but Stephen didn't take in any sail, he flirted with the sea instead, meeting the waves head on, defying them. And then, for no apparent reason, he turned *Maria Nina* broadside and waited to be engulfed.

As the yacht capsized, he realised, vaguely, that he had not lashed himself to the helm as he usually did when he was sailing outside the heads on his own. He could have clung to the yacht too, but he didn't, and again he wondered vaguely why as he was swept away from *Maria Nina*.

Instinctively he struggled for survival, swallowing water, gagging, feeling panic rise within him. Then he looked at the far-off lights of Sydney. Far too far to swim. He relaxed a little, thinking for a moment of Susan, hoping she'd understand; she was the only one he was leaving behind.

Heavy as the swell was, the waves were not white-tipped and angry. He discovered that if he went with the motion of the sea, he bobbed like a cork upon the crest of each wave and slid down into the trough behind, to be lifted once more, bobbing again like a plaything on the crest of the following wave. It was not an unfriendly feeling, the sea was not set upon killing him cruelly. They said that drowning was not an unpleasant death, so long as one relaxed; it was panic and the ensuing suffocation that made it so terrible, they said. He could bob around for hours, he thought. For hours and hours, just thinking about Mark, and the love that he bore his son.

'He did it deliberately,' Charles said to Susan from his bed in Sydney Hospital. *Maria Nina* had been found a week ago, wrecked upon the rocks of the Gap at Watsons Bay, but the body of

Stephen Kendle had not been washed ashore until two days later. His death had been recorded as accidental drowning, but Charles knew better. So did Susan.

'He did it deliberately to spite me,' Charles said.

'Oh for God's sake, Father, why should he kill himself to spite you?' Susan kept her voice down, conscious of the fact that in the corner of Charles's private room the nurse was arranging the flowers which Susan had brought for her father. But she wanted to hit the old man. His broken femur and the reports that he'd never walk again roused no sympathy in Susan. Despite his physical debilitation and the loss of his son and grandson, her father was as callous and as cruel as ever, and she felt no guilt at her sense of loathing.

'He'd just heard of his son's death,' she hissed. 'What the hell could his suicide have had to do with you?'

The nurse finished arranging the flowers. Despite Susan's forced whisper, she'd heard every word. What a hideous woman, she thought, to talk so harshly to an old man so ill. She cast a baleful look at Susan as she left.

'Everything,' Charles snarled, 'it had everything to do with me. The man wasn't even fifty years old, he could have sired more children, he owed it to the family, but no, he has to kill himself instead. That's why he did it. To spite me. To cheat the family of its name.'

'Did you say anything to him that night?' Susan demanded.

'Of course I did. I told him he was useless. Killed the one and only son he ever managed to sire, that's what I told him.' Charles started muttering to himself, not caring whether Susan was listening or not. 'He's always been useless to this family. Useless. The whole of his life.'

'You said that to him the night he learned that Mark was dead?' Susan asked, horrified.

'Of course I did.' The voice that barked at her didn't belong to the emaciated body in the bed. 'That's why he killed himself, I tell you, to spite me.'

Susan felt sickened. She'd supposed, when she'd heard the news, that grief had killed her brother, but perhaps after all it had been the old man's contempt which had driven him to his death.

'What did he do, Father?' She kept her voice steady, she had to know. 'When you said that to him, what did he do?'

'He walked away,' the old man sneered, and Susan could have cheered out loud. It was what she had told her brother to do, time and again. 'Walk away from him, Stephen,' she'd said. 'Walk away. He can do nothing if you turn your back on him.' 'He didn't say a word,' Charles confirmed, 'didn't have the guts. Just walked away like the coward he is. Like the coward he's always been.'

'Good for you, Stephen,' she said quietly.

Charles didn't hear. Or possibly he chose not to, there was nothing wrong with his hearing.

'There's only one solution,' he said.

'Solution to what?'

'The Kendle name of course. What the hell do you think we've been talking about? You're a Kendle, Susan. And so is your son.' Charles's eyes glowed fanatically in the yellow-skinned skull of his face. 'You must convince Lionel. He must change his name, he is a Kendle.'

Susan had an insane desire to laugh. 'He thinks he's a Napier, and so does his father.'

'I'm serious, damn you, girl.' Charles struggled his weight onto one sticklike elbow. 'There's money in it for him. I'll make him my sole beneficiary.'

'He doesn't want your money,' Susan replied coldly.

'But there's wealth and property,' Charles protested. He was feeling weak, his elbow couldn't support his weight, but he had to convince her. 'And prestige. Above all, there's prestige. Kendle and Streatham! He'd be one half of Kendle and Streatham, you tell him that!'

'He's already one half of Napier and Son.'

Excited spittle dribbled from the corner of the old man's mouth. Any moment he'd collapse with exhaustion, but Susan felt no pity whatsoever.

'Napier and Son is one of the most prestigious law firms in Melbourne,' she continued, 'as you no doubt know. Furthermore, Lionel is running for the seat of Collingwood in the next election. I doubt whether there is anything much you could offer him, Father.'

'Kendle!' The word rasped painfully from the very depths of

Charles's chest. 'Kendle! I can offer him the name Kendle!'

'Kendle!' Susan exploded. 'Kendle?' And in the laughter which followed there was a touch of madness to match her father's. 'Shall I tell you what Lionel thinks of the name Kendle, Father? He loathes and abhors it, just as he loathes and abhors me. Do you know what he said to me once? He said, "The best thing you ever did for this family was to change your name back to Kendle."' She laughed again at the sheer irony of it. 'Those were his exact words. "You and your father are two of a kind," he said, "you're both Kendles and you're both fanatics."'

Susan felt light-headed and dizzy with a sense of release. 'I'm a megalomaniac, Lionel says, just like you. An unnatural parent with a lust for power, cold and hard and incapable of human affection.

'It seems we have a lot in common after all,' she said, gathering up her bag from the chair by the bed, 'not least of all that we are both despised by our offspring. I hope you like the flowers. I shan't be coming to see you any more.

'I'm very much afraid, Father,' she said as she opened the door to leave, 'that you will have to resign yourself to the certainty that, when you die, the name Kendle will die with you.'

Five weeks later, on 11 November, an evening performance of the Sydney production of *Katinka* starring Gladys Moncrieff was interrupted and the audience informed that the Armistice had been signed. In the auditorium, on the stage and behind the scenes in the wings, people stood and cheered. As theatregoers danced in the aisles, actors and stagehands wept and hugged one another.

At approximately the same time in Melbourne. Mr Phillip Wirth stepped into the main ring during a performance of Wirth's Circus and announced that the war was officially over. As one, the crowd leapt to its feet and sang the national anthem.

In cities and towns throughout Australia news of the Armistice was greeted with wild and emotional jubilation, pride and sheer relief.

Here and there, impromptu firework displays lit up the sky, particularly in Melbourne where excited hordes surged into the Chinese quarter and ransacked the stores for firecrackers. The following day, the press published an official appeal by the Defence Department urging people not to explode bungers, 'in the interest of invalided soldiers and particularly those suffering from shell shock'.

And, in Sydney, throughout the night sirens screamed and whistles shrieked as people jammed the streets, cheering, singing and shouting with joy, while the sonorous horns of ferries reverberated across the harbour.

From his bedroom at Kendle Lodge, Charles could see, through the open balcony doors, the lights which fanned the sky, and he could hear the ferry horns and the riotous celebration in the city streets. Sydney has gone mad, he thought.

He was quite alone, the servants hadn't even asked his permission before racing out to join the throng. The nurse had at least had the courtesy to inform him of the reason for the chaos.

'It's the Armistice, sir,' she'd said—as if he hadn't guessed—'they've signed the Armistice,' and she'd stepped briefly out onto the balcony, obviously longing to be a part of it all.

'Well go on, go on,' he said, his voice an angry whisper, he could barely speak these days, 'leave me alone, see if I care.'

'Just for a minute sir, I promise.' And she'd dived out the door before he could withdraw his permission.

She'd been gone for hours now, or so it felt to Charles, he had little concept of time and he couldn't see the hands of the clock on the mantel. He'd rung the silver bell which he held constantly to his chest at least a dozen times, but no-one had come, and the effort of ringing had exhausted him.

It was a plot, he thought. They'd left him alone deliberately. They wanted him to die whilst the rest of the world was celebrating, damn them.

The sound of the festivities angered him. He wanted to scream at them all to shut up, he had nothing to celebrate.

What had Susan said? 'You will have to resign yourself to the certainty that, when you die, the name Kendle will die with you.'

Well, he wouldn't die. Not yet. There was still time. Money could buy anything. Of course. That was it! He would find a young man of good stock who would be only too willing to accept the Kendle name for a healthy sum, hundreds'd queue up for such an opportunity. Background and breeding would have to be thoroughly investigated, but he could employ someone to do that ...

He tried to concentrate on his plan, but it was difficult to catch hold of his swirling thoughts with all the noise which swelled from the streets. And his mouth was dry, he needed a drink. He looked at the jug on his bedside table, the full glass of water beside it, and feebly he reached out, only to hear the bell fall from the bed, and then discover that he couldn't reach the glass anyway.

He tried to swallow but his mouth was so dry he couldn't. He was panting now, small birdlike gasps. He needed to keep calm, he told himself, and to concentrate on his plan, but the noise was growing louder. And louder. His head was throbbing with the sound of celebration.

For the first time in his life Charles felt afraid, shockingly afraid. As the cheers and laughter, the sirens and ferry horns grew to a screaming pitch in his brain, he sensed suddenly that they were all directed at him. There was no time left, that's what they were saying. His whole life's work had been in vain, they were saying. There was no-one left to glorify his achievements, no Kendle remained to carry his name.

As the tumultuous joy of thousands mocked him, he clawed at the bedclothes, trying to close his ears to their voices, but he couldn't. The whole city of Sydney was laughing at him, Charles Kendle, and the travesty of his life.

Nearly sixty-two thousand men had died, the newspapers reported. More than one in five of those who had served overseas. For a nation boasting an entire population of less than five million, such loss was devastating. A generation of young men had been decimated and, with them, their thousands of unborn children. Generation upon generation which should have existed, wiped out in four bloody years.

And amongst those who returned were the wounded. Thousands and thousands of limbless, blinded, shell-shocked men. For them the war would never be over.

Such men were living proof of the unbelievable horror from which, for the most part, the general public had been protected. War correspondents at the front had been advised of the need for censorship, photographers had been forbidden to take pictures of dead bodies, and even official war artists, who could have pleaded exemption on the grounds of artistic interpretation, had avoided painting the grisly truth. The policy of censorship was practised for the sake of the war effort, but in reality, those called upon to record the events openly admitted to the impossibility of describing the indescribable.

Laurence Binyon's verses 'For the Fallen' had been embraced throughout the war, and afterwards remained to serve as a remembrance of the Anzacs; a more reassuring and comforting tribute to heroism than the recollection of things too awful to contemplate.

They shall grow not old, as we that are left grow old:
Age shall not weary them, nor the years condemn.
At the going down of the sun and in the morning
We will remember them.

But the facts of this war, though unspoken, could never be denied. It had been the war to end all wars, they said and, for the future of mankind, it must never, never happen again.

Chapter Thirteen

'It is my melancholy duty to inform you officially that, in consequence of a persistence by Germany in her invasion of Poland, Great Britain has declared war on her and that, as a result, Australia is now also at war.'

Millions gathered around their wireless sets at nine o'clock on Sunday night 3 September, 1939 to hear Prime Minister Robert Gordon Menzies's broadcast to the nation. And amongst the millions were many who wondered at the fact that it was less than twenty-one years since the war to end all wars.

But, even as they wondered, there were none who questioned the validity of the war in Europe, or Australia's responsibility in once more allying herself to Britain. They had weathered the Great Depression which had followed the stock market collapse of 1929 and they had rallied to rebuild their country. They were weary. They did not welcome another war, but they were resigned to its inevitability. The policy of aggression adopted by Adolf Hitler and his Nazi Party was a direct attack upon human rights, a clear-cut case of good against evil and, as women who had lost their husbands prepared to watch their sons march off to war, and others who had lost their fathers waved goodbye to their husbands, none argued the reason why.

It was a different nation which now prepared for another war. The news was greeted with none of the excitement and patriotic fervour which had welcomed the prospect of battle in 1914. Pragmatism prevailed, and the mood of the people was composed and purposeful.

Enemy aliens were rounded up and interned, amateur radio operations were banned and, although overseas service remained voluntary, the government introduced compulsory military training for defence of the home front.

This would be a war fought on land, sea and air that would spill out of Europe to Asia and the Pacific; a global battle which would creep ever closer to home.

When the HMAS *Sydney* sank off the coast of Western Australia following a gunnery duel with the German raider *Kormoran*, Australians were aghast to learn that all 645 on board had died, the greatest loss in their country's naval history.

But less than a month later, on 8 December, 1941, when Prime Minister John Curtin announced that Australia was at war with Japan, for the first time in their short history, Australians realised that their country was under threat of direct attack. Air raid precautions were adopted. City hospitals were evacuated, shelters were built, trenches dug and blackout laws enforced. Home defence conscription ages were immediately extended. Single men from 18 to 45 and married men from 18 to 35 were called up for full-time duty. The vast and vulnerable coastlines of Australia must somehow be defended.

The Allies, too, looked south. Australia could now serve a purpose other than the supply of troops and materials. She could prove an invaluable military base.

Fourteen days after the bombing of Pearl Harbor, American troops arrived in Brisbane, and on 17 March, 1942, General Douglas MacArthur landed at Batchelor Field, south of Darwin. A week and a half later, the city of Sydney received its first shipload of US servicemen, over 8,000 in all.

'But it's Friday,' Ada insisted, 'and you promised you'd come this Friday.' The Yanks had been in town for a whole six weeks and Ada and her girlfriends had danced the night away at the Trocadero each Friday since. 'Oh please, Caroline. Please.' Caroline remained silent as they walked from the tram-stop down William Street, but Ada refused to give up. 'You promised me on Monday that you would.'

'I said I might.'

'You didn't. You said "I'll come with you this Friday". It was a promise.'

Caroline sighed. She probably had promised, in fact she now remembered that she had, simply to appease Ada at the time. When Ada had a bee in her bonnet, she was relentless. Caroline supposed she would have to give in some time and it might as well be tonight.

'All right, I'll come,' she said with ill-humour. She really didn't want to go to the Trocadero but Ada was her best friend, and a promise was a promise.

They turned the corner into Bourke Street, and walked down the hill into Woolloomooloo, avoiding the piles of sand dumped here and there by the City Council for fire-fighting use in the event of incendiary bombs. Ada ignored her friend's petulance as she skipped along the pavement with girlish excitement, dodging both the sand and the passers-by. Despite the fact that she was twenty-four years old, two years younger than Caroline, there was a disarmingly childlike quality about Ada.

'You won't regret coming, honestly you won't. The Yanks are gentlemen, and they dance much better than our boys.'

A group of American sailors was walking up from the docks. Ada stopped skipping and walked sedately and demurely down the hill, aware that she looked attractive in the stylish little felt hat which she wore pertly tilted to one side. She'd made the hat herself from squares of material normally used for toymaking. She was aware, too, that her knee-length skirt and her high-heeled shoes effectively showed off her neat calves and ankles. Despite the austere wartime fashion, Ada managed, by way of meticulous improvisation, to retain a touch of thirties glamour.

Hatless and in a plain, belted cotton dress, Caroline, too, looked attractive, but unlike her friend she was neither a slave to fashion, nor apparently aware of the admiring glances she and Ada regularly drew from men in the street.

The American sailors raised their caps, 'Afternoon ladies,' several of them said, and Ada flashed a coquettish dimpled smile as she nodded back. Caroline also nodded, but walked briskly on.

'They've got a darn sight more manners than our boys too,' Ada said when they'd passed, and she'd caught up once again with Caroline.

'I know, I know, I've seen them around town.' And a darn sight more money, which they were only too happy to throw about,

Caroline thought, feeling sorry for the Aussie blokes who couldn't compete. Caroline found the Americans a bit flashy, but then she hadn't met any, so she supposed she really shouldn't judge.

Five minutes later, they parted company outside Caroline's house. 'I'll be at your place at seven,' Ada said, skipping down the road, she lived just around the corner, 'don't be late.'

Caroline O'Shea and Ada Bird had grown up together, children of Woolloomooloo. Like Caroline, Ada's family had lived in the Loo for four generations and, with six children in the current crop, it was quite likely they'd live there for four more, the Birds were a fixture of Woolloomooloo.

When Caroline had completed her Stott's Business Course for Women in shorthand and typing, she had been an inspiration to Ada who had immediately followed suit. And when, a year or so after the war broke out, Caroline had resigned from the small insurance company where she worked as a clerk to accept a secretarial position at H. Small & Company, it had been only natural for Ada to apply for a position there also. Caroline had been most encouraging.

'It's a very patriotic company, Ada,' she boasted. 'Seventy-five percent of Small's Club Chocolate is sold to the armed services, so we'll be helping the war effort.' Ada was most impressed. 'And they're employing factory workers for their new cocoa department,' she added, 'so they're bound to need more office staff.'

She'd been right and Ada had had no trouble in getting a clerical job with H. Small & Company in Bridge Road, Stanmore. Ada and Caroline were a pride and joy to their respective families. Two Woolloomooloo lasses who'd made good.

'I'm going dancing at the Trocadero with Ada tonight,' Caroline said to her grandmother as she walked into the kitchen and plonked her handbag on the table.

'Good.' Kathleen was pleased. She wanted to say 'it's about time you went out and had fun', but she didn't.

'I don't want to,' Caroline said a little sulkily, 'I'm only going because she made me promise last week.'

'Well, I'm very glad she did.'

'I won't stay long.'

'Of course you won't if you're not having a good time, that'd be silly wouldn't it?'

Caroline looked suspiciously at her grandmother, but Kathleen ignored her as she stirred the stew in the iron pot. 'But then who knows,' she continued, putting the lid back on the pot, 'a miracle might happen.' She turned to her granddaughter. 'You might actually have fun.'

Caroline frowned. She'd been right, her grandmother was teasing her.

Kathleen laughed, her magnificent eyes disappearing into crinkles amidst the fleshy folds of her still handsome face. It was an infectious laugh, full of warmth, humour and affection, but Caroline stood her ground. She didn't like being teased.

'Wipe that frown off, missy,' Kathleen said as she had for the past twenty years, 'before the wind changes.'

'Don't, Gran,' Caroline frowned all the more, 'don't treat me like a . . .'

'Why not? You're behaving like one.' Kathleen's smile faded and she looked concerned. 'Sit down, darling. Please.' Caroline begrudgingly sat at the kitchen table and Kathleen, too, pulled up a chair. 'You're cross because Ada's twisted your arm, but what am I expected to say? "Go to the dance and have a miserable time?" You know what I want to say, of course, but you'll get cross with me if I say that too.'

Caroline nodded. She looked down at the floor, but she was no longer sulking. 'I'm sorry,' she said.

Kathleen knew her granddaughter only too well. Obstinate as Caroline could be, she was by nature a good-humoured and sensible young woman. If she could not be joked out of a bad mood, she could invariably be made to see commonsense.

'I'm going to say it anyway,' Kathleen warned, and she took a deep breath. 'It's nearly eighteen months since Ian died, and you're nearly twenty-seven years old, and it's high time you met someone else. A young woman your age needs a husband.'

Caroline looked up. She rarely laughed out loud, but when she smiled her generous smile she needed no voice, her whole face lit up with laughter. She smiled now. 'When you say it, you really say it, don't you?'

Kathleen smiled back. Never a day passed for Kathleen without feeling a rush of love for her granddaughter, or seeing Robbie in the strength of that brow and the depth of those black-brown eyes.

Caroline sprang from her chair, good humour restored. 'I'll try to have a good time,' she promised, 'really I will, but I'm not going to flirt with the Yanks like Ada does. Do you know, she went out with one for a while. He gave her an orchid each time he picked her up, and each time she sold it back to the florist the next morning for half price.'

'How very practical.' Kathleen stood and eased her back, feeling a touch of rheumatism. At sixty-seven years of age she tended to do things slowly now, though no less deliberately. 'Go and get washed up,' she said, 'tea at six o'clock. Unless you're dining out with Ada.'

'And miss your Friday stew?' Caroline called as she ran up the stairs.

Kathleen busied herself peeling the potatoes. She was genuinely pleased that Ada had persuaded Caroline to go to the dance hall. It wouldn't change things overnight, she was sure, but it was a start.

Caroline's fiancé, a pilot with the RAAF, had successfully survived action in Europe but, after the fall of France and Italy's entry into the war in 1940, No. 3 squadron had been transferred to the Middle East, and he'd died within the week. It had taken Caroline a full year to come to terms with his death. She no longer seemed to be grieving, but she simply didn't care to socialise, and that, according to Kathleen, wasn't healthy for a young woman.

Kathleen had meant what she said. Even in this modern age, with women forging careers of their own, doing men's work, even joining the services, the truth remained that a young woman needed a husband. It was as simple as that. She put the potatoes on to boil.

Half an hour later, she stepped out onto the back porch. 'Tea's ready, Stefan,' she called.

Stefan Brandt was the lodger who rented the room Otto had built out the back for the boys, and he dined regularly with Kathleen and Caroline on Friday and Sunday nights. His Dutch accent reminded Kathleen of Otto. It was probably why she had chosen him as a tenant, she often thought, she found his voice comforting.

Otto had died seven years previously. During the Depression, he'd been forced to sell his beloved store for a trifle of its true value, and he'd accepted whatever menial labour he could find.

Anything to ensure that Kathleen could keep her cottage and that Caroline would not spend her teenage years in abject poverty. Times had been hard, but through Otto's self-sacrifice, they'd survived far better than many who'd lost everything they owned and who'd struggled for their very existence. When he'd reached his three score years and ten, Otto had died peacefully in his sleep, never knowing there was another war around the corner. For that Kathleen was thankful, but she missed him dreadfully.

There was much about Stefan Brandt which reminded Kathleen of the younger Otto De Haan. He was big in build, not given to idle chatter, he was mild and harmless and yet he, too, had been persecuted at the outbreak of the war.

Stefan had only recently moved in to Kathleen's at the time and there had been those in the neighbourhood who had reported him as an alien. Kathleen had been angry, it was not the Woolloomooloo way to report on one's neighbours, and didn't they know he was Dutch? She'd said as much to the policemen when they arrived to take Stefan to an internment camp.

'He's Dutch for goodness' sake, can't you tell the difference?'

They couldn't, and they'd insisted on seeing his papers. When all had appeared to be in order, they apologised to Kathleen as vociferously as they had to Stefan himself, clearly impressed by her defence of the lodger.

Stefan had been very grateful, and a pleasant relationship had evolved. Kathleen had no idea what Stefan did for a living and she didn't enquire; he paid his rent on the dot each Friday and on Sundays he insisted upon doing whatever odd jobs needed to be done about the house and, like Otto, he was a good handyman. When he shared their meals, Kathleen and Caroline chatted away, with very little comment from the Dutchman; he obviously preferred it that way.

'Tea's ready,' Kathleen called up the stairs.

'You are pretty,' Stefan said when Caroline appeared. He was sitting at the kitchen table having his pre-dinner beer, he only ever had one. 'You go out?'

'Thank you. Yes. To the Trocadero.'

'Very pretty indeed,' Kathleen agreed as Caroline twirled about in her pink floral dress, the waves of her raven-black hair bouncing as if with a life of their own against her bare neck and shoulders.

But Caroline wasn't 'pretty', she thought, not according to the fashion of the day, her looks were too dramatic to be 'pretty'. Radiant and animated as she was now, Caroline was beautiful, Kathleen thought with pride.

The Trocadero was crowded and noisy. It always was, but nobody minded, the clamour and din were all part of the excitement. Men were predominantly in uniform, but so too were many women, the government's initial reluctance to accept females into the services having undergone a rapid revision when Japan entered the war.

On the dance floor, hundreds of couples embraced, some clumsily swaying, some twirling with expert synchronisation to the melodies of Cole Porter or Irving Berlin. And on the sidelines, hordes of onlookers crammed together, chatting and calling out to each other at the tops of their voices in order to be heard above the swing of the big band.

'You two go in ahead,' Ada said to her girlfriends when they met up together outside. 'I'll look after Caroline.'

Bev and Enid disappeared into the throng and Ada, obviously searching for a familiar face, looked about at the dozens of soldiers milling in the street.

'Come on,' she finally called above the hubbub, taking Caroline's hand and jostling her way inside. They checked their handbags and wraps into the foyer cloakroom and, the moment they were through the doors and into the main hall, Ada was swept onto the dance floor by an American soldier. The one she'd been looking for outside, Caroline assumed, judging by her delighted giggle. And for an instant, amidst the frantic festivity which surrounded her, Caroline felt very alone. But only for an instant.

'Wanna dance?'

'Hi, may I have the pleasure?'

Two servicemen had swooped upon her, the first an Aussie, the second a Yank. Caroline looked from one to the other and immediately chose the Australian. The Aussie smirked triumphantly at the Yank who, undeterred, shrugged and offered his arm to another girl standing nearby.

For the next three hours, Caroline barely drew breath. She'd forgotten how much she loved to dance. Ian had too, she thought briefly, recalling their Saturday nights at the Palais de Dance in

Bondi. But there was no time to dwell on Ian now, the band was playing 'Begin the Beguine' and she was being led yet again onto the dance floor. She'd stopped discriminating against the Americans and, feeling a little disloyal, had to admit that the Yanks were the better dancers.

Refusing a dance simply to catch her breath, Caroline found Ada was doing the same. But even as Ada was catching her breath, she was with the American soldier who'd been waiting for her. She introduced him as Steve. He was in the US Marine Corps, she proudly announced, and Caroline wondered if it was Steve who'd given her the orchids.

'This is my buddy Gene,' Steve said. 'Gene, this is Caroline.'

'Hello,' she said.

'Hi. Care to dance?' He offered his arm.

Caroline scraped her damp hair back from her face. She could feel the trickle of perspiration between her breasts. She must look a fright, she thought, but she didn't care. 'I was having a breather,' she smiled and took his arm, 'but why not?'

It was the smile that did it. Gene was smitten.

Three consecutive dances later, Caroline finally called a halt, and she and Gene joined Ada and Steve on the sidelines.

'Thanks, Gene,' Caroline gasped, struggling to regain her breath; the last number had been a jitterbug. 'You're a really beaut dancer,' she said with genuine admiration.

'You're not too bad yourself.'

She gave him another of her winning smiles and turned to Ada. 'Eleven o'clock, time I went home. You coming, Ada?'

Ada exchanged a glance with Steve who in turn exchanged a glance with Gene.

'We thought we'd go on to the Roosevelt for supper,' Gene said. 'Will you join us, Caroline?'

'Oh, I don't think so. Thanks anyway.' Caroline's refusal was automatic. She'd had a wonderful, carefree evening, but if she were to accept the American's offer she would be obliged to chat to him, to get to know him, and she wasn't sure if she wanted to do that. He was certainly handsome, just like the Americans in the pictures, tall and tanned with white teeth. She'd supposed all Americans were like that until the Yanks had arrived in Sydney. He was very courteous too, and his voice was pleasant; he was not brash and his accent was not harsh like some of the others. Perhaps he was a little too courteous, she thought, she wasn't used to such good manners. 'Wanna come to the pictures Saturday arvo, Caroline?' That was the customary invitation. No, the Yank was too smooth for Caroline.

'Goodnight, Gene,' she said.

'Let's go to the powder room before we leave.' Ada had taken her arm and was firmly leading her away. 'Won't be a tick,' she called back to the men.

As they crammed themselves into a corner of the crowded powder room, Ada rummaged in her purse for her lipstick. 'You have to come with us, Caroline,' she begged, 'I won't be able to go if you don't.' She had to raise her voice above the surrounding babble of female voices.

'Why?'

'Because Brian's home on leave and he got really snaky when Mum told him I'd been out with a Yank.'

Brian was the oldest of Ada's three brothers. The younger two had volunteered and were serving overseas but Brian, considering himself the responsible male member of the Bird family, their father being prone to the bottle and gambling, served with the Home Defence in Brisbane and came down to Sydney on leave whenever he could. 'With the Yanks in town now, a bloke's got to look after his sisters,' he told his mother.

'He doesn't even like me going out dancing with the girls,' Ada said, 'he reckons Bev and Enid are common.'

'You keep away from girls like that, Ada, they're loose,' Brian had told her. 'Floosies they are.'

'They are not!' She'd been outraged at such an accusation, she'd been to school with Bev, she knew her well, and both Bev and Enid had respectable jobs. 'They're good girls and they work for the war effort,' she'd protested angrily, 'Bev's at the services canteen above Woolies and Enid's at the munitions and you've got no right to talk about them like that. They're not loose, and they're not floosies!'

'Well, they look it,' he'd muttered defensively, taken aback by her explosion and aware that he'd overstepped the mark. 'You should be going out with Caroline, she's a cut above those other mates of yours.' Brian Bird had always fancied Caroline O'Shea. Caroline O'Shea had class.

'If I tell him I went to the Roosevelt with you,' Ada said to the mirror, expertly applying her lipstick whilst she talked, 'it'll be OK. He won't even mind if we're out with a couple of Yanks, 'cos he reckons you're real classy.'

The American jargon was contagious, Caroline thought as she combed her hair, Ada was acquiring more and more of it lately. Then a thought occurred to her.

'When did Brian get back?'

'Last weekend.'

'So that's why you made me promise to come out with you tonight.'

'I've been nagging you to come out with me for weeks,' Ada said airily, 'you know I have.' She put her lipstick away and fluffed up her fair, curly hair with her fingers.

'And you knew you were meeting Steve, and you knew he'd have a friend, and you knew they'd ask us on to the Roosevelt.'

'Well, last Friday Steve sort of mentioned ...'

'You knew. And you didn't tell me.'

Ada stopped avoiding the issue. She nodded. Then she pleaded unashamedly. 'Just for an hour, Caroline. Please! The Roosevelt's great, real classy, you'll love it.'

'All right, all right,' Caroline gave up, 'just for an hour. So long as you stop talking like a Yank.'

Ada squealed and hugged her, and as they walked out of the powder room Caroline asked, 'Is Steve the one who gave you the orchids?' She'd been longing to know.

'Oh good heavens no. He started wanting to go too far so I told him to get lost. Sorry,' she said, aware she'd just used another American expression.

Outside the powder room, Ada put her hand on her friend's arm and leant her mouth close to Caroline's ear. She had to talk loudly above the din, and she didn't want others to hear her advice. 'That's the trick, Caroline, you don't get too serious. They've got lots of money and they like to have a good time and they like to give you presents so you let them, but when they want to go too far you tell them you're a nice girl and you don't do that, and then they move on to the next one. It's easy.'

Caroline threw back her head and gave one of her amazing silent laughs, which Ada found so stylish. It was a sort of throaty gurgle then an intake of breath. Ada had practised it often in front of the bathroom mirror, but she'd never been able to master it, so she'd given up and accepted the fact that she was a squealer and a giggler. Oh well, men seemed to like her that way, so she supposed it didn't matter.

'It's true, Caroline,' she said, encouraged by her friend's obvious delight. 'Bev and Enid have taught me all the tricks, they told me about selling the orchids, everybody's doing it. The Yanks'll give you perfume and nylons and cigarettes and liquor, you can keep them or sell them, but it all adds up.'

As they linked arms and pushed their way through the crowd, Ada thought it was astonishing that someone as classy as Caroline could be so naive, and Caroline thought it was astonishing that someone as worldly as Ada had maintained her innocence.

Caroline and Ada didn't speak intimately any more, they hadn't for a long time, Caroline had not encouraged it. When she and Ian had become engaged, shortly before he'd left for Europe, the girlish, giggling secrets she and Ada had shared had become meaningless. Caroline had known a man and he had known her, and to talk of their love was sacrilege. She had been aware that she'd changed, and she had known that Ada sensed it. But to her credit, Ada had never asked, and Caroline never told her. That had been nearly two years ago now, and Caroline had assumed that Ada, with her flirtatiousness and vivacity and sophisticated chatter, had succumbed to one of the men whose attentions she'd welcomed. Ada was always popular with men.

As they joined the Americans, Caroline looked fondly at her friend. 'Only for an hour,' Ada was saying, her dimples spontaneously working overtime, 'but we'd love to come, wouldn't we, Caroline?'

'Yes,' she said, 'we'd love to.'

An ugly scene was taking place as they stepped out into the street.

'What are you letting niggers in for? What kinda joint is this?'

Two American Negro servicemen, in private's uniform, had been about to enter the Trocadero. The doorman, who had been only too willing to admit them, was being harassed by three white American soldiers.

'Do your job, buddy,' the ringleader insisted, 'tell the niggers to buzz off.' He was a big man, bull-like and pugnacious. He turned to the black American nearest him. 'Go on, boy,' he ordered, 'there's a club in Kings Cross for blacks, this is whites only.'

'No it's not, mate.' Unintimidated, Clive Carter stood his ground, it was why they paid him to work the door. He, too, was a big man, and just as bull-like and pugnacious. An ex-professional boxer, Clive was afraid of no-one. 'Come on in, lads.' He gave a beckoning wave to the two black Americans who stood bewildered, obviously confused as to the rules.

The big white American swaggered up to Clive. 'You let the niggers in, me and my pals just might wreck your dance hall.'

'Oh yeah?' Clive folded his massive arms over his chest. 'You won't get inside, mate. I don't like your sort of bloke. You step one foot in this door and I'll chuck you out on your head.'

The other two men stepped up beside their companion. 'Let's teach the nigger-lover a lesson, Marvin,' one of them threatened.

'You wanna teach me a lesson yourself, Marvin?' Clive asked, ignoring the other two. 'Or do you need your pals to lend a hand?'

Marvin signalled his friends to stand back, and the two big men squared up to each other.

Gene and Steve edged the girls well clear of the mob which was gathering to watch, some merely interested in the outcome, others taking sides. The Aussies started booing the Americans. 'Go home Yank,' they chanted. Sick of the Yanks flashing their money about, they decided that this was as good an excuse as any to pick a fight.

Goaded by the heckling, the Yanks responded. As Marvin's jaw collected a perfect uppercut from Clive's right fist, the argument was no longer about colour prejudice. The boys in uniform were just itching for a fight.

Elroy Brown and Jimmy J. Smith, who were resigned to segregation laws in their home country and who had had no intention of starting trouble, headed for the Booker T Club in the Cross. The Booker T had been established for the exclusive entertainment of Negro American troops. It was safer at the Booker T, they decided.

Caroline, Ada, Steve and Gene also headed for Kings Cross. Whilst Steve hurried the girls away from the Trocadero, Gene dived out into the street and hailed a taxicab. 'The Roosevelt,' he said, and they all piled in.

'Rightio, the Roosevelt it is.'

The taxicab crawled off at a snail's pace. In the enforced semi-blackout conditions, all motorists drove slowly at night. Headlights were shielded, every second streetlight turned off, and the roads were dim and gloomy. But the cabbie was driving far more slowly than usual as he peered into his side view mirror to watch the fight. It was no contest, he could see that in an instant. Big Clive Carter had a bloke pinned to the ground and was belting the hell out of him. Now who the heck'd have the nerve to take on Clive, the cabbie wondered. Then he saw that the bloke was a Yank. Poor bugger, someone should have told him. Clive 'Killer' Carter had never lost a fight in his heyday.

'There's going to be a real barney,' Ada said, twisting around to peer through the back window. Caroline said nothing, but the ugliness of the episode had shaken her a little and, seated beside her, Gene sensed it.

'We're not all like that,' he said quietly, 'they're from the South those guys, they've got strong feelings about blacks in the South.'

Caroline appreciated his concern, but she changed the subject nevertheless. 'Where are you from?'

'Maine. A little town called Casco, by Sabbathday Lake. Peaceful,' he shrugged, 'pretty, but nothing much happens.'

He smiled and she noticed that the perfect white teeth in his handsome tanned face were slightly crooked. She rather liked that.

Kings Cross was the centre of Sydney's nightlife. Along the breadth of Darlinghurst Road flashed the gaudy lights of girlie bars and strip joints, and in Macleay Street, for the more wealthy and selective, the hotels boasted cabarets starring international celebrities. During the day, the fashionable open-air cafes of Bayswater Road were home to the bohemian society of writers and painters and poets, many of whom lived in the Cross.

The taxicab pulled up in Orwell Street outside the Roosevelt Hotel. Of all the nightclubs in Kings Cross, and there were many, the Roosevelt was the most fashionable and the most popular.

Steve and Gene protectively guided the girls through the crowds at the doors. Once inside, they led them around the periphery of the packed dance floor, amongst the potted palms and the waiters with silver trays, to the stairs which led to the upper-level balconies. They'd never get a table, surely, Caroline thought, and she wanted to say as much, but she would have had to yell to be heard above the noise of the swing band and the excited chatter of the crowd, so she obediently followed as Gene and Steve led them up the stairs.

To her astonishment, a waiter greeted them effusively and, in an instant, ushered them to a table right at the front overlooking the dance floor. How amazing, she thought. Then Steve handed the man a five-pound note. Quite openly, nothing furtive about it. Five quid! Caroline was shocked. A whole week's wages! For her, anyway, and over half a week's wages for the average man. Then she noticed that nearly all of the tables on the upper level were taken by American servicemen. There were several men in 'civvies' but not one Aussie uniform was present at the upstairs supper tables.

She leant over the railing and peered down at the dance floor, sensing the antagonism in the Aussie servicemen dancing and milling about below, and she couldn't help feeling guilty, sitting up there with the Yanks.

Ada drank Coca-Cola, she'd discovered a passion for Coke, it was addictive she said, particularly with a dash of bourbon. And Caroline, who'd never tasted bourbon and Coke, had to agree.

Steve offered his packet of Lucky Strikes to Ada and, to Caroline's amazement, she accepted one. She posed elegantly as he leaned close to light it for her and then, to Caroline's further amazement, inhaled like an expert. Since when had Ada smoked?

'No thank you.' Gene was offering her his packet of Camels, and it appeared, a little suspiciously to Caroline, as if a cigarette was something shared between 'couples'. 'I don't smoke.' She smiled apologetically as she said it, not wanting to seem rude.

'But you have to try,' Ada brightly insisted, 'it's the fashionable thing to do. Besides,' she added, hoping the men hadn't noticed her kick Caroline none too gently under the table, 'you'll enjoy it, it's very relaxing.'

Caroline gathered there was a hidden agenda which Ada would later explain and accepted a Camel, careful not to inhale as Gene lit it for her. She puffed tentatively, hating the taste, 'thank you,' she said.

The supper was excellent. The girls had salmon, the men steaks and each of them followed up with the Roosevelt speciality, a rich dessert made with full cream. The chef obviously had an 'in' with the black market, Caroline thought. The government was already announcing the imminent issue of ration books.

It was late when the men escorted them home, for Caroline anyway, after two o'clock in the morning, and she hoped her grandmother was not worried.

'We can walk from here,' she insisted outside the Roosevelt as Gene raised his arm to hail a taxicab. By now Caroline felt thoroughly guilty about the money they'd spent. 'We only live in the Loo.'

Gene and Steve exchanged a glance of amusement. They'd heard the Pommie soldiers refer to lavatories as loos, and they'd found it difficult to come to terms with the fact that the dockland suburb where their ships were berthed was known as 'the Loo'. No pun appeared intentional from the Sydneysiders however, so they didn't openly mock the name.

'OK, let's walk,' Gene agreed.

The four of them parted company at the corner of Bourke and Plunkett Streets, Steve walking Ada home and Gene accompanying Caroline.

Outside Kathleen's house, Caroline shook his hand. 'Thank you very much,' she said as formally as she could, praying that he wouldn't try to kiss her. 'It's been a lovely evening.' Americans might be gentlemen as Ada professed them to be, but they were still men when all was said and done, and Caroline had fought off the unwelcome attentions of many a suitor in the past.

'It sure has, Caroline.' His returning handshake was warm and unthreatening. 'May I call on you? Tomorrow maybe? We could go out and dine.'

'Oh.' She wasn't sure what to say. She'd felt self-conscious walking back from the Cross with a Yank, but Ada's lack of inhibition had made it seem acceptable. She didn't want to go out with Gene on her own. She wished Ada was with them now.

He sensed her reluctance, and felt he knew why. 'Perhaps we could repeat tonight,' he said. 'We could go to the Trocadero with Ada and Steve.' His suggestion sounded casual, but Gene was desperate. Don't let her say no, he was inwardly praying. Please don't let her say no.

'Two nights in a row'd be a bit much for me,' she said, and she meant it, three Coca-Colas laced with bourbon had gone to her head, she wasn't used to hard liquor. She wasn't even used to Coca-Cola.

'Next Friday then?' Please, he was begging, please.

'All right,' she said after a moment's hesitation. Then she smiled, not wishing to appear ungracious. 'I'd love that. Like I said, you're a beaut dancer.'

Gene laughed out loud. She delighted him. She looked like a film star and yet she was guileless. Most beautiful women played games, he'd found, he'd never met anyone quite like Caroline O'Shea.

'I'll come by and pick you up in a cab. Say, seven o'clock, or eight maybe?'

'No. No, I'll meet you outside the Troc.' She had that wary look in her eyes again, he noticed. 'Do you mind?' she asked.

'Not at all,' he said as airily as he could. 'Eight o'clock OK?'

'Yep. Eight o'clock's fine.'

Gene pulled out an unopened packet of Camel cigarettes from his pocket and placed them in her hand. 'Just a little present,' he said, 'I wish I had some flowers, but . . .'

'No, please,' she protested, trying to give them back. 'I don't smoke, really I don't.'

'I know that.' He took her hand in both of his and folded her fingers over the packet. 'Looked to me like that kick Ada gave you under the table packed quite a punch.' She frowned. 'Hey, no offence taken,' he hastily added, 'Ada's quite right, cigarettes are a valuable commodity. But you don't have to pretend to smoke.'

'I didn't have a cigarette so that you'd give me a whole packet,' she said, annoyed that Ada's hidden agenda had been so readable to everyone but herself.

'I know that too,' he insisted, charmed again by her candour. 'Come on now, it's only a gift, if you don't want to sell them, then give them to a friend.' He squeezed her hand gently. 'Goodnight Caroline. I'll see you next Friday.'

'Goodnight.' She stood, holding the packet of Camels, and watched for a moment as he strode briskly up the hill towards William Street. Fair enough, she thought, she'd share the cigarettes around at work on Monday. Many of her workmates smoked, and she'd seen them preserve the tobacco from their used butts to roll up in airmail paper when they'd saved enough for a fag.

'You most certainly will not give them away,' Kathleen said over breakfast the following morning. 'We can swap them for coffee and sugar.'

'Oh. All right,' Caroline agreed.

'He might give you two packets next week, and maybe some nylons and flowers, who knows?' Kathleen's eyes gleamed mischievously, but Caroline knew that her grandmother wasn't altogether joking. Kathleen De Haan was an eminently practical woman and her household wanted for nothing. Various commodities were already in short supply as the war progressed, and Kathleen unashamedly bartered this for that.

Although there was little ready cash, Kathleen refusing to accept any more than two pounds of Caroline's meagre weekly salary, and the rent from Stefan Brandt being half that amount, Kathleen's supply of items for barter seemed endless. Mostly household goods, they came directly from Caroline's godfather, Tim Kendall.

Caroline adored Tim. She'd adored him for as long as she could remember. Tim Kendall was the father she'd never had, and, although he now had children of his own, the eldest only four years younger than she herself, Caroline had remained his 'princess', and he remained her hero.

Wealthy and successful as Tim Kendall now was, he still called in regularly, at least once a fortnight, to check on his 'princess', and these days, more than ever, he brought presents.

At first, Kathleen had been suspicious. It had been shortly after Otto had died that Tim, attentive and solicitous of both Kathleen and Caroline, had arrived with a brand new wireless set.

'I appreciate the thought, Tim,' she'd said, 'but I can't possibly accept that.'

'Why not?'

'Because it's brand new and it's worth a fortune.'

'So?'

'And it's stolen, it has to be, that's why not.'

He laughed out loud. 'Do you read the newspapers?' he asked.

'Of course I do.' She'd been quite defensive. She might be getting old, but she kept herself abreast of the times.

'But not the business pages I'll bet.'

'No,' she admitted.

'Kendall Markets,' he said, bursting with pride. 'I've announced the opening of three more stores, and one day there'll be a whole chain of them, just like Coles and Woolies, you wait and see.'

'Oh Tim, that's wonderful.'

She'd known that he'd gone into the retail business. 'Specialist shops and variety stores,' he'd said at the time, 'in the suburbs. The days of the big city family stores are coming to an end, you mark my words.' But she'd thought it was just youthful boasting.

'You see I was right, Kathleen,' he said as he handed her the wireless set. 'This is just the beginning.'

And it had been. Tim Kendall now owned fifteen stores throughout suburban Sydney, the depressed property market having worked to the advantage of a quick-thinking battler like Tim. And, despite the war, business was thriving. He'd been right about the big city stores too. Still recovering from their losses during the Depression, they were now suffering from the effects of the war. Staff shortages and blackouts were crippling the big stores and it was predicted that rationing might see the end of many. The Foy family was struggling and rumour had it that Kendle and Streatham's was on the brink of closure.

Tim had done well for himself and Kathleen was inordinately proud. For, just as he was a father to Caroline, Tim Kendall was a son to Kathleen De Haan.

The following Saturday morning, Kathleen discovered a shoulder spray of orchids and two packets of Camels sitting on the kitchen table. She pottered about getting breakfast, careful not to wake Caroline, who had been out until three in the morning. Kathleen knew exactly the time of her return. She'd lain awake, just as she had the preceding week, waiting to hear the click of the front door and her granddaughter's feet on the stairs. She didn't mean to spy, and she wasn't particularly worried, but old habits died hard.

Kathleen neither approved nor disapproved of Caroline going out with a Yank, appearances had always been of little importance to her, if people wanted to point and make judgements, let them. Kathleen was only too relieved to see her granddaughter being a young woman again, dancing and enjoying the attentions of a young man, albeit a Yank; it was healthy.

'No nylons?' she asked when Caroline emerged at ten o'clock, tousled and still a little sleepy.

Caroline gave a throaty chortle, she'd always chortled, even as a child, Kathleen found it most infectious. 'I tried, Gran,' she said, 'I did my best. I told him that my grandmother wanted flowers, two packets of cigarettes and some nylons.'

'You did not!' Kathleen grinned delightedly, it was exactly what Caroline would do.

'Oh yes I did, I told him all about you. And he said to tell you that, in his opinion, nylon stockings were a little too personal for a second date, but if I'd go out with him next week, he'd promise to bring along a pair just for my grandmother.'

Kathleen guffawed. 'I hope you accepted the offer.'

'I did.' Caroline sat at the table. 'I asked him to tea on Friday, is that all right?'

Oh dear. A sudden, sobering thought occurred to Kathleen. She placed a mug of tea in front of Caroline and busied herself with the pot of porridge on the stove. 'Does this mean it's serious?' she asked, trying to sound unconcerned. Surely Caroline wasn't about to fall in love with a Yank, she thought. Oh dear, oh dear.

'No,' Caroline scoffed, 'of course it's not serious.' She sipped her tea and said solemnly, after a moment or so, 'He's leaving soon.' Kathleen turned, a bowl of porridge in each hand, and gave Caroline her full attention. 'He hasn't told me exactly what day, or where they're going of course, but I thought a meal in someone's home before he left. You know . . .'

'I think that's an excellent idea.' Kathleen set the bowls in front of them and sat at the head of the table.

'Besides,' Caroline changed the subject and chatted on in a lighter vein, 'I get so guilty at the way he spends money. I don't mind the presents,' she said, 'because you don't see him buying them, but the way he chucks money around like there's no tomorrow. Honestly Gran, they all do,' she said through a mouthful of porridge, 'it's embarrassing in front of the Aussie blokes.'

'How do you do, Mrs De Haan.' He stood at the front door and formally saluted her. 'Lieutenant Gene Hamilton, United States Marines.' She was taken aback. Was he serious? 'And I believe these are for you.' He held out the three slim packets of nylon stockings which he'd been hiding behind his back.

Kathleen laughed, and ushered him into the front room just as Caroline bounded down the stairs. 'Hello, Gene,' she said, 'are these the nylons?' She took them from her grandmother. 'Heavens above, three pairs!'

'Sit down, Gene, please. Would you like a beer?' Kathleen offered. 'I'm afraid we don't have anything stronger.'

Gene was halfway into an armchair when Caroline grabbed him by the hand. 'Don't try and be formal, Gran,' she said, dragging the American into the kitchen where Stefan Brandt was seated at the far end of the table having his pre-dinner beer. 'Gene, this is Stefan. Stefan, Gene.'

The Dutchman rose and shook Gene's hand. 'How do you do,' he said in his thick guttural accent, and Kathleen noticed Gene's slight reaction. Possibly he thought the man was German, as many others did, well she'd clear up that misconception right from the start, she thought.

'Stefan's Dutch,' she said briskly, 'he's from Holland.'

'That is where I was born,' Stefan corrected her, 'but most recent I am from Java,' he smiled at Gene, 'where I work for the Dutch East India Company.'

Kathleen and Caroline exchanged a look. It was more information than Stefan had ever imparted, he was obviously impressed by an officer in the US Marines.

'Sit down, everyone. Gene, you're here.' Kathleen patted the chair at the head of the table which was normally reserved for her. He was certainly handsome, she thought as she fetched him a beer. Rather like Douglas Fairbanks only taller.

'The lace tablecloth,' Caroline remarked as she sat, 'Gran's showing off.' A present from Tim Kendall which Kathleen was loath to barter, the lace tablecloth rarely saw the light of day.

'For three pairs of nylons why not?' Kathleen placed Gene's beer in front of him and started to serve the stew.

'She was going to cook you something fancy,' Caroline said, 'but I made her promise to do a stew, Gran's famous for her stews, isn't that right, Stefan?'

'Ja. They are very good.' He beamed uncharacteristically at Gene. 'Kathleen cook a stew every Friday. Always good.'

Gene gave a polite smile by way of return, he wasn't accustomed to socialising with foreigners. Not foreigners like Stefan anyway. But he tried his hardest to be polite.

'You're right, Stefan,' he said when he tasted the stew, 'it's excellent.'

The Dutchman beamed back at him as he piled potatoes and

silver beet onto his plate. 'Ja. The vegetable too is good,' he pushed the bowl in Gene's direction, 'You try. Kathleen is very good cook.'

Kathleen and Caroline exchanged amused glances, never had they seen Stefan so animated. He seemed fascinated by the American.

'Where you are from, Gene?' Stefan asked.

Gene hesitated for a second, automatically baulking at the foreigner's interrogation.

'Casco, by Sabbathday Lake,' Caroline chimed in, aware that Gene's reluctance to answer may have appeared rude to Stefan, who was obviously trying his best to be friendly.

Kathleen, too, had noted the hesitation. But then she'd also observed that Gene had remained wary of Stefan even after being informed that he was Dutch. Having been married to a man who had suffered persecution, Kathleen was particularly protective of Stefan. She said nothing, but she was starting to view the American through different eyes. For all of his charm and good looks, it seemed to Kathleen that Lieutenant Gene Hamilton was somewhat of a bigot.

'Yes,' Gene said, aware that his hesitation had seemed rude. 'Casco, it's a little town in Maine.'

'Peaceful and pretty, but nothing much happens,' Caroline said.

Gene relaxed and smiled at her. 'I guess that about sums it up,' he said.

'You like Sydney?' Stefan asked.

'Yes, very much,' Gene politely replied. He wished the man would stop questioning him.

'American soldier have been here two months now, they all like Sydney I think.'

'Yes, I'm sure they do.'

They finished their stew and Kathleen served tinned peaches in little glass bowls for dessert.

'I'm crazy about tinned peaches,' Gene said with his Douglas Fairbanks smile, but Kathleen, sensing the American's dislike of Stefan, was no longer so easy to charm.

'That's good, I'm glad,' she said, pleasantly enough.

Caroline cleared the table and served the coffee. 'Full cream milk,' she said proudly, placing the jug on the table. Then she raised her cup. 'To your safe return, Gene,' she said.

Kathleen raised her cup also, 'Godspeed,' she said.

Gene nodded his thanks and the three of them sipped their coffee, but Stefan seemed unaware of the solemnity of the toast.

'Ah, you go away,' he said, intrigued. 'When you go?'

'In several days,' Gene answered evasively, trying hard not to let his irritation show.

'Where you go?'

Gene felt his hackles rise. 'I'm afraid that's classified information,' he said coldly, this time not bothering to disguise his annoyance.

Even Kathleen had to admit that Stefan's questioning was a little insensitive. She was about to offer more coffee, but the Dutchman continued, apparently oblivious to the American's anger.

'You leave on the USS *Chicago*?' he asked.

'What the hell business is it of yours?' Gene was more than angry now, he was deeply suspicious, this could well be the enemy seated opposite him, he thought. 'Why are you asking me all these questions?' he demanded.

Caroline was appalled. 'Please, Gene,' she said, 'I'm sure Stefan didn't mean ...'

'The USS *Chicago* is in the harbour,' Stefan shrugged and looked about the table, seemingly unaware how he could have offended. 'I like to look at the big ships in the harbour.'

'I'm sorry Mrs De Haan, I'm afraid I must leave.' Gene rose from the table.

'Very well.' Kathleen rose too. She didn't try to stop him, or to mollify the situation. Tasteless as the Dutchman's questions might have been, they were innocent enough. The American owed Stefan an apology, she thought, indeed he owed them all an apology.

'Thank you for an excellent meal.'

'I'm glad you enjoyed it.'

'Gran, please ...' Caroline jumped up from the table, dismayed. Why was her grandmother being so cold? Why wasn't Gene apologising? 'Gene ...'

'Caroline, see the Lieutenant to the door,' Kathleen instructed. 'Thank you very much for the stockings,' she added, she certainly wasn't giving the bigot back his nylons, she wasn't that proud.

'My pleasure, ma'am.'

Caroline was confused and distressed. 'What happened, Gene?'

she said at the front door. 'What went wrong? Why ...'

But he stopped her, kissing her very gently on the lips. It was the first time he'd done so. The previous Friday he'd given her a chaste peck on the cheek when he'd said goodnight.

'Goodbye Caroline,' he said. 'I hope to see you when I return to Sydney.' He looked over her shoulder towards the kitchen. 'I hope nothing is wrong,' he said, 'for your sake, I very much hope so.' And abruptly he left, before Caroline could ask him what he meant.

When she returned to the kitchen, Stefan seemed as confused as she was. 'What I do wrong?' he asked. 'I talk, I ask questions, what I do wrong?'

'Nothing, Stefan,' Kathleen said brusquely, 'you did nothing wrong. But I think it's time we all said goodnight.'

'I am sorry, Caroline,' Stefan turned apologetically at the back door. 'I do not wish to anger your American.'

'It doesn't matter.' But it did matter, she thought. Of all the nights Stefan had to get talkative, he had to choose tonight. Inwardly, she cursed the Dutchman, but she tried to sound pleasant. 'Goodnight.'

When he'd gone, she said to her grandmother, 'Why didn't you ask him to stay? Why did you ... ?'

'Why didn't he apologise?' Kathleen demanded.

Caroline had no answer for that. 'He would have, I'll bet,' she said sulkily, 'if you'd been a bit nicer.'

'Why should I be nice to a bigot?'

'He's not.'

'Yes he is, he's a bigot. I could tell from the moment he walked in, and I'm not going to discuss it any further.'

Kathleen turned her back and started stacking the dishes in the sink, and Caroline slouched off upstairs without offering to help with the washing up. On the odd occasion when she and her grandmother had a genuine disagreement, neither one would give in to the other.

Tim Kendall was seated on his Elizabeth Bay balcony, sipping a cup of Milo and listening to Glenn Miller's rendition of 'Night and Day' playing softly on the gramophone in the lounge room behind him. It was half past eleven on a Sunday evening and his wife,

Ruth, had retired, leaving him alone on the balcony with his night-cap and his music.

He'd reread the letter he'd received that morning from his daughter who had recently left university to join the land army. She was stationed at Bathurst and was picking asparagus at Edgell, she wrote. The work was hard, she was up at three every morning, six days a week, and every bone in her body was aching. But the countryside was beautiful, the very light itself distinctively different from that in the city. 'Just like the Banjo says, Dad, "... the air, so dry and so clear and bright, refracts the sun with a wondrous light".' Tim smiled to himself; 'In the Droving Days' had always been their favourite of Banjo Paterson's poems.

In the whole of her tender nineteen years, Kitty Kendall had never been outside the city of Sydney, and she'd always wanted to see the countryside. Well, she was sure as hell seeing it now, Tim thought. He never worried about Kitty, she'd always land on her feet. It was young Robert he worried about. Robert was off at the war. He'd volunteered, the stupid bugger, and Tim worried about him constantly. It didn't make sense. He thought he'd fought the war to end all wars. He looked out at the harbour and silently prayed that his son would survive.

Tim Kendall had named his firstborn after Robbie O'Shea. It was twenty-five years since Robbie's death, but he was never far from Tim's mind. In fact, with young Robert off at the war, Robbie O'Shea featured more and more in Tim's thoughts these days.

If Robbie had survived, Tim reflected, sipping on his Milo, they would have gone into partnership. Like him, Robbie would now be a wealthy man. He'd hold the controlling interest in a chain of retail stores; he'd own shares in media outlets, both newspaper and radio, and he'd even boast a string of rental properties in Macleay Street. What a joke; Robbie would have loved it.

'Not bad for two boys from Surry Hills and the Loo,' Tim could hear him say. And he'd be right. Despite the fact that Tim mingled with the powerful and influential these days, he never lost sight of his roots. There was always Robbie's voice in his ear saying, 'Don't forget where you came from, Tim Kendall.'

His thoughts turned to Kathleen and Caroline. He hadn't seen Robbie's mother and daughter for a whole three weeks, longer than usual, but he'd been very busy. He'd recently switched his affiliation from the staid, family-run Fairfax press to Frank Packer's brash, more adventurous consortium and the necessary negotiations had taken up a great deal of his time. He must pay a visit to his princess, he told himself, and he must take Kathleen some more goods for barter, she would be running short by now. It was the only way in which Tim could help support them, he knew Kathleen would never accept money.

He tucked Kitty's letter into his pocket, turned off the balcony light and drained the last of his Milo. He stood in the darkness for a moment, savouring a last look at the harbour lights before retiring, and then it happened.

There was a muffled explosion and, before his very eyes, the near side of Garden Island ignited. There was another muffled explosion. What the hell was it, an air raid? But there were no planes in the sky. An invasion? But there were no foreign ships in the harbour.

In a matter of seconds, warning sirens began screaming. Searchlights swept the waters and tracer bullets gleamed red as patrol vessels swung into action. Machine-gun fire cracked the air, then the sounds of heavy artillery, the whistle of shells, the muffled detonations of depth charges. The harbour was a battlefield, but the enemy was invisible.

'What the hell's happening?' Ruth yelled, running to his side.

'I don't know,' he yelled back, drawing her close as they watched from the balcony.

Kathleen dragged Caroline from her bed at the first scream of the sirens. 'Air raid,' she said, 'get downstairs.' It was probably another military exercise, Kathleen thought, damn them, but one had to play safe.

In the Bird household, Brian took charge. 'Ada, look after Betsy,' he yelled as he grabbed his gasmask and rifle.

'It's an invasion,' his mother was screaming hysterically. 'The Japs have invaded!'

'I reckon it's just an exercise, Mum,' Brian said, trying to keep her calm. It sure as hell didn't sound like one, he thought. 'I'll go out and check.'

Ada grabbed ten-year-old Betsy. 'Shut up Mum!' she yelled. Her mother was no use, and neither was her father, out like a light on the front room sofa. 'Come on Betsy,' she said to her little sister who was whimpering with fear, 'get under the table, we'll play cubbies.'

She pushed Betsy under the kitchen table and dragged the mattress Brian kept for such emergencies over the top. Then she crawled under the table herself and hugged her little sister. 'See, love? It's a cubby.'

Ada listened and, above the sound of the sirens and the gunfire and explosions, she heard her mother trying to rouse her father. 'The Japs are coming!' her mother was yelling. 'For God's sake, Norm, wake up! The Japs are coming!'

The Japs are coming! Ada tried hard to concentrate on Brian's words—'I reckon it's just an exercise, Mum,' he'd said. 'Just an exercise', she told herself, that's all it was. Ada trusted Brian. But she knew what was happening, she read the newspapers. The Japs had bombed Darwin, they'd scuttled ships outside Sydney, they were getting closer and closer. And she'd heard the stories too. If they invaded ... well, young women were the plums weren't they? Rape and murder, that's what they said. If the yellow peril got into Sydney, she and her lot'd be the first to cop it.

'It's all right, Betsy,' she yelled above the sirens and the guns as her little sister screamed with terror, 'play cubbies with me, it's just an exercise, that's all. Just an exercise.'

Japanese midget submarines had attacked Sydney Harbour, the newspapers announced. One had even been sighted by passengers on a ferry between Garden Island and Bradleys Head. Another, entangled in the boom net at the entrance to the main harbour, had exploded. Garden Island had been shelled and the HMAS *Kuttabul*, a converted ferry serving as an accommodation ship, had been sunk, killing twenty-one sleeping sailors and wounding ten.

Fear and speculation abounded. How many subs were there? Had numbers of Japanese been landed ashore? Was the enemy hiding out around Woolloomooloo and the Cross?

It was eventually reported to the public that there had been only three midget submarines. They had been launched from outside the heads by mother ships, one of which later shelled Bondi Beach. midget 1-27 was caught in the boom net and destroyed by its own suicide crew. Midget 1-22 fired two torpedoes at USS *Chicago*, one passing under the American cruiser to explode harmlessly on the eastern shore of Garden Island, the other sinking the *Kuttabul*. Midget 1-24, observed by the ferry passengers, passed safely out of the harbour, never to be seen again.

The public was assured that all was safe, but the damage had been done. Convinced that the Japanese were hiding out in buildings close to the docks, people moved out in droves. Tim Kendall, like other landlords around the Cross, found it impossible to rent properties, twenty-eight flats in the Macleay Regis alone remaining vacant until the hubbub eventually died down.

The day after the raid, two plainclothes police officers called upon Kathleen.

'Mrs De Haan?' one of them asked.

'Yes.'

'May we come in, please?' Senior Detective Sergeant Walton showed his ID and the two officers stepped into the front room as she opened the door for them.

'We believe you are harbouring one Stefan Brandt.' His partner standing silently to one side, it was obvious that Senior Detective Sergeant Walton did all the talking.

'I'm not "harbouring" him,' Kathleen retorted. Dear God, they're going to hound the poor man all over again, she thought. 'He's a lodger, he rents a room from me.'

'Is he in?'

'No. He hasn't been home for two days.' Kathleen had actually been concerned about Stefan. It was the first time in the whole of the two years he'd been living at her house that he'd not come home of a night. She'd presumed he'd met a woman, but she'd worried a little nonetheless. What if he'd had an accident, or met with foul play?

'Where is his room?'

'Out the back.'

'We'd like to take a look at it.'

'Well, you can't.' How dare they, she thought.

'We have a warrant.' Senior Detective Sergeant Walton nodded to his partner, who took a piece of paper from his upper pocket.

Kathleen waved aside the document which the policeman held out, she had no reason to disbelieve them, but she was outraged nonetheless. 'What gives you the right,' she demanded, 'Stefan's not an enemy alien, his papers are in order, he's a Dutchman from Java, and he works for the Dutch East India Company.'

'I'm afraid you're wrong, Mrs De Haan.'

'Oh?'

'He doesn't work for the Dutch East India Company . . .'

'Well, he did.'

'. . . he has never worked for the Dutch East India Company, his papers are not in order, and he does not come from Java.'

The policeman was watching her closely. They both were, reading her every reaction.

'Furthermore,' the policeman concluded, 'he's not Dutch and his name is not Stefan Brandt.' Kathleen looked, dumbfounded, from one to the other. 'Now if you'd be good enough to show us his room?'

Silently, she led them out the back and unlocked the door to Stefan's room, then she stood to one side as they searched.

It took them only minutes to find what they were after. A radio transmitter in the cupboard, in the top drawer of the desk numerous photographs of warships and carriers, and rolled up on the little desk in the corner, an intricate map of Sydney Harbour with military and naval installations circled in red. Secure in the knowledge that Kathleen would never intrude upon his privacy, Stefan had gone to no pains to find secret hiding places.

Kathleen accompanied the policemen back inside. She led them into the front room. 'What is he? Who is he?' she asked, fearful of the answer.

'He's German,' Walton answered, 'we're not sure of his name, we know several aliases he's used over the years. All of them Dutch.'

Kathleen felt sick, and suddenly unsteady on her feet, she sat down on the sofa. Not only had she housed an enemy spy, she'd defended and protected him. 'The Japanese submarines?' She looked up at the two men who stood before her, and her voice, too, was a little unsteady.

'Possibly. They certainly had advance information.' Walton felt sorry for the woman, he was sure she was telling the truth, but she'd have to be investigated nevertheless.

He wondered himself just how key a figure Brandt might have been. They should have picked him up on Saturday morning, he thought, the moment the Yank had reported him as a suspect, but they'd decided to leave it until Monday, nobody wanted extra paperwork on a Saturday. Walton wondered whether it might have had an effect upon the Japanese raid if they'd picked Brandt up. Oh well, he supposed they'd never know.

'We'd like you to come with us and answer some questions, Mrs De Haan,' he said, not unkindly. 'Is there someone you'd like to telephone? Someone who could help you?'

She telephoned Tim Kendall.

The Japanese submarine attack on Sydney Harbour was the final straw for Susan Kendle. Time to leave, she decided. She was seventy-four years of age and far too old for this. She detested the war but, in all honesty, she couldn't argue against its necessity. She hadn't been able to even at the outset. And now that Australia was threatened, she was frustrated at being unable to help. If she were younger she would have been one of the driving forces behind women's involvement in the war. No longer did women sit around sewing socks for men being needlessly slaughtered; now they drove lorries and taxis, they worked the land to feed the people and they joined the forces to protect their country. Women were proving their worth and being recognised for it, and Susan was proud of her sex. If only she could do more. God, how she hated being old.

Susan Kendle's financial contribution to the war effort had been invaluable but, money being meaningless to her, she'd lost sight of that fact.

Susan had been astonished to discover that, with the exception of his partnership in Kendle and Streatham, her father had left everything to her. Kendle and Streatham was indeed the bulk of his wealth, but there was much else besides. Mostly property, including Kendle Lodge itself, together with various trust accounts, shares and investments. Susan had presumed that, after her condemnation at his hospital bedside, he'd leave his money to someone else. But then who was there? He'd never give it to charity. She could only assume that, even on his deathbed, Charles had hoped his money might force her hand. That, through the sheer guilt of her inheritance, she would persuade her son to embrace the Kendle name.

Charles had been desperate to preserve his name under any

circumstances. His will instructed that, in leaving his share of the controlling interest in Kendle and Streatham to Godfrey, the name of the company was never to be changed. 'Kendle' must remain forever. If his name was not to be carried on by his blood then it must be sustained by his business interests.

Ironically enough, even that contingency had been destined to fail, Susan thought. She saw the Streathams a lot and she knew the difficulties they were suffering. Godfrey Streatham III was a young man of the utmost integrity, just like his father and grandfather before him, and he would most certainly have honoured his commitment had he been able. But it had been impossible to preserve Charles Kendle's name simply because it had been impossible to preserve Kendle and Streatham itself. The stores had been sold and were shortly to be converted to office space.

Only Kendle Lodge remained and, as a gesture to her father, Susan had maintained the name. In the late thirties she had made a personal visit to the Wunderlich Company to arrange an emblem to be erected above the main doors of the Lodge.

Wunderlichs had barely scraped through the Depression, their Redfern factory reduced to a skeleton staff, but they had survived by the sheer ingenuity of the brothers and the diversified range of building products they supplied. The outbreak of war, however, brought about substantial changes to the company. The production of essential goods and contracts with the American and Australian Armed forces saw their profits rise and Wunderlichs was once more a force to be reckoned with. The company had remained a family concern, run principally by the offspring of the original brothers, but to Susan's surprise it was Alfred Wunderlich himself who had personally overseen the design of the Kendle Lodge emblem.

The old man must have been well into his seventies, she'd thought as they sat in his office, yet, lean and fit, he looked a good decade younger.

'Moulded zinc is still the best,' he said. Alfred Wunderlich loved his work with a passion and he had no intention of retiring, there were another twenty years in him yet. 'And we should keep the motif of a yacht, I think, like the original emblem we designed for Kendle and Streatham.'

'Yes,' she agreed, 'Father loved his yachts.'

'I suggest something large and impressive.'

'Most certainly,' Susan agreed, and they shared a smile. Mr Wunderlich appeared to know her father well, she thought. Charles Kendle had not been a man given to subtlety.

Once erected, the sign indeed proved most impressive. A magnificent yacht in full sail was emblazoned with the words 'Kendle Lodge', beneath which, in smaller lettering, was 'War Veterans' Hospice'.

Susan had spent a vast amount of her father's money converting the old family mansion to a convalescent home for returned soldiers. She'd set up a charity trust, in perpetuity, to be operated by the Red Cross Society, with one proviso only: that the hospice always remain known as Kendle Lodge.

Her father's name lived on as he'd wished, she'd made sure of that. But, most delicious of all ironies, it served an altruistic purpose. She knew that he wouldn't have thanked her for that.

Susan waddled up the gangplank and onto the Manly ferry. She'd become bigger than ever in her latter years and it made getting about rather difficult. This would be her last ride on a Manly ferry, and the thought saddened her a little. But she was ready to leave. Tomorrow she was heading south to Tasmania aboard an apple steamer bound for Hobart. Tasmania, Susan was convinced, was the only remaining escape, the war was everywhere. Besides, she needed to get away from this heat. She swept her dampened, unruly hair from her face. It would be Christmas soon, and Sydney's December swelter was insufferable. Well, for fat old ladies anyway.

She gazed out at the Bridge, saddened also by the knowledge that she would never see it again. To Susan, as to many, the Sydney Harbour Bridge was a symbol of triumph.

Australians had embraced many distractions during the Depression. Radio had become increasingly innovative, and to crowd around the wireless set of an evening was a welcome escape for families who lived a miserable existence. And then there were the 'talkies'. Many would spend their last precious pennies to elude reality in a darkened picture house. Other distractions were the sporting heroes, not least of all Donald Bradman who carried Australia on his back each time he went in to bat. And the great Melbourne Cup winner, Phar Lap, whose triumphs were eagerly followed throughout the country, and whose untimely demise in America stimulated endless debate in dole queues and pubs.

But for Sydneysiders there was, above all else, the Bridge. Completed at the height of the Depression, it had created jobs for thousands, and given hope and pride to the city's people. As its mighty span grew, foot by foot, over the eight years of its construction, it came to symbolise more and more the triumph and endurance of its people.

I will miss the Bridge, Susan thought. As she watched the giant steel coathanger recede into the distance she thought of her father. He'd been on her mind a lot of late. Probably because she was leaving Sydney. For better or for worse, her family had had an impact upon this city, and this city had had an impact upon them. She wondered whether, as the last of the Kendles, she should feel guilty at abandoning Sydney.

She walked to the starboard side of the ferry and looked at Manly Pier looming ahead. No, she didn't feel guilty. Not even a little. She'd done her bit.

Chapter Fourteen

'Gene!' Caroline opened the front door to Lieutenant Gene Hamilton of the US Marines.

'Hello, Caroline.'

It had been eighteen months, but he was as handsome as she remembered. His composure seemed a little ruffled, however, as if he wasn't sure as to how he would be received.

'Come in,' Caroline opened the door wide, 'we're having a cup of tea in the kitchen.' Of course, Gene thought, when were Aussies not having a cup of tea in the kitchen. 'Gran'll be thrilled to see you. She always said that she owes you an apology.'

That smile. She was irresistible. He wished he could suggest they just go for a walk, he longed to be alone with her. 'A cup of tea'd be great,' he said as he stepped reluctantly inside. Kathleen De Haan owed him an apology? He'd all but accused the woman of being a spy.

'It's nice to see you again, Gene,' Kathleen shook his hand warmly. 'I owe you an apology, you were right about Stefan.'

'I know, I heard.' Confused by the warmth of his reception, Gene wondered whether she knew it was he who'd reported Brandt; she certainly couldn't know that he'd also reported her as a possible accessory.

'You thought my Gran was a spy, didn't you?' said Caroline, embarrassing him. 'That's what the police told us.'

'Caroline, stop it,' Kathleen ordered.

'They interrogated us for hours,' she continued, ignoring the admonishment, aware of Gene's discomfort. She didn't intend to be cruel, but he should have come to see them at the time, she thought, so she decided to make him squirm, just for a moment. 'We only got off the hook because we had Tim Kendall for a character witness.'

'Gene, sit down, please,' Kathleen interrupted.

'Kendall Markets, do you know them?' Caroline asked.

'Of course,' Gene nodded.

'He's my godfather, Tim Kendall, the police were very impressed.'

'Would you like some tea?' Kathleen asked. It was time for Caroline to shut up, she'd had her fun.

'I'm sorry.' Gene directed his apology to Kathleen. 'I didn't intend to cause trouble.'

'Of course you didn't,' she said. Of course he did, she thought. If he'd suspected her, as he obviously had, then his very intention had been to cause trouble. And so it should have been. 'You did the right thing, now sit down and I'll get you some tea.'

'What about a beer instead?' Caroline suggested and, before he could answer, she'd fetched a bottle from the icebox.

Gene didn't much like Australian beer, he was a bourbon man himself. But he drank the beer, and joined in the conversation and, to his amazement, an hour later, the three of them were laughing about the fact that he'd thought Kathleen might have been a spy. This Aussie beer had quite an effect after all, he realised, feeling rather light-headed and enjoying the women's company, but most particularly Caroline's.

Gene had chosen to spend his furloughs in Brisbane over the past eighteen months. He'd even had an affair with a girl there. Convinced that he would no longer be welcome in the De Haan household, he had decided to put Caroline O'Shea out of his mind. But it had been impossible. And when he'd found himself posted to Sydney he hadn't been able to resist visiting the little old house in Woolloomooloo.

And now here she was, enchanting him once more with her beauty, delighting him all over again with her candour and earthy humour. How could he ever have thought he could put such a creature out of his mind? Gene Hamilton was more smitten than ever. In fact, he had to admit it, he was head over heels in love.

'How long are you on leave, Gene?' Caroline asked, hoping it would be long enough for him to ask her out, she'd forgotten how attractive he was.

'Well, I'm not actually. I'm on secondment to the Aussies.'

'Oh?'

'Which means I'm in Sydney for a month.'

'Oh.'

'Would you like to go out to dinner? Or the theatre maybe?' Then he recalled that she didn't like being seen out alone with a Yank, so he quickly added, 'or we could go to The Trocadero with your friend ... er ...'

'Ada?'

'Yeah, Ada, that's right. We could go dancing with Ada.'

'I think dinner would be nice.' Caroline was less self-conscious these days. The Yanks had been in town for so long now that people accepted Aussie girls in their company. Besides, dinner with the urbane American would make a welcome change from the Saturday arvo pictures with Ada's big brother Brian.

'How about tonight?'

'Why not?' she grinned.

They dined out that night, and when he brought her home, he kissed her on the lips. Chastely, his hands resting gently on her shoulders, resisting the urge to take her in his arms and feel her body against his.

'Sunday, tomorrow,' he said, 'would you like to go out for the day? I could hire a car. A drive into the countryside maybe?' He was rushing her, he knew it, she wouldn't wish to spend the whole weekend in his company, but he didn't want her out of his sight, he'd spend every minute with her if he possibly could.

'How about the beach? We could go to Bondi.'

'No taxis, Gene,' she said the following morning, and she took his hand as they walked up William Street. 'Everybody catches the Bondi tram, it's what going to the beach is all about.'

She was right, Gene thought, as the tram turned the corner and he caught his first sight of Bondi Beach. The broad sweep of sandy bay and rocky headland was spectacular viewed from the front seat of the tram which rattled down the hill at an alarming speed.

He was a good swimmer, she noted, admiring his athleticism from the distant safety of her deckchair up near the sea-wall.

Caroline enjoyed the beach, but was no water baby, preferring to plonk herself in the ocean every now and then simply in order to cool off.

She studied him more closely as he started to run up the beach towards her. Naturally olive-skinned, his body was as tanned as his face. Broad-shouldered, slim-hipped, his was the physique of a soldier, fit and well toned. She closed her eyes as he joined her.

'That was fantastic,' he said, sprawling panting and soaking wet in the sand, 'absolutely fantastic.'

'Oh you're back,' she opened her eyes, 'I must have dozed off. Don't you want a towel?' She leaned down to pull a towel from the bag.

'No, I like the feel of hot sand on my skin, I'll rinse it off later.'

They bought icecreams and ate them sitting on the stone steps which led down to the beach, gazing out over the endless hordes of sunworshippers burning to a crisp in the baking-hot summer afternoon. Then they had a dip together, Caroline allowing herself to be teased out of her depth in order to feel Gene's body against hers as he supported her in the water.

After they'd dried off and dressed in their respective changing rooms at the Pavilion, they walked hand in hand up the grassy knoll towards Campbell Parade where they sat in the corner shop eating pies and watching the passers-by promenade in the cool of the late afternoon, the breeze whisking in from the sea.

'Would you like to come in for a cup of tea?' Caroline asked when they returned home in the early dusk. 'Or a coffee, or a beer?'

'No thanks,' Gene said. 'I'm still carrying a bit of sand around, think I'll go back to the hotel and clean up.' Much as he enjoyed Kathleen De Haan's company he didn't think he could bear to share Caroline with anyone. Not right now. Not after the day they'd had. 'It was a perfect day, Caroline.' It seemed natural to take her in his arms.

'Yes it was.' She responded wholeheartedly to his kiss until, aware of their conspicuousness on Kathleen's front porch, she drew away, a little out of breath.

'May I call on you Tuesday? Dinner? The theatre?'

'Whatever,' Caroline said, 'Tuesday'd be beaut.'

She closed the door behind her, then opened it to watch him

striding off down the street. She had been taken aback by her response. Did it happen as quickly as this? Was she falling in love with the man, she wondered as she relished the tingle of sea salt on her skin, her body felt so alive.

Three weeks later she had no doubts whatsoever. She was desperately in love with Gene Hamilton. And he with her, she knew it. If he'd asked her to go back to his hotel room she would have agreed. But he didn't. He always kissed her goodnight on the front porch, both of them by now fully aware of the other's desire. But never once did he suggest they go to his hotel.

Gene was in a dilemma. He knew full well that Caroline would sleep with him, but he'd already made one terrible mistake. Less than two months ago, the girl in Brisbane with whom he'd been having an affair had fallen pregnant. They'd been careful, as careful as they could be, but it had happened. He'd given the girl enough money for a proper abortion by a qualified medical doctor. A number of general practitioners were carrying out the illegal procedure and it cost ten times as much as a backstreet job, but at least it was safe, most of the time.

He'd breathed a sigh of relief when all had gone smoothly, but he'd felt riddled with guilt nonetheless. Abortion went directly against his Wesleyan Methodist upbringing, but at least he'd been honest. He'd never told the girl that he loved her, he'd never promised he'd marry her and take her to America like many of his friends had told their Australian girls. And when she'd become pregnant, he hadn't lied and told her he'd come back for her and the baby. He'd been honest he'd told himself over and over, but it hadn't made him feel any better.

And now here was Caroline, willing to give herself to him, and he loved her deeply. Of course he would marry her in a second, he only wished that he could. But that wouldn't solve the dilemma at all. He was leaving shortly on active service. After Guadalcanal Gene knew exactly what to expect. It was quite likely he would not return. What if Caroline was left with a child? What kind of life was that to wish upon the woman he loved?

Each time he kissed her goodnight, Gene struggled with his passion and his conscience, and each time his conscience won out. He would not risk destroying her.

'Where is it you're going to?' she asked the Sunday before he left. It was a balmy night and they were sitting on the back porch. Kathleen, having cooked one of her stews, had discreetly retired early to leave them together.

'Oh, you don't need to know that,' he answered casually as though it really didn't matter, and she realised that she should have known better than to have asked. He never spoke about military matters. In fact he rarely even spoke about the war.

'What's the point?' he'd say, 'we've just got to get through it and one day it'll all be over.' So they'd talk about their respective childhoods instead, asking endless questions, each wanting to know everything about the other.

As only children they'd both had lonely childhoods, they discovered.

'Gran's been everything to me,' Caroline told him. 'Mother, father, best friend. When I was about fifteen she told me my mother was still alive, said if I wanted to meet her she'd try and find out where she was.'

'And did you?'

'Nope. I decided if my mother didn't want to know me then I didn't want to know her.'

'We're two of a kind then, my mom didn't want to know me either.'

'At least you were brought up with a silver spoon,' Caroline laughed. 'Posh boarding schools and riding camps. Your own car when you were eighteen! My God, what a Woolloomooloo boy wouldn't have given for that.'

'I'd've swapped them all for someone like your gran.'

'Yep, you're right, I'm lucky.'

Gene's father had been a racing car driver, and as a boy Gene had been left in boarding school whilst his mother accompanied the famous Brad Hamilton on the international circuit, from one Grand Prix to the next.

'I idolised my father,' Gene said. 'He was every boy's hero. Taught me how to drive when I was ten. I was racing as an amateur at Indianapolis when I was eighteen. All my buddies were envious, they wanted a dad like mine. Course I didn't dare tell them that I never really knew him. The only thing we shared was a love of racing cars.

'But then,' Gene shrugged, 'I can't hold that against him, I guess it's all he had to offer. I was twenty-one when he died. A crash in the Indy 500. Killed instantly. Mom went to pieces for a while, then she took up with a buddy of Dad's, another driver, and she was back following the circuit again. So I finished my engineering course at Harvard and joined the army. I had to get away from home and I figured the marines sounded pretty adventurous.'

'Caroline,' he said now as they sat on the porch and he took her hand in both of his, 'I love you, you know that don't you?'

'Yes.'

'And you love me too.'

'Yes.'

It hadn't been a question, he knew that she loved him, but the simplicity of her reply and the fervour in her eyes thrilled him beyond measure.

'When the war's over, will you marry me?'

'Yes.'

They stood and embraced and, returning his kiss, her body responded alarmingly as it did these days at his very touch.

'Gene,' she whispered as their mouths parted, 'if you want to . . .'

'We leave on Tuesday,' he said brusquely, 'but I won't see you tomorrow, there's a lot to be done, so I'll say my goodbyes now.'

'Oh.' She quelled the sick feeling in her stomach, she hadn't known it was so soon. 'Some time next week,' that's what he'd said. 'I don't suppose you know how long you'll be gone?' she asked, trying to sound as matter of fact as she could.

'No.'

'Godspeed then.'

He nodded and left abruptly before she could see him to the front door.

It turned out to be three months. Three months, one week and two days to be precise. Caroline had counted.

She met his train at Central Station and, after escaping the swarming crowds on the railway platform, they stood outside trying to hail a taxi. In the teeming rain it was impossible.

'It's been raining for days,' she yelled above the din and clamour of people yelling for taxis and cars honking their horns, 'it always does in April.'

But they didn't care. Gene gave up trying to get a cab and they gave up trying to keep dry. They clung to each other in the pouring rain and kissed and laughed for pure joy. Then Gene shouldered his backpack and they walked through the deluge, his arm around her, rivulets of water cascading from her best felt hat, now soggy and ruined.

They dined that night at the Roosevelt—for old times' sake, he said, and she remembered the night they'd first met, as she peered over the balcony railing at the couples on the dance floor below.

Caroline launched into her attack just after the steaks had arrived. 'You asked me to marry you, right?' she demanded.

'And you said yes.' Those compelling brown eyes with their depth of seriousness and their hint of laughter were mesmerising him. God, but it was wonderful to be with her again.

'I did,' she affirmed, nodding briskly. 'After the war, that's what you said.'

'Correct.'

'Well I'm reneging on the offer, it's not good enough.'

'Oh?' He wanted to laugh, she delighted him so.

'Now, Gene.' The banter was gone. 'Marry me now.'

He looked down at the steak on his plate, it was suddenly unappetising. How could he tell her what he'd been through? How could he explain that it would happen again before the war was over? Again he'd watched his comrades die and each moment of each day he'd wonder if he was the next in line.

'Caroline,' he said haltingly, 'when I go away . . .'

'I know.'

'If I don't come back . . .'

'I know that too. Let's risk it, Gene. I'm willing if you are, in fact I'll go mad if we don't.' He looked up from the steak he'd been toying with. Her eyes were begging him. 'Please,' she said, 'please marry me.'

'When?'

'Now. Right now.' She grinned. 'You're not enjoying that steak anyway. We'll bash on some priest's door and make him marry us in the middle of the night with two witnesses we've grabbed off the street, just like they do in the movies.'

He laughed, he couldn't help it. 'Oh no we won't, we'll do it the proper way.'

'What way's that?'

'With my Commanding Officer's permission and your grandmother's blessing.'

A week later Caroline O'Shea married Gene Hamilton in the Registry Office of Births, Deaths and Marriages and their witnesses were Kathleen De Haan and Ada Bird.

Any lingering misgivings Kathleen might have harboured disappeared as she watched them exchange vows. They were so deeply in love it would have been wrong if they'd not married, and she prayed that Gene would return unscathed from the war.

Ada wept throughout the short service. Caroline looked so beautiful and Gene so handsome. Fancy Caroline marrying a Yank, how adventurous of her.

Ada had changed her opinions about the Yanks since she'd met her GI, Pete. Pete wasn't just for good times and presents, Pete was mad about her. He hadn't lost interest when she'd refused to sleep with him. In fact he wanted to marry her, to take her to America after the war and have a big white wedding with his family. Ada hadn't seriously considered marriage, however, he was a Yank after all. But if Caroline was marrying a Yank, then why shouldn't she? She'd always followed Caroline's example, right from when she'd enrolled in Stott's Secretarial College. Marriage to Pete suddenly held a strong appeal, he'd be home on leave in a month, she'd give it some serious thought.

'I now pronounce you man and wife.'

Ada burst into fresh tears as Gene kissed his new bride.

Gene had hired a suite at the Hotel Australia and they barely left the bedroom for the entire week of their honeymoon.

'What a terrible waste of money,' Caroline said, surveying the spacious sitting room and balcony. So he made love to her then and there on the floor.

'Shall we try the balcony next?' he said, when she lay sated in his arms, and she gave one of her wicked gurgles of laughter. An hour later he took her back into the bedroom, he wouldn't put it past Caroline to take him up on his suggestion.

Then the week was over and Gene was gone. She didn't ask him where he was going or for how long, she was a soldier's wife now and knew better. And she didn't cry or allow her fear to show. She simply said 'Godspeed my love.'

Caroline knew from the moment she saw Ada's face that Ada was no longer a virgin. Gone was the giggling coquette, she was glowing with womanly fulfilment. 'You slept with Pete, didn't you?' True to form Caroline jumped straight to the point.

'Yes.' Ada couldn't wait to admit it, she desperately needed to tell someone, and Caroline was her only possible confidante. She knew that Bev and Enid slept with men, they openly discussed it, and she'd sometimes felt jealous of them, wondering what it would be like. She was nearly twenty-six years old, it was high time she lost her virginity. But, now that it had happened, she couldn't tell Bev and Enid about Pete, they wouldn't understand. 'Oh Caroline, it was wonderful,' she said. 'I love him so much, and I know he loves me.'

Any advice Caroline might have been contemplating went out the window. She hugged her friend. 'I'm happy for you,' she said.

It was obvious to Caroline that Pete loved Ada. Every leave he could get he raced to Sydney to see his Ladybird.

'Where's my Ladybird?' he'd say, standing at the front door of the Bird house, his arms laden with chocolates and flowers, and little Betsy would run squealing inside.

'He's here Ada, he's here!'

Eleven-year-old Betsy adored Pete, and Pete adored Betsy, so it was a fair exchange. But then Pete seemed genuinely fond of the whole Bird family, even Norm who, having fallen captive to the American's charm, seemed to remain sober longer when Pete was around. Most people ignored Norm. Pete didn't. Norm liked that.

Caroline, too, couldn't help but like Pete. He was attractive in his own way. A little on the short side and not handsome in the conventional sense, but he had dimples which danced, rather like Ada's, she thought, and a cheeky appeal which was irresistible. Furthermore, he treated Ada like a princess.

'We're going to be married, Caroline,' Ada announced proudly. 'We'll be having a ceremony here before we leave for America, will you be my matron of honour?'

'Of course, I'd be dead snaky if you asked anyone else.'

The Allies had invaded northern France. On 8 June, 1944 the Australian press screamed the news and, all over the country, millions listened to the long-awaited announcement by General

Eisenhower, broadcast by the BBC. Surely it was only a matter of time till the war ended. But it dragged on.

Gene was home for Christmas. It had been a whole seven months and Caroline was shocked when she saw him, drawn and haggard. She had read the newspaper reports of the battles in the Pacific, and she had worried continuously, but in his letters he had mentioned nothing of the hardship and she'd hoped that he might have escaped the worst of it. She asked no questions but clung to him tightly, telling him over and over that she loved him, wishing that she could do something to ease his mind.

He didn't speak of his ordeal, but the announcement he made said it all. 'When the war's over I'm leaving the army,' he told her.

'Good,' she whispered, holding him close.

They celebrated Christmas as if there were no war. Pete was on leave too, and he and Ada joined Caroline and Gene for the midday feast which Kathleen prepared, the luxuries having been provided by the men. Tinned ham from Gene and, surprisingly, a fresh turkey from Pete.

'Where the hell did you get that?' Kathleen asked when he'd arrived on Christmas Eve with the bird, wrapped in brown paper, tucked under his arm.

'Ask me no questions ...' and he tapped his nose. So Kathleen didn't. Pete was a resourceful young man and she was only too happy to accept his illicit gift.

Kathleen had slaved all morning over the old wood stove and, as it was a sweltering day, they ate gathered around the small table on the back porch to get away from the heat of the kitchen and take advantage of what little breeze they could.

They toasted each other with the champagne Gene had brought and they scoffed back Kathleen's plum pudding with brandy sauce, and nobody mentioned the war.

Kathleen insisted upon getting the coffee. 'No, no,' she said refusing Caroline's and Ada's help, 'you young ones sit and chat.' God knows, they needed to grab every moment they could. 'The four of you can do the washing up later.'

So they sat and chatted, Pete lighting up one of his cigars and regaling them with plans for the wedding. 'A big white wedding at the ranch,' he said, 'all the family'll be there. Ma'll be so proud of my Ladybird.'

Ada sat on his lap, her arm draped around his shoulder. 'Pete's parents own a ranch in North Carolina,' she explained proudly to Gene. 'Is that anywhere near Maine?'

The men laughed. 'Not exactly,' Gene said. Ada was a bit giddy maybe, but he couldn't help liking her. Gene felt a contentment he'd not known in months. Caroline was happily cuddled up against him, and the steaming jungles of Saipan and Palau seemed very far away.

Less than five months later the war in Europe was over. On 8 May, 1945, VE day was celebrated throughout Australia, but there was a dampener to the enthusiasm. The war in the Pacific continued. 'Wait until all the fellows are home and the men of the 8th division swing down Martin Place,' one Sydney digger was quoted as saying. 'That will be the day!'

'I got your letter,' Tim said. 'Thanks. I'm sorry I didn't come around earlier, but . . .' He gave a weary shrug, leaned his elbows on his knees and stared at the knuckles of his clasped hands.

'I knew you'd come when you were ready.'

Tim and Kathleen were sitting on the back porch, Caroline having discreetly made her departure shortly after his arrival.

'I'm so sorry, Tim,' Caroline had said.

'Yes. Thank you.' He hadn't hugged her as he always did, and he hadn't called her his princess. He hadn't even noticed she was pregnant and, at five months now, she was showing. Caroline knew he needed to be alone with Kathleen.

'I'm going to the shops, Gran, do you want anything?'

Kathleen had shaken her head and smiled her thanks as she took Tim out onto the porch.

'Oh Tim,' she now said. 'Oh Tim.'

She rose from her chair and he felt the coolness of her hands against his cheeks as she gently lifted his head so that their eyes could meet.

In the fleshy folds of her aged face, Kathleen's eyes remained magnificent, and in them was a wealth of love and compassion. Tim felt a tide of emotion rising in him. His wife hadn't looked at him like this. Which wasn't her fault, he knew. He hadn't been able to share his pain with her, and she had the burden of her own sorrow to bear. His remoteness was driving a wedge between them which was destroying their marriage. But Tim knew that he could share his pain with Kathleen. Kathleen understood.

He put his arms around her waist and sobbed like a baby, his face nestled against her ample bosom as she stroked his hair and said 'there, there', over and over.

He hadn't been able to cry for the whole four months. His wife had. And he'd felt guilty for not crying with her. He'd said all the right words, or he'd thought he had.

'It's the risk he ran,' he'd said. 'He was a soldier, a professional, he died for his country.' But he'd known the words sounded empty.

They'd sounded empty because they were. The endless enquiries Tim had made, without Ruth's knowledge, had been to no avail. It appeared there had been no witnesses to Robert's death, and all Tim could think of was the fear, the sheer terror his son might have known. Did he die in agony? Was he crying like a baby when he died? Had his body been blown to shreds the way Robbie's had been? Had young Robert awakened from the brief and nasty dream of war to see his intestines ripped from his body and his blood spilled in a pool about him? If he had, Tim prayed that there might have been some friend nearby, some friend who might have blown his son's brains out. If he'd been there himself he would have done it. Tim had never regretted sparing Robbie O'Shea the hideousness of his death, and he would not have hesitated to do the same for his son.

It had all come back. The images, vivid and remorseless, would not leave him alone. But they were no longer images of Robbie, they were images of his son. History repeating itself. Not his boy, he prayed. Not Robert. Please God, don't let it have been that way.

And now there was Kathleen, and he could cry. Without words. He could just cry.

'I'll get us a cup of tea, shall I?' Kathleen asked when his sobs had subsided.

'Yes.' He felt no embarrassment, and when she brought the tea, he said, 'So this is what it's like to lose your son in a war.'

'Yes.'

They held hands for a moment and Tim felt a deep sense of gratitude. The wall he'd built around himself had crumbled, and he knew now that he would be able to give his wife the support she so sorely needed.

'Kitty's come home,' he said.

'Good, that'll help.'

'She's going back to university. Reckons she wants to be a writer and change the world.'

'She's the sort who could,' Kathleen agreed. She'd not seen Tim's daughter since childhood, but even as a little girl Kitty Kendall had had guts.

They were comfortable in their silence, and then Tim added, 'I'm going to see Billy tomorrow, he's in Kendle Lodge.'

'Yes, I saw him last week.'

'You knew?' He looked at her, surprised; he'd presumed that she received all the news directly from him.

'Of course, I read the casualty lists every day. I spoke to Marge and she told me.'

Billy Kendall's son, Tom, had been reported dead only days after the death of young Robert. And, ironically, both had died barely two months before the war had ended in Europe.

The death of his younger son had driven Billy over the edge. He'd been unstable for years, and when both of his sons had enlisted, his wife had thought he would never recover.

'They're too old, for God's sake,' he'd ranted. 'They're in their thirties, they should have more sense, leave it to the younger ones.'

The thought that his sons might go through what he had was driving Billy to madness. But Wally and Tom were determined. They were going off to war, just as their father had. And their cousin Tim Kendall. And Robbie O'Shea. And the Putmans, and all the others who'd known the glory of war. 'You did it, why shouldn't we?' was their argument, and there was nothing Billy could say which could possibly change their minds.

And now Tom was dead, and Billy had lost the last flimsy hold he had on reality. He needed constant medical care and, as Marge was no longer able to look after him, he had been admitted to Kendle Lodge.

'You haven't seen him yet?' Kathleen asked. Billy had been at the hospice for two months.

Tim shook his head. 'I didn't think I could face him.' He rose and smiled at her gratefully. 'I can now.'

Tim Kendall was only eleven years younger than his uncle Billy. He could remember how he'd joked to Robbie O'Shea when they'd all enlisted at Victoria Barracks. 'A bloke feels a bit of a dill signing up with his uncle,' he'd said. But Billy had never really been an uncle to Tim, more like a big brother. The best big brother a man could have, and it broke Tim's heart to see him now. At sixty-three years of age, Billy looked ninety. Frail and near death. But it was the fear in his eyes and the nervous tics which were most disturbing.

'He likes to sit here,' the nurse had said after she'd wheeled his chair down the specially designed path to the arbour at the bottom of Kendle Lodge gardens. 'He enjoys the view, don't you, dear?' There'd been no answer from Billy and she hadn't waited for one. 'Give me a call if you need anything,' and then she was gone, leaving Tim alone with Billy.

Billy paid no heed to his visitor as he stared out at the view. There'd been a flicker of recognition when Tim had first arrived, but that was all. 'He's there when he wants to be,' the nurse had said in answer to Tim's querying look.

Now Tim sat on the garden bench beside his uncle, who was rocking back and forth in his chair, and watched the fingers of Billy's left hand, constantly weaving and twisting and entwining with each other, the stump of his right wrist moving restlessly upon his knee as if he wished he could twist the fingers of his missing hand too. And Tim watched the remorseless movement of Billy's clenched jaw, and listened to the grinding of his teeth. Billy was a soul in torment.

Tim forced himself to look away. 'It's a big place now all right,' he said, staring out over Woolloomooloo to the tangle of the city beyond and the giant span of the Harbour Bridge. 'A city on any world map, I reckon.'

Billy said nothing, but remained rocking back and forth.

'It must be good to have Wally home.' Wally had visited his father immediately upon his return; it had really broken him up, Marge had said, seeing his dad that way.

'Wally,' Billy stopped rocking. His fingers remained in incessant motion but he stopped clenching his jaw and grinding his teeth. He started to rapidly nod his head instead. 'Wally, Wally, Wally, Wally,' he said very quickly, over and over. Nod, nod, nod, nod. 'Wally, Wally, Wally, Wally.'

Tenuous as it was, Tim was glad of the breakthrough. 'I'm going to offer him a job, what do you reckon?' For the first time Billy turned his head to look at him. 'We'll find a top place for him in the company, a junior partner he'll be.' The head had stopped nodding, the jaw remained unclenched and the movement of the fingers had visibly slowed. 'It's a family company, Billy,' Tim said enthusiastically, 'and that's what we are. We're family, and the Kendalls look after their own.'

'Tim.' The eyes, fearful as they were, were alert, intelligent.

'Yes?'

'Bloody silly, war you know.'

'Yes.'

'Nobody ever wins.'

Tim once more nodded his agreement. He'd heard these words before. A poem, written by a veteran of the Great War at the outbreak of World War II. He didn't know the poet, but he and Billy had admired the verses. He finished the brief quote:

' "Men fight and die, and twenty years on their sons repeat their sins." '

Billy's fragile face cracked into the vestige of a smile and, for just one moment, the old Billy Kendall was there. 'Good poem. Simple. Says it all, doesn't it?' Then he looked out at the harbour and his fingers once more picked up their pace.

Billy showed no other reaction for the rest of the visit, but Tim was glad of that one moment. As he left, he hoped that Billy would die soon.

'Fellow citizens, the war is over.' The announcement was made by Australia's new Prime Minister, Joseph Benedict Chifley. The indefatigable John Curtin, the man General Douglas MacArthur described as 'one of the Great of the Earth', had succumbed to a heart attack barely six weeks before the unconditional surrender of Japan on 14 August, 1945.

A two-day holiday was proclaimed, and victory in the Pacific was celebrated throughout the country with all the exuberance Australians could muster. An effigy of a Japanese soldier was burned in Martin Place, the hokey-pokey was danced in the city streets, and endless conga lines were formed by soldiers and sailors, nurses and airmen whilst loudspeakers blasted out 'Rule Britannia' and 'Roll Out the Barrel'. Girls exchanged kisses for servicemen's hats, and kerbside pedlars quickly sold out of their supplies of streamers, flags, rattles and whistles.

Her baby due in three weeks, Caroline did not risk the rowdiness of the streets and the jostling crowds, but she and Kathleen toasted the end of the war and Gene's safe return.

'He'll cop a bit of a shock, won't he?' Caroline smiled at Kathleen, trying to sound braver than she felt. 'He probably won't get home until after the baby's born.' She hadn't mentioned her pregnancy in her letters, not wishing to burden him with any added cause for anxiety.

'It'll be a surprise, all right,' Kathleen agreed, smiling back at her granddaughter. She knew Caroline's bravado was a front, that she was really sick with worry. There'd been no word from Gene for over a month.

'No news is good news,' Kathleen had said, and Caroline had brightly agreed, neither woman daring to voice her true concern.

A week or so later, Tim Kendall called upon Kathleen and Caroline and asked them out to dinner. He knew Caroline worried for her husband's safety, bravely as she disguised the fact, and his invitation was by way of distraction. 'A family affair,' he said, 'it's time you got to know Ruth and Kitty. And my cousin Wally'll be there too. I've booked a balcony table at Henri's this Friday and I won't take no for an answer.'

Kathleen was glad to see the old Tim Kendall was back. Confident, in charge, he was a different man from the haunted creature who'd sobbed against her bosom only a month or so ago.

'Henri's. How posh,' Caroline raised a mock eyebrow but she was impressed. Henri's was a very chic and very expensive restaurant in Roslyn Gardens, 'can Ada come too?'

'Caroline,' Kathleen gently rebuked, 'Tim hardly knows Ada.'

But Tim laughed, Caroline delighted him when she was brazen, which was often. 'Of course Ada can come.' He'd met Caroline's friend briefly on several occasions, 'the more the merrier.'

'Thanks, Tim.' Caroline was not being perverse in inviting Ada along, she wanted to cheer her friend up. Ada too needed distraction. She'd received word from Pete that he was safe, but she was missing him dreadfully.

As Caroline threw her arms around his neck and hugged him, Tim could feel the fullness of her belly. 'I hope you'll be there yourself,' he said, breaking from the embrace and looking her up and down.

'Oh, I've got a full two weeks to go yet,' Caroline said. 'Well nearly,' she added, stroking her stomach. 'Anyway, she wouldn't dare get in the way of a night at Henri's, she's far too well mannered for that.'

'She?'

'We're both convinced it's a girl,' Kathleen explained, 'a boy would have kicked more.'

'Well, that's what they say, isn't it?' Caroline insisted. 'I'm going around to Ada's to tell her about Friday.'

Tim watched as Caroline waddled off with none of her customary grace. The image of the little girl who used to sit on his knee and tell him about her day at great length and with great solemnity flashed through his mind. It was strange to see his princess about to become a mother.

The following day, Caroline was dozing off in the upstairs front bedroom, Kathleen having insisted they swap bedrooms several weeks ago. 'A pregnant woman needs space to move,' she'd maintained, 'being cooped up in that tiny back room is not good for the baby,' and she'd swapped their belongings over, ignoring Caroline's attempt to argue the point.

As she dozed, Caroline didn't hear the knock at the front door. She didn't hear Kathleen's exclamation of heartfelt relief.

'You're back.' Kathleen, who rarely cried, felt the tears spring to her eyes as she embraced him. 'Oh my dear you're back, thank God.'

'I'm sorry I couldn't get word to you,' Gene said, 'I knew you'd both be worried, but it was impossible.'

Kathleen briskly wiped away the tears with the back of her hand. 'Come in, come in,' she said, hauling him inside. 'Heavens above, we'll have to get some fat back on those bones, you're so thin.'

'I sent a letter out with a buddy, but I heard later that he didn't make it back. Has Caroline been distressed? I worried that . . .'

'She's been very brave, she knew you'd come home. I'll pop upstairs and get her, she's having a lie-down.'

'She's not ill?' Gene looked alarmed, Caroline never rested during the day.

'No, no, she's not ill. You go into the kitchen and put the kettle on, there's a good boy.' And Kathleen disappeared up the stairs.

Gene did as he was told. He filled the kettle and lit the stove, and then he heard her enter behind him. He turned. His wife stood, radiant, in the full bloom of her pregnancy, framed in the kitchen doorway.

'Caroline,' he whispered, unable to move.

'I hope you don't mind,' she said. Then she flung herself at him, crying tears of joy, laughing, kissing, hugging him fiercely.

'Careful,' Gene warned, disentangling himself from her. 'Be careful, the baby ...'

'Don't worry about the baby, it's a Hamilton, it's tough.'

So Gene held her to him as tightly as he dared, feeling the swell of her belly and marvelling at the thought of his child in her womb.

They didn't stop talking for the rest of that day. In the upstairs front bedroom, between kissing and caressing, laughing and feeling the baby kick, they talked of their lives together. The war was over and Gene had plans.

Caroline was thrilled to learn that he was being demobbed in Sydney. 'So you don't have to go back to the States to leave the army?' she asked.

'Nope, they give you a choice, so of course I said Sydney. And we're not going to live in America either, is that OK with you?'

Caroline nodded, she couldn't care where they lived so long as they were together. 'And it'll be more than OK with Gran.'

'It'll probably be Melbourne though.'

'Well, she can't complain about that, Melbourne's closer to Sydney than Maine.' He was excited, she could tell. 'So come on, don't keep me in suspense. What's so attractive about Melbourne?'

'General Motors-Holden.' She looked blankly at him. 'General Motors in the US has formed a partnership with the Aussies,' he explained. 'They're setting up a plant just outside Melbourne to work on the planning stages of a new Australian-made car.'

'And you think you could get a job with them?'

'Matt says it's a cinch. Matt's my Commanding Officer and his brother's a big wheel in General Motors. He said they'd be begging for guys with my qualifications and experience and he's given me contacts. Even said he'd recommend me to his brother as soon as he got back home.' Gene's exuberance sobered a little. 'Of course we weren't exactly talking across a desk. It was the sort of talk guys have when they're in the thick of it. Plans for the future and all that. Big promises. A lot of the time it's just a load of hot air.'

She said nothing. It was the first time he had even hinted at the action he'd seen.

'But Matt's no phoney,' he added with genuine confidence, giving her a reassuring grin. 'General Motors-Holden here I come. A top-ranking, top-paying job, I'll accept nothing less.' He winked. 'But I won't let them know it's a job I'd pay to do.'

'My godfather Tim'll be disappointed.'

'The mighty Tim Kendall? Why?'

'Because he'll want to offer you a job. He likes to have a say in our lives, mine and Gran's. Don't get me wrong,' she hastily assured him, 'Tim's a beaut bloke and you'll really like him. But when you come to dinner with us on Friday, I'll bet you five bob he offers you a job, and I'll bet you another five bob he says "I won't take no for an answer".'

'M'sieur Kendall. Welcome. Welcome.'

Ada was hugely impressed by the reception afforded Tim Kendall. 'That's Henri,' she whispered to Caroline. She'd been to Henri's once before, Pete had taken her, and she'd found the Frenchman wildly sophisticated.

Henri, a hardnosed little Parisian who was aware that affectation impressed his diners, offered a welcoming nod, bordering on a bow, to each of them, and when it came to Ada's turn, she nodded in reply. 'Bonsoir, M'sieur' she said, just as Pete had taught her.

'Mademoiselle, mademoiselle,' and to Ada's great delight he bowed over her hand and kissed it. Then he personally escorted them to their table on the balcony, overlooking the park at Rushcutters Bay.

'M'sieur Kendall,' Henri pulled out the chair at the head of the table for Tim and clicked his fingers at two waiters who hurriedly rushed to assist the ladies. After he had fussed about for a suitably impressive amount of time and ordered the waiter in attendance to look after his 'very special guests', Henri disappeared.

The Frenchman's showmanship produced varied reactions from the assembled company, Tim noted. Having dined there often, Ruth and Kitty took him for granted; a comfortable walk up the hill from the Kendall home, Henri's had become one of their local haunts. Gene Hamilton, too, with eyes for no-one but his wife, appeared barely to notice the man, but Kathleen found Henri pretentious, and Wally Kendall was basking in the fact that the people at the other two tables situated on the balcony were looking at them with interest.

But then Wally was a larrikin with a bit of flair. Not unlike his father, Tim had been pleased to discover, recalling the days at the push pubs when little Tim 'Tiny Tot' Kendall had longed to emulate his uncle Billy. He'd have to watch Wally in business though, Wally could well turn cocky. He'd have a talk with his younger cousin, Tim decided. 'Never forget your roots, Wally,' he'd say. 'Never forget where you came from.'

Then of course there were Caroline and Ada. It was their reactions which most fascinated Tim. Ada, pretty, petite, having gone to great pains to dress for the occasion, was revelling in the attention. And down-to-earth, unpretentious Caroline, who couldn't herself have given a damn about Henri and his airs, was relishing her friend's enjoyment. Tim shared a special smile with Caroline which did not go unnoticed by his daughter, Kitty.

Kitty Kendall did not feel threatened, however, secure as she was in her father's admiration and affection. Unlike her mother, Kitty had never felt jealous of Tim Kendall's relationship with Kathleen and her granddaughter. But then, unlike her mother, Kitty had met Kathleen and Caroline on several occasions when, as children, her father had taken her and her brother to visit the De Haan household. He had never once taken his wife.

Kitty glanced at her mother. Ruth was discreetly assessing Kathleen De Haan, as Kitty had known she would. There appeared no animosity in her however, not even an element of criticism that Kitty could see. And, correct and proper as she was, her mother was very often critical of others. It was a regular bone of contention between Kitty's mother and father.

'Live and let live, Ruth,' Tim would say, 'live and let live,' and he'd walk away, refusing to listen to Ruth's criticisms. Which wasn't very fair of him, Kitty often thought, her mother was not malicious, she never intended to be cruel. Ruth Kendall was merely the product of her neat and tidy middle-class upbringing, just as her husband was the product of his layabout, Surry Hills childhood. That was her dad, Kitty thought, with affection, working class and proud of it. Little did he know that, like others of his kind, he could be the biggest snob of them all.

Although her father was her hero, Kitty loved both her parents and, analytical as she was—as she had been all her life—their relationship was of constant interest to her. Something had happened between them. Very recently, she guessed. Her brother's death had nearly destroyed her parents' already tenuous marriage, but in the past month, they had appeared more comfortable, more affectionate with each other than they had in years. Kitty wondered what it was that had brought about the change.

The entrées arrived, and Henri bustled up to ensure that all was in order, his waxed moustache twitching as busily as his hands which fluttered like butterflies, fingers tapping against his chest one minute, clasped the next, then palms rapturously exposed either side of his face as he extolled the virtues of this or that dish.

Kitty leaned across the table when Henri had flitted through the balcony doors to the interior of the restaurant, and, with a comical raise of her eyebrows, she whispered, 'he's such a silly little man isn't he?'

Tim, Kathleen, Gene and Wally all shared grins of agreement, whilst Ada looked dutifully shocked and Ruth Kendall glanced self-consciously at Henri's receding back to make sure he'd not heard. Only Caroline laughed.

Or was it a laugh? Kitty couldn't be sure. A sort of gurgling intake of breath, accompanied by a radiant smile of sheer enjoyment. That a woman as beautiful as Caroline Hamilton should have such a ridiculous laugh was to Kitty not only contradictory, but highly infectious. She couldn't help it. She threw back her head and laughed herself. And there was nothing silent about Kitty's laugh, like everything else about Kitty Kendall, her laugh was bold and rebellious.

'Kitty, please,' her mother whispered, but it was no use. Kitty had set Caroline off again and she continued to gurgle wickedly, which only made Kitty laugh all the more. Then the others joined in, Ada's sense of propriety disappeared altogether in a fit of the giggles, and even Ruth was unable to resist a smile, having checked that Henri was safely out of sight.

The ice had been well and truly broken by the time they pulled themselves together, but, throughout the evening, whenever Henri bustled up to the table, Caroline and Kitty had to fight for control.

As the evening progressed, Tim basked in the exchange between his daughter and his princess. Of course they liked one another, he had known that they would, they shared the most admirable trait a human being could possess in his opinion—honesty. And he felt such pride in twenty-two-year-old Kitty as he watched her. The boyish face, framed by its mane of chestnut hair, and the lithe, toned body, reminded him of a racehorse, well bred, strong and intelligent. Strange how like her mother she looked, and yet how unlike Ruth she was in character. He glanced at his wife who was listening politely to Wally expounding some new promotional idea for the business.

It had been Ruth's patrician quality which had first attracted Tim, and it had certainly been helpful to the company, Ruth could be most impressive. An excellent businesswoman, and a partner in the family firm, she and Tim had made an efficient team from the very start.

As the waiters collected the main course dishes, Wally looked up at one of them and asked loudly, 'Where's the dunny mate?'

Ruth blanched, Wally had been drinking too much.

'Left at the top of the stairs,' Tim said. He grinned as he rose from the table, 'I think I'll join you,' then to appease his wife, 'Excuse me dear, nature calls.'

Gene also stood and excused himself from the company.

Ruth nodded politely and turned her attention to her daughter who was telling Caroline, Kathleen and Ada about the current Sydney University revue. Its content was highly satirical and Kitty was being outrageous, but since the women found her funny Ruth didn't feel too embarrassed or concerned. She looked about, hoping those at the nearby tables couldn't hear. They couldn't. Ruth, thankfully, relaxed.

In the men's room, as Gene joined Tim at the basins and they rinsed their hands and wiped them on the linen hand towels provided, Tim thought now was as good a time as any to make his approach. Gene Hamilton seemed a nice enough bloke, and not short of a quid it was obvious. But Tim didn't like the idea of the Yank whisking his princess off to America.

'What are you going to do now the war's over, Gene?' Tim's approach was as blunt as usual.

'I've got plans,' Gene said pleasantly, smiling to himself.

'You could come and work for me, we need a man with your qualifications.'

'Do we?' Wally joined them at the basins, it was news to him, he didn't even know what Gene's qualifications were.

'I'm sure we do.' Tim wasn't sure at all, he'd have to talk to his foreman but Caroline had told him Gene had an engineering degree, they'd find a job for the man somewhere in Kendall Markets.

'We can always do with a man of Gene's calibre,' he said, his eyes telling Wally to 'bugger off'. Wally bid a hasty retreat, leaving them alone together.

'Thanks, it's a generous offer.'

'I won't take no for an answer,' Tim insisted.

'I'll think about it, Tim,' the American replied. 'Thanks.'

'I owe you ten bob,' Gene whispered to Caroline as the men rejoined the party.

Champagne was served with the dessert and it was, surprisingly, Ruth who proposed the first toast. She'd had three glasses of wine, which was far more than she was accustomed to drinking, but she wasn't drunk. She was more relaxed and at ease than she had been for a very long time, and it had nothing to do with the wine.

'I should like to propose a toast,' she said, rising from her chair.

Seated beside her, Tim looked up at his wife in surprise, but she didn't return his look, her eyes were fixed upon the handsome old woman on the opposite side of the table. 'To Kathleen,' she said as she raised her glass. The others raised theirs, happy to oblige, and Kathleen wondered what on earth it was all about. 'I should like to thank Kathleen for being such a fine mother to Tim.'

'Kathleen,' they all said with bonhomie, rising to their feet and sipping their champagne, only too ready to embark on any number of toasts, it had been a good evening. Mystified, Kathleen sat there surrounded by them all, wondering if Ruth intended to humiliate her. Why, she wondered, she'd never met the woman. She looked at Tim, but Tim was sharing the moment with his wife. They exchanged a smile and he took Ruth's hand as they sat.

Kitty was watching her parents, she knew they were holding hands under the table. How long had it been since they'd held hands, she wondered. And it had something to do with Kathleen De Haan. She'd probably never know, but whatever it was, Kitty was grateful.

Ruth looked at Kathleen. 'Thank you,' she said, and her smile was so genuine that Kathleen's cynicism vanished in an instant. She had no idea what she might have done to deserve such gratitude, but she smiled warmly in return.

Ruth recalled the early evening, not very long ago, when Tim had come home from Kendle Lodge. By all reports Billy Kendall was close to death, and she'd worried a little at the effect seeing his Uncle Billy might have upon Tim. For all of his remoteness, she knew that Tim was grieving over the death of his son, he didn't need any added pain. If only he could share Robert's death with her, she'd thought time and again. But he couldn't, and she had to accept that.

She'd taken extra pains with the meal that night, and was prepared to comfort him. But, to her surprise, it was he who comforted her. He embraced her as soon as he walked in the door.

'I'm so sorry,' he said. 'I'm so sorry about our son.' And he held her as she clung to him and wept her thankful tears, suddenly overcome by the compassion she'd been seeking for months. 'There, there,' he said, stroking her with such tenderness, 'there, there.' She'd thought, gratefully, that it was the visit to Billy which had brought about the breakthrough.

But when they sat together on the sofa, his arm protectively around her, and she finally asked, 'How is he? Billy?' Tim had seemed surprised by the question.

'Oh. Not good,' he said, dismissively. 'I hope he dies soon.' It was not the callousness of the remark, but the distraction with which he made it that surprised Ruth, his mind had obviously been elsewhere. She waited patiently for him to explain.

'I visited Kathleen before I went to Kendle Lodge ...' he said, having no idea of the impact of his statement.

Kathleen! His arm around her felt like a dead weight.

'... and I cried like a baby,' he said, bemused, he wasn't sure himself how it had happened. 'It all came out somehow.'

You cried like a baby! With Kathleen! It all came out somehow! With Kathleen! His arm on her shoulder weighed a ton.

'I know I've closed you out these past few months, Ruth, and I'm sorry . . .'

These past few months! What about the last twenty years! He was stroking her wrist with his other hand and his fingers felt like ice.

'. . . I know I've been selfish, we should have been able to share our grief.' He pulled her closer to him, wanting so much to give her the strength and support she'd been deprived of, trying so hard to make up for her months of lonely suffering.

His arm was weighing her down and the hand which clasped her shoulder felt like a giant claw.

'But we can now,' he said, 'I can help you now.'

'Now that you've seen Kathleen.'

'Yes.'

He didn't register the monotone of her voice, he didn't recognise the danger signs. But then he rarely listened to her anyway, she thought.

'And what did Kathleen say?'

'Nothing. She didn't need to.' He recalled Kathleen's eyes and the knowledge he'd seen in them. The unspoken knowledge of the agony he was going through. It was something he couldn't explain. 'And then she held me,' he shrugged, 'and like I said, I cried like a baby.'

'Jesus Christ!' She wrenched herself free of his smothering embrace and crossed to the balcony windows, her heart pounding, her whole body shaking. With what? Rage? Humiliation? She didn't know.

Tim was amazed. His wife never blasphemed. 'Ruth?' Bewildered, he joined her at the windows, and she turned the full force of her frustration and anger upon him.

'How much more do you expect me to take?' she yelled. 'For over twenty years I've watched you go to this woman. "My best friend's mother", that's the only explanation you've ever given me. And every time you come home you're a different man. You're fulfilled! You're content! "I saw Kathleen today" you tell me. And I'm supposed to be happy for you! Happy that some other woman can give you something I can't! Well to hell with you!' she screamed. The years of neglect and emotional insecurity having finally caught up with her, she'd lost all control. 'To hell with you and your precious Kathleen!'

'God Almighty, Ruth, the woman's nearly twenty years older than me.' Had she been thinking Kathleen was his mistress all these years? It was ludicrous, if she wasn't so hysterical he might well laugh out loud.

'I know, I know, and she's your best friend's mother, I know that too.' He put out his hand to comfort her but she shrank away, still screaming hysterically, 'the only thing I don't know is whether you slept with her or not and I frankly don't care! All I do know is that you share your love with her and you don't with me!'

Tim stared at her, the truth of her words finally hitting home. Ruth had been so much a part of his business empire, that it was true he'd neglected her as a wife. The love had been reserved for his children, and indeed for Kathleen and Caroline.

Her body sagged against the door frame. She couldn't scream any more, her energy and her rage were spent, but her chest heaved as she tried to regain her breath. 'And now you even share the grief of your son's death with her, Kathleen can hold you and you cry like a baby.' She gave a helpless, pitiful shrug. 'He was my son too, Tim, why couldn't you cry with me?'

'I don't know.' He shook his head hopelessly. 'I wanted to, but I couldn't.' He felt overwhelmed with remorse. What could he possibly do or say to assuage her? 'Please Ruth, come and sit down.'

She was too tired to argue, and he led her out onto the balcony. It was dark now and the lights of the ferries dotted the harbour, and the houses on the nearby promontory gave off a homely glow. One could practically see all the happy people sitting down to their dinners, Ruth thought as she looked across the bay. She was dried up, empty, spent.

He wracked his brains. Something special. He had to give her something special, something only they could share.

Tell her, a voice said. Was it his, or was it Robbie's? Tell her, you know you can trust her, give her that much at least. Go on, the voice said, tell her. Did he dare, he wondered, he might regret it, but he knew he had no alternative.

'I want to tell you something about Kathleen,' he said.

'I don't want to hear,' she stared over the water at the houses, imagining them, the happy people, sitting down to their meals, laughing, enjoying being a family. 'I don't want to know anything about Kathleen.'

He'd tell her anyway. And if she didn't accept his offer of trust, he'd hate himself for having told her. And he'd probably hate her too. But he'd tell her anyway, it was his only chance.

'I was with Kathleen's son Robbie when he died.'

'I know,' she said, dully, 'you told me.' He had, briefly, in the early days. Robbie was Kathleen's only child, he'd told her, 'I was with him when he died,' he'd said, 'we were best mates, and I think Kathleen sees me as a son.' And in the early days, she'd accepted the explanation.

'Kathleen needed desperately to know that Robbie hadn't died in pain,' Tim said, his eyes picking out the lights of a Manly ferry. He focused on it.

So? Ruth thought, unmoved as she watched the houses. What the hell did he think she'd been going through herself? It was the agony which plagued her daily.

'I told her he didn't know what hit him,' he said. 'One minute he was running, and the next he was dead.' Tim's eyes followed the ferry lights as it tracked its way across the black water. 'That's what I told her.'

Well, bully for you, she thought, that was thirty years ago.

'What I didn't tell her was that I killed him.'

What had he said? The houses and the happy families forgotten, she turned to him.

Tim was unaware whether he had her attention or not, but it didn't really matter, he'd started now, there was no turning back. Detached, remote, he stared at the ferry and said out loud the words that he had thought he would never say. *Could* never say.

'He was a mangled mess. Unconscious. Dying. I thought he was dead at first. Then he started to come to.' Tim turned his head slightly, following the path of the ferry as it headed for Circular Quay, and saw his wife in his peripheral vision.

'I took the bayonet off my rifle,' he said. 'And I held the muzzle to Robbie's temple. And I blew his brains out.'

That was it, he'd said it. He turned to her. 'So you see you know something that Kathleen doesn't, that no-one ever will.' He waited to see how she'd receive it, but she said nothing. 'It doesn't undo twenty years of neglect, Ruth, but it does show that I trust you. There's no-one else I would ever tell, and it's all I have to offer.'

'I understand.' She didn't know what else to say. 'We won't ever talk about it again.' Was he regretting having told her? She hoped not. Horrific as the story was, the belief in her trust was a declaration and she treasured it.

She did understand, he thought, thank God. 'Good,' he said, 'forget that I told you, I'd like it that way.' But there was one thing more he needed to say. 'I said I wanted to tell you something about Kathleen, and I do. It's no excuse, and I don't offer it as one ...' He searched for the right words, help me, Robbie, he thought. 'When Kathleen looks at me,' he said slowly, 'she sees a son ...'

She nodded. It made sense. Anyone who could offer her comfort about the death of her own son would have her lifelong gratitude and affection.

'... but when I look at her, I see Robbie,' he continued, 'and I see Robbie when I look at Caroline. Not all the time of course, I love them both for the women they are. Real friends. Good, honest friends. But they're everything that Robbie was. He's a part of them, he's always there.'

He took her hand in his, and this time she didn't shrink from the caress. 'He lets me know it too,' he added. 'Robbie haunts me, Ruth.'

Her look was one of concern, but he smiled comfortingly. 'Oh, he does it in the best of ways, believe me. He gives me advice, keeps me on the straight and narrow, reminds me of my roots, he's a bugger of a bloke like that.'

She returned his smile, entwining her fingers in his, and Tim was thankful that he'd told her. He was thankful to Robbie too, Robbie had come to his rescue. Good on you, mate, he thought. The rest would be up to him, Tim knew. He must work on his marriage, give more to his wife, but, for the moment, Robbie had saved the day. 'If I've closed you out all these years, and I realise now that I have, then perhaps we can blame Robbie?' He smiled hopefully.

'We will,' she said. 'Are you hungry?'

'Starving.'

Tim gently squeezed Ruth's hand, beneath the lace cloth of the table. She squeezed his fingers back, then removed her hand, as propriety dictated she should. He glanced at her fondly. Whatever demonstrative passion may be lacking in their marriage, he could not want for a more loyal wife, his trust in her was infinite. Not only would Ruth never tell a soul of his secret, she would never remind him that he had told her. Unlike many of the wives of men he knew, she would not make him suffer for a confidence shared. They would not even talk of the toast she had made tonight, she would not want him to. But it was a gesture of forgiveness to him, and a genuine tribute to Kathleen, he could tell.

Tim could have laughed out loud at Kathleen's bewilderment though, and he could well picture what would happen when next he saw her.

'What in God's name did I do to deserve such a toast?' she'd demand.

'Ruth likes you,' he'd say, 'that's obvious.' He knew that he'd love to add, 'which is surprising because she's thought for twenty years we were having an affair,' just to see Kathleen's face and hear her guffaw of laughter. But of course he wouldn't say that, out of loyalty to Ruth.

Tim looked around the table at his guests. It had been a night of nights, he thought happily. He caught his daughter's eye and Kitty gave him a wink. He winked back, Kitty never missed a trick.

The waiter was clearing the dessert dishes. 'Anyone for a port with their coffee?' Tim asked. 'A port? A cognac?'

Wally nodded to both. He'd had the very best night, scoffing back wine like there was no tomorrow, and he was noticeably drunk, a little loud and a little uncoordinated. Ruth looked disapprovingly at him every now and then, but nobody else seemed to mind.

'When do you go back to America, Gene?' Ada asked, sipping tentatively at her port, aware that she'd had quite enough alcohol already. She knew she behaved a little foolishly when she got squiffy, and she'd had too splendid an evening to risk spoiling it now. Kitty was shrieking and Caroline gurgling with laughter at a slightly off-colour joke of Wally's and Ada decided to make polite conversation with Gene in order to appear on her best behaviour.

'I don't.'

'Pardon?'

'I don't go back to the States. Well, maybe just briefly, in a few months' time to ship my gear over and tie up some family business, but Caroline and I are staying in Australia.' Gene's telephone enquiries had been well received and his application to General Motors-Holden readily invited, but he had no intention of discussing his plans, not until a contract had been signed.

'But you'll need to go back to be demobbed, won't you?'

'No, I can be demobbed in Sydney, they give us the choice.'

'Oh.' Ada pushed away her glass, the alcohol was definitely going to her head, she suddenly didn't feel very well. Or perhaps it was just the disappointment that officers in the US Marines had advantages over ordinary GIs. It wasn't fair, she thought, that Pete didn't have the same choice. She felt a little maudlin, which she put down to the port. She shouldn't have succumbed, she never drank port.

'I'm just popping into the powder room,' she whispered to Caroline a moment or so later.

'It's to the right at the top of the stairs,' Caroline instructed, she'd made three trips already herself, as her pregnancy demanded.

Ada was gone for some time. When she returned she was subdued.

'Are you all right?' Caroline whispered. Ada had been bubbling merrily away throughout the night, and Caroline was concerned.

'Shh,' Ada said, worried that the others might think she was a little the worse for wear, 'just a bit of a headache that's all.'

'Thank you so much for a wonderful evening, Mr Kendall,' she said outside in the street, while Gene organised a taxi and Wally staggered about a bit trying to help.

'My pleasure, Ada,' he said effusively, 'I'm glad you could come.' It had indeed been an excellent evening, he thought, as he assisted the women into the car. 'We'll walk,' Tim had insisted, 'we always do.'

They waved goodbye to the taxi, then strolled down the hill, the three of them, Tim in the middle, his arms around Ruth and Kitty.

They were behaving like drunken sailors, Ruth thought, conscious that those coming up the hill had to make way for them, walking three abreast as they were, Tim and Kitty chattering at the tops of their voices, it was most undignified. But she swallowed her pride and didn't say a word, nothing must spoil this night.

*

Three days later, at two o'clock in the morning, there was a thunderous pounding on Kathleen's front door.

'Wake up!' a female voice screamed. 'Caroline, wake up!'

In the upstairs bedroom, Caroline and Gene were instantly awake. It had been agreed that, until the baby was born, they would stay at Kathleen's. Gene raced down the stairs and threw open the door.

It was Ada's friend, Bev, in a state of hysteria, terrified at the sight of him.

'What is it? What's happened?' he demanded.

'It's Ada,' she gasped, 'it's Ada.' She backed away as if he might strike her.

'It's all right, Bev, I'm here.' Caroline appeared beside Gene and led Bev into the front room and sat her on the sofa in an effort to calm her. 'What is it, tell us, what's happened?'

'It's Ada,' Bev sobbed, 'she's dying. I didn't know what to do. I didn't know how to stop it.'

Gene pulled the woman to her feet. 'Where is she?'

'She's dying I tell you, she's dying!'

He slapped her face hard and the sobs subsided to a whimper. 'Where is she?'

'In a room at the Cross, Kellett Street.'

Gene grabbed his coat from the peg on the back of the door and hauled it over his pyjamas. 'Take me there.' He dragged her by the arm out onto the front porch.

'She's calling for Caroline,' Bev babbled, hysteria once more mounting. 'She wants Caroline.'

'Don't be stupid, woman, look at her. She's going to have a baby any minute.'

'I'm coming with you,' Caroline said.

'No, you're not, you're staying here,' and Gene half-carried, half-dragged Bev into the street.

It was a sordid, dingy little room. Peeling paint, naked lightbulb, bed in one corner, not much else. It was a room prostitutes used. Or drug addicts. Or backstreet abortionists. The landlord owned many such rooms and hired them out for a standard fee.

Bev had had an abortion in a room just like this, and it had worked out all right for her. But it was the luck of the draw they said, and it hadn't worked out all right for Ada.

Gene was sickened by the sight. Ada was lying on the bed, her legs splayed, wearing her chemise and nothing more, her torso propped up by pillows, and a plastic sheet spread beneath her. The sheet was draped over the bed-end, forming a pool to catch the blood and the aborted foetus. She was unconscious. Or dead.

'He said it wouldn't take long,' Bev babbled. 'We just had to wait, that's what he said. But it wouldn't stop. The bleeding wouldn't stop . . .'

Gene gathered Ada up in his arms. She gained consciousness as he did so, mumbling, 'Caroline, where's Caroline?'

'She'll be with you soon, Ada, don't you worry.'

Bev remained at the door, still babbling. 'It's not supposed to happen like this, he said . . .'

Gene elbowed the woman out of the way and clambered down the narrow, darkened stairwell, holding Ada's head protectively to his shoulder.

'St Vincent's,' he said to the taxi driver who'd been waiting for them to return.

'Hey, steady on, mate, you can't put her in here.' The woman was covered in blood. The taxi driver had seen it all before in Kings Cross, and he wanted no part in this.

'I said St Vincent's Hospital, you bastard!'

The driver took one look at Gene, hedged his bets and drove, as fast as he could.

Caroline pulled the chair up beside the hospital bed. Ada had survived, although the doctor said that if Gene had not arrived when he did, she would most certainly have died from the loss of blood.

'She's one of the lucky ones,' he told Gene and Caroline. 'Half of these wretched backstreet jobs leave them either dead or infertile, but there's no reason why Miss Bird should not bear children in the future.'

Caroline drew the curtains around Ada's bed to give them some privacy from the other five women in the six-bed ward, all of whom were middle-aged and were peering at them curiously. The women had gossiped amongst themselves when Ada had been brought in from surgery several days previously and, from the respectable security of their hysterectomies and prolapsed bladder operations, they'd concluded that the girl had had an abortion.

After all, no husband came to visit her, only family and friends. It had to be an abortion, they'd all agreed disapprovingly.

As Caroline eased herself into the chair, she felt another of the pains. She'd felt the first one as Gene had helped her into the motor car he'd hired. The baby was due any day now and he refused to let her walk anywhere. He was waiting outside in the car even now, whilst Caroline had her private chat with Ada. The contraction passed quickly enough and Caroline ignored it, there was plenty of time.

'Why, Ada?' she asked gently. 'Why did you do it?'

'Gene . . .'

Caroline leaned over the bed in order to hear what she was saying. Her voice was as weak and lifeless as her poor face on the pillow. Ada was defeated in spirit, Caroline thought. Poor, dear, pretty little Ada.

'At the restaurant,' Ada murmured, listlessly staring into space. 'Gene said he was being demobbed in Sydney.'

'Yes?' Caroline willed her to continue.

'I thought perhaps only officers were allowed to do that, but I checked the next day, and every American soldier's given the choice.'

Caroline said nothing and Ada was forced to look at her. 'So why didn't Pete choose to be demobbed in Sydney?'

'Because he was going home first,' Caroline stroked the hand which rested on the bedcovers, 'he told you that. He was going home to see his family and get things in order, and then he was coming back to take you to America, that's what he told you.'

'No, it's not.' Tears slowly welled in Ada's eyes. 'I asked him to come to Sydney as soon as the war was over. I didn't want us to be apart all that time, I said I'd go to America with him while he was being demobbed. I didn't need things to be in order.' The tears started to stream down her cheeks. 'He said, "I would if only I could, Ladybird, but they have to send me home first, it's the way the army does things." '

Pete had deserted her, and Ada knew it. Nothing could be gained by trying to deny the truth.

Caroline dried Ada's tears and stayed with her for another hour, ignoring the pains which were becoming more insistent. She stroked her friend's hand until, exhausted, Ada dozed off.

'Knock, knock,' came a voice from behind the curtains.

Gene, oh hell, she'd forgotten he was waiting in the car.

'I'm sorry, love,' she whispered as she parted the curtains. But he wasn't in the least cross. Gene had the patience of a saint.

'She all right?' he asked.

'Asleep,' Caroline nodded. Then, out in the corridor, away from the prying eyes of the hysterectomies and the prolapsed bladders, she said, 'I think I'm about to have a baby.'

It became Gene's proud boast over the years. 'Caroline's perfect timing,' he called it. 'The gynaecological ward of a hospital, that's where she chose to go into labour.'

It was an easy birth with no complications, and just as Caroline had predicted, it was a girl. They called her Emma.

One month later, Gene left for Melbourne. Excited as he was at the prospect of his new job, he was loath to leave Caroline and the baby.

'It'll only be for a couple of months, love,' she said as she helped him pack. 'You get things all set up for us and we'll be there before you know it.' They'd agreed that she'd join him when Emma was three months old.

She waved goodbye to him at Central Railway Station as the train pulled out. The three of them were there to see him off, Caroline, Emma and Kathleen. Gene leaned from the window and watched them for as long as he could.

'You've got a bloody hide.' It was six weeks later and Pete had come back.

'What the hell's going on, Caroline?' The American was dishevelled, and he seemed in a state of shock. 'What's happened? Where's Ada? I went to her house and her brother Brian threw me out into the street. He said if I came back he'd kill me.'

'You're lucky he didn't.'

'But why?' Pete begged. 'What the hell's going on?'

Caroline didn't beat about the bush. 'Ada had an abortion, it nearly killed her.'

'Oh Jesus,' Pete whispered, 'oh Jesus.'

'So now you know why her brother chucked you into the street.' Caroline made to close the front door in his face, but Pete's hand flashed out.

'I had no idea, I swear it,' he pushed heavily against the door, it was impossible for Caroline to close it. 'Why didn't she tell me?'

'She probably didn't know herself,' Caroline's voice was scathing, 'it takes a while for a woman to know she's pregnant. But I'll tell you something, Pete,' she said with the full weight of accusal, 'Ada would never have got rid of that baby if she'd thought you were coming back. Now let me close the door.'

'No,' he refused, 'where is she? I'm not leaving until you tell me where she is.'

Pete recalled Norm's words at the Bird house. Uncharacteristically sober, Norm had screamed through the window, 'Bugger off you bastard, she's not here!' Norm of all people, he'd thought briefly, he'd always been pals with Norm. Then he'd been thrown into the street.

'Have they sent her somewhere?' Pete was becoming desperate. 'Where? You have to tell me, Caroline!' he begged. 'Please!'

'Why did you do it, Pete?' She stopped resisting and allowed the door to swing open. 'Why did you lie to her? Why did you tell her you had to go to America to be demobbed?'

'I thought it was the only way.' So he was admitting to the lie, Caroline thought, that was a start. 'I never would have told her that if I'd known she was pregnant.'

'You'd better come in,' she said grudgingly, thankful that Kathleen was out shopping and she had the house to herself.

They sat in the front room—only friends were invited into the kitchen—and she rocked Emma in her cradle whilst Pete told his story.

There'd been a lot of lies, he admitted. In fact just about everything he'd told Ada had been a lie. Except for the fact that he loved her. He came from North Carolina, it was true, but his parents didn't own a property there, and he didn't come from a large family as he'd said he did. The truth was he had neither parents nor family to speak of. Just a grandmother who'd begrudgingly brought up her daughter's illegitimate son.

'She did the right thing as she saw it in God's eyes,' he said. 'She was a religious woman and it was her duty, but she couldn't wait for me to leave home. So I did. When I was fifteen. I haven't seen her since. I don't even know if she's still alive. Which is wrong of me, I guess. I owe her.'

'Why didn't you tell Ada all this?'

'I wanted her to like me,' he said. 'I wanted to sound interesting. That's how it started anyway.' He looked bewildered, he wasn't quite sure himself how it had happened. 'Then it kind of got out of hand. I was so crazy about her I said just about anything to get her to marry me.'

'Like a big white family wedding on your parents' ranch in North Carolina?'

He nodded miserably.

'You're a fool, Pete.' A bloody fool, Caroline thought. Ada would have married you in a backyard dunny, you stupid, stupid man.

'I know. Then I started to worry that maybe she was only marrying me to come to America and live on the ranch and all that.' He picked nervously at his thumbnail. 'I didn't know what to do. So I figured I'd go home and sort everything out, and then I'd come back and . . .' He tailed off lamely.

'And then you'd tell her you wanted to get married here and settle in Sydney instead,' she finished for him.

'I guess so.'

'And then of course you'd have the ready-made big family you wanted, young Betsy mad about you, old Norm thinking you're the bee's knees,' Caroline sounded brutal, the man was pathetic, 'and naturally you'd be able to talk the brothers around once you were married.'

There was a large element of truth in what Caroline was saying and Pete knew it. He ached to be a part of a big family, a family just like the Birds. But she was making it sound as if he'd used Ada. And that wasn't true.

He stopped picking at his thumbnail. 'I love Ada, Caroline,' he said. 'I know I've done everything wrong, but I love her, and that's the truth.'

'Where are all your belongings?' Caroline asked after a pause. 'All the stuff you brought with you to settle in Sydney?'

Pete answered miserably, 'There's not much, it's in storage at Central Railway.'

'Well I suggest you leave it there when you get the train to Bowral.' He stared at her, hardly daring to hope. 'She's at Bowral, staying with her married sister.

'Good luck, Pete,' Caroline said at the door as she handed him the address she'd written on a piece of paper. 'I don't know if she'll take you back.' She would, Caroline knew it, but let him suffer a bit longer. 'Just tell her the truth and see what happens.'

She must be getting old, Kathleen thought, she never cried. Well, she was old, wasn't she, she should be allowed to cry if she wanted to, and she sure as hell wanted to. But it wasn't fair on Caroline, so she mopped up the stray tear as she heaved the old suitcase from the back of the wardrobe. She lifted out the book, pulled herself together, and went downstairs with it clutched to her chest.

'You must have this,' she said, placing Hannah's journal on the kitchen table.

'What a beautiful thing,' Caroline exclaimed, running her fingers over the old leather. 'What is it?'

'My grandmother's diary,' Kathleen said, opening the cover. 'You must make your first entry.'

As Kathleen bustled off to find a pen, Caroline traced with her finger the names and dates on the flyleaf page. There was the neat copperplate writing of young Hannah Kendall. 'This journal is the property of Hannah Kendall,' Caroline read to herself, 'given her by her mother, Emily, on her sixteenth birthday, the 13th of April in this year of 1831.'

Then below Hannah's writing, in the childish scrawl of a seven-year-old, was 'Kathleen O'Shea, 1 October, 1882.' Below that, the dates of the birth and the death of her own father. 'Robert Daniel O'Shea' it said, with 'Robbie' written in brackets. Then, below her father's name, was her own name and date of birth, and below that, the date of the death of Otto De Haan.

'It's a family tree,' she said as Kathleen returned.

'Yes, I suppose you could call it that. You must write your first entry. Emma's birth.' She handed Caroline the pen. 'And when I die you must record my death. I'm not being maudlin,' she hastily assured her granddaughter. 'It's a fine family record to have, and I want you to promise me.'

'Of course I will, Gran. I promise.'

Caroline took the pen and neatly wrote 'Emma Jane Hamilton, born to Caroline Hamilton (nee O'Shea) and Gene Bradford Hamilton, 20 September 1945.'

'Excellent,' Kathleen said, closing the book. Then she picked it up and ceremoniously held it out to Caroline. 'There you are. It's yours.'

'Don't be silly, it belongs here with you.' Caroline could sense her grandmother was upset. 'It's only a year's contract, Gran, I'll be back in nine months.'

'It's a whole new career for him, Caroline,' Kathleen said brusquely, angry with herself at the fresh threat of tears. 'If your husband needs to stay in Melbourne for his job, then you and Emma must stay with him.'

'Of course we will if needs be. And if that's the case, then I'll come and see you once a year, and you can come and see me. Heavens above,' she laughed, trying to cheer her grandmother up, 'Gene works for General Motors-Holden, and this is the age of the motor car, Gran, we're only a drive away.'

Kathleen successfully quelled the tears. 'Yes, of course you are,' she said, 'but I still wish you'd take the book.'

'No, Gran.' For some strange reason Kathleen was being maudlin, and Caroline would have none of it. 'Hannah's journal belongs here,' she said adamantly. 'With you. In this house.'

They always took turns in bossing each other about, they had for years.

'Yes,' Kathleen agreed, knowing her granddaughter was right. 'It belongs here with me,' and she put the book back down on the table. 'Are you all packed? Tim'll be here any minute.'

'I'm all packed.'

'Good, then I'll put the kettle on, we'll have time for a quick cup of tea before he takes us to the station.' Kathleen busied herself at the stove. 'And fetch the biscuits, will you, Tim likes those shortbread ones.'

Kitty Kendall was with her father when he arrived. 'You didn't think you'd get out of this town without a proper farewell, did you?' she said to Caroline as she opened the champagne she'd brought. Since the night at Henri's she and Caroline had become firm friends. 'Here's to friendship,' she said. 'The lifelong kind.'

Kathleen laughed and chatted with Tim and Kitty. They drove together to Central Station and waved at the train as it disappeared down the track, and all the time she told herself she was being foolish. But try as she might, she could not dispel her fears. And later that day, alone in her little house in Woolloomooloo, Kathleen De Haan gave in to her tears, convinced that she would never see her granddaughter again.

BOOK FOUR

THE DREAM

Chapter Fifteen

'Now tell me, Artie,' Ron Benson asked, 'what sort of job would you like?'

Arturo studied the employment officer for a moment or two. The man seemed friendly enough, certainly, and his use of the diminutive was an attempt to sound casual and obliging. A number of Australians he'd met had told him Arturo was impossible to pronounce—'the way you say it anyway, mate'—so he'd accepted Artie as a gesture of friendship. It was certainly preferable to wog, wop or dago, terms with which he'd become all too familiar over the past year.

But Arturo could sense the man's disinterest, he'd seen it before. 'If I tell you what it is I would like, that would make a difference?' he asked.

The Italian was being neither insolent nor rebellious, Ron Benson realised; there was no impudence in his eyes, no sullen tone to his voice. But his question, which was more of a statement, was challenging. He was clearly an intelligent young man.

Tall for an Italian—but then he was probably from the north, and Ron was accustomed to dealing with the more stocky southerners—he had a certain style. He was well mannered and his English was excellent. In fact, apart from his obviously Italian appearance, which could hardly be helped, the bloke seemed exceptionally well assimilated.

There was something about Arturo Farinelli that commanded respect, and to his surprise, Ron found himself telling the truth.

'No,' he said, 'it probably wouldn't make any difference, but they tell us to ask you what job you'd like. I suppose because it makes us sound good.'

Arturo nodded. At least they understood each other. 'So I go where you send me.'

They sent him to the Snowy Mountains, to work on the Hydro-Electric Scheme.

Arturo Farinelli had emigrated in 1949, heeding, along with thousands of his fellow countrymen, the irresponsible advice of Italy's Prime Minister, Alcide De Gasperi, who exhorted Italians to learn a foreign language and emigrate. Italy had no employment for its workers and Australia beckoned as a friendly, hospitable land. A land of endless wealth and limitless prospects.

It was all propaganda, they were shocked to discover. The Australian Immigration Department had spent much money and effort in order to attract European migrants, but upon their arrival, very little was offered by way of assistance. Like many, Arturo was quickly disenchanted, but he did not scrimp and save for his fare home like so many others unable to accept the sordid conditions and the isolation. Arturo had no intention of running back to his starving country, his tail between his legs. If the Australians would not come to him, then he would go to the Australians.

Ron Benson was right. Arturo was intelligent. Observant and quick to learn. He had taught himself the basics of English before coming to Australia, and he quickly soaked up the classes at Bonegilla, the former internment camp which had been hastily converted for temporary migrant accommodation.

Men languished at Bonegilla, situated near Albury on the Victorian–New South Wales border, while they awaited employment, frustrated and helpless in their isolation. Many had young wives and families to whom the dank huts were depressing, the ill-taught English lessons confusing, and the stink of cooking lard in the canteen and the fatty taste of mutton foreign and abominable. The standard of teaching was so poor that Artie and Nick Steriakos, who had lived in London for three years and spoke fluent English, coached the less fortunate.

Artie and Nick the Greek became very good friends and shared their confined space amicably. Surprisingly enough, most of the migrants did. Arturo was constantly amazed at the lack of conflict between the many nationalities gathered at Bonegilla. Italians,

Austrians, Greeks, Czechs, Poles, Russians, the most devout and the most orthodox of Catholics and Jews, all had no trouble getting on together. Yet, when they were sent out to work as seasonal labourers on nearby properties, the Australians' antipathy was palpable. What were they afraid of?

'Are they frightened of us?' he asked Rube one night.

Artie had the greatest of respect for Hermann Rubenstein. Rube was a very cultured man, a concert musician. Or he had been at one time, many years ago, a violinist with the Vienna Philharmonic Orchestra no less. Now retired, he was a music teacher by trade. At least he had been, he said, until Hitler had decided otherwise.

Rube knew everything, or so it seemed. It wasn't that he was showing off, Arturo knew that, he just liked to talk. Well, to him and Nick. Rube would talk about any subject under the sun to him and Nick. Apart from himself or his family. And Artie and Nick knew why, they'd seen the tattoo on his wrist.

Hermann Rubenstein was a Jew, a Pole from Warsaw, and he'd been through all that the Holocaust had to offer. Except death. His own anyway, the daily prayers he'd made in that direction having remained unanswered during his final weeks at Auschwitz.

Rube could have told them such stories. He could have told them about the ghettoes and the stand that the Jews of Warsaw had taken. He'd been a leader then and proud of it. He could have told them about Eichmann's Final Solution. The term mystified Rube, it sounded so pure. It should have referred to the clarification of a long-lost algebraic formula, not to the extermination of a race of people. He could have told Nick and Artie about the cattle trucks. And the gas chambers. And more. Much more. But he didn't. And of course Nick and Artie didn't ask him.

But that was all behind him now, and Rube had decided that he would not give up after all. He was going to Melbourne, he told Artie and Nick, where he would teach music. There was a big Jewish community in Melbourne, and he'd heard that Melbourne was a civilised city. More or less. By Australian standards.

Nick wasn't interested in Melbourne. Nick the Greek was going to Sydney. He had a cousin there who owned a fishing boat. As soon as he'd made some money he was going to join up with his cousin, 'and we'll have a fleet of boats, you just wait and see'.

With the exception of Nick and Artie, Rube kept fairly much to himself, which was a pity really, Arturo thought, because he spoke six languages and could have been helpful to the others. He suggested as much to Rube.

'No, Arturo,' was the blunt response. Rube felt no obligation to assist the peasant migrants with their problems, they must fight their own fight as he had his. 'It is good that you help them with their English, but I am too old, I have taught enough.' Which was strange, because several times a week he gave Artie writing lessons, Artie having never mastered the art of writing English. It was because of the talks, Artie realised. Rube liked the talks that went with the lessons.

So, tonight, as Arturo sat with Hermann Rubenstein and Nick Steriakos on the benches outside the camp theatre, watching the Italians throw bocce balls, he asked Rube. 'Why? Why are the Australians frightened of us?'

'Human nature,' Rube said, sipping the black, treacly coffee he always drank from the tin mug with his initials on the side. 'We are different. People fear that which is different.'

'But we are all different here at Bonegilla,' Nick argued, 'and there is no friction between us.'

'Europe is our bond.'

Artie wasn't buying that one. 'How can you say that, you of all people? Europe has been at war for centuries. We have been torn apart by our differences.'

'Exactly. That is our bond.' He drained his coffee and dabbed at the grey-bearded corners of his mouth with his pocket handkerchief. 'This country has never known war upon its own soil, God forbid that it ever should. But we have, and it draws us together. Perhaps Australia does not wish to shelter the war-wounded like us, perhaps we are reminders of the fact that hatred and persecution exist, who can tell,' he shrugged, 'but we are most certainly different.'

'Australians have been as isolated from us,' Rube continued, 'as we here at Bonegilla are isolated from them.' He gave a cynical shake of his head. 'You think that you feel animosity out here in the country? Just you wait until you get to the city, my friends. They will insult you in the streets, they will not want you as their neighbours, they will not welcome your children in their schools.'

Nick cast a dubious glance in Artie's direction. The perennial optimist, Nick did not choose to believe Rube's dour predictions.

'I am right, you will see.' Rube eased himself up from the bench, it would soon be dark and he always went to bed early so that he would be asleep, or could at least pretend to be, before his room-mate retired. A young Finn, his room-mate was a pleasant enough fellow, Rube didn't dislike him, but he always wanted to practise his fractured English. Of course Rube could have told the young man that he himself spoke Finnish but, selfishly, he had neglected to do so, having little time for conversation which did not interest him.

'It will change however,' he said. 'In time.' He smiled his lugubrious smile, he hadn't really intended to be so depressing. 'And it is my advice to young men like you to bring about the change. You are strong and resilient. You must embrace the Australians, and one day they will embrace you. One day. You'll see. Good-night, my friends.'

Rube left for Melbourne shortly after that, and several months later, Nick went to Sydney. Artie stayed on for a while at Bonegilla, but it wasn't long before he too was off. To the Snowy Mountains.

Conditions for the vast numbers of unskilled labourers employed to work on the Snowy Mountains Hydro-Electric Scheme were not much better than at Bonegilla and much more dangerous—a man died for each mile of the tunnel's completion. But, a year later, Artie's decision to leave was not prompted by fear, he enjoyed the physical labour and the camaraderie. He would miss the many friends he'd made, but if he were to pursue his ambitions he knew he must leave.

Artie had forgotten neither Rube's predictions nor his advice and, in the Snowy, he had found himself surrounded by fellow migrant workers. If he was to embrace Australians and have them embrace him back, he decided, then he must risk the big cities. He decided upon Sydney.

A friend, a Calabrian from Terranova called Franco, gave him the address of his brother-in-law.

'Luigi has been in Sydney for fifteen years,' Franco said. 'He is very successful, he has a pastry shop in Leichhardt. He will show you about.'

Luigi was indeed successful. His was more than a pastry shop, it was a miniature factory. He employed three chefs in his kitchen out the back and sold not only from his shopfront but also delivered regular supplies to a number of Italian restaurants and clubs, of which there were many in the inner-city areas.

A stocky man in his late thirties, Luigi was boisterous and likeable, and his greeting was most effusive.

'Arturo,' he said, embracing Artie, 'Franco wrote to me that you were coming, welcome to Sydney.'

He gave Artie a job as a kitchen hand and rented him one of the rooms above the shop. Luigi and his family didn't live on the premises, they had a four-bedroom house several blocks away.

Artie was grateful and the two men becamc good friends, Luigi enjoying their lively conversations and regularly inviting Artie to his home. 'For some good Italian home cooking,' he insisted, 'Australians know nothing of food.' A fact with which Artie readily agreed.

On his first visit to Luigi's home, Artie was astonished to discover that Luigi had never met his brother-in-law, Franco. He had married Maria only eighteen months previously. An arranged marriage, he had paid for her passage from Italy, having met neither her nor her family. He had, however, received a photograph.

'And she is even prettier than her photograph.' He draped his arm proudly around the shoulder of his young pregnant wife, 'I am not disappointed. She is beautiful, yes? Maria, embrace Arturo, he is a friend of your brother Franco.'

Maria shyly embraced Artie.

'Hello, Maria,' he said. She looked so young.

'Any friend of Maria's family is a friend of mine,' Luigi said giving Artie a slap on the shoulder. 'We look after our family, don't we, Maria? Now you be a good girl and bring me my son.'

Maria obediently left the room to fetch one-year-old Alfio.

'She is a good wife,' Luigi confided in Artie as soon as she'd gone. 'A man needs a good wife and a family. We have been married only eighteen months,' he winked, 'and already she has given me a son, and is halfway through carrying a second child.' He laughed boisterously. 'I work so hard for so many years to make a success that I nearly leave it too late, but she is twenty-three years old, there will be many more sons. I am a lucky man, do you not agree?'

Artie agreed, and dutifully admired young Alfio when he arrived, and later he ate a huge bowl of ravioli, the best meal he'd had in two years he truthfully told Maria.

Over the ensuing months, Artie befriended the young Italian woman. He felt sorry for her, he could tell she was desperately lonely. Luigi was a good man who worked hard and was an excellent provider, but he was an Italian of the old school. He never took his wife out with him when he socialised, he drank with his male friends at the Italian clubs and restaurants, and Maria was expected to fraternise with her own circle of female friends. But she had none. She spoke not a word of English, and Luigi, whose English was fluent, never bothered to teach her.

Artie did. 'You need to speak English, Maria,' he urged. He'd been out to the shops with her—to help her carry home the groceries, he'd said, but he'd really wanted to see how she coped. She'd been fine at the fruiterer and the grocery store, she'd chosen the two that were run by Italians, but her embarrassment at the butcher's shop had been painful. The butcher was an Australian. She'd pointed at the tray of mince in the display counter, and when he'd picked up a fistful of the meat and said 'a pound?' she'd flushed and nodded, and then accepted without question the change he offered from the note she gave him.

That was when Artie had interrupted. 'Excuse me,' he said, 'you've given the lady the wrong change.'

The shop was fairly crowded and Artie had stood at the back, the man had not even seen him.

Another dago, the butcher thought, and he gave a dismissive shrug to the Australian customers, most of whom were thinking the same thing. They all looked at Maria and Artie. 'Wog.' It was written on their faces. 'Dago.' 'Go home to your own country,' their eyes were saying.

Without a word of apology, the butcher handed over the correct change, and Maria, flushed with embarrassment, fled from the shop.

She wished Artie hadn't done that. She'd always hated going to the butcher's shop, and for a long time now she had suspected him of giving her the wrong change. She never counted her money in public, it took too long and people would know that she had trouble with Australian money. But when she got home, she meticulously counted every penny of her housekeeping allowance, and always she found less than she had expected. She was sure it wouldn't be the Italian shopkeepers, it had to be the butcher who was robbing her, but she would rather die than draw attention to herself by pointing out any error. Now Artie had done so, and she could never go back to the butcher's shop again. What would she do? Where would she buy their meat? What would she tell Luigi? She eventually solved the problem by finding another butcher's shop, seven blocks away.

'You must learn English,' Artie continued to urge. 'I will teach you.'

She tried. As hard as she could. But the lessons were stressful, she did not have a natural ear, and English was such a difficult language.

Although her progress was slow, one major benefit resulted from Maria's weekly English lessons with Artie. She talked to him. Finally, she had a confidant.

It had been so bad at one time, she said, that she'd contemplated ending it all. 'An accident,' she told him, 'just an accident, God couldn't blame me for that. I could trip in the street, and I could fall under a tram, it could happen to anyone. I knew deep down that of course God would know, but my husband would not. Nor his friends. He could hold his head high at my funeral, he could grieve with dignity if it was an accident.'

'Why didn't you do it?'

'I thought I might be with child,' she said. 'They examine you when you are dead and, even if it was an accident, Luigi would hate me for killing his child. And he would be right to do so. He brings me to this country to be his wife and to give him children, and I do something terrible like that. Oh no,' she shuddered, 'Luigi would never forgive me. And neither would God.'

Artie tried to broach the subject with Luigi. He knew he was interfering, but he couldn't help himself.

'I think Maria is lonely,' he said one night at the Cafe Francatelli over a glass of wine. He rarely accepted Luigi's invitations to join him at the Cafe Francatelli, one of the older, more well-established Italian haunts where an illicit drink could always be bought. A favourite meeting place for bachelors, young men gathered outside the cafe doors to ogle and make gestures at the women passing in the street.

They meant no harm, Artie knew, but it was the sort of behaviour which gave Italians a bad name. And the cafe itself he found claustrophobic. Too many Italians trying to create their own little Italy, he thought. But tonight he wanted to talk about Maria's problem and Luigi's home was not the right place, there he was too much a king in his castle. For a subject as delicate as Maria's loneliness, Artie needed surroundings which were a little more impersonal.

'Lonely?' Luigi scoffed. 'No, no, she enjoys her own company, she tells me so.'

'She's saying what she thinks you want to hear, Luigi.' Artie knew he was treading on dangerous ground. 'She needs help.'

Artie was right. It was dangerous ground.

'She needs help? Hah!' Luigi scoffed. 'Maria has it easy, believe me my friend. And if she does not wish to help herself, so be it. She can stay at home and be a good wife and mother.'

Luigi tossed back the remnants of his red wine and picked up the bottle to pour himself another glass. The flash of irritation he'd felt at Artie's interference had passed in an instant. Arturo knew no better, he told himself. Arturo was ignorant. He had been in Sydney for how many months?

'Arturo,' he said, filling his glass and topping up Artie's. 'I have been in this city for more than fifteen years. I have nothing when I come here. No family, no friends, no home, I speak no English. Maria, she has everything. A home, a husband, a family, more money than she would ever have known back in her village.'

Artie knew that he'd overstepped the mark. Luigi had taken his comments as a criticism upon his marriage and such a criticism to a man like Luigi was inexcusable. Fortunately, however, the man's basic good nature had won over. Artie was being forgiven on the grounds of his youth and ignorance, he realised. Wisely, he kept quiet and listened.

'I will tell you a story, Arturo,' Luigi said. He took a large swig of his wine and settled back in his chair. 'I was interned during the war. They were hard times for Italians in Sydney, the Government, they think we are all Fascists. Or Nazis. Or Communists. Or all of these things together. I appeal against this imprisonment. Me and many of my friends appeal, and at the Aliens Tribunal hearings we are all cross-examined by lawyers. Smart men, you know?

'One of my friends, Gaetano, a shopkeeper, he have some

pamphlets from the Fascist Club. He is not a Fascist himself, but his brother-in-law is, and he keeps sending Gaetano these pamphlets. They are addressed to him "Caro Camarata". Gaetano is not interested, he throws them away or they lie around in his shop, who cares? And when his brother-in-law visits and they have coffee in his shop, Gaetano tells him "we don't talk about politics, I am not interested". So they don't.

'But the smart men, the lawyers, they don't believe this. "You are a member of the Fascist Party," they tell him, "you are a 'comrade'. 'Caro Camarata', this mean 'Dear Comrade'," they say. Gaetano, he tells them that it means "Dear Brother".

'"He address the pamphlets to me 'Dear Brother'," Gaetano says. "He is my brother-in-law. My family".

'"If you do not agree with his politics," the smart lawyers say, "why do you have coffee with him in your shop?"

'"Because he is my brother-in-law," Gaetano says. "He is my family."

'The Australians do not understand, you see?' Luigi gave an expressive shrug. 'They do not understand about family. They do not understand our tradition, that family is important above all else. So Gaetano goes back to the camp for the rest of the war. It is not fair.'

Artie agreed.

'Maria, she has the most important thing in the world, right here in Sydney, Arturo,' Luigi said. 'She has family. She has tradition.'

Artie couldn't disagree with that. They toasted to 'famiglia' and finished the bottle, and Artie never broached the subject again.

But he thought a great deal about it over the ensuing months. The unarguable values of family and tradition aside, the Italians were going about things the wrong way. As were the Australians. Both sides must make allowances. Luigi and his ilk were deceiving themselves by adhering so strictly to tradition, by trying to recreate their village lifestyle in a country so foreign. And the Australians were being unrealistic in expecting the Italians to cast aside their customs and attitudes, their language and culture, indeed their very heritage in order to 'assimilate'.

Artie left his job at Luigi's pastry shop in early 1952 to work for *La Fiamma*, the Italian newspaper whose headquarters were in Leichhardt, and he shifted into a small inner-city bachelor flat, catching the tram to work each morning. His parting with Luigi was most amicable and he promised to visit them often.

'You must keep up your English lessons, Maria,' he said as he embraced her. She nodded, but he knew it was unlikely that she would.

After several of his articles on Italian integration were published by *La Fiamma*, Artie's typesetting and editing duties soon included regular reportage, and in July he was sent to Bonegilla for two days to cover the riot there.

Two thousand Italians had rioted against the camp conditions, the lack of work, and most importantly, the lack of assistance in finding it. Artie was proud of his fellow countrymen for standing up for their rights in this new country, but he feared that such an approach would not find much favour with the Australians.

Whilst he worked hard to enlighten migrants about their rights, in his private life Artie distanced himself from the closed community of Italians. He enrolled in an advanced English course at night school and, during his free hours, frequented Australian pubs and cafes.

At first he sat quietly, not wishing to be noticed, just absorbing the atmosphere. Sometimes he was aware of animosity, and could even hear the odd mutterings. 'What's he doing here? Why doesn't he go to one of the dago hangouts?' Occasionally, however, he found the Australians surprisingly welcoming. One night he was at the Hero of Waterloo, a tough pub in the Rocks where they were accustomed to foreigners. Many sailors drank at the Hero of Waterloo. Four Aussies were clustered at the end of the bar. 'Come and have a beer, mate,' one of them said.

'Thank you.' Artie joined them.

'Bob's the name,' his new friend said, offering his hand.

'Artie.'

'Work on the site, do you, Artie?' Bob asked. The bloke didn't look like a labourer, but there were a lot of dagos working on the nearby building site, maybe he was one of the bosses.

'No, I work for *La Fiamma*.'

'Oh.'

'It is an Italian newspaper.'

'Right.' It didn't create much interest, and the four Australians talked amongst themselves, Artie trying to follow the conversation without success. It was mainly about horse racing and football.

Another beer was placed in front of him.

'Thank you,' he said.

Then, ten minutes later, another. When a fourth arrived, Artie shook his head.

'Come on, mate, drink up,' the man insisted. Apparently it was impolite not to, so Artie did, sipping slowly, the taste now sour on his tongue.

Fifteen minutes went by. There was a lull in the conversation it seemed, although Artie had given up trying to follow it.

Then, 'Your shout, mate,' one of the Aussies said.

'Excuse me?'

'Another beer, mate,' the man tapped his empty glass on the bar. 'It's your shout.' All four empty glasses sat tellingly on the bar, but Artie didn't get the point.

'No, thank you,' he said. He had to go home, he wasn't feeling very well.

'It's your bloody shout, you dago bludger,' the man said belligerently, squaring up to Artie.

Artie stared at him blankly. Something was expected of him, but what?

It was starting to look ugly when Bob stepped in. 'Give him a break, Knocker, he doesn't understand.'

Bob explained the situation to Artie. 'We go by rounds here, mate. It's your shout, see? Your turn to buy.'

Embarrassed, Artie bought a round of beers and left ten minutes later, but it had been an education. There were many lessons to be learned, particularly of Australian men and their drinking habits.

Over time, Artie gradually discovered the places where the conversation was at its most stimulating and where he would be accepted. Indeed, where anyone could be accepted. He discovered the bohemian circle of Sydney.

Amongst the eclectic mixture of artists, down-and-out writers, actors, journalists and general layabouts, there were two principal groups. The Push—colourfully garbed and outrageous, the Push drank heavily, played musical instruments, discussed literature and read each other's poetry—and the Libertarians. More drab of dress and less aesthetically inclined than the Push, the Libertarians were more intense and, for the most part, politically motivated.

Artie wasn't sure as to the true value of either; there seemed to be a lot of talk and very little action. Their conversation, however, was stimulating and, better still, no-one cared that he was Italian. They were only too happy to listen to his views, to discuss, argue and endlessly debate with him. Artie liked that.

There was another thing the Push and the Libertarians had in common—they were sexually promiscuous. In fact, sexual promiscuity seemed a prerequisite.

Artie loved women, and it had been a long time. He'd visited a brothel on his arrival in Sydney, but he didn't like brothels. In brothels, conversation was limited and, to Artie, conversation with a good-looking woman was part of the lovemaking process. Now, amongst the women of the Push and the Libertarians, Artie was offered a smorgasbord of conversation and sex, and he was only too happy to participate in both.

He found it a little disconcerting, however, that the women appeared interested only in one-night stands. Some even preferred to remain nameless, which seemed to Artie a very clinical and detached method of engaging in a practice as intimate as lovemaking. But it was the women's standard approach that he found most unsettling of all.

'Let's fuck,' a woman would say after they'd engaged in passionate discussion for an hour or so. 'Your place or mine?'

It always came as a shock to Artie. Not only the obscenity, but the usurping of his masculine prerogative. Couldn't the woman have waited for him to seduce her?

And when, after they'd made love, he'd try to arrange to meet her the following day, she'd become evasive. And when he saw her again at one of the regular hangouts, she'd be in earnest discussion with her next conquest. The pattern became somewhat predictable and Artie found it disappointing, but he supposed he shouldn't complain, not whilst conversation and sex were so plentiful.

Tonight was different though, he knew it.

'What is your name?' he asked the woman seated at the bar. The Tudor Hotel in Phillip Street, a favourite watering hole for the Push, was one of the few hotels where the licensee allowed women to drink at the bar.

'Red,' the woman said, and she shrugged disinterestedly. Then he bought her a beer. 'What's yours?' she asked.

'Arturo. People call me Artie.'

'Why? Arturo's a beautiful name.'

Artie was pleased, she pronounced it perfectly. 'Arturo Farinelli,' he said.

'Arturo Farinelli.' She stretched it out, rolling the r's sensually, as if she was eating the words. She was terribly sexy. And beautiful. Copper-coloured hair, cropped short, framed the fine bones of her face like the border of a lovely painting.

'So I suppose you're a Scot,' she said with a slow smile.

They talked for a good hour after that, and when they rose to leave he noticed that she was tall. In her high-heeled ankle boots, she was as tall as he was.

They went to the Greek's for a cheap meal in the upstairs room where many of the Push gathered. There were people there they both knew, but she ignored them all and gave him her full attention. At first they talked about journalism; she worked for *Smith's Weekly* and was as passionate as he was about the responsibility of journalists as the voice of the people. Then she asked about him, and she seemed so interested that Artie found himself telling her his whole life story.

One o'clock in the morning saw them sitting on a bench in Hyde Park, looking at the Archibald Fountain, swigging from a bottle of wine they'd brought with them from the Greek's.

Artie could barely see Red in the dark, just her profile as she looked up at the moon. He placed the near-empty bottle of wine on the ground and, leaning towards her, his face close to hers, he caressed her cheek as she stared up at the sky. She turned to him. Her lips parted. They kissed. It was a thrilling kiss. Tender and sensual, and Artie was lost in the smell and the taste of her.

When, finally, he opened his eyes, he discovered that she was staring at him. Then she smiled, her lips wet and luscious. 'I could do with a fuck,' she said. 'How about you?'

The moment was shattered.

'No,' Artie said, deeply disappointed. 'I would rather not fuck.'

'Oh?' Red asked, surprised. 'Why on earth not?' She reached up and placed both of her hands behind his head. Her fingers entwined in his thick black hair, she gently drew his face to hers and they kissed again.

Once more the sensation was overwhelming and Artie couldn't help himself, he responded passionately.

'However,' he said a little breathlessly as their lips parted, 'if you would allow me to seduce you, I would be most honoured.'

She threw back her head and laughed, and there appeared no mockery in her laughter. It was a bold, delighted laugh, and Artie found himself grinning back at her.

'What is your real name?' he asked.

'Kitty,' she said. 'Kitty Kendall.'

They went back to his flat and made love. Twice. And she didn't skulk off in the dead of night as many of the other women had. He awoke to find her still sleeping blissfully beside him.

He studied her naked body in the early morning light, admiring the curve of her back and the arch of her hip and the graceful length of her thigh. When she rolled over and opened her eyes to discover him, propped on one elbow, examining her, she didn't cover herself.

'Good morning, Arturo,' she said, then she, in turn, examined him, tracing her finger along his shoulder, down his arm, across his chest, over the flat of his stomach and the curve of his hipbone. And they made love again.

'Why do you approach men the way you do?' he asked as he lay sated, watching her light up one of her Turkish cigarettes.

Kitty tossed the matches onto the table and flopped back on the bed. 'What way?' she said, exhaling and watching the smoke furl its way towards the ceiling.

' "Do you want a fuck?", why do you say that? Is it to shock?'

'No.' She turned her head on the pillow and faced him. 'It's because I want to fuck.'

Her answer was so simple, so direct and honest, that Artie knew he'd already lost the argument.

'Couldn't you say "make love",' he suggested lamely.

'Why? That's not what I mean. I mean that I want to fuck. I want to have sex, nothing more.' Kitty grinned knowingly. 'You don't like us taking the initiative, do you?' He shrugged, but he was cornered and they both knew it. 'Come on now, Arturo, admit it.'

'No, I don't like it.' She was being honest with him, she deserved honesty back. 'I like a woman to desire me of course. But I like to make the opening move,' he said a little defensively. 'What is wrong with that?'

'Everything,' Kitty replied. She took another puff of her cigarette. 'This is the age of sexual liberation, Arturo; women no longer have to sit around and wait to be asked, we can take the initiative, and some of us do.'

He looked so serious. 'I'll make a bargain with you,' she said. 'I'll never say "fuck" again. Not to you.' She sat up, stubbed her cigarette out in the ashtray on the bedside table and reached her hand down towards his groin. 'You and I will always make love.'

Artie laughed as he took her hand in his. 'We will not make love now,' he said, 'not for a little while.'

Kitty Kendall had not really changed, although her parents thought she had. She was merely rebelling, as she had always done.

When she'd moved out of the family home to live with a dubious collection of bohemian types in a seedy terrace house in the Cross, her mother had been deeply shocked.

'They're so drab,' she said to Tim, 'and ill-kempt. They look positively unwashed. What in heaven's name does she see in such people?'

'Well there must be something to them, Kitty's an intelligent young woman.' Tim had tried to defend his daughter at first. 'And you must remember, my dear, that clothes do not make the man.' He knew he sounded pompous and condescending, but he always felt the need to puncture Ruth's ego when she behaved like a snob.

Although he didn't want to admit it, however, Tim secretly agreed with Ruth. Kitty had everything at her fingertips, why would she want to live like a pauper and mingle with a crowd like that? She refused to accept any money from him, and she steadfastly resisted any offer of help in finding employment.

'Just youthful rebellion,' he said to his wife, 'she'll get over it.' But when Kitty tried to tell him about the Libertarians, their anarchistic political leanings, their belief in equality and freedom of choice, he could only accuse her of turning her back on life's opportunities, knowing even as he did so that he was alienating her, and gradually Kitty had stopped visiting the family home.

The truth was, Kitty loved her parents and didn't intend to hurt them. But she needed to break away from the comfort and the restriction of her middle-class existence. She needed to be free of it in order to ask questions, to seek answers, even, possibly, to make a statement with her life. All the youthful, passionate beliefs the Libertarians appeared to espouse.

But she was soon disenchanted with the Libertarians, particularly in their attitude towards sexual liberation. If the Libertarians were so devoted to individuality and freedom of choice, then why was promiscuity essential? They seemed to equate promiscuity with radicalism. If you slept with a different partner every night, you were a progressive thinker, you were living out a radical philosophy. Well, Kitty didn't agree. The Libertarians were not liberated at all, she decided, they'd simply come up with a new set of rules.

So she'd swapped her dark trousers and men's jackets for bright scarves and an antiquated pair of ankle boots, and had begun exploring the Push instead, moving out of the seedy Kings Cross terrace into a decaying, two-storey mansion in Frenchman's Road, Randwick, which she shared with eight others.

She found the Push stimulating at first. They didn't have the answers, it was true, but then she was rapidly discovering that no-one did. Those who gathered at the Stink'n Lincoln on a Saturday afternoon, however, to talk art, philosophy, occasional politics and much sex, were witty and amusing.

The Lincoln Inn coffee shop, a converted cellar in a narrow, crowded lane near Martin Place, had become home to many of Sydney's students, artists and actors, as well as the unemployed who pretended to be. From there they would gravitate to the Tudor Hotel and drink as heavily as they could until closing time. Then they'd move on to one of the many houses Push members shared, very often to Frenchman's Road where up to twenty people might party until dawn before passing out on the mattresses and sleeping bags which littered each dusty room of the once fine mansion.

As with the Libertarians, promiscuity was rife, but it was not mandatory. Many an affair was given time to blossom before it withered and died. So Kitty embraced her sexual liberation and slept with whom she liked, even falling in love now and then. Or, in any event, becoming briefly infatuated.

One such infatuation was Lou. A tall, thin, aesthetic young man with a head of wild, long hair and an impressive beard, Lou looked like a biblical character. He wore a *djellabah* and carried a small silver snuff box in his top pocket from which he sniffed on the hour. He wrote passable poetry, refused to work and played the guitar in the back rooms of pubs in return for beer, cigarettes and meals which 'tourists', who found him colourful, bought him. The tourists, as Lou termed those who liked to gawk and to mingle on the fringe of the Push, paid as much for the intensity of his conversation as they did for his musical prowess, and Lou would happily talk for hours to those who had contributed enough to his wellbeing to be named benefactor.

'My benefactor,' he would say expansively in his rich, fruity voice when the fifth beer and a fresh packet of cigarettes arrived, 'I thank you.' And the tourist would glow with pride.

Lou was the undisputed head of the Randwick Push, and when he set his eye upon her and decided that this newcomer was his, Kitty was flattered.

'Red,' he said as he ran his fingers through her thick, cropped hair, 'I shall call you Red.'

He read his poetry to her and taught her the lyrics to his songs. Kitty sang, her voice thin but not unpleasing, when he played in the pubs and, along with the free food and beer, they even acquired cash from time to time. Lou encouraged her to dress seductively and to flirt with the benefactors, which helped, and Kitty had the feeling he wouldn't have minded at all if she'd slept with them, provided they paid well. Many of the Push women exchanged sex for sustenance or cash. So long as their benefactor was attractive of course, Push women were not whores.

But the inevitable day came when more money was required, and Lou made a drastic choice. He was going to work for the Water Board, he announced, in order to augment the coffers of the Randwick household. The others agreed it was a noble gesture, and Lou donned a pair of trousers and went off to sign up as a Water Board labourer.

He came home with his hair shorn short and his beard shaved off. They wouldn't take him with all that hair, they said, those were the rules.

Kitty fell out of love the moment she saw him. Lou had no chin. And furthermore, no crown to his head. Where was the fine, biblical figure? A pasty, characterless little face sat atop a skinny beanpole of a body. How could she have been so deceived?

She worried for a moment that her disenchantment made her shallow. Was she really that superficial? Well yes, she must be, she decided, and she dumped Lou immediately, shifting to a room upstairs and thinking no more about it. She was a liberated woman, superficiality was her prerogative. She was not hunting for a husband after all.

Then one night she met Jim. Jim was a tourist and she normally avoided sex with tourists, but he was quite attractive in a beefy, rugby-playing way, and she was considering whether or not to sleep with him. The Tudor had closed and she'd taken him to Repins coffee house in King Street and he'd spiked her coffees, and the coffees of her friends, with the Scotch he'd bought at the pub. Jim was generous and affable.

When he suggested they go for a drive, Kitty agreed. They waved goodbye to the gang and left, deciding upon Clovelly, where they could sit on the rocks and polish off the Scotch.

But it was obvious when they got to Clovelly that a storm was brewing. There was an ominous stillness. Heavy clouds gathered overhead, and the night was unwelcoming, black and moonless.

'Let's sit in the car,' Kitty suggested. 'It's going to pour down any minute.'

Jim, however, insisted they walk out to the rocky headland which jutted into the sea. 'Where's your sense of adventure? We can always belt back to the car.'

Kitty clambered over the rocks, stumbling in the dark, cursing him, but it was a long way home.

They stood for a moment staring out at the black, still sea, the rockface behind them, and Jim put down the bottle of Scotch.

'This'll do,' he said.

Then he grabbed her. One strong hand behind her back, the other fumbling at her breasts, he ground himself against her. 'Come on, slut,' he said, 'come on,' and she felt the rocks dig into her spine as he pushed her against them and started hitching up her skirt.

'Cut it out, Jim,' she said, 'not here, we can go back to my place.' Over her dead body, Kitty thought, any sexual inclination she might have had having instantly vanished. But the man was about to rape her, she had to lull him into a false sense of security. 'Give us a break,' she said as she felt his hand thrust between her thighs, 'we'll do it at my place.'

'Oh no we won't, slut,' he rasped angrily, 'we'll do it here. I know your sort,' she felt the crotch of her panties tear apart, 'take a bloke's money and then don't come up with the goods.' One hand at her throat, he pinned her against the rocks as he fumbled with his trousers. 'Think you're better than us, don't you, you lot. Well, you're just whores, that's all you are. I spent a packet on you tonight, you owe me.'

'Well, if that's the way you feel, let's at least make it enjoyable.' Adrenalin was pumping through Kitty and her heart was pounding with a mixture of fear and anger. No bastard was going to rape her. 'Here, let me help.'

She put her hands on his belt and unclasped the buckle. He took his hand from her throat and undid his trousers, and that was when Kitty made her move. He was too close for her to knee him in the groin, so with both hands she shoved him in the chest as hard as she could. He staggered and, the trousers which had fallen to his knees impeding him, fell heavily onto his backside. It was all the time Kitty needed. In an instant she was across the brief stretch of rock and had hurled herself into the sea.

He stood, horrified, pulling up his trousers. Then he walked to the edge of the rocks and looked out at the blackness. He could see nothing.

'Oh shit,' she heard him mutter as she shivered in the still, icy water. She'd swum clumsily around the outcrop, her clothes and her boots threatening to drag her under, and wedged herself into the rocks. She could see his silhouette against the dark sky as she looked up from her niche.

'Red!' he yelled. 'Red, get back here for Christ's sake! I won't hurt you, I promise.'

He spent several frantic minutes searching. Each time he came near, Kitty ducked under the water and held onto the rocks.

Jim was terrified. What if she drowned? They'd all seen him leave that coffee house with her. All those loony, arty types she mixed with, she'd told them he was taking her for a drive to the beach. If her body was washed up in the morning, he'd be in deep trouble. 'Oh shit,' he muttered.

'Red!' he yelled. 'Red, where are you?' But there was nothing out there. Nothing but blackness. And a sudden fork of lightning. 'Oh shit.' Well, they didn't know his name, did they; none of that crazy mob knew who he was or where he came from, they probably wouldn't be able to trace him.

He gave up and headed back to the car. There was a rumble of thunder and the rain started. 'Oh shit.' He'd only gone to the place because a mate of his had said that if you bought one of the crazy sheilas a beer and a meal, more often than not they'd sleep with you. Oh shit, he hoped she wasn't dead.

Kitty watched him staggering over the rocks. She hauled herself out of the water and spent several minutes dragging off her sodden boots. A vivid streak of lightning forked the sky, the storm was overhead now. She walked around the point to where she could see his car, her clothes clinging uncomfortably to her body. The headlights were on. The car reversed, turned, and was gone.

It was a long way home to Randwick, and as Kitty walked, barefoot and bedraggled, through the pelting rain, thunder bellowing and lightning cracking all around her, she decided that she'd learned a lesson.

She moved out of the Randwick house the following day and into an upstairs bedsit in East Sydney. She had just enough money for one week's rent. Five days later she got a job on *Smith's Weekly*.

'You're Tim Kendall's daughter, aren't you?' she was asked at the job interview. Damn, she thought, she'd wondered why her application had been so readily accepted.

'Yes,' she said, and had nearly walked out of the interview.

'Good bloke, your dad.' Ned Clarke had only met Tim Kendall the once, but everyone knew Tim Kendall was a good bloke.

'Yes.'

She hadn't walked out. And she was glad that she hadn't. She liked *Smith's Weekly*. She admired the newspaper's satire and irreverence. Humour, she thought, that was the way to reach the people.

A week or two after she began work her father turned up at the bedsit.

'I was pleased to hear that you're working.' Tim sat awkwardly on the mothy little sofa. Why the hell was she in a place like this when she could come home and live in comfort? He didn't understand, but he knew better than to ask. And where on earth was the bed? He was probably sitting on it, he thought, and shifted uncomfortably. 'Ned tells me you're doing a good job.'

'So that's how you found me.'

'Yes. Ned telephoned, said he'd taken you on.' He didn't tell her how humiliated he'd felt having to ask a man he barely knew for his own daughter's address. But Kitty knew.

'I'm sorry, Dad. I would have got in touch with you soon, honestly I would.' She would have too. Damn Ned. He'd been only too quick to pick up the telephone, trying to ingratiate himself with the almighty Tim Kendall.

'I'm sorry.' She plonked herself down on the sofa beside her father and gave him a heartfelt hug.

Encouraged by her display of affection, Tim threw caution to the wind and dived right in. 'Why, Kitty, for God's sake? Why?'

She heaved an inward sigh, he was going to ask all those questions again, the ones she couldn't answer. Certainly not without hurting him anyway.

'Why can't you come home? Or if you want to live on your own, why can't you let me get you a decent flat?'

Tim was frustrated by her silence, and an edge of irritation crept into his voice. 'How long is this going to go on, this search for whatever it is you're after? Good God, girl, you're only a couple of years off thirty, you've got to grow up some time.'

Exasperated, Kitty got up from the sofa.

'What the hell is it you're looking for?' Tim demanded.

I don't know! she wanted to yell. *Maybe myself!* 'I can't come home, Dad,' she said evenly. How many times did she have to say it? 'And I don't want you to get me a flat.'

'Well what am I supposed to do then?' Tim's helplessness was making him angry. 'Just sit around and let my daughter live in a pigsty?'

You can let your daughter live her own life. 'I'm earning good money now, Dad, I'll get a better place soon.'

Tim rose to leave. 'You're making a big mistake, Kitty, there's so much I could do for you.'

It's my mistake, let me make it. 'I know, Dad, and thanks for the offer.'

She went downstairs with him and hugged him goodbye in the street. 'I'll ring once a week, I promise, and I'll come and see you more often.'

'Good girl. Your mother'll be pleased.'

Surprisingly enough, Kitty knew that her mother's questions would be much easier to field. Ruth would be interested in one thing, and one thing only. Was there a prospective husband on the horizon? 'Do you have a young man?' she could hear her ask. 'You must bring him home, we'd like to meet him.'

Her father's questions were always the difficult ones. God, if only she knew what it was she was looking for, what it was she was doing with her life.

Her work at the newspaper did interest her, very much, but it was not enough. Kitty still didn't know where she belonged. She got on well with her workmates at *Smith's Weekly* and enjoyed the camaraderie over a few beers on Fridays, but she soon drifted back to the freedom of her Push friends. It had remained an empty existence, however. Until she met Arturo.

'I want to bring a friend over for dinner, Mum.'

She telephoned her mother the day she and Artie moved into the new flat. It was three months to the very day since they'd met, and they'd made love on the carpet amongst the milk crates and cardboard boxes. Afterwards she'd said, 'Who will we call?'

Sitting naked on the floor, they'd both looked at the telephone. Their very own phone. Neither of them had had their own telephone before. She picked up the receiver.

'The first call, who will it be?'

'Your parents,' he said. She looked surprised. 'I would like to meet your parents.'

There was a moment's hesitation on the other end of the line. Was her mother holding her breath, Kitty wondered.

'A male friend?' Ruth asked tentatively.

'Yes.'

'You're seeing someone?' There was eager anticipation in her voice.

'Yes.'

'Oh darling, I'm so glad. Tim,' Kitty heard her mother call to her father, 'Tim, Kitty's bringing a young man over for dinner.' Then, into the phone, 'Tonight?'

'Well, no, I thought tomorrow, Sunday, if that's all right.'

'Yes, of course it is, darling.'

'He wants to meet you.'

Artie was sitting behind her, cradling her between his thighs, fondling her breasts, nuzzling her neck with his lips, and he could hear clearly the reaction on the other end of the line.

'He wants to meet us.' Ruth's hand over the receiver was ineffective. 'She said he wants to meet us.' Then back into the phone, 'Well, how delightful, and of course we'd love to meet him. What's his name, dear?'

'Arr-turr-o Fa-rrr-ine-lll-i.' Kitty dragged out the name, rolling her r's outrageously. Artie nudged her to stop.

'Oh.' Quite a long pause, then, 'He's an Italian, is he?'

Kitty couldn't resist. 'No, he's a Scot.' Artie jumped to his feet and she looked up at him. He was shaking his head vigorously. 'Oh, what does it matter anyway,' she said, as much to him as to her mother. 'You'll meet him tomorrow. Seven o'clock all right?'

'Yes. Seven o'clock will be fine.'

'That was cruel,' he said when she'd hung up.

'I don't think so. Better for her to be prepared. Mother hates surprises.'

Kitty was right, Artie realised, the instant he met Ruth Kendall.

'Arturo, isn't it? How nice to meet you.' She was poised, impeccably dressed and coiffed, and quite beautiful. Artie could see where Kitty got her looks. But she was, without doubt, a woman to whom surprises were not welcome. She had definitely prepared herself.

'How do you do, Mrs Kendall,' he said.

Her husband stood beside her. So this was Tim Kendall, Artie thought. The labourer's son who had become a self-made millionaire. Artie admired such men.

'My friends call me Artie, Mr Kendall,' he said.

'G'day, Artie. Call me Tim.' Tim offered his hand. 'Artie, just as well, eh, mate? Can't get my tongue around those Italian names.'

Kitty sensed her mother cringe a little, and she agreed with her. Her father was playing hail-fellow-well-met. It was fake and, in its own way, more hypocritical than her mother's distant charm. Tim was out to prove he was a good all-round bloke with not a discriminatory bone in his body. Which Kitty knew to be untrue: Tim Kendall was as suspicious of foreigners as the next person.

'I think Arturo's a beautiful name,' she said.

Her father ignored her. 'Come on in, Artie, do you want a beer?' Handsome bugger, Tim thought, but the bloke was as dago-looking as his name. Why the hell couldn't she have found an Aussie?

Despite Tim's hearty attempt at mateship, it was Ruth who put Artie at his ease. Throughout dinner she encouraged him to talk about himself, and guilelessly he did. He told her about his family. His father was a stonemason, he said, from Tuscany. And his grandfather, and his grandfather's father.

'I am a disappointment to my family,' he said. 'I decide to emigrate. But I have four brothers who continue the family tradition, so . . .' He shrugged and added with a smile, 'There must always be one black sheep, yes?'

Kitty was unusually quiet, studying her mother and father. Ruth was being charming and gracious, obviously thankful for Artie's good manners, but praying that her daughter was not seriously interested in him. And Tim, having let his wife take centre stage, was sizing up the Italian, finding him foreign and unacceptable, Kitty could tell. Oh, in the workplace her father would be the most racially tolerant of men, Tim Kendall was a good bloke, everyone knew that. But his daughter going out with a dago? That was something altogether different. Kitty could sense her father's antagonism, and she felt an overwhelming desire to shock.

'Arturo and I are living together,' she declared, when the maid brought the dessert.

There was a stunned silence. Her father stared at her and her mother glanced at the maid to see if she'd heard. She had.

Artie was annoyed with Kitty. They'd agreed that they would wait until her parents had accepted him before telling them the truth.

'Is that so?' Tim turned to Artie, unable to disguise his hostility, not even trying to.

'I would like very much to marry your daughter, Mr Kendall,' Artie said.

Tim couldn't trust himself to answer. Did the boy think that made things better, his daughter marrying a dago? Over his dead body!

'Over my dead body!' It was Kitty who said it. She, in turn, was annoyed with Artie. Why was he playing her parents' conventional games, why did he feel the necessity of mentioning marriage? They'd never spoken of it, she didn't believe in marriage. 'We're not getting married,' she said to her parents, 'we don't believe in it.'

'I do,' Artie said.

'Since when?'

'Since always.'

It went downhill after that. Tim glowered, Kitty sulked, and Ruth bravely behaved as if nothing had happened. Artie would have preferred to discuss the whole situation openly. Marriage, ethnic integration, why couldn't they discuss it all like civilised people? But he was hardly in a position to make such a suggestion, and he must not rush them, he thought, he must give them time. He decided it was probably wisest to retreat.

'I think perhaps we will leave now, Mrs Kendall,' he said when she offered coffee. 'It is Monday tomorrow and we both start work early. Kitty?'

'Yes, let's skip coffee.' She jumped up from her chair. 'Thanks for dinner, Mum, it was wonderful as usual.' She kissed her mother on the cheek, didn't look at her father. 'Bye,' she said, and left the three of them sitting at the table.

Artie hastily rose. He thanked them both, Tim gave a brusque nod in return, and Ruth saw him to the front door.

Kitty was waiting outside. They caught a taxi back to the flat in Leichhardt and Kitty tried to argue all the way, Artie refusing to join in.

'You didn't tell me you wanted to get married.'

'I did not know until tonight.'

'Oh rubbish, you only said it because it was the conventional thing to say under the circumstances.'

'Perhaps. I am a conventional man.'

'Well, I don't want to get married, I can tell you that right here and now. And I never will.'

'Fine,' he shrugged, 'then we will not marry.'

He was obviously not going to be drawn into an argument, so Kitty turned her hostility upon her parents instead.

'They behaved just the way I expected them to,' she said, then started to systematically tear them apart. Her mother was a snob to whom nothing but appearances mattered, but her father was much worse. Her father was a bigot who pretended not to be.

'Good old Tim Kendall,' she said, 'a bonza bloke! Everybody's mate! The working-class boy who made good, but never forgot his roots! Well, bully for him, he's the biggest hypocrite of them all.'

Artie paid off the taxi and she was still berating her father when they entered the flat.

He turned the lights on to reveal the chaos—they hadn't finished unpacking the previous day.

'He disappointed you,' Artie said.

'What?'

'Your father. He disappointed you.'

'No,' she said defensively, 'I knew he'd behave like that.'

'But you hoped that he would not.'

Kitty's lower lip quivered a little, suddenly she wanted to cry. It was true. She'd been disappointed. Her heart had sunk the moment her father had gone into his 'g'day mate' act. Kitty loved her father dearly, and she had hoped that he would recognise her love for Arturo. She had hoped that he would genuinely welcome him into the family.

Artie put his arms around her. 'Poor Kitty,' he said, 'you have got yourself all worked up . . .' she sniffled against his shoulder, '. . . and for no reason at all.' She raised her head, about to argue the point. 'No, no,' he said quickly, 'I will not fight with you. But I will talk with you if you wish.'

They did. Around midnight Artie opened a bottle of red wine. By then he'd convinced her that her father was not really a bigot.

'Your father is afraid. He fears that which is different,' Artie had explained, recalling Rube's words at Bonegilla and how, time and again, they had proven to be so true. 'But he is a good man, he will learn to accept me in time. And I do not need to be Italian for him to dislike me.' He laughed at her puzzled expression. 'I am your lover, Kitty, every father is jealous of his daughter's lover.'

He'd defended her mother too. He had found Ruth a most gracious woman, he said. 'You must learn acceptance yourself, Kitty. You too must accept that which is different in others.'

It was then he had suggested they share a bottle of wine, and she sat on the bed as he opened it, waiting, impatiently, for him to continue.

'Your mother and father were trying hard in their own ways

tonight. You must accept that your mother's social graces are important to her. And you must accept that it is important to your father that he is—how did you say it?—a bonza bloke. It is the way they wish others to perceive them, there is nothing wrong in that.'

He poured the wine and joined her on the bed. 'And I must accept that which is different in you.' He smiled. 'The way you initiate sex, and the way you say "fuck".'

'I don't say "fuck" any more.'

'I appreciate that.'

'And what is different in you that I must accept, Arturo?' She rolled over on her stomach and looked up at him as he leaned back against the bedhead.

'Everything,' he laughed. 'And you do. It is what I most love about you.'

They talked until four in the morning. Then they made love and slept for two hours before getting up to go to work.

Artie was right. Kitty not only accepted, unequivocally, his differences, she loved him for them. She loved his dark, foreign looks and his accent. She loved the Italian music he played, and the pasta he ate, and his passion for conversation and sex. Never in her life, she thought, had she met a person as vibrant, and as honest, as Arturo Farinelli.

But she was well aware of the malice they attracted as they walked down the street. The Australians didn't like seeing an Aussie girl with a dago. And she could feel the animosity when they walked into one of the Italian restaurants which they regularly frequented. The Italians didn't like seeing one of their kind with his arm around an Australian woman.

Artie turned a blind eye. He said he didn't notice it any more, and that it didn't bother him. So Kitty did the same. She ignored the hostility. It was difficult for her at first. At first she felt belligerent, she wanted to confront those who sneered at them. 'What's your problem, mate?' she wanted to demand. 'Spit it out, what don't you like?' But she resisted the urge. And eventually, like Artie, the prejudice which confronted them daily ceased to bother her.

It was then that Kitty realised she had learned another lesson in acceptance. She had learned to accept herself. No longer did she need to shock and to make statements. No longer did she need to search amongst the bohemian fringe for a reason as to her existence. The very life she now led made a statement.

Once a fortnight Kitty rang her mother. 'May I bring Arturo to dinner?' she asked. And of course Ruth always said yes. Kitty and Artie had agreed that it was the way to go about things. 'We'll wear them down,' Kitty said.

And they did to a degree. Certainly Ruth was won over. She was only too thankful that Artie had led her daughter back to the fold. It was a pity he was so foreign-looking, certainly, but his manners were impeccable, he was obviously intelligent and, over a period of time, Ruth found that she liked him. And he liked her, she could tell.

Once the bond was sealed, Ruth was his ally. Arturo was a handsome, civilised man of the world, after all. And that was exactly what she would tell her acquaintances who might differ, though she would not tell them that he lived with her daughter.

Tim was a more difficult case. He had reluctantly accepted that his daughter was in love with an Italian and that there was little he could do about it. But as he saw the friendship developing between his wife and Artie, he became more and more alienated. Why wasn't the dago trying to win him over? That's what a bloke was supposed to do.

Artie knew nothing of the Australian male ego. He didn't realise that he was expected to drink beer and discuss the footie with Tim. He didn't like beer and he knew little about football, and it didn't occur to him to pretend otherwise.

Kitty observed it all, and at first she was amused by her father's piqued ego. Let him stew, she thought, and she said nothing. Then she realised that a tension was building between her parents and Artie was the cause. Reluctantly, she decided that Artie would have to play the game.

'Go and have a beer with Dad,' she said one Saturday after lunch when Tim had retired to the balcony with a bottle and a glass.

'But he is listening to the radio,' Artie said. Tim Kendall always listened to the radio on a Saturday afternoon. 'It would be rude to interrupt.'

'It's just the footie,' she said.

Artie knew of this Rugby League game. Sydneysiders, it

appeared, had a passion for it. Even some of his Italian friends at *La Fiamma* avidly followed the matches each Saturday.

'So?' he asked.

'So let him tell you about it,' Kitty said. 'Here,' and she thrust an empty glass into his hand, 'ask him for a beer and talk about the footie.'

'I know nothing about football.'

'It doesn't matter. He does.'

Artie stepped tentatively out onto the balcony. 'May I join you?' he asked, holding up the glass.

'Yes, of course, Artie, take a seat, there's the bottle.'

Artie poured himself a beer and pulled up a chair, and Tim turned down the volume on the radio.

'Please do not do that on my account,' Artie said, but Tim did anyway.

'It's a lousy match,' he said. 'A walkover, the Rabbitohs are getting slaughtered.'

'Rapidos?' Artie was surprised. A Rugby League team with an Italian name, how strange. 'They are an Italian team?'

'Eh?'

'*Rapido*, it is Italian for swift.'

'No. Rabbitoh. It's a bloke who used to sell rabbits off a cart in the old days.'

'Oh.' What a strange name for a rugby team, Artie thought. Rapidos would have been better.

'Yeah, they're a South Sydney club, good team normally but they've lost it today.'

'I know very little about Australian Rugby League,' Artie said, 'but I have friends who follow the game. It is very popular in Sydney.'

'Yep,' Tim nodded. Then after a brief pause, 'Play any sport yourself, Artie?'

'Soccer, yes. I play soccer a great deal in Italy.'

'Ah. Good game, soccer,' Tim said. 'Skilful.'

'Very skilful,' Artie agreed with enthusiasm.

'Can't get away with a trick in soccer.'

Artie shook his head.

'Have to have all your ball skills about you there.' Tim thought for a moment. 'Slow scoring game, though, a bit frustrating I'd think.'

'It is the frustration that gives the game its passion,' Artie said.

'Oh.' Tim hadn't thought about it like that.

'A whole match played for perhaps just one winning goal,' Artie said. 'It makes for great intensity.'

Half an hour later the men came inside with their glasses. 'It's easier if I show you on paper.' Tim took a pad and pencil from the sideboard drawer and sat down at the large coffee table. 'Kitty, grab us another beer, will you?'

'Your father is explaining Rugby League to me,' Artie said, and Kitty grinned as she left for the kitchen.

Was it really this easy, Artie wondered as he sat beside Tim and watched him draw a map. It was more than the beer and the rugby, he realised, it was the offer of mateship. But it certainly appeared that the Australian male ego, once offended, was very easily appeased.

In his country, Artie thought, it was difficult to truly offend. Men shouted and screamed and made gestures, but it meant little. If, however, a man did take offence, it might be a whole lifetime before he forgave. Perhaps never. A son might even carry on his father's vendetta without any knowledge as to the original offence. Yet here in Australia it appeared that if you accepted a man's offer of a beer, all was forgiven. The Australian way was quite possibly the better, he thought.

Artie had been in the country for well over three years, but there was still so much to be learned.

'I'm pregnant.' As usual Kitty didn't waste any time getting to the point. But she watched closely for his reaction. Did he want the baby? She would abort if he didn't. She had no problem with abortion, she was mistress of her own body, she believed.

'How wonderful.' Artie was glowing. There was no other word for it, he was glowing with unashamed happiness.

Kitty tried not to show it, tried not to acknowledge it even to herself, but she felt an overriding sense of joy that he wanted the baby, deep down she had hoped that he would.

'*Cara mia.*' He held her to him and laughed delightedly. 'A child, how wonderful.'

'I can get rid of it if you don't want it.' The old Kitty Kendall couldn't help coming to the fore.

He refused to be shocked, he knew her too well. 'We will get married,' he said.

'Oh no we will not. You know the way I feel about marriage.'

Artie was suddenly serious. He sat her on the bed. Lecture time, she thought. Well, she wouldn't listen. She could be tamed only so much.

'And how will your child ... *our* child, Kitty ... how will *our* child feel about marriage?'

'It can form its own opinion,' she said with a touch of defiance, 'nothing to do with me.'

'Do you not think it will have enough troubles?' Rube's words returned, as they always did at such times: *They will not want you as their neighbours, they will not welcome your children in their schools.*

'Society will be cruel to this child,' he said. 'Do not add to its burden, Kitty. Marry me.'

She knew she was going to give in, but she pushed just that little bit further. 'You want me to succumb to convention?' she frowned.

And Artie, in turn, knew that he'd won. 'Of course,' he said. 'I am a conventional man.'

Kitty dropped all her defences and laughed. 'A conventional man doesn't emigrate,' she said, 'and if he does, he brings out a conventional wife from Italy and he settles in a conventional Italian community. You are not a conventional man, Arturo,' she draped her arms around his neck and kissed him, 'but you insist upon making me a conventional woman.'

'Yes.'

They married before her pregnancy showed, and Ruth Kendall couldn't have been happier. And when their son was born they named him Robert after Kitty's brother who had died in the war. Tim Kendall couldn't have been happier.

It was Artie's idea to call the child Robert.

'You sly bugger,' Kitty said. 'You're just doing it to get him on side. And all this time I thought there wasn't a devious bone in your body.'

'It is only right that I should give my father-in-law, who has lost his only son, a grandson who bears the same name. It is my duty.'

He said it so seriously that Kitty wasn't sure whether it was an Italian tradition or not. And for once she didn't push for an answer. She had loved her brother and it was a damn good idea. But she didn't want Artie to be disappointed that his son did not bear an Italian name.

'All right,' she agreed, 'Robert it is.' Suddenly she had an even better idea: 'Let's make it Roberto and then he'll know he's half Italian.'

CHAPTER SIXTEEN

Kathleen De Haan's premonition had been right. She had never seen her granddaughter again. Kathleen died eight months after Caroline left for Melbourne.

'There was nothing you could have done, Caroline,' Tim said when she came home for the funeral, 'it was an accident. One of those stupid, senseless accidents; no-one could have prevented it.'

Kathleen had fallen down the steep, narrow stairs of her Woolloomooloo house. There would have been no pain, the doctor said, her neck had been instantly broken. Tim told Caroline as much, but it didn't seem to absolve her sense of guilt.

'If only I'd been there,' she agonised. 'If I'd been there it might not have happened.'

'Of course it would have happened,' Tim insisted. Grieving as he was himself over Kathleen's death, it was obvious Caroline needed reassurance. 'Your grandmother was seventy-one years old, she was unsteady on her feet, she would have fallen whether or not you'd been there.'

His words didn't seem to comfort her, however. Even Kitty could not break through the wall of Caroline's guilt. But then, Caroline was five months pregnant and, in Tim's experience, pregnant women were often unable to grasp reason.

Tim did not understand. Much as he had been Caroline's childhood hero, and to a certain extent a father-figure, the only real family she had ever known was her grandmother. And, as Caroline had grown to adulthood, Kathleen had become her friend, her confidante, and mentor. It had seemed that Kathleen would always be there, and her death had come as a terrible shock.

Kathleen had left the house to her, and at first Caroline found the burden unbearable. She couldn't bring herself to sift through her grandmother's belongings, and she did not want any stranger to do so. She decided to leave the place locked up, to gather dust, until she felt strong enough to face it. Perhaps after the baby was born. All she wanted now was to go back to Gene, regretting that she'd insisted he stay in Melbourne to look after Emma.

Then the perfect solution presented itself. She would lease the house to Ada and Pete. They were married now and living with Ada's parents. They wanted to start a family and needed a place of their own.

'I'll look after the house,' Ada promised. 'I'll keep everything the way it was.' And knowing how fond Ada had been of Kathleen, Caroline trusted her.

She went back to Melbourne. General Motors-Holden had offered Gene a long-term contract, and she was relieved to be out of Sydney, glad of the distance. She could not possibly have lived in the Woolloomooloo house, the memories of her childhood and of Kathleen were too fresh, they would have haunted her.

'I'll come back after the baby's born,' she had promised Ada, 'I'll come back and sort things out then.'

But she hadn't. It was sixteen years before Caroline returned to Woolloomooloo, a widow with three children, in the summer of early '62.

Gene had met his death on a car racing track. Just like his father. And, just like his father, he'd been killed instantly. The blame did not rest with General Motors-Holden, as Kitty had first presumed when she'd heard the horrifying news. He had not been conducting a test run for the company, as he'd so often told her on the occasions when he'd return home with cuts and bruises, and once even with a broken arm.

'My own stupid mistake,' he'd insist. 'Nothing to worry about sweetheart, honest. The test runs are very safely conducted, it was driver's error, my own damn fault, and it'll never happen again, I promise.'

But it had. And this time the price had been his life. That's when Caroline had discovered that, throughout the whole of their marriage, her husband had been racing cars on the weekends when he'd said he was working. His life with her had been a lie, and Caroline could see it no other way.

Those who loved her, and who rallied upon hearing the news, were shocked at the change in Caroline when she returned to Sydney. She looked weary and drawn, which was to be expected, but it was her manner which was most alarming. She was remote, aloof, even cold towards them.

Tim went to Melbourne to bring her and the children home, and Kitty met them all at the station and drove them to Woolloomooloo. Ada had prepared the old house for Caroline's return, Ada and Pete, now with two children of their own, having moved to a terrace cottage several blocks away.

'I've tried to put everything back just the way it was.' Ada chatted on as she always did when she felt self-conscious and insecure, while Kitty merely watched from the sidelines.

Tim had taken seventeen-year-old Emma and the two boys out shopping for supplies, leaving Caroline with the women. He felt that she might need female company since she'd not been forthcoming at all with him.

'Well, as close to the way it was as I can remember,' Ada went on, 'sixteen years is a long time.'

Caroline wandered about the house, Ada following like a puppy seeking approval, and Kitty busied herself in the kitchen making tea.

Kitty had wondered if it was wise for Caroline to move into the old home which held so many memories. Gene had left her adequately provided for, she could have set herself up in a whole new life, made a fresh start for herself and her children. But Caroline had been insistent.

Yes, it did all look the same, Caroline thought as she wandered amongst the familiar rooms. The old counterpanes, which Ada had had laundered and stored away, were back on the beds, and the lace tablecloth back in the front parlour. She'd returned the furniture to pretty much the same way as it had been in Kathleen's time. She'd even resurrected the old pots and pans and hung them back on the pegs of the kitchen walls.

Some things were different, Caroline noticed, accepting the cup of tea Kitty handed her. A refrigerator stood where the icebox had been, and the old wood stove had been replaced with a gas one, but with Kathleen's iron cooking pot sitting on the top, somehow it all looked the same.

She was touched. It made her feel comfortable in a vague sort of way. 'I'm home,' she said, but with the same aloofness she'd displayed from the moment she'd arrived.

She dutifully drank tea with Kitty and Ada, but was grateful when Kitty said, 'Would you like a little while on your own before Dad comes home with the kids?'

'Yes. Thank you. Thank you both.'

When they'd gone, Caroline sat for a moment in the kitchen, just soaking up the old house and its memories. Then she went upstairs to the bedrooms.

In the little back room the old cupboard was still there, with Kathleen's things neatly stored inside. One by one she lifted them out. The knitted hot-water bottle cover which Kathleen had made herself. Clumsily crafted, Kathleen had been no expert with knitting needles. But Caroline remembered its thick cosy comfort as a child when the nights were cold. And Otto's old dressing gown which Kathleen herself had worn after his death. Ada had had it cleaned and it sat folded, pristine, in its tissue paper wrapping. Dear Ada, Caroline thought. And the tattered photograph album with the faded picture of her father on the first page, and others, equally faded, of Otto and his son Johann, and many of herself as a child, and then as a young woman. A history of the family.

She lifted the old suitcase from out of the back of the wardrobe, and there was Hannah's journal. Only then did she realise that she'd forgotten to record Kathleen's death as she'd promised she would.

She carried the book downstairs, fetched a pen, and sat at the kitchen table.

'Kathleen De Haan (nee O'Shea), died 3 August 1946' she wrote. Then, directly beneath, 'Gene Bradford Hamilton, died 10 January, 1962.' She stared at the entries for quite a long time, but she didn't cry. The two people she cared most about in the world had died senseless, unnecessary deaths. It angered her.

Then she realised that there were two more entries to be made, and that she'd got them out of order. She should have recorded the births of her sons before the death of her husband. Oh well, it was a mishmash of a list anyway, and she added 'James Francis

Hamilton, born 18 November 1946' and 'Bruce Anthony Hamilton, born 7 June 1948'.

She carried the journal upstairs and returned it to the suitcase in the back of the cupboard, praying that she would never make another entry in its pages. God forbid that she should ever be called upon to record the death of one of her children, they were all she had to live for now.

As the months passed, both Tim and Kitty, and Ada too, worried about Caroline. The children, grieving as they were, seemed to have accepted the loss of their father but Caroline remained bitter and remote, and when anyone attempted to break through her barriers she closed off and was sullen.

It was Kitty who decided upon the drastic approach. She called on Caroline unexpectedly one afternoon, taking Artie and nine-year-old Robert with her. She hadn't telephoned, knowing full well that Caroline would avoid her if she did.

'Caroline.' Kitty knew in an instant that Caroline was not pleased to see them, but she ignored the fact, offering no apology for the intrusion, and warmly hugged her. 'I thought it was time you met my husband and son. This is Arturo and Rob.'

'Hello,' Caroline said as she shook hands with them both. So this was the Italian Kitty had married. Well, you didn't get much more Italian than that, and the boy had inherited his father's looks. How like Kitty, always the rebel; it would have been a surprise to no-one if Kitty Kendall had married a black man. Caroline wondered idly if she loved her husband, or if she'd married him for the shock value.

Artie was aware he was being given the once-over, and he too sensed that their visit was not welcome.

'Perhaps you would like to talk alone together,' he said meaningfully to Kitty. 'Rob and I can go for a walk in the park.'

'No, no,' Kitty ignored him, 'I want Rob to meet the children.' She said to Caroline, 'May we come in?'

'Yes, of course, I'm sorry,' Caroline replied distractedly, appearing to notice for the first time that they were standing on the porch. 'Come in, I'll make us some tea.

'They're not here,' she said, leading the way to the kitchen. 'The boys play footie on Saturday afternoon and Emma's at the pictures with a girlfriend.'

'Oh what a shame, do you have any photographs?'

'Upstairs.'

'Well, I'll put the kettle on while you go and get them.'

Caroline reluctantly went upstairs and Arturo muttered to Kitty in Italian, 'Why do you boss her about? She does not want us here, we must go.'

'Have a quick cup of tea and then leave us alone together.' Kitty automatically replied in Italian. When they were on their own with their son, they invariably spoke Italian, forcing the boy to follow suit. 'Do you want to go to the park, Rob?' she asked as she filled up the kettle.

'Yes, can we go now?' Rob was bored already, he didn't want to sit around drinking tea.

'In a few minutes,' Kitty said. 'Be patient.' She winked at Artie. 'You can take him to see the Archibald Fountain.' Artie smiled back, recalling the first night they'd met.

As she reached the bottom of the stairs, Caroline heard the three of them chatting in Italian. Were they talking about her, she momentarily wondered. But then the boy was joining in, and she heard the Archibald Fountain mentioned. No, she was just being paranoid, and she really must make some effort, she'd been churlish and probably rude. Still, they could have telephoned. Then she could have avoided them altogether.

'You speak Italian, Kitty, I'm very impressed,' she said, forcing a smile as she put the photographs on the table.

'Sorry, didn't mean to be rude.' Kitty dumped the kettle on the stove. 'We always speak Italian with Rob, it's become a bit of a habit. We want him to grow up bilingual, although he's not too sure about it himself, are you, Rob?'

Rob shrugged as if he didn't care, but he did really. Very much. He'd never admit to the kids at school that he spoke Italian. He had enough trouble with the way he looked as it was. And he insisted that his name was Robert, not Roberto.

'Here, I'll do that,' Caroline said as Kitty lit the stove, 'you sit down.'

Artie dutifully admired the photographs of the children, Kitty pointing out how pretty Emma was, and Artie marvelling at his wife's capacity for small talk. It was a talent Kitty rarely displayed. As soon as they could make good their escape, Artie and Robert disappeared off to the park.

Caroline wrapped up some bread. 'You can feed the pigeons,' she said to Rob.

'Thanks.' He was a handsome little boy when he smiled, she thought.

Caroline relaxed a little after they'd gone. 'You're deliberately pushing me, aren't you, Kitty? You haven't changed,' she said. Caroline had always admired Kitty's boldness. 'You haven't changed a bit.'

'You have,' Kitty said, 'you've changed a lot.'

'Yes.' Straight to the point, Caroline thought, typically Kitty.

'You're very unhappy, aren't you?'

Caroline gave a snort of derision. 'Do you blame me?'

'Of course not.' Strange, Kitty thought, how Caroline's beauty had been destroyed from within. She was a little weightier, it was true, but the handsome brow was still clearly defined, the mouth still luscious, she should have been a handsome woman. But dissatisfaction and resentment had marred her looks.

'You have every right to be unhappy,' she agreed, 'but why are you so bitter?'

Caroline was confronted. Just as Kitty intended her to be. No-one had spoken to her this way. She'd had endless condolences and offers of help, but no-one really understood. They thought they did. A woman grieving for her husband, and left with three children too. Sad. Tragic. But they didn't understand at all. She wondered if Kitty might. She obviously wanted to try.

'He died such a senseless death,' Caroline began. 'It shouldn't have happened. He shouldn't have died the way he did.'

'What way?'

Caroline's dark eyes glared with irritation. 'Senselessly,' she snapped. 'Stupidly, uselessly, unnecessarily.'

'But he didn't. Gene didn't die a senseless death. He died doing what he loved most. He smashed himself up in a racing car.' Ignoring Caroline's anger, Kitty barged on relentlessly.

'Would a heart attack have been better? Or a stroke? Cancer perhaps?'

'Yes!' Caroline yelled. 'Yes! Yes! Yes! Any one of the above! Or all of them! All of them would have been better!'

'Why?'

'Because they wouldn't have been his decision!' She screamed it out. 'What right did he have to take risks like that? What right did he have to leave me alone? To leave his children without a father? What right?' She was shaking now, enraged far more with her dead husband than with Kitty's goading.

Kitty sat in silence for a moment, watching Caroline fight to regain her control. And when she had, Kitty said quietly, 'He didn't *mean* to do it, Caroline. He didn't *mean* to die and leave you alone.'

'I know.' Caroline's anger had evaporated and once more she was cold and distant. 'But don't glorify his death to me, Kitty. He died ignominiously on a seedy little racetrack in country Victoria and his life with me was one whole lie.'

Caroline's icy statement had the desired effect. Kitty lapsed into silence. So now we get to the truth, she thought, as she waited for her friend to continue.

'I never knew he was racing, you see. In all the years of our marriage he never told me. He lied every time he went to a race meeting, and he lied every time he came home.' Caroline had told no-one the real reason for her pain and there was a sense of relief in saying it out loud.

'But he'd been brought up with racing cars,' Kitty's voice was gentle now, no longer provocative, 'you told me that when we first met. And his father had been killed in the Indianapolis 500, you told me that, too.'

'Yes.'

'So surely, by keeping you in ignorance he was being protective. I should imagine it would have taken a great deal of self-control for Gene to keep quiet about his racing.'

Caroline gave a derisive snort, but Kitty continued in earnest. 'No, listen to me, Caroline, please! How many men who live dangerous lives would go home and brag to their wives? Or if not brag, at least feel the need to talk about the danger, get it out of their system? But Gene didn't. He knew that if he had, you would have been living in daily terror.'

Kitty was right, Caroline realised, feeling drained and exhausted, but somehow calmer than she had in months. 'Why did he have to do it at all, though? It was so selfish. Why did he have to take the risks?'

'Because racing was in his blood. And because it was his life and he had to live it his way.' Kitty smiled to soften her words as she added, 'And it would have been selfish of you not to let him.'

Caroline was overwhelmed with a sense of relief. Tomorrow she might once more blame Gene for cheating her of their life together, who could tell, but for now Kitty's words were a great comfort. 'You're a clever woman, Kitty Kendall,' she said.

'I'm Kitty Farinelli now.'

'Of course.' It was Caroline's turn to be direct. 'Do you love him?'

'More than I ever thought humanly possible.'

'Oh I am glad. I thought he might be a gesture.'

Kitty gave a hoot of laughter.

Ten minutes later, when Artie returned from the park with his son, he found Caroline Hamilton a different woman altogether.

'Arturo,' she said and she smiled apologetically, 'I'm sorry I was rude, I have my bad days and this was one of them.'

That smile. He hadn't noticed she was beautiful.

'What did you do?' he asked Kitty when they left.

'Taught her a bit about acceptance, I think,' she grinned. 'You would have been proud of me.'

Kitty hoped that she'd helped. She wondered how she would cope if Arturo died, and she shuddered at the thought. Life must be very hard for Caroline.

Kitty's own life had not been without its problems. Early in her marriage she had suffered two miscarriages and, just five years previously, a premature labour which, at seven months, had cost not only the life of her baby, a girl, but very nearly her own. Since then she and Artie had stopped trying to have more children. It was sad; she knew that Arturo would have liked a large family, and she regretted the fact that Roberto had no sibling, but Kitty herself bore the loss with fortitude. Her body had rebelled; it refused to bear more children and, after a period of grief over the loss of her baby, she accepted the fact and got on with her life.

It was a good life too, and Kitty lived it with her customary zest. She had given up full-time employment before Roberto's birth and wrote freelance now from their home at Bondi Beach. They had shifted to Bondi shortly after their marriage in order to be near the water. Having lived by the harbour all her childhood, Kitty missed the water, and with the baby due and the need for a bigger flat, why not rent one by the beach? Artie had no objections, and they had started to hunt for a place they could afford.

Then Tim Kendall had entered the picture, announcing that he was going to buy them a house as a wedding present. Kitty's refusal to accept his offer led to open war between them. She'd never accepted his assistance before, she said, and she didn't intend to start now.

'It's a wedding present, for God's sake!' he roared, but she wouldn't listen.

Ruth joined in. 'Please, darling,' she begged, taking Kitty aside. Father and daughter couldn't be in the same room together when they disagreed, neither listened and neither would back down. 'Please accept your father's offer, if not for yourself, then for the baby.'

'My baby will not be brought up in the manner to which my father wishes it to become accustomed,' Kitty said with the mulish arrogance she always adopted when taking a stand. 'My baby will be brought up in the manner which Arturo and I can afford, we do not need somebody else's money.'

'That "somebody else" is your father,' Ruth said, exasperated, 'and he wishes to give you a wedding present.' But her plea fell on deaf ears.

Ruth appealed to Artie. 'Please, Arturo, help me.'

Artie, however, had decided to keep well out of it. He wasn't sure if Kitty was just being stubborn, or whether this perverse family pride was yet another Australian trait about which he had yet to learn.

Then Tim Kendall himself sought Artie's help.

'It's up to you, Artie,' he said over a beer on the balcony, turning the radio down, even though the Rabbitohs were winning. 'You have to get her to accept the house.'

'I think this is between you and Kitty,' Artie said, backing off.

'Oh no it's not.' Tim had thought long and hard, and Artie was his only hope. 'In an Italian village, if a bloke gets married, doesn't he accept a few goats or something from the bride's father?' He was being blunt, he knew it, but he didn't mean to be condescending, and he hoped Artie wouldn't take offence.

Artie didn't at all. 'Yes,' he said, 'or a cow or some sheep, that is most common. It is her dowry.'

'Exactly. Well, that's what the house is. A dowry. Don't you understand?'

'Yes, of course I understand.' So some customs remained the same in their two countries, Artie thought, and the knowledge pleased him.

'A house is hardly a cow!' Kitty exploded when he told her.

'It is not the point, Kitty, and you know it, now accept your father's offer.'

She was taken aback. 'But I was refusing mainly on your behalf,' she said, 'I thought you realised that.' Arturo was a man to whom self-respect was of the utmost importance. Kitty had assumed that he would be insulted, that to him the offer of a house would imply he was not a good provider. 'I thought you'd be too proud to accept his help.'

'It is not his help, it is his gift. And there is a difference between pride and perversity. You are being perverse in refusing your father's gift, you should accept it with pride.'

It was as simple as that. The next day, much to her father's astonishment, she graciously accepted his offer, though she politely refused to allow her parents any say in her choice.

Tim didn't mind. 'Just remember,' he said, 'that money's no object,' but Ruth was deeply disappointed. She would have so loved to have done the rounds of the harbourside homes for sale and to have picked the most gracious with the most splendid view.

'Bondi Beach!' she said a week later. 'But I thought you wanted a harbour view.'

'No, just water. It looks out over the ocean, it's lovely.'

'But it's a holiday suburb, people go there to swim. Nobody *lives* at Bondi Beach.'

'Oh yes they do, Mum,' Kitty laughed. 'Just wait till you see it.'

'My God, it's a shop!' Tim exclaimed as he and Ruth stood with Artie and Kitty in the middle of Campbell Parade looking up at the dilapidated three-storey building.

'Well, it was once, downstairs,' Kitty said as her parents gazed with horror at the gutted shopfront, 'and it probably will be again. I'm thinking of opening a sort of bookshop.'

'A bookshop on Bondi Beach?' Her father looked horrified. 'You're joking.'

'Not a mainstream bookshop. I'd stock the sort of stuff that gets lost in commercial outlets.' It was sounding worse by the minute, Tim thought. 'It'd be a sort of meeting place, a cafe, I thought, with a reading room where people can sit and talk.'

'Nobody reads in Bondi Beach, you'd go broke in a week.'

'Oh, it wouldn't be run to make a profit, just a hobby really, and it won't be for ages yet, not until well after the baby's born.' She fumbled about in her handbag for the front door keys. 'But I'll have to do something with my time eventually. Arturo'll be at work all day and I know I'll go mad just being a housewife.' She found the keys. 'Come on,' she said, 'I'll show you upstairs, the rooms are big and the view's spectacular.'

Kitty unlocked the door and Ruth followed her inside.

'What do you think, Artie?' Tim asked.

'I like the house very much.'

'No, about this other business.'

Artie wasn't quite sure himself whether Kitty had thought her project through properly. Was she trying to set up a Bondi Beach Push, he wondered. But he was happy to see her so excited by the prospect, even if it never eventuated.

'If anyone could make it work,' he answered diplomatically, 'I am sure that person would be Kitty.'

When Roberto was two, Kitty embarked upon her project. As a bookshop it proved a dismal failure, but as a meeting place it gradually grew very popular. Many of both Kitty's and Artie's friends were struggling writers, mostly working journalists with minor published works, and Kitty's intention had been to give them a centre from which to market and sell their works. The writers themselves came. They sat, they drank coffee, they read and discussed each other's work, but they rarely made a purchase, and the general public appeared completely disinterested.

The habitués of Kitty's, as the place became known, although there was no sign to indicate it, sat around for so long that Kitty decided they needed to be fed more than coffee and biscuits. She applied for a licence from the local council and set up a kitchen downstairs from which she served big bowls of pasta with hunks of fresh bread for five shillings a pop. She did the cooking herself. Arturo had taught her the basics, but her culinary skills had long since outstripped his. She made just the one pasta a day, but she varied it throughout the week, and the aroma of garlic, herbs, onions and tomatoes which wafted each morning down Campbell Parade attracted many a passer-by.

On the window tables overlooking the beach, she set up a chess and a chequerboard, and both were always in use. And on days when the breeze was not too strong or the sun not too glaringly hot, many lifted their chairs outside and sat on the pavement to look out over the ocean.

Determined to cater to all, Kitty continued to stock a limited selection of obscure writers' works in a reading room out the back. The room led onto a small courtyard where people sat in the sun and read the daily newspapers, which Kitty also supplied. And then second-hand books appeared. They grew in number until a book-exchange-cum-miniature library materialised in the reading room.

It was a bizarre place, and it attracted an eclectic clientele. Some would come up from a morning's sunbake on the beach, others would step fresh off the Bondi tram; whilst some came for the food and some for the conversation, there were those who came simply because they knew they would meet others of their kind and that they would be free to speak their own language without being glared at.

Business was thriving, and eventually Kitty hired a cook and a waitress. The cook was Italian, a man in his sixties, and the waitress a nineteen-year-old Czech from Prague. Then, a year later, Kitty hired a manager, a Frenchman, Jean-Claude, and retired upstairs to write. She'd proved her point, she thought. Potpourri it may be, unusual, even outlandish to some, but, in four years, she had made a success of Kitty's.

'You actually make a profit?' her father asked.

'Yep. Enough.'

'Well, I'll be damned.' Strange sort of place, he thought, but she'd made a go of it. 'Good on you,' he said.

Ruth had a few misgivings, however. 'It's a most admirable effort, darling . . .' she said, and Kitty waited for the 'but', '. . . but I'm not sure it's quite the right sort of setting in which to bring up a child.'

'We don't bring him up in the shop, Mum.' Kitty had mellowed of late, she refused to feel even slightly irritated.

'No, no, dear, I'm aware of that. But no doubt he occasionally mingles downstairs . . .'

If only you knew how much ...

'... and they really are a rather motley crowd.'

... and that's exactly what's good for him.

'I don't for one minute suggest that you sell the shop ...'

You're praying for me to do just that. Kitty wanted to laugh out loud.

'... heavens above no, dear, I'm so proud of you, really I am. But do you not think that ... well, perhaps you should consider leasing upstairs and moving to another house?'

'Nope. We're perfectly happy where we are.'

'But Roberto ...'

'And Rob's perfectly happy too. Have to go now, Mum, bye.'

Roberto Farinelli did indeed have a happy childhood. Kitty taught him to swim in the shallow rockpool at the north end of the beach almost before he could walk, and by the time he was six he was body surfing the smaller waves. Kitty would sit on the beach and watch. He was like a dolphin in the water, she thought with pride.

He was a happy little boy, feted by the customers in the shop. Bilingual, he chatted to the Italians who gathered there; when he was little, the writers in the back room read him stories; and when he was a bit older, the Hungarians at the corner table taught him to play chess; then when he was eight years old, thrill of all thrills, two young Aussies who regularly came up from the beach for a bowl of minestrone taught him to ride a surfboard.

But once he started his first year at Bondi State Primary School things started to go wrong. He'd had no trouble in Infants School, but this was different.

'You're the dago kid from that crazy place in Campbell Parade, aren't you?'

There were three of them. Tough little locals, and they backed Roberto into a corner of the schoolyard.

'My dad reckons they ought to clear that place out. It's a breeding ground for foreign scum, he says. Dagos just like you.'

'I'm not a dago, I'm Australian.'

'Oh yeah? You don't look like one.'

'Well, I am. I was born here, I'm as Australian as you.'

Secure in their strength of numbers, the boys didn't like the dago kid talking back, he was supposed to be frightened.

'Show him, Max,' one of them said, and the ringleader, a ginger-haired boy quite big for his age, stepped up to Roberto.

'Dago,' he said, 'dago wop scum.' It sounded good, just like the way his dad said it. Good and tough. And he shoved Roberto in the chest.

Roberto staggered back a little, caught off balance. Then, maddened, he threw himself at the boy, taking him completely by surprise, and they fell to the ground, Roberto on top.

The other two boys watched on in stunned amazement, they hadn't expected the kid to fight. Roberto hadn't expected to either. He'd never been in a fight in his life, but then he'd never felt such anger. And, despite the fact that he was smaller than the ginger-haired boy, his anger gave him the upper edge as the two of them rolled in the dirt.

The scuffle didn't last long. A minute or so later, two strong hands grabbed each of the boys by the scruff of the neck and hauled them to their feet.

'You causing trouble again, Max?' Bob 'Barker' Shaw, PT instructor and star rugby league player, was every boy's hero. Max could have told him the dago had started it, which was sort of true, but he knew that he wouldn't score any points with Barker if he dobbed the kid in, so he stood his ground.

'All right, who started it?'

Max waited for the kid to say, 'He called me a dago'. But he didn't. He stood silent, along with the others.

Barker turned to Max's mates. 'You boys see who started it?' Both boys shook their head, they knew the rules.

'Right,' Barker was pleased, he didn't like dobbers, 'you can both spend your lunchtime doing lines. Now, shake hands.'

Roberto and Max shook hands and Barker dispersed the group and left.

At lunchtime they sat together in the empty classroom writing 'I will not fight in the playground' over and over on their pads, and, after ten minutes or so, Max turned to Roberto. 'What's your name?' he asked.

'Robert.' Roberto shrugged. 'Or Rob. Whatever.' Anything but Roberto, he decided then and there.

'I'm Max. Want to go for a swim after school?'

'Can you ride a surfboard?'

'Nup.'

'I can.'

'You're kidding.' Max had admired the surfboard riders who occasionally gathered at the southern end of the beach, but kids didn't ride surfboards.

'I've got a board.' It was true, his proud grandfather had given him one for Christmas. Tim had had it specially made, about half the size of an adult board. Rob had no trouble catching waves on the huge boards the men rode, but he was not strong enough to swim them back out through the surf. He handled his own custom-made board with ease. 'I'll show you if you like.'

Max Brown and Rob Farinelli became good mates after that, though Max never quite mastered the surfboard, strong swimmer as he was. They swam together daily, explored the rockpools for crabs and, on still days, fished off the reef. But neither boy asked the other to his home.

Max would have liked to. But what would his dad say? He'd probably call Rob a dago or a wop. And if he found out that Rob lived above the crazy place in Campbell Parade, his dad'd go on about the foreign scum invading Bondi.

And Rob didn't ask Max to his home because, for the first time in his life, he was ashamed of it. Why couldn't his parents live in a normal house? And why did they have to speak Italian, why couldn't they speak English? His mum wasn't even Italian in the first place. And why did they have to have all those foreigners around?

Rob would sneak in the front door of their home, hoping that none of his schoolmates would see him, embarrassed that he lived above the place where the foreigners gathered.

Kitty and Artie noticed the change in their son. He was often sullen these days. And he insisted they stop calling him Roberto.

'What's wrong, Rob?' Kitty asked. 'Is it school?'

Rob shrugged. How could he tell them? 'I got called a dago,' he said, 'but that was ages ago, I'm good mates with the kid now.' Let them think it was school, it was easier that way.

'Why do you not ask this mate of yours home?' Artie suggested. 'We would like to meet him.'

'Yeah, maybe I will.'

But Artie had seen the look in his son's eyes. 'And we will meet his family when we come to the Parents and Citizens meeting next month,' he said.

'You're not going to come, are you?' The boy's horror confirmed Artie's suspicions.

'Not if you do not wish me to.' Artie felt hurt, but he understood.

'Of course you'll come,' Kitty said. 'We're going together, we agreed, I want us to meet the teachers, why on earth wouldn't you come?'

Kitty was missing the point. 'Perhaps your mother will go on her own,' Artie said to his son.

'Yeah.' Rob hated seeing the hurt in his father's eyes. But much as he loved his dad, the thought of him meeting his friends' parents made Rob cringe with embarrassment.

'Yeah, it'd be good if Mum came.' He couldn't look at his father as he said it.

Artie knew that Kitty was about to argue. 'Go and do your homework,' he said. And Rob gratefully went to his room.

'He's ashamed of us!' Kitty wasn't in the least bit hurt, she was angry.

'Of me, yes.'

'Well, we'll soon put a stop to that, why did you let him get away with it?'

'You will go to the meeting on your own, Kitty.'

'Like hell I will. You're his father, for God's sake. So he's half Italian, so what? He should be proud of the fact.'

Artie smiled. Kitty would never change. 'He is Australian, Kitty, and it is difficult to be different when you are nine.'

Kitty went to the meeting alone. But she was deliberately provocative when she got there. She made it known that she ran 'that place on Campbell Parade' and she noted the reactions of several parents. Particularly the father of Rob's friend Max.

Max had girded his loins and taken the plunge. 'This is my mate, Rob,' he'd said to his dad.

What was his son doing being mates with a dago? Mick Brown thought. Then he met the mother. Good looker, and an Aussie, that wasn't so bad. And the kid spoke like an Aussie, so Mick was prepared to forgive. Then the mother said, 'You must bring Max around one Saturday afternoon, we run the cafe down in Campbell

Parade, the one with the chessboard in the front.' Just like that! So she was the one.

'You're not to see that kid again,' Mick told his son when they got home. 'Bad blood there. You can't mix the races like that, it's not natural. And that place of hers, should be cleared out, it should, too many foreigners. You keep away from that kid.'

'My dad said I'm not allowed to be mates with you any more,' Max told Rob the following day.

'Fair enough,' Rob replied coldly, as if he didn't care. He didn't blame Max, he'd expected as much. He'd been present during the exchange between his mum and Max's dad, and he'd hated his mother for saying what she had, knowing that she'd done it deliberately. He'd said nothing to her, but he'd sworn to himself that he would never forgive her. Never. And now, because of her, he'd lost his best friend. Rob hated his mother.

'But I don't care what Dad says.' Max was a gutsy little bloke. 'I want us to be mates.'

Rob couldn't disguise his pleasure. 'Me too,' he said.

'Can I come to your place after school?' His father's dire warnings had intrigued Max, he wanted to have a closer look at this place in Campbell Parade. 'Come on, Rob, be a sport, we're best mates.'

Rob agreed, with reluctance, hoping that it wouldn't be the end of their friendship.

There was an autumn nip in the air but it was a fine day, and outside the cafe people had lifted their chairs onto the pavement. Rob led Max through the shop.

One of the men hunched over the chessboard in the corner gave a nod and said, 'Roberto, *jo napot*,' and Rob said 'hello' back. He could have said it in Hungarian, he usually did to old Franz who'd been coming to Kitty's for years, but he was self-conscious in front of Max. He gave a wave to Jean-Claude who was behind the counter and walked through to the kitchen.

'G'day, Guiseppe, this is my mate Max.'

'Hello, Max,' said old Guiseppe the chef, then in Italian to Rob, 'You want some ravioli for you and your friend?' Kitty was always more than happy for Guiseppe to prepare a snack for Rob when he got home from school. It filled in the gap until dinner. Lately, however, Rob had been dodging upstairs for a glass of milk and some biscuits, avoiding the cafe altogether. Guiseppe was pleased to see him. And with a friend too.

'Thanks, Guiseppe, ravioli would be good.' Rob had answered in Italian before he knew it. He was conscious of Max's look of astonishment and cursed himself. 'We'll be out the back,' he said in English, 'give us a yell when it's ready,' and he led the way past the reading room and into the courtyard. It was four o'clock on a weekday afternoon and business was slow, so they had the place to themselves.

'Was that Italian,' Max asked, 'what you said?' Rob nodded, and Max waited for an explanation but none was forthcoming. 'So what did you say?' he queried impatiently.

'Guiseppe asked if we wanted something to eat and I said yes.'

'Gee, I didn't know you spoke Italian.'

'Well, of course I do, my dad's Italian.'

'Yeah, I knew that.' Max had tended to forget that fact lately.

'So that makes me half Italian.'

'Yeah.' Max had forgotten that too. He'd completely forgotten that Rob was different.

Guiseppe brought their meals out himself. 'You will enjoy this,' he said in Italian, ceremoniously placing a bowl and a spoon before each of the boys. 'It is very good, the sauce is of mushroom and peppers.'

'Thanks, Guiseppe.'

'What did he say?' Max asked.

'He said it's very good.'

Max studied the food in the bowl, it looked pretty dodgy to him. Lumps of dough with gooey stuff over the top, not like the real meals he got at home. He tentatively lifted the spoon to his mouth. It didn't taste like the real meals he got at home either. In fact he'd never tasted anything like it. He spooned in another mouthful, and then another.

'Do you like it?' Rob asked.

He nodded vigorously, his mouth full. 'Beaut,' he said. 'What is it?'

'Ravioli. Pasta with meat inside and sauce on top.'

When they'd finished, they took their empty bowls back into the kitchen.

'How do you say beaut in Italian?' Max muttered.

'Eh?'

'I want to tell Guiseppe it was beaut, how do I say it in Italian?'

'*Molto buono.*'

Max whispered it to himself a few times. 'Hey Guiseppe,' he said, as they put their bowls in the sink, 'that was mollto borno.'

'*Gracie*, Max,' Guiseppe replied; then, in his heavily accented English, 'you come back any time, I give you more "mollto borno" Italian food.' He grinned at Rob and said in Italian, 'It is good you bring your friend.'

Max became a regular after that, and gradually other schoolmates trooped along, until there was a tribe of half a dozen or so nine-year-olds regularly scoffing bowls of pasta in Kitty's courtyard after school.

They came for the food at first, it was as good as Max had told them, but, like Max, they ended up loving the place.

'You should come on Saturdays,' Rob said proudly. He'd forgotten that he was ashamed of his home. He'd forgotten that he hated his mother and that he'd never forgive her. 'On Saturdays there's music.'

The boys told lies to their parents, most of whom would have been horrified to discover their young sons were mingling with foreigners, eating their strange food, even learning their strange languages.

They conferred, the boys. On Saturday arvo they'd be late home from footie, they told their parents, because the gang was going to Steve's. Or to Tom's, or to Benny's. They varied it. And their parents never knew that from four until six each Saturday, their sons were in Kitty's back courtyard eating bowls of spaghetti and listening to two Russian fiddlers. And when they queried why the boys weren't hungry after an afternoon's footie, the reply 'Steve's mum cooked us tea,' seemed acceptable.

No-one knew where the Russian fiddlers had come from, they'd just drifted in one day, as many did. The couple didn't speak a word of English, or appeared not to. Indeed, the woman never spoke at all, and the man just muttered to her every now and then in Russian.

Jean-Claude did not pay for their services, they played their fiddles for free food and wine. Jean-Claude sold illicit wine in cheap porcelain coffee mugs, even though Kitty had told him not to. They didn't have a liquor licence and it wasn't worth the risk, but he sold it nonetheless. Kitty decided to turn a blind eye. Jean-Claude was a good manager, and she had little to do with the shop these days, busy as she was with the regular feature articles she wrote for one of the major syndicates. She certainly had no time to find and train another manager.

The Russians played, sometimes for an hour, sometimes until the shop closed, depending upon their mood, but they always gathered a crowd. And the half dozen or so little boys, squatted on the ground in front of them, watched mesmerised.

A little unkempt and always dressed in black, the man and the woman looked like each other. Lank, shoulder-length brown hair, expressionless faces, they sat at the corner table in the courtyard and wordlessly ate their pasta, as if unaware that everyone was waiting for them to play. And then, when they had finished eating, Jean-Claude would move the table away. The man would mutter to the woman, and they would turn their chairs to face each other, take their fiddles from their cases, and everything would change.

Their faces were no longer lacklustre. Their eyes locked together with such intensity that they could have been looking into each other's soul. And they played. Theirs was the music of the Russian peasants, now hauntingly sentimental, now rising wildly to a crescendo of gypsy madness. The woman might lead one moment, the man the next; then they might play a duet which could have been a duel as their frenzied bows cut the air and their fingers darted upon the strings and the sweat poured from their brows. And never once did either player's eyes leave the other's; they seemed barely to blink.

Max and his mates had never seen or heard anything like it.

'Can I come on Saturday?' was the constant request. Word had got around. And Max, as the boss, had to lay down some rules. They'd have to take it in turns, he said, only six at a time, and they had to swear to keep it a secret.

'Cross your heart,' he'd say. 'Spit.' And another boy would be accepted into the gang.

The change in Rob was incredible Artie and Kitty agreed.

'He's made friends,' Kitty said, 'I'm so glad.'

'And his friends accept us,' Artie added, 'that is important to him.'

It was true. Young Rob Farinelli now introduced his dad with pride, and Artie was deeply relieved. He had understood his son's dilemma but, even to Kitty, he had not admitted the hurt he had felt.

'Given time,' Artie recalled Rube had said, 'given time they will accept us.' Perhaps that was what Rube had meant, he thought. The next generation.

Artie said as much to his wife. 'Perhaps it is the next generation which will have the answers, Kitty,' he said. 'Perhaps we do not need to push so hard.'

'Perhaps,' she agreed, 'but I for one certainly intend to give a good shove whenever I can.' Kitty wasn't one to sit around and wait.

Then the inevitable happened. 'Cross your heart and spit' wasn't enough. Excited young boys eventually had to talk, and the word somehow got out.

Tempers were frayed and Mick Brown led the brigade of angry parents. The council was informed and Kitty's was closed down. Neighbours had already complained that the music on Saturday nights was too loud, and when it was discovered that liquor was sold on the premises without a licence, the die was cast. Furthermore, it was a safehouse for illegal immigrants. Two Russians and a number of Hungarians.

Kitty fought, and won, the charge of harbouring illegal immigrants. But she paid the fine for selling liquor without a licence and closed the business, leasing the shopfront to a couple who sold pies and steak sandwiches. At least they were Latvian, she was glad about that, it was still a bit of a statement.

The boys missed Kitty's, but the place on Campbell Parade had formed such a bond that their friendship remained intact. It was something they would take into their adulthood. The year they turned ten, the year they ate Italian food and listened to Russian music. They'd never forget that.

And despite his father's instructions that he was 'never to see that dago kid outside school again', Max Brown and Rob Farinelli remained the closest of mates throughout their lives.

Chapter Seventeen

Billy Kendall's son Wally, whom Tim had taken into partnership after the war just as he'd promised, had proved every bit the lair Tim had anticipated. Tim couldn't help liking him though. Some people didn't, some people found Wally a bit wearing. But over the years Tim had grown very fond of his younger cousin. Which was just as well, age had done little to temper Wally's flashy exuberance.

At fifty-five there was still a lot of the larrikin in Wally Kendall. Grey-haired, overweight, he was still showy, still a snappy dresser, and he still had an eye for the women, much to the chagrin of Darlene, his third wife and twenty years his junior. But whether one liked Wally Kendall or not, one had to admit that he was an excellent host.

Wally loved entertaining. In his first years with Kendall Markets, as soon as he'd been able to scrape together enough money, he'd bought an old house down on the harbour foreshore. It was hardly Point Piper or Vaucluse, but it had cost a packet by Wally's standards, and even then he'd only been able to afford the place because it was falling down. Now, barely eighteen years later, having bought the block next door and pulled down the house which was on it, Wally's home boasted a swimming pool, a grass tennis court, a boatshed and ramp, and a small private beach with a jetty. The perfect venue for entertaining.

Many of Wally's rich friends and associates wondered why he didn't get rid of the old house altogether and build something more lavish and modern. But Wally had never once considered demolishing the old colonial home, he loved it with a passion, and had had it fully restored instead. Now it sat, strangely out of place amidst the surrounding luxury, but magnificent in its own way, overshadowed by a huge Moreton Bay fig, its wooden-shuttered windows and its large verandahs reminders of a bygone era.

Throughout the fifties, Wally's son and two daughters had grown up living the life of Riley. Wallace Junior sailed his yacht with his mates on the harbour, and Lucy and Julia, tomboys the two of them, rowed the little dinghy around the point and picked oysters from the rocks, returning with hands cut and bleeding. In the late afternoons, after school, they bombed each other from the end of the jetty, or, legs dangling over the side, fished for flathead and bream in the early dusk. They built a tree house in the Moreton Bay fig, anyone daring to walk beneath it proving a perfect water pistol target, and they regularly stained themselves purple raiding the neighbour's mulberry tree.

Wally adored his kids and spoiled them rotten, particularly young Wallace, who could do no wrong. Without a mother to control them, the children ran wild, the succession of nannies barely able to control them. Wally's first wife, Mabel, had died of cancer and Wallace, six years old at the time, was the only one of the children who had even the vaguest memory of their mother.

Wally's second wife had only lasted a couple of years, the kids made sure of that. She might have stayed, even accepting Wally's philandering, but she wasn't going to take his monster kids and his women as well. So she decided to take a sizable amount of his money instead. Wally vowed that he'd learned a lesson after that, but he hadn't: three years later he was married again. To pretty, blonde Darlene.

Ever since Wally had had the grass tennis court installed, he'd held a tennis party one Saturday each month throughout the summer, weather depending of course. Unlike his extravagant dinners, the Saturday afternoons were casual affairs. People were encouraged to bring their costumes and to swim if they wished, and all were expected to participate in the tennis matches, which were run like a tournament. Wally took his tennis very seriously, having been an accomplished player in his day, and he insisted that they all wear their whites, that they draw lots as to partners and opponents, and that they play through quarters and semis and finals, depending upon the numbers.

In his inimitable style, Wally had his Saturdays beautifully catered, but very informally so. There were no waiters, people helped themselves to the endless array of sandwiches and finger food which the maid kept replenishing on the verandah tables.

The food sat under lace domes to keep the flies away, and there were coolers packed with iced beer, and champagne and white wine in ice buckets. People were expected to help themselves to the alcohol also, but not too liberally, not until the tennis was over. Wally, who drank with the best of them, considered it bad form to play tennis drunk. He certainly made up for it afterwards though, and for the few hardened partygoers, those without young families in attendance, Wally's Saturday afternoons had been known to go on until midnight.

So family-orientated were Wally's tennis parties that one Saturday afternoon in the November of 1964, at Caroline's suggestion, young Emma Hamilton decided to announce her engagement. They were all there—Tim and Ruth; Artie, Kitty and young Rob, who'd brought along a mate of his called Max; Ada, Pete and their brood were there, and Caroline and hers, and of course Wally and his.

'Shall we tell them?' Caroline whispered to her daughter at the start of the afternoon as they gathered under the shade of the huge umbrellas, all in their tennis whites, Wally handing the tin around for people to draw the names of their partners. Emma nodded.

'Come on then, you two.' Caroline led the way up the steps to the verandah. 'Attention everyone!' she called. 'Attention please!' They stopped and looked up at the verandah. 'Emma has an announcement to make.'

Taking her fiancé's hand, Emma stepped forward, 'Gordon and I are engaged,' she said, 'we're going to be married next April.'

Everyone gave three cheers, poured glasses of champagne and made toasts, and Wally glowered a little because he wanted to get on with the tennis.

'Now don't be sour, Wally.' Wally turned, startled that he'd been caught out. 'I know you want to play your tennis,' Caroline said, 'but it was the only time I could get everybody together. Ten minutes later and they'd all have been off in dinghies or in swimming pools or on the court.'

'Sorry.' Wally relaxed and smiled, he liked Caroline. She'd had a tough life, her husband dying prematurely the way he had. Jesus, Wally thought, the man hadn't even reached fifty and fifty was the prime of life. But Caroline had come through all right. She had a good sense of humour, anyway, and to Wally, a good sense of humour was one of the prime assets a person could possess. A good looking woman too, in a beefy sort of way. Wally Kendall had a soft spot for Caroline. 'She's very young,' he said, looking up at Emma on the verandah, surrounded by well-wishers.

'Twenty,' Caroline said, 'old enough.' There was a hint of regret in her voice. Gordon was a nice bloke but, having just graduated from Sydney University, he'd recently accepted a position in his uncle's law firm. In London.

'But London's so far away,' she said.

'Oh.' So that's why she sounded gloomy.

There wasn't much he could say by way of comfort, so he patted her hand and hurried off to begin the tennis proceedings.

'Emma tells me she and Gordon are going to England.' Kitty joined Caroline on one of the spectator benches beside the court and offered her a glass of champagne.

'Better not,' Caroline said, 'It's ladies' doubles next and I've already had two glasses.'

'Me too. But it's you and me up against Ada and Darlene, why worry?' Kitty gave one of her hoots. Ada and Darlene were hopeless on the court.

Caroline smiled and took the glass. 'I play better drunk anyway.' She took a healthy swig. 'Yes,' she said, 'they leave in May. God only knows for how long.'

'Forty, fifteen,' Ruth called from her umpire's seat above the net. Ruth Kendall was sixty-seven years old, although she still looked in her fifties. Once a superb tennis player, she'd given up playing several years previously and, since then, had been the official umpire at Wally's tournaments, never missing a trick, and looking chic and professional in her white slacks, white shade and dark glasses.

'You'll miss her.'

Caroline gave a heartfelt nod. She would miss Emma dreadfully.

Caroline had adjusted to her life. It was nearly three years since Gene's death and time had healed her wounds. She no longer blamed him or felt bitter. She missed him and was lonely, particularly at night, longing for his touch, recalling the strength and the gentleness of his body.

But there was no point in living in the past, so she'd concentrated her love upon her children instead. The boys had inherited their father's vitality and athleticism, reminding her so often of Gene. And Emma. Well Emma was beautiful. Indulged, Caroline had to admit. But then Emma had a true appreciation of beauty, she loved beautiful things.

'It'll probably do her the world of good to get away from you,' Kitty said in her customary blunt fashion. 'You dote on that girl, you spoil her rotten.'

Caroline gave a low gurgle of laughter. 'Yes, you're right, I do.'

'Fault!'

Kitty and Caroline turned their attention to the game. Wally and eighteen-year-old Wallace Junior were playing Caroline's sons, Jim and Bruce. Jim, the same age as Wallace, was a strong player, and sixteen-year-old Bruce was no slouch with a racquet, but the Hamilton brothers were getting slaughtered by Kendall father and son.

'Double fault!' Ruth called. 'Game to the Kendalls.'

'Bugger it!' Bruce had let himself get rattled, it was the third double fault he'd served and it had cost them the game. 'Sorry, Jim.'

'No worries, mate,' Jim said a little tightly as they changed ends. He didn't blame Bruce, but he hated to lose. 'They get to practise every day,' he muttered. 'If we had our own court, we'd beat the hell out of them.'

'Youth is not everything, you see, boys,' Wally said pompously, puffing like a grampus when he met them at the net. He picked up a hand towel and mopped the sweat which was pouring from his brow. 'Technical know-how, that's what counts.'

Wally was having a splendid day. He hadn't rigged the draw, he never did, but he loved it when he was partnered with his son. They made a fine team, Wallace playing the baseline and doing all the running whilst he stayed at the net and slammed the balls back. Between them, they ran their opponents ragged and there were few who could beat them.

'Technical know-how every time,' he said, and he puffed his way off to the far end of the court.

'He'll give himself a heart attack,' Kitty muttered to Caroline. She waved at Artie who was on the other side of the court, sitting beneath a big umbrella with his father-in-law and Pete.

Tim was seventy-one now and the heat affected him. Not that he looked seventy-one. Despite his silver-white hair, there remained an indecently boyish quality to Tim's face, but he was definitely feeling his age these days.

'So you're all for the war, Pete?' Tim asked Ada's American husband. He was most interested to hear Pete's views on America's involvement in Vietnam.

'Oh, I most definitely am. Communism has to be stamped out, it's America's duty to do just that.'

Life was simple for an American, Tim thought, even for one who'd been away from his home country for so long. 'I'm not sure Australia should be involved though. What do you reckon, Artie?'

Only a month ago Prime Minister Menzies had announced the introduction of selective conscription, and it had created a furore amongst Australians.

'I am against any foreign involvement in the Vietnam War,' Artie said emphatically, and Pete looked at him askance.

'Well, I don't know about the war itself,' Tim said, 'maybe the Americans do need to go in and sort it out.' Pete nodded effusively. 'But this business of conscription, I don't like it. We've never had compulsory overseas service before, and we've been through two world wars and Korea. Surely this isn't a world-wide threat, why put our boys through it?'

'But communism *is* a world-wide threat,' Pete insisted. 'It's our duty to fight it.'

'It is not Australia's war and it is no threat to world peace,' Artie said firmly. 'The South Vietnamese have not even asked for our help; the Australian Government is sending troops merely to appease the Americans. It is not right, the Australians should not be sent.'

Pete bristled. Where did this guy get off thinking that the Americans were wrong? And why was he speaking for the Australians? He was an Italian for Christ's sake.

He was just about to retort when Ruth distracted him by calling 'Game, set and match!'

There was a time when Wally would have hurdled the net but

those days were long gone. Huffing and puffing, he met the Hamilton boys at the net and shook hands with them.

'Good match, boys, well done.' Wally returned the congratulatory wave from Kitty and Caroline on the sidelines. 'Energetic, the both of you, just got to work on the technical aspects of the game.' Then he crossed the court to talk to Tim.

Jim was steaming. 'Sorry,' Wallace said, pretending embarrassment although he was just as delighted as his father that they'd won.

'He's good,' Bruce conceded. 'He's bloody good for an old codger.'

Wallace grinned, he liked Bruce. He'd become good mates with both the Hamilton brothers but, although there was a two-year age difference, he preferred Bruce. He was less intense and competitive than his brother Jim.

'A fat old codger too,' Wallace added to keep side with his mates, and even Jim laughed.

'Good match, eh Tim?' Wally called as he crossed the court, but Tim was so engrossed in conversation that he didn't notice Wally's approach.

'I reckon you're right, Artie, the Aussies shouldn't go,' he was saying. 'At least, not unless they want to. If the silly buggers want to go to war, then let 'em sign up the way we all did in the old days. But just picking a name, that's not on. This conscription business is a bastard.'

Wally's disappointment at not being the star of the day, particularly to Tim who was a bit of a hero to him, disappeared as soon as he heard Tim's words. Wally was angry about conscription.

'They don't pick your name, they pick a date, and if the date's your bloody birthday, you're buggered.' Wally plonked himself down heavily on the bench and leaned his elbows on his knees. He was panting and his face was bright red. 'You're right, Tim, it's a bastard of a thing to do.'

'Good match, Wally,' Tim said, 'You've still got it in you. Why don't you go for a swim?' Wally really shouldn't do this to himself, Tim thought, he was carrying far too much weight.

'Yeah, I reckon I might. But I tell you something,' Wally said as he rose to go, 'they're not sending any bloody kid of mine to Vietnam. Over my dead body!'

*

Wallace William Kendall's name came up the following year. Or rather his birth date did, as did that of James Francis Hamilton.

Jim accepted his lot. He felt excited about it. If the truth be known, he wanted to go to war. He wanted to wear a uniform and carry a rifle and be a hero. Young Wallace, however, had other ideas. He had no intention of going off to risk life and limb for some country he'd hardly even heard of, but he didn't have to admit to that. After all, his father Wally Kendall had determined that, under no circumstances, would his son go to war. So young Wallace, dutiful son as he had always been, bowed to his father's wishes.

Wally had mates in high places and he made discreet enquiries. It appeared that deferment on the grounds of university studies was a common ploy and heavily policed by the authorities. It would have to be medical grounds then. But you couldn't take on the Commonwealth Department of Labour and National Service, you couldn't start at the top, you had to find a little man.

Through a mate, Wally got hold of a letter. Signed by an official with the title 'Registrar', it granted release from national service on the grounds that the bearer did not meet the required standard of fitness.

This was what Wally needed for his son. But it was unlikely that this Registrar bloke was corruptible; even if he was, he was too important, too traceable. Perhaps the person who had typed the letter? But the letter was roneoed.

Somebody had to be responsible for such letters, however, Wally thought as he made his way to the National Service Registration offices. After he'd made some innocuous general enquiries, he asked the man behind the counter where the men's lavatory was and then disappeared for several minutes. Nobody noticed when he reappeared and took a wrong turning.

The typing pool was a long, rectangular room with a number of women, mostly young, little more than girls, seated at desks against the walls. With busy fingers the girls rattled away at their typewriters, the staccato clack of the keys like miniature castanets.

A bespectacled, middle-aged woman sat at a desk on a platform at the far end of the room, like a schoolmistress overseeing her class. Occasionally she left her own typewriter to prowl past the desks, peering at the girls' work and collecting from their out baskets.

Wally enquired after her name at the front counter and left.

Phyllis Pickford was a smart woman. A woman who could have done all the men's jobs in the department. A single woman, she had devoted herself to her career. She was as qualified as the men, more intelligent than most, but because she was a woman she had graduated to head of the typing pool and remained there for fifteen years. Although she enjoyed her position of power within the small area over which she reigned, Phyllis was just a little bitter at her lack of advancement.

'Miss Pickford?' He greeted her as she left the offices two days later. He'd made his enquiries in the interim, and he knew a lot about her.

'Yes.' Phyllis recognised Wally Kendall immediately. She had seen his picture in the business and social pages of the newspapers. In the flesh, despite the extra weight he was carrying, he was far more attractive than the newspaper photographs depicted; he was almost handsome in fact.

'Wally Kendall of Kendall Markets. How do you do.' He offered his hand.

'Mr Kendall,' she said and she shook his hand firmly, briskly, as if she met men of Wally Kendall's ilk every day of the week.

'I wondered whether we might have a cup of coffee,' Wally smiled. 'A little matter I'd like to discuss.' She was about forty-five, he guessed, and could have been attractive if she'd done something about her hair which was greying and scraped back into a severe French roll. And what did she have against makeup? Still, she'd kept her figure. Beneath the beige skirt and brown twin set was a neat little body.

She looked at her watch, pretending she had an appointment. 'Yes,' she agreed, wondering what on earth Wally Kendall could want with her, 'I have time for a quick coffee.'

'I won't beat about the bush,' Wally said as they sat down at the booth in the far end of the coffee lounge. But he did, he needed to soften her up. He told her that his wife had died fourteen years ago, and that he'd been left with three children to rear on his own.

'A son and two daughters,' he said, smiling fondly. 'They were difficult times I can tell you, but I wouldn't swap those years watching them grow up for a thousand quid. 'Course, they're nearly adults now. Well, Wallace is, he's twenty this year.'

He looked even more attractive when he spoke about his

children, Phyllis thought. 'What exactly is it you want of me, Mr Kendall?' She asked the question gently enough, but she was direct, it was time somebody got to the point.

He told her. In no uncertain terms. And Phyllis was shocked. She stared at him, barely able to believe what she was hearing.

'He's my only son, Miss Pickford,' Wally was still playing the fond father. 'I'll do anything to prevent him going to war. His medical examination's next week. When the results come through, it'd be so easy for you, they're only draft letters, and of course I'd make it well worth your while ...'

'I'm sorry, Mr Kendall,' her lips were set in a thin, hard line, 'what you ask is out of the question.' She rose to go.

'Fifty thousand dollars.'

She sat down heavily. It was the shock. She needed to catch her breath. That was twenty-five thousand pounds! Australia had only recently converted to decimal currency and Phyllis still thought in pounds, shillings and pence.

'In cash,' Wally added.

She must leave, the man was outrageous, she could not be bought.

He put his hand over hers. 'Fifty thousand dollars is a lot of money, Phyllis.' There was concern in his voice, kindness, as if her wellbeing were important to him. 'You could buy a house, you could set yourself up for life with fifty thousand.'

'It's not as easy as you think,' she heard herself say. 'It's more than just a draft letter, there is other correspondence, there are records, lists.'

'I'm sure there are, but then you're a very clever woman, Miss Pickford.' Wally smiled winningly. Everyone had their price.

Kitty and Artie were only too grateful that their son Rob was too young to go to war, but they were nonetheless passionate in their anticonscription beliefs.

Kitty joined the SOS, a movement of mothers opposing the conscription of their sons for Vietnam, and she and Artie regularly took part in antiwar marches and sit-ins. They demonstrated alongside the 'flower power' hippies who wore bright kaftans and beads, headbands and sandals. These youngsters reminded Kitty of herself at their age; youth didn't really change all that much, she thought.

Every evening Kitty and Artie sat glued to their television set, watching the American reports on the war, even footage of the combat itself filmed by intrepid teams of cameramen and war correspondents. Since the Australians' clumsy introduction to television in 1956, the medium had grown to become a sophisticated purveyor of the news, and it brought the Vietnam War into people's lounge rooms.

At the commencement of the Tet Offensive on 31 January 1968, when the Vietcong and North Vietnamese troops attacked US military installations throughout South Vietnam, television coverage showed that the Americans were not winning the war as they would have the world believe. People realised that they had been lied to and that the war was far from over.

Students were arrested for handing out 'Don't Register' leaflets, and those draft evaders who openly burned their cards and refused to comply risked a two-year gaol sentence. Many fled the authorities, hiding out in safehouses provided by a network of supporters. One such safehouse was in Campbell Parade, where Kitty and Artie regularly took in conscientious objectors.

By 1971 the Farinellis' house served as more than a refuge. Paul Dundas, a leading figure in the Draft Resisters Union of New South Wales, hid in the rooms upstairs and held secret meetings there. The DRU was only one organisation amongst many actively opposed to conscription, but it had a high profile and its key members were keenly sought by the police.

One morning, after Kitty and Artie had been sheltering Paul for a number of months, the phone rang.

'Quick, get him out. The police are here.'

Kitty recognised the voice of Andy Kaminskis from the pie shop downstairs. Andy had been in the country for fifteen years, but he still had a thick Latvian accent.

She raced to the lounge room and looked out the front windows to the busy street below. She could see no sign of police, but she had no reason to doubt Andy, he was sympathetic to their cause.

'Paul,' she urged, running back to the kitchen, 'the fire escape, quick, Andy reckons they're here.'

It was a Friday afternoon, Artie was at work and eighteen-year-old Rob at university. Thank Christ there hadn't been a meeting in progress.

Paul moved swiftly—two years on the run had taught him to be always at the ready for a quick escape. Shoving a couple of books into his backpack, he said, 'Get rid of any pamphlets, they might have a search warrant,' then he was out through the back kitchen door and onto the small landing which led to the fire escape and the courtyard below.

Kitty grabbed the pamphlets from the drawer in the lounge room, ripped some into shreds and flushed them down the toilet. Then another handful. But they choked the cistern and remained swirling in the bowl.

She dashed into the lounge room and threw the remaining leaflets into the fire grate. Matches, where the hell were the matches, she'd given up cigarettes years ago.

Downstairs, Andy Kaminskis was pretending he had trouble with his English.

'Policemen?' he said, looking the two plain-clothes detectives up and down, as if bewildered by the fact that they were not in uniform. One of them showed his identification. 'Ah,' Andy said and ushered them into his shop.

The man who was doing the talking said something about a search warrant, and Andy made a great show of taking them both through his pie shop and into the kitchen out the back where his wife made the steak sandwiches.

As his dumpy little wife, flustered and genuinely confused, distracted the men in the kitchen, Andy glanced out the back door to the courtyard in time to see Paul throw his backpack over the paling fence.

'You see?' Andy said from the doorway. 'Is all clean, no dirt in my shop.' The policeman tried to step out of the kitchen but Andy barred the way. 'You check the stove,' he insisted, 'you see is all very clean in my shop.'

Senior Detective Fulham was irritated. Bloody immigrants. 'We're not from the Health Department,' he snapped, 'we're Commonwealth police. Now show us the rest of the place.'

'Ah,' Andy nodded, seemingly impressed. 'Commonwealth. Very important.' And he fumbled about for a moment, trying clumsily to get out of their way.

Of course he'd known they were Commonwealth cops, their car had been a dead giveaway. The moment he'd seen it pull up out the front of the shop, Andy had known the HR Holden with the aerial in the middle of the roof was a Commonwealth police car. In the early days, when his papers had not been in order, Andy had learned to recognise any sign that might spell trouble.

By the time the detectives looked out the back, Paul had scaled the fence and disappeared.

The policemen examined the old reading room which had long been closed off and now served as a storeroom. Then, 'Upstairs,' Fulham demanded.

Andy looked blank.

'Show us upstairs.'

'Ah. Upstairs.' Andy grinned. 'Upstairs is not me. Upstairs is Farinelli's.'

The detectives looked at each other. 'Bugger it,' Fulham muttered. They'd been given only a number in Campbell Parade. And the number had been in big, blatant lettering above the shop. They'd presumed the shop was the front for the DRU safe house.

The toilet cistern was still flushing when Kitty let them in. But there was nothing in the bowl. And there were fresh ashes in the grate, still smoking a little.

'December, strange time for a fire,' Fulham said between clenched teeth.

'Just burning off a few bits of rubbish,' Kitty said brazenly, as if daring him to differ.

The men made a perfunctory search of the place, but they found nothing. That bastard foreigner downstairs, Fulham thought. He'd brick the bloke, he'd plant some dirt on him and get his shop closed down. Fulham didn't like being taken for a fool.

'We'll be watching this place from now on,' he warned Kitty.

'I don't know why on earth you'd bother,' she said as she saw them out the door.

She and Artie sent word through the network of supporters that the house in Campbell Parade was no longer safe. But the end was in sight and, barely a year later, there was no longer a need for such refuges.

Nine days after its historic victory, the Whitlam Labor Government withdrew Australia's last remaining military advisers from Vietnam. The troops would soon be on their way home.

*

Amongst the first wave of conscriptees, Jim Hamilton served two terms in Vietnam, surviving the Battle of Long Tan and the early horrors of the war, during which the Australian troops experienced the majority of their casualties.

He returned to Sydney a changed man. Physically uninjured he was nonetheless a casualty of the war. The army offered no form of counselling. It simply didn't occur to the military authorities that the aggression and violence which it had so successfully instilled into its raw young recruits might continue unchecked following their discharge.

Not long after his return, Jim and his friend Shorty Barber went to the Bondi RSL. Jim and Shorty, who was six foot four with a build to match, had served together in Vietnam and had become close mates.

They walked straight into the bar, ignoring the grizzled old bloke at the front door who seemed about to ask them something.

They plonked themselves down on the bar stools and Jim called out, 'Two schooners, mate, whatever's on tap.'

The barman looked up from the glass he was wiping and past them to the old bloke who'd appeared at the door.

'You boys members?' the barman asked.

'Course we are,' Jim said and he looked at Shorty who nodded. But behind them the old bloke was shaking his head.

'Sorry, can't serve you if you're not members,' and the barman put down the glass, picked up another from the tray on the bar, and continued wiping.

'You what?' The glint in Jim's eye was dangerous.

'Gotta be a member, mate, or you gotta be signed in by one.'

Jim looked around at the bar and lounge. There were half a dozen old men in the place, one bloke propped at the end of the bar, the others sitting in lounge chairs sipping their beers. 'R ... S ... L,' Jim spelled out slowly. 'Returned ... Servicemen's ... League.'

Shorty recognised the signs. The calm before the storm. 'Come on, Jim,' he said, 'let's go.'

But Jim ignored him. 'This is a club for returned soldiers, right?'

'Yep,' the barman nodded.

'So I'm a returned soldier, mate,' Jim snarled. 'How about you?' He stood and turned to face the men in the lounge. 'How many of you old bastards have been to war?' he yelled at the top of his voice.

Probably most of them, Shorty thought. 'Hey, Jim . . .' He tried to interrupt but, as usual, there was no stopping Jim once he'd started.

'Well I've been to bloody war, I've fought for this fucking country!' Jim shouted. 'I've fought so that old bludgers like you can sit on your fat fucking arses and do bugger-all all day!' He picked up two beer glasses out of the tray, one in each hand, and he hurled one, with all of his might, at the mirror behind the bar.

'Fucking bastards!' he yelled as the glass smashed and the mirror cracked. Then he hurled the other glass. 'Fucking bastards!'

He grabbed two more glasses.

'Get your mate out of here,' the barman said to Shorty as the old man at the door ducked out to call the police.

Shorty dragged Jim out of the bar. 'Come on, mate, let's get you home.'

One of the old men ducked as a glass careered past, and they all sat watching silently whilst Jim was hauled, screaming, through the door.

'Fucking bastards!' And the final glass smashed against the wall outside.

The nights were bad for Jim. Regularly he woke in a sweat, paralysed with fear, reliving his terror. He was lying in the mud of a riverbank. He could hear their voices. Four of them, Vietcong, not far away, getting closer now. And closer. Death was preferable to being taken alive, and the muzzle of his rifle was in his mouth, his finger on the trigger. Now? Should he do it now? Surely they could see him, their voices were directly above. But he daren't look up, he daren't make the slightest movement. Now? Slowly, his finger moved on the trigger. That was when he woke up.

There were the images, too, and the smell. The charred bodies, barely recognisable as human, the acrid stench of burning flesh, but worst by far were the heads on spikes.

In the dead of the night, the sheets sticky with his sweat, Jim saw the American's head. A sergeant he'd been, or that's what the Yanks who'd known him had said, and his severed penis had been stuffed into his mouth. A young American soldier Jim had met, just a kid, his helmet too big for his head, had had an obsession about doing the same thing to the Gooks. Every dead Gook he found, he cut its head off and shoved its dick into its mouth.

Jim often awoke gagging, the nights were bad for him. In fact Jim Hamilton was a bit of a mess altogether. As some soldiers aptly put it when describing casualties like Jim, the war had 'fucked his brain'.

Caroline knew that her son was suffering, but she was powerless to help. If she tried, he became irritable and accused her of fussing, so she left him alone. But her son's alienation was the final stamp upon Caroline's awful loneliness. Emma had been living in London for over three years, and Bruce had shifted from the Woolloomooloo house into a flat in Kensington with two other students. She understood, of course. He needed to be closer to New South Wales University where he was studying economics.

Caroline was extremely proud of Bruce, he would be the first of their family to achieve a university degree. How proud Kathleen would have been. But she sorely missed her youngest son. And perhaps if he'd been living at home, he could have helped Jim. Although Caroline knew, deep down, that nothing could help Jim.

Thankfully, Kitty visited often. Caroline wished she could be like Kitty, passionate and committed. Every day was full and exciting to Kitty. But Caroline found passion in nothing, and her days were empty and dull.

When the weather was fine, she idled away the hours walking through the Botanic Gardens and down to Circular Quay where she sat and gazed at the boats on the harbour and marvelled at the ever-expanding city.

The expansion was as much upward as outward. The AMP building had led the brigade in 1962, and others had soon followed—the State Office Block, Australia Square, like termite mounds, they clustered about the Quay, towering competitively to increasingly dizzy heights.

On Bennelong Point the country's most controversial building was slowly taking shape. Opinions were divided about the Sydney Opera House and its inflated cost. Some said it was an indulgence, and when its designer Joern Utzon had resigned from the project in 1966, the denigrators had been quick to label the thing a disaster. But there were those who loved its design and followed its progress with interest. Caroline was one.

On days when the weather was inclement, Caroline sat in front of the television set, taking little note of what she was watching but finding the midday American soap operas, and the noise in general, somehow comforting.

Kitty was most disapproving when she arrived to find Caroline in her dressing gown curled up on the sofa, mindlessly watching TV commercials which advocated to housewives the advantages of this or that soap powder for a whiter wash.

'For goodness' sake, Caroline, how can you?' Daytime television was a sin to Kitty. In fact she wasn't too sure about the evening variety, with the exception of the news.

Kitty would then switch the set off and make them a coffee, and Caroline would say, 'You're so bossy,' but she was always pleased to see Kitty. Kitty Farinelli was a breath of fresh air.

It was early in '73 Tim Kendall died, or rather, in Kitty's opinion, gave up. Not long before his eightieth birthday he retired from the company and took to his bed. He'd served his purpose, he told his daughter as she sat by his bedside. He enjoyed talking to Kitty, he could be honest with her.

He couldn't with Ruth. Ruth would nag him, but then he could tell she was frightened. 'For goodness' sake, Tim,' she'd say, 'get up and have a walk, just a gentle one, get some fresh air in your lungs. It's what the doctor recommends.' Poor Ruth, still vigorous and young for her years, she didn't know what it was like to feel constantly worn out and exhausted.

Tim was not enjoying old age. He hated the fact that his body was letting him down, that he no longer had the stamina to run the company and call the shots. He was not one to enjoy sitting with a book, or listening to music, or taking a gentle walk now and then.

He'd tied up all the loose ends. There were trust accounts and property investments left to Ruth and Kitty so that they would be wealthy in their own right.

'But I'm leaving my shares in the company to Wally and the partners,' he told Kitty. 'They've worked hard, they've earned it.'

'You're giving up, aren't you, Dad?'

Kitty knew, he thought gratefully. But then Kitty always knew, there'd never been secrets between them. And he did so love the way she cut to the chase.

'Yes,' he admitted.
'Why?'
'Because I'm bored,' he said. 'Tired, and very, very bored.'
A week later, Tim Kendall died in his sleep.

Having escaped the war, young Wallace Kendall had gone from strength to strength. Old Tim Kendall had died and Wallace's own father, Wally, in ill health and rapidly aging, had retired. So, at the tender age of twenty-seven, Wallace Kendall had become the driving force behind the successful chain of Kendall Markets.

Gradually, over several years, Wallace replaced the older board members, retiring them prematurely with healthy payouts and replacing them with younger members, among them, his friend Bruce Hamilton.

Then Wally Kendall had a stroke. In 1975, at sixty-six years of age, grossly overweight, his body had finally succumbed to the years of cigars, heavy drinking and general good living.

It was a debilitating stroke and the doctor said he would never recover; in fact it was quite likely a further stroke would follow. So a live-in nurse was hired to meet Wally's every need, and the family, his wife Darlene in particular, watched and waited for the inevitable.

Wally was reduced to a pathetic figure. Confined to a wheelchair, with no movement save for the fingers of his left hand which twitched and trembled continuously. Everything about him was twisted, grotesque: his crippled spine, his drooping right eye, his dribbling mouth. So impaired was his speech that the words he bravely struggled to muster came out as an indiscernible growl. But, unbeknown to his family, beneath the pitiful exterior, Wally's mind was intact. His brain was as alert as ever, and his inability to communicate this was torture.

He could hear them talking about him as if he wasn't there.

'The lawyer said everything's in order,' Lucy informed her sister Julia and her stepmother Darlene, whilst Wally listened from his wheelchair only yards away. 'Daddy kept his will up to date. Joe wouldn't give me the details of course, but he said it's most equitable.'

Good on you, Joe. He'd like to see Joe, Wally thought.

Wally's lawyer, friend and ally of thirty years, Joe Davison, had visited him in the hospital, and again shortly after his return home, but he'd not been back for the past several weeks.

Bugger it, I want to see Joe. Can one of you bloody women get Joe?

Wally scowled and his eyes flashed angrily, but if any of the women noticed, they put his grimaces down to his affliction.

'Right we are, pet, time for our walk.' It was the nurse, come to wheel him out onto the verandah as she did every late afternoon.

The nurse, the bloody nurse, she was the worst of the lot. An old battleaxe. Couldn't they have found a pretty one?

'Comfy are we?' she said. She always spoke at him, never to him. She never looked into his eyes for any response, expecting none.

She shoved a pill into his mouth and poured water down his throat until he gagged. Sometimes she even massaged his throat to help the pill go down, just as if he was a dog. Christ how he wished they'd get rid of her. *Sack her. Sack her.* Wally practised and practised the words over and over, but they always came out the same growl, and people had given up taking any notice.

To her credit, Julia had tried at first. 'What is it, Dad? Something you want?' But his vocal contortions sounded so like groans, that she invariably called the nurse who gave him a painkiller or a hot-water bottle, or simply adjusted his cushions and scolded him.

But Wally never stopped practising in private. He practised blinking, learning to control the involuntary fluttering of his eyelids, and he practised specific movements with the fingers of his left hand, that they might be read as messages. But most of all he practised his words. *Get Joe.* He concentrated on just the two.

As he thought of the words he fought desperately to move his tongue. *Get Joe.* But his tongue sat in his mouth like a useless piece of dead meat. Wally inwardly cursed, but he didn't give up. *Get Joe.* And gradually, a month or so after his stroke, he found he could make some contact between the back of his tongue and his soft palate, producing a sort of guttural consonant.

He waited for Wallace's visit. The women saw him too regularly to notice any difference, they'd given up looking.

'G'day, Dad,' Wallace said as he joined him on the verandah, bending low over the stooped form in the wheelchair in order to see his father's face. 'And how are we today?' he asked loudly.

I'm not a moron, you dumb bastard, and I'm not deaf. Even his son spoke to him like he was a halfwit.

He blinked. Three times. Very hard. And he didn't make a sound as he stared at his son.

Wallace was taken aback. Where were the groans? Where were the flickering eyelids? Then he saw the forefinger of his father's left hand. He was no longer clutching feebly at the rug on his knees. He was tapping his forefinger. Three times he tapped. Then he stopped.

'Dad?' Wallace knelt by the chair. His father was trying to make contact, he knew it.

Got him. Wally fought to position his tongue, but he didn't make a sound until he could see his son's face very close to his.

Then 'Heh . . . Hoe,' he said, with all the force he could muster. *Bugger it, it didn't sound right.*

This was more than the customary groan, Wallace thought, there was a definite sound there, his father was trying to say something.

'I'm here, Dad, I'm here,' he said. 'What is it you want to say?'

Jesus Christ, boy, if only it was that simple. Wally forced himself not to make a sound. He wanted to. In his frustration, he wanted to groan and growl as loudly as he could. But he didn't. His son was watching him, that was all he needed. He blinked his eyes. Three times, quickly. Three times, slowly. Then three times, quickly again. *SOS, you stupid bugger.*

Wallace got the message. 'Oh Jesus, Dad, you're talking to me.'

Bloody right I am.

'You want help?'

Wally sighed with relief.

Blink once for yes, Wallace said, and Wally did.

'Oh God, Dad, what can I do?'

Wally concentrated on the lump of useless tongue in his mouth. 'Heh . . . Hoe.'

'Heck hoe?'

Oh shit! Wally tensed his throat muscles, and with all of his might he thrust the back of his tongue against his soft palate. 'Geh . . .' *Triumph. He'd made a real sound.* 'Geh . . . Hoe.' The tip of his tongue wouldn't work. He couldn't make the 't' or the 'j'.

'You want me to get you something, Dad?'

Wally made no movement, his eyes starting to water as he stared at his son, forcing his eyelids not to flutter.

'Someone. You want me to get someone.'

Wally blinked. Just once. For yes. He mustn't get excited. And he tapped the forefinger of his left hand.

'Joe. You want me to get Joe.'

Oh you beautiful boy. The tears welled in Wally's eyes. He blinked. Once.

'Time for our medication.' The nurse was there with the pills. But neither of them took any notice. Wallace was staring into his father's eyes as he knelt on the floor beside him.

'Excuse me, Mr Kendall,' the nurse said, 'it's time for our medication.'

'Ach . . . her,' Wally said. Wallace concentrated upon his father's eyes. They rolled up into his head, as if Wally were raising his face to look at the nurse, which he couldn't of course, but the eyes said it all. Then they rolled back in their sockets. 'Ach . . . her,' Wally said, staring at his son.

'Rightio, Dad.' Wallace winked. 'I'll sack her,' he murmured, 'and we'll get you a pretty one, right?'

Wally wept unreservedly that night. God how he loved his son.

Wallace immediately replaced the nurse, giving no reason to his sisters and Darlene other than the fact that his father should have someone prettier to look after him, seeing as he always had an eye for the women. Which didn't go down at all well with Darlene, but when he insisted upon footing the nursing expenses himself, she agreed without further argument. And several days later Joe Davison visited.

Wallace deliberately chose a Saturday when the house would be empty. He gave the new nurse the afternoon off, and as he led Joe into the study he told the maid not to disturb them. He'd told no-one but Joe of the contact he'd made with his father.

Communication didn't take long with Joe. He'd brought along an alphabet chart which he sat on Wally's lap. All Wally had to do was point, with his left forefinger, at the letters he wanted.

Joe was moved by the sight of his old friend trying so desperately to communicate, and more than a little guilt-ridden. 'I'm sorry I haven't been to see you for a while, Wally, but I didn't think there was much point. I didn't know.' His shrug was deeply apologetic.

'O ... K.' Wally laboriously pointed at the letters.

Joe had been mystified as to the need for secrecy. 'But the girls'll be thrilled to know they can talk to their father,' he'd said over the phone when Wallace had suggested they say nothing to them for the moment.

'Oh, of course I intend to tell them, but it only happened the other day, and Dad decided one thing at a time. He thought that everybody crowding in at once might be a bit much, and you're the first person he wants to see.' Joe had been flattered until Wallace had added, 'Oh, and he'd like you to bring along his will.'

'I believe it's your decision not to tell the girls?' Joe studied Wally's eyes for any sign of surprise; he didn't trust young Wallace for an instant. 'I believe that you wanted to see me first?'

Wally pointed to 'Y' for yes. He wasn't sure about the decision not to tell the girls, he'd simply gone along with Wallace's suggestion, but he'd certainly wanted to see Joe. Now more than ever.

'There's some changes you want made in your will, I believe?'

'Y' for yes.

'Of course.' Joe didn't like it one bit. 'Wallace, if you'd mind leaving us.'

Wallace hesitated and looked at his father.

'Y' for yes. *Go on, boy. Out.* Joe, a stickler for protocol, would never discuss a will in the presence of one of the beneficiaries, or anyone else for that matter. *Good old Joe. Straight as a die.*

Wallace reluctantly left the room.

Forty minutes later, Joe closed the study door behind him and joined Wallace in the lounge room.

'I could refuse to accept this will on the grounds that your father was not of sound mind when he changed it.' He saw the fear in Wallace's eyes. 'But of course he is of sound mind, and we both know it. And with his present mental abilities, I doubt you'd have much difficulty gaining medical opinion to that effect.'

Wallace relaxed.

'But you'll have no cause to do so,' Joe continued. 'Your father wishes to change his will and I cannot convince him otherwise. Although it will cause an irreparable split in your family, Wallace. I hope you realise that.'

'I don't know what you're talking about, Joe,' Wallace feigned surprise. 'My father's will is his own affair.'

Cheeky young bastard, Joe thought. God only knew how he'd done it. But then even as a boy Wallace had always been able to wrap his old man around his little finger.

'I suggest you let the girls know they can speak to their father,' Joe said. 'I'll be ringing Darlene tomorrow to tell her as much myself.'

'Oh, I intend to tell them tonight, Joe. Of course. Like you say, they'll be thrilled.'

Wally Kendall died of a massive stroke two months later. His shares in Kendall Markets, his cash and his property investments, were all divided equally between his wife and three children. But it was Wallace Kendall who, alone, inherited the family home.

Julia and Lucy were horrified. It had been common knowledge that their father had intended to leave the old house to all three of his children. It wasn't so much the money, although the property was worth a fortune. The three of them had made an agreement that the old home would remain intact, even if one sibling purchased it from the others. Their children and their children's children, they had all agreed, would be free to experience the idyllic childhood they themselves had had in the old house down on the harbour.

'Why did he do it?' Julia demanded.

'You were always his favourite, Wallace,' Lucy said. 'Perhaps that's why.'

To the credit of both women, neither of them blamed Wallace. But even as he shook his head, mystified and apologetic, he could have told them why.

'I love this place, Dad,' he'd said during the several afternoons he'd had Wally all to himself, before Joe's visit. He'd looked out at the harbour and the tennis court, the jetty and the swimming pool. 'The times we've had here, eh? I tell you, I wouldn't change this place for a million quid.'

Good on you, boy. Wally loved hearing his son talk like this, it brought back all the memories.

'Remember the time I fell out of the mulberry tree and broke my nose?' Wallace knelt in front of the wheelchair and wiggled his nose comically. 'See, it never healed straight.' It was true, Wallace's crooked nose was at odds with his otherwise handsome face.

There were many such reminiscences during those afternoons,

until Wallace dropped the bombshell. 'Pity the girls want to demolish the house,' he said, fondly patting the verandah railing upon which he was sitting. 'Whatever they put up, it'll never be the same.'

What? His father's horrified eyes blinked twice for no.

'Yeah, it's a bugger, isn't it?' Wallace agreed. 'But you know women, they like modern things.'

Two more blinks. And his father's breathing was becoming agitated.

'I'm sorry, Dad, I didn't mean to upset you.' He knelt by the wheelchair. 'But there's nothing I can do.'

Oh yes there bloody well is. One blink. For yes.

Wallace looked puzzled for a moment or so, and then realisation appeared to dawn. 'Well, yes,' he said slowly, 'I suppose there is. I suppose if you left the place to me, then we'd know that it'd be safe.'

One blink.

Easy. It had been that easy.

Three years after his father's death, Wallace demolished the old family home to build his harbourside mansion, and in doing so alienated his sisters forever.

It was very unrealistic of them, Wallace thought. Who on earth maintained such architectural dinosaurs? Who on earth kept hold of rambling old colonial houses on harbourside frontages where every square metre of land was worth a fortune? Romantic rubbish. His sisters were businesswomen, they should recognise progress.

But Julia and Lucy wanted nothing more to do with their brother. As members of the Kendall Markets board of directors, they were forced to deal with him however. That changed a few years later when all ties were severed. It seemed that the family business was not enough for Wallace, he wanted to expand. He had ambitious ideas which could make millions for Kendall Markets if the board wished to be adventurous.

But they didn't. Kendall Markets had no desire to invest in Wallace's entrepreneurial schemes. So he sold his shares, mortgaged his mansion and, with a healthy cash base and breakthrough concepts, was welcomed with open arms by the Tricontinental Merchant Bank.

Chapter Eighteen

As a borrower, Wallace Kendall met Tricontinental's guidelines to perfection. He had the ideas and the cashflow and Tricontinental, unlike other merchant banks, was prepared to be as supportive as necessary.

This was 1980 after all. Gone were the days when people borrowed at low, and realistic, interest rates. Now, with financial deregulation, credit was unlimited and the banks encouraged their clients to borrow heavily. There was money enough for everyone, they would all grow wealthy together.

When Wallace left Kendall Markets, he took with him his fellow board member and lifelong friend, Bruce Hamilton. He needed Bruce's sound financial commonsense to temper the flamboyance of Jason Bruford.

Jason Bruford, Harvard-educated corporate lawyer, thirty-three years of age, just one year younger than Wallace, was confident, groomed and smooth-talking. He'd made a deep impression on Wallace from the moment they'd first met, which was at one of Packer's lavish annual functions designed to impress his publishing syndicate's major clients and associates.

'Good God, man, you have all these assets, all this cash at your fingertips, and you're not expanding?' Jason had appeared horror-struck with disbelief. 'You should move with the times.'

It had been Jason Bruford who had inspired Wallace. Indeed, the man remained a force to be reckoned with throughout the rapid growth of what was to become the Kendall Corporation. But Wallace remained the power behind the throne, despite the fact that he modelled himself upon Jason. Within only months of their meeting, Wallace had dropped his earthy Australian image. Gone were the casual work clothes and in their place sleek designer suits. These days Wallace dressed impeccably, and carried a slim, black briefcase wherever he went, just as Jason did, though he drew the line at growing a pencil moustache like Jason's. A pager was always at the ready in the top pocket of his jacket, and he wore dark glasses when it wasn't necessary.

His friend's change of image irritated Bruce Hamilton enormously. He refused to call Jason 'JB' as Wallace did, loathing the American use of acronyms, and when Wallace had had the effrontery to refer to him as 'BH', he had made his thoughts on the matter quite clear.

'What do you think, BH?' Wallace had asked innocently enough.

'Oh for God's sake, Wallace, my name's Bruce and you bloody well know it.' He glared at Wallace and Jason across the boardroom table. 'Call me BH once more, either of you, and you'll cop Wal and Jase from me, and you won't like that in public, will you?'

But even Bruce had to admit that the three of them made a formidable team. Wallace Kendall, Chairman of the Board, bold, innovative; Jason Bruford, Managing Director, expert on the state of the market, knowing when to buy up a failing company, when to sell; and he, Bruce Hamilton, keeping the other two in check, tempering their enthusiasm with sound financial management.

Bruce Hamilton wasn't too sure if he liked Jason Bruford, but perhaps that was because Jason Bruford was a homosexual, a fact which made Bruce a little uncomfortable. Jason went to no pains to disguise his persuasion. In fact he even seemed boastful of it, which Bruce had to admit was brave. Sydney might be becoming a city of poofters as some said, and homos were certainly a dime a dozen, particularly in the eastern suburbs, but in the corporate world it was wisest to keep quiet if one was homosexual.

Bruce was a good bloke by most people's standards, one who rarely took a dislike to others, and he tried to be fair. It was because Jason had turned Wallace into a bit of a poseur, that was it, he decided. He didn't like Jason Bruford because the man was manipulative. Not that it mattered, he had the feeling that Jason considered him a touch plebeian and didn't much like him either.

It was Shangri-La Chalets which put Kendall Enterprises well and truly on the map.

'They're broke and they're desperate. The place is only four years old, in perfect nick and we can buy it for half its market value,' Jason said.

Shangri-La was a five-star resort in Queensland. Superbly designed, it sat on green, hilly slopes and was surrounded by rainforest. The resort consisted of forty split-level luxury chalets, hidden amongst the hills, each private, secluded and complete with spa and sundeck.

Nestled in the valley below was a superb cordon bleu restaurant with its own wine cellar, a large piano bar overlooking the valley, and a cigar lounge with an open log fireplace at one end. Even in Queensland the winter nights could be chilly.

The resort also boasted an eighteen-hole golf course, two tennis courts, an Olympic-size swimming pool and a gymnasium for those who liked to temper their hedonism with a healthy workout. So why had the owners gone bankrupt?

'The hills,' Wallace said. 'It's the hills. No-one's going to pay five-star prices to walk up hills.'

'A miniature railway system?' Bruce suggested. 'Or cable cars?'

'No, no,' Jason said dismissively, 'mini-mokes. A guest simply picks up a phone and dials a mini-moke and a driver. They'd have to be on tap twenty-four hours a day of course, so—'

'Too expensive, too complicated, and there's a much better way,' Wallace interrupted.

His idea was simple. Pure genius.

The place was converted into a health resort. The hills were marketed as 'incidental exercise'. Shangri-La had been deliberately designed, the guests were told, to ensure that they received a daily workout as they walked from their luxury chalets to the restaurant or the lecture room—the converted bar—where expert advice on nutrition, diet and exercise was offered, or to the pampering lounge—the cigar room—where beauticians administered facials and massages. 'Incidental exercise', they were informed with all due seriousness, was as important to their stay at Shangri-La Chalets as was the daily regime of tai chi, meditation, circuit training and swimming.

Wallace poached the manager from a popular health resort in

the Blue Mountains, offered the personal trainer of an Olympic marathon runner twice what the Olympian could afford, and hired a top nutritionist and chef, as well as several beauticians and masseurs. After a fanfare of publicity and marketing hype, Shangri-La Chalets never looked back.

With Jason's shrewd eye, Bruce's tough financial negotiation, and the limitless support of Tricontinental, Wallace acquired other properties which had lost their way, and set about creating a series of thematic resorts to appeal to specific markets. That was what it was all about. Marketing. Target your market correctly and you couldn't go wrong.

The Kendall Family Resort on the Gold Coast was the next acquisition. No flashy name, no flashy prices. Well within the working man's budget, the Kendall Family Resort offered not only value for money but all the beauty and comfort of a five-star resort. Brand new, it boasted rooms with verandahs or terraces, for all the world like luxury suites. The massive swimming pool was landscaped with an island in the middle, and even the children's wading pool had a miniature fountain, a smiling dolphin which squirted water on the toddlers as they crawled about.

Regular competitions were run, prior to the resort's opening, for lucky families to win a week's holiday at the luxurious Kendall Family Resort. When interviewed by the press, the families agreed that the Kendall Family Resort was every bit as impressive as the glossy brochures had boasted.

But, shoddily built with cheap materials, its gloss would not last long, and the Kendall Corporation sold it after three years, ensuring that its new owners would be blamed for its eventual shabbiness.

The Kendall Corporation had gone public with a massive publicity campaign, and the company's stockmarket value steadily rose as small buyers queued up for shares in such a substantial commodity. It was heartening to the small stockholder to be able to see where his money was going. To witness the opulence and success of the Kendall resorts and to know that he owned a small part of it all.

'Wealth certainly doesn't buy good taste. He's made a monstrosity of that beautiful family property, no wonder his sisters won't speak to him.'

Bruce Hamilton heaved a sigh. Kitty Farinelli was at it again. As soon as she'd arrived at his mother's house, she'd dived on the topic and worried it like a dog did a bone. As a lad, Bruce had found Kitty exciting. He'd fancied her. He and his brother Jim both had. Kitty Farinelli had been sexy and bold. She'd held passionate views on the most controversial of subjects like free love and abortion, and the Hamilton boys had found her slightly shocking and very attractive.

Bruce found her neither shocking nor attractive these days, although he had to admit that she was pretty damn good for her age. A little hatchet-faced perhaps, but still lean and lithe. Good God, she'd have to be in her late fifties and yet she had the body of a woman half her years. But he found her dogmatic and, at times, downright aggressive. Towards him, anyway.

To be fair, Bruce knew that Kitty picked on him because she was worried about his mother, but he wished she'd lay off. There was little he could do about his mother's predicament and he'd told Kitty as much when she'd delivered her lecture over six months ago. He'd called in to see Caroline and discovered the two women in the kitchen, where they'd been playing Scrabble.

'Do you want a lift home in my new car?' he'd asked Kitty, with all the eager pride of a ten-year-old. He loved showing off his new Mercedes Benz.

'But you've only been here ten minutes,' Kitty said.

'I know, just time for a quick cuppa, but I've got to dash.' He looked at his watch as he put his cup down. 'Big bad world of finance beckons. Mum understands, don't you, Mum?' He kissed Caroline on the cheek as he rose from the kitchen table.

'Of course I do, dear.' Caroline smiled proudly at Kitty. 'He's doing so well, he just got back from America last week.'

'I know, you told me.' Kitty smiled tightly at Bruce. 'You were there for a whole month, I believe.' So now that you're back, you could stay with your mother for longer than ten minutes surely, she thought. 'I am impressed,' she added a little archly.

'Bye, Mum,' Bruce said, wondering what he'd done to put Kitty's nose out of joint. 'I'll pop in next week. Want that lift, Kitty?'

'Well, I don't need a lift,' she'd driven as usual, 'but I'll accept a drive around the block in your brand new car.'

Damn, that hadn't been the offer at all. 'Okay,' he said pleasantly enough. 'Have to be a quick one though, I've got a meeting at three.'

Kitty hugged Caroline goodbye. She looked so old, Kitty thought, unhealthily bloated, her skin patchy, her poor hands like talons, crippled as they were with arthritis. Stoic as always, Caroline never complained, but Kitty worried terribly about her.

'Very impressive,' Kitty said as Bruce opened the passenger door. Then, as soon as they'd pulled out from the kerb, she got straight to the point.

'You should see more of your mother, Bruce, she's not well and she's lonely ...'

'I see her once a week when I'm in town, Kitty,' he said mildly, although he found the criticism a little offensive.

'... she needs you,' she barged on regardless. 'Emma barely even phones any more ...'

If the truth be known, it was Emma who really raised Kitty's ire. Selfish little bitch. Her husband earned a fortune, they holidayed twice annually with business friends, St Moritz in the winter, the south of France in the summer, and yet she'd been home to see her mother just once in the last five years.

Caroline always came to Emma's defence of course. 'Gordon is feting his clients,' she'd say, 'he needs his wife with him. And there's an open offer for me to visit them at any time. They even sent me a first-class return ticket.'

Well that was so easy for them, wasn't it? And they bloody well knew she'd never take them up on it. The one trip she'd made to London had nearly killed her. Her sciatica was so bad she hadn't been able to walk for three days after she'd got there, and then for another week after she'd got back. Emma was a selfish little bitch.

'... and Jim,' Kitty continued, 'well, Jim's of no use. It's up to you to—'

'I visit Jim once a week too,' Bruce interrupted. They were turning from Macleay Street into Darlinghurst Road at the top of the Cross and she hadn't once commented on the car or even looked out the window. 'I visit Jim and I visit Mum, both of them, once a week whenever I can,' he continued evenly, 'and I'm a very busy man, it's all the time I can afford.'

Christ, what did the woman expect of him? He'd offered to buy his mother a new house, but she didn't want to move. He'd helped support his poor, pathetic brother for years. A drunk who lived alone on a war pension, his wife having deserted him, and who could blame her. Christ alive, he felt sorry for both his mother and his brother, and he helped them in every way he could, but he had a highly successful and demanding career, he couldn't sit around and hold their hands all day. Jesus, he didn't even have time for a social life, he didn't even have a girlfriend.

'But surely you can spare a little more than ten minutes when you visit her, Bruce?' Kitty never knew when to stop. 'A little more time, that's all I'm asking.'

'Time is the one commodity I don't have, Kitty,' he said stuffily as they turned into William Street; he couldn't wait to get her out of the car. 'I don't think you quite understand. I work in the corporate world, I have responsibilities to my companies, to my stockholders.'

Kitty knew she'd annoyed him with her nagging. She hadn't meant to. But he'd changed. Dear, nice, mild Bruce Hamilton had grown pompous and self-important. What a pity. Bruce had always been one of those good all-round blokes Kitty had thought would never change.

They sat in silence, each deep in thought, until they returned to the house in Woolloomooloo. Bruce said, 'Kitty, I didn't mean to sound . . .' just as Kitty began, 'I didn't mean to nag . . .'

They smiled at each other. 'I do care,' Bruce said. 'I love Mum very much and I care a great deal.'

'I know you do.' She patted his hand; perhaps the old Bruce Hamilton was there underneath. And she had been pushy. She'd grown cantankerous of late. Arturo's illness hadn't helped. Nor the fact that he'd wished her to keep it a secret. He didn't want people's sympathy, he'd said.

Caroline was the only person she'd told. Artie had undergone a series of radiation treatments, and the cancer was currently in remission, but nothing was certain and they lived on the knife-edge of hope.

She got out of the car. 'I know you love her, Bruce,' she said. Before she closed the door, she bent down and added through the open window, 'Just spare a little more time for her, that's all I ask.'

Bruce had shaken his head as he'd driven off. Kitty Farinelli just couldn't bloody help herself.

'It's an eyesore, an absolute eyesore. Wallace should be shot for such desecration.'

And here was Kitty, going on again.

'He's bought the property next door, you know,' Bruce said just to shock her.

'The pretty one with the terraces down to the water?'

'Yep.'

'Oh well, that's tasteful enough.'

'He's going to mow it down and build a three-storey mansion with a helipad on the roof.'

'A what?'

'A helipad, so that he can land his helicopter on top of his home.'

Kitty's face was laughable, a picture of horror, and Caroline smiled at Bruce, aware that he was baiting her.

Bruce grinned back at his mother, but he shook his head as he said, 'It's no joke, Mum, it's a fact.'

'My God,' Caroline laughed, 'the man's a megalomaniac.'

'What do his neighbours have to say about this helipad thing?' Kitty demanded to know.

'Oh there'll be complaints, I'm sure, and they'll try to stop him, but Wallace has the council in his pocket, I reckon he'll pull it off.'

That wasn't quite true, there was one councillor who was proving a lot of trouble. Bernard Williams couldn't be bought, and he was heavily on the side of the local residents. Bruce secretly admired the man for his stance, but Jason had said he'd look after it, and Bruce had no doubt that, through whatever nefarious means he chose, Jason Bruford would do exactly that.

'Wallace is a very powerful man now, Kitty,' Bruce continued, 'very powerful and very wealthy.'

Kitty refused to be impressed. 'He's still a vulgarian. Like I said, money doesn't buy good taste. What he's done to that beautiful property's downright disgraceful, and now it appears he's going to repeat the exercise. Somebody must stop him. The harbourside should belong to the people of Sydney, not to the rich vulgarians who want to desecrate—'

'I have to go,' Bruce interrupted, kissing Caroline on the cheek. 'Bye, Mum.'

'No, no,' Kitty insisted, rising from her chair, 'you stay, I can always come back tomorrow. I have plenty of time to share with your mother . . .'

Was that a deliberate dig, Bruce wondered.

'Kitty,' he said firmly, 'I've been here for an hour and a half, I have to go!'

'Oh all right.' Unperturbed, Kitty sat down again. An hour and a half, well that was better than ten minutes.

'He's a good son,' Caroline said pointedly when he'd gone.

'Yes, I know.'

'And you're a bugger of a friend.' Caroline never found Kitty offensive, brittle and aggressive as she could be. The poor woman was a bundle of nerves, and who could blame her? Caroline wished she could have told her son the truth about Artie, but she'd been sworn to secrecy. 'You'll frighten the poor boy off the way you carry on,' she smiled. 'Honestly, Kitty, if there was one poor sheep alone in a paddock, you'd worry it to death, I swear you would.'

Fifty-year-old Bernard Williams was a man with a conscience. Not only had he never accepted a bribe, he had never made use of privileged information to gain or sell a property, as many of his colleagues had, nor had he ever traded information for favours. Bernard was scrupulously ethical.

A devoted Rotarian and tireless charity worker, he was an unprepossessing little man in appearance. Grey-haired, bespectacled and somewhat colourless. But he was not meek when challenged and, over the years, he had achieved quite a reputation in the press. Unintentionally of course, he did not seek headlines, but one bright journalist had called him 'the mild-mannered tiger' and the name had stuck.

He was voicing the views of local residents when he opposed Wallace Kendall's monstrous three-storey mansion, and the helicopter landing pad, which guaranteed noise pollution for all. Over his dead body, Bernard said in an interview with the local *Wentworth Courier*.

'Which could be arranged,' Jason muttered to Wallace with such deadly humour that Wallace wondered whether perhaps he was serious. 'But there are other ways,' Jason added.

'Whatever,' Wallace said. 'Just do it.'

Mike Lowe, talkback radio king and darling to the millions who hung on his every insincere word, had opened his breakfast programme with the subject of Sydney's Gay Mardi Gras.

'Should it be banned?' he demanded, as if he cared. 'Should it be encouraged?' The voice of command had just the right edge of concern and query; Mike was keen to hear his listeners' views, he said. Then the patronising ploy (he could afford to be patronising, few of his fans were poofters): 'And, should it, I ask you, be called 'Gay and Lesbian'? Why not just 'Gay'? Surely 'gay' means homosexual persons of both gender?'

Mike was pleased, the Gay Mardi Gras was a nicely controversial subject to get the morning up and going. People were bound to ring up and complain about Sodom and Gomorrah, as they had for the past eight years since the parade's inception. He'd booked the Reverend Fred Nile for eleven o'clock. Fred'd have a lot to say about such unnatural, deviant behaviour, which would get the militant poofters riled. It promised to be an exciting morning.

'I'm ringing about Councillor Bernard Williams,' the male caller said.

'Yes, what about him?' It was an hour and a half later and, with the exception of one lesbian caller who had taken offence at Mike's suggestion that lesbians be labelled 'female gays', all the calls had been one-sided. 'Have the thing banned'; 'It makes me ashamed to be a Sydneysider,' 'Bloody disgraceful, that's what it is'. The show was becoming boring. Mike had expected a bit more feedback from the militant homosexuals out there; maybe he'd cancel the interview with Nile.

'It's his duty,' the male caller said. 'His duty to stand up and be counted.'

'Counted as what?'

'Gay, that's what.'

Mike glanced up at his producer on the other side of the recording booth's glass panels. They shared a brisk nod and the producer dialled Mike's investigator; they'd need to do some research for Mike to back up the story in his weekly newspaper column.

'Ummm . . .' ponderous tone, '. . . may I ask who's calling?'

'I'd rather not give my name,' the voice with the effeminate twang replied, 'but I can promise you I have my facts straight. And, for the sake of we, the gay minority, people like Bernard Williams should come out of their closets and back our cause.'

'Why?' Mike adopted the voice of concern whilst he incited the caller. 'If indeed your claim is correct, and of course it may well be slanderous, why should Councillor Williams expose his private life for public examination?'

'Because we, the gay minority, will never win social acceptance whilst there are those like Bernard Williams who hide their homosexuality as if it was something to be ashamed of.'

'I see, I see,' Mike said, delighted with the turn the show had taken. The switchboard was lit up with incoming calls. 'Well, if you'd like to stay on the line, we'll get back to you shortly.'

He wouldn't, at least not until the radio station had checked with their legal eagles, they didn't want to risk a law suit.

'In the meantime,' he said, 'we have a number of calls waiting, in fact the switchboard is going mad.' Voice of command once more. 'What do you think, all you out there listening? Do you believe in "outing"? I'm Mike Lowe and I'm waiting to hear from you. Yes, Gwenneth?'

'Cheers,' Jason said. 'To talkback radio, and to the idiots who rule the airwaves, long may they live.' He and Wallace clinked glasses.

They were sitting by Wallace's pool, in their Speedos, celebrating, just the two of them, taking advantage of the lull in proceedings before chaos took over and the bulldozers arrived to demolish the property next door. Wallace would move into his city penthouse when they did. They hadn't asked Bruce Hamilton to join them, because he hadn't approved of their tactics.

'Do you know what your pal Bruce said to me?' Jason remarked as he swigged back his Bollinger. 'He said,' and he adopted a heavy ocker accent, ' "You've ruined that poor bloody man's life." '

Jason laughed as he topped up their glasses from the bottle in the ice bucket. 'Dear God, Wallace, I don't know how you maintain a friendship with that man, he's so square. I mean, really, pet, there's such a thing as being altogether *too* straight.'

'Yeah, well he's got a point,' Wallace growled, 'we did ruin the man's life.'

Bernard Williams had been forced to retire from council office after twenty-five years of loyal service. But Wallace didn't really give a shit whether they'd ruined Bernard's life or not—Jesus, they'd ruined enough lives, bankrupted enough people, why the hell start feeling guilty now? What annoyed him was that Jason was camping it up in his presence and such effeminacy, directed at him, seemed to intimate that the two of them shared something in common. Well they bloody didn't. Just because, on a few drunken occasions, rat-arsed with booze and high on cocaine, he'd let Jason muck around a bit meant nothing. It wasn't as if they'd had sex or anything. A little mutual masturbation, that was all, schoolboys did it behind dunny doors. He'd let Jason go down on him a few times too, but that didn't mean a thing either. Christ, Wallace thought, when he was high on coke and randy as hell, he couldn't give a fuck who sucked him off.

'Oh, she's getting titchy, is she?' Jason said in reply to Wallace's taciturn growl. He was deliberately goading him, aware that the more he queened it up, the more defensive Wallace would become, and the more butch and aggressive his manner. All of which was very amusing to Jason. Even a bit of a turn-on too. They'd had two bottles of Bollinger and, what with the late afternoon sun beating down on their seminaked bodies, Jason was feeling quite horny. 'Oh dear, she's turning a bit, I do declare.'

'Shut the fuck up, Jason.'

'Want another bottle?'

'No, it'll put me to sleep. I'm going to the opera with Melanie tonight, it'll be hard enough to stay awake as it is.'

'What about a line of coke then?' Jason dropped the queen act altogether. 'That'll wake you up,' he gave a lewd wink and played masculine camaraderie, 'put you in the mood for Melanie later on.'

'Yeah.' Wallace grinned. He'd had the best sex with Melanie when he was coked up, he didn't actually find her all that attractive when he wasn't. Still, he wasn't marrying her for her sex appeal. He needed a wife and she had all the right qualifications: she had class and her father was a judge.

'You cut it up while I have a dip,' he said, diving into the pool and powering his way to the other end.

As he sat watching, Jason wondered whether Wallace would ever admit that he was gay. Probably not. He would most likely play it straight for a few years, batting occasionally for the other side; he'd sire a family, then years down the track discover that his 'adventures' with men were far more appealing than his wife, but even then he wouldn't admit to homosexuality. Jason had seen it all before.

Hell, he thought, Melanie was one of the best looking women in Sydney. A splendid creature. Raven-haired, tall, slim, and elegant. Jason was a great admirer of beauty. If Wallace preferred a torrid, coked-up night with him, as Jason knew he did, rather than a fuck with his magnificent fiancée, then what was the prognosis for their future marital passion? Oh well, Melanie would find out in time. And by then she'd be more than compensated by the generous trust accounts set up for herself and whatever children she'd borne. Which was why Wallace was marrying her after all.

Funny, Jason thought, as he rose from his chair, that it had been good old, straight, square Bruce Hamilton who had inadvertently led Wallace to the altar.

'You need to set up some family trust accounts, Wallace,' Bruce had said. 'What about your sisters?'

'Bugger them,' Wallace had replied.

'Well, their children then.'

'Bugger them too.' Wallace had decided to take a wife instead.

Funny, Jason thought, that good old, straight, square Bruce Hamilton had no idea his mate Wallace was a poofter. Jason went inside to cut up the coke.

Melanie Kendall respected her husband. She respected what he'd done with his life, amassing a fortune, heading a corporation, befriending the world's rich and famous. She wasn't sure if she loved him, but she loved the life he offered her.

Their wedding had received the fanfare of publicity such an extravaganza demanded. The guest list had been straight out of *Who's Who*, and Melanie's bridal gown had been designed by Gucci. They had honeymooned in Rome, a suite at the Hassler, then Milan and Paris for some shopping. Then, en route home, a week in the penthouse at Hong Kong's Peninsula Hotel.

Melanie had loved it all, and on their return to Sydney the whirlwind of her life hadn't lessened. If anything it had intensified. True, she didn't see much of her husband, but that was to be expected, he was a very busy man. In the meantime there were the gala opening nights, the charity premieres, the formal dinners and balls. She was invited by the doyens of Sydney society to be on several high-profile committees; she presented the Humanitarian of the Year Award at the Variety Club's Christmas dinner and was guest speaker at the Black and White Committee's annual businesswomen's luncheon. As Wallace Kendall's wife, and an elegant and beautiful woman, Melanie was feted by all.

Pregnancy disrupted the pattern of her life, but not for long. Shortly after the birth of her daughter, the women's magazines boasted pictures of 'the Kendall Rose'. Little Rose Kendall, born with her mother's raven hair and violet eyes, was pictured in Melanie's arms. Mother and daughter, dressed in beige satin and lace, gazed out at the reader. Both serene. Both beautiful.

Several months later, with an army of nannies to protect her from the more sordid and mundane aspects of motherhood, Melanie continued her fairytale existence.

So when did it start to go wrong? Melanie couldn't be sure. Around the time Rose was two, she supposed.

It wasn't the lack of sex, she'd become accustomed to that, even grateful. For quite a while now Wallace had demanded anal sex, which she detested, but to which she submitted. When he'd told her that, since childbirth, she'd become 'looser' and less exciting, and that he enjoyed 'a tighter fit', she'd supposed it was her duty to comply. Fortunately, he wasn't demanding.

But Wallace's whole demeanour had changed. He'd become tense and irritable, and she presumed it was something to do with business. The sharemarket crash in late '87? But it hadn't appeared to affect them too badly. She queried Jason about it.

'No, no, we have Tricontinental on our side,' he assured her. 'We can weather any storm, believe me.' He patted her hand reassuringly. 'Don't you worry about Wallace, sweetheart, he's just got a few things on his mind.'

It wasn't that Melanie was stupid, far from it, but they had kept her well out of the picture. Her profile as devoted mother and wife, tireless charity worker and glamorous socialite served a far more valuable purpose than any corporate involvement might have done.

It was in fact Bruce Hamilton who was making Wallace tense. They'd weathered the storm of the share crash it was true, but Bruce had been keeping a close eye on Tricontinental.

'They're going to go under, Wallace,' he insisted, 'or they're going to have to call in repayments at a moment's notice. They have a commitment to just twenty-six clients which exceeds thirty per cent of their entire capital base. It's unrealistic. If those borrowers go under, then Tricontinental goes with them.'

'Rubbish! They're owned by the State bloody Bank of Victoria, how can they go broke?' But Wallace worried nevertheless. Christ knew where Bruce got his information, but he was good at his job. The Kendall Corporation was built like a house of cards—if one came down, the others would tumble. Wallace needed Tricontinental's endless credit.

Bruce was right. By March '89 the amount lent to Tricontinental's thirteen biggest clients, of which the Kendall Corporation was one, had risen to an incredible $1.7 billion, and their parent, the State Bank of Victoria, was in crisis. Wallace and Jason had to move quickly.

Melanie was given just one week to organise the packing of the family's clothes and personal possessions. These were to be shipped on ahead, together with whatever valuables and furnishings Wallace could discreetly remove. He'd already transferred money overseas. They were leaving in ten days, he told her, a night flight, with hand luggage only. And she was to tell no-one.

A month after the Kendalls' departure, Bruce Hamilton was arrested. Wallace and Jason hadn't told him of their plans, he'd been deliberately left behind as a smokescreen. Bruce realised as much, but made no attempt to escape, staying instead to answer the charges.

Jason Bruford had travelled on a false passport and could not be traced, the newspapers said. Not at the moment anyway, but it was only a matter of time. Wallace Kendall was safely ensconced with his family in Brazil, living a life of luxury while his companies crumbled. But again, the newspapers reassuringly reported, it was only a matter of time before he would be extradited, the government had given its assurance of that.

By the time Bruce Hamilton was finally sentenced, the thousands of small stockholders who had put their trust in the Kendall Corporation, and whose life savings had been wiped out, had to be satisfied with his six-year gaol term. Jason Bruford had not been found, and Wallace Kendall had not been extradited. Justice had not been served, the stockholders protested. But there was little they could do about it.

Chapter Nineteen

Rob Farinelli was taking his parents to lunch. They'd met him at Wodin and Wodin, Solicitors, in the Australia Square Building so that he could show them his new offices, complete with reception room and personal secretary. Rob had worked for the massive law firm for ten years, but it had taken him all this time to get a plush office like the other senior lawyers. He knew exactly why, but he didn't care.

'Pretty impressive, eh?'

'About time too,' Kitty said, 'you've certainly earned it.'

They said goodbye to Samantha, blonde, twenty-three and very pretty, and as they stepped into the lift Artie said, 'Joanna cannot be too happy about a secretary like that.'

'She wasn't at first. "Swap her for an old one", that's what she told me.' Rob laughed. His wife was certainly feisty, she reminded him a little of his mother, that's why he'd married her. Well, they said men married their mothers, didn't they?

'But she and Sam get on really well now,' he added. 'Sometimes they even gang up on me.'

Kitty and Artie had presumed they'd be dining somewhere in the central business district, but instead they took a water taxi from Circular Quay to Watsons Bay on the southern harbour headland. Rob had booked a table at Doyle's Restaurant, by the beach, where they could sit and enjoy the panoramic view of Sydney.

'Your farewell lunch,' he said. 'Had to make it special. I've taken the afternoon off work.'

'But we are having a farewell dinner tomorrow with you and the family,' Artie said.

'Yes, I know, and you'll spend all your time playing Grandma and Grandpa. This way we get to talk.'

Kitty nodded her approval. They didn't have their son all to themselves very often. Arturo always enjoyed playing with his two grandchildren, but Kitty found the combined energies of a four- and five-year-old a little wearing. And she and her daughter-in-law were very competitive.

It was a hot January afternoon, and Kitty and Artie were flying to Europe in two days' time. The occasion was not a particularly happy one, being the funeral of one of Artie's older brothers, but his death had not been unexpected, he'd been ill for some time. They'd decided to stay in Europe for six months, to visit family and to holiday in Tuscany throughout the spring and into the summer. They hadn't been overseas since Artie's diagnosis.

Rob took his father's wrist to steady him as they stepped together from the water taxi onto the jetty at Watsons Bay. It disturbed him to see his father's once handsome face so gaunt and sunken, and to feel the bones of his wrist so very brittle and thin. Artie had been given a clean bill of health, his cancer having been in remission for the requisite five years, but no-one seemed able to explain his inability to gain weight. He was as appallingly haggard and thin as he had been when the cancer was ravaging his body. He always said he felt fine, but he obviously didn't; he was weak, and sometimes in pain, Kitty suspected, although the doctors could find nothing wrong.

They ordered a seafood platter, as the waiter opened a bottle of white wine, then Rob proposed the first toast. 'I congratulated you on the phone, Dad, but we haven't made it official yet. Here's to *Son of a Migrant*,' he said raising his glass, 'may it be a bestseller.'

They toasted Artie's novel, the third he had written and the first to finally be published.

It had been Kitty's encouragement which had given Artie the strength to persevere through his despondency; indeed, it had been Kitty's idea which had formed the very basis of the book.

'Write about the next generation, Arturo,' she'd said. 'Write about your son and his life and the work that he does, there's a story in that.' She'd been right.

During his illness, Artie had left his job and worked from home, devoting himself to his books, which, although works of fiction, had been loosely autobiographical. Of his first two, the publishers had said that, well written as they were, there was nothing new in them. European immigrants' stories were old hat. The story of Arturo's son, however, was a different matter. And Rob didn't mind being the fictional hero in his father's book. He was flattered. Nevertheless, he meticulously proofread the manuscript to ensure that his character and those of the other protagonists were suitably disguised.

Rob Farinelli, fresh out of university, had been an up and coming member of the Labor Party in the mid-seventies. Devoted as he was to the left's policies, particularly the formal abolition of the White Australia Policy, and to the Prime Minister's personal beliefs in Aboriginal rights and multiculturalism, Rob had been shocked and disillusioned by the dismissal of the Whitlam Government in 1975. So disillusioned in fact that he quit all thoughts of a political career and accepted a position with a successful law firm instead.

He quickly became disillusioned there too. He was expected to make unpalatable compromises and to constantly take the easy way out. 'But we can win this case,' he'd argue. 'Let's go in and fight.'

'Accept the out-of-court settlement and shut up, Rob,' he would be told by the senior partners.

Things finally came to a head when he was handling a negligence claim for a wharfie. The defence brought up Rob's friendship with the militant trade unionist, Max Brown, and a picture of the two of them appeared in the newspapers. The intimation that there was some nefarious aspect to their friendship meant little in court, but the newspaper innuendoes had done their damage, as had been intended, and Rob's credibility had been undermined.

Refusing to obey his superiors' instructions, Rob neither denied the friendship nor maintained his silence. He issued a furious statement to the press instead. 'Max Brown and I went to Bondi Beach Public School together,' he was quoted as saying. 'We were childhood friends, we were friends throughout our youth, we are friends today, and we will remain friends, God willing, through our old age until our respective deaths, and anyone who wishes to make something of that can go to hell!'

He and the law firm parted company. He was unrealistic, they told him. He was willing neither to make concessions nor to turn a blind eye, nor, as was evident from his statement to the press, to practise diplomacy when necessary. In fact, it appeared he lacked all the skills of compromise required by a proficient lawyer.

Rob started to wonder whether perhaps law, like politics, had been an incorrect career choice on his part. He'd honestly wished to do some good.

'I don't expect to change the world, Dad,' he'd said to Artie at the time, 'but I'd like to serve a useful purpose.' He could only suppose now that that made him naive.

The problem with Rob Farinelli was his parents. There was too much of Artie and Kitty in him. The lethal mixture of his father's idealism and his mother's attack and tenacity was confronting to most people.

He was just the idealist Wodin and Wodin had been looking for. 'It won't be big money,' he was warned, 'you'll be handling minority cases.'

'Minority cases', he soon discovered, were 'underdog' cases, which at that time appeared to refer in the main to the Vietnamese boat people. The legal quandary raised by the boatloads of tragic and desperate refugees who were landing in droves on the north and north-western shores of the continent was receiving a lot of attention in the press. Such cases were worth little money to Wodin and Wodin, but as a public relations exercise they were invaluable.

The government had accepted the firm's caring offer of assistance, but the partners were having trouble finding someone who was willing to go. They discovered just the man in Rob Farinelli.

Rob was sent to Darwin where he was on his own. 'Do what you can to assist the government's legal aid,' he was instructed, 'but make sure the company's name appears regularly in the press.'

At the refugee camp Rob befriended a young Vietnamese-born Chinese girl. She was a student, just turned twenty, and she'd been at the camp for a month, having arrived on a boat with thirty-seven others, including three babies, seven children under ten, and four men and women over sixty.

'There was a four' baby,' she told Rob, 'but she die, we bury her at sea.'

Mai Wang Lee was a godsend, she spoke excellent English.

'It is my English that save me,' she said. 'They don' kill me because of my English.'

At one point in the voyage, she said, when their engine had broken down and they had drifted for over three weeks, having run out of food and being short of water, the people had become very frightened. She heard them talking about eating the first one of them who died. Then, at the end of the fourth week, she heard them discussing who they might kill. A woman it should be, the men were needed to do the hard work.

Mai was the only person aboard who was travelling without any family and, with no-one to defend her, she knew she would be the first choice. Then she heard them say they could not kill Mai Wang Lee because she was useful, she spoke English.

'But they kill no-one,' she said, 'because the nex' day the winds come. They make a big sail from women's clo's. My blouse,' she hugged her arms around her thin chest, 'is terrible, I am so shy.' She shrugged off her shame and got on with her story. 'The nex' day the rains come, and we catch the water in a raincoat. And then, two days, we find land. You see?' she smiled. Mai Wang Lee had the most charming smile. 'The gods are kind.'

Rob and Mai became allies. Not only was she an invaluable interpreter, but he watched with admiration as she calmed, advised and counselled her fellow refugees. She was a strong, intelligent young woman. She would be an asset to this country, he maintained, using her as a prime example when presenting the emotional aspects of his argument.

With Mai's help, Rob achieved much success and Mai was the first amongst a number of the refugees granted residency in Australia. Although his own name featured minimally in the press, 'legal representation by Wodin and Wodin' appeared so regularly that his superiors congratulated themselves upon their choice.

There were other 'minority cases' to be addressed. Following the collapse of Pol Pot's regime in 1979, Cambodian refugees sought settlement in Australia and other Western countries, and who better qualified to represent them than Rob Farinelli of Wodin and Wodin?

But a case much closer to home raised its head in the late eighties. It had started in 1982 when Eddie Mabo, a Torres Strait Islander, made legal claim to eight hectares of government land on his native home of Mer Island off the northernmost tip of Queensland. It was the first challenge to the legal basis of white settlement, and the outcome, should Eddie Mabo prove successful, was bound to create a precedent for other such claims to follow.

Wodin and Wodin had found a prime PR issue with which to become associated. And now they had just the man to represent their caring commitment to the cause. Even his name was perfect. Farinelli. And he looked so Italian too. Son of a European immigrant fighting for the rights of the indigenous people. Couldn't be better. Finally they gave Rob Farinelli his own plush office and his own personal secretary.

Rob was fully aware he was being used, but he didn't give a damn. He believed wholeheartedly in Aboriginal land rights, so he took up the banner and used Wodin and Wodin right back.

Having thoroughly toasted *Son of a Migrant*, and having demolished the seafood platter, Rob ordered a second bottle and the conversation turned to Bruce Hamilton.

'Caroline told me you visited him last week,' Kitty said. 'I'm glad. He needs a friend.' Of course it was Caroline she was really worried about. With Emma in England and Jim an empty shell of a man, Bruce was the only family Caroline had, and his imprisonment had left her distraught. Although she had accepted the fact of his guilt, she would not hear a word against her son's character.

'He made a mistake, certainly, but he stayed and faced the music like a man,' she said defiantly, daring anyone else to differ. 'Not like those other two cowardly bastards.'

Kitty readily agreed, which was a comfort to Caroline who so valued her opinion. But now Kitty was worried—she was leaving, and who would visit Caroline and fill in the lonely void of her days?

'You will visit Caroline regularly, won't you?' she said to Rob as the waiter opened the second bottle of wine.

'Yes, I promised you I would.' He'd promised about ten times.

'And you'll take her to see Bruce once a week?'

'I promised you I'd do that too.'

'I've arranged Meals on Wheels . . .'

'Yes, so you told me.'

'. . . more for the company than anything, at least she'll have someone popping in daily . . .'

'Shall we order dessert?' Artie suggested, changing the subject. Kitty's worries about Caroline had become an obsession. When they'd discussed the possibility of extending their overseas trip, she'd carried on to such a degree that Artie had suggested it would be simpler if he went on his own. 'My place is by my husband's side,' Kitty had insisted. Artie had raised an eyebrow, normally Kitty resisted such platitudes, but she'd continued oblivious, '... and you need a holiday. We're going to Italy for six months as we planned and I'll hear no more on the subject.' But it didn't stop her going on about Caroline.

Not that Artie minded really, he could forgive Kitty anything. She had saved his life. Quite literally, he often thought.

At the lowest depths of his illness, Artie had been prepared to give up. He'd accepted the fact that his cancer would kill him, but he'd been unable to accept the fact that his life had been meaningless. When his second book, two years in the writing, had been rejected by all the leading publishers, he'd become demoralised and, in his weakened physical condition, deeply depressed.

He had retreated further and further into himself, despondent, refusing to burden his wife with his unhappiness. But she hadn't given up, she'd nagged at him until finally he had told her the truth.

'What have I lived for?' he said, hating the fact that it sounded like self-pity. 'I wanted to do so much with my life, Kitty, but I leave behind nothing. I have served no purpose.'

'You call Roberto "nothing"?' Kitty said. That got his attention. 'You call the fact that he's lived his life by your example "no purpose"?' Kitty could have held him to her and comforted him, but it was not her way. Kitty was a fighter. 'I wanted to change the world too, Arturo, but I didn't know how until I met you. Both Rob and I have lived by your example. And the next generation will live by his. If that isn't changing the world then I don't know what is.'

She knew she was making sense. Strange, she thought, Arturo had always been the one with the sound advice, she the headstrong and irresponsible one. It was true, she had learned from him, and now it was his turn to listen to her.

'You always said that perhaps the next generation would have the answers. Well, how do they get their answers without learning through us? Don't you see, Arturo, Rob wouldn't be the man he is, he wouldn't be doing the work he does, if it weren't for you.'

It was then that the idea had hit her, the perfect solution. 'So why don't you write about the next generation,' she'd said, 'why don't you write about your son?'

'Yes, I'll go dessert, Dad.' Rob was thankful for the change of topic, his mother's preoccupation with Caroline's welfare could be maddening at times. 'The cheesecake here's terrific.'

Both men shared a smile, and then the three of them talked about Italy, and Tuscany in the spring, and they all felt a little giddy with the wine and the sun and their love for each other.

On the trip back to Circular Quay Artie dozed off in the stern of the water taxi. Kitty had asked the skipper to go slowly so that she could enjoy the view from the water. Her chin resting on her hands, her elbows on the gunwales, Kitty looked out at the plush harbourside homes as they glided past. Many beautiful, some ugly and pretentious, and of course the most monstrous of them all, Wallace Kendall's twin mansions. Well, they weren't Wallace's any more, they were in the hands of the receivers now. But there they stood, rivalling each other in their ostentation, the larger of the two with a helicopter pad sitting atop it like an unsightly bonnet.

How everything had changed, Kitty thought. She didn't need to close her eyes to see Wally's old house lounging peacefully there on the point, surrounded by cool verandahs, shaded by the huge Moreton Bay fig. She could see them all now, in their tennis whites; she could hear the shrieks of their laughter. But Wally and her parents had gone, and now she and her generation were the next on the way out. Sobering thought.

It had been shock enough turning sixty. Sixty was old. And yet here it was, 1991, in just two years she'd be seventy, and people spoke with such glibness of the year 2000. It sent shivers down her spine. 2000 had always been light years away. She had never contemplated being alive at the turn of the millennium, and yet in a way it was only tomorrow.

Other water taxis sped past them, dodging busily like worker bees amongst the ferries and the yachts. Fort Denison glided past their starboard bow, to the left was Mrs Macquarie's Chair, and dead ahead, sitting in all its magnificence upon Bennelong Point, was the Opera House and beyond that the giant coathanger of steel. Dear God, Kitty thought, how she loved this city.

*

'Hello, Mrs Hamilton. How are you today?'

'I'm fine, dear, I'm fine.'

Caroline Hamilton wasn't fine, far from it. She was so desperately lonely that each evening when she went to bed she hoped she might not wake up. It wasn't a prayer, Caroline was not a religious woman, she simply wished that she could sleep forever. In sleep she could give herself up to her dreams. She could dance with Gene at the Trocadero and watch him running up from the water's edge at Bondi Beach. They could dine at the Roosevelt on oysters and champagne and always, in her dreams, they were young and beautiful.

During her waking hours, Caroline allowed herself to think of Gene only briefly, refusing to wander too long in the past, for that way lay madness, and she intended to keep her wits about her to the very end. But, when she dreamed she was happy, and in sleep she was free of the pain which plagued her waking hours and of the emptiness of her interminable days. Days which stretched forever, broken only by the visit of the cheery young woman from Meals on Wheels.

Sally was fond of old Mrs Hamilton, she never complained like so many of the others, and she was always good for a laugh. Sally always tried to schedule Mrs Hamilton last on her list of deliveries so that they could have the odd game of Scrabble now and then.

'You get the board and I'll clear the table,' Caroline said.

'Aren't you going to have your lunch first?'

'No, I'm not hungry today, the food can wait. Besides,' she called as Sally disappeared into the front room, 'I'm hardly malnourished.'

'It's lack of exercise,' Sally said, returning with the Scrabble set to see Caroline easing her bulky body into the chair at the head of the table.

It was difficult to imagine someone as old and as fat as Mrs Hamilton ever having been young. Sally wondered if she'd been pretty. Quite possibly. Her hair, though now white, was thick, and her eyes, amidst the folds of her face, were the deepest brown.

'You really should try and get out for a walk now and then,' she said.

If only she could, Caroline thought. Every single movement

caused her pain. 'I know, I know, dear. I'm thinking of taking up jogging. In those little tight shorts and a sweatband.'

Sally laughed. Old Mrs Hamilton was always good for a laugh.

Caroline played a similar game with Rob Farinelli when he visited her, and particularly with Kitty during their weekly telephone calls.

Kitty rang at the same time each Saturday, and the conversation always started the same way.

'Are you well?'

'Yes, I'm fine. Went for a five-mile hike this morning.'

'Now don't be silly. Are you all right? Really?'

'Really, yes, I'm fighting fit.'

'Has Rob visited?'

'Yes, on Thursday, as usual.'

'Is there anything you need?'

'Rob asked me that. There's nothing, Kitty, truly. I'm perfectly happy.' Then Caroline would change the subject. 'I got your postcard. San Gimignano looks beautiful.' She was on safe ground there, Kitty would wax lyrical about the glories of Tuscany, the countryside and the medieval towns for a full ten minutes.

'And Artie,' Caroline would ask before they said goodbye, 'how's Artie?'

Kitty was always a little guarded in her reply. She didn't dare raise her hopes too much. 'He hasn't gained any weight and he doesn't seem any stronger, but he's loving being here. It's good for him, Caroline, he's happy, I can tell.'

'Oh my dear, I'm so glad.'

Then came the phone call three weeks before Kitty and Artie's planned return.

'My God, the time's flown,' Kitty said, 'it seems only yesterday we stepped onto the plane ...'

Really? Caroline thought. To her the days and the months had dragged by, each day seeming longer than the last, each morning bringing with it the disappointing discovery that she was still alive.

'... and now we'll be home in three weeks. I can't wait to see you.'

Caroline longed to see Kitty too, just once, to say goodbye. She had a feeling it wouldn't be long now. She'd stopped eating to help speed up the process. She was simply being practical. She knew she would never survive long enough to see her son out of gaol, so what was the point in hanging around any longer than was necessary. The meals Sally brought her she wrapped in plastic bags and put in the outside rubbish bin. But she was amazed at how efficiently the body could cope without food, it had been a whole two weeks.

'You don't look well, Mrs Hamilton,' Sally had remarked only yesterday. 'Shall I call the doctor?'

'No, dear, I'm perfectly fine, and I can call him myself if I feel the need. Leave the food on the bench, there's a good girl. Do you have time for Scrabble? I feel a winning streak coming on.'

A thought occurred to Caroline as Kitty chatted away. Was she coming home just because of her? If so, how terrible.

'Kitty,' she said, broaching the subject with care, 'if Artie is responding well, then surely you should stay in Italy longer.'

'Oh good heavens no, it's time to come home. Besides, I'm missing everyone.' Then the hoot of Kitty's laughter down the line as she truthfully admitted, 'Well, you and Rob anyway, the rest can go to buggery.'

Yes, Caroline thought, Kitty Farinelli was returning to Sydney for the sole purpose of looking after her friend. Her friend who didn't want to be looked after, who dearly wished to leave this mortal coil. Well, that was it, Caroline decided, she had a little less than three weeks in which to do it.

'There's someone at the door, Kitty, I have to go. I'll speak to you next Saturday.'

Caroline brought up the subject of funerals with Rob when he called the following Thursday. He gave her the perfect opening. 'I'm calling the doctor,' he said the moment he saw her. 'You don't look at all well, Caroline.'

'He's already been, dear,' she replied quite airily, 'this morning.'

'What did he say?'

'I'm just a little run-down, that's all. I'm seventy-six, I'm allowed to be. And Rob,' she said before he could interrupt, 'if I do drop dead, I want you to know that I don't believe in the fuss of funerals, I'm not a religious woman.'

Caroline had thought it all out. She didn't want to leave a note of instruction that Kitty was not to return for her funeral, it might look as if she'd suicided, and she had no intention of doing that.

'For instance,' she continued, 'I would simply loathe the thought of Kitty galloping home to sit on a hard church pew and listen to a perfect stranger saying sickeningly nice things about me. I detest funerals, I don't go to them myself and I don't expect others to come to mine.'

'All right, Caroline, I get the message.'

'Kitty's a practical woman, she'd feel the same way.'

Rob was sure she would. In fact Caroline sounded just like his mother.

Sally let herself in. She'd had her own key for weeks now, it saved Mrs Hamilton having to come to the front door. If the old lady was in her bedroom, it took her a month of Sundays to get downstairs.

'Mrs Hamilton! I'm here!' Sally called.

The old lady wasn't in the kitchen. She'd be upstairs again, like she had been yesterday. 'Just having a bit of a lie-down,' she'd said. 'Leave the food, there's a dear, it's not a good day today.' Poor old thing, she really wasn't well.

'It's me, Mrs Hamilton,' Sally whispered as she pushed open the bedroom door.

Caroline was in bed, propped up against the pillows, an open book resting upon her chest, her reading glasses halfway down her nose, the bedside lamp still switched on. She'd fallen asleep while she was reading, as she very often did. Only this time she hadn't woken up.

Oh, Sally thought, how sad. But then was it? Old Mrs Hamilton looked so beautifully peaceful.

Caroline's timing had been perfect. It was still a full ten days before the Farinellis' return, plenty of time for Kitty to alter her arrangements.

'The funeral's on Wednesday,' Rob said when he rang his mother with the news, 'and she didn't want you to come home for it, she was adamant about that.' He relayed his conversation with Caroline word for word. 'She obviously knew she was going to die soon.'

'If only she'd told me,' Kitty said, distraught. 'If I'd known, I would have come home.'

'That's why she didn't tell you.'

Kitty was crying and Rob was shocked by the sound. Never in

his life had he seen or heard his mother cry. 'I saw her, Mum,' he said gently. 'The girl who found her, Sally, she had my phone number for emergencies and she called me. I was there before the doctor arrived. She looked so peaceful, I wish you could have seen her. She died in her sleep, a mild heart attack.'

'Good.' Kitty pulled herself together. 'That's good, I'm glad.'

'So don't come home, it's not what she wanted.'

'No, I won't. Caroline was quite right, it wouldn't be practical.' Rob could hear her blowing her nose. 'The plane trip would be uncomfortable for Arturo,' she said briskly, 'and I won't leave him here on his own. In fact I think we'll stay in Italy for several more months, it's doing your father the world of good. You'll look after everything, won't you?'

'Of course,' Rob reassured her. 'I've arranged Bruce's prison release for the funeral, and I'm collecting Jim on the day, although God only knows what condition he'll be in, he was drunk as a skunk when I told him the news.'

'You did all this before phoning to tell me she'd died?' Kitty asked in a tone of disbelief.

'The time difference, Mum, remember? I didn't want to wake you at three in the morning . . .'

'The time's neither here nor there, I should have been—'

'. . . besides, I knew you'd want to know things were being looked after, so I used the time to arrange it all before phoning you at a reasonable hour.' So there, his voice said.

A pause. 'How very practical. You don't just take after your father, do you?'

'Nope.'

They could sense each other's smile on the other end of the phone. Then, 'What about Emma?' Kitty asked.

'She's not coming home for the funeral.'

'What?'

'Says she can't.'

'I'll ring her,' Kitty said. And she did.

'Why aren't you going to your mother's funeral, Emma?' she asked bluntly.

How rude, Emma thought. 'Because it's on Wednesday, I'd have to leave tomorrow.'

'So?'

'Well it's too short notice. My husband has engagements, commitments we both need to honour.'

'What a pity your mother couldn't have given you a little more notice of her death.'

'I beg your pardon.' A touch of outrage down the line.

'I presume you'll be going to Sydney some time shortly, at your convenience of course, to look after your mother's possessions. Your brothers are hardly in a position to do so.'

'Naturally.' Emma's tone was as icy as Kitty's. 'I shall look after my mother's property in due course and I shall pay my respects when I do so. Right now, however—'

'Good, you do that.' Selfish little bitch, Kitty thought as she slammed down the receiver.

Three months after the funeral Rob rang his mother with further news. 'There's a for sale sign up at Caroline's house,' he said.

'Oh, so Emma's been home and sorted things out,' Kitty replied. 'Well at least that's something.'

'No, she hasn't,' he said. 'I checked at the real estate office. Caroline left her house and everything in it to her three children and they've put the whole lot on the market as a deceased estate. Everything's been left there, lock, stock and barrel, and the agent's opening the place for inspection next week.'

'Oh my God,' Kitty breathed, 'the cow.' Then she hastily instructed, 'Get in there, Rob. Get hold of her personal belongings before some stranger buys the place.'

'I'll need permission . . .'

'Bugger it, pretend you're a prospective buyer, that's what I'd do. Just get in there, and get her things out. Hang on to them for me until I get home. Your father and I will be back in a month.'

Rob didn't go off half cocked as his mother would have done. He got written permission from two of the owners instead. Bruce was deeply grateful for Rob's intervention, and Jim had no idea what he was signing, but two out of three owners meant that all was in order, and Rob set off to explore the old house in Woolloomooloo.

At the front door the real estate agent searched through the dozens of keys dangling from the huge metal ring he held in his hands, and he warned Rob as he did so that, upon instructions from the owners' solicitors in London, the house was to be sold with furnishings, and that he'd advertised it as such.

'Don't you worry,' Rob assured him, 'I won't be removing anything of any value, just the old lady's personal possessions. And if you'd like to make an inventory before I do . . .'

'I already have.' Henry Shortall stepped into the front room behind Rob. 'Well, you never know, do you?' he hastily added, not wishing to offend the smart young lawyer.

'Of course.'

'The place wasn't going to be open for inspection until Monday,' Henry said, 'my wife was going to clear out the old lady's clothes on the weekend . . .'

'Well she won't need to now, will she, that's why I'm here.'

Rob stood for a moment waiting for the man to leave, but it appeared he didn't intend to. 'Would you mind?' he asked politely. 'I'd like to look around on my own.'

'Oh. Yes. Well, the door isn't self-locking you see.' A pause. Rob said nothing. 'I could leave you a key, I suppose.' The man was obviously loath to do so. 'You could drop it back to the office.'

'I'll tell you what, Mr Shortall. Why don't you go back to the office and I'll ring you when I'm finished? Then I'll wait for you to come back and lock up. How'd that be?'

'The phone's not on.'

'I've got a mobile.' Rob put his briefcase on the table, opened it, and took out his mobile telephone.

'Oh.' Henry was extremely impressed. 'Yes, well, I suppose that'd be all right.'

'I might be some time,' Rob said. The man hesitated. 'You can lock me in if you like, I don't mind.'

Henry Shortall gave a self-conscious laugh as if Rob was joking, and then left, pulling the door closed behind him.

It was eerie, standing there in the gloom. The traffic noises from the street outside seemed strangely distant, and Rob could feel the ghosts of the past as he looked about at the lace-clothed table, the antimacassared sofa and the hardback chairs, all immaculate. A china cabinet against one wall housed Caroline's best harlequin tea set and a collection of porcelain ornaments, and on the corner mantelpiece, above the small fireplace, sat silver-framed photographs of her children. This was the formal room, unused by the family, reserved for visitors.

Rob wandered through to the kitchen. Pots and pans and utensils hung from the walls; a china teapot and mugs and tin canisters sat on shelves, and a very old, well-loved wooden table took up most of the space. Yes, this was where the family had lived. Where they had probably lived for generations, he thought. With the exception of the gas stove and refrigerator, it was obvious that little had changed over the years.

He climbed the narrow staircase to the bedrooms. The small back room was for guests, he supposed. Bare and characterless, with little else but a bed and an old stained-wood wardrobe, it had not been used for years. He gave a cursory glance around then continued on to the front bedroom.

This room was a different matter altogether. Lace curtains fluttered lightly in the afternoon breeze which found its way through the cracks in the French windows leading to the small balcony. A bright hand-crocheted bedspread dominated the room, a little out of place with the pastel wallpaper, curtains and furnishings, but cheery nevertheless.

The dressing table was scattered with an assortment of perfume bottles and atomisers, a bowl of powder, a hairbrush, a hand mirror, a clothes brush and comb. A feminine array. And on the large chest of drawers was a collection of framed photographs. At least a dozen or so. In the centre was a wedding photo of Caroline and Gene, and carefully arranged around it were pictures of their children. Gene with Emma in his arms, Bruce captaining his school rugby team, Jim in his army uniform, Emma and Gordon with their wedding cake. A family shrine.

Rob opened the wardrobe. Inside, Caroline's clothes hung neatly, the shelves to one side housing hats and scarves. He lifted them all out and put them on the bed, then he laid everything else on top. The articles from the dressing table, the photographs, Caroline's undergarments from the drawers of the dresser. He felt shockingly intrusive. A daughter should be doing this. His mother was right, Emma was a bitch.

As he was about to go downstairs to fetch the plastic bags from his briefcase, he decided that he'd better check the spare room, just to be sure.

Thank goodness he had, he thought, when he opened the door of the old stained-wood wardrobe. For here, he guessed, was Caroline's treasure trove of yesterdays. He lifted out the tattered photo album, the hand-knitted hot-water bottle cover, the man's dressing gown wrapped in tissue paper, probably her husband's, he thought.

There were baby dolls and teddy bears and children's books. Dozens of them. How sad that she needed to preserve them. Deserted by her children in their adulthood, she'd had nothing left to cherish but their childhood things. How lonely she must have been.

Having cleared everything else out, he discovered the battered suitcase at the very back of the wardrobe. Inside was a leather-bound journal. Very old by the looks of it. He sat on the bed and opened the cover to the flyleaf page.

Hannah Kendall. 1831. It was a young girl's diary. Written over a hundred and sixty years ago. A collector's item.

Beneath the neat copperplate, a rough family tree was recorded in an eclectic and clumsy mixture of handwriting. Rob turned the next page and started to read. This was no ordinary young girl's diary, he quickly discovered. Hannah told him so in her very first sentence.

> *This is not to be the girlish diary my mother presumes it will be*, Hannah wrote, *nor will I ever allow it to become so. This is to be a journal for the recording of special events. And I begin with the story of Grandpa Thomas, as told to my brother William and my cousin James.*

The story of Thomas Kendall and Wolawara unfolded before Rob's eyes. Although it was told in a childlike manner, it was meticulous in detail.

> *I was there in the front parlour with Mother and Aunt Mary when Grandpa Thomas returned home with William and James*, Hannah wrote. *I have never witnessed anger such as Aunt Mary displayed that day. She was like a*

madwoman. I could tell that James and Phoebe were terrified.

It was a winter afternoon and dusk was setting in early. Rob switched on the overhead light and read on.

There is a schism in the family. Aunt Mary and Grandpa Thomas are at war. Grandpa Thomas informed Uncle Richard that he is giving to Wolawara and his kinspeople the land adjoining theirs at Parramatta. Aunt Mary is furious, but there is little she can do about it. Grandpa Thomas himself told me so. It is his land to do with as he wishes, he said, and he wishes to give it to Wolawara. 'For as long as Wolawara and his descendants wish to live upon it,' that's what he told me. 'And your Aunt Mary can go to the devil.' Grandpa Thomas tells me everything. He knows I write it all down in my journal, but he says that is admirable.

'Mr Farinelli?' Rob started at the sound of the real estate agent calling up the stairs.

'Yes, I'm up here,' he called. 'I'm terribly sorry, Mr Shortall,' he said, stepping out onto the landing, the journal under his arm, to discover the man peering up at him, 'I completely lost track of the time.'

Henry Shortall was secretly relieved. He'd had the horrible feeling that perhaps the whole thing had been a set-up after all and that the fancy lawyer with his fancy mobile phone had ransacked the place and scarpered.

'Yes. Well. I thought that perhaps you might have tried to get through to me at the office.'

'No, I didn't try to ring you at all, I'm afraid, I completely forgot. Just look at this.' Rob galloped down the stairs two at a time.

Henry Shortall had turned on the downstairs lights and he watched as Rob placed a large book on the table and opened to the first page.

'A journal,' Rob said, 'written by a young girl in 1831. It'll have to go to the Mitchell Library of course, but I got carried away. Fascinating, isn't it?'

'Oh. Yes. Well. It looks very old.'

The man had no interest in it whatsoever. Rob closed the book and said, 'I've sorted through the old lady's things, Mr Shortall, but would you mind if I came back tomorrow to collect them?' He had to get home and finish the journal.

'Yes. Well. I suppose that'd be all right. It's a bit late now anyway, isn't it?' For a fancy lawyer with a mobile phone, he seemed pretty excited, Henry thought.

'Fine, I'll call into your office at ten.'

Rob played with the children for a half an hour when he got home, then he begged off dinner and went to his study.

'You can eat in there if you have to,' Joanna said, exasperated, 'it's just pasta and a salad, I'll bring it in to you.'

'That'll be fine, thanks, darling.'

But she knew what would happen. He was excited. On one of his 'missions'. He'd stay up all night and the meal she'd left him would be untouched in the morning.

She was right. Rob read on into the early hours, studying Hannah's every word.

> *Wolawara has died. I was with Grandpa Thomas when Uncle Richard brought the news.*

Hannah was obviously a young woman now. Her writing style was less self-conscious and there was a maturity to her observations.

> *I could tell Grandpa Thomas was moved, but he refused to show the depth of his emotions in front of Uncle Richard. Uncle Richard is an ineffectual man, and I think that Grandpa Thomas secretly despises him. It is a sad thing for a man to despise his own son.*
>
> *He has asked me to accompany him to the Aboriginal camp at Parramatta. In a month or so, he says, when the mourning period is over. He wishes to convey his sympathies to Wolawara's wife and family.*

It was the entry, a month later, which excited Rob Farinelli most of all.

> *My grandfather dictates to me as I write this*, Hannah wrote, and then followed the words of Thomas Kendall himself. *'Wolawara was an elder of the Gadigal tribe, a people whose very language is dying. This is his story, to be recorded for the future by my granddaughter, Hannah Kendall.'*

Much of the story Rob had already read in Hannah's first entry. But now he heard it in Thomas's words. Brief and concise. The rushcutting bay massacre, the interview with Governor Phillip, the secret bond shared between Thomas and Wolawara for the rest of their lives. Then, upon Wolawara's death, Thomas's attempt to explain to his widow the fact that the Parramatta lands belonged to her and her kinspeople.

> *'I have tried to communicate to Wiriwa that the land belongs to the Gadigal people. Legally. Under the white man's law. But I do not have the Dharug words, if indeed such words exist, and why should they? But my gift to Wolawara was no empty offer to exist only for the duration of my own lifetime or his. WR Patterson and Son, Solicitors, handled the conveyancing, and the Parramatta lands, so recorded in the title and deeds, remain the property, in perpetuity, of the people of the Gadigal tribe.'*

When he'd finished the journal, Rob read it again, making notes as he went. Dates, places, times, names. His wife delivered him coffee at seven in the morning. She said nothing but gave him one of her looks as she collected the untouched pasta and salad.

After a series of examinations and tests, the specialists at Christies verified the authenticity of Hannah's journal. Finding proof of Thomas's transfer of land to the Gadigal people proved a little more difficult, the original records of deed and title having been destroyed, along with land occupancy records from the beginning of the colony, in the Garden Palace fire of 1883.

A search for the solicitors who had handled the conveyancing also proved fruitless. WR Patterson and Son had long ceased to exist, fading into obscurity during World War I. Rob refused to give up, however. If needs be, he would go into battle with nothing but Hannah's journal, though he was sure there would be records somewhere. There had to be.

He found them in the Westpac archives. Extracts from the original document initialled by Thomas and a surveyor's plans with measurements to the inch. WR Patterson and Son had been very thorough. There was even a note, written by Thomas Kendall himself.

His was no neat copperplate hand like that of his granddaughter. His was the clumsy hand of a self-taught man, but his message was concise and to the point.

> *I have no doubt that, upon my death, my daughter-in-law, Mary Kendle, will attempt to reclaim Wolawara's land as her own. Should she, or her offspring, make any such attempt, either to run stock on the aforesaid land, or to construct any form of building upon it, she is to be prevented at all costs.*

Rob visited Parramatta to discover that the area mapped out in the surveyor's report was preserved as public parkland. Further enquiries disclosed that the vacant land had been used for so long as a common walkway that the council had finally converted it into a public park.

All that was left to do now was to convince the government to open its own investigation into the rights of the Gadigal tribe to the lands given them by Thomas Kendall.

It took Rob Farinelli five years, for the issue was delicate. The country was in turmoil over the granting of native land rights, some suggesting that if this case succeeded, there would be nothing to stop claims to suburban backyards.

Rob patiently argued that this was not an indigenous land rights claim at all, but the simple return of property to its legally documented owners. He curbed his anger and frustration as he did so. He wanted to scream, 'If this was a white person's claim, there'd be no question of ownership, would there?' but he didn't, it would serve no purpose. Perhaps he had at last learned the value of diplomacy.

With reluctance, the government finally agreed to an investigation. In the lengthy course of the proceedings, the Black Town case was cited as a precedent for refusing the claim.

In 1920, the land at Black Town which had been originally granted by Governor Macquarie to the members of the Dharruk tribe was taken over by the Aboriginal Protection Board and the descendants of the grantees evicted. Many years later, it was decided that the grantees had abandoned their rights by moving off the land.

Rob turned the case to his advantage. The Dharruk descendants had been forcibly removed, he said, and by the Aboriginal 'Protection' Board, the same board which had systematically taken children from their parents to be raised by white families, more often than not as unpaid workers.

It was 1998 and the issue of the 'stolen generation' was inflaming the nation. Should the Australian government make an official apology to the thousands of Aborigines who had been taken from their families in the 1950s and 60s? Children, now adults, who had been cheated not only of filial love, but of their culture and their very identity? Many believed an apology was essential.

But such inhumanity was practised long before the 50s and 60s, Rob argued. 'Well over a hundred years earlier,' he said, 'Aboriginal families were being torn apart by the do-gooders of white society. What better way to make some gesture of reparation than to grant the Gadigal people the land which is legally theirs?'

A year later, the government took action. The eyes of the world being upon Sydney, host city to the 2000 Olympics, a humane gesture to the country's indigenous people was considered politically advantageous. And in the spring of 1999, Thomas Kendall's land at Parramatta was finally restored to its rightful owners.

Chapter Twenty

Kitty Farinelli stood beside her son as the assembled company awaited the arrival of the Premier of New South Wales and the commencement of the formal ceremony. A marquee had been erected in the park, and waiters were handing around trays of champagne. People chatted in groups, eminent faces smiled for television cameras, and journalists and photographers roamed amongst the crowd. Ranging down the gentle slope of the hill were rows of chairs facing a platform and podium, beside which was a cloth-covered commemorative plaque which the premier would unveil after his speech.

Kitty looked about her. With the exception of several footpaths and the odd bench here and there, the land had been left very much in its original state.

Two magpies warbled from a nearby sugar-scented gum; galahs exchanged larrikin screeches as they flew overhead, and from distant trees came the cackle of kookaburras proclaiming their territory. It was a glorious day, the river at the bottom of the hill sparkling in the clear spring sunlight.

Beneath a Moreton Bay fig squatted four Aboriginal boys, no more than sixteen or seventeen years of age. Three of them tapped their sticks in unison to the steady, pulsating rhythm of the didgeridoo played by the fourth member of their team. They were to give an exhibition of tribal dance after the ceremony. Not far from the boys, the two Gadigal elders, representatives of their people, stood in silence, every now and then nodding their heads to the beat of the music.

If she ignored the marquee, Kitty thought, and the crowd of guests and the press and the officials . . . If she blocked her ears to the social chat and the clink of champagne glasses . . . If she watched the boys and the elders and concentrated on the birds and the pulse of the didgeridoo . . . Could it perhaps have been like this in Wolawara's time?

She looked at Rob. He too was watching the boys and listening to their music, and she knew he was thinking the same thing.

'Excuse me, Mr Farinelli.' A young female reporter broke into their respective thoughts. 'If you wouldn't mind, could we have a picture of you with the Gadigal elders?'

Kitty watched the two old men's faces break into smiles as they posed with Rob, one on each side, arms linked, patting him on the back, calling him brother.

She wandered down to sit on a chair in the very front row. Rob would be seated in one of the official chairs beside the podium, facing the audience during the ceremony, and Kitty wanted to be sure she didn't miss a thing.

Several minutes later Rob joined her. The television cameras, the photographers and press were now concentrating their attention on the arrival of the guests of honour, two Aboriginal athletes who were to represent Australia in the forthcoming Olympics. Rob had approved the marketing company's choice. In fact he had approved the whole marketing hype. If the government wished to advertise its good work with a media bunfight, then fine, it all helped the cause. He himself had tracked down and invited the Gadigal elders, but the addition of the athletes he'd found an excellent idea. Bound to ensure even more coverage. Rob was learning. So long as you were batting for the right team, he'd decided, what was wrong with using all the tricks? They worked.

The press had already had a field day with the story. The government's official handover of the land to the Gadigal people had been a major news item for months. It was discussed by television panels, lauded by newspaper editors and argued by diehards who insisted it created a dangerous precedent.

'You're responsible for all this, Rob,' Kitty murmured, as the government vehicles pulled up at the top of the hill and the premier's party alighted. 'I'm so proud of you.' If only Arturo could be here with them. He'd been dead a whole five years now, although it never seemed it. 'And your father would have been proud,' she added, 'very very proud.' Fearing the onset of tears, she added briskly, 'Of course he knew that you'd win. From the moment you took up the fight he said that you'd win.'

'I know,' Rob smiled. 'He told me.'

Kitty studied her son's face. She could see the young Arturo in his eyes. 'You've changed the world, Rob,' she said in all seriousness. 'Just as your father always wanted to. Just as I wanted to myself.'

As Rob returned her gaze he could hear his father's voice. 'It is young men like you who can bring about change,' Arturo had said. 'Strong, resilient young men. Someone once said that same thing to me, very many years ago. And now, when I look at you and the work that you do, I know that such young men exist, and that such change is possible. You will win, Roberto.'

Rob put his arms around Kitty. 'If I've changed the world, Mum,' he said, holding her tight for a moment, 'then it's because of you and Arturo Farinelli.'

That was it, Kitty gave up trying to play tough. What was the point? Besides, old women were allowed a sentimental tear, weren't they?

She found it easy to control her emotions throughout the ceremony, however. There were three speakers, including the premier, and Rob Farinelli's name was mentioned just once, and then only in passing. It appeared you didn't get any thanks for changing the world, Kitty thought crossly.

Just before the unveiling of the commemorative plaque, she caught Rob's eye and, from the knowing smile and the slight shake of his head, she knew she'd been scowling through the whole proceedings. And now that she was old, she looked so ferocious when she scowled. But what the hell, they should have paid credit where credit was due; they should have thanked her son from the very bottom of their hearts.

Kitty gave a defiant shrug back, and Rob nearly laughed out loud. God, but his mother was a terror.

Young Jarrod, future Olympian and just seventeen years old, found the whole ceremony rather overwhelming. He'd found it overwhelming from the moment he'd arrived. He wasn't accustomed to all this attention, so he'd stuck close to Cathy's side. Cathy Freeman was his hero. But then Cathy Freeman was everybody's hero. She'd been world champion and knew how to handle this sort of stuff.

Realising he was unnerved, Cathy had given him a smile and a wink. 'You'll get used to it, Jarrod,' she'd whispered, 'don't you worry.'

'I dunno, do you reckon?' he'd said nervously, 'It's all a bit much.'

'You have to get used to it, mate.' Her smile was still warm, still friendly, but he could tell she was serious. 'All of this is good for us. Good for our people.'

Jarrod had thought a little after she said that. He was just an athlete, he'd never expected to become a symbol to his people. He wondered whether, after the Olympic Games, they'd expect him to be a spokesperson like Cathy. Pretty scary.

During the ceremony, when the attention was no longer focused upon them, Jarrod relaxed. He even got a bit bored by the speeches. He and Cathy were seated with the official party to the side of the podium, facing the audience, and instead of concentrating dutifully upon the speakers, Jarrod allowed his mind to wander.

He turned his head and gazed at the willow tree drooping over the riverbank. But he wasn't really seeing it. He was seeing the Olympic Stadium. In a few months now it'd be the year 2000, the year of the Sydney Olympics. And he'd be there. In that stadium. Running the two hundred metres with the best of them. And he'd win a medal, he'd told his dad he would. He'd be a hero too, just like Cathy Freeman. He'd be a hero to his people.

Cathy dug her elbow into young Jarrod's side. The premier had just been introduced and yet still Jarrod took no notice, craning his head in the opposite direction as he had for the past five minutes.

'Sorry,' Jarrod murmured.

The premier was going on about the Gadigal people. 'My mob's Gadigal,' Jarrod whispered proudly. He hadn't really thought about it before. It meant a lot to his dad, he knew, but it hadn't meant much to him, his mob being Gadigal. It did now though. It felt good.

When the speeches were over, Jarrod and Cathy posed beside

the bronze commemorative plaque with the premier and the elders, then with the officials and the television personalities, and it was a full half hour or so before, together, they stood back and read the actual words on the plaque.

'THIS PARKLAND BELONGS TO THE GADIGAL PEOPLE. GIVEN THEM BY THOMAS KENDALL IN THE YEAR 1831, IT SHALL FOREVER REMAIN THEIR PROPERTY.'

'Gadigal people,' Jarrod said with pride. 'My people. I own part of this park.' He read the sign again. Then 'Hey, Cathy, look at that,' he said loudly, 'Thomas Kendall. I've got the same name.'

Cathy laughed. Jarrod was an engaging kid. 'Hardly, mate, it's not spelt the same.'

'Sounds the same though,' he said. 'Sounds exactly the same.'

If only he'd known. But no-one did. No-one would ever know that Jarrod Kendle carried the blood of both Wolawara, elder of the Gadigal tribe, and Thomas Kendall, the warrener from Norwich.

BONUS CHAPTER SAMPLER

JUDY NUNN

Territory

He didn't talk of the war or the missions he'd flown, but of his home in Australia. The Northern Territory, he called it. And the cattle station. 'Bullalalla'. She thought it was a beautiful name.

Territory is the story of Henrietta Southern, a young Englishwoman who trades her war-torn homeland for a place of wild tropical storms and searing heat, crocodile-infested rivers and barren red wilderness. Six months after the bombing of Darwin, she joins her new husband, Spitfire pilot Terence Galloway, at his family cattle station, just as he is faced with the desperate defence of the Top End against the Imperial Japanese Air Force.

It is also the story of their sons. Of Malcolm and Kit, two brothers who grow up in the harsh but beautiful environment, and share a baptism of fire as young men in the jungles of Vietnam.

And what of the Dutch East Indies treasure ship which foundered off Western Australia in 1629? How is the Galloway family's destiny linked with *Batavia*'s horrific tale of mutiny and murder . . .?

From the blazing inferno that was Darwin on 19 February 1942 to the devastation of Cyclone Tracy, from the red desert to the tropical shore, *Territory* is a mile-a-minute read from one of Australia's best loved writers.

PROLOGUE

Lieutenant Akira Nakajima felt a deep pride at the spectacle which surrounded him. The clear blue sky of early morning was alive with action. Threatening, lethal and all-powerful. Through his cockpit windows Akira could see Val dive-bombers, just like his. And Kate high-level bombers. And Zero fighters. Two hundred and forty-two aircraft in all. A magnificent sight. Today would be another splendid victory for the Japanese Imperial Air Force. He glanced to his right and shared a smile with his young copilot who grinned back, barely able to contain his own excitement.

Toshiro Kurasoto was honoured to be a member of Nakajima's team. Lieutenant Nakajima had been a bomber commander in the force which had so triumphantly attacked Pearl Harbor. It was most regrettable that the Lieutenant's regular copilot had been wounded in the attack, Toshiro had agreed, but silently he had thanked the gods for his own good fortune. Soon he, Toshiro Kurasoto, barely twenty-three years of age, would share a similar glory to that of the heroes of Pearl Harbor.

Through their headsets nothing could be heard but the muffled throb of the powerful engines. Since their departure from Ambon, radio silence had been maintained, but it would not be long before their headsets would be crackling with the voices of command.

Paul Trewinnard leaned back in his large wicker armchair, sipped at his tea, and looked out across the harbour from the windows of his room on the first floor of the Hotel Darwin. The overhead ceiling fan created the comforting illusion of breeze, but at barely nine o'clock in the morning the air was already hot and still, clammy with the humidity of the monsoon season. Today was his birthday, 19 February. Born shortly after the turn of the century, he was forty-two years old today and he felt every bit of it. No, that wasn't at all true, he felt twenty years older.

What would he do with the day, he wondered vaguely as he watched two boys playing football on the harbourside oval. He could complete his regular editorial article for the *Northern Standard*, or he could start on his reportage of the situation in the Pacific which he regularly forwarded to the *London Times*, but he didn't feel like embarking upon either. At the best of times his writing was only a way of filling in the days, of giving his life some sense of purpose. He didn't need the money; the quarterly remittances that regularly arrived from the family law firm in London were more than enough to sustain him. No, to hell with journalistic responsibilities, he'd visit his good friend Foong Lee. Perhaps they'd get drunk together. Well, perhaps he would; Foong Lee never seemed to get drunk, no matter how much alcohol he appeared to imbibe. And that was it of course. Foong Lee always 'appeared' to do things. Like a magician, a master of the sleight of hand, he was the perfect manipulator, a fact which most failed to recognise. Most, particularly Europeans, saw only a squat, jovial businessman who somewhat resembled a Chinese penguin. A man who spoke like them and enjoyed a good laugh. Paul, however, knew better.

It had been Foong Lee's wisdom which had helped Paul Trewinnard through what he called his 'dark years', the years of despair when he'd first come to Darwin to escape the horror of his life. And Darwin was a good part of the world to escape to, a remote outpost where no questions were asked and no judgements made.

These days, no longer in need of escape, Paul based himself principally in Darwin simply because he loved both the place and its people. For many years now the Hotel Darwin had become intermittent home to Paul Trewinnard, and Foong Lee had become his closest friend.

He raked his thick greying hair back from his brow, his forehead already damp. Not that the heat particularly bothered him. To Paul, the human body's perpetual state of perspiration throughout the aptly named 'wet' season was all part and parcel of Darwin's sensuality. He'd go down to the dining room and have a light breakfast, he decided, easing his gangly frame up out of the wicker chair. That would at least get the day started.

In her small weatherboard house on the Esplanade, not far from the Hotel Darwin, thirty-two-year-old Aggie Marshall, school teacher, sat at her desk completing her newsletter for the Country Women's Association. She applied herself diligently to the task despite the fact that there was no-one to send it to, all the members of the CWA having evacuated Darwin, along with the majority of women and children, and many of the men too, following the fall of Hong Kong on Christmas Day. The fall of Singapore only four days ago had made those who'd stayed even more aware of their precarious existence and the Government had evacuated the last boatload of people at noon just the previous day. The Japs could attack at any moment, many said.

Aggie had stayed in Darwin for the simple reason that she had nowhere else to go. Which wasn't exactly true, she could have returned to her elderly parents in Perth, they telephoned regularly begging her to do so, but the thought of being in the same city as her ex-husband made the prospect unbearable. And Perth was hardly a city in the true sense of the word, more like a large country town; it was not unrealistic to presume he would hear of her return and seek her out. For the first twelve months after she'd come to Darwin, Aggie had lived in fear that he might even have followed her north. Now, five years later, having reverted to her maiden name, her hideous marriage a thing of the past, Darwin had claimed Aggie. She'd discovered herself here, found a strength of her own she'd never known existed, and even the threat of a Japanese invasion could not drive her away. Darwin was where she belonged.

The school at which Aggie taught had been closed down so she'd set herself up as a one person secretarial office doing volunteer work for the war effort. She corresponded with various branches of the Red Cross, coordinating the parcels to be sent overseas, she typed endless circulars and lists of supplies and necessities, and she steadfastly continued to write her CWA newsletters. Mainly about courage in the face of adversity, now and then including a frivolous observation to boost morale, and she posted them up on noticeboards, in the post office and anywhere else she thought people might see them. It was something to do.

Aggie gathered together the pages of her newsletter. She was looking forward to a hearty chat with her friends at the post office. So few of her old acquaintances remained in Darwin, and the armed forces seemed to have completely taken over the town lately, but she enjoyed the company of the new friends she'd made at the post office. Many of them were recruits who had responded to the call for staff in this time of need, and they were young, vital and stimulating company.

She jammed on the brown felt hat that had seen better

days without bothering to check in the mirror—Aggie cared little about appearances. Her lack of vanity surprised some people because Aggie was a rather good-looking woman, tall and strong-boned. But she chose to wear her dark hair in an unfashionable bob (it was more practical that way), took little time with her dress (thank goodness trousers were acceptable, they were far more comfortable than skirts or frocks), and with the exception of a touch of lipstick (in the evenings, and when she remembered) she eschewed makeup.

As she opened the front door, Aggie noted that the wall clock said only nine-thirty. No, she decided, closing the door, she'd give it another fifteen or twenty minutes. Just until the post office had set up for the business of the day, then the staff would have time for a chat.

In Cavenagh Street, Foong Lee was carefully arranging his display of goods preparatory to opening his shop. Under normal circumstances he would have opened the shutters for business much earlier, or rather his eighteen-year-old son would have, Foong Lee himself having left before seven o'clock to visit the wharves or the market gardens or the number of subcontractors with whom he traded. But things had changed. Since the evacuation of Darwin business was poor, and his son Albert was in Adelaide looking after the rest of the family whom Foong Lee had sent south.

Most of the Chinese community had fled Darwin. As was to be expected, Foong Lee thought, the Chinese were not stupid, and he would most certainly have accompanied his family had it not been for the fragile condition of his father, who was unfit to travel. Foong Lee persuaded himself, with his characteristic commonsense, that it was just as well he had remained in Darwin, to protect not only his own interests but those of his friends.

Foong Lee was a highly successful businessman and leader of his community, not only loved and respected by the Chinese but recognised by the Europeans, which was unusual in Darwin where the two communities rarely intermingled.

Despite the fact that he was always well dressed (which was to be expected, since amongst his many interests he owned one of the major tailor's shops in Darwin) Foong Lee didn't look like an influential businessman. He looked and behaved more like 'one of the boys'. But a tai pan he was, nonetheless.

Born in Darwin on 22 January 1901, he had taken his first breath, he said, 'in the same hour that Queen Victoria took her last'. At times he spoke like a colonial Englishman, and at others like an outback Aussie, depending upon the occasion and who he was talking to. As a result, in the eyes of the European community, Foong Lee so contradicted the image of the inscrutable Oriental that he qualified unreservedly, albeit a little patronisingly, as a good all-round chap by some, and a bonzer bloke by others. In actuality, Foong Lee was perceived by all exactly the way Foong Lee wished to be perceived.

Having prepared his shopfront display—an extraordinary selection of goods, both European and Chinese, from general groceries and photographic supplies to silks and lanterns and Eastern delicacies—Foong Lee walked through to the living quarters at the rear. Perhaps his father may want some breakfast, it might be one of the old man's good days. But it wasn't.

In the living area which looked out over the large back courtyard, Foong Shek Mei was a crumpled heap on the sofa. He'd slept there last night. Again. As he had for the past week or so. When the family had been present he had at least attempted to scrape himself up from the sofa and retire to his bed. It saddened Foong Lee beyond measure to see his father reduced to a skeleton, his eyes dim and befuddled, his mind obscured by the phantoms which haunted it.

Foong Shek Mei's addiction was no secret amongst the

elders of the Chinese community. There were a number like him, remnants of the old days, habitues of the opium divans of Hong Kong and Singapore, who secretly fed their habits behind closed doors in little rooms at the rear of shops and shanty dwellings in Chinatown. Although the Darwin Chinese upheld the law and indeed did not approve of the opium trade, they sympathised with those few elders amongst them to whom, throughout their lives, the drug had been readily and legally available and whose inner peace could now only be attained by 'chasing the dragon'.

The once-strong body of Foong Shek Mei, the body which had served him so well when he'd arrived from Singapore in the nineties to work as a coolie on the goldfields, was now a wasted skeleton. A lifetime of opium abuse had taken its toll, and over the past decade his mind too had decayed to the point where he'd become childlike, dependent. Foong Lee now purchased the opium necessary to assuage the relentless demands of his father's addiction. He was reluctant to do so but aware that he had no option. Foong Shek Mei was too far gone, and the opium was now necessary to ease him into a painless death.

Foong Lee warmed some soup and sat beside the old man, cradling the emaciated body against his. Gently, he touched the bowl to the parched lips.

'*Lei yiu yam, Baba.*'

Foong Shek Mei's eyes slowly opened. But glazed, unfocussed, they saw nothing.

'*Lei yiu yam,*' Foong Lee repeated, imploring his father to drink.

The old man's head leaned forward slightly, the cracked lips parted and, like an obedient child, he sipped. Very gently. Twice. Then he rested his head back on his son's shoulder and his gaze focussed on the hand which held the bowl. His eyes slowly became alive and he turned to look at Foong Lee.

'*Lei hai ho jai, Foong Lee,*' he said. Both the voice and the smile were gentle. Faded and distant, as if they came from far away, but they were genuine nonetheless. Foong Lee was indeed a good son and Foong Shek Mei wished very much to tell him so.

Foong Lee smiled fondly back. '*Lei yiu yam, Baba. Ho gan yue.*'

But the old man's head lolled against his son's shoulder, he'd fallen asleep.

Foong Lee rose. He eased his father's head comfortably back upon the sofa, then he walked through the house to the shop to prepare for his morning stroll. It was his custom these days to walk the streets of Chinatown, to greet those few of his friends who remained in Darwin and to check on the properties of those who had left. The closed and shuttered shops were an advertisement to the lawless element who might wish to take advantage of the current situation. Foong Lee considered it his duty to keep his eye on things, to check the shopfronts for any sign of forced entry which may have taken place under the veil of night.

Before embarking on his walk, he checked the day's 'specials'. Despite the fact that business was poor, Foong Lee liked to vary the array and to have some tantalising offer displayed daily out front. Satisfied that all was in order, he stepped into the street. He would open the shutters for business upon his return.

Toshiro Kurasoto flinched. He couldn't help it. The voice that cracked like a whip through his headset momentarily startled him. It shouldn't have done so, he'd been expecting the break in radio silence from the moment their flight path had approached Bathurst Island. Fifty miles north-north-west of Darwin, Bathurst Island was the point at which the attack force was to receive its specific orders. After the continuous monotone of the engine, however, the sudden sharp noise caused Toshiro to flinch, involuntarily and barely perceptibly, but he cast a glance to his left nevertheless, hoping his commander had not observed his inappropriate reaction.

Lieutenant Akira Nakajima was far too intent upon the information and instruction he was receiving to take any notice whatsoever of his young copilot. The US destroyer *Peary* had returned to the port of Darwin for refuelling within the past hour. It was a stroke of luck. Her presence had not been anticipated when the attack plans had first been laid out. And she was to be Nakajima's prime target. After the initial high-level assault upon Darwin, the dive-bombers would take control of the attack. And Akira Nakajima determined that it would be he who would eradicate the US destroyer. The whole of Darwin would be under attack and its installations annihilated, that was the plan, but the *Peary* would be the personal jewel in Akira's crown.

Having breakfasted, Paul Trewinnard lounged about in the luxury of the Hotel Darwin foyer observing, through the potted palms, the comings and goings of the few remaining guests and staff. It was one of his favourite pastimes, studying human behaviour. After ten minutes or so, he decided to wander down to the wharf to look at the warships. The US destroyer *Peary* had arrived this morning, the desk clerk had told him.

'Huge thing,' the clerk had said, 'quite terrifying really.'

She'd be worth a look at, Paul thought, donning his Panama hat. He nodded to the uniformed doorman as he stepped out into the glare of the morning.

Aggie Marshall walked down the Esplanade on her way to the post office. The Esplanade formed the harbourside boundary of Darwin's township, sweeping down the coastline and turning in an L-shape north-east at the wharves.

The streets of Darwin were busy, mainly with military personnel. Many of the older buildings along the

Esplanade had been commandeered by the military, and men went about their business. The streets leading off to the left from the Esplanade and into the town centre were busy too. The civilians who had remained in the town were also going about their business.

Foong Lee stepped out of his shop and started down the broad avenue of Cavenagh Street, walking beneath the welcome shade of the endless verandahed shops and crossing the small laneways which dissected the major streets of Chinatown. Just ahead, to his right, was Gordon's Don Hotel on the corner of Bennet Street and beyond that, to his left, was the *yung si*, the massive banyan tree which stood at the far end of Cavenagh Street only half a block from the wharf end of the Esplanade. The *yung si* was a dominant feature of Chinatown, particularly to the children who played amongst its branches. Foong Lee made a habit of turning into Bennet Street just before he got to the *yung si*, then he'd walk up Smith Street and back into Cavenagh to complete his around-the-block stroll. It was a pleasant twenty-minute walk in all, at a leisurely pace.

The attack force had crossed the coast of the mainland to the east of Darwin. Upon instruction, they swung round to approach the town from the south-east, with the sun behind them. Far in the distance, and from twenty thousand feet up in the sky, Darwin Harbour looked magnificent. And vulnerable. Ships of every description sat like tiny dots on the vast blue water. Forty-five in number. And tucked away, on its tiny peninsula within the massive harbour, was Darwin itself. Most vulnerable of all. Innocently waiting. Undefended. A lamb to the slaughter, Akira Nakajima thought.

'Tora!' The command barked through Nakajima's headset. 'Tora! Tora!'

Akira Nakajima commenced his dive.

Paul Trewinnard had strolled down Lover's Walk to the wharves and was studying the ships in the harbour when he heard the warning sirens. He thought it was a military exercise at first. Until he looked up.

Aggie Marshall was outside the Hotel Darwin and just about to cross Herbert Street when she heard the wail of the sirens. An awful sound, it always unnerved her, even when she knew it was only an exercise of some sort. Then she looked up.

Having turned the corner from Bennet into Smith Street, Foong Lee was outside the Bank of New South Wales when the sirens sounded. An air raid, he thought in the instant he heard them. He shaded his eyes and looked up.

The whole of Darwin looked up. It was two minutes before ten o'clock on a Thursday morning and people stood in the street staring up at the sky in disbelief, unable to comprehend what their eyes perceived.

Time stopped as the menacing horde swooped down from the sun. For the hundreds watching from the town, it seemed an eternity. Then, suddenly, the planes were overhead, so many they all but obliterated the sun. The light seemed to dim, the sky no longer seemed blue, and by ten o'clock, Darwin was under massive attack from the Japanese Imperial Air Force.

The *Peary* was hit aft by a dive-bomber. Her bridge ignited and the crew worked valiantly to extinguish the flames. Then again, another direct hit. But she fought on. Upon her captain's orders her guns still fired as she drifted ablaze on the harbour waters.

The *Neptuna*, berthed at Main Jetty, was hit amidships. She burned fiercely. A time bomb, the intense heat threatening at any moment to ignite the heavy ammunition and depth charges she carried.

The *Zealandia* and the *British Motorist*, both at anchor, were hit and sank at their moorings. The harbour was an inferno, erupting in pockets of flame and belching black smoke and, as shells screamed through the air and explosions showered the shoreline with debris, the township of Darwin too became a blaze of destruction.

Foong Lee ran up Smith Street. His one aim was to get back to his father whom he knew would be in a state of utter terror and confusion. People were screaming in the streets, panic-stricken. He passed C.J. Cashman's store and, halfway up the block, the force of an explosion caused him to stagger. He fell to his knees, hauled himself back up on his feet and looked over his shoulder. Cashman's had been hit. Sheets of galvanised iron had been hurled across the street and smoke billowed from the windows of the gutted building. Two bodies were sprawled on the pavement. Foong Lee ran on.

Paul Trewinnard made no attempt at all to run for cover. What was the point? In his opinion there seemed no specific place in Darwin any safer than another. There had been no preparation for an event such as this, although there damn well should have been, he thought. Where were the Government-built bunkers? Where was the massive defence force which should have been present to drive away the marauders? He was as fearful as the next man, he'd be the first to admit, as he sqatted, covering his head with his arms, water and debris showering about him, but he might as well stay where he was. If he was going to be killed then he'd watch the spectacle first.

And as he watched, Paul's fear was mingled with awe. Out on the harbour, the *Peary*, already twice hit and adrift, her guns still bravely blazing, suddenly destructed. The vessel's magazine exploded and, in the instant before she was engulfed in flames, Paul could swear he saw men flying through the air. Black oil flooded the harbour, black smoke billowed up into the morning air and the once-proud *Peary*, now a massive ball of fire, burned on the water. His own fear now forgotten, Paul thought of the men who, only seconds previously, had been firing those guns. This was Armageddon, he thought. The annihilation was total.

After the first hideous moments of shock, Aggie Marshall ran for cover. The post office was only a block away, on the bend of the Esplanade, so she headed there. If she was to die then at least she'd be with people she knew. She crossed Bennet Street, the post office was right ahead of her. Then she was thrown backwards by a force so strong it lifted her off her feet. The noise was deafening. Surely her eardrums must have burst, she thought briefly. Then she knew nothing as she hit the pavement and was showered with rubble.

Foong Lee ran down Knuckey Street to the corner of Cavenagh. All about him others were running, screaming, wailing, terrified, and the air was thick with smoke and the sickening smell of cordite. It seemed to him that the whole of Darwin was exploding. He looked up Cavenagh Street. His shop was a block away. He stepped from the kerb. But he had barely crossed Knuckey Street before the force of another explosion threw him to the ground.

When the smoke had cleared and he'd struggled to his feet, there was no shop a block away. There was no block at all. Just wasteland. Amidst the pall of smoke and dust, there was no delineation of streets and houses. There was nothing but rubble. Half of Chinatown had been obliterated.

Foong Lee walked towards where his shop and his home had been. As he walked, he ignored the mayhem which surrounded him. He ignored the fire which crackled about his feet, licking at the dried timbers which had once been verandah posts. He walked slowly, there was no point in running. He'd check the wreckage, he thought numbly, then he must help the others, those who lay maimed and bleeding amongst the ruins. He prayed that Foong Shek Mei had not awakened from his drug-induced state, he prayed that the gods had been kind and that his father had known no terror. As he stepped over the threshold into the smouldering remains of the small room which had once served as his office he saw the valuables safe. It sat upright, still locked and unscarred, apparently impervious to the Japanese bombs. With a numb sense of irony, Foong Lee walked past the safe and commenced the search for his father's remains amongst the destruction.

At 10.40 a.m. the all-clear sounded. The Japanese attack force had departed as quickly as it had appeared, and Darwin lay devastated in its wake.

Fire engines and ambulances screamed through the streets. Rescue work started immediately; there were those trapped beneath rubble, the wounded and the dying.

Foong Lee went to the aid of a child. A little boy. He was badly burned and, as Foong Lee gently lifted him, the child's skin came away in his hands. Mercifully, the boy was dead. Foong Lee was not a man given to the expression of emotion, but he fell to his knees and wept for the human race.

It was an army Landrover, serving as an ambulance, which transported Aggie Marshall to the hospital. She regained consciousness as they lifted her from where she lay in the street and, as she did, she realised that she was not in pain, but she couldn't seem to move. Her body was a dead weight and yet she felt extremely light-headed. A strange combination.

Good heavens, she thought when she saw the firemen fighting the flames which were devouring the post office. It's gone. The post office has gone. She wondered if all of her friends who worked there had gone too, surely nobody could have survived such destruction. She wanted to ask one of the two kind men who were so gently carrying her what had happened to her friends. She raised her head and opened her mouth to say something, but then she noticed the blood. All over the stretcher, all over her clothes. Such a lot of blood. Was it hers? And she seemed to have lost her left shoe, she noticed as they laid her gently in the back of the Landrover. But then she seemed to have lost most of her left foot as well. She couldn't really tell for the blood.

Whilst emergency rescue work and firefighting continued there was no time to ponder what had happened, or even to mourn the dead. There was so much to do that it seemed the battle was still being fought and, as if to emphasise the point, the time bomb berthed at Main Jetty suddenly exploded.

The *Neptuna* had been burning fiercely for close to an hour and, at 11.15, the heat aboard the 6,000-ton vessel reached such an intensity that the high explosives aboard finally ignited.

Giant jets of flame propelled wreckage high into the sky like an erupting volcano, showering the harbour with smouldering debris. In the town the force of the explosion shattered the windows of those buildings left standing as the whole of Darwin trembled from the impact of the shock waves.

The gigantic black cloud which followed the explosion billowed over the harbour and the township like a huge exclamation mark. Surely it indicated the end to the battle, to the unspeakable events of the morning. But it didn't. Barely thirty minutes later a fresh horror presented itself.

At 11.58, two hours after the initial assault on Darwin, fifty-four unescorted land-based bombers attacked the RAAF base four miles north-east of the town. The attack lasted twenty-five minutes and the base was virtually annihilated. The gateway to the north lay ruined. The Japanese had successfully destroyed all RAAF strength in the north-western area of Australia, known as the Top End. The vast land to the south was now more vulnerable than ever.

Khaki Town

Judy Nunn's new no.1 bestseller was inspired by a true wartime story that remained a well-kept secret for over seventy years.

It seems to have happened overnight, Val thought.
How extraordinary. We've become a khaki town.

It's March 1942. Singapore has fallen. Darwin has been bombed. Australia is on the brink of being invaded by the Imperial Japanese Forces. And Val Callahan, publican of The Brown's Bar in Townsville, could not be happier as she contemplates the fortune she's making from lonely, thirsty soldiers.

Overnight the small Queensland city is transformed into the transport hub for 70,000 American and Australian soldiers destined for combat in the South Pacific. Barbed wire and gun emplacements cover the beaches. Historic buildings are commandeered. And the dance halls are in full swing with jazz, jitterbug and jive.

The Australian troops begrudge the confident, well-fed 'Yanks' who have taken over their town and their women. There's growing conflict, too, within the American ranks, because black GIs are enjoying the absence of segregation. And the white GIs don't like it.

As racial violence explodes through the ranks of the military, a young United States Congressman, Lyndon Baines Johnson, is sent to Townsville by his president to investigate. 'Keep a goddamned lid on it, Lyndon,' he is told, 'lest it explode in our faces . . .'

Other titles by Judy Nunn

The Glitter Game

Edwina Dawling is the golden girl of Australian television. The former pop singer is now the country's most popular actress, an international star thanks to the hit TV soap *The Glitter Game*. But behind the seductive glamour of television is a cutthroat world where careers are made or destroyed with a word in the right ear . . . or a night in the right bed.

The Glitter Game is a delicious exposé of the glitzy world of television, a scandalous behind-the-scenes look at what goes on when the cameras stop rolling.

Centre Stage

Alex Rainford has it all. He's sexy, charismatic and adored by fans the world over. But he is not all he seems. What spectre from the past is driving him? And who will fall under his spell? Madeleine Frances, beautiful stage and screen actress? Susannah Wright, the finest classical actress of her generation? Or Imogen McLaughlin, the promising young actress whose biggest career break could be her greatest downfall . . .

Centre Stage is a tantalising glimpse into the world of theatre and what goes on when the spotlight dims and the curtain falls.

Other titles by Judy Nunn

Araluen

On a blistering hot day in 1850, brothers George and Richard Ross take their first steps on Australian soil after three long months at sea. All they have is each other.

A decade on, and they are the owners of successful vineyard, Araluen, nestled in a beautiful valley near Adelaide. Now a successful businessman, George has laid down the roots of a Ross dynasty, born of the New World. But building a family empire – whatever the cost – can have a shattering effect on the generations to come . . .

Pacific

Australian actress Samantha Lindsay is thrilled when she scores her first Hollywood movie role, playing a character loosely based on World War II heroine Mamma Tack.

But on location in Vanuatu, uncanny parallels between history and fiction emerge and Sam begins a quest for the truth. Just who was the real Mamma Tack?

Other titles by Judy Nunn

Kal

Kalgoorlie. It grew out of the red dust of the desert over the world's richest vein of gold . . . From the heady early days of the gold rush, to the horrors of the First World War in Gallipoli and France, to the shame and confrontation of the post-war riots, *Kal* tells the story of Australia itself and the people who forged a nation out of a harsh and unforgiving land.

Heritage

In the 1940s refugees from more than seventy nations gathered in Australia to forge a new identity – and to help realise one man's dream: the mighty Snowy Mountains Hydro-Electric Scheme. From the ruins of Berlin to the birth of Israel, from the Italian Alps to the Australian high country, *Heritage* is a passionate tale of rebirth, struggle, sacrifice and redemption.

Other titles by Judy Nunn

Floodtide

Floodtide traces the fortunes of four men and four families over four memorable decades in the mighty 'Iron Ore State' of Western Australia. The prosperous 1950s when childhood is idyllic in the small city of Perth . . . The turbulent 60s when youth is caught up in the Vietnam War . . . The avaricious 70s when WA's mineral boom sees a new breed of entrepreneurs . . . The corrupt 80s, when greedy politicians and powerful businessmen bring the state to its knees . . .

Maralinga

Maralinga, 1956. A British airbase in the middle of nowhere, a top-secret atomic testing ground . . . *Maralinga* is the story of Lieutenant Daniel Gardiner, who accepts a posting to the wilds of South Australia on a promise of rapid promotion, and of adventurous young English journalist Elizabeth Hoffmann, who travels halfway around the world in search of the truth.

Other titles by Judy Nunn

Tiger Men

Van Diemen's Land was an island of stark contrasts: a harsh penal colony, an English idyll for its gentry, and an island so rich in natural resources it was a profiteer's paradise . . . *Tiger Men* is a sweeping saga of three families who lived through Tasmania's golden era and the birth of Federation and then watched with pride as their sons marched off to fight for King and Country.

Elianne

A captivating story of wealth, power, privilege and betrayal, set on a grand sugar cane plantation in Queensland. In 1881 'Big Jim' Durham ruthlessly creates for Elianne Desmarais, his young French wife, the finest of the great sugar mills of the Southern Queensland cane fields, and names it in her honour. The massive estate becomes a self-sufficient fortress and home to hundreds of workers, but 'Elianne' and the Durham Family, have dark and distant secrets; secrets that surface in the wildest of times, the 1960s . . .

Other titles by Judy Nunn

Spirits of the Ghan

It is 2001 and as the world charges into the new Millennium, a century-old dream is about to be realised in the Red Centre of Australia: the completion of the mighty Ghan railway, a long-lived vision to create the 'backbone of the continent', a line that will finally link Adelaide with the Top End. But construction of the final leg between Alice Springs and Darwin will not be without its complications, for much of the desert it will cross is Aboriginal land . . .

Sanctuary

On a barren island off the coast of Western Australia, a rickety wooden dinghy runs aground. Aboard are nine people who have no idea where they are. Strangers before the violent storm that tore their vessel apart. While they remain undiscovered on the deserted island, they dare to dream of a new life . . . But forty kilometres away on the mainland lies the tiny fishing port of Shoalhaven. Here everyone knows everyone, and everyone has their place. In Shoalhaven things never change. Until now . . .